Agatha Christie is known throughout the world as the Queen of Crime. Her books have sold over a billion copies in English with another billion in 100 foreign countries. She is the most widely published author of all time and in any language, outsold only by the Bible and Shakespeare. She is the author of 80 crime novels and short story collections, 19 plays, and six novels written under the name of Mary Westmacott.

Agatha Christie's first novel, *The Mysterious Affair at Styles*, was written towards the end of the First World War, in which she served as a VAD. In it she created Hercule Poirot, the little Belgian detective who was destined to become the most popular detective in crime fiction since Sherlock Holmes. It was eventually published by The Bodley Head in 1920.

In 1926, after averaging a book a year, Agatha Christie wrote her masterpiece. *The Murder of Roger Ackroyd* was the first of her books to be published by Collins and marked the beginning of an author-publisher relationship which lasted for 50 years and well over 70 books. *The Murder of Roger Ackroyd* was also the first of Agatha Christie's books to be dramatised – under the name *Alibi* – and to have a successful run in London's West End. *The Mousetrap*, her most famous play of all, opened in 1952 and is the longest-running play in history.

Agatha Christie was made a Dame in 1971. She died in 1976, since when a number of books have been published posthumously: the bestselling novel *Sleeping Murder* appeared later that year, followed by her autobiography and the short story collections *Miss Marple's Final Cases*, *Problem at Pollensa Bay* and *While the Light Lasts*. In 1998 *Black Coffee* was the first of her plays to be novelised by another author, Charles Osborne.

THE AGATHA CHRISTIE COLLECTION

The Man in the Brown Suit
The Secret of Chimneys
The Seven Dials Mystery
The Mysterious Mr Quin
The Sittaford Mystery
The Hound of Death
The Listerdale Mystery
Why Didn't They Ask Evans?
Parker Pyne Investigates
Murder is Easy
And Then There Were None
Towards Zero
Death Comes as the End
Sparkling Cyanide
Crooked House
They Came to Baghdad
Destination Unknown
Ordeal by Innocence
The Pale Horse
Endless Night
Passenger to Frankfurt
Problem at Polensa Bay
While the Light Lasts

Poirot
The Mysterious Affair at Styles
Murder on the Links
Poirot Investigates
The Murder of Roger Ackroyd
The Big Four
The Mystery of the Blue Train
Peril at End House
Lord Edgware Dies
Murder on the Orient Express
Three-Act Tragedy
Death in the Clouds
The ABC Murders
Murder in Mesopotamia
Cards on the Table
Murder in the Mews
Dumb Witness
Death on the Nile
Appointment with Death
Hercule Poirot's Christmas
Sad Cypress
One, Two, Buckle My Shoe
Evil Under the Sun
Five Little Pigs
The Hollow
The Labours of Hercules
Taken at the Flood
Mrs McGinty's Dead
After the Funeral
Hickory Dickory Dock
Dead Man's Folly
Cat Among the Pigeons
The Adventure of the Christmas Pudding
The Clocks
Third Girl
Hallowe'en Party
Elephants Can Remember
Poirot's Early Cases
Curtain: Poirot's Last Case

Marple
The Murder at the Vicarage
The Thirteen Problems
The Body in the Library
The Moving Finger
A Murder is Announced
They Do It With Mirrors
A Pocket Full of Rye
The 4.50 from Paddington
The Mirror Crack'd from Side to Side
A Caribbean Mystery
At Bertram's Hotel
Nemesis
Sleeping Murder
Miss Marple's Final Cases

Tommy & Tuppence
The Secret Adversary
Partners in Crime
N or M?
By the Pricking of My Thumbs
Postern of Fate

Published as Mary Westmacott
Giant's Bread
Unfinished Portrait
Absent in the Spring
The Rose and the Yew Tree
A Daughter's a Daughter
The Burden

Memoirs
An Autobiography

Published as Agatha Christie Mallowan
Come, Tell Me How You Live

Play Collections
The Mousetrap and Selected Plays
Witness for the Prosecution and
Selected Plays

Play adaptations by Charles Osborne
Black Coffee (Poirot)
Spider's Web
The Unexpected Guest

Agatha Christie

the complete quin & satterthwaite

LOVE DETECTIVES

HarperCollins*Publishers*

HarperCollins*Publishers*
77–85 Fulham Palace Road,
Hammersmith, London W6 8JB
www.harpercollins.co.uk

This edition first published 2004
1 3 5 7 9 8 6 4 2

ISBN 0 00 717155 3

Typeset by Palimpsest Book Production Limited,
Polmont, Stirlingshire

Printed and bound in Great Britain by
Clays Ltd, St Ives plc

Author's Foreword

The Mr Quin stories were not written as a series. They were written one at a time at rare intervals. Mr Quin, I consider, is an epicure's taste.

A set of Dresden figures on my mother's mantelpiece fascinated me as a child and afterwards. They represented the Italian *commedia dell'arte*: Harlequin, Columbine, Pierrot, Pierette, Punchinello, and Punchinella. As a girl I wrote a series of poems about them, and I rather think that one of the poems, *Harlequin's Song*, was my first appearance in print. It was in the *Poetry Review*, and I got a guinea for it!

After I turned from poetry and ghost stories to crime, Harlequin finally reappeared; a figure invisible except when he chose, not quite human, yet concerned with the affairs of human beings and particularly of lovers. He is also the advocate for the dead.

Though each story about him is quite separate, yet the collection, written over a considerable period of years, outlines in the end the story of Harlequin himself.

With Mr Quin there has been created little Mr Satterthwaite, Mr Quin's friend in this mortal world: Mr Satterthwaite, the gossip, the looker-on at life, the little man who without ever touching the depths of joy and sorrow himself, recognizes drama when he sees it, and is conscious that he has a part to play.

Of the Mr Quin stories, my favourites are: *World's End*, *The Man from the Sea*, and *Harlequin's Lane*.

Agatha Christie

Publisher's Note

This edition gathers together all the stories by Agatha Christie featuring the enigmatic Harley Quin and the snobbish Mr Satterthwaite, two of the unlikeliest heroes who together made a crime-fighting *tour de force*. It should be noted that Mr Satterthwaite makes only a cameo appearance in the novella *Dead Man's Mirror*, which is included for the sake of completeness.

Contents

The Mysterious Mr Quin 1

The Coming of Mr Quin 3
The Shadow on the Glass 20
At the 'Bells and Motley' 40
The Sign in the Sky 57
The Soul of the Croupier 73
The Man from the Sea 89
The Voice in the Dark 115
The Face of Helen 132
The Dead Harlequin 149
The Bird with the Broken Wing 171
The World's End 190
Harlequin's Lane 209

Three-Act Tragedy 231

First Act: Suspicion 233
Second Act: Certainty 267
Third Act: Discovery 321

Dead Man's Mirror 421

The Love Detectives 501

The Harlequin Tea Set 523

THE MYSTERIOUS MR QUIN

To Harlequin the Invisible

CHAPTER 1

The Coming of Mr Quin

It was New Year's Eve.

The elder members of the house party at Royston were assembled in the big hall.

Mr Satterthwaite was glad that the young people had gone to bed. He was not fond of young people in herds. He thought them uninteresting and crude. They lacked subtlety and as life went on he had become increasingly fond of subtleties.

Mr Satterthwaite was sixty-two – a little bent, dried-up man with a peering face oddly elflike, and an intense and inordinate interest in other people's lives. All his life, so to speak, he had sat in the front row of the stalls watching various dramas of human nature unfold before him. His role had always been that of the onlooker. Only now, with old age holding him in its clutch, he found himself increasingly critical of the drama submitted to him. He demanded now something a little out of the common.

There was no doubt that he had a flair for these things. He knew instinctively when the elements of drama were at hand. Like a war horse, he sniffed the scent. Since his arrival at Royston this afternoon, that strange inner sense of his had stirred and bid him be ready. Something interesting was happening or going to happen.

The house party was not a large one. There was Tom Evesham, their genial good-humoured host, and his serious political wife who had been before her marriage Lady Laura Keene. There was Sir Richard Conway, soldier, traveller and sportsman, there were six or seven young people whose names Mr Satterthwaite had not grasped and there were the Portals.

It was the Portals who interested Mr Satterthwaite.

He had never met Alex Portal before, but he knew all about him. Had known his father and his grandfather. Alex Portal ran pretty true to type. He was a man of close on forty, fair-haired, and blue-eyed like all the Portals, fond of sport, good at games, devoid of imagination. Nothing unusual about Alex Portal. The usual good sound English stock.

But his wife was different. She was, Mr Satterthwaite knew, an Australian. Portal had been out in Australia two years ago, had met her out there and had married her and brought her home. She had never been to England previous to her marriage. All the same, she wasn't at all like any other Australian woman Mr Satterthwaite had met.

He observed her now, covertly. Interesting woman – very. So still, and yet so – alive. Alive! That was just it! Not exactly beautiful – no, you wouldn't call her beautiful, but there was a kind of calamitous magic about her that you couldn't miss – that no man could miss. The masculine side of Mr Satterthwaite spoke there, but the feminine side (for Mr Satterthwaite had a large share of femininity) was equally interested in another question. *Why did Mrs Portal dye her hair?*

No other man would probably have known that she dyed her hair, but Mr Satterthwaite knew. He knew all those things. And it puzzled him. Many dark women dye their hair blonde; he had never before come across a fair woman who dyed her hair black.

Everything about her intrigued him. In a queer intuitive way, he felt certain that she was either very happy or very unhappy – but he didn't know which, and it annoyed him not to know. Furthermore there was the curious effect she had upon her husband.

'He adores her,' said Mr Satterthwaite to himself, 'but sometimes he's – yes, afraid of her! That's very interesting. That's uncommonly interesting.'

Portal drank too much. That was certain. And he had a curious way of watching his wife when she wasn't looking.

'Nerves,' said Mr Satterthwaite. 'The fellow's all nerves. She knows it too, but she won't do anything about it.'

He felt very curious about the pair of them. Something was going on that he couldn't fathom.

He was roused from his meditations on the subject by the solemn chiming of the big clock in the corner.

'Twelve o'clock,' said Evesham. 'New Year's Day. Happy New Year – everybody. As a matter of fact that clock's five minutes fast . . . I don't know why the children wouldn't wait up and see the New Year in?'

'I don't suppose for a minute they've really gone to bed,' said his wife placidly. 'They're probably putting hairbrushes or something in our beds. That sort of thing does so amuse them. I can't think why. We should never have been allowed to do such a thing in my young days.'

'*Autre temps, autres moeurs*,' said Conway, smiling.

He was a tall soldierly-looking man. Both he and Evesham were much of the same type – honest upright kindly men with no great pretensions to brains.

'In my young days we all joined hands in a circle and sang "Auld Lang Syne",' continued Lady Laura. '"Should auld acquaintance be forgot" – so touching, I always think the words are.'

Evesham moved uneasily.

'Oh! drop it, Laura,' he muttered. '*Not here*.'

He strode across the wide hall where they were sitting, and switched on an extra light.

'Very stupid of me,' said Lady Laura, *sotto voce*. 'Reminds him of poor Mr Capel, of course. My dear, is the fire too hot for you?'

Eleanor Portal made a brusque movement.

'Thank you. I'll move my chair back a little.'

What a lovely voice she had – one of those low murmuring echoing voices that stay in your memory, thought Mr Satterthwaite. Her face was in shadow now. What a pity.

From her place in the shadow she spoke again.

'Mr – Capel?'

'Yes. The man who originally owned this house. He shot himself you know – oh! very well, Tom dear, I won't speak of it unless you like. It was a great shock for Tom, of course, because he was here when it happened. So were you, weren't you, Sir Richard?'

'Yes, Lady Laura.'

An old grandfather clock in the corner groaned, wheezed, snorted asthmatically, and then struck twelve.

'Happy New Year, Tom,' grunted Evesham perfunctorily.

Lady Laura wound up her knitting with some deliberation.

'Well, we've seen the New Year in,' she observed, and added, looking towards Mrs Portal, 'What do you think, my dear?'

Eleanor Portal rose quickly to her feet.

'Bed, by all means,' she said lightly.

'She's very pale,' thought Mr Satterthwaite, as he too rose, and began busying himself with candlesticks. 'She's not usually as pale as that.'

He lighted her candle and handed it to her with a funny little old-fashioned bow. She took it from him with a word of acknowledgment and went slowly up the stairs.

Suddenly a very odd impulse swept over Mr Satterthwaite. He wanted to go after her – to reassure her – he had the strangest feeling that she was in danger of some kind. The impulse died down, and he felt ashamed. *He* was getting nervy too.

She hadn't looked at her husband as she went up the stairs, but now she turned her head over her shoulder and gave him a long searching glance which had a queer intensity in it. It affected Mr Satterthwaite very oddly.

He found himself saying goodnight to his hostess in quite a flustered manner.

'I'm sure I hope it *will* be a happy New Year,' Lady Laura was saying. 'But the political situation seems to me to be fraught with grave uncertainty.'

'I'm sure it is,' said Mr Satterthwaite earnestly. 'I'm sure it is.'

'I only hope,' continued Lady Laura, without the least change of manner, 'that it will be a dark man who first crosses the threshold. You know that superstition, I suppose, Mr Satterthwaite? No? You surprise me. To bring luck to the house it must be a dark man who first steps over the door step on New Year's Day. Dear me, I hope I shan't find anything *very* unpleasant in my bed. I never trust the children. They have such very high spirits.'

Shaking her head in sad foreboding, Lady Laura moved majestically up the staircase.

With the departure of the women, chairs were pulled in closer round the blazing logs on the big open hearth.

'Say when,' said Evesham, hospitably, as he held up the whisky decanter.

When everybody had said when, the talk reverted to the subject which had been tabooed before.

'You knew Derek Capel, didn't you, Satterthwaite?' asked Conway.

'Slightly – yes.'

'And you, Portal?'

'No, I never met him.'

So fiercely and defensively did he say it, that Mr Satterthwaite looked up in surprise.

'I always hate it when Laura brings up the subject,' said Evesham slowly. 'After the tragedy, you know, this place was sold to a big manufacturer fellow. He cleared out after a year – didn't suit him or something. A lot of tommy rot was talked about the place being haunted of course, and it gave the house a bad name. Then, when Laura got me to stand for West Kidleby, of course it meant living up in these parts, and it wasn't so easy to find a suitable house. Royston was going cheap, and – well, in the end I bought it. Ghosts are all tommy rot, but all the same one doesn't exactly care to be reminded that you're living in a house where one of your own friends shot himself. Poor old Derek – we shall never know why he did it.'

'He won't be the first or the last fellow who's shot himself without being able to give a reason,' said Alex Portal heavily.

He rose and poured himself out another drink, splashing the whisky in with a liberal hand.

'There's something very wrong with him,' said Mr Satterthwaite, to himself. 'Very wrong indeed. I wish I knew what it was all about.'

'Gad!' said Conway. 'Listen to the wind. It's a wild night.'

'A good night for ghosts to walk,' said Portal with a reckless laugh. 'All the devils in Hell are abroad tonight.'

'According to Lady Laura, even the blackest of them would bring us luck,' observed Conway, with a laugh. 'Hark to that!'

The wind rose in another terrific wail, and as it died away there came three loud knocks on the big nailed doorway.

Everyone started.

'Who on earth can that be at this time of night?' cried Evesham.

They stared at each other.

'I will open it,' said Evesham. 'The servants have gone to bed.'

He strode across to the door, fumbled a little over the heavy bars, and finally flung it open. An icy blast of wind came sweeping into the hall.

Framed in the doorway stood a man's figure, tall and slender. To Mr Satterthwaite, watching, he appeared by some curious effect of the stained glass above the door, to be dressed in every colour of the rainbow. Then, as he stepped forward, he showed himself to be a thin dark man dressed in motoring clothes.

'I must really apologize for this intrusion,' said the stranger, in a pleasant level voice. 'But my car broke down. Nothing much, my chauffeur is putting it to rights, but it will take half an hour or so, and it is so confoundedly cold outside –'

He broke off, and Evesham took up the thread quickly.

'I should think it was. Come in and have a drink. We can't give you any assistance about the car, can we?'

'No, thanks. My man knows what to do. By the way, my name is Quin – Harley Quin.'

'Sit down, Mr Quin,' said Evesham. 'Sir Richard Conway, Mr Satterthwaite. My name is Evesham.'

Mr Quin acknowledged the introductions, and dropped into the chair that Evesham had hospitably pulled forward. As he sat, some effect of the firelight threw a bar of shadow across his face which gave almost the impression of a mask.

Evesham threw a couple more logs on the fire.

'A drink?'

'Thanks.'

Evesham brought it to him and asked as he did so:

'So you know this part of the world well, Mr Quin?'

'I passed through it some years ago.'

'Really?'

'Yes. This house belonged then to a man called Capel.'

'Ah! yes,' said Evesham. 'Poor Derek Capel. You knew him?'

'Yes, I knew him.'

Evesham's manner underwent a faint change, almost imperceptible to one who had not studied the English character. Before, it had contained a subtle reserve, now this was laid aside. Mr Quin had known Derek Capel. He was the friend of a friend, and, as such, was vouched for and fully accredited.

'Astounding affair, that,' he said confidentially. 'We were just talking about it. I can tell you, it went against the grain, buying this place. If there had been anything else suitable, but there wasn't you see. I was in the house the night he shot himself – so was Conway, and upon my word, I've always expected his ghost to walk.'

'A very inexplicable business,' said Mr Quin, slowly and deliberately, and he paused with the air of an actor who has just spoken an important cue.

'You may well say inexplicable,' burst in Conway. 'The thing's a black mystery – always will be.'

'I wonder,' said Mr Quin, non-committally. 'Yes, Sir Richard, you were saying?'

'Astounding – that's what it was. Here's a man in the prime of life, gay, light-hearted, without a care in the world. Five or six old pals staying with him. Top of his spirits at dinner, full of plans for the future. And from the dinner table he goes straight upstairs to his room, takes a revolver from a drawer and shoots himself. Why? Nobody ever knew. Nobody ever will know.'

'Isn't that rather a sweeping statement, Sir Richard?' asked Mr Quin, smiling.

Conway stared at him.

'What d'you mean? I don't understand.'

'A problem is not necessarily unsolvable because it has remained unsolved.'

'Oh! Come, man, if nothing came out at the time, it's not likely to come out now – ten years afterwards?'

Mr Quin shook his head gently.

'I disagree with you. The evidence of history is against you. The contemporary historian never writes such a true history as the historian of a later generation. It is a question of getting the true perspective, of seeing things in proportion. If you like to call it so, it is, like everything else, a question of relativity.'

Alex Portal leant forward, his face twitching painfully.

'You are right, Mr Quin,' he cried, 'you are right. Time does not dispose of a question – it only presents it anew in a different guise.'

Evesham was smiling tolerantly.

'Then you mean to say, Mr Quin, that if we were to hold, let us say, a Court of Inquiry tonight, into the circumstances of Derek

Capel's death, we are as likely to arrive at the truth as we should have been at the time?'

'*More* likely, Mr Evesham. The personal equation has largely dropped out, and you will remember facts as facts without seeking to put your own interpretation upon them.'

Evesham frowned doubtfully.

'One must have a starting point, of course,' said Mr Quin in his quiet level voice. 'A starting point is usually a theory. One of you must have a theory, I am sure. How about you, Sir Richard?'

Conway frowned thoughtfully.

'Well, of course,' he said apologetically, 'we thought – naturally we all thought – that there must be a woman in it somewhere. It's usually either that or money, isn't it? And it certainly wasn't money. No trouble of that description. So – what else could it have been?'

Mr Satterthwaite started. He had leant forward to contribute a small remark of his own and in the act of doing so, he had caught sight of a woman's figure crouched against the balustrade of the gallery above. She was huddled down against it, invisible from everywhere but where he himself sat, and she was evidently listening with strained attention to what was going on below. So immovable was she that he hardly believed the evidence of his own eyes.

But he recognized the pattern of the dress easily enough – an old-world brocade. It was Eleanor Portal.

And suddenly all the events of the night seemed to fall into pattern – Mr Quin's arrival, no fortuitous chance, but the appearance of an actor when his cue was given. There was a drama being played in the big hall at Royston tonight – a drama none the less real in that one of the actors was dead. Oh! yes, Derek Capel had a part in the play. Mr Satterthwaite was sure of that.

And, again suddenly, a new illumination came to him. This was Mr Quin's doing. It was he who was staging the play – was giving the actors their cues. He was at the heart of the mystery pulling the strings, making the puppets work. He knew everything, even to the presence of the woman crouched against the woodwork upstairs. Yes, he knew.

Sitting well back in his chair, secure in his role of audience, Mr Satterthwaite watched the drama unfold before his eyes. Quietly and naturally, Mr Quin was pulling the strings, setting his puppets in motion.

'A woman – yes,' he murmured thoughtfully. 'There was no mention of any woman at dinner?'

'Why, of course,' cried Evesham. 'He announced his engagement. That's just what made it seem so absolutely mad. Very bucked about it he was. Said it wasn't to be announced just yet – but gave us the hint that he was in the running for the Benedick stakes.'

'Of course we all guessed who the lady was,' said Conway. 'Marjorie Dilke. Nice girl.'

It seemed to be Mr Quin's turn to speak, but he did not do so, and something about his silence seemed oddly provocative. It was as though he challenged the last statement. It had the effect of putting Conway in a defensive position.

'Who else could it have been? Eh, Evesham?'

'I don't know,' said Tom Evesham slowly. 'What did he say exactly now? Something about being in the running for the Benedick stakes – that he couldn't tell us the lady's name till he had her permission – it wasn't to be announced yet. He said, I remember, that he was a damned lucky fellow. That he wanted his two old friends to know that by that time next year he'd be a happy married man. Of course, we assumed it was Marjorie. They were great friends and he'd been about with her a lot.'

'The only thing –' began Conway and stopped.

'What were you going to say, Dick?'

'Well, I mean, it was odd in a way, if it were Marjorie, that the engagement shouldn't be announced at once. I mean, why the secrecy? Sounds more as though it were a married woman – you know, someone whose husband had just died, or who was divorcing him.'

'That's true,' said Evesham. 'If that were the case, of course, the engagement couldn't be announced at once. And you know, thinking back about it, I don't believe he had been seeing much of Marjorie. All that was the year before. I remember thinking things seemed to have cooled off between them.'

'Curious,' said Mr Quin.

'Yes – looked almost as though someone had come between them.'

'Another woman,' said Conway thoughtfully.

'By jove,' said Evesham. 'You know, there was something almost indecently hilarious about old Derek that night. He looked almost drunk with happiness. And yet – I can't quite explain what I mean – but he looked oddly defiant too.'

'Like a man defying Fate,' said Alex Portal heavily.

Was it of Derek Capel he was speaking – or was it of himself? Mr Satterthwaite, looking at him, inclined to the latter view. Yes, that was what Alex Portal represented – a man defying Fate.

His imagination, muddled by drink, responded suddenly to that note in the story which recalled his own secret preoccupation.

Mr Satterthwaite looked up. She was still there. Watching, listening – still motionless, frozen – like a dead woman.

'Perfectly true,' said Conway. 'Capel *was* excited – curiously so. I'd describe him as a man who had staked heavily and won against well nigh overwhelming odds.'

'Getting up courage, perhaps, for what he's made up his mind to do?' suggested Portal.

And as though moved by an association of ideas, he got up and helped himself to another drink.

'Not a bit of it,' said Evesham sharply. 'I'd almost swear nothing of that kind was in his mind. Conway's right. A successful gambler who has brought off a long shot and can hardly believe in his own good fortune. That was the attitude.'

Conway gave a gesture of discouragement.

'And yet,' he said. 'Ten minutes later –'

They sat in silence. Evesham brought his hand down with a bang on the table.

'Something must have happened in that ten minutes,' he cried. 'It must! But what? Let's go over it carefully. We were all talking. In the middle of it Capel got up suddenly and left the room –'

'Why?' said Mr Quin.

The interruption seemed to disconcert Evesham.

'I beg your pardon?'

'I only said: Why?' said Mr Quin.

Evesham frowned in an effort of memory.

'It didn't seem vital – at the time – Oh! of course – the Post. Don't you remember that jangling bell, and how excited we were. We'd been snowed up for three days, remember. Biggest snowstorm for years and years. All the roads were impassable. No newspapers, no letters. Capel went out to see if something had come through at last, and got a great pile of things. Newspapers and letters. He opened the paper to see if there was any news, and then went upstairs with his letters. Three minutes afterwards, we heard a shot . . . Inexplicable – absolutely inexplicable.'

'That's not inexplicable,' said Portal. 'Of course the fellow got some unexpected news in a letter. Obvious, I should have said.'

'Oh! Don't think we missed anything so obvious as that. It was one of the Coroner's first questions. *But Capel never opened one of his letters.* The whole pile lay unopened on his dressing-table.'

Portal looked crestfallen.

'You're sure he didn't open just one of them? He might have destroyed it after reading it?'

'No, I'm quite positive. Of course, that would have been the natural solution. No, every one of the letters was unopened. Nothing burnt – nothing torn up – There was no fire in the room.'

Portal shook his head.

'Extraordinary.'

'It was a ghastly business altogether,' said Evesham in a low voice. 'Conway and I went up when we heard the shot, and found him – It gave me a shock, I can tell you.'

'Nothing to be done but telephone for the police, I suppose?' said Mr Quin.

'Royston wasn't on the telephone then. I had it put in when I bought the place. No, luckily enough, the local constable happened to be in the kitchen at the time. One of the dogs – you remember poor old Rover, Conway? – had strayed the day before. A passing carter had found it half buried in a snowdrift and had taken it to the police station. They recognized it as Capel's, and a dog he was particularly fond of, and the constable came up with it. He'd just arrived a minute before the shot was fired. It saved us some trouble.'

'Gad, that was a snowstorm,' said Conway reminiscently. 'About this time of year, wasn't it? Early January.'

'February, I think. Let me see, we went abroad soon afterwards.'

'I'm pretty sure it was January. My hunter Ned – you remember

Ned? – lamed himself the end of January. That was just after this business.'

'It must have been quite the end of January then. Funny how difficult it is to recall dates after a lapse of years.'

'One of the most difficult things in the world,' said Mr Quin, conversationally. 'Unless you can find a landmark in some big public event – an assassination of a crowned head, or a big murder trial.'

'Why, of course,' cried Conway, 'it was just before the Appleton case.'

'Just after, wasn't it?'

'No, no, don't you remember – Capel knew the Appletons – he'd stayed with the old man the previous Spring – just a week before he died. He was talking of him one night – what an old curmudgeon he was, and how awful it must have been for a young and beautiful woman like Mrs Appleton to be tied to him. There was no suspicion then that she had done away with him.'

'By jove, you're right. I remember reading the paragraph in the paper saying an exhumation order had been granted. It would have been that same day – I remember only seeing it with half my mind, you know, the other half wondering about poor old Derek lying dead upstairs.'

'A common, but very curious phenomenon, that,' observed Mr Quin. 'In moments of great stress, the mind focuses itself upon some quite unimportant matter which is remembered long afterwards with the utmost fidelity, driven in, as it were, by the mental stress of the moment. It may be some quite irrelevant detail, like the pattern of a wallpaper, but it will never be forgotten.'

'Rather extraordinary, your saying that, Mr Quin,' said Conway. 'Just as you were speaking, I suddenly felt myself back in Derek Capel's room – with Derek lying dead on the floor – I saw as plainly as possible the big tree outside the window, and the shadow it threw upon the snow outside. Yes, the moonlight, the snow, and the shadow of the tree – I can see them again this minute. By Gad, I believe I could draw them, and yet I never realized I was looking at them at the time.'

'His room was the big one over the porch, was it not?' asked Mr Quin.

'Yes, and the tree was the big beech, just at the angle of the drive.'

Mr Quin nodded, as though satisfied. Mr Satterthwaite was curiously thrilled. He was convinced that every word, every inflection of Mr Quin's voice, was pregnant with purpose. He was driving at something – exactly what Mr Satterthwaite did not know, but he was quite convinced as to whose was the master hand.

There was a momentary pause, and then Evesham reverted to the preceding topic.

'That Appleton case, I remember it very well now. What a sensation it made. She got off, didn't she? Pretty woman, very fair – remarkably fair.'

Almost against his will, Mr Satterthwaite's eyes sought the kneeling figure up above. Was it his fancy, or did he see it shrink a little as though at a blow. Did he see a hand slide upwards to the table cloth – and then pause.

There was a crash of falling glass. Alex Portal, helping himself to whisky, had let the decanter slip.

'I say – sir, damn' sorry. Can't think what came over me.'

Evesham cut short his apologies.

'Quite all right. Quite all right, my dear fellow. Curious – That smash reminded me. That's what she did, didn't she? Mrs Appleton? Smashed the port decanter?'

'Yes. Old Appleton had his glass of port – only one – each night. The day after his death, one of the servants saw her take the decanter out and smash it deliberately. That set them talking, of course. They all knew she had been perfectly wretched with him. Rumour grew and grew, and in the end, months later, some of his relatives applied for an exhumation order. And sure enough, the old fellow had been poisoned. Arsenic, wasn't it?'

'No – strychnine, I think. It doesn't much matter. Well, of course, there it was. Only one person was likely to have done it. Mrs Appleton stood her trial. She was acquitted more through lack of evidence against her than from any overwhelming proof of innocence. In other words, she was lucky. Yes, I don't suppose there's much doubt she did it right enough. What happened to her afterwards?'

'Went out to Canada, I believe. Or was it Australia? She had an uncle or something of the sort out there who offered her a home. Best thing she could do under the circumstances.'

Mr Satterthwaite was fascinated by Alex Portal's right hand as it clasped his glass. How tightly he was gripping it.

'You'll smash that in a minute or two, if you're not careful,' thought Mr Satterthwaite. 'Dear me, how interesting all this is.'

Evesham rose and helped himself to a drink.

'Well, we're not much nearer to knowing why poor Derek Capel shot himself,' he remarked. 'The Court of Inquiry hasn't been a great success, has it, Mr Quin?'

Mr Quin laughed . . .

It was a strange laugh, mocking – yet sad. It made everyone jump.

'I beg your pardon,' he said. 'You are still living in the past, Mr Evesham. You are still hampered by your preconceived notion. But I – the man from outside, the stranger passing by, see only – facts!'

'Facts?'

'Yes – facts.'

'What do you mean?' said Evesham.

'I see a clear sequence of facts, outlined by yourselves but of which you have not seen the significance. Let us go back ten years and look at what we see – untrammelled by ideas or sentiment.'

Mr Quin had risen. He looked very tall. The fire leaped fitfully behind him. He spoke in a low compelling voice.

'You are at dinner. Derek Capel announces his engagement. You think then it was to Marjorie Dilke. You are not so sure now. He has the restlessly excited manner of a man who has successfully defied Fate – who, in your own words, has pulled off a big coup against overwhelming odds. Then comes the clanging of the bell. He goes out to get the long overdue mail. He doesn't open his letters, but you mention yourselves that *he opened the paper to glance at the news*. It is ten years ago – so we cannot know what the news was that day – a far-off earthquake, a near at hand political crisis? The only thing we do know about the contents of that paper is that it contained one small paragraph – *a paragraph stating that the Home Office had given permission to exhume* the body of Mr Appleton three days ago.'

'What?'

Mr Quin went on.

'Derek Capel goes up to his room, and there he sees something out of the window. Sir Richard Conway has told us that the curtain was not drawn across it and further that it gave on to the drive. What did he see? What could he have seen that forced him to take his life?'

'What do you mean? What did he see?'

'I think,' said Mr Quin, 'that he saw a policeman. A policeman who had come about a dog – But Derek Capel didn't know that – he just saw – a policeman.'

There was a long silence – as though it took some time to drive the inference home.

'My God!' whispered Evesham at last. 'You can't mean that? Appleton? But he wasn't there at the time Appleton died. The old man was alone with his wife –'

'But he may have been there a week earlier. Strychnine is not very soluble unless it is in the form of hydrochloride. The greater part of it, put into the port, would be taken in the last glass, perhaps a week after he left.'

Portal sprung forward. His voice was hoarse, his eyes bloodshot.

'Why did she break the decanter?' he cried. 'Why did she break the decanter? Tell me that!'

For the first time that evening, Mr Quin addressed himself to Mr Satterthwaite.

'You have a wide experience of life, Mr Satterthwaite. Perhaps you can tell us that.'

Mr Satterthwaite's voice trembled a little. His cue had come at last. He was to speak some of the most important lines in the play. He was an actor now – not a looker-on.

'As I see it,' he murmured modestly, 'she – cared for Derek Capel. She was, I think, a good woman – and she had sent him away. When her husband – died, she suspected the truth. And so, to save the man she loved, she tried to destroy the evidence against him. Later, I think, he persuaded her that her suspicions were unfounded, and she consented to marry him. But even then, she hung back – women, I fancy, have a lot of instinct.'

Mr Sattherthwaite had spoken his part.

Suddenly a long trembling sigh filled the air.

'My God!' cried Evesham, starting, 'what was that?'

Mr Satterthwaite could have told him that it was Eleanor Portal in the gallery above, but he was too artistic to spoil a good effect.

Mr Quin was smiling.

'My car will be ready by now. Thank you for your hospitality, Mr Evesham. I have, I hope, done something for my friend.'

They stared at him in blank amazement.

'That aspect of the matter has not struck you? He loved this woman, you know. Loved her enough to commit murder for her sake. When retribution overtook him, as he mistakenly thought, he took his own life. But unwittingly, he left her to face the music.'

'She was acquitted,' muttered Evesham.

'Because the case against her could not be proved. I fancy – it may be only a fancy – that she is still – facing the music.'

Portal had sunk into a chair, his face buried in his hands.

Quin turned to Satterthwaite.

'Goodbye, Mr Satterthwaite. You are interested in the drama, are you not?'

Mr Satterthwaite nodded – surprised.

'I must recommend the Harlequinade to your attention. It is dying out nowadays – but it repays attention, I assure you. Its symbolism is a little difficult to follow – but the immortals are always immortal, you know. I wish you all goodnight.'

They saw him stride out into the dark. As before, the coloured glass gave the effect of motley . . .

Mr Satterthwaite went upstairs. He went to draw down his window, for the air was cold. The figure of Mr Quin moved down the drive, and from a side door came a woman's figure, running. For a moment they spoke together, then she retraced her steps to the house. She passed just below the window, and Mr Satterthwaite was struck anew by the vitality of her face. She moved now like a woman in a happy dream.

'Eleanor!'

Alex Portal had joined her.

'Eleanor, forgive me – forgive me – You told me the truth, but God forgive me – I did not quite believe . . .'

Mr Satterthwaite was intensely interested in other people's

affairs, but he was also a gentleman. It was borne in upon him that he must shut the window. He did so.

But he shut it very slowly.

He heard her voice, exquisite and indescribable.

'I know – I know. You have been in hell. So was I once. Loving – yet alternately believing and suspecting – thrusting aside one's doubts and having them spring up again with leering faces . . . I know, Alex, I know . . . But there is a worse hell than that, the hell I have lived in with you. I have seen your doubt – your fear of me . . . poisoning all our love. That man – that chance passer by, saved me. I could bear it no longer, you understand. Tonight – tonight I was going to kill myself . . . Alex . . . Alex . . .'

CHAPTER 2

The Shadow on the Glass

I

'Listen to this,' said Lady Cynthia Drage.

She read aloud from the journal she held in her hand.

'Mr and Mrs Unkerton are entertaining a party at Greenways House this week. Amongst the guests are Lady Cynthia Drage, Mr and Mrs Richard Scott, Major Porter, D.S.O., Mrs Staverton, Captain Allenson and Mr Satterthwaite.'

'It's as well,' remarked Lady Cynthia, casting away the paper, 'to know what we're in for. But they *have* made a mess of things!'

Her companion, that same Mr Satterthwaite whose name figured at the end of the list of guests, looked at her interrogatively. It had been said that if Mr Satterthwaite were found at the houses of those rich who had newly arrived, it was a sign either that the cooking was unusually good, or that a drama of human life was to be enacted there. Mr Satterthwaite was abnormally interested in the comedies and tragedies of his fellow men.

Lady Cynthia, who was a middle-aged woman, with a hard face and a liberal allowance of make-up, tapped him smartly with the newest thing in parasols which lay rakishly across her knee.

'Don't pretend you don't understand me. You do perfectly. What's more I believe you're here on purpose to see the fur fly!'

Mr Satterthwaite protested vigorously. He didn't know what she was talking about.

'I'm talking about Richard Scott. Do you pretend you've never heard of him?'

'No, of course not. He's the Big Game man, isn't he?'

'That's it – "Great big bears and tigers, etc." as the song says.

Of course, he's a great lion himself just now – the Unkertons would naturally be mad to get hold of him – *and* the bride! A charming child – oh! quite a charming child – but so naïve, only twenty, you know, and he must be at least forty-five.'

'Mrs Scott seems to be very charming,' said Mr Satterthwaite sedately.

'Yes, poor child.'

'Why poor child?'

Lady Cynthia cast him a look of reproach, and went on approaching the point at issue in her own manner.

'Porter's all right – a dull dog, though – another of these African hunters, all sunburnt and silent. Second fiddle to Richard Scott and always has been – life-long friends and all that sort of thing. When I come to think of it, I believe they were together on that trip –'

'Which trip?'

'*The* trip. The Mrs Staverton trip. You'll be saying next you've never heard of Mrs Staverton.'

'I *have* heard of Mrs Staverton,' said Mr Satterthwaite, almost with unwillingness.

And he and Lady Cynthia exchanged glances.

'It's so exactly like the Unkertons,' wailed the latter, 'they are absolutely hopeless – socially, I mean. The idea of asking those two together! Of course they'd heard that Mrs Staverton was a sportswoman and a traveller and all that, and about her book. People like the Unkertons don't even begin to realize what pitfalls there are! I've been running them, myself, for the last year, and what I've gone through nobody knows. One has to be constantly at their elbow. "Don't do that! You can't do this!" Thank goodness, I'm through with it now. Not that we've quarrelled – oh! no, I never quarrel, but somebody else can take on the job. As I've always said, I can put up with vulgarity, but I can't stand meanness!'

After this somewhat cryptic utterance, Lady Cynthia was silent for a moment, ruminating on the Unkertons' meanness as displayed to herself.

'If I'd still been running the show for them,' she went on presently, 'I should have said quite firmly and plainly: "You can't ask Mrs Staverton with the Richard Scotts. She and he were once –"'

She stopped eloquently.

'But were they once?' asked Mr Satterthwaite.

'My dear man! It's well known. That trip into the Interior! I'm surprised the woman had the face to accept the invitation.'

'Perhaps she didn't know the others were coming?' suggested Mr Satterthwaite.

'Perhaps she did. That's far more likely.'

'You think –?'

'She's what I call a dangerous woman – the sort of woman who'd stick at nothing. I wouldn't be in Richard Scott's shoes this week-end.'

'And his wife knows nothing, you think?'

'I'm certain of it. But I suppose some kind friend will enlighten her sooner or later. Here's Jimmy Allenson. Such a nice boy. He saved my life in Egypt last winter – I was so bored, you know. Hullo, Jimmy, come here at once.'

Captain Allenson obeyed, dropping down on the turf beside her. He was a handsome young fellow of thirty, with white teeth and an infectious smile.

'I'm glad somebody wants me,' he observed. 'The Scotts are doing the turtle dove stunt, two required, not three, Porter's devouring the *Field*, and I've been in mortal danger of being entertained by my hostess.'

He laughed. Lady Cynthia laughed with him. Mr Satterthwaite, who was in some ways a little old-fashioned, so much so that he seldom made fun of his host and hostess until after he had left their house, remained grave.

'Poor Jimmy,' said Lady Cynthia.

'Mine not to reason why, mine but to swiftly fly. I had a narrow escape of being told the family ghost story.'

'An Unkerton ghost,' said Lady Cynthia. 'How screaming.'

'Not an Unkerton ghost,' said Mr Satterthwaite. 'A Greenways ghost. They bought it with the house.'

'Of course,' said Lady Cynthia. 'I remember now. But it doesn't clank chains, does it? It's only something to do with a window.'

Jimmy Allenson looked up quickly.

'A window?'

But for the moment Mr Satterthwaite did not answer. He was looking over Jimmy's head at three figures approaching from the direction of the house – a slim girl between two men. There was a superficial resemblance between the men, both were tall and dark with bronzed faces and quick eyes, but looked at more closely the resemblance vanished. Richard Scott, hunter and explorer, was a man of extraordinarily vivid personality. He had a manner that radiated magnetism. John Porter, his friend and fellow hunter, was a man of squarer build with an impassive, rather wooden face, and very thoughtful grey eyes. He was a quiet man, content always to play second fiddle to his friend.

And between these two walked Moira Scott who, until three months ago, had been Moira O'Connell. A slender figure, big wistful brown eyes, and golden red hair that stood out round her small face like a saint's halo.

'That child mustn't be hurt,' said Mr Satterthwaite to himself. 'It would be abominable that a child like that should be hurt.'

Lady Cynthia greeted the newcomers with a wave of the latest thing in parasols.

'Sit down, and don't interrupt,' she said. 'Mr Satterthwaite is telling us a ghost story.'

'I love ghost stories,' said Moira Scott. She dropped down on the grass.

'The ghost of Greenways House?' asked Richard Scott.

'Yes. You know about it?'

Scott nodded.

'I used to stay here in the old days,' he explained. 'Before the Elliots had to sell up. The Watching Cavalier, that's it, isn't it?'

'The Watching Cavalier,' said his wife softly. 'I like that. It sounds interesting. Please go on.'

But Mr Satterthwaite seemed somewhat loath to do so. He assured her that it was not really interesting at all.

'Now you've done it, Satterthwaite,' said Richard Scott sardonically. 'That hint of reluctance clinches it.'

In response to popular clamour, Mr Satterthwaite was forced to speak.

'It's really very uninteresting,' he said apologetically. 'I believe the original story centres round a Cavalier ancestor of the Elliot family. His wife had a Roundhead lover. The husband was killed by the lover in an upstairs room, and the guilty pair fled, but as they fled, they looked back at the house, and saw the face of the dead husband at the window, watching them. That is the legend, but the ghost story is only concerned with a pane of glass in the window of that particular room on which is an irregular stain, almost imperceptible from near at hand, but which from far away certainly gives the effect of a man's face looking out.'

'Which window is it?' asked Mrs Scott, looking up at the house.

'You can't see it from here,' said Mr Satterthwaite. 'It is round the other side but was boarded up from the inside some years ago – forty years ago, I think, to be accurate.'

'What did they do that for? I thought you said the ghost didn't walk.'

'It doesn't,' Mr Satterthwaite assured her. 'I suppose – well, I suppose there grew to be a superstitious feeling about it, that's all.'

Then, deftly enough, he succeeded in turning the conversation. Jimmy Allenson was perfectly ready to hold forth upon Egyptian sand diviners.

'Frauds, most of them. Ready enough to tell you vague things about the past, but won't commit themselves as to the future.'

'I should have thought it was usually the other way about,' remarked John Porter.

'It's illegal to tell the future in this country, isn't it?' said Richard Scott. 'Moira persuaded a gypsy into telling her fortune, but the woman gave her her shilling back, and said there was nothing doing, or words to that effect.'

'Perhaps she saw something so frightful that she didn't like to tell it me,' said Moira.

'Don't pile on the agony, Mrs Scott,' said Allenson lightly. 'I, for one, refuse to believe that an unlucky fate is hanging over you.'

'I wonder,' thought Mr Satterthwaite to himself. 'I wonder . . .'

Then he looked up sharply. Two women were coming from the house, a short stout woman with black hair, inappropriately dressed in jade green, and a tall slim figure in creamy white. The first woman was his hostess, Mrs Unkerton, the second was a woman he had often heard of, but never met.

'Here's Mrs Staverton,' announced Mrs Unkerton, in a tone of great satisfaction. 'All friends here, I think.'

'These people have an uncanny gift for saying just the most awful things they can,' murmured Lady Cynthia, but Mr Satterthwaite was not listening. He was watching Mrs Staverton.

Very easy – very natural. Her careless 'Hullo! Richard, ages since we met. Sorry I couldn't come to the wedding. Is this your wife? You must be tired of meeting all your husband's weather-beaten old friends.' Moira's response – suitable, rather shy. The elder woman's swift appraising glance that went on lightly to another old friend.

'Hullo, John!' The same easy tone, but with a subtle difference in it – a warming quality that had been absent before.

And then that sudden smile. It transformed her. Lady Cynthia had been quite right. A dangerous woman! Very fair – deep blue eyes – not the traditional colouring of the siren – a face almost haggard in repose. A woman with a slow dragging voice and a sudden dazzling smile.

Iris Staverton sat down. She became naturally and inevitably the centre of the group. So you felt it would always be.

Mr Satterthwaite was recalled from his thoughts by Major Porter's suggesting a stroll. Mr Satterthwaite, who was not as a general rule much given to strolling, acquiesced. The two men sauntered off together across the lawn.

'Very interesting story of yours just now,' said the Major.

'I will show you the window,' said Mr Satterthwaite.

He led the way round to the west side of the house. Here there was a small formal garden – the Privy Garden, it was always called, and there was some point in the name, for it was surrounded by high holly hedges, and even the entrance to it ran zigzag between the same high prickly hedges.

Once inside, it was very charming with an old-world charm of formal flower beds, flagged paths and a low stone seat, exquisitely carved. When they had reached the centre of the garden, Mr Satterthwaite turned and pointed up at the house. The length of Greenways House ran north and south. In this narrow west wall there was only one window, a window on the first floor, almost overgrown by ivy, with grimy panes, and which you could just see was boarded up on the inside.

'There you are,' said Mr Satterthwaite.

Craning his neck a little, Porter looked up.

'H'm I can see a kind of discolouration on one of the panes, nothing more.'

'We're too near,' said Mr Satterthwaite. 'There's a clearing higher up in the woods where you get a really good view.'

He led the way out of the Privy Garden, and turning sharply to the left, struck into the woods. A certain enthusiasm of showmanship possessed him, and he hardly noticed that the man at his side was absent and inattentive.

'They had, of course, to make another window, when they boarded up this one,' he explained. 'The new one faces south overlooking the lawn where we were sitting just now. I rather fancy the Scotts have the room in question. That is why I didn't want to pursue the subject. Mrs Scott might have felt nervous if she had realized that she was sleeping in what might be called the haunted room.'

'Yes. I see,' said Porter.

Mr Satterthwaite looked at him sharply, and realized that the other had not heard a word of what he was saying.

'Very interesting,' said Porter. He slashed with his stick at some tall foxgloves, and, frowning, he said: 'She ought not to have come. She ought never to have come.'

People often spoke after this fashion to Mr Satterthwaite. He seemed to matter so little, to have so negative a personality. He was merely a glorified listener.

'No,' said Porter, 'she ought never to have come.'

Mr Satterthwaite knew instinctively that it was not of Mrs Scott he spoke.

'You think not?' he asked.

Porter shook his head as though in foreboding.

'I was on that trip,' he said abruptly. 'The three of us went. Scott and I and Iris. She's a wonderful woman – and a damned fine shot.' He paused. 'What made them ask her?' he finished abruptly.

Mr Satterthwaite shrugged his shoulders.

'Ignorance,' he said.

'There's going to be trouble,' said the other. 'We must stand by – and do what we can.'

'But surely Mrs Staverton –?'

'I'm talking of Scott.' He paused. 'You see – there's Mrs Scott to consider.'

Mr Satterthwaite had been considering her all along, but he did not think it necessary to say so, since the other man had so clearly forgotten her until this minute.

'How did Scott meet his wife?' he asked.

'Last winter, in Cairo. A quick business. They were engaged in three weeks, and married in six.'

'She seems to me very charming.'

'She is, no doubt about it. And he adores her – but that will make no difference.' And again Major Porter repeated to himself, using the pronoun that meant to him one person only: 'Hang it all, she shouldn't have come . . .'

Just then they stepped out upon a high grassy knoll at some little distance from the house. With again something of the pride of the showman, Mr Satterthwaite stretched out his arm.

'Look,' he said.

It was fast growing dusk. The window could still be plainly descried, and apparently pressed against one of the panes was a man's face surmounted by a plumed Cavalier's hat.

'Very curious,' said Porter. 'Really very curious. What will happen when that pane of glass gets smashed some day?'

Mr Satterthwaite smiled.

'That is one of the most interesting parts of the story. That pane of glass has been replaced to my certain knowledge at least eleven times, perhaps oftener. The last time was twelve years ago when the then owner of the house determined to destroy the myth. But it's always the same. *The stain reappears* – not all at once, the discolouration spreads gradually. It takes a month or two as a rule.'

For the first time, Porter showed signs of real interest. He gave a sudden quick shiver.

'Damned odd, these things. No accounting for them. What's the real reason of having the room boarded up inside?'

'Well, an idea got about that the room was – unlucky. The Eveshams were in it just before the divorce. Then Stanley and his wife were staying here, and had that room when he ran off with his chorus girl.'

Porter raised his eyebrows.

'I see. Danger, not to life, but to morals.'

'And now,' thought Mr Satterthwaite to himself, 'the Scotts have it . . . I wonder . . .'

They retraced their steps in silence to the house. Walking almost noiselessly on the soft turf, each absorbed in his own thoughts, they became unwittingly eavesdroppers.

They were rounding the corner of the holly hedge when they heard Iris Staverton's voice raised fierce and clear from the depths of the Privy Garden.

'You shall be sorry – sorry – for this!'

Scott's voice answered low and uncertain, so that the words could not be distinguished, and then the woman's voice rose again, speaking words that they were to remember later.

'Jealousy – it drives one to the Devil – it *is* the Devil! It can drive one to black murder. Be careful, Richard, for God's sake, be careful!'

And then on that she had come out of the Privy Garden ahead of them, and on round the corner of the house without seeing them, walking swiftly, almost running, like a woman hag-ridden and pursued.

Mr Satterthwaite thought again of Lady Cynthia's words. A dangerous woman. For the first time, he had a premonition of tragedy, coming swift and inexorable, not to be gainsaid.

Yet that evening he felt ashamed of his fears. Everything seemed normal and pleasant. Mrs Staverton, with her easy insouciance, showed no sign of strain. Moira Scott was her charming, unaffected self. The two women appeared to be getting on very well. Richard Scott himself seemed to be in boisterous spirits.

The most worried looking person was stout Mrs Unkerton. She confided at length in Mr Satterthwaite.

'Think it silly or not, as you like, there's something giving me the creeps. And I'll tell you frankly, I've sent for the glazier unbeknown to Ned.'

'The glazier?'

'To put a new pane of glass in that window. It's all very well. Ned's proud of it – says it gives the house a tone. I don't like it. I tell you flat. We'll have a nice plain modern pane of glass, with no nasty stories attached to it.'

'You forget,' said Mr Satterthwaite, 'or perhaps you don't know. The stain comes back.'

'That's as it may be,' said Mrs Unkerton. 'All I can say is if it does, it's against nature!'

Mr Satterthwaite raised his eyebrows, but did not reply.

'And what if it does?' pursued Mrs Unkerton defiantly. 'We're not so bankrupt, Ned and I, that we can't afford a new pane of glass every month – or every week if need be for the matter of that.'

Mr Satterthwaite did not meet the challenge. He had seen too many things crumple and fall before the power of money to believe that even a Cavalier ghost could put up a successful fight. Nevertheless, he was interested by Mrs Unkerton's manifest uneasiness. Even she was not exempt from the tension in the atmosphere – only she attributed it to an attenuated ghost story, not to the clash of personalities amongst her guests.

Mr Sattherwaite was fated to hear yet another scrap of conversation which threw light upon the situation. He was going up the wide staircase to bed, John Porter and Mrs Staverton were sitting together in an alcove of the big hall. She was speaking with a faint irritation in her golden voice.

'I hadn't the least idea the Scotts were going to be here. I daresay, if I had known, I shouldn't have come, but I can assure you, my dear John, that now I am here, I'm not going to run away –'

Mr Satterthwaite passed on up the staircase out of earshot. He thought to himself: 'I wonder now – How much of that is true? Did she know? I wonder – what's going to come of it?'

He shook his head.

In the clear light of the morning he felt that he had perhaps been a little melodramatic in his imaginings of the evening before. A moment of strain – yes, certainly – inevitable under the circumstances – but nothing more. People adjusted themselves. His fancy that some great catastrophe was pending was nerves – pure nerves – or possibly liver. Yes, that was it, liver. He was due at Carlsbad in another fortnight.

On his own account he proposed a little stroll that evening just as it was growing dusk. He suggested to Major Porter that they should go up to the clearing and see if Mrs Unkerton had been as good as her word, and had a new pane of glass put in. To himself, he said: 'Exercise, that's what I need. Exercise.'

The two men walked slowly through the woods. Porter, as usual, was taciturn.

'I can't help feeling,' said Mr Satterthwaite loquaciously, 'that we were a little foolish in our imaginings yesterday. Expecting – er – trouble, you know. After all, people have to behave themselves – swallow their feelings and that sort of thing.'

'Perhaps,' said Porter. After a minute or two he added: 'Civilized people.'

'You mean –?'

'People who've lived outside civilization a good deal sometimes go back. Revert. Whatever you call it.'

They emerged on to the grassy knoll. Mr Satterthwaite was breathing rather fast. He never enjoyed going up hill.

He looked towards the window. The face was still there, more life-like than ever.

'Our hostess has repented, I see.'

Porter threw it only a cursory glance.

'Unkerton cut up rough, I expect,' he said indifferently. 'He's the sort of man who is willing to be proud of another family's ghost, and who isn't going to run the risk of having it driven away when he's paid spot cash for it.'

He was silent a minute or two, staring, not at the house, but at the thick undergrowth by which they were surrounded.

'Has it ever struck you,' he said, 'that civilization's damned dangerous?'

'Dangerous?' Such a revolutionary remark shocked Mr Satterthwaite to the core.

'Yes. There are no safety valves, you see.'

He turned abruptly, and they descended the path by which they had come.

'I really am quite at a loss to understand you,' said Mr Satterthwaite, pattering along with nimble steps to keep up with the other's strides. 'Reasonable people –'

Porter laughed. A short disconcerting laugh. Then he looked at the correct little gentleman by his side.

'You think it's all bunkum on my part, Mr Satterthwaite? But there are people, you know, who can tell you when a storm's coming. They feel it beforehand in the air. And other people can foretell trouble. There's trouble coming now, Mr Satterthwaite, big trouble. It may come any minute. It may –'

He stopped dead, clutching Mr Satterthwaite's arm. And in that tense minute of silence it came – the sound of two shots and following them a cry – a cry in a woman's voice.

'My god!' cried Porter, 'it's come.'

He raced down the path, Mr Satterthwaite panting behind him. In a minute they came out on to the lawn, close by the hedge of the Privy Garden. At the same time, Richard Scott and Mr Unkerton came round the opposite corner of the house. They halted, facing each other, to left and right of the entrance to the Privy Garden.

'It – it came from in there,' said Unkerton, pointing with a flabby hand.

'We must see,' said Porter. He led the way into the enclosure. As he rounded the last bend of the holly hedge, he stopped dead. Mr Satterthwaite peered over his shoulder. A loud cry burst from Richard Scott.

There were three people in the Privy Garden. Two of them lay on the grass near the stone seat, a man and a woman. The third was Mrs Staverton. She was standing quite close to them by the holly hedge, gazing with horror-stricken eyes, and holding something in her right hand.

'Iris,' cried Porter. 'Iris. For God's sake! What's that you've got in your hand?'

She looked down at it then – with a kind of wonder, an unbelievable indifference.

'It's a pistol,' she said wonderingly. And then – after what seemed an interminable time, but was in reality only a few seconds, 'I – picked it up.'

Mr Satterthwaite had gone forward to where Unkerton and Scott were kneeling on the turf.

'A doctor,' the latter was murmuring. 'We must have a doctor.'

But it was too late for any doctor. Jimmy Allenson who had complained that the sand diviners hedged about the future, and Moira Scott to whom the gypsy had returned a shilling, lay there in the last great stillness.

It was Richard Scott who completed a brief examination. The iron nerve of the man showed in this crisis. After the first cry of agony, he was himself again.

He laid his wife gently down again.

'Shot from behind,' he said briefly. 'The bullet has passed right through her.'

Then he handled Jimmy Allenson. The wound here was in the breast and the bullet was lodged in the body.

John Porter came towards them.

'Nothing should be touched,' he said sternly. 'The police must see it all exactly as it is now.'

'The police,' said Richard Scott. His eyes lit up with a sudden flame as he looked at the woman standing by the holly hedge. He made a step in that direction, but at the same time John Porter also moved, so as to bar his way. For a moment it seemed as though there was a duel of eyes between the two friends.

Porter very quietly shook his head.

'No, Richard,' he said. 'It looks like it – but you're wrong.'

Richard Scott spoke with difficulty, moistening his dry lips.

'Then why – has she got that in her hand?'

And again Iris Staverton said in the same lifeless tone: 'I – picked it up.'

'The police,' said Unkerton rising. 'We must send for the police – at once. You will telephone perhaps, Scott? Someone should stay here – yes, I am sure someone should stay here.'

In his quiet gentlemanly manner, Mr Satterthwaite offered to do so. His host accepted the offer with manifest relief.

'The ladies,' he explained. 'I must break the news to the ladies, Lady Cynthia and my dear wife.'

Mr Satterthwaite stayed in the Privy Garden looking down on the body of that which had once been Moira Scott.

'Poor child,' he said to himself. 'Poor child . . .'

He quoted to himself the tag about the evil men do living after them. For was not Richard Scott in a way responsible for his innocent wife's death? They would hang Iris Staverton, he supposed, not that he liked to think of it, but was not it at least a part of the blame he laid at the man's door? The evil that men do –

And the girl, the innocent girl, had paid.

He looked down at her with a very deep pity. Her small face, so white and wistful, a half smile on the lips still. The ruffled golden hair, the delicate ear. There was a spot of blood on the lobe of it. With an inner feeling of being something of a detective, Mr Satterthwaite deduced an ear-ring, torn away in her fall. He craned his neck forward. Yes, he was right, there was a small pearl drop hanging from the other ear.

Poor child, poor child.

II

'And now, sir,' said Inspector Winkfield.

They were in the library. The Inspector, a shrewd-looking forceful man of forty odd, was concluding his investigations. He had questioned most of the guests, and had by now pretty well made up his mind on the case. He was listening to what Major Porter and Mr Satterthwaite had to say. Mr Unkerton sat heavily in a chair, staring with protruding eyes at the opposite wall.

'As I understand it, gentlemen,' said the Inspector, 'you'd been for a walk. You were returning to the house by a path that winds round the left side of what they call the Privy Garden. Is that correct?'

'Quite correct, Inspector.'

'You heard two shots, and a woman's scream?'

'Yes.'

'You then ran as fast as you could, emerged from the woods and made your way to the entrance of the Privy Garden. If anybody had left that garden, they could only do so by one entrance. The holly bushes are impassable. If anyone had run out of the garden and turned to the right, he would have been met by Mr Unkerton and Mr Scott. If he had turned to the left, he could not have done so without being seen by you. Is that right?'

'That is so,' said Major Porter. His face was very white.

'That seems to settle it,' said the Inspector. 'Mr and Mrs Unkerton and Lady Cynthia Drage were sitting on the lawn, Mr Scott was in the Billiard Room which opens on to that lawn. At ten minutes past six, Mrs Staverton came out of the house, spoke a word or two to those sitting there, and went round the corner of the house towards the Privy Garden. Two minutes later the shots were heard. Mr Scott rushed out of the house and together with Mr Unkerton ran to the Privy Garden. At the same time you and Mr – er – Satterthwaite arrived from the opposite direction. Mrs Staverton was in the Privy Garden with a pistol in her hand from which two shots had been fired. As I see it, she shot the lady first from behind as she was sitting on the bench. Then Captain Allenson sprang up and went for her, and she shot him in the chest as he came towards her. I understand that there had been a – er – previous attachment between her and Mr Richard Scott –'

'That's a damned lie,' said Porter.

His voice rang out hoarse and defiant. The Inspector said nothing, merely shook his head.

'What is her own story?' asked Mr Satterthwaite.

'She says that she went into the Privy Garden to be quiet for a little. Just before she rounded the last hedge, she heard the shots. She came round the corner, saw the pistol lying at her feet, and picked it up. No one passed her, and she saw no one in the garden but the two victims.' The Inspector gave an eloquent pause. 'That's what she says – and although I cautioned her, she insisted on making a statement.'

'If she said that,' said Major Porter, and his face was still deadly white, 'she was speaking the truth. I know Iris Staverton.'

'Well, sir,' said the Inspector, 'there'll be plenty of time to go into all that later. In the meantime, I've got my duty to do.'

With an abrupt movement, Porter turned to Mr Satterthwaite.

'You! Can't you help? Can't *you* do something?'

Mr Satterthwaite could not help feeling immensely flattered. He had been appealed to, he, most insignificant of men, and by a man like John Porter.

He was just about to flutter out a regretful reply, when the butler, Thompson, entered, with a card upon a salver which he took to his master with an apologetic cough. Mr Unkerton was still sitting huddled up in a chair, taking no part in the proceedings.

'I told the gentleman you would probably not be able to see him, sir,' said Thompson. 'But he insisted that he had an appointment and that it was most urgent.'

Unkerton took the card.

'Mr Harley Quin,' he read. 'I remember, he was to see me about a picture. I did make an appointment, but as things are –'

But Mr Satterthwaite had started forward.

'Mr Harley Quin, did you say?' he cried. 'How extraordinary, how very extraordinary. Major Porter, you asked me if I could help you. I think I can. This Mr Quin is a friend – or I should say, an acquaintance of mine. He is a most remarkable man.'

'One of these amateur solvers of crime, I suppose,' remarked the Inspector disparagingly.

'No,' said Mr Satterthwaite. 'He is not that kind of man at all. But he has a power – an almost uncanny power – of showing you what you have seen with your own eyes, of making clear to you what you have heard with your own ears. Let us, at any rate, give him an outline of the case, and hear what he has to say.'

Mr Unkerton glanced at the Inspector, who merely snorted and looked at the ceiling. Then the former gave a short nod to Thompson, who left the room and returned ushering in a tall, slim stranger.

'Mr Unkerton?' The stranger shook him by the hand. 'I am sorry to intrude upon you at such a time. We must leave our little picture chat until another time. Ah! my friend, Mr Satterthwaite. Still as fond of the drama as ever?'

A faint smile played for a minute round the stranger's lips as he said these last words.

'Mr Quin,' said Mr Satterthwaite impressively, 'we have a drama here, we are in the midst of one, I should like, and my friend, Major Porter, would like, to have your opinion of it.'

Mr Quin sat down. The red-shaded lamp threw a broad band of coloured light over the checked pattern of his overcoat, and left his face in shadow almost as though he wore a mask.

Succinctly, Mr Satterthwaite recited the main points of the tragedy. Then he paused, breathlessly awaiting the words of the oracle.

But Mr Quin merely shook his head.

'A sad story,' he said. 'A very sad and shocking tragedy. The lack of motive makes it very intriguing.'

Unkerton stared at him.

'You don't understand,' he said. 'Mrs Staverton was heard

to threaten Richard Scott. She was bitterly jealous of his wife. Jealousy –'

'I agree,' said Mr Quin. 'Jealousy or Demoniac Possession. It's all the same. But you misunderstand me. I was not referring to the murder of Mrs Scott, but to that of Captain Allenson.'

'You're right,' cried Porter, springing forward. 'There's a flaw there. If Iris had ever contemplated shooting Mrs Scott, she'd have got her alone somewhere. No, we're on the wrong tack. And I think I see another solution. Only those three people went into the Privy Garden. That is indisputable and I don't intend to dispute it. But I reconstruct the tragedy differently. Supposing Jimmy Allenson shoots first Mrs Scott and then himself. That's possible, isn't it? He flings the pistol from him as he falls – Mrs Staverton finds it lying on the ground and picks it up just as she said. How's that?'

The Inspector shook his head.

'Won't wash, Major Porter. If Captain Allenson had fired that shot close to his body, the cloth would have been singed.'

'He might have held the pistol at arm's length.'

'Why should he? No sense in it. Besides, there's no motive.'

'Might have gone off his head suddenly,' muttered Porter, but without any great conviction. He fell to silence again, suddenly rousing himself to say defiantly: 'Well, Mr Quin?'

The latter shook his head.

'I'm not a magician. I'm not even a criminologist. But I will tell you one thing – I believe in the value of impressions. In any time of crisis, there is always one moment that stands out from all the others, one picture that remains when all else has faded. Mr Satterthwaite is, I think, likely to have been the most unprejudiced observer of those present. Will you cast your mind back, Mr Satterthwaite, and tell us the moment that made the strongest impression on you? Was it when you heard the shots? Was it when you first saw the dead bodies? Was it when you first observed the pistol in Mrs Staverton's hand? Clear your mind of any preconceived standard of values, and tell us.'

Mr Satterthwaite fixed his eyes on Mr Quin's face, rather as a schoolboy might repeat a lesson of which he was not sure.

'No,' he said slowly. 'It was not any of those. The moment that I shall always remember was when I stood alone by the bodies –

afterwards – looking down on Mrs Scott. She was lying on her side. Her hair was ruffled. There was a spot of blood on her little ear.'

And instantly, as he said it, he felt that he had said a terrific, a significant thing.

'Blood on her ear? Yes, I remember,' said Unkerton slowly.

'Her ear-ring must have been torn out when she fell,' explained Mr Satterthwaite.

But it sounded a little improbable as he said it.

'She was lying on her left side,' said Porter. 'I suppose it was that ear?'

'No,' said Mr Satterthwaite quickly. 'It was her right ear.'

The Inspector coughed.

'I found this in the grass,' he vouchsafed. He held up a loop of gold wire.

'But my God, man,' cried Porter. 'The thing can't have been wrenched to pieces by a mere fall. It's more as though it had been shot away by a bullet.'

'So it was,' cried Mr Satterthwaite. 'It was a bullet. It must have been.'

'There were only two shots,' said the Inspector. 'A shot can't have grazed her ear and shot her in the back as well. And if one shot carried away the ear-ring, and the second shot killed her, it can't have killed Captain Allenson as well – not unless he was standing close in front of her – very close – facing her as it might be. Oh! no, not even then, unless, that is –'

'Unless she was in his arms, you were going to say,' said Mr Quin, with a queer little smile. 'Well, why not?'

Everyone stared at each other. The idea was so vitally strange to them – Allenson and Mrs Scott – Mr Unkerton voiced the same feeling.

'But they hardly knew each other,' he said.

'I don't know,' said Mr Satterthwaite thoughtfully. 'They might have known each other better than we thought. Lady Cynthia said he saved her from being bored in Egypt last winter, and you' – he turned to Porter – 'you told me that Richard Scott met his wife in Cairo last winter. They might have known each other very well indeed out there . . .'

'They didn't seem to be together much,' said Unkerton.

'No – they rather avoided each other. It was almost unnatural, now I come to think of it –'

They all looked at Mr Quin, as if a little startled at the conclusions at which they had arrived so unexpectedly.

Mr Quin rose to his feet.

'You see,' he said, 'what Mr Satterthwaite's impression has done for us.' He turned to Unkerton. 'It is your turn now.'

'Eh? I don't understand you.'

'You were very thoughtful when I came into this room. I should like to know exactly what thought it was that obsessed you. Never mind if it has nothing to do with the tragedy. Never mind if it seems to you – superstitious –' Mr Unkerton started, ever so slightly. 'Tell us.'

'I don't mind telling you,' said Unkerton. 'Though it's nothing to do with the business, and you'll probably laugh at me into the bargain. I was wishing that my Missus had left well alone and not replaced that pane of glass in the haunted window. I feel as though doing that has maybe brought a curse upon us.'

He was unable to understand why the two men opposite him stared so.

'But she hasn't replaced it yet,' said Mr Satterthwaite at last.

'Yes, she has. Man came first thing this morning.'

'My God!' said Porter, 'I begin to understand. That room, it's panelled, I supposed, not papered?'

'Yes, but what does that –?'

But Porter had swung out of the room. The others followed him. He went straight upstairs to the Scotts' bedroom. It was a charming room, panelled in cream with two windows facing south. Porter felt with his hands along the panels on the western wall.

'There's a spring somewhere – must be. Ah!' There was a click, and a section of the panelling rolled back. It disclosed the grimy panes of the haunted window. One pane of glass was clean and new. Porter stooped quickly and picked up something. He held it out on the palm of his hand. It was a fragment of ostrich feather. Then he looked at Mr Quin. Mr Quin nodded.

He went across to the hat cupboard in the bedroom. There were several hats in it – the dead woman's hats. He took out one with a large brim and curling feathers – an elaborate Ascot hat.

Mr Quin began speaking in a gentle, reflective voice.

'Let us suppose,' said Mr Quin, 'a man who is by nature intensely jealous. A man who has stayed here in bygone years and knows the secret of the spring in the panelling. To amuse himself he opens it one day, and looks out over the Privy Garden. There, secure as they think from being overlooked, he sees his wife and another man. There can be no possible doubt in his mind as to the relations between them. He is mad with rage. What shall he do? An idea comes to him. He goes to the cupboard and puts on the hat with the brim and feathers. It is growing dusk, and he remembers the story of the stain on the glass. Anyone looking up at the window will see as they think the Watching Cavalier. Thus secure he watches them, and at the moment they are clasped in each other's arms, he shoots. He is a good shot – a wonderful shot. As they fall, he fires once more – that shot carries away the ear-ring. He flings the pistol out of the window into the Privy Garden, rushes downstairs and out through the billiard room.'

Porter took a step towards him.

'But he let her be accused!' he cried. 'He stood by and let her be accused. Why? Why?'

'I think I know why,' said Mr Quin. 'I should guess – it's only guess-work on my part, mind – that Richard Scott was once madly in love with Iris Staverton – so madly that even meeting her years afterwards stirred up the embers of jealousy again. I should say that Iris Staverton once fancied that she might love him, that she went on a hunting trip with him and another – and that she came back in love with the better man.'

'The better man,' muttered Porter, dazed. 'You mean –?'

'Yes,' said Mr Quin, with a faint smile. 'I mean you.' He paused a minute, and then said: 'If I were you – I should go to her now.'

'I will,' said Porter.

He turned and left the room.

CHAPTER 3

At the 'Bells and Motley'

Mr Satterthwaite was annoyed. Altogether it had been an unfortunate day. They had started late, there had been two punctures already, finally they had taken the wrong turning and lost themselves amidst the wilds of Salisbury Plain. Now it was close on eight o'clock, they were still a matter of forty miles from Marswick Manor whither they were bound, and a third puncture had supervened to render matters still more trying.

Mr Satterthwaite, looking like some small bird whose plumage had been ruffled, walked up and down in front of the village garage whilst his chauffeur conversed in hoarse undertones with the local expert.

'Half an hour at *least*,' said that worthy pronouncing judgment.

'And lucky at that,' supplemented Masters, the chauffeur. 'More like three quarters if you ask me.'

'What is this – place, anyway?' demanded Mr Satterthwaite fretfully. Being a little gentleman considerate of the feelings of others, he substituted the word 'place' for 'God-forsaken hole' which had first risen to his lips.

'Kirtlington Mallet.'

Mr Satterthwaite was not much wiser, and yet a faint familiarity seemed to linger round the name. He looked round him disparagingly. Kirtlington Mallet seemed to consist of one straggling street, the garage and the post office on one side of it balanced by three indeterminate shops on the other side. Farther down the road, however, Mr Satterthwaite perceived something that creaked and swung in the wind, and his spirits rose ever so slightly.

'There's an Inn here, I see,' he remarked.

'"Bells and Motley",' said the garage man. 'That's it – yonder.'

'If I might make a suggestion, sir,' said Masters, 'why not try it? They would be able to give you some sort of a meal, no doubt – not, of course, what you are accustomed to.' He paused apologetically, for Mr Satterthwaite was accustomed to the best cooking of continental chefs, and had in his own service a *cordon bleu* to whom he paid a fabulous salary.

'We shan't be able to take the road again for another three quarters of an hour, sir. I'm sure of that. And it's already past eight o'clock. You could ring up Sir George Foster, sir, from the Inn, and acquaint him with the cause of our delay.'

'You seem to think you can arrange everything, Masters,' said Mr Satterthwaite snappily.

Masters, who did think so, maintained a respectful silence.

Mr Satterthwaite, in spite of his earnest wish to discountenance any suggestion that might possibly be made to him – he was in that mood – nevertheless looked down the road towards the creaking Inn sign with faint inward approval. He was a man of birdlike appetite, an epicure, but even such men can be hungry.

'The "Bells and Motley",' he said thoughtfully. 'That's an odd name for an Inn. I don't know that I ever heard it before.'

'There's odd folks come to it by all account,' said the local man.

He was bending over the wheel, and his voice came muffled and indistinct.

'Odd folks?' queried Mr Satterthwaite. 'Now what do you mean by that?'

The other hardly seemed to know what he meant.

'Folks that come and go. That kind,' he said vaguely.

Mr Satterthwaite reflected that people who come to an Inn are almost of necessity those who 'come and go'. The definition seemed to him to lack precision. But nevertheless his curiosity was stimulated. Somehow or other he had got to put in three quarters of an hour. The 'Bells and Motley' would be as good as anywhere else.

With his usual small mincing steps he walked away down the road. From afar there came a rumble of thunder. The mechanic looked up and spoke to Masters.

'There's a storm coming over. Thought I could feel it in the air.'

'Crikey,' said Masters. 'And forty miles to go.'

'Ah!' said the other. 'There's no need to be hurrying over this job. You'll not be wanting to take the road till the storm's passed over. That little boss of yours doesn't look as though he'd relish being out in thunder and lightning.'

'Hope they'll do him well at that place,' muttered the chauffeur. 'I'll be pushing along there for a bite myself presently.'

'Billy Jones is all right,' said the garage man. 'Keeps a good table.'

Mr William Jones, a big burly man of fifty and landlord of the 'Bells and Motley', was at this minute beaming ingratiatingly down on little Mr Satterthwaite.

'Can do you a nice steak, sir – *and* fried potatoes, and as good a cheese as any gentleman could wish for. This way, sir, in the coffee-room. We're not very full at present, the last of the fishing gentlemen just gone. A little later we'll be full again for the hunting. Only one gentleman here at present, name of Quin –'

Mr Satterthwaite stopped dead.

'Quin?' he said excitedly. 'Did you say Quin?'

'That's the name, sir. Friend of yours perhaps?'

'Yes, indeed. Oh! yes, most certainly.' Twittering with excitement, Mr Satterthwaite hardly realized that the world might contain more than one man of that name. He had no doubts at all. In an odd way, the information fitted in with what the man at the garage had said. 'Folks that come and go . . .' a very apt description of Mr Quin. And the name of the Inn, too, seemed a peculiarly fitting and appropriate one.

'Dear me, dear me,' said Mr Satterthwaite. 'What a *very* odd thing. That we should meet like this! Mr Harley Quin, is it not?'

'That's right, sir. This is the coffee-room, sir. Ah! here is the gentleman.'

Tall, dark, smiling, the familiar figure of Mr Quin rose from the table at which he was sitting, and the well-remembered voice spoke.

'Ah! Mr Satterthwaite, we meet again. An unexpected meeting!'

Mr Satterthwaite was shaking him warmly by the hand.

'Delighted. Delighted, I'm sure. A lucky breakdown for me. My car, you know. And you are staying here? For long?'

'One night only.'

'Then I am indeed fortunate.'

Mr Satterthwaite sat down opposite his friend with a little sigh of satisfaction, and regarded the dark, smiling face opposite him with a pleasurable expectancy.

The other man shook his head gently.

'I assure you,' he said, 'that I have not a bowl of goldfish or a rabbit to produce from my sleeve.'

'Too bad,' cried Mr Satterthwaite, a little taken aback. 'Yes, I must confess – I do rather adopt that attitude towards you. A man of magic. Ha, ha. That is how I regard you. A man of magic.'

'And yet,' said Mr Quin, 'it is you who do the conjuring tricks, not I.'

'Ah!' said Mr Satterthwaite eagerly. 'But I cannot do them without you. I lack – shall we say – inspiration?'

Mr Quin smilingly shook his head.

'That is too big a word. I speak the cue, that is all.'

The landlord came in at that minute with bread and a slab of yellow butter. As he set the things on the table there was a vivid flash of lightning, and a clap of thunder almost overhead.

'A wild night, gentlemen.'

'On such a night –' began Mr Satterthwaite, and stopped.

'Funny now,' said the landlord, unconscious of the question, 'if those weren't just the words I was going to use myself. It was just such a night as this when Captain Harwell brought his bride home, the very day before he disappeared for ever.'

'Ah!' cried Mr Satterthwaite suddenly. 'Of course!'

He had got the clue. He knew now why the name Kirtlington Mallet was familiar. Three months before he had read every detail of the astonishing disappearance of Captain Richard Harwell. Like other newspaper readers all over Great Britain he had puzzled over the details of the disappearance, and, also like every other Briton, had evolved his own theories.

'Of course,' he repeated. 'It was at Kirtlington Mallet it happened.'

'It was at this house he stayed for the hunting last winter,' said the landlord. 'Oh! I knew him well. A main handsome young gentleman and not one that you'd think had a care on his mind. He was done away with – that's my belief. Many's the time I've seen them come riding home together – he and Miss Le Couteau, and all the village saying there'd be a match come of it – and sure enough, so it did. A very beautiful young lady, and well thought of, for all she was a Canadian and a stranger. Ah! there's some dark mystery there. We'll never know the rights of it. It broke her heart, it did, sure enough. You've heard as she's sold the place up and gone abroad, couldn't bear to go on here with everyone staring and pointing after her – through no fault of her own, poor young dear! A black mystery, that's what it is.'

He shook his head, then suddenly recollecting his duties, hurried from the room.

'A black mystery,' said Mr Quin softly.

His voice was provocative in Mr Satterthwaite's ears.

'Are you pretending that we can solve the mystery where Scotland Yard failed?' he asked sharply.

The other made a characteristic gesture.

'Why not? Time has passed. Three months. That makes a difference.'

'That is a curious idea of yours,' said Mr Satterthwaite slowly. 'That one sees things better afterwards than at the time.'

'The longer the time that has elapsed, the more things fall into proportion. One sees them in their true relationship to one another.'

There was a silence which lasted for some minutes.

'I am not sure,' said Mr Satterthwaite, in a hesitating voice, 'that I remember the facts clearly by now.'

'I think you do,' said Mr Quin quietly.

It was all the encouragement Mr Satterthwaite needed. His general role in life was that of listener and looker-on. Only in the company of Mr Quin was the position reversed. There Mr Quin was the appreciative listener, and Mr Satterthwaite took the centre of the stage.

'It was just over a year ago,' he said, 'that Ashley Grange passed into the possession of Miss Eleanor Le Couteau. It is a beautiful old house, but it had been neglected and allowed to remain empty for many years. It could not have found a better chatelaine. Miss Le Couteau was a French Canadian, her forebears were *émigrés* from the French Revolution, and had handed down to her a collection of almost priceless French relics and antiques. She was a buyer and a collector also, with a very fine and discriminating taste. So much so, that when she decided to sell Ashley Grange and everything it contained after the tragedy, Mr Cyrus G. Bradburn, the American millionaire, made no bones about paying the fancy price of sixty thousand pounds for the Grange as it stood.'

Mr Satterthwaite paused.

'I mention these things,' he said apologetically, 'not because they are relevant to the story – strictly speaking, they are not – but to convey an atmosphere, the atmosphere of young Mrs Harwell.'

Mr Quin nodded.

'Atmosphere is always valuable,' he said gravely.

'So we get a picture of this girl,' continued the other. 'Just twenty-three, dark, beautiful, accomplished, nothing crude and unfinished about her. And rich – we must not forget that. She was an orphan. A Mrs St Clair, a lady of unimpeachable breeding and social standing, lived with her as duenna. But Eleanor Le Couteau had complete control of her own fortune. And fortune-hunters are never hard to seek. At least a dozen impecunious young men were to be found dangling round her on all occasions, in the hunting field, in the ballroom, wherever she went. Young Lord Leccan, the most eligible *parti* in the country, is reported to have asked her to marry him, but she remained heart free. That is, until the coming of Captain Richard Harwell.

'Captain Harwell had put up at the local Inn for the hunting. He was a dashing rider to hounds. A handsome, laughing daredevil of a fellow. You remember the old saying, Mr Quin? "Happy the wooing that's not long doing." The adage was carried out at least in part. At the end of two months, Richard Harwell and Eleanor Le Couteau were engaged.

'The marriage followed three months afterwards. The happy pair went abroad for a two weeks' honeymoon, and then returned to take up their residence at Ashley Grange. The landlord has just told us that it was on a night of storm such as this that they returned to their home. An omen, I wonder? Who can tell? Be that as it may, the following morning very early – about half-past seven, Captain Harwell was seen walking in the garden by one of the gardeners, John Mathias. He was bareheaded, and was whistling. We have a picture there, a picture of light-heartedness, of careless happiness. And yet from that minute, as far as we know, no one ever set eyes on Captain Richard Harwell again.'

Mr Satterthwaite paused, pleasantly conscious of a dramatic moment. The admiring glance of Mr Quin gave him the tribute he needed, and he went on.

'The disappearance was remarkable – unaccountable. It was not till the following day that the distracted wife called in the police. As you know, they have not succeeded in solving the mystery.'

'There have, I suppose, been theories?' asked Mr Quin.

'Oh! theories, I grant you. Theory No. 1, that Captain Harwell had been murdered, done away with. But if so, where was the body? It could hardly have been spirited away. And besides, what motive was there? As far as was known, Captain Harwell had not an enemy in the world.'

He paused abruptly, as though uncertain. Mr Quin leaned forward.

'You are thinking,' he said softly, 'of young Stephen Grant.'

'I am,' admitted Mr Satterthwaite. 'Stephen Grant, if I remember rightly, had been in charge of Captain Harwell's horses, and had been discharged by his master for some trifling offence. On the morning after the homecoming, very early, Stephen Grant was seen in the vicinity of Ashley Grange, and could give no good account of his presence there. He was detained by the police as being concerned in the disappearance of Captain Harwell, but nothing could be proved against him, and he was eventually discharged. It is true that he might be supposed to bear a grudge against Captain Harwell for his summary dismissal, but the motive was undeniably of the flimsiest. I suppose the police felt they must do something. You see, as I said just now, Captain Harwell had not an enemy in the world.'

'As far as was known,' said Mr Quin reflectively.

Mr Satterthwaite nodded appreciatively.

'We are coming to that. What, after all, *was* known of Captain Harwell? When the police came to look into his antecedents they were confronted with a singular paucity of material. Who was Richard Harwell? Where did he come from? He had appeared, literally out of the blue as it seemed. He was a magnificent rider, and apparently well off. Nobody in Kirtlington Mallet had bothered to inquire further. Miss Le Couteau had had no parents or guardians to make inquiries into the prospects and standing of her fiancé. She was her own mistress. The police theory at this point was clear enough. A rich girl and an impudent impostor. The old story!

'But it was not quite that. True, Miss Le Couteau had no parents or guardians, but she had an excellent firm of solicitors in London who acted for her. Their evidence made the mystery deeper. Eleanor Le Couteau had wished to settle a sum outright upon her prospective husband, but he had refused. He himself was well off, he declared. It was proved conclusively that Harwell never had a penny of his wife's money. Her fortune was absolutely intact.

'He was, therefore, no common swindler, but was his object a refinement of the art? Did he propose blackmail at some future date if Eleanor Harwell should wish to marry some other man? I will admit that something of that kind seemed to me the most likely solution. It had always seemed so to me – until tonight.'

Mr Quin leaned forward, prompting him.

'Tonight?'

'Tonight. I am not satisfied with that. How did he manage to disappear so suddenly and completely – at that hour in the morning, with every labourer bestirring himself and tramping to work? Bareheaded, too.'

'There is no doubt about the latter point – since the gardener saw him?'

'Yes – the gardener – John Mathias. Was there anything there, I wonder?'

'The police would not overlook him,' said Mr Quin.

'They questioned him closely. He never wavered in his statement. His wife bore him out. He left his cottage at seven to attend to the greenhouses, he returned at twenty minutes to eight. The servants in the house heard the front door slam at about a quarter after seven. That fixes the time when Captain Harwell left the house. Ah! yes, I know what you are thinking.'

'Do you, I wonder?' said Mr Quin.

'I fancy so. Time enough for Mathias to have made away with his master. But why, man, why? And if so, where did he hide the body?'

The landlord came in bearing a tray.

'Sorry to have kept you so long, gentlemen.'

He set upon the table a mammoth steak and beside it a dish filled to overflowing with crisp brown potatoes. The odour from the dishes was pleasant to Mr Satterthwaite's nostrils. He felt gracious.

'This looks excellent,' he said. 'Most excellent. We have been discussing the disappearance of Captain Harwell. What became of the gardener, Mathias?'

'Took a place in Essex, I believe. Didn't care to stay hereabouts. There were some as looked askance at him, you understand. Not that I ever believe he had anything to do with it.'

Mr Satterthwaite helped himself to steak. Mr Quin followed suit. The landlord seemed disposed to linger and chat. Mr Satterthwaite had no objection, on the contrary.

'This Mathias now,' he said. 'What kind of a man was he?'

'Middle-aged chap, must have been a powerful fellow once but bent and crippled with rheumatism. He had that mortal bad, was laid up many a time with it, unable to do any work. For my part, I think it was sheer kindness on Miss Eleanor's part to keep him on. He'd outgrown his usefulness as a gardener, though his wife managed to make herself useful up at the house. Been a cook she had, and always willing to lend a hand.'

'What sort of a woman was she?' asked Mr Satterthwaite, quickly.

The landlord's answer disappointed him.

'A plain body. Middle-aged, and dour like in manner. Deaf, too. Not that I ever knew much of them. They'd only been here a month, you understand, when the thing happened. They say he'd been a rare good gardener in his time, though. Wonderful testimonials Miss Eleanor had with him.'

'Was she interested in gardening?' asked Mr Quin, softly.

'No, sir, I couldn't say that she was, not like some of the ladies round here who pay good money to gardeners and spend the whole of their time grubbing about on their knees as well. Foolishness I call it. You see, Miss Le Couteau wasn't here very much except in the winter for hunting. The rest of the time she was up in London and away in those foreign seaside places where they say the French ladies don't so much as put a toe into the water for fear of spoiling their costumes, or so I've heard.'

Mr Satterthwaite smiled.

'There was no – er – woman of any kind mixed up with Captain Harwell?' he asked.

Though his first theory was disposed of, he nevertheless clung to his idea.

Mr William Jones shook his head.

'Nothing of that sort. Never a whisper of it. No, it's a dark mystery, that's what it is.'

'And your theory? What do you yourself think?' persisted Mr Satterthwaite.

'What do I think?'

'Yes.'

'Don't know what to think. It's my belief as how he was done in, but who by I can't say. I'll fetch you gentlemen the cheese.'

He stumped from the room bearing empty dishes. The storm, which had been quietening down, suddenly broke out with redoubled vigour. A flash of forked lightning and a great clap of thunder close upon each other made little Mr Satterthwaite jump, and before the last echoes of the thunder had died away, a girl came into the room carrying the advertised cheese.

She was tall and dark, and handsome in a sullen fashion of her own. Her likeness to the landlord of the 'Bells and Motley' was apparent enough to proclaim her his daughter.

'Good evening, Mary,' said Mr Quin. 'A stormy night.'

She nodded.

'I hate these stormy nights,' she muttered.

'You are afraid of thunder, perhaps?' said Mr Satterthwaite kindly.

'Afraid of thunder? Not me! There's little that I'm afraid of. No, but the storm sets them off. Talking, talking, the same thing over and over again, like a lot of parrots. Father begins it. "It reminds me, this does, of the night poor Captain Harwell . . ." And so on, and so on.' She turned on Mr Quin. 'You've heard how he goes on. What's the sense of it? Can't anyone let past things be?'

'A thing is only past when it is done with,' said Mr Quin.

'Isn't this done with? Suppose he wanted to disappear? These fine gentlemen do sometimes.'

'You think he disappeared of his own free will?'

'Why not? It would make better sense than to suppose a kind-hearted creature like Stephen Grant murdered him. What should he murder him for, I should like to know? Stephen had had a drop too much one day and spoke to him saucy like, and got the sack for it. But what of it? He got another place just as good. Is that a reason to murder a man in cold blood?'

'But surely,' said Mr Satterthwaite, 'the police were quite satisfied of his innocence?'

'The police! What do the police matter? When Stephen comes into the bar of an evening, every man looks at him queer like. They don't really believe he murdered Harwell, but they're not sure, and so they look at him sideways and edge away. Nice life for a man, to see people shrink away from you, as though you were something different from the rest of folks. Why won't Father hear of our getting married, Stephen and I? "You can take your pigs to a better market, my girl. I've nothing against Stephen, but – well, we don't know, do we?"'

She stopped, her breast heaving with the violence of her resentment.

'It's cruel, cruel, that's what it is,' she burst out. 'Stephen, that wouldn't hurt a fly! And all through life there'll be people who'll think he did. It's turning him queer and bitter like. I don't wonder, I'm sure. And the more he's like that, the more people think there must have been something in it.'

Again she stopped. Her eyes were fixed on Mr Quin's face, as though something in it was drawing this outburst from her.

'Can nothing be done?' said Mr Satterthwaite.

He was genuinely distressed. The thing was, he saw, inevitable. The very vagueness and unsatisfactoriness of the evidence against Stephen Grant made it the more difficult for him to disprove the accusation.

The girl whirled round on him.

'Nothing but the truth can help him,' she cried. 'If Captain Harwell were to be found, if he was to come back. If the true rights of it were only known –'

She broke off with something very like a sob, and hurried quickly from the room.

'A fine-looking girl,' said Mr Satterthwaite. 'A sad case altogether.

I wish – I very much wish that something could be done about it.'

His kind heart was troubled.

'We are doing what we can,' said Mr Quin. 'There is still nearly half an hour before your car can be ready.'

Mr Satterthwaite stared at him.

'You think we can come at the truth just by – talking it over like this?'

'You have seen much of life,' said Mr Quin gravely. 'More than most people.'

'Life has passed me by,' said Mr Satterthwaite bitterly.

'But in so doing has sharpened your vision. Where others are blind you can see.'

'It is true,' said Mr Satterthwaite. 'I am a great observer.'

He plumed himself complacently. The moment of bitterness was passed.

'I look at it like this,' he said after a minute or two. 'To get at the cause for a thing, we must study the effect.'

'Very good,' said Mr Quin approvingly.

'The effect in this case is that Miss Le Couteau – Mrs Harwell, I mean, is a wife and yet not a wife. She is not free – she cannot marry again. And look at it as we will, we see Richard Harwell as a sinister figure, a man from nowhere with a mysterious past.'

'I agree,' said Mr Quin. 'You see what all are bound to see, what cannot be missed, Captain Harwell in the limelight, a suspicious figure.'

Mr Satterthwaite looked at him doubtfully. The words seemed somehow to suggest a faintly different picture to his mind.

'We have studied the effect,' he said. 'Or call it the *result*. We can now pass –'

Mr Quin interrupted him.

'You have not touched on the result on the strictly material side.'

'You are right,' said Mr Satterthwaite, after a moment or two for consideration. 'One should do the thing thoroughly. Let us say then that the result of the tragedy is that Mrs Harwell is a wife and not a wife, unable to marry again, that Mr Cyrus Bradburn has been able to buy Ashley Grange and its contents for – sixty thousand pounds, was it? – and that somebody in Essex has been able to secure John Mathias as a gardener! For all that we do not suspect "somebody in Essex" or Mr Cyrus Bradburn of having engineered the disappearance of Captain Harwell.'

'You are sarcastic,' said Mr Quin.

Mr Satterthwaite looked sharply at him.

'But surely you agree –?'

'Oh! I agree,' said Mr Quin. 'The idea is absurd. What next?'

'Let us imagine ourselves back on the fatal day. The disappearance has taken place, let us say, this very morning.'

'No, no,' said Mr Quin, smiling. 'Since, in our imagination, at least, we have power over time, let us turn it the other way. Let us say the disappearance of Captain Harwell took place a hundred years ago. That we, in the year two thousand twenty-five are looking back.'

'You are a strange man,' said Mr Satterthwaite slowly. 'You believe in the past, not the present. Why?'

'You used, not long ago, the word atmosphere. There is no atmosphere in the present.'

'That is true, perhaps,' said Mr Satterthwaite thoughtfully. 'Yes, it is true. The present is apt to be – parochial.'

'A good word,' said Mr Quin.

Mr Satterthwaite gave a funny little bow.

'You are too kind,' he said.

'Let us take – not this present year, that would be too difficult, but say – last year,' continued the other. 'Sum it up for me, you who have the gift of the neat phrase.'

Mr Satterthwaite thought for a minute. He was jealous of his reputation.

'A hundred years ago we have the age of powder and patches,' he said. 'Shall we say that 1924 was the age of Crossword Puzzles and Cat Burglars?'

'Very good,' approved Mr Quin. 'You mean that nationally, not internationally, I presume?'

'As to Crossword Puzzles, I must confess that I do not know,' said Mr Satterthwaite. 'But the Cat Burglar had a great innings on the Continent. You remember that series of famous thefts from French châteaux? It is surmised that one man alone could not have done it. The most miraculous feats were performed to gain admission. There was a theory that a troupe of acrobats were concerned – the Clondinis. I once saw their performance – truly masterly. A mother, son and daughter. They vanished from the stage in a rather mysterious fashion. But we are wandering from our subject.'

'Not very far,' said Mr Quin. 'Only across the Channel.'

'Where the French ladies will not wet their toes, according to our worthy host,' said Mr Satterthwaite, laughing.

There was a pause. It seemed somehow significant.

'Why did he disappear?' cried Mr Satterthwaite. 'Why? Why? It is incredible, a kind of conjuring trick.'

'Yes,' said Mr Quin. 'A conjuring trick. That describes it exactly. Atmosphere again, you see. And wherein does the essence of a conjuring trick lie?'

'The quickness of the hand deceives the eye,' quoted Mr Satterthwaite glibly.

'That is everything, is it not? To deceive the eye? Sometimes by the quickness of the hand, sometimes – by other means. There are many devices, the pistol shot, the waving of a red handkerchief, something that seems important, but in reality is not. The eye is diverted from the real business, it is caught by the spectacular action that means nothing – nothing at all.'

Mr Satterthwaite leant forward, his eyes shining.

'There is something in that. It is an idea.'

He went on softly. 'The pistol shot. What was the pistol shot in the conjuring trick we were discussing? What is the spectacular moment that holds the imagination?'

He drew in his breath sharply.

'The disappearance,' breathed Mr Satterthwaite. 'Take that away, and it leaves nothing.'

'Nothing? Suppose things took the same course without that dramatic gesture?'

'You mean – supposing Miss Le Couteau were still to sell Ashley Grange and leave – for no reason?'

'Well.'

'Well, why not? It would have aroused talk, I suppose, there would have been a lot of interest displayed in the value of the contents in – Ah! wait!'

He was silent a minute, then burst out.

'You are right, there is too much limelight, the limelight on

Captain Harwell. And because of that, *she* has been in shadow. *Miss Le Couteau!* Everyone asking "Who was Captain Harwell? Where did he come from?" But because she is the injured party, no one makes inquiries about her. Was she really a French Canadian? Were those wonderful heirlooms really handed down to her? You were right when you said just now that we had not wandered far from our subject – *only across the Channel.* Those so-called heirlooms were stolen from the French châteaux, most of them valuable *objets d'art*, and in consequence difficult to dispose of. She buys the house – for a mere song, probably. Settles down there and pays a good sum to an irreproachable English woman to chaperone her. Then *he* comes. The plot is laid beforehand. The marriage, the disappearance and the nine days' wonder! What more natural than that a broken-hearted woman should want to sell everything that reminds her of her past happiness. The American is a connoisseur, the things are genuine and beautiful, some of them beyond price. He makes an offer, she accepts it. She leaves the neighbourhood, a sad and tragic figure. The great *coup* has come off. The eye of the public has been deceived by the quickness of the hand and the spectacular nature of the trick.'

Mr Satterthwaite paused, flushed with triumph.

'But for you, I should never have seen it,' he said with sudden humility. 'You have a most curious effect upon me. One says things so often without even seeing what they really mean. You have the knack of showing one. But it is still not quite clear to me. It must have been most difficult for Harwell to disappear as he did. After all, the police all over England were looking for him.'

'It would have been simplest to remain hidden at the Grange,' mused Mr Satterthwaite. 'If it could be managed.'

'He was, I think, very near the Grange,' said Mr Quin.

His look of significance was not lost on Mr Satterthwaite.

'Mathias' cottage?' he exclaimed. 'But the police must have searched it?'

'Repeatedly, I should imagine,' said Mr Quin.

'Mathias,' said Mr Satterthwaite, frowning.

'And Mrs Mathias,' said Mr Quin.

Mr Satterthwaite stared hard at him.

'If that gang was really the Clondinis,' he said dreamily, 'there were three of them in it. The two young ones were Harwell and Eleanor Le Couteau. The mother now, was she Mrs Mathias? But in that case . . .'

'Mathias suffered from rheumatism, did he not?' said Mr Quin innocently.

'Oh!' cried Mr Satterthwaite. 'I have it. But could it be done? I believe it could. Listen. Mathias was there a month. During that time, Harwell and Eleanor were away for a fortnight on a honeymoon. For the fortnight before the wedding, they were supposedly in town. A clever man could have doubled the parts of Harwell and Mathias. When Harwell was at Kirtlington Mallet, Mathias was conveniently laid up with rheumatism, with Mrs Mathias to sustain the fiction. Her part was very necessary. Without her, someone might have suspected the truth. As you say, Harwell was hidden in Mathias' cottage. He *was* Mathias. When at last the plans matured, and Ashley Grange was sold, he and his wife gave out they were taking a place in Essex. Exit John Mathias and his wife – for ever.'

There was a knock at the coffee-room door, and Masters entered. 'The car is at the door, sir,' he said.

Mr Satterthwaite rose. So did Mr Quin, who went across to the window, pulling the curtains. A beam of moonlight streamed into the room.

'The storm is over,' he said.

Mr Satterthwaite was pulling on his gloves.

'The Commissioner is dining with me next week,' he said importantly. 'I shall put my theory – ah! – before him.'

'It will be easily proved or disproved,' said Mr Quin. 'A comparison of the objects at Ashley Grange with a list supplied by the French police –!'

'Just so,' said Mr Satterthwaite. 'Rather hard luck on Mr Bradburn, but – well –'

'He can, I believe, stand the loss,' said Mr Quin.

Mr Satterthwaite held out his hand.

'Goodbye,' he said. 'I cannot tell you how much I have appreciated this unexpected meeting. You are leaving here tomorrow, I think you said?'

'Possibly tonight. My business here is done . . . I come and go, you know.'

Mr Satterthwaite remembered hearing those same words earlier in the evening. Rather curious.

He went out to the car and the waiting Masters. From the open door into the bar the landlord's voice floated out, rich and complacent.

'A dark mystery,' he was saying. 'A dark mystery, that's what it is.'

But he did not use the word 'dark'. The word he used suggested quite a different colour. Mr William Jones was a man of discrimination who suited his adjectives to his company. The company in the bar liked their adjectives full flavoured.

Mr Satterthwaite reclined luxuriously in the comfortable limousine. His breast was swelled with triumph. He saw the girl Mary come out on the steps and stand under the creaking Inn sign.

'She little knows,' said Mr Satterthwaite to himself. 'She little knows what *I* am going to do!'

The sign of the 'Bells and Motley' swayed gently in the wind.

CHAPTER 4

The Sign in the Sky

The Judge was finishing his charge to the jury.

'Now, gentlemen, I have almost finished what I want to say to you. There is evidence for you to consider as to whether this case is plainly made out against this man so that you may say he is guilty of the murder of Vivien Barnaby. You have had the evidence of the servants as to the time the shot was fired. They have one and all agreed upon it. You have had the evidence of the letter written to the defendant by Vivien Barnaby on the morning of that same day, Friday, September 13th – a letter which the defence has not attempted to deny. You have had evidence that the prisoner first denied having been at Deering Hill, and later, after evidence had been given by the police, admitted he had. You will draw your own conclusions from that denial. This is not a case of direct evidence. You will have to come to your own conclusions on the subject of motive – of means, of opportunity. The contention of the defence is that some person unknown entered the music room after the defendant had left it, and shot Vivien Barnaby with the gun which, by strange forgetfulness, the defendant had left behind him. You have heard the defendant's story of the reason it took him half an hour to get home. If you disbelieve the defendant's story and are satisfied, beyond any reasonable doubt, that the defendant did, upon Friday, September 13th, discharge his gun at close quarters to Vivien Barnaby's head with intent to kill her, then, gentlemen, your verdict must be Guilty. If, on the other hand, you have any reasonable doubt, it is your duty to acquit the prisoner. I will now ask you to retire to your room and consider and let me know when you have arrived at a conclusion.'

The jury were absent a little under half an hour. They returned the verdict that to everyone had seemed a foregone conclusion, the verdict of 'Guilty'.

Mr Satterthwaite left the court after hearing the verdict, with a thoughtful frown on his face.

A mere murder trial as such did not attract him. He was of too fastidious a temperament to find interest in the sordid details of the average crime. But the Wylde case had been different. Young Martin Wylde was what is termed a gentleman – and the victim, Sir George Barnaby's young wife, had been personally known to the elderly gentleman.

He was thinking of all this as he walked up Holborn, and then plunged into a tangle of mean streets leading in the direction of Soho. In one of these streets there was a small restaurant, known only to the few, of whom Mr Satterthwaite was one. It was not cheap – it was, on the contrary, exceedingly expensive, since it catered exclusively for the palate of the jaded *gourmet*. It was quiet – no strains of jazz were allowed to disturb the hushed atmosphere – it was rather dark, waiters appeared soft-footed out of the twilight, bearing silver dishes with the air of participating in some holy rite. The name of the restaurant was Arlecchino.

Still thoughtful, Mr Satterthwaite turned into the Arlecchino and made for his favourite table in a recess in the far corner. Owing to the twilight before mentioned, it was not until he was quite close to it that he saw it was already occupied by a tall dark man who sat with his face in shadow, and with a play of colour from a stained window turning his sober garb into a kind of riotous motley.

Mr Satterthwaite would have turned back, but just at that moment the stranger moved slightly and the other recognized him.

'God bless my soul,' said Mr Satterthwaite, who was given to old-fashioned expressions. 'Why, it's Mr Quin!'

Three times before he had met Mr Quin, and each time the meeting had resulted in something a little out of the ordinary. A strange person, this Mr Quin, with a knack of showing you the things you had known all along in a totally different light.

At once Mr Satterthwaite felt excited – pleasurably excited. His role was that of the looker-on, and he knew it, but sometimes when in the company of Mr Quin he had the illusion of being an actor – and the principal actor at that.

'This is very pleasant,' he said, beaming all over his dried-up little face. 'Very pleasant indeed. You've no objection to my joining you, I hope?'

'I shall be delighted,' said Mr Quin. 'As you see, I have not yet begun my meal.'

A deferential head waiter hovered up out of the shadows. Mr Satterthwaite, as befitted a man with a seasoned palate, gave his whole mind to the task of selection. In a few minutes, the head waiter, a slight smile of approbation on his lips, retired, and a young satellite began his ministrations. Mr Satterthwaite turned to Mr Quin.

'I have just come from the Old Bailey,' he began. 'A sad business, I thought.'

'He was found guilty?' said Mr Quin.

'Yes, the jury were out only half an hour.'

Mr Quin bowed his head.

'An inevitable result – on the evidence,' he said.

'And yet,' began Mr Satterthwaite – and stopped.

Mr Quin finished the sentence for him.

'And yet your sympathies were with the accused? Is that what you were going to say?'

'I suppose it was. Martin Wylde is a nice-looking young fellow – one can hardly believe it of him. All the same, there have been a good many nice-looking young fellows lately who have turned out to be murderers of a particularly cold-blooded and repellent type.'

'Too many,' said Mr Quin quietly.

'I beg your pardon?' said Mr Satterthwaite, slightly startled.

'Too many for Martin Wylde. There has been a tendency from the beginning to regard this as just one more of a series of the same type of crime – a man seeking to free himself from one woman in order to marry another.'

'Well,' said Mr Satterthwaite doubtfully. 'On the evidence –'

'Ah!' said Mr Quin quickly. 'I am afraid I have not followed all the evidence.'

Mr Satterthwaite's self-confidence came back to him with a rush. He felt a sudden sense of power. He was tempted to be consciously dramatic.

'Let me try and show it to you. I have met the Barnabys, you understand. I know the peculiar circumstances. With me, you will come behind the scenes – you will see the thing from inside.'

Mr Quin leant forward with his quick encouraging smile.

'If anyone can show me that, it will be Mr Satterthwaite,' he murmured.

Mr Satterthwaite gripped the table with both hands. He was uplifted, carried out of himself. For the moment, he was an artist pure and simple – an artist whose medium was words.

Swiftly, with a dozen broad strokes, he etched in the picture of life at Deering Hill. Sir George Barnaby, elderly, obese, purse-proud. A man perpetually fussing over the little things of life. A man who wound up his clocks every Friday afternoon, and who paid his own house-keeping books every Tuesday morning, and who always saw to the locking of his own front door every night. A careful man.

And from Sir George he went on to Lady Barnaby. Here his touch was gentler, but none the less sure. He had seen her but once, but his impression of her was definite and lasting. A vivid defiant creature – pitifully young. A trapped child, that was how he described her.

'She hated him, you understand? She had married him before she knew what she was doing. And now –'

She was desperate – that was how he put it. Turning this way and that. She had no money of her own, she was entirely dependent on this elderly husband. But all the same she was a creature at bay – still unsure of her own powers, with a beauty that was as yet more promise than actuality. And she was greedy. Mr Satterthwaite affirmed that definitely. Side by side with defiance there ran a greedy streak – a clasping and a clutching at life.

'I never met Martin Wylde,' continued Mr Satterthwaite. 'But I heard of him. He lived less than a mile away. Farming, that was his line. And she took an interest in farming – or pretended to. If you ask me, it was pretending. I think that she saw in him her only way of escape – and she grabbed at him, greedily, like a child might have done. Well, there could only be one end to that. We know what that end was, because the letters were read out in court. He kept her letters – she didn't keep his, but from the text of hers one can see that he was cooling off. He admits as much. There was the other girl. She also lived in the village of Deering Vale. Her father was the doctor there. You saw her in court, perhaps? No, I remember, you were not there, you said. I shall have to describe her to you. A fair girl – very fair. Gentle. Perhaps – yes, perhaps a tiny bit stupid. But very restful, you know. And loyal. Above all, loyal.'

He looked at Mr Quin for encouragement, and Mr Quin gave it him by a slow appreciative smile. Mr Satterthwaite went on.

'You heard that last letter read – you must have seen it, in the papers, I mean. The one written on the morning of Friday, September 13th. It was full of desperate reproaches and vague threats, and it ended by begging Martin Wylde to come to Deering Hill that same evening at six o'clock. "*I will leave the side door open for you, so that no one need know you have been here. I shall be in the music room.*" It was sent by hand.'

Mr Satterthwaite paused for a minute or two.

'When he was first arrested, you remember, Martin Wylde denied that he had been to the house at all that evening. His statement was that he had taken his gun and gone out shooting in the woods. But when the police brought forward their evidence, that statement broke down. They had found his finger-prints, you remember, both on the wood of the side door and on one of the two cocktail glasses on the table in the music room. He admitted then that he had come to see Lady Barnaby, that they had had a stormy interview, but that it had ended in his having managed to soothe her down. He swore that he left his gun outside leaning against the wall near the door, and that he left Lady Barnaby alive and well, the time being then a minute or two after a quarter past six. He went straight home, he says. But evidence was called to show that he did not reach his farm until a quarter to seven, and as I have just mentioned, it is barely a mile away. It would not take half an hour to get there. He forgot all about his gun, he declares. Not a very likely statement – and yet –'

'And yet?' queried Mr Quin.

'Well,' said Mr Satterthwaite slowly, 'it's a possible one, isn't it? Counsel ridiculed the supposition, of course, but I think he was wrong. You see, I've known a good many young men, and these emotional scenes upset them very much – especially the dark, nervous type like Martin Wylde. Women now, can go through a scene like that and feel positively better for it afterwards, with all their wits about them. It acts like a safety valve for them, steadies their nerves down and all that. But I can see Martin Wylde going away with his head in a whirl, sick and miserable, and without a thought of the gun he had left leaning up against the wall.'

He was silent for some minutes before he went on.

'Not that it matters. For the next part is only too clear, unfortunately. It was exactly twenty minutes past six when the shot was heard. All the servants heard it, the cook, the kitchen-maid, the butler, the housemaid and Lady Barnaby's own maid. They came rushing to the music room. She was lying huddled over the arm of her chair. The gun had been discharged close to the back of her head, so that the shot hadn't a chance to scatter. At least two of them penetrated the brain.'

He paused again and Mr Quin asked casually:

'The servants gave evidence, I suppose?'

Mr Satterthwaite nodded.

'Yes. The butler got there a second or two before the others, but their evidence was practically a repetition of each other's.'

'So they *all* gave evidence,' said Mr Quin musingly. 'There were no exceptions?'

'Now I remember it,' said Mr Satterthwaite, 'the housemaid was only called at the inquest. She's gone to Canada since, I believe.'

'I see,' said Mr Quin.

There was a silence, and somehow the air of the little restaurant seemed to be charged with an uneasy feeling. Mr Satterthwaite felt suddenly as though he were on the defensive.

'Why shouldn't she?' he said abruptly.

'Why should she?' said Mr Quin with a very slight shrug of the shoulders.

Somehow, the question annoyed Mr Satterthwaite. He wanted to shy away from it – to get back on familiar ground.

'There couldn't be much doubt who fired the shot. As a matter of fact the servants seemed to have lost their heads a bit. There was no one in the house to take charge. It was some minutes before anyone thought of ringing up the police, and when they did so they found that the telephone was out of order.'

'Oh!' said Mr Quin. 'The telephone was out of order.'

'It was,' said Mr Satterthwaite – and was struck suddenly by the feeling that he had said something tremendously important. 'It might, of course, have been done on purpose,' he said slowly. 'But there seems no point in that. Death was practically instantaneous.'

Mr Quin said nothing, and Mr Satterthwaite felt that his explanation was unsatisfactory.

'There was absolutely no one to suspect but young Wylde,' he went on. 'By his own account, even, he was only out of the house three minutes before the shot was fired. And who else could have fired it? Sir George was at a bridge party a few houses away. He left there at half-past six and was met just outside the gate by a servant bringing him the news. The last rubber finished at half-past six exactly – no doubt about that. Then there was Sir George's secretary, Henry Thompson. He was in London that day, and actually at a business meeting at the moment the shot was fired. Finally, there is Sylvia Dale, who after all, had a perfectly good motive, impossible as it seems that she should have had anything to do with such a crime. She was at the station of Deering Vale seeing a friend off by the 6.28 train. That lets her out. Then the servants. What earthly motive could any one of them have? Besides they all arrived on the spot practically simultaneously. No, it must have been Martin Wylde.'

But he said it in a dissatisfied kind of voice.

They went on with their lunch. Mr Quin was not in a talkative mood, and Mr Satterthwaite had said all he had to say. But the silence was not a barren one. It was filled with the growing dissatisfaction of Mr Satterthwaite, heightened and fostered in some strange way by the mere acquiescence of the other man.

Mr Satterthwaite suddenly put down his knife and fork with a clatter.

'Supposing that that young man is really innocent,' he said. 'He's going to be hanged.'

He looked very startled and upset about it. And still Mr Quin said nothing.

'It's not as though –' began Mr Satterthwaite, and stopped. 'Why shouldn't the woman go to Canada?' he ended inconsequently.

Mr Quin shook his head.

'I don't even know what part of Canada she went to,' continued Mr Satterthwaite peevishly.

'Could you find out?' suggested the other.

'I suppose I could. The butler, now. He'd know. Or possibly Thompson, the secretary.'

He paused again. When he resumed speech, his voice sounded almost pleading.

'It's not as though it were anything to do with me?'

'That a young man is going to be hanged in a little over three weeks?'

'Well, yes – if you put it that way, I suppose. Yes, I see what you mean. Life and death. And that poor girl, too. It's not that I'm hard-headed – but, after all – what good will it do? Isn't the whole thing rather fantastic? Even if I found out where the woman's gone in Canada – why, it would probably mean that I should have to go out there myself.'

Mr Satterthwaite looked seriously upset.

'And I was thinking of going to the Riviera next week,' he said pathetically.

And his glance towards Mr Quin said as plainly as it could be said, 'Do let me off, won't you?'

'You have never been to Canada?'

'Never.'

'A very interesting country.'

Mr Satterthwaite looked at him undecidedly.

'You think I ought to go?'

Mr Quin leaned back in his chair and lighted a cigarette. Between puffs of smoke, he spoke deliberately.

'You are, I believe, a rich man, Mr Satterthwaite. Not a millionaire, but a man able to indulge a hobby without counting the expense. You have looked on at the dramas of other people. Have you never contemplated stepping in and playing a part? Have you never seen yourself for a minute as the arbiter of other people's destinies – standing in the centre of the stage with life and death in your hands?'

Mr Satterthwaite leant forward. The old eagerness surged over him.

'You mean – if I go on this wild-goose chase to Canada –?'

Mr Quin smiled.

'Oh! it was your suggestion, going to Canada, not mine,' he said lightly.

'You can't put me off like that,' said Mr Satterthwaite earnestly. 'Whenever I have come across you –' He stopped.

'Well?'

'There is something about you I do not understand. Perhaps I never shall. The last time I met you –'

'On Midsummer's Eve.'

Mr Satterthwaite was startled, as though the words held a clue that he did not quite understand.

'Was it Midsummer's Eve?' he asked confusedly.

'Yes. But let us not dwell on that. It is unimportant, is it not?'

'Since you say so,' said Mr Satterthwaite courteously. He felt that elusive clue slipping through his fingers. 'When I come back from Canada' – he paused a little awkwardly – 'I – I – should much like to see you again.'

'I am afraid I have no fixed address for the moment,' said Mr Quin regretfully. 'But I often come to this place. If you also frequent it, we shall no doubt meet before very long.'

They parted pleasantly.

Mr Satterthwaite was very excited. He hurried round to Cook's and inquired about boat sailings. Then he rang up Deering Hill. The voice of a butler, suave and deferential, answered him.

'My name is Satterthwaite. I am speaking for a – er – firm of solicitors. I wished to make a few inquiries about a young woman who was recently housemaid in your establishment.'

'Would that be Louisa, sir? Louisa Bullard?'

'That is the name,' said Mr Satterthwaite, very pleased to be told it.

'I regret she is not in this country, sir. She went to Canada six months ago.'

'Can you give me her present address?'

The butler was afraid he couldn't. It was a place in the mountains she had gone to – a Scotch name – ah! Banff, that was it. Some of the other young women in the house had been expecting to hear from her, but she had never written or given them any address.

Mr Satterthwaite thanked him and rang off. He was still undaunted. The adventurous spirit was strong in his breast.

He would go to Banff. If this Louisa Bullard was there, he would track her down somehow or other.

To his own surprise, he enjoyed the trip greatly. It was many years since he had taken a long sea voyage. The Riviera, Le Touquet and Deauville, and Scotland had been his usual round. The feeling that he was setting off on an impossible mission added a secret zest to his journey. What an utter fool these fellow travellers of his would think him did they but know the object of his quest! But then – they were not acquainted with Mr Quin.

In Banff he found his objective easily attained. Louisa Bullard was employed in the large Hotel there. Twelve hours after his arrival he was standing face to face with her.

She was a woman of about thirty-five, anaemic looking, but with a strong frame. She had pale brown hair inclined to curl, and a pair of honest brown eyes. She was, he thought, slightly stupid, but very trustworthy.

She accepted quite readily his statement that he had been asked to collect a few further facts from her about the tragedy at Deering Hill.

'I saw in the paper that Mr Martin Wylde had been convicted, sir. Very sad, it is, too.'

She seemed, however, to have no doubt as to his guilt.

'A nice young gentleman gone wrong. But though I wouldn't speak ill of the dead, it was her ladyship what led him on. Wouldn't leave him alone, she wouldn't. Well, they've both got their punishment. There's a text used to hang on my wall when I was a child, "God is not mocked," and it's very true. I knew something was going to happen that very evening – and sure enough it did.'

'How was that?' said Mr Satterthwaite.

'I was in my room, sir, changing my dress, and I happened to glance out of the window. There was a train going along, and the white smoke of it rose up in the air, and if you'll believe me it formed itself into the sign of a gigantic hand. A great white hand against the crimson of the sky. The fingers were crooked like, as though they were reaching out for something. It fair gave me a turn. "Did you ever now?" I said to myself. "That's a sign of something coming" – and sure enough at that very minute I heard the shot. "It's come," I said to myself, and I rushed downstairs and joined Carrie and the others who were in the hall, and we went into the music room and there she was, shot through the head – and the blood and everything. Horrible! I spoke up, I did, and told Sir George how I'd seen the sign beforehand, but he didn't seem to think much of it. An unlucky day, that was, I'd felt it in my bones from early in the morning. Friday, and the 13th – what could you expect?'

She rambled on. Mr Satterthwaite was patient. Again and again he took her back to the crime, questioning her closely. In the end he was forced to confess defeat. Louisa Bullard had told all she knew, and her story was perfectly simple and straightforward.

Yet he did discover one fact of importance. The post in question had been suggested to her by Mr Thompson, Sir George's secretary. The wages attached were so large that she was tempted, and accepted the job, although it involved her leaving England very hurriedly. A Mr Denman had made all the arrangements this end and had also warned her not to write to her fellow-servants in England, as this might 'get her into trouble with the immigration authorities', which statement she had accepted in blind faith.

The amount of wages, casually mentioned by her, was indeed so large that Mr Satterthwaite was startled. After some hesitation he made up his mind to approach this Mr Denman.

He found very little difficulty in inducing Mr Denman to tell all he knew. The latter had come across Thompson in London and Thompson had done him a good turn. The secretary had written to him in September saying that for personal reasons Sir George was anxious to get this girl out of England. Could he find her a job? A sum of money had been sent to raise the wages to a high figure.

'Usual trouble, I guess,' said Mr Denman, leaning back nonchalantly in his chair. 'Seems a nice quiet girl, too.'

Mr Satterthwaite did not agree that this was the usual trouble. Louisa Bullard, he was sure, was not a cast-off fancy of Sir George Barnaby's. For some reason it had been vital to get her out of England. But why? And who was at the bottom of it? Sir George himself, working through Thompson? Or the latter working on his own initiative, and dragging in his employer's name?

Still pondering over these questions, Mr Satterthwaite made the return journey. He was cast down and despondent. His journey had done no good.

Smarting under a sense of failure, he made his way to the *Arlecchino* the day after his return. He hardly expected to be successful the first time, but to his satisfaction the familiar figure was sitting at the table in the recess, and the dark face of Mr Harley Quin smiled a welcome.

'Well,' said Mr Satterthwaite as he helped himself to a pat of butter, 'you sent me on a nice wild-goose chase.'

Mr Quin raised his eyebrows.

'I sent you?' he objected. 'It was your own idea entirely.'

'Whosever idea it was, it's not succeeded. Louisa Bullard has nothing to tell.'

Thereupon Mr Satterthwaite related the details of his conversation with the housemaid and then went on to his interview with Mr Denman. Mr Quin listened in silence.

'In one sense, I was justified,' continued Mr Satterthwaite. 'She was deliberately got out of the way. But why? I can't see it.'

'No?' said Mr Quin, and his voice was, as ever, provocative.

Mr Satterthwaite flushed.

'I daresay you think I might have questioned her more adroitly. I can assure you that I took her over the story again and again. It was not my fault that I did not get what we want.'

'Are you sure,' said Mr Quin, 'that you did not get what you want?'

Mr Satterthwaite looked up at him in astonishment, and met that sad, mocking gaze he knew so well.

The little man shook his head, slightly bewildered.

There was a silence, and then Mr Quin said, with a total change of manner:

'You gave me a wonderful picture the other day of the people in this business. In a few words you made them stand out as clearly as though they were etched. I wish you would do something of that kind for the place – you left that in shadow.'

Mr Satterthwaite was flattered.

'The place? Deering Hill? Well, it's a very ordinary sort of house nowadays. Red brick, you know, and bay windows. Quite hideous outside, but very comfortable inside. Not a very large house. About two acres of ground. They're all much the same, those houses round the links. Built for rich men to live in. The inside of the house is reminiscent of a hotel – the bedrooms are like hotel suites. Baths and hot and cold basins in all the bedrooms and a good many gilded electric-light fittings. All wonderfully comfortable, but not very country-like. You can tell that Deering Vale is only nineteen miles from London.'

Mr Quin listened attentively.

'The train service is bad, I have heard,' he remarked.

'Oh! I don't know about that,' said Mr Satterthwaite, warming to his subject. 'I was down there for a bit last summer. I found it quite convenient for town. Of course the trains only go every hour. Forty-eight minutes past the hour from Waterloo – up to 10.48.'

'And how long does it take to Deering Vale?'

'Just about three-quarters of an hour. Twenty-eight minutes past the hour at Deering Vale.'

'Of course,' said Mr Quin with a gesture of vexation. 'I should have remembered. Miss Dale saw someone off by the 6.28 that evening, didn't she?'

Mr Satterthwaite did not reply for a minute or two. His mind had gone back with a rush to his unsolved problem. Presently he said:

'I wish you would tell me what you meant just now when you asked me if I was sure I had not got what I wanted?'

It sounded rather complicated, put that way, but Mr Quin made no pretence of not understanding.

'I just wondered if you weren't being a little too exacting. After all, you found out that Louisa Bullard was deliberately got out of the country. That being so, there must be a reason. And the reason must lie in what she said to you.'

'Well,' said Mr Satterthwaite argumentatively. 'What did she say? If she'd given evidence at the trial, what could she have said?'

'She might have told what she saw,' said Mr Quin.

'What did she see?'

'A sign in the sky.'

Mr Satterthwaite stared at him.

'Are you thinking of *that* nonsense? That superstitious notion of its being the hand of God?'

'Perhaps,' said Mr Quin, 'for all you and I know it may have been the hand of God, you know.'

The other was clearly puzzled at the gravity of his manner.

'Nonsense,' he said. 'She said herself it was the smoke of the train.'

'An up train or a down train, I wonder?' murmured Mr Quin.

'Hardly an up train. They go at ten minutes to the hour. It must have been a down train – the 6.28 – no, that won't do. She said the shot came immediately afterwards, and we know the shot was fired at twenty minutes past six. The train couldn't have been ten minutes early.'

'Hardly, on that line,' agreed Mr Quin.

Mr Satterthwaite was staring ahead of him.

'Perhaps a goods train,' he murmured. 'But surely, if so –'

'There would have been no need to get her out of England. I agree,' said Mr Quin.

Mr Satterthwaite gazed at him, fascinated.

'The 6.28,' he said slowly. 'But if so, if the shot was fired then, why did everyone say it was earlier?'

'Obvious,' said Mr Quin. 'The clocks must have been wrong.'

'All of them?' said Mr Satterthwaite doubtfully. 'That's a pretty tall coincidence, you know.'

'I wasn't thinking of it as a coincidence,' said the other. 'I was thinking it was Friday.'

'Friday?' said Mr Satterthwaite.

'You did tell me, you know, that Sir George always wound the clocks on a Friday afternoon,' said Mr Quin apologetically.

'He put them back ten minutes,' said Mr Satterthwaite, almost in a whisper, so awed was he by the discoveries he was making. 'Then he went out to bridge. I think he must have opened the note from his wife to Martin Wylde that morning – yes, decidedly he opened it. He left his bridge party at 6.30, found Martin's gun standing by the side door, and went in and shot her from behind. Then he went out again, threw the gun into the bushes where it was found later, and was apparently just coming out of the neighbour's gate when someone came running to fetch him. But the telephone – what about the telephone? Ah! yes, I see. He disconnected it so that a summons could not be sent to the police that way – they might have noted the time it was received.

And Wylde's story works out now. The real time he left was five and twenty minutes past six. Walking slowly, he would reach home about a quarter to seven. Yes, I see it all. Louisa was the only danger with her endless talk about her superstitious fancies. Someone might realize the significance of the train and then – goodbye to that excellent *alibi*.'

'Wonderful,' commented Mr Quin.

Mr Satterthwaite turned to him, flushed with success.

'The only thing is – how to proceed now?'

'I should suggest Sylvia Dale,' said Mr Quin.

Mr Satterthwaite looked doubtful.

'I mentioned to you,' he said, 'she seemed to me a little – er – stupid.'

'She has a father and brothers who will take the necessary steps.'

'That is true,' said Mr Satterthwaite, relieved.

A very short time afterwards he was sitting with the girl telling her the story. She listened attentively. She put no questions to him but when he had done she rose.

'I must have a taxi – at once.'

'My dear child, what are you going to do?'

'I am going to Sir George Barnaby.'

'Impossible. Absolutely the wrong procedure. Allow me to –'

He twittered on by her side. But he produced no impression. Sylvia Dale was intent on her own plans. She allowed him to go with her in the taxi, but to all his remonstrances she addressed a deaf ear. She left him in the taxi while she went into Sir George's city office.

It was half an hour later when she came out. She looked exhausted, her fair beauty drooping like a waterless flower. Mr Satterthwaite received her with concern.

'I've won,' she murmured, as she leant back with half-closed eyes.

'What?' He was startled. 'What did you do? What did you say?'

She sat up a little.

'I told him that Louisa Bullard had been to the police with her story. I told him that the police had made inquiries and that he had been seen going into his own grounds and out again a few minutes after half-past six. I told him that the game was up. He – he went to pieces. I told him that there was still time for him to get away, that the police weren't coming for another hour to arrest him. I told him that if he'd sign a confession that he'd killed Vivien I'd do nothing, but that if he didn't I'd scream and tell the whole building the truth. He was so panicky that he didn't know what he was doing. He signed the paper without realizing what he was doing.'

She thrust it into his hands.

'Take it – take it. You know what to do with it so that they'll set Martin free.'

'He actually signed it,' cried Mr Satterthwaite, amazed.

'He is a little stupid, you know,' said Sylvia Dale. 'So am I,' she added as an afterthought. 'That's why I know how stupid people behave. We get rattled, you know, and then we do the wrong thing and are sorry afterwards.'

She shivered and Mr Satterthwaite patted her hand.

'You need something to pull you together,' he said. 'Come, we are close to a very favourite resort of mine – the *Arlecchino*. Have you ever been there?'

She shook her head.

Mr Satterthwaite stopped the taxi and took the girl into the little restaurant. He made his way to the table in the recess, his heart beating hopefully. But the table was empty.

Sylvia Dale saw the disappointment in his face.

'What is it?' she asked.

'Nothing,' said Mr Satterthwaite. 'That is, I half expected to see a friend of mine here. It doesn't matter. Some day, I expect, I shall see him again . . .'

CHAPTER 5

The Soul of the Croupier

Mr Satterthwaite was enjoying the sunshine on the terrace at Monte Carlo.

Every year regularly on the second Sunday in January, Mr Satterthwaite left England for the Riviera. He was far more punctual than any swallow. In the month of April he returned to England, May and June he spent in London, and had never been known to miss Ascot. He left town after the Eton and Harrow match, paying a few country house visits before repairing to Deauville or Le Touquet. Shooting parties occupied most of September and October, and he usually spent a couple of months in town to wind up the year. He knew everybody and it may safely be said that everybody knew him.

This morning he was frowning. The blue of the sea was admirable, the gardens were, as always, a delight, but the people disappointed him – he thought them an ill-dressed, shoddy crowd. Some, of course, were gamblers, doomed souls who could not keep away. Those Mr Satterthwaite tolerated. They were a necessary background. But he missed the usual leaven of the *élite* – his own people.

'It's the exchange,' said Mr Satterthwaite gloomily. 'All sorts of people come here now who could never have afforded it before. And then, of course, I'm getting old . . . All the young people – the people coming on – they go to these Swiss places.'

But there were others that he missed, the well-dressed Barons and Counts of foreign diplomacy, the Grand Dukes and the Royal Princes. The only Royal Prince he had seen so far was working a lift in one of the less well-known hotels. He missed, too, the beautiful and expensive ladies. There was still a few of them, but not nearly as many as there used to be.

Mr Satterthwaite was an earnest student of the drama called

Life, but he liked his material to be highly coloured. He felt discouragement sweep over him. Values were changing – and he – was too old to change.

It was at that moment that he observed the Countess Czarnova coming towards him.

Mr Satterthwaite had seen the Countess at Monte Carlo for many seasons now. The first time he had seen her she had been in the company of a Grand Duke. On the next occasion she was with an Austrian Baron. In successive years her friends had been of Hebraic extraction, sallow men with hooked noses, wearing rather flamboyant jewellery. For the last year or two she was much seen with very young men, almost boys.

She was walking with a very young man now. Mr Satterthwaite happened to know him, and he was sorry. Franklin Rudge was a young American, a typical product of one of the Middle West States, eager to register impression, crude, but loveable, a curious mixture of native shrewdness and idealism. He was in Monte Carlo with a party of other young Americans of both sexes, all much of the same type. It was their first glimpse of the Old World and they were outspoken in criticism and in appreciation.

On the whole they disliked the English people in the hotel, and the English people disliked them. Mr Satterthwaite, who prided himself on being a cosmopolitan, rather liked them. Their directness and vigour appealed to him, though their occasional solecisms made him shudder.

It occurred to him that the Countess Czarnova was a most unsuitable friend for young Franklin Rudge.

He took off his hat politely as they came abreast of him, and the Countess gave him a charming bow and smile.

She was a very tall woman, superbly made. Her hair was black, so were her eyes, and her eyelashes and eyebrows were more superbly black than any Nature had ever fashioned.

Mr Satterthwaite, who knew far more of feminine secrets than it is good for any man to know, rendered immediate homage to the art with which she was made up. Her complexion appeared to be flawless, of a uniform creamy white.

The very faint bistre shadows under her eyes were most effective. Her mouth was neither crimson nor scarlet, but a subdued wine colour. She was dressed in a very daring creation of black and white and carried a parasol of the shade of pinky red which is most helpful to the complexion.

Franklin Rudge was looking happy and important.

'There goes a young fool,' said Mr Satterthwaite to himself. 'But I suppose it's no business of mine and anyway he wouldn't listen to me. Well, well, I've bought experience myself in my time.'

But he still felt rather worried, because there was a very attractive little American girl in the party, and he was sure that she would not like Franklin Rudge's friendship with the Countess at all.

He was just about to retrace his steps in the opposite direction when he caught sight of the girl in question coming up one of the paths towards him. She wore a well-cut tailor-made 'suit' with a white muslin shirt waist, she had on good, sensible walking shoes, and carried a guide-book. There are some Americans who pass through Paris and emerge clothed as the Queen of Sheba, but Elizabeth Martin was not one of them. She was 'doing Europe' in a stern, conscientious spirit. She had high ideas of culture and art and she was anxious to get as much as possible for her limited store of money.

It is doubtful if Mr Satterthwaite thought of her as either cultured or artistic. To him she merely appeared very young.

'Good morning, Mr Satterthwaite,' said Elizabeth. 'Have you seen Franklin – Mr Rudge – anywhere about?'

'I saw him just a few minutes ago.'

'With his friend the Countess, I suppose,' said the girl sharply.

'Er – with the Countess, yes,' admitted Mr Satterthwaite.

'That Countess of his doesn't cut any ice with me,' said the girl in a rather high, shrill voice. 'Franklin's just crazy about her. *Why* I can't think.'

'She's got a very charming manner, I believe,' said Mr Satterthwaite cautiously.

'Do you know her?'

'Slightly.'

'I'm right down worried about Franklin,' said Miss Martin. 'That boy's got a lot of sense as a rule. You'd never think he'd fall for this sort of siren stuff. And he won't hear a thing, he gets madder than a hornet if anyone tries to say a word to him. Tell me, anyway – is she a real Countess?'

'I shouldn't like to say,' said Mr Satterthwaite. 'She may be.'

'That's the real Ha Ha English manner,' said Elizabeth with signs of displeasure. 'All I can say is that in Sargon Springs – that's our home town, Mr Satterthwaite – that Countess would look a mighty queer bird.'

Mr Satterthwaite thought it possible. He forebore to point out that they were not in Sargon Springs but in the principality of Monaco, where the Countess happened to synchronize with her environment a great deal better than Miss Martin did.

He made no answer and Elizabeth went on towards the Casino. Mr Satterthwaite sat on a seat in the sun, and was presently joined by Franklin Rudge.

Rudge was full of enthusiasm.

'I'm enjoying myself,' he announced with naïve enthusiasm. 'Yes, sir! This is what I call seeing life – rather a different kind of life from what we have in the States.'

The elder man turned a thoughtful face to him.

'Life is lived very much the same everywhere,' he said rather wearily. 'It wears different clothes – that's all.'

Franklin Rudge stared.

'I don't get you.'

'No,' said Mr Satterthwaite. 'That's because you've got a long way to travel yet. But I apologize. No elderly man should permit himself to get into the habit of preaching.'

'Oh! that's all right.' Rudge laughed, displaying the beautiful teeth of all his countrymen. 'I don't say, mind you, that I'm not disappointed in the Casino. I thought the gambling would be different – something much more feverish. It seems just rather dull and sordid to me.'

'Gambling is life and death to the gambler, but it has no great spectacular value,' said Mr Satterthwaite. 'It is more exciting to read about than to see.'

The young man nodded his agreement.

'You're by way of being rather a big bug socially, aren't you?' he asked with a diffident candour that made it impossible to take offence. 'I mean, you know all the Duchesses and Earls and Countesses and things.'

'A good many of them,' said Mr Satterthwaite. 'And also the Jews and the Portuguese and the Greeks and the Argentines.'

'Eh?' said Mr Rudge.

'I was just explaining,' said Mr Satterthwaite, 'that I move in English society.'

Franklin Rudge meditated for a moment or two.

'You know the Countess Czarnova, don't you?' he said at length.

'Slightly,' said Mr Satterthwaite, making the same answer he had made to Elizabeth.

'Now there's a woman whom it's been very interesting to meet. One's inclined to think that the aristocracy of Europe is played out and effete. That may be true of the men, but the women are different. Isn't it a pleasure to meet an exquisite creature like the Countess? Witty, charming, intelligent, generations of civilization behind her, an aristocrat to her finger-tips!'

'Is she?' asked Mr Satterthwaite.

'Well, isn't she? You know what her family are?'

'No,' said Mr Satterthwaite. 'I'm afraid I know very little about her.'

'She was a Radzynski,' explained Franklin Rudge. 'One of the oldest families in Hungary. She's had the most extraordinary life. You know that great rope of pearls she wears?'

Mr Satterthwaite nodded.

'That was given her by the King of Bosnia. She smuggled some secret papers out of the kingdom for him.'

'I heard,' said Mr Satterthwaite, 'that the pearls had been given her by the King of Bosnia.'

The fact was indeed a matter of common gossip, it being reported that the lady had been a *chère amie* of His Majesty's in days gone by.

'Now I'll tell you something more.'

Mr Satterthwaite listened, and the more he listened the more he admired the fertile imagination of the Countess Czarnova. No vulgar 'siren stuff' (as Elizabeth Martin had put it) for her. The young man was shrewd enough in that way, clean living and idealistic. No, the Countess moved austerely through a labyrinth of diplomatic intrigues. She had enemies, detractors – naturally! It was a glimpse, so the young American was made to feel, into the life of the old régime with the Countess as the central figure, aloof, aristocratic, the friend of counsellors and princes, a figure to inspire romantic devotion.

'And she's had any amount to contend against,' ended the young man warmly. 'It's an extraordinary thing but she's never found a woman who would be a real friend to her. Women have been against her all her life.'

'Probably,' said Mr Satterthwaite.

'Don't you call it a scandalous thing?' demanded Rudge hotly.

'N – no,' said Mr Satterthwaite thoughtfully. 'I don't know that I do. Women have got their own standards, you know. It's no good our mixing ourselves up in their affairs. They must run their own show.'

'I don't agree with you,' said Rudge earnestly. 'It's one of the worst things in the world today, the unkindness of woman to woman. You know Elizabeth Martin? Now she agrees with me in theory absolutely. We've often discussed it together. She's only a kid, but her ideas are all right. But the moment it comes to a practical test – why, she's as bad as any of them. Got a real down on the Countess without knowing a darned thing about her, and won't listen when I try to tell her things. It's all *wrong*, Mr Satterthwaite. I believe in democracy – and – what's that but brotherhood between men and sisterhood between women?'

He paused earnestly. Mr Satterthwaite tried to think of any circumstances in which a sisterly feeling might arise between the Countess and Elizabeth Martin and failed.

'Now the Countess, on the other hand,' went on Rudge, 'admires Elizabeth immensely, and thinks her charming in every way. Now what does that show?'

'It shows,' said Mr Satterthwaite dryly, 'that the Countess has lived a considerable time longer than Miss Martin has.'

Franklin Rudge went off unexpectedly at a tangent.

'Do you know how old she is? She told me. Rather sporting of her. I should have guessed her to be twenty-nine, but she told me of her own accord that she was thirty-five. She doesn't look it, does she?' Mr Satterthwaite, whose private estimate of the lady's age was between forty-five and forty-nine, merely raised his eyebrows.

'I should caution you against believing all you are told at Monte Carlo,' he murmured.

He had enough experience to know the futility of arguing with the lad. Franklin Rudge was at a pitch of white hot chivalry when he would have disbelieved any statement that was not backed with authoritative proof.

'Here is the Countess,' said the boy, rising.

She came up to them with the languid grace that so became her. Presently they all three sat down together. She was very charming to Mr Satterthwaite, but in rather an aloof manner. She deferred to him prettily, asking his opinion, and treating him as an authority on the Riviera.

The whole thing was cleverly managed. Very few minutes had elapsed before Franklin Rudge found himself gracefully but unmistakably dismissed, and the Countess and Mr Satterthwaite were left *tête-à-tête*.

She put down her parasol and began drawing patterns with it in the dust.

'You are interested in the nice American boy, Mr Satterthwaite, are you not?'

Her voice was low with a caressing note in it.

'He's a nice young fellow,' said Mr Satterthwaite, noncommittally.

'I find him sympathetic, yes,' said the Countess reflectively. 'I have told him much of my life.'

'Indeed,' said Mr Satterthwaite.

'Details such as I have told to few others,' she continued dreamily. 'I have had an extraordinary life, Mr Satterthwaite. Few would credit the amazing things that have happened to me.'

Mr Satterthwaite was shrewd enough to penetrate her meaning. After all, the stories that she had told to Franklin Rudge *might* be the truth. It was extremely unlikely, and in the last degree improbable, but it was *possible* . . . No one could definitely say: 'That is not so –'

He did not reply, and the Countess continued to look out dreamily across the bay.

And suddenly Mr Satterthwaite had a strange and new impression of her. He saw her no longer as a harpy, but as a desperate creature at bay, fighting tooth and nail. He stole a sideways glance at her. The parasol was down, he could see the little haggard lines at the corners of her eyes. In one temple a pulse was beating.

It flowed through him again and again – that increasing certitude. She was a creature desperate and driven. She would be merciless to him or to anyone who stood between her and Franklin Rudge. But he still felt he hadn't got the hang of the situation. Clearly she had plenty of money. She was always beautifully dressed, and her jewels were marvellous. There could be no real urgency of that kind. Was it love? Women of her age did, he well knew, fall in love with boys. It might be that. There was, he felt sure, something out of the common about the situation.

Her *tête-à-tête* with him was, he recognized, a throwing down of the gauntlet. She had singled him out as her chief enemy. He felt sure that she hoped to goad him into speaking slightingly of her to Franklin Rudge. Mr Satterthwaite smiled to himself. He was too old a bird for that. He knew when it was wise to hold one's tongue.

He watched her that night in the Cercle Privé, as she tried her fortunes at roulette.

Again and again she staked, only to see her stake swept away. She bore her losses well, with the stoical *sang froid* of the old *habitué*. She staked *en plein* once or twice, put the maximum on red, won a little on the middle dozen and then lost it again, finally she backed *manque* six times and lost every time. Then with a little graceful shrug of the shoulders she turned away.

She was looking unusually striking in a dress of gold tissue with an underlying note of green. The famous Bosnian pearls were looped round her neck and long pearl ear-rings hung from her ears.

Mr Satterthwaite heard two men near him appraise her.

'The Czarnova,' said one, 'she wears well, does she not? The Crown jewels of Bosnia look fine on her.'

The other, a small Jewish-looking man, stared curiously after her.

'So those are the pearls of Bosnia, are they?' he asked. '*En vérité*. That is odd.'

He chuckled softly to himself.

Mr Satterthwaite missed hearing more, for at the moment he

turned his head and was overjoyed to recognize an old friend.

'My dear Mr Quin.' He shook him warmly by the hand. 'The last place I should ever have dreamed of seeing you.'

Mr Quin smiled, his dark attractive face lighting up.

'It should not surprise you,' he said. 'It is Carnival time. I am often here in Carnival time.'

'Really? Well, this is a great pleasure. Are you anxious to remain in the rooms? I find them rather warm.'

'It will be pleasanter outside,' agreed the other. 'We will walk in the gardens.'

The air outside was sharp, but not chill. Both men drew deep breaths.

'That is better,' said Mr Satterthwaite.

'Much better,' agreed Mr Quin. 'And we can talk freely. I am sure that there is much that you want to tell me.'

'There is indeed.'

Speaking eagerly, Mr Satterthwaite unfolded his perplexities. As usual he took pride in his power of conveying atmosphere. The Countess, young Franklin, uncompromising Elizabeth – he sketched them all in with a deft touch.

'You have changed since I first knew you,' said Mr Quin, smiling, when the recital was over.

'In what way?'

'You were content then to look on at the drama that life offered. Now – you want to take part – to act.'

'It is true,' confessed Mr Satterthwaite. 'But in this case I do not know what to do. It is all very perplexing. Perhaps –' He hesitated. 'Perhaps you will help me?'

'With pleasure,' said Mr Quin. 'We will see what we can do.'

Mr Satterthwaite had an odd sense of comfort and reliance.

The following day he introduced Franklin Rudge and Elizabeth Martin to his friend Mr Harley Quin. He was pleased to see that they got on together. The Countess was not mentioned, but at lunch time he heard news that aroused his attention.

'Mirabelle is arriving in Monte this evening,' he confided excitedly to Mr Quin.

'The Parisian stage favourite?'

'Yes. I daresay you know – it's common property – she is the King of Bosnia's latest craze. He has showered jewels on her, I believe. They say she is the most exacting and extravagant woman in Paris.'

'It should be interesting to see her and the Countess Czarnova meet tonight.'

'Exactly what I thought.'

Mirabelle was a tall, thin creature with a wonderful head of dyed fair hair. Her complexion was a pale mauve with orange lips. She was amazingly chic. She was dressed in something that looked like a glorified bird of paradise, and she wore chains of jewels hanging down her bare back. A heavy bracelet set with immense diamonds clasped her left ankle.

She created a sensation when she appeared in the Casino.

'Your friend the Countess will have a difficulty in outdoing this,' murmured Mr Quin in Mr Satterthwaite's ear.

The latter nodded. He was curious to see how the Countess comported herself.

She came late, and a low murmur ran round as she walked unconcernedly to one of the centre roulette tables.

She was dressed in white – a mere straight slip of marocain such as a débutante might have worn and her gleaming white neck and arms were unadorned. She wore not a single jewel.

'It is clever, that,' said Mr Satterthwaite with instant approval. 'She disdains rivalry and turns the tables on her adversary.'

He himself walked over and stood by the table. From time to time he amused himself by placing a stake. Sometimes he won, more often he lost.

There was a terrific run on the last dozen. The numbers 31 and 34 turned up again and again. Stakes flocked to the bottom of the cloth.

With a smile Mr Satterthwaite made his last stake for the evening, and placed the maximum on Number 5.

The Countess in her turn leant forward and placed the maximum on Number 6.

'*Faites vos jeux,*' called the croupier hoarsely. '*Rien ne va plus. Plus rien.*'

The ball span, humming merrily. Mr Satterthwaite thought to himself: '*This means something different to each of us. Agonies of hope and despair, boredom, idle amusement, life and death.*'

Click!

The croupier bent forward to see.

'*Numéro cinque, rouge, impair et manque.*'

Mr Satterthwaite had won!

The croupier, having raked in the other stakes, pushed forward Mr Satterthwaite's winnings. He put out his hand to take them. The Countess did the same. The croupier looked from one to the other of them.

'*A madame*,' he said brusquely.

The Countess picked up the money. Mr Satterthwaite drew back. He remained a gentleman. The Countess looked him full in the face and he returned her glance. One or two of the people round pointed out to the croupier that he had made a mistake, but the man shook his head impatiently. He had decided. That was the end. He raised his raucous cry:

'*Faites vos jeux, Messieurs et Mesdames.*'

Mr Satterthwaite rejoined Mr Quin. Beneath his impeccable demeanour, he was feeling extremely indignant. Mr Quin listened sympathetically.

'Too bad,' he said, 'but these things happen.'

'We are to meet your friend Franklin Rudge later. I am giving a little supper party.'

The three met at midnight, and Mr Quin explained his plan.

'It is what is called a "Hedges and Highways" party,' he explained. 'We choose our meeting place, then each one goes out and is bound in honour to invite the first person he meets.'

Franklin Rudge was amused by the idea.

'Say, what happens if they won't accept?'

'You must use your utmost powers of persuasion.'

'Good. And where's the meeting place?'

'A somewhat Bohemian café – where one can take strange guests. It is called Le Caveau.'

He explained its whereabouts, and the three parted. Mr Satterthwaite was so fortunate as to run straight into Elizabeth Martin and he claimed her joyfully. They reached Le Caveau and descended into a kind of cellar where they found a table spread for supper and lit by old-fashioned candles in candlesticks.

'We are the first,' said Mr Satterthwaite. 'Ah! here comes Franklin –'

He stopped abruptly. With Franklin was the Countess. It was

an awkward moment. Elizabeth displayed less graciousness than she might have done. The Countess, as a woman of the world, retained the honours.

Last of all came Mr Quin. With him was a small, dark man, neatly dressed, whose face seemed familiar to Mr Satterthwaite. A moment later he recognized him. It was the croupier who earlier in the evening had made such a lamentable mistake.

'Let me introduce you to the company, M. Pierre Vaucher,' said Mr Quin.

The little man seemed confused. Mr Quin performed the necessary introductions easily and lightly. Supper was brought – an excellent supper. Wine came – very excellent wine. Some of the frigidity went out of the atmosphere. The Countess was very silent, so was Elizabeth. Franklin Rudge became talkative. He told various stories – not humorous stories, but serious ones. And quietly and assiduously Mr Quin passed round the wine.

'I'll tell you – and this is a true story – about a man who made good,' said Franklin Rudge impressively.

For one coming from a Prohibition country he had shown no lack of appreciation of champagne.

He told his story – perhaps at somewhat unnecessary length. It was, like many true stories, greatly inferior to fiction.

As he uttered the last word, Pierre Vaucher, opposite him, seemed to wake up. He also had done justice to the champagne. He leaned forward across the table.

'I, too, will tell you a story,' he said thickly. 'But mine is the story of a man who did not make good. It is the story of a man who went, not up, but down the hill. And, like yours, it is a true story.'

'Pray tell it to us, monsieur,' said Mr Satterthwaite courteously.

Pierre Vaucher leant back in his chair and looked at the ceiling.

'It is in Paris that the story begins. There was a man there, a working jeweller. He was young and light-hearted and industrious in his profession. They said there was a future before him. A good marriage was already arranged for him, the bride not too bad-looking, the dowry most satisfactory. And then, what do you think? One morning he sees a girl. Such a miserable little wisp of a girl, messieurs. Beautiful? Yes, perhaps, if she were not half starved. But anyway, for this young man, she has a magic that he cannot resist. She has been struggling to find work, she is virtuous – or at least that is what she tells him. I do not know if it is true.'

The Countess's voice came suddenly out of the semi-darkness. 'Why should it not be true? There are many like that.'

'Well, as I say, the young man believed her. And he married her – an act of folly! His family would have no more to say to him. He had outraged their feelings. He married – I will call her Jeanne – it was a good action. He told her so. He felt that she should be very grateful to him. He had sacrificed much for her sake.'

'A charming beginning for the poor girl,' observed the Countess sarcastically.

'He loved her, yes, but from the beginning she maddened him. She had moods – tantrums – she would be cold to him one day, passionate the next. At last he saw the truth. She had never loved him. She had married him so as to keep body and soul together. That truth hurt him, it hurt him horribly, but he tried his utmost to let nothing appear on the surface. And he still felt he deserved gratitude and obedience to his wishes. They quarrelled. She reproached him – Mon Dieu, what did she not reproach him with?

'You can see the next step, can you not? The thing that was bound to come. She left him. For two years he was alone, working in his little shop with no news of her. He had one friend – absinthe. The business did not prosper so well.

'And then one day he came into the shop to find her sitting there. She was beautifully dressed. She had rings on her hands. He stood considering her. His heart was beating – but beating! He was at a loss what to do. He would have liked to have beaten her, to have clasped her in his arms, to have thrown her down on the floor and trampled on her, to have thrown himself at her feet. He did none of those things. He took up his pincers and went on with his work. "Madame desires?" he asked formally.

'That upset her. She did not look for that, see you. "Pierre," she said, "I have come back." He laid aside his pincers and looked at her. "You wish to be forgiven?" he said. "You want me to take you back? You are sincerely repentant?" "Do you want me back?" she murmured. Oh! very softly she said it.

'He knew she was laying a trap for him. He longed to seize her in his arms, but he was too clever for that. He pretended indifference.

'"I am a Christian man," he said. "I try to do what the Church directs." "Ah!" he thought, "I will humble her, humble her to her knees."

'But Jeanne, that is what I will call her, flung back her head and laughed. Evil laughter it was. "I mock myself at you, little Pierre," she said. "Look at these rich clothes, these rings and bracelets. I came to show myself to you. I thought I would make you take me in your arms and when you did so, then – *then* I would spit in your face and tell you how I hated you!"

'And on that she went out of the shop. Can you believe, messieurs, that a woman could be as evil as all that – to come back only to torment me?'

'No,' said the Countess. 'I would not believe it, and any man who was not a fool would not believe it either. But all men are blind fools.'

Pierre Vaucher took no notice of her. He went on.

'And so that young man of whom I tell you sank lower and lower. He drank more absinthe. The little shop was sold over his head. He became of the dregs, of the gutter. Then came the war. Ah! it was good, the war. It took that man out of the gutter and taught him to be a brute beast no longer. It drilled him – and sobered him. He endured cold and pain and the fear of death – but he did not die and when the war ended, he was a man again.

'It was then, messieurs, that he came South. His lungs had been affected by the gas, they said he must find work in the South. I will not weary you with all the things he did. Suffice it to say that he ended up as a croupier, and there – there in the Casino one evening, he saw her again – the woman who had ruined his life. She did not recognize him, but he recognized her. She appeared to be rich and to lack for nothing – but messieurs, the eyes of a croupier are sharp. There came an evening when she placed her last stake in the world on the table. Ask me not how I know – I do know – one feels these things. Others might not believe. She still had rich clothes – why not pawn them, one would say? But to do that – pah! your credit is gone at once. Her jewels? Ah no! Was I not a jeweller in my time? Long ago the real jewels have gone. The pearls of a King are sold one by one, are replaced with false. And meantime one must eat and pay one's hotel bill. Yes, and the rich men – well, they have seen one about for many years. Bah! they say – she is over fifty. A younger chicken for my money.'

A long shuddering sigh came out of the windows where the Countess leant back.

'Yes. It was a great moment, that. Two nights I have watched her. Lose, lose, and lose again. And now the end. She put all on one number. Beside her, an English milord stakes the maximum also – on the next number. The ball rolls . . . The moment has come, she has lost . . .

'Her eyes meet mine. What do I do? I jeopardize my place in the Casino. I rob the English milord. "*A Madame*" I say, and pay over the money.'

'Ah!' There was a crash, as the Countess sprang to her feet and leant across the table, sweeping her glass on to the floor.

'Why?' she cried. 'That's what I want to know, *why* did you do it?'

There was a long pause, a pause that seemed interminable, and still those two facing each other across the table looked and looked . . . It was like a duel.

A mean little smile crept across Pierre Vaucher's face. He raised his hands.

'Madame,' he said, 'there is such a thing as pity . . .'

'Ah!'

She sank down again.

'I see.'

She was calm, smiling, herself again.

'An interesting story, M. Vaucher, is it not? Permit me to give you a light for your cigarette.'

She deftly rolled up a spill, and lighted it at the candle and held it towards him. He leaned forward till the flame caught the tip of the cigarette he held between his lips.

Then she rose unexpectedly to her feet.

'And now I must leave you all. Please – I need no one to escort me.'

Before one could realize it she was gone. Mr Satterthwaite would have hurried out after her, but he was arrested by a startled oath from the Frenchman.

'*A thousand thunders!*'

He was staring at the half-burned spill which the Countess had dropped on the table. He unrolled it.

'*Mon Dieu!*' he muttered. 'A fifty thousand franc bank note. You understand? Her winnings tonight. All that she had in the world. And she lighted my cigarette with it! Because she was too proud to accept – pity. Ah! proud, she was always proud as the Devil. She is unique – wonderful.'

He sprang up from his seat and darted out. Mr Satterthwaite and Mr Quin had also risen. The waiter approached Franklin Rudge.

'*La note, monsieur,*' he observed unemotionally.

Mr Quin rescued it from him quickly.

'I feel kind of lonesome, Elizabeth,' remarked Franklin Rudge. 'These foreigners – they beat the band! I don't understand them. What's it all mean, anyhow?'

He looked across at her.

'Gee, it's good to look at anything so hundred per cent American as you.' His voice took on the plaintive note of a small child. 'These foreigners are so *odd*.'

They thanked Mr Quin and went out into the night together. Mr Quin picked up his change and smiled across at Mr Satterthwaite, who was preening himself like a contented bird.

'Well,' said the latter. 'That's all gone off splendidly. Our pair of love birds will be all right now.'

'Which ones?' asked Mr Quin.

'Oh!' said Mr Satterthwaite, taken aback. 'Oh! yes, well, I suppose you are right, allowing for the Latin point of view and all that –'

He looked dubious.

Mr Quin smiled, and a stained glass panel behind him invested him for just a moment in a motley garment of coloured light.

CHAPTER 6

The Man from the Sea

Mr Satterthwaite was feeling old. That might not have been surprising since in the estimation of many people he *was* old. Careless youths said to their partners: 'Old Satterthwaite? Oh! he must be a hundred – or at any rate about eighty.' And even the kindest of girls said indulgently, 'Oh! Satterthwaite. Yes, he's quite old. He *must* be sixty.' Which was almost worse, since he was sixty-nine.

In his own view, however, he was not old. Sixty-nine was an interesting age – an age of infinite possibilities – an age when at last the experience of a lifetime was beginning to tell. But to feel old – that was different, a tired discouraged state of mind when one was inclined to ask oneself depressing questions. What was he after all? A little dried-up elderly man, with neither chick nor child, with no human belongings, only a valuable Art collection which seemed at the moment strangely unsatisfying. No one to care whether he lived or died . . .

At this point in his meditations Mr Satterthwaite pulled himself up short. What he was thinking was morbid and unprofitable. He knew well enough, who better, that the chances were that a wife would have hated him or alternatively that he would have hated her, that children would have been a constant source of worry and anxiety, and that demands upon his time and affection would have worried him considerably.

'To be safe and comfortable,' said Mr Satterthwaite firmly – that was the thing.

The last thought reminded him of a letter he had received that morning. He drew it from his pocket and re-read it, savouring its contents pleasurably. To begin with, it was from a Duchess, and Mr Satterthwaite liked hearing from Duchesses. It is true that the letter began by demanding a large subscription for charity and but for that would probably never have been written, but the terms in which it was couched were so agreeable that Mr Satterthwaite was able to gloss over the first fact.

> *So you've deserted the Riviera*, wrote the Duchess. *What is this island of yours like? Cheap? Cannotti put up his prices shamefully this year, and I shan't go to the Riviera again. I might try your island next year if you report favourably, though I should hate five days on a boat. Still anywhere you recommend is sure to be pretty comfortable – too much so. You'll get to be one of those people who do nothing but coddle themselves and think of their comfort. There's only one thing that will save you, Satterthwaite, and that is your inordinate interest in other people's affairs . . .*

As Mr Satterthwaite folded the letter, a vision came up vividly before him of the Duchess. Her meanness, her unexpected and alarming kindness, her caustic tongue, her indomitable spirit.

Spirit! Everyone needed spirit. He drew out another letter with a German stamp upon it – written by a young singer in whom he had interested himself. It was a grateful affectionate letter.

> '*How can I thank you, dear Mr Satterthwaite? It seems too wonderful to think that in a few days I shall be singing Isolde . . .*'

A pity that she had to make her *début* as Isolde. A charming, hardworking child, Olga, with a beautiful voice but no temperament. He hummed to himself. '*Nay order him! Pray understand it! I command it. I, Isolde.*' No, the child hadn't got it in her – the spirit – the indomitable will – all expressed in that final 'Ich Isoldé!'

Well, at any rate he had done something for somebody. This island depressed him – why, oh! why had he deserted the Riviera which he knew so well and where he was so well known? Nobody here took any interest in him. Nobody seemed to realize that here was *the* Mr Satterthwaite – the friend of Duchesses and Countesses and singers and writers. No one in the island was of any social importance or of any artistic importance either. Most people had been there seven, fourteen, or twenty-one years running and valued themselves and were valued accordingly.

With a deep sigh Mr Satterthwaite proceeded down from the Hotel to the small straggling harbour below. His way lay between an avenue of bougainvillaea – a vivid mass of flaunting scarlet, that made him feel older and greyer than ever.

'I'm getting old,' he murmured. 'I'm getting old and tired.'

He was glad when he had passed the bougainvillaea and was walking down the white street with the blue sea at the end of it. A disreputable dog was standing in the middle of the road, yawning and stretching himself in the sun. Having prolonged his stretch to the utmost limits of ecstasy, he sat down and treated himself to a really good scratch. He then rose, shook himself, and looked round for any other good things that life might have to offer.

There was a dump of rubbish by the side of the road and to this he went sniffing in pleasurable anticipation. True enough, his nose had not deceived him! A smell of such rich putrescence that surpassed even his anticipations! He sniffed with growing appreciation, then suddenly abandoning himself, he lay on his back and rolled frenziedly on the delicious dump. Clearly the world this morning was a dog paradise!

Tiring at last, he regained his feet and strolled out once more into the middle of the road. And then, without the least warning, a ramshackle car careered wildly round the corner, caught him full square and passed on unheeding.

The dog rose to his feet, stood a minute regarding Mr Satterthwaite, a vague dumb reproach in his eyes, then fell over. Mr Satterthwaite went up to him and bent down. The dog was dead. He went on his way, wondering at the sadness and cruelty of life. What a queer dumb look of reproach had been in the dog's eyes. 'Oh! World,' they seemed to say. 'Oh! Wonderful World in which I have trusted. Why have you done this to me?'

Mr Satterthwaite went on, past the palm trees and the straggling white houses, past the black lava beach where the surf thundered and where once, long ago, a well-known English swimmer had been carried out to sea and drowned, past the rock pools were children and elderly ladies bobbed up and down and called it bathing, along the steep road that winds upwards to the top of the cliff. For there on the edge of the cliff was a house, appropriately named La Paz. A white house with faded green shutters tightly closed, a tangled beautiful garden, and a walk between cypress trees that led to a plateau on the edge of the cliff where you looked down – down – down – to the deep blue sea below.

It was to this spot that Mr Satterthwaite was bound. He had developed a great love for the garden of La Paz. He had never entered the villa. It seemed always to be empty. Manuel, the Spanish gardener, wished one good-morning with a flourish and gallantly presented ladies with a bouquet and gentlemen with a single flower as a buttonhole, his dark face wreathed in smiles.

Sometimes Mr Satterthwaite made up stories in his own mind about the owner of the villa. His favourite was a Spanish dancer, once world-famed for her beauty, who hid herself here so that the world should never know that she was no longer beautiful.

He pictured her coming out of the house at dusk and walking through the garden. Sometimes he was tempted to ask Manuel for the truth, but he resisted the temptation. He preferred his fancies.

After exchanging a few words with Manuel and graciously accepting an orange rosebud, Mr Satterthwaite passed on down the cypress walk to the sea. It was rather wonderful sitting there – on the edge of nothing – with that sheer drop below one. It made him think of Tristan and Isolde, of the beginning of the third act with Tristan and Kurwenal – that lonely waiting and of Isolde rushing up from the sea and Tristan dying in her arms. (No, little Olga would never make an Isolde. Isolde of Cornwall, that Royal hater and Royal lover . . .) He shivered. He felt old, chilly, alone . . . What had he had out of life? Nothing – nothing. Not as much as that dog in the street . . .

It was an unexpected sound that roused him from his reverie. Footsteps coming along the cypress walk were inaudible, the first he knew of somebody's presence was the English monosyllable 'Damn.'

He looked round to find a young man staring at him in obvious surprise and disappointment. Mr Satterthwaite recognized him at once as an arrival of the day before who had more or less intrigued him. Mr Satterthwaite called him a young man – because in comparison to most of the die-hards in the Hotel he *was* a young man, but he would certainly never see forty again and was probably drawing appreciably near to his half century. Yet in spite of that, the term young man fitted him – Mr Satterthwaite was usually right about such things – there was an impression of immaturity about him. As there is a touch of puppyhood about many a full grown dog so it was with the stranger.

Mr Satterthwaite thought: 'This chap has really never grown up – not properly, that is.'

And yet there was nothing Peter Pannish about him. He was sleek – almost plump, he had the air of one who has always done himself exceedingly well in the material sense and denied himself no pleasure or satisfaction. He had brown eyes – rather round – fair hair turning grey – a little moustache and rather florid face.

The thing that puzzled Mr Satterthwaite was what had brought him to the island. He could imagine him shooting things, hunting things, playing polo or golf or tennis, making love to pretty women. But in the Island there was nothing to hunt or shoot, no games except Golf-Croquet, and the nearest approach to a pretty woman was represented by elderly Miss Baba Kindersley. There were, of course, artists, to whom the beauty of the scenery made appeal, but Mr Satterthwaite was quite certain that the young man was not an artist. He was clearly marked with the stamp of the Philistine.

While he was resolving these things in his mind, the other spoke, realizing somewhat belatedly that his single ejaculation so far might be open to criticism.

'I beg your pardon,' he said with some embarrassment. 'As a matter of fact, I was – well, startled. I didn't expect anyone to be here.'

He smiled disarmingly. He had a charming smile – friendly – appealing.

'It is rather a lonely spot,' agreed Mr Satterthwaite, as he moved politely a little further up the bench. The other accepted the mute invitation and sat down.

'I don't know about lonely,' he said. 'There always seems to be *someone* here.'

There was a tinge of latent resentment in his voice. Mr

Satterthwaite wondered why. He read the other as a friendly soul. Why this insistence on solitude? A rendezvous, perhaps? No – not that. He looked again with carefully veiled scrutiny at his companion. Where had he seen that particular expression before quite lately? That look of dumb bewildered resentment.

'You've been up here before then?' said Mr Satterthwaite, more for the sake of saying something than for anything else.

'I was up here last night – after dinner.'

'Really? I thought the gates were always locked.'

There was a moment's pause and then, almost sullenly, the young man said:

'I climbed over the wall.'

Mr Satterthwaite looked at him with real attention now. He had a sleuthlike habit of mind and he was aware that his companion had only arrived on the preceding afternoon. He had had little time to discover the beauty of the villa by daylight and he had so far spoken to nobody. Yet after dark he had made straight for La Paz. Why? Almost involuntarily Mr Satterthwaite turned his head to look at the green-shuttered villa, but it was as ever serenely lifeless, close shuttered. No, the solution of the mystery was not there.

'And you actually found someone here then?'

The other nodded.

'Yes. Must have been from the other Hotel. He had on fancy dress.'

'Fancy dress?'

'Yes. A kind of Harlequin rig.'

'What?'

The query fairly burst from Mr Satterthwaite's lips. His companion turned to stare at him in surprise.

'They often do have fancy dress shows at the Hotels, I suppose?'

'Oh! quite,' said Mr Satterthwaite. 'Quite, quite, quite.'

He paused breathlessly, then added:

'You must excuse my excitement. Do you happen to know anything about catalysis?'

The young man stared at him.

'Never heard of it. What is it?'

Mr Satterthwaite quoted gravely: '*A chemical reaction depending for its success on the presence of a certain substance which itself remains unchanged.*'

'Oh,' said the young man uncertainly.

'I have a certain friend – his name is Mr Quin, and he can best be described in the terms of catalysis. His presence is a sign that things are going to happen, because when he is there strange revelations come to light, discoveries are made. And yet – he himself takes no part in the proceedings. I have a feeling that it was my friend you met here last night.'

'He's a very sudden sort of chap then. He gave me quite a shock. One minute he wasn't there and the next minute he was! Almost as though he came up out of the sea.'

Mr Satterthwaite looked along the little plateau and down the sheer drop below.

'That's nonsense, of course,' said the other. 'But it's the feeling he gave me. Of course, really, there isn't the foothold for a fly.' He looked over the edge. 'A straight clear drop. If you went over – well, that would be the end right enough.'

'An ideal spot for a murder, in fact,' said Mr Satterthwaite pleasantly.

The other stared at him, almost as though for the moment he did not follow. Then he said vaguely: 'Oh! yes – of course . . .'

He sat there, making little dabs at the ground with his stick and frowning. Suddenly Mr Satterthwaite got the resemblance he had been seeking. That dumb bewildered questioning. *So had the dog looked who was run over*. His eyes and this young man's eyes asked the same pathetic question with the same reproach. '*Oh! world that I have trusted – what have you done to me*?'

He saw other points of resemblance between the two, the same pleasure-loving easy-going existence, the same joyous abandon to the delights of life, the same absence of intellectual questioning. Enough for both to live in the moment – the world was a good place, a place of carnal delights – sun, sea, sky – a discreet garbage heap. And then – what? A car had hit the dog. What had hit the man?

The subject of these cogitations broke in at this point, speaking, however, more to himself than to Mr Satterthwaite.

'One wonders,' he said, 'what it's All For?'

Familiar words – words that usually brought a smile to Mr

Satterthwaite's lips, with their unconscious betrayal of the innate egoism of humanity which insists on regarding every manifestation of life as directly designed for its delight or its torment. He did not answer and presently the stranger said with a slight, rather apologetic laugh:

'I've heard it said that every man should build a house, plant a tree and have a son.' He paused and then added: 'I believe I planted an acorn once . . .'

Mr Satterthwaite stirred slightly. His curiosity was aroused – that ever-present interest in the affairs of other people of which the Duchess had accused him was roused. It was not difficult. Mr Satterthwaite had a very feminine side to his nature, he was as good a listener as any woman, and he knew the right moment to put in a prompting word. Presently he was hearing the whole story.

Anthony Cosden, that was the stranger's name, and his life had been much as Mr Satterthwaite had imagined it. He was a bad hand at telling a story but his listener supplied the gaps easily enough. A very ordinary life – an average income, a little soldiering, a good deal of sport whenever sport offered, plenty of friends, plenty of pleasant things to do, a sufficiency of women. The kind of life that practically inhibits thought of any description and substitutes sensation. To speak frankly, an animal's life. 'But there are worse things than that,' thought Mr Satterthwaite from the depths of his experience. 'Oh! many worse things than that . . .' This world had seemed a very good place to Anthony Cosden. He had grumbled because everyone always grumbled but it had never been a serious grumble. And then – *this*.

He came to it at last – rather vaguely and incoherently. Hadn't felt quite the thing – nothing much. Saw his doctor, and the doctor had persuaded him to go to a Harley Street man. And then – the incredible truth. They'd tried to hedge about it – spoke of great care – a quiet life, but they hadn't been able to disguise that that was all eyewash – letting him down lightly. It boiled down to this – six months. That's what they gave him. Six months.

He turned those bewildered brown eyes on Mr Satterthwaite. It was, of course, rather a shock to a fellow. One didn't – one didn't somehow, know what do *do*.

Mr Satterthwaite nodded gravely and understandingly.

It was a bit difficult to take in all at once, Anthony Cosden went on. How to put in the time. Rather a rotten business waiting about to get pipped. He didn't feel really ill – not yet. Though that might come later, so the specialist had said – in fact, it was bound to. It seemed such nonsense to be going to die when one didn't in the least want to. The best thing, he had thought, would be to carry on as usual. But somehow that hadn't worked.

Here Mr Satterthwaite interrupted him. Wasn't there, he hinted delicately, any woman?

But apparently there wasn't. There were women, of course, but not that kind. His crowd was a very cheery crowd. They didn't, so he implied, like corpses. He didn't wish to make a kind of walking funeral of himself. It would have been embarrassing for everybody. So he had come abroad.

'You came to see these islands? But why?' Mr Satterthwaite was hunting for something, something intangible but delicate that eluded him and yet which he was sure was there. 'You've been here before, perhaps?'

'Yes.' He admitted it almost unwillingly. 'Years ago when I was a youngster.'

And suddenly, almost unconsciously so it seemed, he shot a quick glance backward over his shoulder in the direction of the villa.

'I remembered this place,' he said, nodding at the sea. '*One step to eternity!*'

'And that is why you came up here last night,' finished Mr Satterthwaite calmly.

Anthony Cosden shot him a dismayed glance.

'Oh! I say – really –' he protested.

'Last night you found someone here. This afternoon you have found me. Your life has been saved – twice.'

'You may put it that way if you like – but damn it all, it's *my* life. I've a right to do what I like with it.'

'That is a cliché,' said Mr Satterthwaite wearily.

'Of course I see your point, said Anthony Cosden generously. 'Naturally you've got to say what you can. I'd try to dissuade a fellow myself, even though I knew deep down that he was right. And you know that I'm right. A clean quick end is better than a lingering one – causing trouble and expense and bother to all. In any case it's not as though I had anyone in the world belonging to me . . .'

'If you had –?' said Mr Satterthwaite sharply.

Cosden drew a deep breath.

'I don't know. Even then, I think, this way would be best. But anyway – I haven't . . .'

He stopped abruptly. Mr Satterthwaite eyed him curiously. Incurably romantic, he suggested again that there was, somewhere, some woman. But Cosden negatived it. He oughtn't, he said, to complain. He had had, on the whole, a very good life. It was a pity it was going to be over so soon, that was all. But at any rate he had had, he supposed, everything worth having. Except a son. He would have liked a son. He would like to know now that he had a son living after him. Still, he reiterated the fact, he had had a very good life –

It was at this point that Mr Satterthwaite lost patience. Nobody, he pointed out, who was still in the larval stage, could claim to know anything of life at all. Since the words *larval stage* clearly meant nothing at all to Cosden, he proceeded to make his meaning clearer.

'You have not begun to live yet. You are still at the beginning of life.'

Cosden laughed.

'Why, my hair's grey. I'm forty –'

Mr Satterthwaite interrupted him.

'That has nothing to do with it. Life is a compound of physical and mental experiences. I, for instance, am sixty-nine, and I am really sixty-nine. I have known, either at first or second hand, nearly all the experiences life has to offer. You are like a man who talks of a full year and has seen nothing but snow and ice! The flowers of Spring, the languorous days of Summer, the falling leaves of Autumn – he knows nothing of them – not even that there are such things. And you are going to turn your back on even this opportunity of knowing them.'

'You seem to forget,' said Anthony Cosden dryly, 'that, in any case, I have only six months.'

'Time, like everything else, is relative,' said Mr Satterthwaite.

'That six months might be the longest and most varied experience of your whole life.'

Cosden looked unconvinced.

'In my place,' he said, 'you would do the same.'

Mr Satterthwaite shook his head.

'No,' he said simply. 'In the first place, I doubt if I should have the courage. It needs courage and I am not at all a brave individual. And in the second place –'

'Well?'

'I always want to know what is going to happen tomorrow.'

Cosden rose suddenly with a laugh.

'Well, sir, you've been very good in letting me talk to you. I hardly know why – anyway, there it is. I've said a lot too much. Forget it.'

'And tomorrow, when an accident is reported, I am to leave it at that? To make no suggestion of suicide?'

'That's as you like. I'm glad you realize one thing – that you can't prevent me.'

'My dear young man,' said Mr Satterthwaite placidly, 'I can hardly attach myself to you like the proverbial limpet. Sooner or later you would give me the slip and accomplish your purpose. But you are frustrated at any rate for this afternoon. You would hardly like to go to your death leaving me under the possible imputation of having pushed you over.'

'That is true,' said Cosden. 'If you insist on remaining here –'

'I do,' said Mr Satterthwaite firmly.

Cosden laughed good-humouredly.

'Then the plan must be deferred for the moment. In which case I will go back to the hotel. See you later perhaps.'

Mr Satterthwaite was left looking at the sea.

'And now,' he said to himself softly, 'what next? There must be a next. I wonder . . .'

He got up. For a while he stood at the edge of the plateau looking down on the dancing water beneath. But he found no inspiration there, and turning slowly he walked back along the path between the cypresses and into the quiet garden. He looked at the shuttered, peaceful house and he wondered, as he had often wondered before, who had lived there and what had taken place within those placid walls. On a sudden impulse he walked up some crumbling stone steps and laid a hand on one of the faded green shutters.

To his surprise it swung back at his touch. He hesitated a moment, then pushed it boldly open. The next minute he stepped back with a little exclamation of dismay. A woman stood in the window facing him. She wore black and had a black lace mantilla draped over her head.

Mr Satterthwaite floundered wildly in Italian interspersed with German – the nearest he could get in the hurry of the moment to Spanish. He was desolated and ashamed, he explained haltingly. The Signora must forgive. He thereupon retreated hastily, the woman not having spoken one word.

He was halfway across the courtyard when she spoke – two sharp words like a pistol crack.

'Come back!'

It was a barked-out command such as might have been addressed to a dog, yet so absolute was the authority it conveyed, that Mr Satterthwaite had swung round hurriedly and trotted back to the window almost automatically before it occurred to him to feel any resentment. He obeyed like a dog. The woman was still standing motionless at the window. She looked him up and down appraising him with perfect calmness.

'You are English,' she said. 'I thought so.'

Mr Satterthwaite started off on a second apology.

'If I had known you were English,' he said, 'I could have expressed myself better just now. I offer my most sincere apologies for my rudeness in trying the shutter. I am afraid I can plead no excuse save curiosity. I had a great wish to see what the inside of this charming house was like.'

She laughed suddenly, a deep, rich laugh.

'If you really want to see it,' she said, 'you had better come in.'

She stood aside, and Mr Satterthwaite, feeling pleasurably excited, stepped into the room. It was dark, since the shutters of the other windows were closed, but he could see that it was scantily and rather shabbily furnished and that the dust lay thick everywhere.

'Not here,' she said. 'I do not use this room.'

She led the way and he followed her, out of the room across a passage and into a room the other side. Here the windows gave on the sea and the sun streamed in. The furniture, like that of the other room, was poor in quality, but there were some worn rugs that had been good in their time, a large screen of Spanish leather and bowls of fresh flowers.

'You will have tea with me,' said Mr Satterthwaite's hostess. She added reassuringly: 'It is perfectly good tea and will be made with boiling water.'

She went out of the door and called out something in Spanish, then she returned and sat down on a sofa opposite her guest. For the first time, Mr Satterthwaite was able to study her appearance.

The first effect she had upon him was to make him feel even more grey and shrivelled and elderly than usual by contrast with her own forceful personality. She was a tall woman, very sunburnt, dark and handsome though no longer young. When she was in the room the sun seemed to be shining twice as brightly as when she was out of it, and presently a curious feeling of warmth and aliveness began to steal over Mr Satterthwaite. It was as though he stretched out thin, shrivelled hands to a reassuring flame. He thought, 'She's so much vitality herself that she's got a lot left over for other people.'

He recalled the command in her voice when she had stopped him, and wished that his protégée, Olga, could be imbued with a little of that force. He thought: 'What an Isolde she'd make! And yet she probably hasn't got the ghost of a singing voice. Life is badly arranged.' He was, all the same, a little afraid of her. He did not like domineering women.

She had clearly been considering him as she sat with her chin in her hands, making no pretence about it. At last she nodded as though she had made up her mind.

'I am glad you came,' she said at last. 'I needed someone very badly to talk to this afternoon. And you are used to that, aren't you?'

'I don't quite understand.'

'I meant people tell you things. You knew what I meant! Why pretend?'

'Well – perhaps –'

She swept on, regardless of anything he had been going to say.

'One could say anything to you. That is because you are half a woman. You know what we feel – what we think – the queer, queer things we do.'

Her voice died away. Tea was brought by a large, smiling Spanish girl. It was good tea – China – Mr Satterthwaite sipped it appreciatively.

'You live here?' he inquired conversationally.

'Yes.'

'But not altogether. The house is usually shut up, is it not? At least so I have been told.'

'I am here a good deal, more than anyone knows. I only use these rooms.'

'You have had the house long?'

'It has belonged to me for twenty-two years – and I lived here for a year before that.'

Mr Satterthwaite said rather inanely (or so he felt): 'That is a very long time.'

'The year? Or the twenty-two years?'

His interest stirred, Mr Satterthwaite said gravely: 'That depends.'

She nodded.

'Yes, it depends. They are two separate periods. They have nothing to do with each other. Which is long? Which is short? Even now I cannot say.'

She was silent for a minute, brooding. Then she said with a little smile:

'It is such a long time since I have talked with anyone – such a long time! I do not apologize. You came to my shutter. You wished to look through my window. And that is what you are always doing, is it not? Pushing aside the shutter and looking through the window into the truth of people's lives. If they will let you. And often if they will not let you! It would be difficult to hide anything from you. You would guess – and guess right.'

Mr Satterthwaite had an odd impulse to be perfectly sincere.

'I am sixty-nine,' he said. 'Everything I know of life I know at second hand. Sometimes that is very bitter to me. And yet, because of it, I know a good deal.'

She nodded thoughtfully.

'I know. Life is very strange. I cannot imagine what it must be like to be that – always a looker-on.'

Her tone was wondering. Mr Satterthwaite smiled.

'No, you would not know. Your place is in the centre of the stage. You will always be the Prima Donna.'

'What a curious thing to say.'

'But I am right. Things have happened to you – will always happen to you. Sometimes, I think, there have been tragic things. Is that so?'

Her eyes narrowed. She looked across at him.

'If you are here long, somebody will tell you of the English swimmer who was drowned at the foot of this cliff. They will tell you how young and strong he was, how handsome, and they will tell you that his young wife looked down from the top of the cliff and saw him drowning.'

'Yes, I have already heard that story.'

'That man was my husband. This was his villa. He brought me out here with him when I was eighteen, and a year later he died – driven by the surf on the black rocks, cut and bruised and mutilated, battered to death.'

Mr Satterthwaite gave a shocked exclamation. She leant forward, her burning eyes focused on his face.

'You spoke of tragedy. Can you imagine a greater tragedy than that? For a young wife, only a year married, to stand helpless while the man she loved fought for his life – and lost it – horribly.'

'Terrible,' said Mr Satterthwaite. He spoke with real emotion. 'Terrible. I agree with you. Nothing in life could be so dreadful.'

Suddenly she laughed. Her head went back.

'You are wrong,' she said. 'There is something more terrible. And that is for a young wife to stand there and hope and long for her husband to drown . . .'

'But good God,' cried Mr Satterthwaite, 'you don't mean –?'

'Yes, I do. That's what it was really. I knelt there – knelt down on the cliff and prayed. The Spanish servants thought I was praying for his life to be saved. I wasn't. I was praying that I might wish him to be spared. I was saying one thing over and over again, "God, help me not to wish him dead. God, help me not to wish him dead." But it wasn't any good. All the time I hoped – hoped – and my hope came true.'

She was silent for a minute or two and then she said very gently in quite a different voice:

'That is a terrible thing, isn't it? It's the sort of thing one can't forget. I was terribly happy when I knew he was really dead and couldn't come back to torture me any more.'

'My child,' said Mr Satterthwaite, shocked.

'I know. I was too young to have that happen to me. Those things should happen to one when one is older – when one is more prepared for – for beastliness. Nobody knew, you know, what he was really like. I thought he was wonderful when I first met him and was so happy and proud when he asked me to marry him. But things went wrong almost at once. He was angry with me – nothing I could do pleased him – and yet I tried so hard. And then he began to like hurting me. And above all to terrify me. That's what he enjoyed most. He thought out all sorts of things . . . dreadful things. I won't tell you. I suppose, really, he must have been a little mad. I was alone here, in his power, and cruelty began to be his hobby.' Her eyes widened and darkened. 'The worst was my baby. I was going to have a baby. Because of some of the things he did to me – it was born dead. My little baby. I nearly died, too – but I didn't. I wish I had.'

Mr Satterthwaite made an inarticulate sound.

'And then I was delivered – in the way I've told you. Some girls who were staying at the hotel dared him. That's how it happened. All the Spaniards told him it was madness to risk the sea just there. But he was very vain – he wanted to show off. And I – I saw him drown – and was glad. God oughtn't to let such things happen.'

Mr Satterthwaite stretched out his little dry hand and took hers. She squeezed it hard as a child might have done. The maturity had fallen away from her face. He saw her without difficulty as she had been at nineteen.

'At first it seemed too good to be true. The house was mine and I could live in it. And no one could hurt me any more! I was an orphan, you know, I had no near relations, no one to care what became of me. That simplified things. I lived on here – in this villa – and it seemed like Heaven. Yes, like Heaven. I've never been so happy since, and never shall again. Just to wake up and know that everything was all right – no pain, no terror, no wondering what he was going to do to me next. Yes, it was Heaven.'

She paused a long time, and Mr Satterthwaite said at last:

'And then?'

'I suppose human beings aren't ever satisfied. At first, just being free was enough. But after a while I began to get – well, lonely, I suppose. I began to think about my baby that died. If only I had had my baby! I wanted it as a baby, and also as a plaything. I wanted dreadfully something or someone to play with. It sounds silly and childish, but there it was.'

'I understand,' said Mr Satterthwaite gravely.

'It's difficult to explain the next bit. It just – well, happened, you see. There was a young Englishman staying at the hotel. He strayed in the garden by mistake. I was wearing Spanish dress and he took me for a Spanish girl. I thought it would be rather fun to pretend I was one, so I played up. His Spanish was very bad but he could just manage a little. I told him the villa belonged to an English lady who was away. I said she had taught me a little English and I pretended to speak broken English. It was such fun – such fun – even now I can remember what fun it was. He began to make love to me. We agreed to pretend that the villa was our home, that we were just married and coming to live there. I suggested that we should try one of the shutters – the one you tried this evening. It was open and inside the room was dusty and uncared for. We crept in. It was exciting and wonderful. We pretended it was our own house.'

She broke off suddenly, looked appealingly at Mr Satterthwaite.

'It all seemed lovely – like a fairy tale. And the lovely thing about it, to me, was that it wasn't true. It wasn't real.'

Mr Satterthwaite nodded. He saw her, perhaps more clearly than she saw herself – that frightened, lonely child entranced with her make believe that was so safe because it wasn't real.

'He was, I suppose, a very ordinary young man. Out for adventure, but quite sweet about it. We went on pretending.'

She stopped, looked at Mr Satterthwaite and said again:

'You understand? We went on pretending . . .'

She went on again in a minute.

'He came up again the next morning to the villa. I saw him from my bedroom through the shutter. Of course he didn't dream I was inside. He still thought I was a little Spanish peasant girl. He stood there looking about him. He'd asked me to meet him. I'd said I would but I never meant to.

'He just stood there looking worried. I think he was worried about me. It was nice of him to be worried about me. He *was* nice . . .'

She paused again.

'The next day he left. I've never seen him again.

'My baby was born nine months later. I was wonderfully happy all the time. To be able to have a baby so peacefully, with no one to hurt you or make you miserable. I wished I'd remembered to ask my English boy his Christian name. I would have called the baby after him. It seemed unkind not to. It seemed rather unfair. He'd given me the thing I wanted most in the world, and he would never even know about it! But of course I told myself that he wouldn't look at it that way – that to know would probably only worry and annoy him. I had been just a passing amusement for him, that was all.'

'And the baby?' asked Mr Satterthwaite.

'He was splendid. I called him John. Splendid. I wish you could see him now. He's twenty. He's going to be a mining engineer. He's been the best and dearest son in the world to me. I told him his father had died before he was born.'

Mr Satterthwaite stared at her. A curious story. And somehow, a story that was not completely told. There was, he felt sure, something else.

'Twenty years is a long time,' he said thoughtfully. 'You've never contemplated marrying again?'

She shook her head. A slow, burning blush spread over her tanned cheeks.

'The child was enough for you – always?'

She looked at him. Her eyes were softer than he had yet seen them.

'Such queer things happen!' she murmured. 'Such queer things . . . You wouldn't believe them – no, I'm wrong, *you* might, perhaps. I didn't love John's father, not at the time. I don't think I even knew what love was. I assumed, as a matter of course, that the child would be like me. But he wasn't. He mightn't have been my child at all. He was like his father – he was like no one but his father. I learnt to know that man – through his child. Through the child, I learnt to love him. I love him now. I always shall love him. You may say that it's imagination, that

I've built up an ideal, but it isn't so. I love the man, the real, human man. I'd know him if I saw him tomorrow – even though it's over twenty years since we met. Loving him has made me into a woman. I love him as a woman loves a man. For twenty years I've lived loving him. I shall die loving him.'

She stopped abruptly – then challenged her listener.

'Do you think I'm mad – to say these strange things?'

'Oh! my dear,' said Mr Satterthwaite. He took her hand again.

'You do understand?'

'I think I do. But there's something more, isn't there? Something that you haven't yet told me?'

Her brow clouded over.

'Yes, there's something. It was clever of you to guess. I knew at once you weren't the sort one can hide things from. But I don't want to tell you – and the reason I don't want to tell you is because it's best for you not to know.'

He looked at her. Her eyes met his bravely and defiantly.

He said to himself: 'This is the test. All the clues are in my hand. I ought to be able to know. If I reason rightly I shall know.'

There was a pause, then he said slowly:

'Something's gone wrong.' He saw her eyelids give the faintest quiver and knew himself to be on the right track.

'Something's gone wrong – suddenly – after all these years.' He felt himself groping – groping – in the dark recesses of her mind where she was trying to hide her secret from him.

'The boy – it's got to do with him. You wouldn't mind about anything else.'

He heard the very faint gasp she gave and knew he had probed correctly. A cruel business but necessary. It was her will against his. She had got a dominant, ruthless will, but he too had a will hidden beneath his meek manners. And he had behind him the Heaven-sent assurance of a man who is doing his proper job. He felt a passing contemptuous pity for men whose business it was to track down such crudities as crime. This detective business of the mind, this assembling of clues, this delving for the truth, this wild joy as one drew nearer to the goal . . . Her very passion to keep the truth from him helped her. He felt her stiffen defiantly as he drew nearer and nearer.

'It is better for me not to know, you say. Better for *me*? But you are not a very considerate woman. You would not shrink from putting a stranger to a little temporary inconvenience. It is more than that, then? If you tell me you make me an accomplice before the fact. That sounds like crime. Fantastic! I could not associate crime with you. Or only one sort of crime. A crime against yourself.'

Her lids drooped in spite of herself, veiled her eyes. He leaned forward and caught her wrist.

'It *is* that, then! You are thinking of taking your life.'

She gave a low cry.

'How did you know? How did you know?'

'But why? You are not tired of life. I never saw a woman less tired of it – more radiantly alive.'

She got up, went to the window, pushing back a strand of her dark hair as she did so.

'Since you have guessed so much I might as well tell you the truth. I should not have let you in this evening. I might have known that you would see too much. You are that kind of man. You were right about the cause. It's the boy. He knows nothing. But last time he was home, he spoke tragically of a friend of his, and I discovered something. If he finds out that he is illegitimate it will break his heart. He is proud – horribly proud! There is a girl. Oh! I won't go into details. But he is coming very soon – and he wants to know all about his father – he wants details. The girl's parents, naturally, want to know. When he discovers the truth, he will break with her, exile himself, ruin his life. Oh! I know the things you would say. He is young, foolish, wrong-headed to take it like that! All true, perhaps. But does it matter what people ought to be? They are what they are. *It will break his heart* . . . But if, before he comes, there has been an accident, everything will be swallowed up in grief for me. He will look through my papers, find nothing, and be annoyed that I told him so little. But he will not suspect the truth. It is the best way. One must pay for happiness, and I have had so much – oh! so much happiness. And in reality the price will be easy, too. A little courage – to take the leap – perhaps a moment or so of anguish.'

'But, my dear child –'

'Don't argue with me.' She flared round on him. 'I won't listen to conventional arguments. My life is my own. Up to now, it has been needed – for John. But he needs it no longer. He wants a mate – a companion – he will turn to her all the more willingly because I am no longer there. My life is useless, but my death will be of use. And I have the right to do what I like with my own life.'

'Are you sure?'

The sternness of his tone surprised her. She stammered slightly.

'If it is no good to anyone – and I am the best judge of that –'

He interrupted her again.

'Not necessarily.'

'What do you mean?'

'Listen. I will put a case to you. A man comes to a certain place – to commit suicide, shall we say? But by chance he finds another man there, so he fails in his purpose and goes away – to live. The second man has saved the first man's life, not by being necessary to him or prominent in his life, but just by the mere physical fact of having been in a certain place at a certain moment. You take your life today and perhaps, some five, six, seven years hence, someone will go to death or disaster simply for lack of your presence in a given spot or place. It may be a runaway horse coming down a street that swerved aside at sight of you and so fails to trample a child that is playing in the gutter. That child may live to grow up and be a great musician, or discover a cure for cancer. Or it may be less melodramatic than that. He may just grow up to ordinary everyday happiness . . .'

She stared at him.

'You are a strange man. These things you say – I have never thought of them . . .'

'You say your life is your own,' went on Mr Satterthwaite. 'But can you dare to ignore the chance that you are taking part in a gigantic drama under the orders of a divine Producer? Your cue may not come till the end of the play – it may be totally unimportant, a mere walking-on part, but upon it may hang the issues of the play if you do not give the cue to another player. The whole edifice may crumple. You as you, may not matter to anyone in the world, but you as a person in a particular place may matter unimaginably.'

She sat down, still staring.

'What do you want me to do?' she said simply.

It was Mr Satterthwaite's moment of triumph. He issued orders.

'I want you at least to promise me one thing – to do nothing rash for twenty-four hours.'

She was silent for a moment or two and then she said: 'I promise.'

'There is one other thing – a favour.'

'Yes?'

'Leave the shutter of the room I came in by unfastened, and keep vigil there tonight.'

She looked at him curiously, but nodded assent.

'And now,' said Mr Satterthwaite, slightly conscious of anti-climax, 'I really must be going. God bless you, my dear.'

He made a rather embarrassed exit. The stalwart Spanish girl met him in the passage and opened a side door for him, staring curiously at him the while.

It was just growing dark as he reached the hotel. There was a solitary figure sitting on the terrace. Mr Satterthwaite made straight for it. He was excited and his heart was beating quite fast. He felt that tremendous issues lay in his hands. One false move –

But he tried to conceal his agitation and to speak naturally and casually to Anthony Cosden.

'A warm evening,' he observed. 'I quite lost count of time sitting up there on the cliff.'

'Have you been up there all this time?'

Mr Satterthwaite nodded. The swing door into the hotel opened to let someone through, and a beam of light fell suddenly on the other's face, illuminating its look of dull suffering, of uncomprehending dumb endurance.

Mr Satterthwaite thought to himself: 'It's worse for him than it would be for me. Imagination, conjecture, speculation – they can do a lot for you. You can, as it were, ring the changes upon pain. The uncomprehending blind suffering of an animal – that's terrible . . .'

Cosden spoke suddenly in a harsh voice.

'I'm going for a stroll after dinner. You – you understand? The third time's lucky. For God's sake don't interfere. I know your interference will be well-meaning and all that – but take it from me, it's useless.'

Mr Satterthwaite drew himself up.

'I never interfere,' he said, thereby giving the lie to the whole purpose and object of his existence.

'I know what you think –' went on Cosden, but he was interrupted.

'You must excuse me, but there I beg to differ from you,' said Mr Satterthwaite. 'Nobody knows what another person is thinking. They may imagine they do, but they are nearly always wrong.'

'Well, perhaps that's so.' Cosden was doubtful, slightly taken aback.

'Thought is yours only,' said his companion. 'Nobody can alter or influence the use you mean to make of it. Let us talk of a less painful subject. That old villa, for instance. It has a curious charm, withdrawn, sheltered from the world, shielding heaven knows what mystery. It tempted me to do a doubtful action. I tried one of the shutters.'

'You did?' Cosden turned his head sharply. 'But it was fastened, of course?'

'No,' said Mr Satterthwaite. 'It was open.' He added gently: 'The third shutter from the end.'

'Why,' Cosden burst out, 'that was the one –'

He broke off suddenly, but Mr Satterthwaite had seen the light that had sprung up in his eyes. He rose – satisfied.

Some slight tinge of anxiety still remained with him. Using his favourite metaphor of a drama, he hoped that he had spoken his few lines correctly. For they were very important lines.

But thinking it over, his artistic judgment was satisfied. On his way up to the cliff, Cosden would try that shutter. It was not in human nature to resist. A memory of twenty odd years ago had brought him to this spot, the same memory would take him to the shutter. And afterwards?

'I shall know in the morning,' said Mr Satterthwaite, and proceeded to change methodically for his evening meal.

It was somewhere round ten o'clock that Mr Satterthwaite set foot once more in the garden of La Paz. Manuel bade him a smiling 'Good morning,' and handed him a single rosebud which

Mr Satterthwaite put carefully into his buttonhole. Then he went on to the house. He stood there for some minutes looking up at the peaceful white walls, the trailing orange creeper, and the faded green shutters. So silent, so peaceful. Had the whole thing been a dream?

But at that moment one of the windows opened and the lady who occupied Mr Satterthwaite's thoughts came out. She came straight to him with a buoyant swaying walk, like someone carried on a great wave of exultation. Her eyes were shining, her colour high. She looked like a figure of joy on a frieze. There was no hesitation about her, no doubts or tremors. Straight to Mr Satterthwaite she came, put her hands on his shoulders and kissed him – not once but many times. Large, dark, red roses, very velvety – that is how he thought of it afterwards. Sunshine, summer, birds singing – that was the atmosphere into which he felt himself caught up. Warmth, joy and tremendous vigour.

'I'm so happy,' she said. 'You darling! How did you know? How *could* you know? You're like the good magician in the fairy tales.'

She paused, a sort of breathlessness of happiness upon her.

'We're going over today – to the Consul – to get married. When John comes, his father will be there. We'll tell him there was some misunderstanding in the past. Oh! he won't ask questions. Oh! I'm so happy – so happy – so happy.'

Happiness did indeed surge from her like a tide. It lapped round Mr Satterthwaite in a warm exhilarating flood.

'It's so wonderful to Anthony to find he has a son. I never dreamt he'd mind or care.' She looked confidently into Mr Satterthwaite's eyes. 'Isn't it strange how things come right and end all beautifully?'

He had his clearest vision of her yet. A child – still a child – with her love of make believe – her fairy tales that ended beautifully with two people 'living happily ever afterwards'.

He said gently:

'If you bring this man of yours happiness in these last months, you will indeed have done a very beautiful thing.'

Her eyes opened wide – surprised.

'Oh!' she said. 'You don't think I'd let him die, do you? After all these years – when he's come to me. I've known lots of people whom doctors have given up and who are alive today. Die? Of course he's not going to die!'

He looked at her – her strength, her beauty, her vitality – her indomitable courage and will. He, too, had known doctors to be mistaken . . . The personal factor – you never knew how much and how little it counted.

She said again, with scorn and amusement in her voice:

'You don't think I'd let him die, do you?'

'No,' said Mr Satterthwaite at last very gently. 'Somehow, my dear, I don't think you will . . .'

Then at last he walked down the cypress path to the bench overlooking the sea and found there the person he was expecting to see. Mr Quin rose and greeted him – the same as ever, dark, saturnine, smiling and sad.

'You expected me?' he asked.

And Mr Satterthwaite answered: 'Yes, I expected you.'

They sat together on the bench.

'I have an idea that you have been playing Providence once more, to judge by your expression,' said Mr Quin presently.

Mr Satterthwaite looked at him reproachfully.

'As if you didn't know all about it.'

'You always accuse me of omniscience,' said Mr Quin, smiling.

'If you know nothing, why were you here the night before last – waiting?' countered Mr Satterthwaite.

'Oh, that –?'

'Yes, that.'

'I had a – commission to perform.'

'For whom?'

'You have sometimes fancifully named me an advocate for the dead.'

'The dead?' said Mr Satterthwaite, a little puzzled. 'I don't understand.'

Mr Quin pointed a long, lean finger down at the blue depths below.

'A man was drowned down there twenty-two years ago.'

'I know – but I don't see –'

'Supposing that, after all, that man loved his young wife. Love can make devils of men as well as angels. She had a girlish adoration for him, but he could never touch the womanhood in her – and that drove him mad. He tortured her because he loved her. Such things happen. You know that as well as I do.'

'Yes,' admitted Mr Satterthwaite, 'I have seen such things – but rarely – very rarely . . .'

'And you have also seen, more commonly, that there is such a thing as remorse – the desire to make amends – at all costs to make amends.'

'Yes, but death came too soon . . .'

'Death!' There was contempt in Mr Quin's voice. 'You believe in a life after death, do you not? And who are you to say that the same wishes, the same desires, may not operate in that other life? If the desire is strong enough – a messenger may be found.'

His voice tailed away.

Mr Satterthwaite got up, trembling a little.

'I must get back to the hotel,' he said. 'If you are going that way.'

But Mr Quin shook his head.

'No,' he said. 'I shall go back the way I came.'

When Mr Satterthwaite looked back over his shoulder, he saw his friend walking towards the edge of the cliff.

CHAPTER 7

The Voice in the Dark

I

'I am a little worried about Margery,' said Lady Stranleigh.

'My girl, you know,' she added.

She sighed pensively.

'It makes one feel terribly old to have a grown-up daughter.'

Mr Satterthwaite, who was the recipient of these confidences, rose to the occasion gallantly.

'No one could believe it possible,' he declared with a little bow.

'Flatterer,' said Lady Stranleigh, but she said it vaguely and it was clear that her mind was elsewhere.

Mr Satterthwaite looked at the slender white-clad figure in some admiration. The Cannes sunshine was searching, but Lady Stranleigh came through the test very well. At a distance the youthful effect was really extraordinary. One almost wondered if she were grown-up or not. Mr Satterthwaite, who knew everything, knew that it was perfectly possible for Lady Stranleigh to have grown-up grandchildren. She represented the extreme triumph of art over nature. Her figure was marvellous, her complexion was marvellous. She had enriched many beauty parlours and certainly the results were astounding.

Lady Stranleigh lit a cigarette, crossed her beautiful legs encased in the finest of nude silk stockings and murmured: 'Yes, I really am rather worried about Margery.'

'Dear me,' said Mr Satterthwaite, 'what is the trouble?'

Lady Stranleigh turned her beautiful blue eyes upon him

'You have never met her, have you? She is Charles' daughter,' she added helpfully.

If entries in 'Who's Who' were strictly truthful, the entries concerning Lady Stranleigh might have ended as follows: *hobbies: getting married.* She had floated through life shedding husbands as she went. She had lost three by divorce and one by death.

'If she had been Rudolph's child I could have understood it,' mused Lady Stranleigh. 'You remember Rudolf? He was always temperamental. Six months after we married I had to apply for those queer things – what do they call them? Conjugal what nots, you know what I mean. Thank goodness it is all much simpler nowadays. I remember I had to write him the silliest kind of letter – my lawyer practically dictated it to me. Asking him to come back, you know, and that I would do all I could, etc., etc., but you never could count on Rudolf, he was so temperamental. He came rushing home at once, which was quite the wrong thing to do, and not at all what the lawyers meant.'

She sighed.

'About Margery?' suggested Mr Satterthwaite, tactfully leading her back to the subject under discussion.

'Of course. I was just going to tell you, wasn't I? Margery has been seeing things, or hearing them. Ghosts, you know, and all that. I should never have thought that Margery could be so imaginative. She is a dear good girl, always has been, but just a shade – dull.'

'Impossible,' murmured Mr Satterthwaite with a confused idea of being complimentary.

'In fact, very dull,' said Lady Stranleigh. 'Doesn't care for dancing, or cocktails or any of the things a young girl ought to care about. She much prefers staying at home to hunt instead of coming out here with me.'

'Dear, dear,' said Mr Satterthwaite, 'she wouldn't come out with you, you say?'

'Well, I didn't exactly press her. Daughters have a depressing effect upon one, I find.'

Mr Satterthwaite tried to think of Lady Stranleigh accompanied by a serious-minded daughter and failed.

'I can't help wondering if Margery is going off her head,' continued Margery's mother in a cheerful voice. 'Hearing voices is a very bad sign, so they tell me. It is not as though Abbot's Mede were haunted. The old building was burnt to the ground in 1836, and they put up a kind of early Victorian château which simply cannot be haunted. It is much too ugly and commonplace.'

Mr Satterthwaite coughed. He was wondering why he was being told all this.

'I thought perhaps,' said Lady Stranleigh, smiling brilliantly upon him, 'that *you* might be able to help me.'

'I?'

'Yes. You are going back to England tomorrow, aren't you?'

'I am. Yes, that is so,' admitted Mr Satterthwaite cautiously.

'And you know all these psychical research people. Of course you do, you know everybody.'

Mr Satterthwaite smiled a little. It was one of his weaknesses to know everybody.

'So what can be simpler?' continued Lady Stranleigh. 'I never get on with that sort of person. You know – earnest men with beards and usually spectacles. They bore me terribly and I am quite at my worst with them.'

Mr Satterthwaite was rather taken aback. Lady Stranleigh continued to smile at him brilliantly.

'So that is all settled, isn't it?' she said brightly. 'You will go down to Abbot's Mede and see Margery, and make all the arrangements. I shall be terribly grateful to you. Of course if Margery is *really* going off her head, I will come home. Ah! here is Bimbo.'

Her smile from being brilliant became dazzling.

A young man in white tennis flannels was approaching them. He was about twenty-five years of age and extremely good-looking.

The young man said simply:

'I have been looking for you everywhere, Babs.'

'What has the tennis been like?'

'Septic.'

Lady Stranleigh rose. She turned her head over her shoulder and murmured in dulcet tones to Mr Satterthwaite: 'It is simply marvellous of you to help me. I shall never forget it.'

Mr Satterthwaite looked after the retreating couple.

'I wonder,' he mused to himself, 'If Bimbo is going to be No. 5.'

II

The conductor of the Train de Luxe was pointing out to Mr Satterthwaite where an accident on the line had occurred a few years previously. As he finished his spirited narrative, the other looked up and saw a well-known face smiling at him over the conductor's shoulder.

'My dear Mr Quin,' said Mr Satterthwaite.

His little withered face broke into smiles.

'What a coincidence! That we should both be returning to England on the same train. You are going there, I suppose.'

'Yes,' said Mr Quin. 'I have business there of rather an important nature. Are you taking the first service of dinner?'

'I always do so. Of course, it is an absurd time – half-past six, but one runs less risk with the cooking.'

Mr Quin nodded comprehendingly.

'I also,' he said. 'We might perhaps arrange to sit together.'

Half-past six found Mr Quin and Mr Satterthwaite established opposite each other at a small table in the dining-car. Mr Satterthwaite gave due attention to the wine list and then turned to his companion.

'I have not seen you since – ah, yes not since Corsica. You left very suddenly that day.'

Mr Quin shrugged his shoulders.

'Not more so than usual. I come and go, you know. I come and go.'

The words seemed to awake some echo of remembrance in Mr Satterthwaite's mind. A little shiver passed down his spine – not a disagreeable sensation, quite the contrary. He was conscious of a pleasurable sense of anticipation.

Mr Quin was holding up a bottle of red wine, examining the label on it. The bottle was between him and the light but for a minute or two a red glow enveloped his person.

Mr Satterthwaite felt again that sudden stir of excitement.

'I too have a kind of mission in England,' he remarked, smiling broadly at the remembrance. 'You know Lady Stranleigh perhaps?'

Mr Quin shook his head.

'It is an old title,' said Mr Satterthwaite, 'a very old title. One of the few that can descend in the female line. She is a Baroness in her own right. Rather a romantic history really.'

Mr Quin settled himself more comfortably in his chair. A waiter, flying down the swinging car, deposited cups of soup before them as if by a miracle. Mr Quin sipped it cautiously.

'You are about to give me one of those wonderful descriptive portraits of yours,' he murmured, 'that is so, is it not?'

Mr Satterthwaite beamed on him.

'She is really a marvellous woman,' he said. 'Sixty, you know – yes, I should say at least sixty. I knew them as girls, she and her sister. Beatrice, that was the name of the elder one. Beatrice and Barbara. I remember them as the Barron girls. Both good-looking and in those days very hard up. But that was a great many years ago – why, dear me, I was a young man myself then.' Mr Satterthwaite sighed. 'There were several lives then between them and the title. Old Lord Stranleigh was a first cousin once removed, I think. Lady Stranleigh's life has been quite a romantic affair. Three unexpected deaths – two of the old man's brothers and a nephew. Then there was the "Uralia". You remember the wreck of the "Uralia"? She went down off the coast of New Zealand. The Barron girls were on board. Beatrice was drowned. This one, Barbara, was amongst the few survivors. Six months later, old Stranleigh died and she succeeded to the title and came into a considerable fortune. Since then she has lived for one thing only – herself! She has always been the same, beautiful, unscrupulous, completely callous, interested solely in herself. She has had four husbands, and I have no doubt could get a fifth in a minute.'

He went on to describe the mission with which he had been entrusted by Lady Stranleigh.

'I thought of running down to Abbot's Mede to see the young lady,' he explained. 'I – I feel that something ought to be done about the matter. It is impossible to think of Lady Stranleigh as an ordinary mother.' He stopped, looking across the table at Mr Quin.

'I wish you would come with me,' he said wistfully. 'Would it not be possible?'

'I'm afraid not,' said Mr Quin. 'But let me see, Abbot's Mede is in Wiltshire, is it not?'

Mr Satterthwaite nodded.

'I thought as much. As it happens, I shall be staying not far from Abbot's Mede, at a place you and I both know.' He smiled. 'You remember that little inn, the "Bells and Motley"?'

'Of course,' cried Mr Satterthwaite; 'you will be there?'

Mr Quin nodded. 'For a week or ten days. Possibly longer. If you will come and look me up one day, I shall be delighted to see you.'

And somehow or other Mr Satterthwaite felt strangely comforted by the assurance.

III

'My dear Miss – er – Margery,' said Mr Satterthwaite, 'I assure you that I should not dream of laughing at you.'

Margery Gale frowned a little. They were sitting in the large comfortable hall of Abbot's Mede. Margery Gale was a big squarely built girl. She bore no resemblance to her mother, but took entirely after her father's side of the family, a line of hard-riding country squires. She looked fresh and wholesome and the picture of sanity. Nevertheless, Mr Satterthwaite was reflecting to himself that the Barrons as a family were all inclined to mental instability. Margery might have inherited her physical appearance from her father and at the same time have inherited some mental kink from her mother's side of the family.

'I wish,' said Margery, 'that I could get rid of that Casson woman. I don't believe in spiritualism, and I don't like it. She is one of these silly women that run a craze to death. She is always bothering me to have a medium down here.'

Mr Satterthwaite coughed, fidgeted a little in his chair and then said in a judicial manner:

'Let me be quite sure that I have all the facts. The first of the – er – phenomena occurred two months ago, I understand?'

'About that,' agreed the girl. 'Sometimes it was a whisper and sometimes it was quite a clear voice but it always said much the same thing.'

'Which was?'

'*Give back what is not yours. Give back what you have stolen.*

On each occasion I switched on the light, but the room was quite empty and there was no one there. In the end I got so nervous that I got Clayton, mother's maid, to sleep on the sofa in my room.'

'And the voice came just the same?'

'Yes – and this is what frightens me – Clayton did not hear it.'

Mr Satterthwaite reflected for a minute or two.

'Did it come loudly or softly that evening?'

'It was almost a whisper,' admitted Margery. 'If Clayton was sound asleep I suppose she would not really have heard it. She wanted me to see a doctor.' The girl laughed bitterly.

'But since last night even Clayton believes,' she continued.

'What happened last night?'

'I am just going to tell you. I have told no one as yet. I had been out hunting yesterday and we had had a long run. I was dead tired, and slept very heavily. I dreamt – a horrible dream – that I had fallen over some iron railings and that one of the spikes was entering slowly into my throat. I woke to find that it was true – there was some sharp point pressing into the side of my neck, and at the same time a voice was murmuring softly: "*You have stolen what is mine. This is death.*"

'I screamed,' continued Margery, 'and clutched at the air, but there was nothing there. Clayton heard me scream from the room next door where she was sleeping. She came rushing in, and she distinctly felt something brushing past her in the darkness, but she says that whatever that something was, it was not anything human.'

Mr Satterthwaite stared at her. The girl was obviously very shaken and upset. He noticed on the left side of her throat a small square of sticking plaster. She caught the direction of his gaze and nodded.

'Yes,' she said, 'it was not imagination, you see.'

Mr Satterthwaite put a question almost apologetically, it sounded so melodramatic.

'You don't know of anyone – er – who has a grudge against you?' he asked.

'Of course not,' said Margery. 'What an idea!'

Mr Satterthwaite started on another line of attack.

'What visitors have you had during the last two months?'

'You don't mean just people for week-ends, I suppose? Marcia Keane has been with me all along. She is my best friend, and just as keen on horses as I am. Then my cousin Roley Vavasour has been here a good deal.'

Mr Satterthwaite nodded. He suggested that he should see Clayton, the maid.

'She has been with you a long time, I suppose?' he asked.

'Donkey's years,' said Margery. 'She was Mother's and Aunt Beatrice's maid when they were girls. That is why Mother has kept her on, I suppose, although she has got a French maid for herself. Clayton does sewing and pottering little odd jobs.'

She took him upstairs and presently Clayton came to them. She was a tall, thin, old woman, with grey hair neatly parted, and she looked the acme of respectability.

'No, sir,' she said in answer to Mr Satterthwaite's inquiries. 'I have never heard anything of the house being haunted. To tell you the truth, sir, I thought it was all Miss Margery's imagination until last night. But I actually felt something – brushing by me in the darkness. And I can tell you this, sir, *it was not anything human*. And then there is that wound in Miss Margery's neck. She didn't do that herself, poor lamb.'

But her words were suggestive to Mr Satterthwaite. Was it possible that Margery could have inflicted that wound herself? He had heard of strange cases where girls apparently just as sane and well-balanced as Margery had done the most amazing things.

'It will soon heal up,' said Clayton. 'It's not like this scar of mine.'

She pointed to a mark on her own forehead.

'That was done forty years ago, sir; I still bear the mark of it.'

'It was the time the "Uralia" went down,' put in Margery. 'Clayton was hit on the head by a spar, weren't you, Clayton?'

'Yes, Miss.'

'What do you think yourself, Clayton,' asked Mr Satterthwaite, 'what do you think was the meaning of this attack on Miss Margery?'

'I really should not like to say, sir.'

Mr Satterthwaite read this correctly as the reserve of the well-trained servant.

'What do you really think, Clayton?' he said persuasively.

'I think, sir, that something very wicked must have been done in this house, and that until that is wiped out there won't be any peace.'

The woman spoke gravely, and her faded blue eyes met his steadily.

Mr Satterthwaite went downstairs rather disappointed. Clayton evidently held the orthodox view, a deliberate 'haunting' as a consequence of some evil deed in the past. Mr Satterthwaite himself was not so easily satisfied. The phenomena had only taken place in the last two months. Had only taken place since Marcia Keane and Roley Vavasour had been there. He must find out something about these two. It was possible that the whole thing was a practical joke. But he shook his head, dissatisfied with that solution. The thing was more sinister than that. The post had just come in and Margery was opening and reading her letters. Suddenly she gave an exclamation.

'Mother is too absurd,' she said. 'Do read this.' She handed the letter to Mr Satterthwaite.

It was an epistle typical of Lady Stranleigh.

Darling Margery (she wrote),

I am so glad you have that nice little Mr Satterthwaite there. He is awfully clever and knows all the big-wig spook people. You must have them all down and investigate things thoroughly. I am sure you will have a perfectly marvellous time, and I only wish I could be there, but I have really been quite ill the last few days. The hotels are so careless about the food they give one. The doctor says it is some kind of food poisoning. I was really very *ill.*

Sweet of you to send me the chocolates, darling, but surely just a wee bit silly, wasn't it? I mean, there's such wonderful confectionery out here.

Bye-bye, darling, and have a lovely time laying the family ghosts. Bimbo says my tennis is coming on marvellously.

Oceans of love.

Yours,

Barbara.

'Mother always wants me to call her Barbara,' said Margery. 'Simply silly, I think.'

Mr Satterthwaite smiled a little. He realized that the stolid conservatism of her daughter must on occasions be very trying to Lady Stranleigh. The contents of her letter struck him in a way in which obviously they did not strike Margery.

'Did you send your mother a box of chocolates?' he asked.

Margery shook her head. 'No, I didn't, it must have been someone else.'

Mr Satterthwaite looked grave. Two things struck him as of significance. Lady Stranleigh had received a gift of a box of chocolates and she was suffering from a severe attack of poisoning. Apparently she had not connected these two things. Was there a connection? He himself was inclined to think there was.

A tall dark girl lounged out of the morning-room and joined them.

She was introduced to Mr Satterthwaite as Marcia Keane. She smiled on the little man in an easy good-humoured fashion.

'Have you come down to hunt Margery's pet ghost?' she asked in a drawling voice. 'We all rot her about that ghost. Hello, here's Roley.'

A car had just drawn up at the front door. Out of it tumbled a tall young man with fair hair and an eager boyish manner.

'Hello, Margery,' he cried. 'Hello, Marcia! I have brought down reinforcements.' He turned to the two women who were just entering the hall. Mr Satterthwaite recognized in the first one of the two the Mrs Casson of whom Margery had spoken just now.

'You must forgive me, Margery, dear,' she drawled, smiling broadly. 'Mr Vavasour told us that it would be quite all right. It was really his idea that I should bring down Mrs Lloyd with me.'

She indicated her companion with a slight gesture of the hand.

'This is Mrs Lloyd,' she said in a tone of triumph. 'Simply the most wonderful medium that ever existed.'

Mrs Lloyd uttered no modest protest, she bowed and remained with her hands crossed in front of her. She was a highly-coloured young woman of commonplace appearance. Her clothes were unfashionable but rather ornate. She wore a chain of moonstones and several rings.

Margery Gale, as Mr Satterthwaite could see, was not too pleased at this intrusion. She threw an angry look at Roley Vavasour, who seemed quite unconscious of the offence he had caused.

'Lunch is ready, I think,' said Margery.

'Good,' said Mrs Casson. 'We will hold a *séance* immediately afterwards. Have you got some fruit for Mrs Lloyd? She never eats a solid meal before a *séance*.'

They all went into the dining-room. The medium ate two bananas and an apple, and replied cautiously and briefly to the various polite remarks which Margery addressed to her from time to time. Just before they rose from the table, she flung back her head suddenly and sniffed the air.

'There is something very wrong in this house. I feel it.'

'Isn't she wonderful?' said Mrs Casson in a low delighted voice.

'Oh! undoubtedly,' said Mr Satterthwaite dryly.

The *séance* was held in the library. The hostess was, as Mr Satterthwaite could see, very unwilling, only the obvious delight of her guests in the proceedings reconciled her to the ordeal.

The arrangements were made with a good deal of care by Mrs Casson, who was evidently well up in those matters, the chairs were set round in a circle, the curtains were drawn, and presently the medium announced herself ready to begin.

'Six people,' she said, looking round the room. 'That is bad. We must have an uneven number, Seven is ideal. I get my best results out of a circle of seven.'

'One of the servants,' suggested Roley. He rose. 'I will rout out the butler.'

'Let's have Clayton,' said Margery.

Mr Satterthwaite saw a look of annoyance pass over Roley Vavasour's good-looking face.

'But why Clayton?' he demanded.

'You don't like Clayton,' said Margery slowly.

Roley shrugged his shoulders. 'Clayton doesn't like me,' he said whimsically. 'In fact she hates me like poison.' He waited a minute or two, but Margery did not give way. 'All right,' he said, 'have her down.'

The circle was formed.

There was a period of silence broken by the usual coughs and fidgetings. Presently a succession of raps were heard and then the voice of the medium's control, a Red Indian called Cherokee.

'Indian Brave says you Good evening ladies and gentlemen. Someone here very anxious speak. Someone here very anxious give message to young lady. I go now. The spirit say what she come to say.'

A pause and then a new voice, that of a woman, said softly:

'Is Margery here?'

Roley Vavasour took it upon himself to answer.

'Yes,' he said, 'she is. Who is that speaking?'

'I am Beatrice.'

'Beatrice? Who is Beatrice?'

To everyone's annoyance the voice of the Red Indian Cherokee was heard once more.

'I have message for all of you people. Life here very bright and beautiful. We all work very hard. Help those who have not yet passed over.'

Again a silence and then the woman's voice was heard once more.

'This is Beatrice speaking.'

'Beatrice who?'

'Beatrice Barron.'

Mr Sattherwaite leaned forward. He was very excited.

'Beatrice Barron who was drowned in the "Uralia"?'

'Yes, that is right. I remember the "Uralia". I have a message – for this house – *Give back what is not yours*.'

'I don't understand,' said Margery helplessly. 'I – oh, are you really Aunt Beatrice?'

'Yes, I am your aunt.'

'Of course she is,' said Mrs Casson reproachfully. 'How can you be so suspicious? The spirits don't like it.'

And suddenly Mr Satterthwaite thought of a very simple test. His voice quivered as he spoke.

'Do you remember Mr Bottacetti?' he asked.

Immediately there came a ripple of laughter.

'Poor old Boatsupsetty. Of course.'

Mr Sattherwaite was dumbfounded. The test had succeeded.

It was an incident of over forty years ago which had happened when he and the Barron girls had found themselves at the same seaside resort. A young Italian acquaintance of theirs had gone out in a boat and capsized, and Beatrice Barron had jestingly named him Boatsupsetty. It seemed impossible that anyone in the room could know of this incident except himself.

The medium stirred and groaned.

'She is coming out,' said Mrs Casson. 'That is all we will get out of her today, I am afraid.'

The daylight shone once more on the room full of people, two of whom at least were badly scared.

Mr Satterthwaite saw by Margery's white face that she was deeply perturbed. When they had got rid of Mrs Casson and the medium, he sought a private interview with his hostess.

'I want to ask you one or two questions, Miss Margery. If you and your mother were to die who succeeds to the title and estates?'

'Roley Vavasour, I suppose. His mother was Mother's first cousin.'

Mr Satterthwaite nodded.

'He seems to have been here a lot this winter,' he said gently. 'You will forgive me asking – but is he – fond of you?'

'He asked me to marry him three weeks ago,' said Margery quietly. 'I said No.'

'Please forgive me, but are you engaged to anyone else?'

He saw the colour sweep over her face.

'I am,' she said emphatically. 'I am going to marry Noel Barton. Mother laughs and says it is absurd. She seems to think it is ridiculous to be engaged to a curate. Why, I should like to know! There are curates and curates! You should see Noel on a horse.'

'Oh, quite so,' said Mr Satterthwaite. 'Oh, undoubtedly.'

A footman entered with a telegram on a salver. Margery tore it open. 'Mother is arriving home tomorrow,' she said. 'Bother. I wish to goodness she would stay away.'

Mr Satterthwaite made no comment on this filial sentiment. Perhaps he thought it justified. 'In that case,' he murmured, 'I think I am returning to London.'

IV

Mr Satterthwaite was not quite pleased with himself. He felt that he had left this particular problem in an unfinished state. True that, on Lady Stranleigh's return, his responsibility was ended, yet he felt assured that he had not heard the last of the Abbot's Mede mystery.

But the next development when it came was so serious in its character that it found him totally unprepared. He learnt of it in the pages of his morning paper. 'Baroness Dies in her Bath,' as the *Daily Megaphone* had it. The other papers were more restrained and delicate in their language, but the fact was the same. Lady Stranleigh had been found dead in her bath and her death was due to drowning. She had, it was assumed, lost consciousness, and whilst in that state her head had slipped below the water.

But Mr Satterthwaite was not satisfied with that explanation. Calling for his valet he made his toilet with less than his usual care, and ten minutes later his big Rolls-Royce was carrying him out of London as fast as it could travel.

But strangely enough it was not for Abbot's Mede he was bound, but for a small inn some fifteen miles distant which bore the rather unusual name of the 'Bells and Motley'. It was with great relief that he heard that Mr Harley Quin was still staying there. In another minute he was face to face with his friend.

Mr Satterthwaite clasped him by the hand and began to speak at once in an agitated manner.

'I am terribly upset. You must help me. Already I have a dreadful feeling that it may be too late – that that nice girl may be the next to go, for she is a nice girl, nice through and through.'

'If you will tell me,' said Mr Quin, smiling, 'what it is all about?'

Mr Satterthwaite looked at him reproachfully.

'You know. I am perfectly certain that you know. But I will tell you.'

He poured out the story of his stay at Abbot's Mede and, as always with Mr Quin, he found himself taking pleasure in his narrative. He was eloquent and subtle and meticulous as to detail.

'So you see,' he ended, 'there must be an explanation.'

He looked hopefully at Mr Quin as a dog looks at his master.

'But it is you who must solve the problem, not I,' said Mr Quin. 'I do not know these people. You do.'

'I knew the Barron girls forty years ago,' said Mr Satterthwaite with pride.

Mr Quin nodded and looked sympathetic, so much so that the other went on dreamily.

'That time at Brighton now, Bottacetti-Boatsupsetty, quite a silly joke but how we laughed. Dear, dear, I was young then. Did a lot of foolish things. I remember the maid they had with them. Alice, her name was, a little bit of a thing – very ingenuous. I kissed her in the passage of the hotel, I remember, and one of the girls nearly caught me doing it. Dear, dear, how long ago that all was.'

He shook his head again and sighed. Then he looked at Mr Quin.

'So you can't help me?' he said wistfully. 'On other occasions –'

'On other occasions you have proved successful owing entirely to your own efforts,' said Mr Quin gravely. 'I think it will be the same this time. If I were you, I should go to Abbot's Mede now.'

'Quite so, quite so,' said Mr Satterthwaite, 'as a matter of fact that is what I thought of doing. I can't persuade you to come with me?'

Mr Quin shook his head.

'No,' he said, 'my work here is done. I am leaving almost immediately.'

At Abbot's Mede, Mr Satterthwaite was taken at once to Margery Gale. She was sitting dry-eyed at a desk in the morning-room on which were strewn various papers. Something in her greeting touched him. She seemed so very pleased to see him.

'Roley and Maria have just left. Mr Satterthwaite, it is not as the doctors think. I am convinced, absolutely convinced, that Mother was pushed under the water and held there. She was murdered, and whoever murdered her wants to murder me too. I am sure of that. That is why –' she indicated the document in front of her.

'I have been making my will,' she explained. 'A lot of the money and some of the property does not go with the title, and there is my father's money as well. I am leaving everything I can to Noel. I know he will make a good use of it and I do not trust Roley, he has always been out for what he can get. Will you sign it as a witness?'

'My dear young lady,' said Mr Satterthwaite, 'you should sign a will in the presence of two witnesses and they should then sign themselves at the same time.'

Margery brushed aside this legal pronouncement.

'I don't see that it matters in the least,' she declared. 'Clayton saw me sign and then she signed her name. I was going to ring for the butler, but you will do instead.'

Mr Satterthwaite uttered no fresh protest, he unscrewed his fountain pen and then, as he was about to append his signature, he paused suddenly. The name, written just above his own, recalled a flow of memories. Alice Clayton.

Something seemed to be struggling very hard to get through to him. Alice Clayton, there was some significance about that. Something to do with Mr Quin was mixed up with it. Something he had said to Mr Quin only a very short time ago.

Ah, he had it now. Alice Clayton, that was her name. *The little bit of a thing*. People changed – yes, *but not like that*. And the Alice Clayton he knew had had brown eyes. The room seemed whirling round him. He felt for a chair and presently, as though from a great distance, he heard Margery's voice speaking to him anxiously. 'Are you ill? Oh, what is it? I am sure you are ill.'

He was himself again. He took her hand.

'My dear, I see it all now. You must prepare yourself for a great shock. The woman upstairs whom you call Clayton is not Clayton at all. The real Alice Clayton was drowned on the "Uralia".'

Margery was staring at him. 'Who – who is she then?'

'I am not mistaken, I cannot be mistaken. The woman you call Clayton is your mother's sister, Beatrice Barron. You remember telling me that she was struck on the head by a spar? I should imagine that that blow destroyed her memory, and that being the case, your mother saw the chance –'

'Of pinching the title, you mean?' asked Margery bitterly. 'Yes, she would do that. It seems dreadful to say that now she is dead, but she was like that.'

'Beatrice was the elder sister,' said Mr Satterthwaite. 'By your uncle's death she would inherit everything and your mother would get nothing. Your mother claimed the wounded girl as her *maid*, not as her *sister*. The girl recovered from the blow and believed, of course, what was told her, that she was Alice Clayton, your mother's maid. I should imagine that just lately her memory had begun to return, but that the blow on the head, given all these years ago, has at last caused mischief on the brain.'

Margery was looking at him with eyes of horror.

'She killed Mother and she wanted to kill me,' she breathed.

'It seems so,' said Mr Satterthwaite. 'In her brain there was just one muddled idea – that her inheritance had been stolen and was being kept from her by you and your mother.'

'But – but Clayton is so old.'

Mr Satterthwaite was silent for a minute as a vision rose up before him – the faded old woman with grey hair, and the radiant golden-haired creature sitting in the sunshine at Cannes. Sisters! Could it really be so? He remembered the Barron girls and their likeness to each other. Just because two lives had developed on different tracks –

He shook his head sharply, obsessed by the wonder and pity of life . . .

He turned to Margery and said gently: 'We had better go upstairs and see her.'

They found Clayton sitting in the little workroom where she sewed. She did not turn her head as they came in for a reason that Mr Satterthwaite soon found out.

'Heart failure,' he murmured, as he touched the cold rigid shoulder. 'Perhaps it is best that way.'

CHAPTER 8

The Face of Helen

I

Mr Satterthwaite was at the Opera and sat alone in his big box on the first tier. Outside the door was a printed card bearing his name. An appreciator and a connoisseur of all the arts, Mr Satterthwaite was especially fond of good music, and was a regular subscriber to Covent Garden every year, reserving a box for Tuesdays and Fridays throughout the season.

But it was not often that he sat in it alone. He was a gregarious little gentleman, and he liked filling his box with the élite of the great world to which he belonged, and also with the aristocracy of the artistic world in which he was equally at home. He was alone tonight because a Countess had disappointed him. The Countess, besides being a beautiful and celebrated woman, was also a good mother. Her children had been attacked by that common and distressing disease, the mumps, and the Countess remained at home in tearful confabulation with exquisitely starched nurses. Her husband, who had supplied her with the aforementioned children and a title, but who was otherwise a complete nonentity, had seized at the chance to escape. Nothing bored him more than music.

So Mr Satterthwaite sat alone. *Cavalleria Rusticana* and *Pagliacci* were being given that night, and since the first had never appealed to him, he arrived just after the curtain went down, on Santuzza's death agony, in time to glance round the house with practised eyes, before everyone streamed out, bent on paying visits or fighting for coffee or lemonade. Mr Satterthwaite adjusted his opera glasses, looked round the house, marked down his prey and sallied forth with a well mapped out plan of campaign ahead of him. A plan, however, which he did not put into execution, for just outside his box he cannoned into a tall dark man, and recognized him with a pleasurable thrill of excitement.

'Mr Quin,' cried Mr Satterthwaite.

He seized his friend warmly by the hand, clutching him as though he feared any minute to see him vanish into thin air.

'You must share my box,' said Mr Satterthwaite determinedly. 'You are not with a party?'

'No, I am sitting by myself in the stalls,' responded Mr Quin with a smile.

'Then, that is settled,' said Mr Satterthwaite with a sigh of relief.

His manner was almost comic, had there been anyone to observe it.

'You are very kind,' said Mr Quin.

'Not at all. It is a pleasure. I didn't know you were fond of music?'

'There are reasons why I am attracted to – *Pagliacci.*'

'Ah! of course,' said Mr Satterthwaite, nodding sapiently, though, if put to it, he would have found it hard to explain just why he had used that expression. 'Of course, you would be.'

They went back to the box at the first summons of the bell, and leaning over the front of it, they watched the people returning to the stalls.

'That's a beautiful head,' observed Mr Satterthwaite suddenly.

He indicated with his glasses a spot immediately beneath them in the stalls circle. A girl sat there whose face they could not see – only the pure gold of her hair that fitted with the closeness of a cap till it merged into the white neck.

'A Greek head,' said Mr Satterthwaite reverently. 'Pure Greek.' He sighed happily. 'It's a remarkable thing when you come to think of it – how very few people have hair that *fits* them. It's more noticeable now that everyone is shingled.'

'You are so observant,' said Mr Quin.

'I see things,' admitted Mr Satterthwaite. 'I do see things. For instance, I picked out that head at once. We must have a look at her face sooner or later. But it won't match, I'm sure. That would be a chance in a thousand.'

Almost as the words left his lips, the lights flickered and went down, the sharp rap of the conductor's baton was heard, and the opera began. A new tenor, said to be a second Caruso, was singing that night. He had been referred to by the newspapers as a Jugo Slav, a Czech, an Albanian, a Magyar, and a Bulgarian, with a beautiful impartiality. He had given an extraordinary concert at the Albert Hall, a programme of the folk songs of his native hills, with a specially tuned orchestra. They were in strange half-tones and the would-be musical had pronounced them 'too marvellous'. Real musicians had reserved judgment, realizing that the ear had to be specially trained and attuned before any criticism was possible. It was quite a relief to some people to find this evening that Yoaschbim could sing in ordinary Italian with all the traditional sobs and quivers.

The curtain went down on the first act and applause burst out vociferously. Mr Satterthwaite turned to Mr Quin. He realized that the latter was waiting for him to pronounce judgment, and plumed himself a little. After all, he *knew*. As a critic he was well-nigh infallible.

Very slowly he nodded his head.

'It is the real thing,' he said.

'You think so?'

'As fine a voice as Caruso's. People will not recognize that it is so at first, for his technique is not yet perfect. There are ragged edges, a lack of certainty in the attack. But the voice is there – magnificent.'

'I went to his concert at the Albert Hall,' said Mr Quin.

'Did you? I could not go.'

'He made a wonderful hit with a Shepherd's Song.'

'I read about it,' said Mr Satterthwaite. 'The refrain ends each time with a high note – a kind of cry. A note midway between A and B flat. Very curious.'

Yoaschbim had taken three calls, bowing and smiling. The lights went up and the people began to file out. Mr Satterthwaite leant over to watch the girl with the golden head. She rose, adjusted her scarf, and turned.

Mr Satterthwaite caught his breath. There were, he knew, such faces in the world – faces that made history.

The girl moved to the gangway, her companion, a young man, beside her. And Mr Satterthwaite noticed how every man in the vicinity looked – and continued to look covertly.

'Beauty!' said Mr Satterthwaite to himself. 'There is such a thing. Not charm, nor attraction, nor magnetism, nor any of the things we talk about so glibly – just sheer beauty. The shape of a face, the line of an eyebrow, the curve of a jaw. He quoted softly under his breath: '*The face that launched a thousand ships.*' And for the first time he realized the meaning of those words.

He glanced across at Mr Quin, who was watching him in what seemed such perfect comprehension that Mr Satterthwaite felt there was no need for words.

'I've always wondered,' he said simply, 'what such women were really like.'

'You mean?'

'The Helens, the Cleopatras, the Mary Stuarts.'

Mr Quin nodded thoughtfully.

'If we go out,' he suggested, 'we may – see.'

They went out together, and their quest was successful. The pair they were in search of were seated on a lounge half-way up the staircase. For the first time, Mr Satterthwaite noted the girl's companion, a dark young man, not handsome, but with a suggestion of restless fire about him. A face full of strange angles; jutting cheek-bones, a forceful, slightly crooked jaw, deep-set eyes that were curiously light under the dark, overhanging brows.

'An interesting face,' said Mr Satterthwaite to himself. 'A real face. It means something.'

The young man was leaning forward talking earnestly. The girl was listening. Neither of them belonged to Mr Satterthwaite's world. He took them to be of the 'Arty' class. The girl wore a rather shapeless garment of cheap green silk. Her shoes were of soiled, white satin. The young man wore his evening clothes with an air of being uncomfortable in them.

The two men passed and re-passed several times. The fourth time they did so, the couple had been joined by a third – a fair young man with a suggestion of the clerk about him. With his coming a certain tension had set in. The newcomer was fidgetting with his tie and seemed ill at ease, the girl's beautiful face was turned gravely up towards him, and her companion was scowling furiously.

'The usual story,' said Mr Quin very softly, as they passed.

'Yes,' said Mr Satterthwaite with a sigh. 'It's inevitable, I suppose. The snarling of two dogs over a bone. It always has been, it always will be. And yet, one could wish for something different. Beauty –' he stopped. Beauty, to Mr Satterthwaite, meant something very wonderful. He found it difficult to speak of it. He looked at Mr Quin, who nodded his head gravely in understanding.

They went back to their seats for the second act.

At the close of the performance, Mr Satterthwaite turned eagerly to his friend.

'It is a wet night. My car is here. You must allow me to drive you – er – somewhere.'

The last word was Mr Satterthwaite's delicacy coming into play. 'To drive you home' would, he felt, have savoured of curiosity. Mr Quin had always been singularly reticent. It was extraordinary how little Mr Satterthwaite knew about him.

'But perhaps,' continued the little man, 'you have your own car waiting?'

'No,' said Mr Quin, 'I have no car waiting.'

'Then –'

But Mr Quin shook his head.

'You are most kind,' he said, 'but I prefer to go my own way. Besides,' he said with a rather curious smile, 'if anything should – happen, it will be for you to act. Goodnight, and thank you. Once again we have seen the drama together.'

He had gone so quickly that Mr Satterthwaite had no time to protest, but he was left with a faint uneasiness stirring in his mind. To what drama did Mr Quin refer? *Pagliacci* or another?'

Masters, Mr Satterthwaite's chauffeur, was in the habit of waiting in a side street. His master disliked the long delay while the cars drew up in turn before the Opera house. Now, as on previous occasions, he walked rapidly round the corner and along the street towards where he knew he should find Masters awaiting him. Just in front of him were a girl and a man, and even as he recognized them, another man joined them.

It all broke out in a minute. A man's voice, angrily uplifted. Another man's voice in injured protest. And then the scuffle. Blows, angry breathing, more blows, the form of a policeman appearing majestically from nowhere – and in another minute Mr

Satterthwaite was beside the girl where she shrank back against the wall.

'Allow me,' he said. 'You must not stay here.'

He took her by the arm and marshalled her swiftly down the street. Once she looked back.

'Oughtn't I –?' she began uncertainly.

Mr Satterthwaite shook his head.

'It would be very unpleasant for you to be mixed up in it. You would probably be asked to go along to the police station with them. I am sure neither of your – friends would wish that.'

He stopped.

'This is my car. If you will allow me to do so, I shall have much pleasure in driving you home.'

The girl looked at him searchingly. The staid respectability of Mr Satterthwaite impressed her favourably. She bent her head.

'Thank you,' she said, and got into the car, the door of which Masters was holding open.

In reply to a question from Mr Satterthwaite, she gave an address in Chelsea, and he got in beside her.

The girl was upset and not in the mood for talking, and Mr Satterthwaite was too tactful to intrude upon her thoughts. Presently, however, she turned to him and spoke of her own accord.

'I wish,' she said pettishly, 'people wouldn't be so silly.'

'It is a nuisance,' agreed Mr Satterthwaite.

His matter-of-fact manner put her at her ease, and she went on as though feeling the need of confiding in someone.

'It wasn't as though – I mean, well, it was like this. Mr Eastney and I have been friends for a long time – ever since I came to London. He's taken no end of trouble about my voice, and got me some very good introductions, and he's been more kind to me than I can say. He's absolutely music mad. It was very good of him to take me tonight. I'm sure he can't really afford it. And then Mr Burns came up and spoke to us – quite nicely, I'm sure, and Phil (Mr Eastney) got sulky about it. I don't know why he should. It's a free country, I'm sure. And Mr Burns is always pleasant, and good-tempered. Then just as we were walking to the Tube, he came up and joined us, and he hadn't so much as said two words before

Philip flew out at him like a madman. And – Oh! I don't like it.'

'Don't you?' asked Mr Satterthwaite very softly.

She blushed, but very little. There was none of the conscious siren about her. A certain measure of pleasurable excitement in being fought for there must be – that was only nature, but Mr Satterthwaite decided that a worried perplexity lay uppermost, and he had the clue to it in another moment when she observed inconsequently:

'I do hope he hasn't hurt him.'

'Now which is "him"?' thought Mr Satterthwaite, smiling to himself in the darkness.

He backed his own judgment and said:

'You hope Mr – er – Eastney hasn't hurt Mr Burns?'

She nodded.

'Yes, that's what I said. It seems so dreadful. I wish I knew.'

The car was drawing up.

'Are you on the telephone?' he asked.

'Yes.'

'If you like, I will find out exactly what has happened, and then telephone to you.'

The girl's face brightened.

'Oh, that would be very kind of you. Are you sure it's not too much bother?'

'Not in the least.'

She thanked him again and gave him her telephone number, adding with a touch of shyness: 'My name is Gillian West.'

As he was driven through the night, bound on his errand, a curious smile came to Mr Satterthwaite's lips.

He thought: 'So that is all it is . . . "*The shape of a face, the curve of a jaw!*"'

But he fulfilled his promise.

II

The following Sunday afternoon Mr Satterthwaite went to Kew Gardens to admire the rhododendrons. Very long ago (incredibly long ago, it seemed to Mr Satterthwaite) he had driven down to Kew Gardens with a certain young lady to see the bluebells. Mr Satterthwaite had arranged very carefully beforehand in his own mind exactly what he was going to say, and the precise words he would use in asking the young lady for her hand in marriage. He was just conning them over in his mind, and responding to her raptures about the bluebells a little absent-mindedly, when the shock came. The young lady stopped exclaiming at the bluebells and suddenly confided in Mr Satterthwaite (as a true friend) her love for another. Mr Satterthwaite put away the little set speech he had prepared, and hastily rummaged for sympathy and friendship in the bottom drawer of his mind.

Such was Mr Satterthwaite's romance – a rather tepid early Victorian one, but it had left him with a romantic attachment to Kew Gardens, and he would often go there to see the bluebells, or, if he had been abroad later than usual, the rhododendrons, and would sigh to himself, and feel rather sentimental, and really enjoy himself very much indeed in an old-fashioned, romantic way.

This particular afternoon he was strolling back past the tea houses when he recognized a couple sitting at one of the small tables on the grass. They were Gillian West and the fair young man, and at that same moment they recognized him. He saw the girl flush and speak eagerly to her companion. In another minute he was shaking hands with them both in his correct, rather prim fashion, and had accepted the shy invitation proffered him to have tea with them.

'I can't tell you, sir,' said Mr Burns, 'how grateful I am to you for looking after Gillian the other night. She told me all about it.'

'Yes, indeed,' said the girl. 'It was ever so kind of you.'

Mr Satterthwaite felt pleased and interested in the pair. Their naïveté and sincerity touched him. Also, it was to him a peep into a world with which he was not well acquainted. These people were of a class unknown to him.

In his little dried-up way, Mr Satterthwaite could be very sympathetic. Very soon he was hearing all about his new friends. He noted that Mr Burns had become Charlie, and he was not unprepared for the statement that the two were engaged.

'As a matter of fact,' said Mr Burns with refreshing candour, 'it just happened this afternoon, didn't it, Gil?'

Burns was a clerk in a shipping firm. He was making a fair salary, had a little money of his own, and the two proposed to be married quite soon.

Mr Satterthwaite listened, and nodded, and congratulated.

'An ordinary young man,' he thought to himself, 'a very ordinary young man. Nice, straightforward young chap, plenty to say for himself, good opinion of himself without being conceited, nice-looking without being unduly handsome. Nothing remarkable about him and will never set the Thames on fire. And the girl loves him . . .'

Aloud he said: 'And Mr Eastney –'

He purposely broke off, but he had said enough to produce an effect for which he was not unprepared. Charlie Burns's face darkened, and Gillian looked troubled. More than troubled, he thought. She looked afraid.

'I don't like it,' she said in a low voice. Her words were addressed to Mr Satterthwaite, as though she knew by instinct that he would understand a feeling incomprehensible to her lover. 'You see – he's done a lot for me. He's encouraged me to take up singing, and – and helped me with it. But I've known all the time that my voice wasn't really good – not first-class. Of course, I've had engagements –'

She stopped.

'You've had a bit of trouble too,' said Burns. 'A girl wants someone to look after her. Gillian's had a lot of unpleasantness, Mr Satterthwaite. Altogether she's had a lot of unpleasantness. She's a good-looker, as you can see, and – well, that often leads to trouble for a girl.'

Between them, Mr Satterthwaite became enlightened as to various happenings which were vaguely classed by Burns under the heading of 'unpleasantness'. A young man who had shot himself, the extraordinary conduct of a Bank Manager (who was a married man!), a violent stranger (who must have been balmy!), the wild behaviour of an elderly artist. A trail of violence and tragedy that Gillian West had left in her wake, recited in the commonplace tones of Charles Burns. 'And it's my opinion,' he ended, 'that this fellow Eastney is a bit cracked. Gillian would have had trouble with him if I hadn't turned up to look after her.'

His laugh sounded a little fatuous to Mr Satterthwaite, and no responsive smile came to the girl's face. She was looking earnestly at Mr Satterthwaite.

'Phil's all right,' she said slowly. 'He cares for me, I know, and I care for him like a friend – but – but not anything more. I don't know how he'll take the news about Charlie, I'm sure. He – I'm so afraid he'll be –'

She stopped, inarticulate in face of the dangers she vaguely sensed.

'If I can help you in any way,' said Mr Satterthwaite warmly, 'pray command me.'

He fancied Charlie Burns looked vaguely resentful, but Gillian said at once: 'Thank you.'

Mr Satterthwaite left his new friends after having promised to take tea with Gillian on the following Thursday.

When Thursday came, Mr Satterthwaite felt a little thrill of pleasurable anticipation. He thought: 'I'm an old man – but not too old to be thrilled by a face. A face . . .' Then he shook his head with a sense of foreboding.

Gillian was alone. Charlie Burns was to come in later. She looked much happier, Mr Satterthwaite thought, as though a load had been lifted from her mind. Indeed, she frankly admitted as much.

'I dreaded telling Phil about Charles. It was silly of me. I ought to have known Phil better. He was upset, of course, but no one could have been sweeter. Really sweet he was. Look what he sent me this morning – a wedding present. Isn't it magnificent?'

It was indeed rather magnificient for a young man in Philip Eastney's circumstances. A four-valve wireless set, of the latest type.

'We both love music so much, you see,' explained the girl. 'Phil said that when I was listening to a concert on this, I should always think of him a little. And I'm sure I shall. Because we have been such friends.'

'You must be proud of your friend,' said Mr Satterthwaite gently. 'He seems to have taken the blow like a true sportsman.'

Gillian nodded. He saw the quick tears come into her eyes.

'He asked me to do one thing for him. Tonight is the anniversary of the day we first met. He asked me if I would stay at home quietly this evening and listen to the wireless programme – not to go out with Charlie anywhere. I said, of course I would, and that I was very touched, and that I would think of him with a lot of gratitude and affection.'

Mr Satterthwaite nodded, but he was puzzled. He was seldom at fault in his delineation of character, and he would have judged Philip Eastney quite incapable of such a sentimental request. The young man must be of a more banal order than he supposed. Gillian evidently thought the idea quite in keeping with her rejected lover's character. Mr Satterthwaite was a little – just a little – disappointed. He was sentimental himself, and knew it, but he expected better things of the rest of the world. Besides sentiment belonged to his age. It had no part to play in the modern world.

He asked Gillian to sing and she complied. He told her her voice was charming, but he knew quite well in his own mind that it was distinctly second-class. Any success that could have come to her in the profession she had adopted would have been won by her face, not her voice.

He was not particularly anxious to see young Burns again, so presently he rose to go. It was at that moment that his attention was attracted by an ornament on the mantelpiece which stood out among the other rather gimcrack objects like a jewel on a dust heap.

It was a curving beaker of thin green glass, long-stemmed and graceful, and poised on the edge of it was what looked like a gigantic soap-bubble, a ball of iridescent glass. Gillian noticed his absorption.

'That's an extra wedding present from Phil. It's rather pretty, I think. He works in a sort of glass factory.'

'It is a beautiful thing,' said Mr Satterthwaite reverently. 'The glass blowers of Murano might have been proud of that.'

He went away with his interest in Philip Eastney strangely stimulated. An extraordinarily interesting young man. And yet the girl with the wonderful face preferred Charlie Burns. What a strange and inscrutable universe!

It had just occurred to Mr Satterthwaite that, owing to the remarkable beauty of Gillian West, his evening with Mr Quin had somehow missed fire. As a rule, every meeting with that mysterious individual had resulted in some strange and unforeseen happening. It was with the hope of perhaps running against the man of mystery that Mr Satterthwaite bent his steps towards the *Arlecchino* Restaurant where once, in the days gone by, he had met Mr Quin, and which Mr Quin had said he often frequented.

Mr Satterthwaite went from room to room at the *Arlecchino*, looking hopefully about him, but there was no sign of Mr Quin's dark, smiling face. There was, however, somebody else. Sitting at a small table alone was Philip Eastney.

The place was crowded and Mr Satterthwaite took his seat opposite the young man. He felt a sudden strange sense of exultation, as though he were caught up and made part of a shimmering pattern of events. He was in this thing – whatever it was. He knew now what Mr Quin had meant that evening at the Opera. There was a drama going on, and in it was a part, an important part, for Mr Satterthwaite. He must not fail to take his cue and speak his lines.

He sat down opposite Philip Eastney with the sense of accomplishing the inevitable. It was easy enough to get into conversation. Eastney seemed anxious to talk. Mr Satterthwaite was, as always, an encouraging and sympathetic listener. They talked of the war, of explosives, of poison gases. Eastney had a lot to say about these last, for during the greater part of the war he had been engaged in their manufacture. Mr Satterthwaite found him really interesting.

There was one gas, Eastney said, that had never been tried. The Armistice had come too soon. Great things had been hoped for it. One whiff of it was deadly. He warmed to animation as he spoke.

Having broken the ice, Mr Satterthwaite gently turned the conversation to music. Eastney's thin face lit up. He spoke with the passion and abandon of the real music lover. They discussed Yoaschbim, and the young man was enthusiastic. Both he and Mr Satterthwaite agreed that nothing on earth could surpass a really fine tenor voice. Eastney as a boy had heard Caruso and he had never forgotten it.

'Do you know that he could sing to a wine-glass and shatter it?' he demanded.

'I always thought that was a fable,' said Mr Satterthwaite smiling.

'No, it's gospel truth, I believe. The thing's quite possible. It's a question of resonance.'

He went off into technical details. His face was flushed and his eyes shone. The subject seemed to fascinate him, and Mr Satterthwaite noted that he seemed to have a thorough grasp of what he was talking about. The elder man realized that he was talking to an exceptional brain, a brain that might almost be described as that of a genius. Brilliant, erratic, undecided as yet as to the true channel to give it outlet, but undoubtedly genius.

And he thought of Charlie Burns and wondered at Gillian West.

It was with quite a start that he realized how late it was getting, and he called for his bill. Eastney looked slightly apologetic.

'I'm ashamed of myself – running on so,' he said. 'But it was a lucky chance sent you along here tonight. I – I needed someone to talk to this evening.'

He ended his speech with a curious little laugh. His eyes were still blazing with some subdued excitement. Yet there was something tragic about him.

'It has been quite a pleasure,' said Mr Satterthwaite. 'Our conversation has been most interesting and instructive to me.'

He then made his funny, courteous little bow and passed out of the restaurant. The night was a warm one and as he walked slowly down the street a very odd fancy came to him. He had the feeling that he was not alone – that someone was walking by his side. In vain he told himself that the idea was a delusion – it persisted. Someone was walking beside him down that dark, quiet street, someone whom he could not see. He wondered what it was that brought the figure of Mr Quin so clearly before his mind. He felt exactly as though Mr Quin were there walking beside him, and yet he had only to use his eyes to assure himself that it was not so, that he was alone.

But the thought of Mr Quin persisted, and with it came

something else: a need, an urgency of some kind, an oppressive foreboding of calamity. There was something he must do – and do quickly. There was something very wrong, and it lay in his hands to put it right.

So strong was the feeling that Mr Satterthwaite forebore to fight against it. Instead, he shut his eyes and tried to bring that mental image of Mr Quin nearer. If he could only have asked Mr Quin – but even as the thought flashed through his mind he knew it was wrong. It was never any use asking Mr Quin anything. 'The threads are all in your hands' – that was the kind of thing Mr Quin would say.

The threads. Threads of what? He analysed his own feeling and impressions carefully. That presentiment of danger, now. Whom did it threaten?

At once a picture rose up before his eyes, the picture of Gillian West sitting alone listening to the wireless.

Mr Satterthwaite flung a penny to a passing newspaper boy, and snatched at a paper. He turned at once to the London Radio programme. Yoaschbim was broadcasting tonight, he noted with interest. He was singing 'Salve Dimora', from Faust and, afterwards, a selection of his folk songs. 'The Shepherd's Song', 'The Fish', 'The Little Deer', etc.

Mr Satterthwaite crumpled the paper together. The knowledge of what Gillian was listening to seemed to make the picture of her clearer. Sitting there alone . . .

An odd request, that, of Philip Eastney's. Not like the man, not like him at all. There was no sentimentality in Eastney. He was a man of violent feeling, a dangerous man, perhaps –

Again his thought brought up with a jerk. A dangerous man – that meant something. '*The threads are all in your hands.*' That meeting with Philip Eastney tonight – rather odd. A lucky chance, Eastney had said. Was it chance? Or was it part of that interwoven design of which Mr Satterthwaite had once or twice been conscious this evening?

He cast his mind back. There must be *something* in Eastney's conversation, some clue there. There must, or else why this strange feeling of urgency? What had he talked about? Singing, war work, Caruso.

Caruso – Mr Satterthwaite's thoughts went off at a tangent.

Yoaschbim's voice was very nearly equal to that of Caruso. Gillian would be sitting listening to it now as it rang out true and powerful, echoing round the room, setting glasses ringing –

He caught his breath. Glasses ringing! Caruso, singing to a wine-glass and the wine-glass breaking. Yoachbim singing in the London studio and in a room over a mile away the crash and tinkle of glass – not a wine-glass, a thin, green, glass beaker. A crystal soap bubble falling, a soap bubble that perhaps was not empty . . .

It was at that moment that Mr Satterthwaite, as judged by passers-by, suddenly went mad. He tore open the newspaper once more, took a brief glance at the wireless announcements and then began to run for his life down the quiet street. At the end of it he found a crawling taxi, and jumping into it, he yelled an address to the driver and the information that it was life or death to get there quickly. The driver, judging him mentally afflicted but rich, did his utmost.

Mr Satterthwaite lay back, his head a jumble of fragmentary thoughts, forgotten bits of science learned at school, phrases used by Eastney that night. Resonance – natural periods – if the period of the force coincides with the natural period – there was something about a suspension bridge, soldiers marching over it and the swing of their stride being the same as the period of the bridge. Eastney had studied the subject. Eastney knew. And Eastney was a genius.

At 10.45 Yoaschbim was to broadcast. It was that now. Yes, but the Faust had to come first. It was the 'Shepherd's Song', with the great shout after the refrain that would – that would – do what?

His mind went whirling round again. Tones, overtones, half-tones. He didn't know much about these things – but Eastney knew. Pray heaven he would be in time!

The taxi stopped. Mr Satterthwaite flung himself out and raced up the stone stairs to a second floor like a young athlete. The door of the flat was ajar. He pushed it open and the great tenor voice welcomed him. The words of the 'Shepherd's Song' were familiar to him in a less unconventional setting.

'Shepherd, see they horse's flowing main –'

He was in time then. He burst open the sitting-room door. Gillian was sitting there in a tall chair by the fireplace.

'Bayra Mischa's daughter is to wed today:
To the wedding I must haste away.'

She must have thought him mad. He clutched at her, crying out something incomprehensible, and half pulled, half dragged her out till they stood upon the stairway.

'To the wedding I must haste away –
Ya-ha!'

A wonderful high note, full-throated, powerful, hit full in the middle, a note any singer might be proud of. And with it another sound, the faint tinkle of broken glass.

A stray cat darted past them and in through the flat door. Gillian made a movement, but Mr Satterthwaite held her back, speaking incoherently.

'No, no – it's deadly: no smell, nothing to warn you. A mere whiff, and it's all over. Nobody knows quite how deadly it would be. It's unlike anything that's ever been tried before.'

He was repeating the things that Philip Eastney had told him over the table at dinner.

Gillian stared at him uncomprehendingly.

III

Philip Eastney drew out his watch and looked at it. It was just half-past eleven. For the past three-quarters of an hour he had been pacing up and down the Embankment. He looked out over the Thames and then turned – to look into the face of his dinner companion.

'That's odd,' he said, and laughed. 'We seem fated to run into each other tonight.'

'If you call it Fate,' said Mr Satterthwaite.

Philip Eastney looked at him more attentively and his own expression changed.

'Yes?' he said quietly.

Mr Satterthwaite went straight to the point.

'I have just come from Miss West's flat.'

'Yes?'

The same voice, with the same deadly quiet.

'We have – taken a dead cat out of it.'

There was silence, then Eastney said:

'Who are you?'

Mr Satterthwaite spoke for some time. He recited the whole history of events.

'So you see, I was in time,' he ended up. He paused and added quite gently:

'Have you anything – to say?'

He expected something, some outburst, some wild justification. But nothing came.

'No,' said Philip Eastney quietly, and turned on his heel and walked away,

Mr Satterthwaite looked after him till his figure was swallowed up in the gloom. In spite of himself, he had a strange fellow-feeling for Eastney, the feeling of an artist for another artist, of a sentimentalist for a real lover, of a plain man for a genius.

At last he roused himself with a start and began to walk in the same direction as Eastney. A fog was beginning to come up. Presently he met a policeman who looked at him suspiciously.

'Did you hear a kind of splash just now?' asked the policeman.

'No,' said Mr Satterthwaite.

The policeman was peering out over the river.

'Another of these suicides, I expect,' he grunted disconsolately. 'They will do it.'

'I suppose,' said Mr Satterthwaite, 'that they have their reasons.'

'Money, mostly,' said the policeman. 'Sometimes it's a woman,' he said, as he prepared to move away. 'It's not always their fault, but some women cause a lot of trouble.'

'Some women,' agreed Mr Satterthwaite softly.

When the policeman had gone on, he sat down on a seat with the fog coming up all around him, and thought about Helen of Troy, and wondered if she were a nice, ordinary woman, blessed or cursed with a wonderful face.

CHAPTER 9

The Dead Harlequin

Mr Satterthwaite walked slowly up Bond Street enjoying the sunshine. He was, as usual, carefully and beautifully dressed, and was bound for the Harchester Galleries where there was an exhibition of the paintings of one Frank Bristow, a new and hitherto unknown artist who showed signs of suddenly becoming the rage. Mr Satterthwaite was a patron of the arts.

As Mr Satterthwaite entered the Harchester Galleries, he was greeted at once with a smile of pleased recognition.

'Good morning, Mr Satterthwaite, I thought we should see you before long. You know Bristow's work? Fine – very fine indeed. Quite unique of its kind.'

Mr Satterthwaite purchased a catalogue and stepped through the open archway into the long room where the artist's works were displayed. They were water colours, executed with such extraordinary technique and finish that they resembled coloured etchings. Mr Satterthwaite walked slowly round the walls scrutinizing and, on the whole, approving. He thought that this young man deserved to arrive. Here was originality, vision, and a most severe and exacting technique. There were crudities, of course. That was only to be expected – but there was also something closely allied to genius. Mr Satterthwaite paused before a little masterpiece representing Westminster Bridge with its crowd of buses, trams and hurrying pedestrians. A tiny thing and wonderfully perfect. It was called, he noted, The Ant Heap. He passed on and quite suddenly drew in his breath with a gasp, his imagination held and riveted.

The picture was called The Dead Harlequin. The forefront of it represented a floor of inlaid squares of black and white marble. In the middle of the floor lay Harlequin on his back with his arms outstretched, in his motley of black and red. Behind him was a window and outside that window, gazing in at the figure on the floor, was what appeared to be the same man silhouetted against the red glow of the setting sun.

The picture excited Mr Satterthwaite for two reasons, the first was that he recognized, or thought that he recognized, the face of the man in the picture. It bore a distinct resemblance to a certain Mr Quin, an acquaintance whom Mr Satterthwaite had encountered once or twice under somewhat mystifying circumstances.

'Surely I can't be mistaken,' he murmured. 'If it *is* so – what does it mean?'

For it had been Mr Satterthwaite's experience that every appearance of Mr Quin had some distinct significance attaching to it.

There was, as already mentioned, a second reason for Mr Satterthwaite's interest. He recognized the scene of the picture.

'The Terrace Room at Charnley,' said Mr Satterthwaite. 'Curious – and very interesting.'

He looked with more attention at the picture, wondering what exactly had been in the artist's mind. One Harlequin dead on the floor, another Harlequin looking through the window – or was it the same Harlequin? He moved slowly along the walls gazing at other pictures with unseeing eyes, with his mind always busy on the same subject. He was excited. Life, which had seemed a little drab this morning, was drab no longer. He knew quite certainly that he was on the threshold of exciting and interesting events. He crossed to the table where sat Mr Cobb, a dignitary of the Harchester Galleries, whom he had known for many years.

'I have a fancy for buying no. 39,' he said, 'if it is not already sold.'

Mr Cobb consulted a ledger.

'The pick of the bunch,' he murmured, 'quite a little gem, isn't it? No, it is not sold.' He quoted a price. 'It is a good investment, Mr Satterthwaite. You will have to pay three times as much for it this time next year.'

'That is always said on these occasions,' said Mr Satterthwaite, smiling.

'Well, and haven't I been right?' demanded Mr Cobb. 'I don't believe if you were to sell your collection, Mr Satterthwaite, that a single picture would fetch less than you gave for it.'

'I will buy this picture,' said Mr Satterthwaite. 'I will give you a cheque now.'

'You won't regret it. We believe in Bristow.'

'He is a young man?'

'Twenty-seven or -eight, I should say.'

'I should like to meet him,' said Mr Satterthwaite. 'Perhaps he will come and dine with me one night?'

'I can give you his address. I am sure he would leap at the chance. Your name stands for a good deal in the artistic world.'

'You flatter me,' said Mr Satterthwaite, and was going on when Mr Cobb interrupted:

'Here he is now. I will introduce you to him right away.'

He rose from behind his table. Mr Satterthwaite accompanied him to where a big, clumsy young man was leaning against the wall surveying the world at large from behind the barricade of a ferocious scowl.

Mr Cobb made the necessary introductions and Mr Satterthwaite made a formal and gracious little speech.

'I have just had the pleasure of acquiring one of your pictures – The Dead Harlequin.'

'Oh! Well, you won't lose by it,' said Mr Bristow ungraciously. 'It's a bit of damned good work, although I say it.'

'I can see that,' said Mr Satterthwaite. 'Your work interests me very much, Mr Bristow. It is extraordinarily mature for so young a man. I wonder if you would give me the pleasure of dining with me one night? Are you engaged this evening?'

'As a matter of fact, I am not,' said Mr Bristow, still with no overdone appearance of graciousness.

'Then shall we say eight o'clock?' said Mr Satterthwaite. 'Here is my card with the address on it.'

'Oh, all right,' said Mr Bristow. 'Thanks,' he added as a somewhat obvious afterthought.

'A young man who has a poor opinion of himself and is afraid that the world should share it.'

Such was Mr Satterthwaite's summing up as he stepped out into the sunshine of Bond Street, and Mr Satterthwaite's judgment of his fellow men was seldom far astray.

Frank Bristow arrived about five minutes past eight to find his host and a third guest awaiting him. The other guest was introduced as a Colonel Monckton. They went in to dinner almost immediately. There was a fourth place laid at the oval mahogany table and Mr Satterthwaite uttered a word of explanation.

'I half expected my friend, Mr Quin, might drop in,' he said. 'I wonder if you have ever met him. Mr Harley Quin?'

'I never meet people,' growled Bristow.

Colonel Monckton stared at the artist with the detached interest he might have accorded to a new species of jelly fish. Mr Satterthwaite exerted himself to keep the ball of conversation rolling amicably.

'I took a special interest in that picture of yours because I thought I recognized the scene of it as being the Terrace Room at Charnley. Was I right?' As the artist nodded, he went on. 'That is very interesting. I have stayed at Charnley several times myself in the past. Perhaps you know some of the family?'

'No, I don't!' said Bristow. 'That sort of family wouldn't care to know me. I went there in a charabanc.'

'Dear me,' said Colonel Monckton for the sake of saying something. 'In a charabanc! Dear me.'

Frank Bristow scowled at him.

'Why not?' he demanded ferociously.

Poor Colonel Monckton was taken aback. He looked reproachfully at Mr Satterthwaite as though to say:

'These primitive forms of life may be interesting to you as a naturalist, but why drag *me* in?'

'Oh, beastly things, charabancs!' he said. 'They jolt you so going over the bumps.'

'If you can't afford a Rolls Royce you have got to go in charabancs,' said Bristow fiercely.

Colonel Monckton stared at him. Mr Satterthwaite thought:

'Unless I can manage to put this young man at his ease we are going to have a very distressing evening.'

'Charnley aways fascinated me,' he said. 'I have been there only once since the tragedy. A grim house – and a ghostly one.'

'That's true,' said Bristow.

'There are actually two authentic ghosts,' said Monckton. 'They say that Charles I walks up and down the terrace with his head under his arm – I have forgotten why, I'm sure. Then there is the Weeping Lady with the Silver Ewer, who is always seen after one of the Charnleys dies.'

'Tosh,' said Bristow scornfully.

'They have certainly been a very ill-fated family,' said Mr Satterthwaite hurriedly. 'Four holders of the title have died a violent death and the late Lord Charnley committed suicide.'

'A ghastly business,' said Monckton gravely. 'I was there when it happened.'

'Let me see, that must be fourteen years ago,' said Mr Satterthwaite, 'the house has been shut up ever since.'

'I don't wonder at that,' said Monckton. 'It must have been a terrible shock for a young girl. They had been married a month, just home from their honeymoon. Big fancy dress ball to celebrate their home-coming. Just as the guests were starting to arrive Charnley locked himself into the Oak Parlour and shot himself. That sort of thing isn't done. I beg your pardon?'

He turned his head sharply to the left and looked across at Mr Satterthwaite with an apologetic laugh.

'I am beginning to get the jimjams, Satterthwaite. I thought for a moment there was someone sitting in that empty chair and that he said something to me.

'Yes,' he went on after a minute or two, 'it was a pretty ghastly shock to Alix Charnley. She was one of the prettiest girls you could see anywhere and cram full of what people call the joy of living, and now they say she is like a ghost herself. Not that I have seen her for years. I believe she lives abroad most of the time.'

'And the boy?'

'The boy is at Eton. What he will do when he comes of age I don't know. I don't think, somehow, that he will reopen the old place.'

'It would make a good People's Pleasure Park,' said Bristow.

Colonel Monckton looked at him with cold abhorrence.

'No, no, you don't really mean that,' said Mr Satterthwaite. 'You wouldn't have painted that picture if you did. Tradition and atmosphere are intangible things. They take centuries to build up and if you destroyed them you couldn't rebuild them again in twenty-four hours.'

He rose. 'Let us go into the smoking-room. I have some photographs there of Charnley which I should like to show you.'

One of Mr Satterthwaite's hobbies was amateur photography. He was also the proud author of a book, 'Homes of My Friends'. The friends in question were all rather exalted and the book itself showed Mr Satterthwaite forth in rather a more snobbish light than was really fair to him.

'That is a photograph I took of the Terrace Room last year,' he said. He handed it to Bristow. 'You see it is taken at almost the same angle as is shown in your picture. That is rather a wonderful rug – it is a pity that photographs can't show colouring.'

'I remember it,' said Bristow, 'a marvellous bit of colour. It glowed like a flame. All the same it looked a bit incongruous there. The wrong size for that big room with its black and white squares. There is no rug anywhere else in the room. It spoils the whole effect – it was like a gigantic blood stain.'

'Perhaps that gave you your idea for your picture?' said Mr Satterthwaite.

'Perhaps it did,' said Bristow thoughtfully. 'On the face of it, one would naturally stage a tragedy in the little panelled room leading out of it.'

'The Oak Parlour,' said Monckton. 'Yes, that is the haunted room right enough. There is a Priests' hiding hole there – a movable panel by the fireplace. Tradition has it that Charles I was concealed there once. There were two deaths from duelling in that room. And it was there, as I say, that Reggie Charnley shot himself.'

He took the photograph from Bristow's hand.

'Why, that is the Bokhara rug,' he said, 'worth a couple of thousand pounds, I believe. When I was there it was in the Oak Parlour – the right place for it. It looks silly on that great expanse of marble flags.'

Mr Satterthwaite was looking at the empty chair which he had drawn up beside his. Then he said thoughtfully: 'I wonder when it was moved?'

'It must have been recently. Why, I remember having a conversation about it on the very day of the tragedy. Charnley was saying it really ought to be kept under glass.'

Mr Satterthwaite shook his head. 'The house was shut up immediately after the tragedy and everything was left exactly as it was.'

Bristow broke in with a question. He had laid aside his aggressive manner.

'Why did Lord Charnley shoot himself?' he asked.

Colonel Monckton shifted uncomfortably in his chair.

'No one ever knew,' he said vaguely.

'I suppose,' said Mr Satterthwaite slowly, 'that it *was* suicide.'

The Colonel looked at him in blank astonishment.

'Suicide,' he said, 'why, of course it was suicide. My dear fellow, I was there in the house myself.'

Mr Satterthwaite looked towards the empty chair at his side and, smiling to himself as though at some hidden joke the others could not see, he said quietly:

'Sometimes one sees things more clearly years afterwards than one could possibly at the time.'

'Nonsense,' spluttered Monckton, 'arrant nonsense! How can you possibly see things better when they are vague in your memory instead of clear and sharp?'

But Mr Satterthwaite was reinforced from an unexpected quarter.

'I know what you mean,' said the artist. 'I should say that possibly you were right. It is a question of proportion, isn't it? And more than proportion probably. Relativity and all that sort of thing.'

'If you ask me,' said the Colonel, 'all this Einstein business is a lot of dashed nonsense. So are spiritualists and the spook of one's grandmother!' He glared round fiercely.

'Of course it was suicide,' he went on. 'Didn't I practically see the thing happen with my own eyes?'

'Tell us about it,' said Mr Satterthwaite, 'so that we shall see it with our eyes also.'

With a somewhat mollified grunt the Colonel settled himself more comfortably in his chair.

'The whole thing was extraordinarily unexpected,' he began. 'Charnley had been his usual normal self. There was a big party staying in the house for this ball. No one could ever have guessed he would go and shoot himself just as the guests began arriving.'

'It would have been better taste if he had waited until they had gone,' said Mr Satterthwaite.

'Of course it would. Damned bad taste – to do a thing like that.'

'Uncharacteristic,' said Mr Satterthwaite.

'Yes,' admitted Monckton, 'it wasn't like Charnley.'

'And yet it *was* suicide?'

'Of course it was suicide. Why, there were three or four of us there at the top of the stairs. Myself, the Ostrander girl, Algie Darcy – oh, and one or two others. Charnley passed along the hall below and went into the Oak Parlour. The Ostrander girl said there was a ghastly look on his face and his eyes were staring – but, of course, that is nonsense – she couldn't even see his face from where we were – but he did walk in a hunched way, as if he had the weight of the world on his shoulders. One of the girls called to him – she was somebody's governess, I think, whom Lady Charnley had included in the party out of kindness. She was looking for him with a message. She called out "Lord Charnley, Lady Charnley wants to know –" He paid no attention and went into the Oak Parlour and slammed the door and we heard the key turn in the lock. Then, one minute after, *we heard the shot.*

'We rushed down to the hall. There is another door from the Oak Parlour leading into the Terrace Room. We tried that but it was locked, too. In the end we had to break the door down. Charnley was lying on the floor – dead – with a pistol close beside his right hand. Now, what could that have been but suicide? Accident? Don't tell me. There is only one other possibility – murder – and you can't have murder without a murderer. You admit that, I suppose.'

'The murderer might have escaped,' suggested Mr Satterthwaite.

'That is impossible. If you have a bit of paper and a pencil I will draw you a plan of the place. There are two doors into the Oak Parlour, one into the hall and one into the Terrace Room. Both these doors were locked in the inside *and the keys were in the locks.*'

'The window?'

'Shut, and the shutters fastened across it.'

There was a pause.

'So that is that,' said Colonel Monckton triumphantly.

'It certainly seems to be,' said Mr Satterthwaite sadly.

'Mind you,' said the Colonel, 'although I was laughing just

now at the spiritualists, I don't mind admitting that there was a deuced rummy atmosphere about the place – about that room in particular. There are several bullet holes in the panels of the walls, the results of the duels that took place in that room, and there is a queer stain on the floor, that always comes back though they have replaced the wood several times. I suppose there will be another blood stain on the floor now – poor Charnley's blood.'

'Was there much blood?' asked Mr Satterthwaite.

'Very little – curiously little – so the doctor said.'

'Where did he shoot himself, through the head?'

'No, through the heart.'

'That is not the easy way to do it,' said Bristow. 'Frightfully difficult to know where one's heart is. I should never do it that way myself.'

Mr Satterthwaite shook his head. He was vaguely dissatisfied. He had hoped to get at something – he hardly knew what. Colonel Monckton went on.

'It is a spooky place, Charnley. Of course, *I* didn't see anything.'

'You didn't see the Weeping Lady with the Silver Ewer?'

'No, I did not, sir,' said the Colonel emphatically. 'But I expect every servant in the place swore they did.'

'Superstition was the curse of the Middle Ages,' said Bristow. 'There are still traces of it here and there, but thank goodness, we are getting free from it.'

'Superstition,' mused Mr Satterthwaite, his eyes turned again to the empty chair. 'Sometimes, don't you think – it might be useful?'

Bristow stared at him.

'Useful, that's a queer word.'

'Well, I hope you are convinced now, Satterthwaite,' said the Colonel.

'Oh, quite,' said Mr Satterthwaite. 'On the face of it, it seems odd – so purposeless for a newly-married man, young, rich, happy, celebrating his home-coming – curious – but I agree there is no getting away from the facts.' He repeated softly, 'The facts,' and frowned.

'I suppose the interesting thing is a thing we none of us will ever know,' said Monckton, 'the story behind it all. Of course there were rumours – all sorts of rumours. You know the kind of things people say.'

'But no one *knew* anything,' said Mr Satterthwaite thoughtfully.

'It's not a best seller mystery, is it?' remarked Bristow. 'No one gained by the man's death.'

'No one except an unborn child,' said Mr Satterthwaite.

Monckton gave a sharp chuckle. 'Rather a blow to poor Hugo Charnley,' he observed. 'As soon as it was known that there was going to be a child he had the graceful task of sitting tight and waiting to see if it would be a girl or boy. Rather an anxious wait for his creditors, too. In the end a boy it was and a disappointment for the lot of them.'

'Was the widow very disconsolate?' asked Bristow.

'Poor child,' said Monckton, 'I shall never forget her. She didn't cry or break down or anything. She was like something – frozen. As I say, she shut up the house shortly afterwards and, as far as I know, it has never been reopened since.'

'So we are left in the dark as to motive,' said Bristow with a slight laugh. 'Another man or another woman, it must have been one or the other, eh?'

'It seems like it,' said Mr Satterthwaite.

'And the betting is strongly on another woman,' continued Bristow, 'since the fair widow has not married again. I hate women,' he added dispassionately.

Mr Satterthwaite smiled a little and Frank Bristow saw the smile and pounced upon it.

'You may smile,' he said, 'but I do. They upset everything. They interfere. They get between you and your work. They – I only once met a woman who was – well, interesting.'

'I thought there would be one,' said Mr Satterthwaite.

'Not in the way you mean. I – I just met her casually. As a matter of fact – it was in a train. After all,' he added defiantly, 'why shouldn't one meet people in trains?'

'Certainly, certainly,' said Mr Satterthwaite soothingly, 'a train is as good a place as anywhere else.'

'It was coming down from the North. We had the carriage to ourselves. I don't know why, but we began to talk. I don't know her name and I don't suppose I shall ever meet her again. I don't know that I want to. It might be – a pity.' He paused, struggling to express himself. 'She wasn't quite real, you know. Shadowy. Like one of the people who come out of the hills in Gaelic fairy tales.'

Mr Satterthwaite nodded gently. His imagination pictured the scene easily enough. The very positive and realistic Bristow and a figure that was silvery and ghostly – shadowy, as Bristow had said.

'I suppose if something very terrible had happened, so terrible as to be almost unbearable, one might get like that. One might run away from reality into a half world of one's own and then, of course, after a time, one wouldn't be able to get back.'

'Was that what had happened to her?' asked Mr Satterthwaite curiously.

'I don't know,' said Bristow. 'She didn't tell me anything, I am only guessing. One has to guess if one is going to get anywhere.'

'Yes,' said Mr Satterthwaite slowly. 'One has to guess.'

He looked up as the door opened. He looked up quickly and expectantly but the butler's words disappointed him.

'A lady, sir, has called to see you on very urgent business. Miss Aspasia Glen.'

Mr Satterthwaite rose in some astonishment. He knew the name of Aspasia Glen. Who in London did not? First advertised as the Woman with the Scarf, she had given a series of matinées single-handed that had taken London by storm. With the aid of her scarf she had impersonated rapidly various characters. In turn the scarf had been the coif of a nun, the shawl of a mill-worker, the head-dress of a peasant and a hundred other things, and in each impersonation Aspasia Glen had been totally and utterly different. As an artist, Mr Satterthwaite paid full reverence to her. As it happened, he had never made her acquaintance. A call upon him at this unusual hour intrigued him greatly. With a few words of apology to the others he left the room and crossed the hall to the drawing-room.

Miss Glen was sitting in the very centre of a large settee upholstered in gold brocade. So poised she dominated the room. Mr Satterthwaite perceived at once that she meant to dominate the situation. Curiously enough, his first feeling was one of repulsion. He had been a sincere admirer of Aspasia Glen's art. Her personality, as conveyed to him over the footlights, had been appealing and sympathetic. Her effects there had been wistful and suggestive rather than commanding. But now, face to face with the woman herself, he received a totally different impression. There was something hard – bold – forceful about her. She was tall and dark, possibly about thirty-five years of age. She was undoubtedly very good-looking and she clearly relied upon the fact.

'You must forgive this unconventional call, Mr Satterthwaite,' she said. Her voice was full and rich and seductive.

'I won't say that I have wanted to know you for a long time, but I *am* glad of the excuse. As for coming tonight' – she laughed – 'well, when I want a thing, I simply can't wait. When I want a thing, I simply *must* have it.'

'Any excuse that has brought me such a charming lady guest must be welcomed by me,' said Mr Satterthwaite in an old-fashioned gallant manner.

'How nice you are to me,' said Aspasia Glen.

'My dear lady,' said Mr Satterthwaite, 'may I thank you here and now for the pleasure you have so often given me – in my seat in the stalls.'

She smiled delightfully at him.

'I am coming straight to the point. I was at the Harchester Galleries today. I saw a picture there I simply couldn't live without. I wanted to buy it and I couldn't because you had already bought it. So' – she paused – 'I do want it so,' she went on. 'Dear Mr Satterthwaite, I simply *must* have it. I brought my cheque book.' She looked at him hopefully. 'Everyone tells me you are so frightfully kind. People *are* kind to me, you know. It is very bad for me – but there it is.'

So these were Aspasia Glen's methods. Mr Satterthwaite was inwardly coldly critical of this ultra-femininity and of this spoilt child pose. It ought to appeal to him, he supposed, but it didn't. Aspasia Glen had made a mistake. She had judged him as an elderly dilettante, easily flattered by a pretty woman. But Mr Satterthwaite behind his gallant manner had a shrewd and critical mind. He saw people pretty well as they were, not as they wished to appear to him. He saw before him, not a charming woman pleading for a whim, but a ruthless egoist determined to get her own way for some reason which was obscure to him. And he knew quite certainly that Aspasia Glen was not going to get her own way. He was not going to give up the picture of the Dead Harlequin to her. He sought rapidly in his mind for the best way of circumventing her without overt rudeness.

'I am sure,' he said, 'that everyone gives you your own way as often as they can and is only too delighted to do so.'

'Then you are really going to let me have the picture?'

Mr Satterthwaite shook his head slowly and regretfully.

'I am afraid that is impossible. You see' – he paused – 'I bought that picture for a lady. It is a present.'

'Oh! but surely –'

The telephone on the table rang sharply. With a murmured word of excuse Mr Satterthwaite took up the receiver. A voice spoke to him, a small, cold voice that sounded very far away.

'Can I speak to Mr Satterthwaite, please?'

'It is Mr Satterthwaite speaking.'

'I am Lady Charnley, Alix Charnley. I daresay you don't remember me Mr Satterthwaite, it is a great many years since we met.'

'My dear Alix. Of course, I remember you.'

'There is something I wanted to ask you. I was at the Harchester Galleries at an exhibition of pictures today, there was one called The Dead Harlequin, perhaps you recognized it – it was the Terrace Room at Charnley. I – I want to have that picture. It was sold to you.' She paused. 'Mr Satterthwaite, for reasons of my own I want that picture. Will you resell it to me?'

Mr Satterthwaite thought to himself: 'Why, this is a miracle.' As he spoke into the receiver he was thankful that Aspasia Glen could only hear one side of the conversation. 'If you will accept my gift, dear lady, it will make me very happy.' He heard a sharp exclamation behind him and hurried on. 'I bought it for you. I did indeed. But listen, my dear Alix, I want to ask you to do me a great favour, if you will.'

'Of course. Mr Satterthwaite, I am so *very* grateful.'

He went on. 'I want you to come round now to my house, at once.'

There was a slight pause and then she answered quietly:

'I will come at once.'

Mr Satterthwaite put down the receiver and turned to Miss Glen.

She said quickly and angrily:

'That was the picture you were talking about?'

'Yes,' said Mr Satterthwaite, 'the lady to whom I am presenting it is coming round to this house in a few minutes.'

Suddenly Aspasia Glen's face broke once more into smiles. 'You will give me a chance of persuading her to turn the picture over to me?'

'I will give you a chance of persuading her.'

Inwardly he was strangely excited. He was in the midst of a drama that was shaping itself to some foredoomed end. He, the looker-on, was playing a star part. He turned to Miss Glen.

'Will you come into the other room with me? I should like you to meet some friends of mine.'

He held the door open for her and, crossing the hall, opened the door of the smoking-room.

'Miss Glen,' he said, 'let me introduce you to an old friend of mine, Colonel Monckton. Mr Bristow, the painter of the picture you admire so much.' Then he started as a third figure rose from the chair which he had left empty beside his own.

'I think you expected me this evening,' said Mr Quin. 'During your absence I introduced myself to your friends. I am so glad I was able to drop in.'

'My dear friend,' said Mr Satterthwaite, 'I – I have been carrying on as well as I am able, but –' He stopped before the slightly sardonic glance of Mr Quin's dark eyes. 'Let me introduce you. Mr Harley Quin, Miss Aspasia Glen.'

Was it fancy – or did she shrink back slightly. A curious expression flitted over her face. Suddenly Bristow broke in boisterously. 'I have got it.'

'Got what?'

'Got hold of what was puzzling me. There is a likeness, there is a distinct likeness.' He was staring curiously at Mr Quin. 'You see it?' – he turned to Mr Satterthwaite – 'don't you see a distinct likeness to the Harlequin of my picture – the man looking in through the window?'

It was no fancy this time. He distinctly heard Miss Glen

draw in her breath sharply and even saw that she stepped back one pace.

'I told you that I was expecting someone,' said Mr Satterthwaite. He spoke with an air of triumph. 'I must tell you that my friend, Mr Quin, is a most extraordinary person. He can unravel mysteries. He can make you see things.'

'Are you a medium, sir?' demanded Colonel Monckton, eyeing Mr Quin doubtfully.

The latter smiled and slowly shook his head.

'Mr Satterthwaite exaggerates,' he said quietly. 'Once or twice when I have been with him he has done some extraordinarily good deductive work. Why he puts the credit down to me I can't say. His modesty, I suppose.'

'No, no,' said Mr Satterthwaite excitedly. 'It isn't. You make me see things – things that I ought to have seen all along – that I actually have seen – but without knowing that I saw them.'

'It sounds to me deuced complicated,' said Colonel Monckton.

'Not really,' said Mr Quin. 'The trouble is that we are not content just to see things – we will tack the wrong interpretation on to the things we see.'

Aspasia Glen turned to Frank Bristow.

'I want to know,' she said nervously, 'what put the idea of painting that picture into your head?'

Bristow shrugged his shoulders. 'I don't quite know,' he confessed. 'Something about the place – about Charnley, I mean, took hold of my imagination. The big empty room. The terrace outside, the idea of ghosts and things, I suppose. I have just been hearing the tale of the last Lord Charnley, who shot himself. Supposing you are dead, and your spirit lives on? It must be odd, you know. You might stand outside on the terrace looking in at the window at your own dead body, and you would see everything.'

'What do you mean?' said Aspasia Glen. '*See* everything?'

'Well, you would see what happened. You would see –'

The door opened and the butler announced Lady Charnley.

Mr Satterthwaite went to meet her. He had not seen her for nearly thirteen years. He remembered her as she once was, an eager, glowing girl. And now he saw – a Frozen Lady. Very fair, very pale, with an air of drifting rather than walking, a snowflake driven at random by an icy breeze. Something unreal about her. So cold, so far away.

'It was very good of you to come,' said Mr Satterthwaite.

He led her forward. She made a half gesture of recognition towards Miss Glen and then paused as the other made no response.

'I am so sorry,' she murmured, 'but surely I have met you somewhere, haven't I?'

'Over the footlights, perhaps,' said Mr Satterthwaite. 'This is Miss Aspasia Glen, Lady Charnley.'

'I am very pleased to meet you, Lady Charnley,' said Aspasia Glen.

Her voice had suddenly a slight trans-Atlantic tinge to it. Mr Satterthwaite was reminded of one of her various stage impersonations.

'Colonel Monckton you know,' continued Mr Satterthwaite, 'and this is Mr Bristow.'

He saw a sudden faint tinge of colour in her cheeks.

'Mr Bristow and I have met too,' she said, and smiled a little. 'In a train.'

'And Mr Harley Quin.'

He watched her closely, but this time there was no flicker of recognition. He set a chair for her, and then, seating himself, he cleared his throat and spoke a little nervously. 'I – this is rather an unusual little gathering. It centres round this picture. I – I think that if we liked we could – clear things up.'

'You are not going to hold a *séance*, Satterthwaite?' asked Colonel Monckton. 'You are very odd this evening.'

'No,' said Mr Satterthwaite, 'not exactly a *séance*. But my friend, Mr Quin, believes, and I agree, that one can, by looking back over the past, see things as they were and not as they appeared to be.'

'The past?' said Lady Charnley.

'I am speaking of your husband's suicide, Alix. I know it hurts you –'

'No,' said Alix Charnley, 'it doesn't hurt me. Nothing hurts me now.'

Mr Satterthwaite thought of Frank Bristow's words. '*She was not quite real you know. Shadowy. Like one of the people who come out of hills in Gaelic fairy tales.*'

'Shadowy,' he had called her. That described her exactly. A shadow, a reflection of something else. Where then was the real Alix, and his mind answered quickly: '*In the past.* Divided from us by fourteen years of time.'

'My dear,' he said, 'you frighten me. You are like the Weeping Lady with the Silver Ewer.'

Crash! The coffee cup on the table by Aspasia's elbow fell shattered to the floor. Mr Satterthwaite waved aside her apologies. He thought: 'We are getting nearer, we are getting nearer every minute – but nearer to what?'

'Let us take our minds back to that night fourteen years ago,' he said. 'Lord Charnley killed himself. For what reason? No one knows.'

Lady Charnley stirred slightly in her chair.

'Lady Charnley knows,' said Frank Bristow abruptly.

'Nonsense,' said Colonel Monckton, then stopped, frowning at her curiously.

She was looking across at the artist. It was as though he drew the words out of her. She spoke, nodding her head slowly, and her voice was like a snowflake, cold and soft.

'Yes, you are quite right. I *know*. That is why as long as I live I can never go back to Charnley. That is why when my boy Dick wants me to open the place up and live there again I tell him it can't be done.'

'Will you tell us the reason, Lady Charnley?' said Mr Quin.

She looked at him. Then, as though hypnotised, she spoke as quietly and naturally as a child.

'I will tell you if you like. Nothing seems to matter very much now. I found a letter among his papers and I destroyed it.'

'What letter?' said Mr Quin.

'The letter from the girl – from that poor child. She was the Merriams' nursery governess. He had – he had made love to her – yes, while he was engaged to me just before we were married. And she – she was going to have a child too. She wrote saying so, and that she was going to tell me about it. So, you see, he shot himself.'

She looked round at them wearily and dreamily like a child who has repeated a lesson it knows too well.

Colonel Monckton blew his nose.

'My God,' he said, 'so that was it. Well, that explains things with a vengeance.'

'Does it?' said Mr Satterthwaite, 'it doesn't explain one thing. *It doesn't explain why Mr Bristow painted that picture.*'

'What do you mean?'

Mr Satterthwaite looked across at Mr Quin as though for encouragement, and apparently got it, for he proceeded:

'Yes, I know I sound mad to all of you, but that picture is the focus of the whole thing. We are all here tonight because of that picture. That picture *had* to be painted – that is what I mean.'

'You mean the uncanny influence of the Oak Parlour?' began Colonel Monckton.

'No,' said Mr Satterthwaite. '*Not* the Oak Parlour. The Terrace Room. That is it! The spirit of the dead man standing outside the window and looking in and seeing his own dead body on the floor.'

'Which he couldn't have done,' said the Colonel, 'because the body was in the Oak Parlour.'

'Supposing it wasn't,' said Mr Satterthwaite, 'supposing it was exactly where Mr Bristow saw it, saw it imaginatively, I mean on the black and white flags in front of the window.'

'You are talking nonsense,' said Colonel Monckton, 'if it was there we shouldn't have found it in the Oak Parlour.'

'Not unless someone carried it there,' said Mr Satterthwaite.

'And in that case how could we have seen Charnley going in at the door of the Oak Parlour?' inquired Colonel Monckton.

'Well, you didn't see his face, did you?' asked Mr Satterthwaite. 'What I mean is, you saw a man going into the Oak Parlour in fancy dress, I suppose.'

'Brocade things and a wig,' said Monckton.

'Just so, and you thought it was Lord Charnley because the girl called out to him as Lord Charnley.'

'And because when we broke in a few minutes later there was only Lord Charnley there dead. You can't get away from that, Satterthwaite.'

'No,' said Mr Satterthwaite, discouraged. 'No – unless there was a hiding-place of some kind.'

'Weren't you saying something about there being a Priests' hole in that room?' put in Frank Bristow.

'Oh!' cried Mr Satterthwaite. 'Supposing –?' He waved a hand for silence and sheltered his forehead with his other hand and then spoke slowly and hesitatingly.

'I have got an idea – it may be just an idea, but I think it hangs together. Supposing someone shot Lord Charnley. Shot him in the Terrace Room. Then he – and another person – dragged the body into the Oak Parlour. They laid it down there with the pistol by its right hand. Now we go on to the next step. It must seem absolutely certain that Lord Charnley has committed suicide. I think that could be done very easily. The man in his brocade and wig passes along the hall by the Oak Parlour door and someone, to make sure of things, calls out to him as Lord Charnley from the top of the stairs. He goes in and locks both doors and fires a shot into the woodwork. There were bullet holes already in that room if you remember, one more wouldn't be noticed. He then hides quietly in the secret chamber. The doors are broken open and people rush in. It seems certain that Lord Charnley has committed suicide. No other hypothesis is even entertained.'

'Well, I think that is balderdash,' said Colonel Monckton. 'You forget that Charnley had a motive right enough for suicide.'

'A letter found afterwards,' said Mr Satterthwaite. 'A lying cruel letter written by a very clever and unscrupulous little actress who meant one day to be Lady Charnley herself.'

'You mean?'

'I mean the girl in league with Hugo Charnley,' said Mr Satterthwaite. 'You know, Monckton, everyone knows, that that man was a blackguard. He thought that he was certain to come into the title.' He turned sharply to Lady Charnley. 'What was the name of the girl who wrote that letter?'

'Monica Ford,' said Lady Charnley.

'Was it Monica Ford, Monckton, who called out to Lord Charnley from the top of the stairs?'

'Yes, now you come to speak of it, I believe it was.'

'Oh, that's impossible,' said Lady Charnley. 'I – I went to her about it. She told me it was all true. I only saw her once afterwards, but surely she couldn't have been acting the whole time.'

Mr Satterthwaite looked across the room at Aspasia Glen.

'I think she could,' he said quietly. 'I think she had in her the makings of a very accomplished actress.'

'There is one thing you haven't got over,' said Frank Bristow, 'there would be blood on the floor of the Terrace Room. Bound to be. They couldn't clear that up in a hurry.'

'No,' admitted Mr Satterthwaite, 'but there is one thing they could do – a thing that would only take a second or two – they could throw over the blood-stains the Bokhara rug. Nobody ever saw the Bokhara rug in the Terrace Room before that night.'

'I believe you are right,' said Monckton, 'but all the same those blood-stains would have to be cleared up some time?'

'Yes,' said Mr Satterthwaite, 'in the middle of the night. A woman with a jug and basin could go down the stairs and clear up the blood-stains quite easily.'

'But supposing someone saw her?'

'It wouldn't matter,' said Mr Satterthwaite. 'I am speaking now of things as they *are*. I said a woman with a jug and basin. But if I had said a Weeping Lady with a Silver Ewer that is what they would have *appeared* to be.' He got up and went across to Aspasia Glen. 'That is what you did, wasn't it?' he said. 'They call you the "Woman with the Scarf" now, but it was that night you played your first part, the "Weeping Lady with the Silver Ewer". That is why you knocked the coffee cup off that table just now. You were afraid when you saw that picture. You thought someone knew.'

Lady Charnley stretched out a white accusing hand.

'Monica Ford,' she breathed. 'I recognize you now.'

Aspasia Glen sprang to her feet with a cry. She pushed little Mr Satterthwaite aside with a shove of the hand and stood shaking in front of Mr Quin.

'So I was right. Someone *did* know! Oh, I haven't been deceived by this tomfoolery. This pretence of working things out.' She pointed at Mr Quin. '*You* were there. *You* were there outside the window looking in. You saw what we did, Hugo and I. I *knew* there was someone looking in, I felt it all the time. And yet when I looked up, there was nobody there. I knew someone was watching us. I thought once I caught a glimpse of a face at the window. It has frightened me all these years. Why did you break silence now? That is what I want to know?'

'Perhaps so that the dead may rest in peace,' said Mr Quin.

Suddenly Aspasia Glen made a rush for the door and stood there flinging a few defiant words over her shoulder.

'Do what you like. God knows there are witnesses enough to what I have been saying. I don't care, I don't care. I loved Hugo and I helped him with the ghastly business and he chucked me afterwards. He died last year. You can set the police on my tracks if you like, but as that little dried-up fellow there said, I am a pretty good actress. They will find it hard to find me.' She crashed the door behind her, and a moment later they heard the slam of the front door, also.

'Reggie,' cried Lady Charnley, 'Reggie.' The tears were streaming down her face. 'Oh, my dear, my dear, I can go back to Charnley now. I can live there with Dickie. I can tell him what his father was, the finest, the most splendid man in all the world.'

'We must consult very seriously as to what must be done in the matter,' said Colonel Monckton. 'Alix, my dear, if you will let me take you home I shall be glad to have a few words with you on the subject.'

Lady Charnley rose. She came across to Mr Satterthwaite, and laying both hands on his shoulders, she kissed him very gently.

'It is so wonderful to be alive again after being so long dead,' she said. 'It was like being dead, you know. Thank you, dear Mr Satterthwaite.' She went out of the room with Colonel Monckton. Mr Satterthwaite gazed after them. A grunt from Frank Bristow whom he had forgotten made him turn sharply round.

'She is a lovely creature,' said Bristow moodily. 'But she's not nearly so interesting as she was,' he said gloomily.

'There speaks the artist,' said Mr Satterthwaite.

'Well, she isn't,' said Mr Bristow. 'I suppose I should only get the cold shoulder if I ever went butting in at Charnley. I don't want to go where I am not wanted.'

'My dear young man,' said Mr Satterthwaite, 'if you will think a little less of the impression you are making on other people, you will, I think, be wiser and happier. You would also do well to disabuse your mind of some very old-fashioned notions, one of which is that birth has any significance at all in our modern conditions. You are one of those large proportioned young men whom women always consider good-looking, and you have possibly, if not certainly, genius. Just say that over to yourself ten times before you go to bed every night and in three months' time go and call on Lady Charnley at Charnley. That is my advice to you, and I am an old man with considerable experience of the world.'

A very charming smile suddenly spread over the artist's face.

'You have been thunderingly good to me,' he said suddenly. He seized Mr Sattherthwaite's hand and wrung it in a powerful grip. 'I am no end grateful. I must be off now. Thanks very much for one of the most extraordinary evenings I have ever spent.'

He looked round as though to say goodbye to someone else and then started.

'I say, sir, your friend has gone. I never saw him go. He is rather a queer bird, isn't he?'

'He goes and comes very suddenly,' said Mr Satterthwaite. 'That is one of his characteristics. One doesn't always see him come and go.'

'Like Harlequin,' said Frank Bristow, 'he is invisible,' and laughed heartily at his own joke.

CHAPTER 10

The Bird with the Broken Wing

I

Mr Satterthwaite looked out of the window. It was raining steadily. He shivered. Very few country houses, he reflected, were really properly heated. It cheered him to think that in a few hours' time he would be speeding towards London. Once one had passed sixty years of age, London was really much the best place.

He was feeling a little old and pathetic. Most of the members of the house party were so young. Four of them had just gone off into the library to do table turning. They had invited him to accompany them, but he had declined. He failed to derive any amusement from the monotonous counting of the letters of the alphabet and the usual meaningless jumble of letters that resulted.

Yes, London was the best place for him. He was glad that he had declined Madge Keeley's invitation when she had rung up to invite him over to Laidell half an hour ago. An adorable young person, certainly, but London was best.

Mr Satterthwaite shivered again and remembered that the fire in the library was usually a good one. He opened the door and adventured cautiously into the darkened room.

'If I'm not in the way –'

'Was that N or M? We shall have to count again. No, of course not, Mr Satterthwaite. Do you know, the most exciting things have been happening. The spirit says her name is Ada Spiers, and John here is going to marry someone called Gladys Bun almost immediately.'

Mr Satterthwaite sat down in a big easy chair in front of the fire. His eyelids drooped over his eyes and he dozed. From time to time he returned to consciousness, hearing fragments of speech.

'It can't be P A B Z L – not unless he's a Russian. John, you're shoving. I *saw* you. I believe it's a new spirit come.'

Another interval of dozing. Then a name jerked him wide awake.

'Q-U-I-N. Is that right?' 'Yes, it's rapped once for "Yes." Quin. Have you a message for someone here? Yes. For me? For John? For Sarah? For Evelyn? No – but there's no one else. Oh! it's for Mr Satterthwaite, perhaps? It says "Yes." Mr Satterthwaite, it's a message for you.'

'What does it say?'

Mr Satterthwaite was broad awake now, sitting taut and erect in his chair, his eyes shining.

The table rocked and one of the girls counted.

'LAI – it can't be – that doesn't make sense. No word begins LAI.'

'Go on,' said Mr Satterthwaite, and the command in his voice was so sharp that he was obeyed without question.

'LAIDEL? and another L – Oh! that seems to be all.'

'Go on.'

'Tell us some more, please.'

A pause.

'There doesn't seem to be any more. The table's gone quite dead. How silly.'

'No,' said Mr Satterthwaite thoughtfully. 'I don't think it's silly.'

He rose and left the room. He went straight to the telephone. Presently he was through.

'Can I speak to Miss Keeley? Is that you, Madge, my dear? I want to change my mind, if I may, and accept your kind invitation. It is not so urgent as I thought that I should get back to town. Yes – yes – I will arrive in time for dinner.'

He hung up the receiver, a strange flush on his withered cheeks. Mr Quin – the mysterious Mr Harley Quin. Mr Satterthwaite counted over on his fingers the times he had been brought into contact with that man of mystery. Where Mr Quin was concerned – things happened! What had happened or was going to happen – at Laidell?

Whatever it was, there was work for him, Mr Satterthwaite, to do. In some way or other, he would have an active part to play. He was sure of that.

Laidell was a large house. Its owner, David Keeley, was one of those quiet men with indeterminate personalities who seem to count as part of the furniture. Their inconspicuousness has nothing to do with brain power – David Keeley was a most brilliant mathematician, and had written a book totally incomprehensible to ninety-nine hundreds of humanity. But like so many men of brilliant intellect, he radiated no bodily vigour or magnetism. It was a standing joke that David Keeley was a real 'invisible man'. Footmen passed him by with the vegetables, and guests forgot to say how do you do or goodbye.

His daughter Madge was very different. A fine upstanding young woman, bursting with energy and life. Thorough, healthy and normal, and extremely pretty.

It was she who received Mr Satterthwaite when he arrived.

'How nice of you to come – after all.'

'Very delightful of you to let me change my mind. Madge, my dear, you're looking very well.'

'Oh! I'm always well.'

'Yes, I know. But it's more than that. You look – well, blooming is the word I have in mind. Has anything happened my dear? Anything – well – special?'

She laughed – blushed a little.

'It's too bad, Mr Satterthwaite. You always guess things.'

He took her hand.

'So it's that, is it? Mr Right has come along?'

It was an old-fashioned term, but Madge did not object to it. She rather liked Mr Satterthwaite's old-fashioned ways.

'I suppose so – yes. But nobody's supposed to know. It's a secret. But I don't really mind your knowing, Mr Satterthwaite. You're always so nice and sympathetic.'

Mr Satterthwaite thoroughly enjoyed romance at second hand. He was sentimental and Victorian.

'I mustn't ask who the lucky man is? Well, then all I can say is that I hope he is worthy of the honour you are conferring on him.'

Rather a duck, old Mr Satterthwaite, thought Madge.

'Oh! we shall get on awfully well together, I think,' she said.

'You see, we like doing the same things, and that's so awfully important, isn't it? We've really got a lot in common – and we know all about each other and all that. It's really been coming on for a long time. That gives one such a nice safe feeling, doesn't it?'

'Undoubtedly,' said Mr Satterthwaite. 'But in my experience one can never really know all about anyone else. That is part of the interest and charm of life.'

'Oh! I'll risk it,' said Madge, laughing, and they went up to dress for dinner.

Mr Satterthwaite was late. He had not brought a valet, and having his things unpacked for him by a stranger always flurried him a little. He came down to find everyone assembled, and in the modern style Madge merely said: 'Oh! here's Mr Satterthwaite. I'm starving. Let's go in.'

She led the way with a tall grey-haired woman – a woman of striking personality. She had a very clear rather incisive voice, and her face was clear cut and rather beautiful.

'How d'you do, Satterthwaite,' said Mr Keeley.

Mr Satterthwaite jumped.

'How do you do,' he said. 'I'm afraid I didn't see you.'

'Nobody does,' said Mr Keeley sadly.

They went in. The table was a low oval of mahogany. Mr Satterthwaite was placed between his young hostess and a short dark girl – a very hearty girl with a loud voice and a ringing determined laugh that expressed more the determination to be cheerful at all costs than any real mirth. Her name seemed to be Doris, and she was the type of young woman Mr Satterthwaite most disliked. She had, he considered, no artistic justification for existence.

On Madge's other side was a man of about thirty, whose likeness to the grey-haired woman proclaimed them mother and son.

Next to him –

Mr Satterthwaite caught his breath.

He didn't know what it was exactly. It was not beauty. It was something else – something much more elusive and intangible than beauty.

She was listening to Mr Keeley's rather ponderous dinner-table conversation, her head bent a little sideways. She was there, it seemed to Mr Satterthwaite – and yet she was not there! She was somehow a great deal less substantial than anyone else seated round the oval table. Something in the droop of her body sideways was beautiful – was more than beautiful. She looked up – her eyes met Mr Satterthwaite's for a moment across the table – and the word he wanted leapt to his mind.

Enchantment – that was it. She had the quality of enchantment. She might have been one of those creatures who are only half-human – one of the Hidden People from the Hollow Hills. She made everyone else look rather too real . . .

But at the same time, in a queer way, she stirred his pity. It was as though semi-humanity handicapped her. He sought for a phrase and found it.

'A bird with a broken wing,' said Mr Satterthwaite.

Satisfied, he turned his mind back to the subject of Girl Guides and hoped that the girl Doris had not noticed his abstraction. When she turned to the man on the other side of her – a man Mr Satterthwaite had hardly noticed, he himself turned to Madge.

'Who is the lady sitting next to your father?' he asked in a low voice.

'Mrs Graham? Oh, no! you mean Mabelle. Don't you know her? Mabelle Annesley. She was a Clydesley – one of the illfated Clydesleys.'

He started. The ill-fated Clydesleys. He remembered. A brother had shot himself, a sister had been drowned, another had perished in an earthquake. A queer doomed family. This girl must be the youngest of them.

His thoughts were recalled suddenly. Madge's hand touched his under the table. Everyone else was talking. She gave a faint inclination of her head to her left.

'That's him,' she murmured ungrammatically.

Mr Satterthwaite nodded quickly in comprehension. So this young Graham was the man of Madge's choice. Well, she could hardly have done better as far as appearances went – and Mr Satterthwaite was a shrewd observer. A pleasant, likeable, rather matter-of-fact young fellow. They'd make a nice pair – no non-sense about either of them – good healthy sociable young folk.

Laidell was run on old-fashioned lines. The ladies left the

dining-room first. Mr Satterthwaite moved up to Graham and began to talk to him. His estimate of the young man was confirmed, yet there was something that struck him as being not quite true to type. Roger Graham was distrait, his mind seemed far away, his hand shook as he replaced the glass on the table.

'He's got something on his mind,' thought Mr Satterthwaite acutely. 'Not nearly as important as he thinks it is, I dare say. All the same, I wonder what it is.'

Mr Satterthwaite was in the habit of swallowing a couple of digestive pastilles after meals. Having neglected to bring them down with him, he went up to his room to fetch them.

On his way down to the drawing-room, he passed along the long corridor on the ground floor. About half-way along it was a room known as the terrace room. As Mr Satterthwaite looked through the open doorway in passing, he stopped short.

Moonlight was streaming into the room. The latticed panes gave it a queer rhythmic pattern. A figure was sitting on the low window sill, drooping a little sideways and softly twanging the string of a ukelele – not in a jazz rhythm, but in a far older rhythm, the beat of fairy horses riding on fairy hills.

Mr Satterthwaite stood fascinated. She wore a dress of dull dark blue chiffon, ruched and pleated so that it looked like the feathers of a bird. She bent over the instrument crooning to it.

He came into the room – slowly, step by step. He was close to her when she looked up and saw him. She didn't start, he noticed, or seem surprised.

'I hope I'm not intruding,' he began.

'Please – sit down.'

He sat near her on a polished oak chair. She hummed softly under her breath.

'There's a lot of magic about tonight,' she said. 'Don't you think so?'

'Yes, there was a lot of magic about.'

'They wanted me to fetch my uke,' she explained. 'And as I passed here, I thought it would be so lovely to be alone here – in the dark and the moon.'

'Then I –' Mr Satterthwaite half rose, but she stopped him.

'Don't go. You – you fit in, somehow. It's queer, but you do.'

He sat down again.

'It's been a queer sort of evening,' she said. 'I was out in the woods late this afternoon, and I met a man – such a strange sort of man – tall and dark, like a lost soul. The sun was setting, and the light of it through the trees made him look like a kind of Harlequin.'

'Ah!' Mr Satterthwaite leant forward – his interest quickened.

'I wanted to speak to him – he – he looked so like somebody I know. But I lost him in the trees.'

'I think I know him,' said Mr Satterthwaite.

'Do you? He is – interesting, isn't he?'

'Yes, he is interesting.'

There was a pause. Mr Satterthwaite was perplexed. There was something, he felt, that he ought to do – and he didn't know what it was. But surely – surely, it had to do with this girl. He said rather clumsily:

'Sometimes – when one is unhappy – one wants to get away –'

'Yes. That's true.' She broke off suddenly. 'Oh! I see what you mean. But you're wrong. It's just the other way round. I wanted to be alone because I'm happy.'

'Happy?'

'Terribly happy.'

She spoke quite quietly, but Mr Satterthwaite had a sudden sense of shock. What this strange girl meant by being happy wasn't the same as Madge Keeley would have meant by the same words. Happiness, for Mabelle Annesley, meant some kind of intense and vivid ecstasy . . . something that was not only human, but more than human. He shrank back a little.

'I – didn't know,' he said clumsily.

'Of course you couldn't. And it's not – the actual thing – I'm not happy yet – but I'm going to be.' She leaned forward. 'Do you know what it's like to stand in a wood – a big wood with dark shadows and trees very close all round you – a wood you might never get out of – and then, suddenly – just in front of you, you see the country of your dreams – shining and beautiful – you've only got to step out from the trees and the darkness and you've found it . . .'

'So many things look beautiful,' said Mr Satterthwaite, 'before we've reached them. Some of the ugliest things in the world look the most beautiful . . .'

There was a step on the floor. Mr Satterthwaite turned his head. A fair man with a stupid, rather wooden face, stood there. He was the man Mr Satterthwaite had hardly noticed at the dinner-table.

'They're waiting for you, Mabelle,' he said.

She got up, the expression had gone out of her face, her voice was flat and calm.

'I'm coming, Gerard,' she said. 'I've been talking to Mr Satterthwaite.'

She went out of the room, Mr Satterthwaite following. He turned his head over his shoulder as he went and caught the expression on her husband's face. A hungry, despairing look.

'Enchantment,' thought Mr Satterthwaite. 'He feels it right enough. Poor fellow – poor fellow.'

The drawing-room was well lighted. Madge and Doris Coles were vociferous in reproaches.

'Mabelle, you little beast – you've been ages.'

She sat on a low stool, tuned the ukelele and sang. They all joined in.

'Is it possible,' thought Mr Satterthwaite, 'that so many idiotic songs could have been written about My Baby.'

But he had to admit that the syncopated wailing tunes were stirring. Though, of course, they weren't a patch on the old-fashioned waltz.

The air got very smoky. The syncopated rhythm went on.

'No conversation,' thought Mr Satterthwaite. 'No good music. No *peace*.' He wished the world had not become definitely so noisy.

Suddenly Mabelle Annesley broke off, smiled across the room at him, and began to sing a song of Grieg's.

'My swan – my fair one . . .'

It was a favourite of Mr Satterthwaite's. He liked the note of ingenuous surprise at the end.

'Wert only a swan then? A swan then?'

After that, the party broke up. Madge offered drinks whilst her father picked up the discarded ukelele and began twanging it absent-mindedly. The party exchanged goodnights, drifted nearer and nearer to the door. Everyone talked at once. Gerard Annesley slipped away unostentatiously, leaving the others.

Outside the drawing-room door, Mr Satterthwaite bade Mrs Graham a ceremonious goodnight. There were two staircases, one close at hand, the other at the end of a long corridor. It was by the latter that Mr Satterthwaite reached his room. Mrs Graham and her son passed by the stairs near at hand whence the quiet Gerard Annesley had already preceded them.

'You'd better get your ukelele, Mabelle,' said Madge. 'You'll forget it in the morning if you don't. You've got to make such an early start.'

'Come on, Mr Satterthwaite,' said Doris Coles, seizing him boisterously by one arm. 'Early to bed – etcetera.'

Madge took him by the other arm and all three ran down the corridor to peals of Doris's laughter. They paused at the end to wait for David Keeley, who was following at a much more sedate pace, turning out electric lights as he came. The four of them went upstairs together.

II

Mr Satterthwaite was just preparing to descend to the dining-room for breakfast on the following morning, when there was a light tap on the door and Madge Keeley entered. Her face was dead white, and she was shivering all over.

'Oh, Mr Satterthwaite.'

'My dear child, what's happened?' He took her hand.

'Mabelle – Mabelle Annesley . . .'

'Yes?'

What had happened? What? Something terrible – he knew that. Madge could hardly get the words out.

'She – she hanged herself last night . . . On the back of her door. Oh! it's too horrible.' She broke down – sobbing.

Hanged herself. Impossible. Incomprehensible!

He said a few soothing old-fashioned words to Madge, and

hurried downstairs. He found David Keeley looking perplexed and incompetent.

'I've telephoned to the police, Satterthwaite. Apparently that's got to be done. So the doctor said. He's just finished examining the – the – good lord, it's a beastly business. She must have been desperately unhappy – to do it that way – Queer that song last night. Swan song, eh? She looked rather like a swan – a black swan.'

'Yes.'

'Swan Song,' repeated Keeley. 'Shows it was in her mind, eh?'

'It would seem so – yes, certainly it would seem so.'

He hesitated, then asked if he might see – if, that is . . .

His host comprehended the stammering request.

'If you want to – I'd forgotten you have a *penchant* for human tragedies.'

He led the way up the broad staircase. Mr Satterthwaite followed him. At the head of the stairs was the room occupied by Roger Graham and opposite it, on the other side of the passage, his mother's room. The latter door was ajar and a faint wisp of smoke floated through it.

A momentary surprise invaded Mr Satterthwaite's mind. He had not judged Mrs Graham to be a woman who smoked so early in the day. Indeed, he had had the idea that she did not smoke at all.

They went along the passage to the end door but one. David Keeley entered the room and Mr Satterthwaite followed him.

The room was not a very large one and showed signs of a man's occupation. A door in the wall led into a second room. A bit of cut rope still dangled from a hook high up on the door. On the bed . . .

Mr Satterthwaite stood for a minute looking down on the heap of huddled chiffon. He noticed that it was ruched and pleated like the plumage of a bird. At the face, after one glance, he did not look again.

He glanced from the door with its dangling rope to the communicating door through which they had come.

'Was that open?'

'Yes. At least the maid says so.'

'Annesley slept in there? Did he hear anything?'

'He says – nothing.'

'Almost incredible,' murmured Mr Satterthwaite. He looked back at the form on the bed.

'Where is he?'

'Annesley? He's downstairs with the doctor.'

They went downstairs to find an Inspector of police had arrived. Mr Satterthwaite was agreeably surprised to recognize in him an old acquaintance, Inspector Winkfield. The Inspector went upstairs with the doctor, and a few minutes later a request came that all members of the house party should assemble in the drawing-room.

The blinds had been drawn, and the whole room had a funereal aspect. Doris Coles looked frightened and subdued. Every now and then she dabbed her eyes with a handkerchief. Madge was resolute and alert, her feelings fully under control by now. Mrs Graham was composed, as always, her face grave and impassive. The tragedy seemed to have affected her son more keenly than anyone. He looked a positive wreck this morning. David Keeley, as usual, had subsided into the background.

The bereaved husband sat alone, a little apart from the others. There was a queer dazed looked about him, as though he could hardly realize what had taken place.

Mr Satterthwaite, outwardly composed, was inwardly seething with the importance of a duty shortly to be performed.

Inspector Winkfield, followed by Dr Morris, came in and shut the door behind him. He cleared his throat and spoke.

'This is a very sad occurrence – very sad, I'm sure. It's necessary, under the circumstances, that I should ask everybody a few questions. You'll not object, I'm sure. I'll begin with Mr Annesley. You'll forgive my asking, sir, but had your good lady ever threatened to take her life?'

Mr Satterthwaite opened his lips impulsively, then closed them again. There was plenty of time. Better not speak too soon.

'I – no, I don't think so.'

His voice was so hesitating, so peculiar, that everyone shot a covert glance at him.

'You're not sure, sir?'

'Yes – I'm – quite sure. She didn't.'

'Ah! Were you aware that she was unhappy in any way?'

'No. I – no, I wasn't.'

'She said nothing to you. About feeling depressed, for instance?'

'I – no, nothing.'

Whatever the Inspector thought, he said nothing. Instead he proceeded to his next point.

'Will you describe to me briefly the events of last night?'

'We – all went up to bed. I fell asleep immediately and heard nothing. The housemaid's scream aroused me this morning. I rushed into the adjoining room and found my wife – and found her –'

His voice broke. The Inspector nodded.

'Yes, yes, that's quite enough. We needn't go into that. When did you last see your wife the night before?'

'I – downstairs.'

'Downstairs?'

'Yes, we all left the drawing-room together. I went straight up leaving the others talking in the hall.'

'And you didn't see your wife again? Didn't she say goodnight when she came up to bed?'

'I was asleep when she came up.'

'But she only followed you a few minutes later. That's right, isn't it, sir?' He looked at David Keeley, who nodded.

'She hadn't come up half an hour later.'

Annesley spoke stubbornly. The Inspector's eyes strayed gently to Mrs Graham.

'She didn't stay in your room talking, Madam?'

Did Mr Satterthwaite fancy it, or was there a slight pause before Mrs Graham said with her customary quiet decision of manner:

'No, I went straight into my room and closed the door. I heard nothing.'

'And you say, sir' – the Inspector had shifted his attention back to Annesley – 'that you slept and heard nothing. The communicating door was open, was it not?'

'I – I believe so. But my wife would have entered her room by the other door from the corridor.'

'Even so, sir, there would have been certain sounds – a choking noise, a drumming of heels on the door –'

'*No.*'

It was Mr Satterthwaite who spoke, impetuously, unable to stop himself. Every eye turned towards him in surprise. He himself became nervous, stammered, and turned pink.

'I – I beg your pardon, Inspector. But I must speak. You are on the wrong track – the wrong track altogether. Mrs Annesley did not kill herself – I am sure of it. She was murdered.'

There was a dead silence, then Inspector Winkfield said quietly:

'What leads you to say that, sir?'

'I – it is a feeling. A very strong feeling.'

'But I think, sir, there must be more than that to it. There must be some particular reason.'

Well, of course there *was* a particular reason. There was the mysterious message from Mr Quin. But you couldn't tell a police inspector that. Mr Satterthwaite cast about desperately, and found nothing.

'Last night – when we were talking together, she said she was very happy. Very happy – just that. That wasn't like a woman thinking of committing suicide.'

He was triumphant. He added:

'She went back to the drawing-room to fetch her ukelele, so that she wouldn't forget it in the morning. That didn't look like suicide either.'

'No,' admitted the Inspector. 'No, perhaps it didn't.' He turned to David Keeley. 'Did she take the ukelele upstairs with her?'

The mathematician tried to remember.

'I think – yes, she did. She went upstairs carrying it in her hand. I remember seeing it just as she turned the corner of the staircase before I turned off the light down here.'

'Oh!' cried Madge. 'But it's here now.'

She pointed dramatically to where the ukelele lay on a table.

'That's curious,' said the Inspector. He stepped swiftly across and rang the bell.

A brief order sent the butler in search of the housemaid whose business it was to do the rooms in the morning. She came, and was quite positive in her answer. The ukelele had been there first thing that morning when she had dusted.

Inspector Winkfield dismissed her and then said curtly:

'I would like to speak to Mr Satterthwaite in private, please. Everyone may go. But no one is to leave the house.'

Mr Satterthwaite twittered into speech as soon as the door had closed behind the others.

'I – I am sure, Inspector, that you have the case excellently in hand. Excellently. I just felt that – having, as I say, a very strong feeling –'

The Inspector arrested further speech with an upraised hand.

'You're quite right, Mr Satterthwaite. The lady was murdered.'

'You knew it?' Mr Satterthwaite was chagrined.

'There were certain things that puzzled Dr Morris.' He looked across at the doctor, who had remained, and the doctor assented to his statement with a nod of the head. 'We made a thorough examination. The rope that was round her neck wasn't the rope that she was strangled with – it was something much thinner that did the job, something more like a wire. It had cut right into the flesh. The mark of the rope was superimposed on it. She was strangled and then hung up on the door afterwards to make it look like suicide.'

'But who –?'

'Yes,' said the Inspector. 'Who? That's the question. What about the husband sleeping next door, who never said goodnight to his wife and who heard nothing? I should say we hadn't far to look. Must find out what terms they were on That's where you can be useful to us, Mr Satterthwaite. You've the *ongtray* here, and you can get the hang of things in a way we can't. Find out what relations there were between the two.'

'I hardly like –' began Mr Satterthwaite, stiffening.

'It won't be the first murder mystery you've helped us with. I remember the case of Mrs Strangeways. You've got a *flair* for that sort of thing, sir. An absolute *flair*.'

Yes, it was true – he *had a flair*. He said quietly:

'I will do my best, Inspector.'

Had Gerard Annesley killed his wife? Had he? Mr Satterthwaite recalled that look of misery last night. He loved her – and he was suffering. Suffering will drive a man to strange deeds.

But there was something else – some other factor. Mabelle had spoken of herself as coming out of a wood – she was looking forward to happiness – not a quiet rational happiness – but a happiness that was irrational – a wild ecstasy . . .

If Gerard Annesley had spoken the truth, Mabelle had not come to her room till at least half an hour later than he had done. Yet David Keeley had seen her going up those stairs. There were two other rooms occupied in that wing. There was Mrs Graham's, and there was her son's.

Her son's. But he and Madge . . .

Surely Madge would have guessed . . . But Madge wasn't the guessing kind. All the same, no smoke without fire – Smoke!

Ah! he remembered. *A wisp of smoke curling out through Mrs Graham's bedroom door.*

He acted on impulse. Straight up the stairs and into her room. It was empty. He closed the door behind him and locked it.

He went across to the grate. A heap of charred fragments. Very gingerly he raked them over with his finger. His luck was in. In the very centre were some unburnt fragments – fragments of letters . . .

Very disjointed fragments, but they told him something of value.

'Life can be wonderful, Roger darling. I never knew . . . all my life has been a dream till I met you, Roger . . .'

'. . . Gerard knows, I think . . . I am sorry but what can I do? Nothing is real to me but you, Roger . . . We shall be together, soon.'

'What are you going to tell him at Laidell, Roger? You write strangely – but I am not afraid . . .'

Very carefully, Mr Satterthwaite put the fragments into an envelope from the writing-table. He went to the door, unlocked it and opened it to find himself face to face with Mrs Graham.

It was an awkward moment, and Mr Satterthwaite was momentarily out of countenance. He did what was, perhaps, the best thing, attacked the situation with simplicity.

'I have been searching your room, Mrs Graham. I have found something – a packet of letters imperfectly burnt.'

A wave of alarm passed over her face. It was gone in a flash, but it had been there.

'Letters from Mrs Annesley to your son.'

She hesitated for a minute, then said quietly: 'That is so. I thought they would be better burnt.'

'For what reason?'

'My son is engaged to be married. These letters – if they had been brought into publicity through the poor girl's suicide – might have caused much pain and trouble.'

'Your son could burn his own letters.'

She had no answer ready for that. Mr Satterthwaite pursued his advantage.

'You found these letters in his room, brought them into your room and burnt them. Why? You were afraid, Mrs Graham.'

'I am not in the habit of being afraid, Mr Satterthwaite.'

'No – but this was a desperate case.'

'Desperate?'

'Your son might have been in danger of arrest – for murder.'

'Murder!'

He saw her face go white. He went on quickly:

'You heard Mrs Annesley go into your son's room last night. He had told her of his engagement? No, I see he hadn't. He told her then. They quarrelled, and he –'

'That's a lie!'

They had been so absorbed in their duel of words that they had not heard approaching footsteps. Roger Graham had come up behind them unperceived by either.

'It's all right, Mother. Don't – worry. Come into my room, Mr Satterthwaite.'

Mr Sattherwaite followed him into his room. Mrs Graham had turned away and did not attempt to follow them. Roger Graham shut the door.

'Listen, Mr Satterthwaite, you think I killed Mabelle. You think I strangled her – here – and took her along and hung her up on that door – later – when everyone was asleep?'

Mr Satterthwaite stared at him. Then he said surprisingly:

'No, I do not think so.'

'Thank God for that. I couldn't have killed Mabelle. I – I loved her. Or didn't I? I don't know. It's a tangle that I can't explain. I'm fond of Madge – I always have been. And she's such a good sort. We suit each other. But Mabelle was different. It was – I can't explain it – a sort of enchantment. I was, I think – afraid of her.'

Mr Satterthwaite nodded.

'It was madness – a kind of bewildering ecstasy . . . But it was impossible. It wouldn't have worked. That sort of thing – doesn't last. I know what it means now to have a spell cast over you.'

'Yes, it must have been like that,' said Mr Satterthwaite thoughtfully.

'I – I wanted to get out of it all. I was going to tell Mabelle – last night.'

'But you didn't?'

'No, I didn't,' said Graham slowly. 'I swear to you, Mr Satterthwaite, that I never saw her after I said goodnight downstairs.'

'I believe you,' said Mr Satterthwaite.

He got up. It was not Roger Graham who had killed Mabelle Annesley. He could have fled from her, but he could not have killed her. He had been afraid of her, afraid of that wild intangible fairy-like quality of hers. He had known enchantment – and turned his back on it. He had gone for the safe sensible thing that he had known 'would work' and had relinquished the intangible dream that might lead him he knew not where.

He was a sensible young man, and, as such, uninteresting to Mr Satterthwaite, who was an artist and a connoisseur in life.

He left Roger Graham in his room and went downstairs. The drawing-room was empty. Mabelle's ukelele lay on a stool by the window. He took it up and twanged it absent-mindedly. He knew nothing of the instrument, but his ear told him that it was abominably out of tune. He turned a key experimentally.

Doris Coles came into the room. She looked at him reproachfully.

'Poor Mabelle's uke,' she said.

Her clear condemnation made Mr Satterthwaite feel obstinate.

'Tune it for me,' he said, and added: 'If you can.'

'Of course I can,' said Doris, wounded at the suggestion of incompetence in any direction.

She took it from him, twanged a string, turned a key briskly – and the string snapped.

'Well, I never. Oh! I see – but how extraordinary! It's the wrong string – a size too big. It's an A string. How stupid to put that on. Of course it snaps when you try to tune it up. How stupid people are.'

'Yes,' said Mr Satterthwaite. 'They are – even when they try to be clever . . .'

His tone was so odd that she stared at him. He took the ukelele from her and removed the broken string. He went out of the room holding it in his hand. In the library he found David Keeley.

'Here,' he said.

He held out the string. Keeley took it.

'What's this?'

'A broken ukelele string.' He paused and then went on: '*What did you do with the other one?*'

'The other one?'

'*The one you strangled her with.* You were very clever, weren't you? It was done very quickly – just in that moment we were all laughing and talking in the hall.

'Mabelle came back into this room for her ukelele. You had taken the string off as you fiddled with it just before. You caught her round the throat with it and strangled her. Then you came out and locked the door and joined us. Later, in the dead of night, you came down and – and disposed of the body by hanging it on the door of her room. And you put another string on the ukelele – *but it was the wrong string*, that's why you were stupid.'

There was a pause.

'But why did you do it?' said Mr Satterthwaite. 'In God's name, *why*?'

Mr Keeley laughed, a funny giggling little laugh that made Mr Satterthwaite feel rather sick.

'It was so very simple,' he said. 'That's why! And then – nobody ever noticed me. Nobody ever noticed what I was doing. I thought – I thought I'd have the laugh of them . . .'

And again he gave that furtive little giggle and looked at Mr Satterthwaite with mad eyes.

Mr Satterthwaite was glad that at that moment Inspector Winkfield came into the room.

III

It was twenty-four hours later, on his way to London, that Mr Satterthwaite awoke from a doze to find a tall dark man sitting opposite to him in the railway carriage. He was not altogether surprised.

'My dear Mr Quin!'

'Yes – I am here.'

Mr Satterthwaite said slowly: 'I can hardly face you. I am ashamed – I failed.'

'Are you sure of that?'

'I did not save her.'

'But you discovered the truth?'

'Yes – that is true. One or other of those young men might have been accused – might even have been found guilty. So, at any rate, I saved a man's life. But, she – she – that strange enchanting creature . . .' His voice broke off.

Mr Quin looked at him.

'Is death the greatest evil that can happen to anyone?'

'I – well – perhaps – No . . .'

Mr Satterthwaite remembered . . . Madge and Roger Graham . . . Mabelle's face in the moonlight – its serene unearthly happiness . . .

'No,' he admitted. 'No – perhaps death is not the greatest evil . . .'

He remembered the ruffled blue chiffon of her dress that had seemed to him like the plumage of a bird . . . A bird with a broken wing . . .

When he looked up, he found himself alone. Mr Quin was no longer there.

But he had left something behind.

On the seat was a roughly carved bird fashioned out of some dim blue stone. It had, possibly, no great artistic merit. But it had something else.

It had the vague quality of enchantment.

So said Mr Satterthwaite – and Mr Satterthwaite was a connoisseur.

CHAPTER 11

The World's End

Mr Satterthwaite had come to Corsica because of the Duchess. It was out of his beat. On the Riviera he was sure of his comforts, and to be comfortable meant a lot to Mr Satterthwaite. But though he liked his comfort, he also liked a Duchess. In his way, a harmless, gentlemanly, old-fashioned way, Mr Satterthwaite was a snob. He liked the best people. And the Duchess of Leith was a very authentic Duchess. There were no Chicago pork butchers in her ancestry. She was the daughter of a Duke as well as the wife of one.

For the rest, she was rather a shabby-looking old lady, a good deal given to black bead trimmings on her clothes. She had quantities of diamonds in old-fashioned settings, and she wore them as her mother before her had worn them: pinned all over her indiscriminately. Someone had suggested once that the Duchess stood in the middle of the room whilst her maid flung brooches at her haphazard. She subscribed generously to charities, and looked well after her tenants and dependents, but was extremely mean over small sums. She cadged lifts from her friends, and did her shopping in bargain basements.

The Duchess was seized with a whim for Corsica. Cannes bored her and she had a bitter argument with the hotel proprietor over the price of her rooms.

'And you shall go with me, Satterthwaite,' she said firmly. 'We needn't be afraid of scandal at our time of life.'

Mr Satterthwaite was delicately flattered. No one had ever mentioned scandal in connection with him before. He was far too insignificant. Scandal – and a Duchess – delicious!

'Picturesque you know,' said the Duchess. 'Brigands – all that sort of thing. And extremely cheap, so I've heard. Manuel was positively impudent this morning. These hotel proprietors need putting in their place. They can't expect to get the best people if they go on like this. I told him so plainly.'

'I believe,' said Mr Satterthwaite, 'that one can fly over quite comfortably. From Antibes.'

'They probably charge you a pretty penny for it,' said the Duchess sharply. 'Find out, will you?'

'Certainly, Duchess.'

Mr Satterthwaite was still in a flutter of gratification despite the fact that his role was clearly to be that of a glorified courier.

When she learned the price of a passage by Avion, the Duchess turned it down promptly.

'They needn't think I'm going to pay a ridiculous sum like that to go in one of their nasty dangerous things.'

So they went by boat, and Mr Satterthwaite endured ten hours of acute discomfort. To begin with, as the boat sailed at seven, he took it for granted that there would be dinner on board. But there was no dinner. The boat was small and the sea was rough. Mr Satterthwaite was decanted at Ajaccio in the early hours of the morning more dead than alive.

The Duchess, on the contrary, was perfectly fresh. She never minded discomfort if she could feel she was saving money. She waxed enthusiastic over the scene on the quay, with the palm trees and the rising sun. The whole population seemed to have turned out to watch the arrival of the boat, and the launching of the gangway was attended with excited cries and directions.

'*On dirait*,' said a stout Frenchman who stood beside them, '*que jamais avant on n'a fait cette manoeuvre là!*'

'That maid of mine has been sick all night,' said the Duchess. 'The girl's a perfect fool.'

Mr Satterthwaite smiled in a pallid fashion.

'A waste of good food, I call it,' continued the Duchess robustly.

'Did she get any food?' asked Mr Satterthwaite enviously.

'I happened to bring some biscuits and a stick of chocolate on board with me,' said the Duchess. 'When I found there was no dinner to be got, I gave the lot to her. The lower classes always make such a fuss about going without their meals.'

With a cry of triumph the launching of the gangway was accomplished. A Musical Comedy chorus of brigands rushed aboard and wrested hand-luggage from the passengers by main force.

'Come on, Satterthwaite,' said the Duchess. 'I want a hot bath and some coffee.'

So did Mr Satterthwaite. He was not wholly successful, however. They were received at the hotel by a bowing manager and were shown to their rooms. The Duchess's had a bathroom attached. Mr Satterthwaite, however, was directed to a bath that appeared to be situated in somebody else's bedroom. To expect the water to be hot at that hour in the morning was, perhaps, unreasonable. Later he drank intensely black coffee, served in a pot without a lid. The shutters and the window of his room had been flung open, and the crisp morning air came in fragrantly. A day of dazzling blue and green.

The waiter waved his hand with a flourish to call attention to the view.

'*Ajaccio*,' he said solemnly. '*Le plus beau port du monde!*'

And he departed abruptly.

Looking out over the deep blue of the bay, with the snowy mountains beyond, Mr Satterthwaite was almost inclined to agree with him. He finished his coffee, and lying down on the bed, fell fast asleep.

At *déjeuner* the Duchess was in great spirits.

'This is just what will be good for you, Satterthwaite,' she said. 'Get you out of all those dusty little old-maidish ways of yours.' She swept a *lorgnette* round the room. 'Upon my word, there's Naomi Carlton Smith.'

She indicated a girl sitting by herself at a table in the window. A round-shouldered girl, who slouched as she sat. Her dress appeared to be made of some kind of brown sacking. She had black hair, untidily bobbed.

'An artist?' asked Mr Satterthwaite.

He was always good at placing people.

'Quite right,' said the Duchess. 'Calls herself one anyway. I knew she was mooching around in some queer quarter of the globe. Poor as a church mouse, proud as Lucifer, and a bee in her bonnet like all the Carlton Smiths. Her mother was my first cousin.'

'She's one of the Knowlton lot then?'

The Duchess nodded.

'Been her own worst enemy,' she volunteered. 'Clever girl too. Mixed herself up with a most undesirable young man. One of that Chelsea crowd. Wrote plays or poems or something unhealthy. Nobody took 'em, of course. Then he stole somebody's jewels and got caught out. I forget what they gave him. Five years, I think. But you must remember? It was last winter.'

'Last winter I was in Egypt,' explained Mr Satterthwaite. 'I had 'flu very badly the end of January, and the doctors insisted on Egypt afterwards. I missed a lot.'

His voice rang with a note of real regret.

'That girl seems to me to be moping,' said the Duchess, raising her *lorgnette* once more. 'I can't allow that.'

On her way out, she stopped by Miss Carlton Smith's table and tapped the girl on the shoulder.

'Well, Naomi, you don't seem to remember me?'

Naomi rose rather unwillingly to her feet.

'Yes, I do, Duchess. I saw you come in. I thought it was quite likely you mightn't recognize me.'

She drawled the words lazily, with a complete indifference of manner.

'When you've finished your lunch, come and talk to me on the terrace,' ordered the Duchess.

'Very well.'

Naomi yawned.

'Shocking manners,' said the Duchess, to Mr Satterthwaite, as she resumed her progress. 'All the Carlton Smiths have.'

They had their coffee outside in the sunshine. They had been there about six minutes when Naomi Carlton Smith lounged out from the hotel and joined them. She let herself fall slackly on to a chair with her legs stretched out ungracefully in front of her.

An odd face, with its jutting chin and deep-set grey eyes. A clever, unhappy face – a face that only just missed being beautiful.

'Well, Naomi,' said the Duchess briskly. 'And what are you doing with yourself?'

'Oh, I dunno. Just marking time.'

'Been painting?'

'A bit.'

'Show me your things.'

Naomi grinned. She was not cowed by the autocrat. She was amused. She went into the hotel and came out again with a portfolio.

'You won't like 'em, Duchess,' she said warningly. 'Say what you like. You won't hurt my feelings.'

Mr Satterthwaite moved his chair a little nearer. He was interested. In another minute he was more interested still. The Duchess was frankly unsympathetic.

'I can't even see which way the things ought to be,' she complained. 'Good gracious, child, there was never a sky that colour – or a sea either.'

'That's the way I see 'em,' said Naomi placidly.

'Ugh!' said the Duchess, inspecting another. 'This gives me the creeps.'

'It's meant to,' said Naomi. 'You're paying me a compliment without knowing it.'

It was a queer vorticist study of a prickly pear – just recognizable as such. Grey-green with slodges of violent colour where the fruit glittered like jewels. A swirling mass of evil, fleshy – festering. Mr Satterthwaite shuddered and turned his head aside.

He found Naomi looking at him and nodding her head in comprehension.

'I know,' she said. 'But it *is* beastly.'

The Duchess cleared her throat.

'It seems quite easy to be an artist nowadays,' she observed witheringly. 'There's no attempt to copy things. You just shovel on some paint – I don't know what with, not a brush, I'm sure –'

'Palette knife,' interposed Naomi, smiling broadly once more.

'A good deal at a time,' continued the Duchess. 'In lumps. And there you are! Everyone says: "How clever." Well, I've no patience with that sort of thing. Give me –'

'A nice picture of a dog or a horse, by Edwin Landseer.'

'And why not?' demanded the Duchess. 'What's wrong with Landseer?'

'Nothing,' said Naomi. 'He's all right. And you're all right. The tops of things are always nice and shiny and smooth. I respect you, Duchess, you've got force. You've met life fair and square and you've come out on top. But the people who are underneath see the under side of things. And that's interesting in a way.'

The Duchess stared at her.

'I haven't the faintest idea what you're talking about,' she declared.

Mr Satterthwaite was still examining the sketches. He realized, as the Duchess could not, the perfection of technique behind them. He was startled and delighted. He looked up at the girl.

'Will you sell me one of these, Miss Carlton Smith?' he asked.

'You can have any one you like for five guineas,' said the girl indifferently.

Mr Satterthwaite hesitated a minute or two and then he selected a study of prickly pear and aloe. In the foreground was a vivid blur of yellow mimosa, the scarlet of the aloe flower danced in and out of the picture, and inexorable, mathematically underlying the whole, was the oblong pattern of the prickly pear and the sword motif of the aloe.

He made a little bow to the girl.

'I am very happy to have secured this, and I think I have made a bargain. Some day, Miss Carlton Smith, I shall be able to sell this sketch at a very good profit – if I want to!'

The girl leant forward to see which one he had taken. He saw a new look come into her eyes. For the first time she was really aware of his existence, and there was respect in the quick glance she gave him.

'You have chosen the best,' she said. 'I – I am glad.'

'Well, I suppose you know what you're doing,' said the Duchess. 'And I daresay you're right. I've heard that you are quite a connoisseur. But you can't tell me that all this new stuff is art, because it isn't. Still, we needn't go into that. Now I'm only going to be here a few days and I want to see something of the island. You've got a car, I suppose, Naomi?'

The girl nodded.

'Excellent,' said the Duchess. 'We'll make a trip somewhere tomorrow.'

'It's only a two-seater.'

'Nonsense, there's a dickey, I suppose, that will do for Mr Satterthwaite?'

A shuddering sigh went through Mr Satterthwaite. He had observed the Corsican roads that morning. Naomi was regarding him thoughtfully.

'I'm afraid my car would be no good to you,' she said. 'It's a terribly battered old bus. I bought it second-hand for a mere song. It will just get me up the hills – with coaxing. But I can't take passengers. There's quite a good garage, though, in the town. You can hire a car there.'

'Hire a car?' said the Duchess, scandalized. 'What an idea. Who's that nice-looking man, rather yellow, who drove up in a four-seater just before lunch?'

'I expect you mean Mr Tomlinson. He's a retired Indian judge.'

'That accounts for the yellowness,' said the Duchess. 'I was afraid it might be jaundice. He seems quite a decent sort of man. I shall talk to him.'

That evening, on coming down to dinner, Mr Satterthwaite found the Duchess resplendent in black velvet and diamonds, talking earnestly to the owner of the four-seater car. She beckoned authoritatively.

'Come here, Mr Satterthwaite, Mr Tomlinson is telling me the most interesting things, and what do you think? – he is actually going to take us on an expedition tomorrow in his car.'

Mr Satterthwaite regarded her with admiration.

'We must go in to dinner,' said the Duchess. 'Do come and sit at our table, Mr Tomlinson, and then you can go on with what you were telling me.'

'Quite a decent sort of man,' the Duchess pronounced later.

'With quite a decent sort of car,' retorted Mr Satterthwaite.

'Naughty,' said the Duchess, and gave him a resounding blow on the knuckles with the dingy black fan she always carried. Mr Satterthwaite winced with pain.

'Naomi is coming too,' said the Duchess. 'In her car. That girl wants taking out of herself. She's very selfish. Not exactly self-centred, but totally indifferent to everyone and everything. Don't you agree?'

'I don't think that's possible,' said Mr Satterthwaite, slowly. 'I mean, everyone's interest must go *somewhere*. There are, of course, the people who revolve round themselves – but I agree with you, she's not one of that kind. She's totally uninterested in herself. And yet she's got a strong character – there must be *something*. I thought at first it was her art – but it isn't. I've never met anyone so detached from life. That's dangerous.'

'Dangerous? What do you mean?'

'Well, you see – it must mean an obsession of some kind, and obsessions are always dangerous.'

'Satterthwaite,' said the Duchess, 'don't be a fool. And listen to me. About tomorrow –'

Mr Satterthwaite listened. It was very much his role in life.

They started early the following morning, taking their lunch with them. Naomi, who had been six months in the island, was to be the pioneer. Mr Satterthwaite went over to her as she sat waiting to start.

'You are sure that – I can't come with you?' he said wistfully.

She shook her head.

'You'll be much more comfortable in the back of the other car. Nicely padded seats and all that. This is a regular old rattle trap. You'd leap in the air going over the bumps.'

'And then, of course, the hills.'

Naomi laughed.

'Oh, I only said that to rescue you from the dickey. The Duchess could perfectly well afford to have hired a car. She's the meanest woman in England. All the same, the old thing is rather a sport, and I can't help liking her.'

'Then I could come with you after all?' said Mr Satterthwaite eagerly.

She looked at him curiously.

'Why are you so anxious to come with me?'

'Can you ask?' Mr Satterthwaite made his funny old-fashioned bow.

She smiled, but shook her head.

'That isn't the reason,' she said thoughtfully. 'It's odd . . . But you can't come with me – not today.'

'Another day, perhaps,' suggested Mr Satterthwaite politely.

'Oh, another day!' she laughed suddenly, a very queer laugh, Mr Satterthwaite thought. 'Another day! Well, we'll see.'

They started. They drove through the town, and then round the long curve of the bay, winding inland to cross a river and then back to the coast with its hundreds of little sandy coves. And then they began to climb. In and out, round nerve-shattering curves, upwards, ever upwards on the tortuous winding road. The blue bay was far below them, and on the other side of it Ajaccio sparkled in the sun, white, like a fairy city.

In and out, in and out, with a precipice first one side of them, then the other. Mr Satterthwaite felt slightly giddy, he also felt slightly sick. The road was not very wide. And still they climbed.

It was cold now. The wind came to them straight off the snow peaks. Mr Satterthwaite turned up his coat collar and buttoned it tightly under his chin.

It was very cold. Across the water, Ajaccio was still bathed in sunlight, but up here thick grey clouds came drifting across the face of the sun. Mr Satterthwaite ceased to admire the view. He yearned for a steam-heated hotel and a comfortable armchair.

Ahead of them Naomi's little two-seater drove steadily forward. Up, still up. They were on top of the world now. On either side of them were lower hills, hills sloping down to valleys. They looked straight across to the snow peaks. And the wind came tearing over them, sharp, like a knife. Suddenly Naomi's car stopped, and she looked back.

'We've arrived,' she said. 'At the World's End. And I don't think it's an awfully good day for it.'

They all got out. They had arrived in a tiny village, with half a dozen stone cottages. An imposing name was printed in letters a foot high.

'Coti Chiaveeri.'

Naomi shrugged her shoulders.

'That's its official name, but I prefer to call it the World's End.'

She walked on a few steps, and Mr Satterthwaite joined her. They were beyond the houses now. The road stopped. As Naomi had said, this was the end, the back of beyond, the beginning of nowhere. Behind them the white ribbon of the road, in front of them – nothing. Only far, far below, the sea . . .

Mr Satterthwaite drew a deep breath.

'It's an extraordinary place. One feels that anything might happen here, that one might meet – anyone –'

He stopped, for just in front of them a man was sitting on a boulder, his face turned to the sea. They had not seen him till this moment, and his appearance had the suddenness of a conjuring trick. He might have sprung from the surrounding landscape.

'I wonder –' began Mr Satterthwaite.

But at that minute the stranger turned, and Mr Satterthwaite saw his face.

'Why, Mr Quin! How extraordinary. Miss Carlton Smith, I want to introduce my friend Mr Quin to you. He's the most unusual fellow. You are, you know. You always turn up in the nick of time –'

He stopped, with the feeling that he had said something awkwardly significant, and yet for the life of him he could not think what it was.

Naomi had shaken hands with Mr Quin in her usual abrupt style.

'We're here for a picnic,' she said. 'And it seems to me we shall be pretty well frozen to the bone.'

Mr Satterthwaite shivered.

'Perhaps,' he said uncertainly, 'we shall find a sheltered spot?'

'Which this isn't,' agreed Naomi. 'Still, it's worth seeing, isn't it?'

'Yes, indeed.' Mr Satterthwaite turned to Mr Quin. 'Miss Carlton Smith calls this place the World's End. Rather a good name, eh?'

Mr Quin nodded his head slowly several times.

'Yes – a very suggestive name. I suppose one only comes once in one's life to a place like that – a place where one can't go on any longer.'

'What do you mean?' asked Naomi sharply.

He turned to her.

'Well, usually, there's a choice, isn't there? To the right or to the left. Forward or back. Here – there's the road behind you and in front of you – nothing.'

Naomi stared at him. Suddenly she shivered and began to retrace her steps towards the others. The two men fell in beside her. Mr Quin continued to talk, but his tone was now easily conversational.

'Is the small car yours, Miss Carlton Smith?'

'Yes.'

'You drive yourself? One needs, I think, a good deal of nerve to do that round here. The turns are rather appalling. A moment of inattention, a brake that failed to hold, and – over the edge – down – down – down. It would be – very easily done.'

They had now joined the others. Mr Satterthwaite introduced his friend. He felt a tug at his arm. It was Naomi. She drew him apart from the others.

'Who is he?' she demanded fiercely.

Mr Satterthwaite gazed at her in astonishment.

'Well, I hardly know. I mean, I have known him for some years now – we have run across each other from time to time, but in the sense of knowing actually –'

He stopped. These were futilities that he was uttering, and the girl by his side was not listening. She was standing with her head bent down, her hands clenched by her sides.

'He knows things,' she said. 'He knows things . . . How does he know?'

Mr Satterthwaite had no answer. He could only look at her dumbly, unable to comprehend the storm that shook her.

'I'm afraid,' she muttered.

'Afraid of Mr Quin?'

'I'm afraid of his eyes. He sees things . . .'

Something cold and wet fell on Mr Satterthwaite's cheek. He looked up.

'Why, it's snowing,' he exclaimed, in great surprise.

'A nice day to have chosen for a picnic,' said Naomi.

She had regained control of herself with an effort.

What was to be done? A babel of suggestions broke out. The snow came down thick and fast. Mr Quin made a suggestion and everyone welcomed it. There was a little stone Cassecroute at the end of the row of houses. There was a stampede towards it.

'You have your provisions,' said Mr Quin, 'and they will probably be able to make you some coffee.'

It was a tiny place, rather dark, for the one little window did little towards lighting it, but from one end came a grateful glow of warmth. An old Corsican woman was just throwing a handful of branches on the fire. It blazed up, and by its light the newcomers realized that others were before them.

Three people were sitting at the end of a bare wooden table. There was something unreal about the scene to Mr Satterthwaite's eye, there was something even more unreal about the people.

The woman who sat at the end of the table looked like a duchess – that is, she looked more like a popular conception of a duchess. She was the ideal stage *grande dame*. Her aristocratic head was held high, her exquisitely dressed hair was of a snowy white. She was dressed in grey – soft draperies that fell about her in artistic folds. One long white hand supported her chin, the other was holding a roll spread with *pâté de foie gras*. On her right was a man with a very white face, very black hair, and horn-rimmed spectacles. He was marvellously and beautifully dressed. At the moment his head was thrown back, and his left arm was thrown out as though he were about to declaim something.

On the left of the white-haired lady was a jolly-looking little man with a bald head. After the first glance, nobody looked at him.

There was just a moment of uncertainty, and then the Duchess (the authentic Duchess) took charge.

'Isn't this storm too dreadful?' she said pleasantly, coming forward, and smiling a purposeful and efficient smile that she had found very useful when serving on Welfare and other committees. 'I suppose you've been caught in it just like we have? But Corsica is a marvellous place. I only arrived this morning.'

The man with the black hair got up, and the Duchess with a gracious smile slipped into his seat.

The white-haired lady spoke.

'We have been here a week,' she said.

Mr Satterthwaite started. Could anyone who had once heard that voice ever forget it? It echoed round the stone room, charged with emotion – with exquisite melancholy. It seemed to him that she had said something wonderful, memorable, full of meaning. She had spoken from her heart.

He spoke in a hurried aside to Mr Tomlinson.

'The man in spectacles is Mr Vyse – the producer, you know.'

The retired Indian judge was looking at Mr Vyse with a good deal of dislike.

'What does he produce?' he asked. 'Children?'

'Oh, dear me, no,' said Mr Satterthwaite, shocked by the mere mention of anything so crude in connection with Mr Vyse. 'Plays.'

'I think,' said Naomi, 'I'll go out again. It's too hot in here.'

Her voice, strong and harsh, made Mr Satterthwaite jump. She made almost blindly, as it seemed, for the door, brushing Mr Tomlinson aside. But in the doorway itself she came face to face with Mr Quin, and he barred her way.

'Go back and sit down,' he said.

His voice was authoritative. To Mr Satterthwaite's surprise the girl hesitated a minute and then obeyed. She sat down at the foot of the table as far from the others as possible.

Mr Satterthwaite bustled forward and button-holed the producer.

'You may not remember me,' he began, 'my name is Satterthwaite.'

'Of course!' A long bony hand shot out and enveloped the other's in a painful grip. 'My dear man. Fancy meeting you here. You know Miss Nunn, of course?'

Mr Satterthwaite jumped. No wonder that voice had been familiar. Thousands, all over England, had thrilled to those wonderful emotion-laden tones. Rosina Nunn! England's greatest emotional actress. Mr Satterthwaite too had lain under her spell. No one like her for interpreting a part – for bringing out the finer shades of meaning. He had thought of her always as an intellectual actress, one who comprehended and got inside the soul of her part.

He might be excused for not recognizing her. Rosina Nunn was volatile in her tastes. For twenty-five years of her life she had been a blonde. After a tour in the States she had returned with the locks of the raven, and she had taken up tragedy in earnest. This 'French Marquise' effect was her latest whim.

'Oh, by the way, Mr Judd – Miss Nunn's husband,' said Vyse, carelessly introducing the man with the bald head.

Rosina Nunn had had several husbands, Mr Satterthwaite knew. Mr Judd was evidently the latest.

Mr Judd was busily unwrapping packages from a hamper at his side. He addressed his wife.

'Some more *pâté*, dearest? That last wasn't as thick as you like it.'

Rosina Nunn surrendered her roll to him, as she murmured simply:

'Henry thinks of the most enchanting meals. I always leave the commissariat to him.'

'Feed the brute,' said Mr Judd, and laughed. He patted his wife on the shoulder.

'Treats her just as though she were a dog,' murmured the melancholy voice of Mr Vyse in Mr Satterthwaite's ear. 'Cuts up her food for her. Odd creatures, women.'

Mr Satterthwaite and Mr Quin between them unpacked lunch. Hard-boiled eggs, cold ham and Gruyère cheese were distributed round the table. The Duchess and Miss Nunn appeared to be deep in murmured confidences. Fragments came along in the actress's deep contralto.

'The bread must be lightly toasted, you understand? Then just a *very* thin layer of marmalade. Rolled up and put in the oven for one minute – not more. Simply delicious.'

'That woman lives for food,' murmured Mr Vyse. 'Simply lives for it. She can't think of anything else. I remember in Riders to the Sea – you know "and it's the fine quiet time I'll be having." I could *not* get the effect I wanted. At last I told her to think of peppermint creams – she's very fond of peppermint creams. I got the effect at once – a sort of far-away look that went to your very soul.'

Mr Satterthwaite was silent. He was remembering.

Mr Tomlinson opposite cleared his throat preparatory to entering into conversation.

'You produce plays, I hear, eh? I'm fond of a good play myself. Jim the Penman, now, that was a play.'

'My God,' said Mr Vyse, and shivered down all the long length of him.

'A tiny clove of garlic,' said Miss Nunn to the Duchess. 'You tell your cook. It's wonderful.'

She sighed happily and turned to her husband.

'Henry,' she said plaintively, 'I've never even *seen* the caviare.'

'You're as near as nothing to sitting on it,' returned Mr Judd cheerfully. 'You put it behind you on the chair.'

Rosina Nunn retrieved it hurriedly, and beamed round the table.

'Henry is too wonderful. I'm so terribly absent-minded. I never know where I've put anything.'

'Like the day you packed your pearls in your sponge bag,' said Henry jocosely. 'And then left it behind at the hotel. My word, I did a bit of wiring and phoning that day.'

'They were insured,' said Miss Nunn dreamily. 'Not like my opal.'

A spasm of exquisite heartrending grief flitted across her face.

Several times, when in the company of Mr Quin, Mr Satterthwaite had had the feeling of taking part in a play. The illusion was with him very strongly now. This was a dream. Everyone had his part. The words 'my opal' were his own cue. He leant forward.

'Your opal, Miss Nunn?'

'Have you got the butter, Henry? Thank you. Yes, my opal. It was stolen, you know. And I never got it back.'

'Do tell us,' said Mr Satterthwaite.

'Well – I was born in October – so it was lucky for me to wear opals, and because of that I wanted a real beauty. I waited a long time for it. They said it was one of the most perfect ones known. Not very large – about the size of a two-shilling piece – but oh! the colour and the fire.'

She sighed. Mr Satterthwaite observed that the Duchess was fidgeting and seemed uncomfortable, but nothing could stop Miss Nunn now. She went on, and the exquisite inflections of her voice made the story sound like some mournful Saga of old.

'It was stolen by a young man called Alec Gerard. He wrote plays.'

'Very good plays,' put in Mr Vyse professionally. 'Why, I once kept one of his plays for six months.'

'Did you produce it?' asked Mr Tomlinson.

'Oh, *no*,' said Mr Vyse, shocked at the idea. 'But do you know, at one time I actually thought of doing so?'

'It had a wonderful part in it for me,' said Miss Nunn. 'Rachel's Children, it was called – though there wasn't anyone called Rachel in the play. He came to talk to me about it – at the theatre. I liked him. He was a nice-looking – and very shy, poor boy. I remember' – a beautiful far-away look stole over her face – 'he bought me some peppermint creams. The opal was lying on the dressing-table. He'd been out in Australia, and he knew something about opals. He took it over to the light to look at it. I suppose he must have slipped it into his pocket then. I missed it as soon as he'd gone. There *was* a to-do. You remember?'

She turned to Mr Vyse.

'Oh, I remember,' said Mr Vyse with a groan.

'They found the empty case in his rooms,' continued the actress. 'He'd been terribly hard up, but the very next day he was able to pay large sums into his bank. He pretended to account for it by saying that a friend of his had put some money on a horse for him, but he couldn't produce the friend. He said he must have put the case in his pocket by mistake. I think that was a terribly weak thing to say, don't you? He might have thought of something better than that . . . I had to go and give evidence. There were pictures of me in all the papers. My press agent said it was very good publicity – but I'd much rather have had my opal back.'

She shook her head sadly.

'Have some preserved pineapple?' said Mr Judd.

Miss Nunn brightened up.

'Where is it?'

'I gave it to you just now.'

Miss Nunn looked behind her and in front of her, eyed her grey silk pochette, and then slowly drew up a large purple silk bag that was reposing on the ground beside her. She began to turn the contents out slowly on the table, much to Mr Satterthwaite's interest.

There was a powder puff, a lip-stick, a small jewel case, a skein of wool, another powder puff, two handkerchiefs, a box of chocolate creams, an enamelled paper knife, a mirror, a little dark brown wooden box, five letters, a walnut, a small square of mauve crêpe de chine, a piece of ribbon and the end of a *croissant*. Last of all came the preserved pineapple.

'*Eureka*,' murmured Mr Satterthwaite softly.

'I beg your pardon?'

'Nothing,' said Mr Satterthwaite hastily. 'What a charming paper knife.'

'Yes, isn't it? Somebody gave it to me. I can't remember who.'

'That's an Indian box,' remarked Mr Tomlinson. 'Ingenious little things, aren't they?'

'Somebody gave me that too,' said Miss Nunn. 'I've had it a long time. It used always to stand on my dressing-table at the theatre. I don't think it's very pretty, though, do you?'

The box was of plain dark brown wood. It pushed open from the side. On the top of it were two plain flaps of wood that could be turned round and round.

'Not pretty, perhaps,' said Mr Tomlinson with a chuckle. 'But I'll bet you've never seen one like it.'

Mr Satterthwaite leaned forward. He had an excited feeling.

'Why did you say it was ingenious?' he demanded.

'Well, isn't it?'

The judge appealed to Miss Nunn. She looked at him blankly.

'I suppose I mustn't show them the trick of it – eh?' Miss Nunn still looked blank.

'What trick?' asked Mr Judd.

'God bless my soul, don't you know?'

He looked round the inquiring faces.

'Fancy that now. May I take the box a minute? Thank you.'

He pushed it open.

'Now then, can anyone give me something to put in it – not too big. Here's a small piece of Gruyère cheese. That will do capitally. I place it inside, shut the box.'

He fumbled for a minute or two with his hands.

'Now see –'

He opened the box again. It was empty.

'Well, I never,' said Mr Judd. 'How do you do it?'

'It's quite simple. Turn the box upside down, and move the left hand flap half-way round, then shut the right hand flap. Now to bring our piece of cheese back again we must reverse that. The right hand flap half-way round, and the left one closed, still keeping the box upside down. And now – Hey Presto!'

The box slid open. A gasp went round the table. The cheese was there – but so was something else. A round thing that blinked forth every colour of the rainbow.

'*My opal!*'

It was a clarion note. Rosina Nunn stood upright, her hands clasped to her breast.

'My opal! How did it get there?'

Henry Judd cleared his throat.

'I – er – I rather think, Rosy, my girl, you must have put it there yourself.'

Someone got up from the table and blundered out into the air. It was Naomi Carlton Smith. Mr Quin followed her.

'But when? Do you mean –?'

Mr Satterthwaite watched her while the truth dawned on her. It took over two minutes before she got it.

'You mean last year – at the theatre.'

'You know,' said Henry apologetically. 'You *do* fiddle with things, Rosy. Look at you with the caviare today.'

Miss Nunn was painfully following out her mental processes.

'I just slipped it in without thinking, and then I suppose I turned the box about and did the thing by accident, but then – but then –' At last it came. 'But then Alec Gerard didn't steal it after all. Oh!' – a full-throated cry, poignant, moving – 'How dreadful!'

'Well,' said Mr Vyse, 'that can be put right now.'

'Yes, but he's been in prison a year.' And then she startled them. She turned sharp on the Duchess. 'Who is that girl – that girl who has just gone out?'

'Miss Carlton Smith,' said the Duchess, 'was engaged to Mr Gerard. She – took the thing very hard.'

Mr Satterthwaite stole softly away. The snow had stopped, Naomi was sitting on the stone wall. She had a sketch book in her hand, some coloured crayons were scattered around. Mr Quin was standing beside her.

She held out the sketch book to Mr Satterthwaite. It was a very rough affair – but it had genius. A kaleidoscopic whirl of snowflakes with a figure in the centre.

'Very good,' said Mr Satterthwaite.

Mr Quin looked up at the sky.

'The storm is over,' he said. 'The roads will be slippery, but I do not think there will be any accident – now.'

'There will be no accident,' said Naomi. Her voice was charged with some meaning that Mr Satterthwaite did not understand. She turned and smiled at him – a sudden dazzling smile. 'Mr Satterthwaite can drive back with me if he likes.'

He knew then to what length desperation had driven her.

'Well,' said Mr Quin, 'I must bid you goodbye.'

He moved away.

'Where is he going?' said Mr Satterthwaite, staring after him.

'Back where he came from, I suppose,' said Naomi in an odd voice.

'But – but there isn't anything there,' said Mr Satterthwaite, for Mr Quin was making for that spot on the edge of the cliff where they had first seen him. 'You know you said yourself it was the World's End.'

He handed back the sketch book.

'It's very good,' he said. 'A very good likeness. But why – er – why did you put him in Fancy Dress?'

Her eyes met his for a brief second.

'I see him like that,' said Naomi Carlton Smith.

CHAPTER 12

Harlequin's Lane

Mr Satterthwaite was never quite sure what took him to stay with the Denmans. They were not of his kind – that is to say, they belonged neither to the great world, nor to the more interesting artistic circles. They were Philistines, and dull Philistines at that. Mr Satterthwaite had met them first at Biarritz, had accepted an invitation to stay with them, had come, had been bored, and yet strangely enough had come again and yet again.

Why? He was asking himself that question on this twenty-first of June, as he sped out of London in his Rolls Royce.

John Denman was a man of forty, a solid well-established figure respected in the business world. His friends were not Mr Satterthwaite's friends, his ideas even less so. He was a man clever in his own line but devoid of imagination outside it.

Why am I doing this thing? Mr Satterthwaite asked himself once more – and the only answer that came seemed to him so vague and so inherently preposterous that he almost put it aside. For the only reason that presented itself was the fact that one of the rooms in the house (a comfortable well-appointed house), stirred his curiosity. That room was Mrs Denman's own sitting-room.

It was hardly an expression of her personality because, so far as Mr Satterthwaite could judge, she had no personality. He had never met a woman so completely expressionless. She was, he knew, a Russian by birth. John Denman had been in Russia at the outbreak of the European war, he had fought with the Russian troops, had narrowly escaped with his life on the outbreak of the Revolution, and had brought this Russian girl with him, a penniless refugee. In face of strong disapproval from his parents he had married her.

Mrs Denman's room was in no way remarkable. It was well and

solidly furnished with good Hepplewhite furniture – a trifle more masculine than feminine in atmosphere. But in it there was one incongruous item: a Chinese lacquer screen – a thing of creamy yellow and pale rose. Any museum might have been glad to own it. It was a collector's piece, rare and beautiful.

It was out of place against that solid English background. It should have been the key-note of the room with everything arranged to harmonize subtly with it. And yet Mr Satterthwaite could not accuse the Denmans of lack of taste. Everything else in the house was in perfectly blended accord.

He shook his head. The thing – trivial though it was – puzzled him. Because of it, so he verily believed, he had come again and again to the house. It was, perhaps, a woman's fantasy – but that solution did not satisfy him as he thought of Mrs Denman – a quiet hard-featured woman, speaking English so correctly that no one would ever have guessed her a foreigner.

The car drew up at his destination and he got out, his mind still dwelling on the problem of the Chinese screen. The name of the Denman's house was 'Ashmead', and it occupied some five acres of Melton Heath, which is thirty miles from London, stands five hundred feet above sea level and is, for the most part, inhabited by those who have ample incomes.

The butler received Mr Satterthwaite suavely. Mr and Mrs Denman were both out – at a rehearsal – they hoped Mr Satterthwaite would make himself at home until they returned.

Mr Satterthwaite nodded and proceeded to carry out these injunctions by stepping into the garden. After a cursory examination of the flower beds, he strolled down a shady walk and presently came to a door in the wall. It was unlocked and he passed through it and came out into a narrow lane.

Mr Satterthwaite looked to left and right. A very charming lane, shady and green, with high hedges – a rural lane that twisted and turned in good old-fashioned style. He remembered the stamped address: ASHMEAD, HARLEQUIN'S LANE – remembered too, a local name for it that Mrs Denman had once told him.

'Harlequin's Lane,' he murmured to himself softly. 'I wonder –'

He turned a corner.

Not at the time, but afterwards, he wondered why this time he felt no surprise at meeting that elusive friend of his: Mr Harley Quin. The two men clasped hands.

'So *you're* down here,' said Mr Satterthwaite.

'Yes,' said Mr Quin. 'I'm staying in the same house as you are.'

'Staying there?'

'Yes. Does it surprise you?'

'No,' said Mr Satterthwaite slowly. 'Only – well, you never stay anywhere for long, do you?'

'Only as long as is necessary,' said Mr Quin gravely.

'I see,' said Mr Satterthwaite.

They walked on in silence for some minutes.

'This lane,' began Mr Satterthwaite, and stopped.

'Belongs to me,' said Mr Quin.

'I thought it did,' said Mr Satterthwaite. 'Somehow, I thought it must. There's the other name for it, too, the local name. They call it the "Lovers' Lane". You know that?'

Mr Quin nodded.

'But surely,' he said gently, 'there is a "Lovers' Lane" in every village?'

'I suppose so,' said Mr Satterthwaite, and he sighed a little.

He felt suddenly rather old and out of things, a little dried-up wizened old fogey of a man. Each side of him were the hedges, very green and alive.

'Where does this lane end, I wonder?' he asked suddenly.

'It ends – *here*,' said Mr Quin.

They came round the last bend. The lane ended in a piece of waste ground, and almost at their feet a great pit opened. In it were tin cans gleaming in the sun, and other cans that were too red with rust to gleam, old boots, fragments of newspapers, a hundred and one odds and ends that were no longer of account to anybody.

'A rubbish heap,' exclaimed Mr Satterthwaite, and breathed deeply and indignantly.

'Sometimes there are very wonderful things on a rubbish heap,' said Mr Quin.

'I know, I know,' cried Mr Satterthwaite, and quoted with just a trace of self-consciousness: '*Bring me the two most beautiful things in the city, said God.* You know how it goes, eh?'

Mr Quin nodded.

Mr Satterthwaite looked up at the ruins of a small cottage perched on the brink of the wall of the cliff.

'Hardly a pretty view for a house,' he remarked.

'I fancy this wasn't a rubbish heap in those days,' said Mr Quin. 'I believe the Denmans lived there when they were first married. They moved into the big house when the old people died. The cottage was pulled down when they began to quarry the rock here – but nothing much was done, as you can see.'

They turned and began retracing their steps.

'I suppose,' said Mr Satterthwaite, smiling, 'that many couples come wandering down this lane on these warm summer evenings.'

'Probably.'

'Lovers,' said Mr Satterthwaite. He repeated the word thoughtfully and quite without the normal embarrassment of the Englishman. Mr Quin had that effect upon him. 'Lovers . . . You have done a lot for lovers, Mr Quin.'

The other bowed his head without replying.

'You have saved them from sorrow – from worse than sorrow, from death. You have been an advocate for the dead themselves.'

'You are speaking of yourself – of what *you* have done – not of me.'

'It is the same thing,' said Mr Satterthwaite. 'You know it is,' he urged, as the other did not speak. 'You have acted – through me. For some reason or other you do not act directly – yourself.'

'Sometimes I do,' said Mr Quin.

His voice held a new note. In spite of himself Mr Satterthwaite shivered a little. The afternoon, he thought, must be growing chilly. And yet the sun seemed as bright as ever.

At that moment a girl turned the corner ahead of them and came into sight. She was a very pretty girl, fair-haired and blue-eyed, wearing a pink cotton frock. Mr Satterthwaite recognized her as Molly Stanwell, whom he had met down here before.

She waved a hand to welcome him.

'John and Anna have just gone back,' she cried. 'They thought you must have come, but they simply had to be at the rehearsal.'

'Rehearsal of what?' inquired Mr Satterthwaite.

'This masquerade thing – I don't quite know what you'll call it. There is singing and dancing and all sorts of things in it. Mr Manly, do you remember him down here? He had quite a good tenor voice, is to be Pierrot, and I am Pierrette. Two professionals are coming down for the dancing – Harlequin and Columbine, you know. And then there is a big chorus of girls. Lady Roscheimer is so keen on training village girls to sing. She's really getting the thing up for that. The music is rather lovely – but very modern – next to no tune anywhere. Claude Wickam. Perhaps you know him?'

Mr Satterthwaite nodded, for, as has been mentioned before, it was his *métier* to know everybody. He knew all about that aspiring genius Claude Wickam, and about Lady Roscheimer who was a fat Jewess with a *penchant* for young men of the artistic persuasion. And he knew all about Sir Leopold Roscheimer who liked his wife to be happy and, most rare among husbands, did not mind her being happy in her own way.

They found Claude Wickam at tea with the Denmans, cramming his mouth indiscriminately with anything handy, talking rapidly, and waving long white hands that had a double-jointed appearance. His short-sighted eyes peered through large horn-rimmed spectacles.

John Denman, upright, slightly florid, with the faintest possible tendency to sleekness, listened with an air of bored attention. On the appearance of Mr Satterthwaite, the musician transferred his remarks to him. Anna Denman sat behind the tea things, quiet and expressionless as usual.

Mr Satterthwaite stole a covert glance at her. Tall, gaunt, very thin, with the skin tightly stretched over high cheek bones, black hair parted in the middle, a skin that was weather-beaten. An out of door woman who cared nothing for the use of cosmetics. A Dutch Doll of a woman, wooden, lifeless – and yet . . .

He thought: 'There *should* be meaning behind that face, and yet there isn't. That's what's all wrong. Yes, all wrong.' And to Claude Wickam he said: 'I beg your pardon? You were saying?'

Claude Wickam, who liked the sound of his own voice, began all over again. 'Russia,' he said, 'that was the only country in the world worth being interested in. They experimented. With lives, if you like, but still they experimented. Magnificent!'

He crammed a sandwich into his mouth with one hand, and added a bite of the chocolate éclair he was waving about in the other. 'Take,' he said (with his mouth full), 'the Russian Ballet.' Remembering his hostess, he turned to her. What did *she* think of the Russian Ballet?

The question was obviously only a prelude to the important point – what Claude Wickam thought of the Russian Ballet, but her answer was unexpected and threw him completely out of his stride.

'I have never seen it.'

'What?' He gazed at her open-mouthed. 'But – surely –'

Her voice went on, level and emotionless.

'Before my marriage, I was a dancer. So now –'

'A busman's holiday,' said her husband.

'Dancing.' She shrugged her shoulders. 'I know all the tricks of it. It does not interest me.'

'Oh!'

It took but a moment for Claude to recover his aplomb. His voice went on.

'Talking of lives,' said Mr Satterthwaite, 'and experimenting in them. The Russian nation made one costly experiment.'

Claude Wickam swung round on him.

'I know what you are going to say,' he cried. 'Kharsanova! The immortal, the only Kharsanova! You saw her dance?'

'Three times,' said Mr Satterthwaite. 'Twice in Paris, once in London. I shall – not forget it.'

He spoke in an almost reverent voice.

'I saw her, too,' said Claude Wickam. 'I was ten years old. An uncle took me. God! I shall never forget it.'

He threw a piece of bun fiercely into a flower bed.

'There is a statuette of her in a Museum in Berlin,' said Mr Satterthwaite. 'It is marvellous. That impression of fragility – as though you could break her with a flip of the thumb nail. I have seen her as Columbine, in the Swan, as the dying Nymph.' He paused, shaking his head. 'There was genius. It will be long years before such another is born. She was young too. Destroyed ignorantly and wantonly in the first days of the Revolution.'

'Fools! Madmen! Apes!' said Claude Wickam. He choked with a mouthful of tea.

'I studied with Kharsanova,' said Mrs Denman. 'I remember her well.'

'She was wonderful?' said Mr Satterthwaite.

'Yes,' said Mrs Denman quietly. 'She was wonderful.'

Claude Wickam departed and John Denman drew a deep sigh of relief at which his wife laughed.

Mr Satterthwaite nodded. 'I know what you think. But in spite of everything, the music that that boy writes *is* music.'

'I suppose it is,' said Denman.

'Oh, undoubtedly. How long it will be – well, that is different.'

John Denman looked at him curiously.

'You mean?'

'I mean that success has come early. And that is dangerous. Always dangerous.' He looked across at Mr Quin. 'You agree with me?'

'You are always right,' said Mr Quin.

'We will come upstairs to my room,' said Mrs Denman. 'It is pleasant there.'

She led the way, and they followed her. Mr Satterthwaite drew a deep breath as he caught sight of the Chinese screen. He looked up to find Mrs Denman watching him.

'You are the man who is always right,' she said, nodding her head slowly at him. 'What do you make of my screen?'

He felt that in some way the words were a challenge to him, and he answered almost haltingly, stumbling over the words a little.

'Why, it's – it's beautiful. More, it's unique.'

'You're right.' Denman had come up behind him. 'We bought it early in our married life. Got it for about a tenth of its value, but even then – well, it crippled us for over a year. You remember, Anna?'

'Yes,' said Mrs Denman, 'I remember.'

'In fact, we'd no business to buy it at all – not then. Now, of course, it's different. There was some very good lacquer going at Christie's the other day. Just what we need to make this room perfect. All Chinese together. Clear out the other stuff. Would you believe it, Satterthwaite, my wife wouldn't hear of it?'

'I like this room as it is,' said Mrs Denman.

There was a curious look on her face. Again Mr Satterthwaite felt challenged and defeated. He looked round him, and for the first time he noticed the absence of all personal touch. There were no photographs, no flowers, no knick-knacks. It was not like a woman's room at all. Save for that one incongruous factor of the Chinese screen, it might have been a sample room shown at some big furnishing house.

He found her smiling at him.

'Listen,' she said. She bent forward, and for a moment she seemed less English, more definitely foreign. 'I speak to you for you will understand. We bought that screen with more than money – with love. For love of it, because it was beautiful and unique, we went without other things, things we needed and missed. These other Chinese pieces my husband speaks of, those we should buy with money only, we should not pay away anything of ourselves.'

Her husband laughed.

'Oh, have it your own way,' he said, but with a trace of irritation in his voice. 'But it's all wrong against this English background. This other stuff, it's good enough of its kind, genuine solid, no fake about it – but mediocre. Good plain late Hepplewhite.'

She nodded.

'Good, solid, genuine English,' she murmured softly.

Mr Satterthwaite stared at her. He caught a meaning behind these words. The English room – the flaming beauty of the Chinese screen . . . No, it was gone again.

'I met Miss Stanwell in the lane,' he said conversationally. 'She tells me she is going to be Pierrette in this show tonight.'

'Yes,' said Denman. 'And she's awfully good, too.'

'She has clumsy feet,' said Anna.

'Nonsense,' said her husband. 'All women are alike, Satterthwaite. Can't bear to hear another woman praised. Molly is a very good-looking girl, and so of course every woman has to have their knife into her.'

'I spoke of dancing,' said Anna Denman. She sounded faintly surprised. 'She is very pretty, yes, but her feet move clumsily. You cannot tell me anything else because I know about dancing.'

Mr Satterthwaite intervened tactfully.

'You have two professional dancers coming down, I understand?'

'Yes. For the ballet proper. Prince Oranoff is bringing them down in his car.'

'Sergius Oranoff?'

The question came from Anna Denman. Her husband turned and looked at her.

'You know him?'

'I used to know him – in Russia.'

Mr Satterthwaite thought that John Denman looked disturbed.

'Will he know you?'

'Yes. He will know me.'

She laughed – a low, almost triumphant laugh. There was nothing of the Dutch Doll about her face now. She nodded reassuringly at her husband.

'Sergius. So he is bringing down the two dancers. He was always interested in dancing.'

'I remember.'

John Denman spoke abruptly, then turned and left the room. Mr Quin followed him. Anna Denman crossed to the telephone and asked for a number. She arrested Mr Satterthwaite with a gesture as he was about to follow the example of the other two men.

'Can I speak to Lady Roscheimer. Oh! it is you. This is Anna Denman speaking. Has Prince Oranoff arrived yet? What? *What?* Oh, my dear! But how ghastly.'

She listened for a few moments longer, then replaced the receiver. She turned to Mr Satterthwaite.

'There has been an accident. There would be with Sergius Ivanovitch driving. Oh, he has not altered in all these years. The girl was not badly hurt, but bruised and shaken, too much to dance tonight. The man's arm is broken. Sergius Ivanovitch himself is unhurt. The devil looks after his own, perhaps.'

'And what about tonight's performance?'

'Exactly, my friend. Something must be done about it.'

She sat thinking. Presently she looked at him.

'I am a bad hostess, Mr Satterthwaite. I do not entertain you.'

'I assure you that it is not necessary. There's one thing though, Mrs Denman, that I would very much like to know.'

'Yes?'

'How did you come across Mr Quin?'

'He is often down here,' she said slowly. 'I think he owns land in this part of the world.'

'He does, he does. He told me so this afternoon,' said Mr Satterthwaite.

'He is –' She paused. Her eyes met Mr Satterthwaite's. 'I think you know what he is better than I do,' she finished.

'I?'

'Is it not so?'

He was troubled. His neat little soul found her disturbing. He felt that she wished to force him further than he was prepared to go, that she wanted him to put into words that which he was not prepared to admit to himself.

'*You* know!' she said. 'I think you know most things, Mr Satterthwaite.'

Here was incense, yet for once it failed to intoxicate him. He shook his head in unwonted humility.

'What can anyone know?' he asked. 'So little – so very little.'

She nodded in assent. Presently she spoke again, in a queer brooding voice, without looking at him.

'Supposing I were to tell you something – you would not laugh? No, I do not think you would laugh. Supposing, then, that to carry on one's' – she paused – 'one's trade, one's profession, one were to make use of a fantasy – one were to pretend to oneself something that did not exist – that one were to imagine a certain person . . . It is a pretence, you understand, a make believe – nothing more. But one day –'

'Yes?' said Mr Satterthwaite.

He was keenly interested.

'The fantasy came true! The thing one imagined – the impossible thing, the thing that could not be – was real! Is that madness? Tell me, Mr Satterthwaite. Is that madness – or do you believe it too?'

'I –' Queer how he could not get the words out. How they seemed to stick somewhere at the back of his throat.

'Folly,' said Anna Denman. 'Folly.'

She swept out of the room and left Mr Satterthwaite with his confession of faith unspoken.

He came down to dinner to find Mrs Denman entertaining a guest, a tall dark man approaching middle age.

'Prince Oranoff – Mr Satterthwaite.'

The two men bowed. Mr Satterthwaite had the feeling that some conversation had been broken off on his entry which would not be resumed. But there was no sense of strain. The Russian conversed easily and naturally on those objects which were nearest to Mr Satterthwaite's heart. He was a man of very fine artistic taste, and they soon found that they had many friends in common. John Denman joined them, and the talk became localized. Oranoff expressed regret for the accident.

'It was not my fault. I like to drive fast – yes, but I am a good driver. It was Fate – chance' – he shrugged his shoulders – 'the masters of all of us.'

'There speaks the Russian in you, Sergius Ivanovitch,' said Mrs Denman.

'And finds an echo in you, Anna Mikalovna,' he threw back quickly.

Mr Satterthwaite looked from one to the other of the three of them. John Denman, fair, aloof, English, and the other two, dark, thin, strangely alike. Something rose in his mind – what was it? Ah! he had it now. The first Act of the Walküre. Siegmund and Sieglinde – so alike – and the alien Hunding. Conjectures began to stir in his brain. Was this the meaning of the presence of Mr Quin? One thing he believed in firmly – wherever Mr Quin showed himself – there lay drama. Was this it here – the old hackneyed three-cornered tragedy?

He was vaguely disappointed. He had hoped for better things.

'What has been arranged, Anna?' asked Denman. 'The thing will have to be put off, I suppose. I heard you ringing the Roscheimers up.'

She shook her head.

'No – there is no need to put it off.'

'But you can't do it without the ballet?'

'You certainly couldn't have a Harlequinade without Harlequin and Columbine,' agreed Anna Denman drily. 'I'm going to be Columbine, John.'

'You?' He was astonished – disturbed, Mr Satterthwaite thought.

She nodded composedly.

'You need not be afraid, John. I shall not disgrace you. You forget – it was my profession once.'

Mr Satterthwaite thought: 'What an extraordinary thing a voice is. The things it says – and the things it leaves unsaid and means! I wish I knew . . .'

'Well,' said John Denman grudgingly, 'that solves one half of the problem. What about the other? Where will you find Harlequin?'

'I *have* found him – there!'

She gestured towards the open doorway where Mr Quin had just appeared. He smiled back at her.

'Good lord, Quin,' said John Denman. 'Do you know anything of this game? I should never have imagined it.'

'Mr Quin is vouched for by an expert,' said his wife. 'Mr Satterthwaite will answer for him.'

She smiled at Mr Satterthwaite, and the little man found himself murmuring:

'Oh, yes – I answer for Mr Quin.'

Denman turned his attention elsewhere.

'You know there's to be a fancy dress dance business afterwards. Great nuisance. We'll have to rig you up, Satterthwaite.'

Mr Satterthwaite shook his head very decidedly.

'My years will excuse me.' A brilliant idea struck him. A table napkin under his arm. 'There I am, an elderly waiter who has seen better days.'

He laughed.

'An interesting profession,' said Mr Quin. 'One sees so much.'

'I've got to put on some fool pierrot thing,' said Denman gloomily. 'It's cool anyway, that's one thing. What about you?' He looked at Oranoff.

'I have a Harlequin costume,' said the Russian. His eyes wandered for a minute to his hostess's face.

Mr Satterthwaite wondered if he was mistaken in fancying that there was just a moment of constraint.

'There might have been three of us,' said Denman, with a laugh. 'I've got an old Harlequin costume my wife made me when we were first married for some show or other.' He paused, looking down on his broad shirt front. 'I don't suppose I could get into it now.'

'No,' said his wife. 'You couldn't get into it now.'

And again her voice said something more than mere words.

She glanced up at the clock.

'If Molly doesn't turn up soon, we won't wait for her.'

But at that moment the girl was announced. She was already wearing her Pierrette dress of white and green, and very charming she looked in it, so Mr Satterthwaite reflected.

She was full of excitement and enthusiasm over the forthcoming performance.

'I'm getting awfully nervous, though,' she announced, as they drank coffee after dinner. 'I know my voice will wobble, and I shall forget the words.'

'Your voice is very charming,' said Anna. 'I should not worry about it if I were you.'

'Oh, but I do. The other I don't mind about – the dancing, I mean. That's sure to go all right. I mean, you can't go very far wrong with your feet, can you?'

She appealed to Anna, but the older woman did not respond. Instead she said:

'Sing something now to Mr Satterthwaite. You will find that he will reassure you.'

Molly went over to the piano. Her voice rang out, fresh and tuneful, in an old Irish ballad.

'Shiela, dark Shiela, what is it that you're seeing?
What is it that you're seeing, that you're seeing in the fire?'
'I see a lad that loves me – and I see a lad that leaves me,
And a third lad, a Shadow Lad – and he's the lad that
grieves me.'

The song went on. At the end, Mr Satterthwaite nodded vigorous approval.

'Mrs Denman is right. Your voice is charming. Not, perhaps, very fully trained, but delightfully natural, and with that unstudied quality of youth in it.'

'That's right,' agreed John Denman. 'You go ahead, Molly, and don't be downed by stage fright. We'd better be getting over to the Roscheimers now.'

The party separated to don cloaks. It was a glorious night and they proposed to walk over, the house being only a few hundred yards down the road.

Mr Satterthwaite found himself by his friend.

'It's an odd thing,' he said, 'but that song made me think of you. *A third lad – a Shadow Lad* – there's mystery there, and wherever there's mystery I – well, think of you.'

'Am I so mysterious?' smiled Mr Quin.

Mr Satterthwaite nodded vigorously.

'Yes, indeed. Do you know, until tonight, I had no idea that you were a professional dancer.'

'Really?' said Mr Quin.

'Listen,' said Mr Satterthwaite. He hummed the love motif from the Walküre. 'That is what has been ringing in my head all through dinner as I looked at those two.'

'Which two?'

'Prince Oranoff and Mrs Denman. Don't you see the difference in her tonight? It's as though – as though a shutter had suddenly been opened and you see the glow within.'

'Yes,' said Mr Quin. 'Perhaps so.'

'The same old drama,' said Mr Satterthwaite. 'I am right, am I not? Those two belong together. They are of the same world, think the same thoughts, dream the same dreams . . . One sees how it has come about. Ten years ago Denman must have been very good-looking, young, dashing, a figure of romance. And he saved her life. All quite natural. But now – what is he, after all? A good fellow – prosperous, successful – but – well, mediocre, Good honest English stuff – very much like that Hepplewhite furniture upstairs. As English – and as ordinary – as that pretty English girl with her fresh untrained voice. Oh, you may smile, Mr Quin, but you cannot deny what I am saying.'

'I deny nothing. In what you see you are always right. And yet –'

'Yet what?'

Mr Quin leaned forward. His dark melancholy eyes searched for those of Mr Satterthwaite.

'Have you learned so little of life?' he breathed.

He left Mr Satterthwaite vaguely disquieted, such a prey to meditation that he found the others had started without him owing to his delay in selecting a scarf for his neck. He went out by the garden, and through the same door as in the afternoon. The lane was bathed in moonlight, and even as he stood in the doorway he saw a couple enlaced in each other's arms.

For a moment he thought –

And then he saw. *John Denman and Molly Stanwell.* Denman's voice came to him, hoarse and anguished.

'I can't live without you. What are we to do?'

Mr Satterthwaite turned to go back the way he had come, but a hand stayed him. Someone else stood in the doorway beside him, someone else whose eyes had also seen.

Mr Satterthwaite had only to catch one glimpse of her face to know how wildly astray all his conclusions had been.

Her anguished hand held him there until those other two had passed up the lane and disappeared from sight. He heard himself speaking to her, saying foolish little things meant to be comforting, and ludicrously inadequate to the agony he had divined. She only spoke once.

'Please,' she said, 'don't leave me.'

He found that oddly touching. He was, then, of use to someone. And he went on saying those things that meant nothing at all, but which were, somehow, better than silence. They went that way to the Roscheimers. Now and then her hand tightened on his shoulder, and he understood that she was glad of his company. She only took it away when they finally came to their destination. She stood very erect, her head held high.

'Now,' she said, 'I shall dance! Do not be afraid for me, my friend. I shall dance.'

She left him abruptly. He was seized upon by Lady Roscheimer, much bediamonded and very full of lamentations. By her he was passed on to Claude Wickam.

'Ruined! Completely ruined. The sort of thing that always happens to me. All these country bumpkins think they can dance. I was never even consulted –' His voice went on – went on interminably. He had found a sympathetic listener, a man who *knew*. He gave himself up to an orgy of self-pity. It only ended when thc first strains of music began.

Mr Satterthwaite came out of his dreams. He was alert, once more the critic. Wickam was an unutterable ass, but he could write music – delicate gossamer stuff, intangible as a fairy web – yet with nothing of the pretty pretty about it.

The scenery was good. Lady Roscheimer never spared expense when aiding her protégés. A glade of Arcady with lighting effects that gave it the proper atmosphere of unreality.

Two figures dancing as they had danced through time immemorial. A slender Harlequin flashing spangles in the moonlight with magic wand and masked face . . . A white Columbine pirouetting like some immortal dream . . .

Mr Satterthwaite sat up. He had lived through this before. Yes, surely . . .

Now his body was far away from Lady Roscheimer's drawing-room. It was in a Berlin Museum at a statuette of an immortal Columbine.

Harlequin and Columbine danced on. The wide world was theirs to dance in . . .

Moonlight – and a human figure. Pierrot wandering through the wood, singing to the moon. Pierrot who has seen Columbine and knows no rest. The Immortal two vanish, but Columbine looks back. She has heard the song of a human heart.

Pierrot wandering on through the wood . . . darkness . . . his voice dies away in the distance . . .

The village green – dancing of village girls – pierrots and pierrettes. Molly as Pierrette. No dancer – Anna Denman was right there – but a fresh tuneful voice as she sings her song 'Pierrette dancing on the Green'.

A good tune – Mr Satterthwaite nodded approval. Wickham wasn't above writing a tune when there was a need for it. The majority of the village girls made him shudder, but he realized that Lady Roscheimer was determinedly philanthropical.

They press Pierrot to join the dance. He refuses. With white face he wanders on – the eternal lover seeking his ideal. Evening falls. Harlequin and Columbine, invisible, dance in and out of the unconscious throng. The place is deserted, only Pierrot, weary, falls asleep on a grassy bank. Harlequin and Columbine dance round him. He wakes and sees Columbine. He woos her in vain, pleads, beseeches . . .

She stands uncertain. Harlequin beckons to her to begone. But she sees him no longer. She is listening to Pierrot, to his song of love outpoured once more. She falls into his arms, and the curtain comes down.

The second Act is Pierrot's cottage. Columbine sits on her hearth. She is pale, weary. She listens – for what? Pierrot sings to her – woos her back to thoughts of him once more. The evening darkens. Thunder is heard . . . Columbine puts aside her spinning wheel. She is eager, stirred . . . She listens no longer to Pierrot. It is her own music that is in the air, the music of Harlequin and Columbine . . . She is awake. She remembers.

A crash of thunder! Harlequin stands in the doorway. Pierrot cannot see him, but Columbine springs up with a glad laugh. Children come running, but she pushes them aside. With another crash of thunder the walls fall, and Columbine dances out into the wild night with Harlequin.

Darkness, and through it the tune that Pierrette has sung. Light comes slowly. The cottage once more. Pierrot and Pierrette grown old and grey sit in front of the fire in two armchairs. The music is happy, but subdued. Pierrette nods in her chair. Through the window comes a shaft of moonlight, and with it the motif of Pierrot's long-forgotten song. He stirs in his chair.

Faint music – fairy music . . . Harlequin and Columbine outside. The door swings open and Columbine dances in. She leans over the sleeping Pierrot, kisses him on the lips . . .

Crash! A peal of thunder. She is outside again. In the centre of the stage is the lighted window and through it are seen the two figures of Harlequin and Columbine dancing slowly away, growing fainter and fainter . . .

A log falls. Pierrette jumps up angrily, rushes across to the window and pulls the blind. So it ends, on a sudden discord . . .

Mr Satterthwaite sat very still among the applause and vociferations. At last he got up and made his way outside. He came upon Molly Stanwell, flushed and eager, receiving compliments. He saw John Denman, pushing and elbowing his way through the throng, his eyes alight with a new flame. Molly came towards him, but, almost unconsciously, he put her aside. It was not her he was seeking.

'My wife? Where is she?'

'I think she went out in the garden.'

It was, however, Mr Satterthwaite who found her, sitting on a stone seat under a cypress tree. When he came up to her, he did an odd thing. He knelt down and raised her hand to his lips.

'Ah!' she said. 'You think I danced well?'

'You danced – as you always danced, Madame Kharsanova.'

She drew in her breath sharply.

'So – you have guessed.'

'There is only one Kharsanova. No one could see you dance and forget. But why – why?'

'What else is possible?'

'You mean?'

She had spoken very simply. She was just as simple now. 'Oh! but you understand. You are of the world. A great dancer – she can have lovers, yes – but a husband, that is different. And he – he did not want the other. He wanted me to belong to him as – as Kharsanova could never have belonged.'

'I see,' said Mr Satterthwaite. 'I see. So you gave it up?'

She nodded.

'You must have loved him very much,' said Mr Satterthwaite gently.

'To make such a sacrifice?' She laughed.

'Not quite that. To make it so light-heartedly.'

'Ah, yes – perhaps – you are right.'

'And now?' asked Mr Satterthwaite.

Her face grew grave.

'Now?' She paused, then raised her voice and spoke into the shadows.

'Is that you, Sergius Ivanovitch?'

Prince Oranoff came out into the moonlight. He took her hand and smiled at Mr Satterthwaite without self-consciousness.

'Ten years ago I mourned the death of Anna Kharsanova,' he said simply. 'She was to me as my other self. Today I have found her again. We shall part no more.'

'At the end of the lane in ten minutes,' said Anna. 'I shall not fail you.'

Oranoff nodded and went off again. The dancer turned to Mr Satterthwaite. A smile played about her lips.

'Well – you are not satisfied, my friend?'

'Do you know,' said Mr Satterthwaite abruptly, 'that your husband is looking for you?'

He saw the tremor that passed over her face, but her voice was steady enough.

'Yes,' she said gravely. 'That may well be.'

'I saw his eyes. They –' he stopped abruptly.

She was still calm.

'Yes, perhaps. For an hour. An hour's magic, born of past memories, of music, of moonlight – That is all.'

'Then there is nothing that I can say?' He felt old, dispirited.

'For ten years I have lived with the man I love,' said Anna Kharsanova. 'Now I am going to the man who for ten years has loved me.'

Mr Satterthwaite said nothing. He had no arguments left. Besides it really seemed the simplest solution. Only – only, somehow, it was not the solution he wanted. He felt her hand on his shoulder.

'I know, my friend, I know. But there is no third way. Always one looks for one thing – the lover, the perfect, the eternal lover . . . It is the music of Harlequin one hears. No lover ever satisfies one, for all lovers are mortal. And Harlequin is only a myth, an invisible presence . . . unless –'

'Yes,' said Mr Satterthwaite. 'Yes?'

'Unless – his name is – Death!'

Mr Satterthwaite shivered. She moved away from him, was swallowed up in the shadows . . .

He never knew quite how long he sat on there, but suddenly he started up with the feeling that he had been wasting valuable time. He hurried away, impelled in a certain direction almost in spite of himself.

As he came out into the lane he had a strange feeling of unreality. Magic – magic and moonlight! And two figures coming towards him . . .

Oranoff in his Harlequin dress. So he thought at first. Then, as they passed him, he knew his mistake. That lithe swaying figure belonged to one person only – Mr Quin . . .

They went on down the lane – their feet light as though they were treading on air. Mr Quin turned his head and looked back, and Mr Satterthwaite had a shock, for it was not the face of Mr Quin as he had ever seen it before. It was the face of a stranger – no, not quite a stranger. Ah! he had it now, it was the face of John Denman as it might have looked before life went too well with him. Eager, adventurous, the face at once of a boy and a lover . . .

Her laugh floated down to him, clear and happy . . . He looked after them and saw in the distance the lights of a little cottage. He gazed after them like a man in a dream.

He was rudely awakened by a hand that fell on his shoulder and he was jerked round to face Sergius Oranoff. The man looked white and distracted.

'Where is she? Where is she? She promised – and she has not come.'

'Madam has just gone up the lane – alone.'

It was Mrs Denman's maid who spoke from the shadow of the door behind them. She had been waiting with her mistress's wraps.

'I was standing here and saw her pass,' she added.

Mr Satterthwaite threw one harsh word at her.

'Alone? Alone, did you say?'

The maid's eyes widened in surprise.

'Yes, sir. Didn't you see her off?'

Mr Satterthwaite clutched at Oranoff.

'Quickly,' he muttered. 'I'm – I'm afraid.'

They hurried down the lane together, the Russian talking in quick disjointed sentences.

'She is a wonderful creature. Ah! how she danced tonight. And that friend of yours. Who is he? Ah! but he is wonderful – unique. In the old days, when she danced the Columbine of Rimsky Korsakoff, she never found the perfect Harlequin. Mordoff, Kassnine – none of them were quite perfect. She had her own little fancy. She told me of it once. Always she danced with a dream Harlequin – a man who was not really there. It was Harlequin himself, she said, who came to dance with her. It was that fancy of hers that made her Columbine so wonderful.'

Mr Satterthwaite nodded. There was only one thought in his head.

'Hurry,' he said. 'We must be in time. Oh! we must be in time.'

They came round the last corner – came to the deep pit and to something lying in it that had not been there before, the body of a woman lying in a wonderful pose, arms flung wide and head thrown back. A dead face and body that were triumphant and beautiful in the moonlight.

Words came back to Mr Satterthwaite dimly – Mr Quin's words: '*wonderful things on a rubbish heap*' . . . He understood them now.

Oranoff was murmuring broken phrases. The tears were streaming down his face.

'I loved her. Always I loved her.' He used almost the same words that had occurred to Mr Satterthwaite earlier in the day. 'We were of the same world, she and I. We had the same thoughts, the same dreams. I would have loved her always . . .'

'How do you know?'

The Russian stared at him – at the fretful peevishness of the tone.

'How do you know?' went on Mr Satterthwaite. 'It is what all lovers think – what all lovers say . . . There is only one lover –'

He turned and almost ran into Mr Quin. In an agitated manner, Mr Satterthwaite caught him by the arm and drew him aside.

'It was *you*,' he said. 'It was *you* who were with her just now?'

Mr Quin waited a minute and then said gently:

'You can put it that way, if you like.'

'And the maid didn't see you?'

'The maid didn't see me.'

'But *I* did. Why was that?'

'Perhaps, as a result of the price you have paid, you see things that other people – do not.'

Mr Satterthwaite looked at him uncomprehendingly for a minute or two. Then he began suddenly to quiver all over like an aspen leaf.

'What is this place?' he whispered. 'What is this place?'

'I told you earlier today. It is *My* lane.'

'A Lovers' Lane,' murmured Mr Satterthwaite. 'And people pass along it.'

'Most people, sooner or later.'

'And at the end of it – what do they find?'

Mr Quin smiled. His voice was very gentle. He pointed at the ruined cottage above them.

'The house of their dreams – or a rubbish heap – who shall say?'

Mr Satterthwaite looked up at him suddenly. A wild rebellion surged over him. He felt cheated, defrauded.

'But *I* –' His voice shook. '*I* have never passed down your lane . . .'

'And do you regret?'

Mr Satterthwaite quailed. Mr Quin seemed to have loomed to enormous proportions . . . Mr Satterthwaite had a vista of something at once menacing and terrifying . . . Joy, Sorrow, Despair.

And his comfortable little soul shrank back appalled.

'Do you regret?' Mr Quin repeated his question. There was something terrible about him.

'No,' Mr Satterthwaite stammered. 'N-no.'

And then suddenly he rallied.

'But I see things,' he cried. 'I may have been only a looker-on at Life – but I see things that other people do not. You said so yourself, Mr Quin . . .'

But Mr Quin had vanished.

THREE-ACT TRAGEDY

Dedicated to
My Friends, Geoffrey and Violet Shipston

Directed by
Sir Charles Cartwright

Assistant Directors
Mr Satterthwaite
Miss Hermione Lytton Gore

Clothes by
Ambrosine Ltd

Illumination by
Hercule Poirot

First Act

SUSPICION

CHAPTER 1

Crow's Nest

Mr Satterthwaite sat on the terrace of 'Crow's Nest' and watched his host, Sir Charles Cartwright, climbing up the path from the sea.

Crow's Nest was a modern bungalow of the better type. It had no half timbering, no gables, no excrescences dear to a third-class builder's heart. It was a plain white solid building – deceptive as to size, since it was a good deal bigger than it looked. It owed its name to its position, high up, overlooking the harbour of Loomouth. Indeed from one corner of the terrace, protected by a strong balustrade, there was a sheer drop to the sea below. By road Crow's Nest was a mile from the town. The road ran inland and then zigzagged high up above the sea. On foot it was accessible in seven minutes by the steep fisherman's path that Sir Charles Cartwright was ascending at this minute.

Sir Charles was a well-built, sunburnt man of middle age. He wore old grey flannel trousers and a white sweater. He had a slight rolling gait, and carried his hands half closed as he walked. Nine people out of ten would say, 'Retired Naval man – can't mistake the type.' The tenth, and more discerning, would have hesitated, puzzled by something indefinable that did not ring true. And then perhaps a picture would rise, unsought: the deck of a ship – but not a real ship – a ship curtailed by hanging curtains of thick rich material – a man, Charles Cartwright, standing on that deck, light that was not sunlight streaming down on him, the hands half clenched, the easy gait and a voice – the easy pleasant voice of an English sailor and gentleman, a great deal magnified in tone.

'No, sir,' Charles Cartwright was saying, 'I'm afraid I can't give you any answer to that question.'

And swish fell the heavy curtains, up sprang the lights, an

orchestra plunged into the latest syncopated measure, girls with exaggerated bows in their hair said, 'Chocolates? Lemonade?' The first act of *The Call of the Sea*, with Charles Cartwright as Commander Vanstone, was over.

From his post of vantage, looking down, Mr Satterthwaite smiled.

A dried-up little pipkin of a man, Mr Satterthwaite, a patron of art and the drama, a determined but pleasant snob, always included in the more important house-parties and social functions (the words 'and Mr Satterthwaite' appeared invariably at the tail of a list of guests). Withal a man of considerable intelligence and a very shrewd observer of people and things.

He murmured now, shaking his head, 'I wouldn't have thought it. No, really, I wouldn't have thought it.'

A step sounded on the terrace and he turned his head. The big grey-haired man who drew a chair forward and sat down had his profession clearly stamped on his keen, kindly, middle-aged face. 'Doctor' and 'Harley Street'. Sir Bartholomew Strange had succeeded in his profession. He was a well-known specialist in nervous disorders, and had recently received a knighthood in the Birthday Honours list.

He drew his chair forward beside that of Mr Satterthwaite and said:

'What wouldn't you have thought? Eh? Let's have it.'

With a smile Mr Satterthwaite drew attention to the figure below rapidly ascending the path.

'I shouldn't have thought Sir Charles would have remained contented so long in – er – exile.'

'By Jove, no more should I!' The other laughed, throwing back his head. 'I've known Charles since he was a boy. We were at Oxford together. He's always been the same – a better actor in private life than on the stage! Charles is always acting. He can't help it – it's second nature to him. Charles doesn't go out of a room – he "makes an exit" – and he usually has to have a good line to make it on. All the same, he likes a change of part – none better. Two years ago he retired from the stage – said he wanted to live a simple country life, out of the world, and indulge his old fancy for the sea. He comes down here and builds this place. His idea of a simple country cottage. Three bathrooms and all the latest gadgets! I was like you, Satterthwaite, I didn't think it would last. After all, Charles is human – he needs his audience. Two or three retired captains, a bunch of old women and a parson – that's not much of a house to play to. I thought the "simple fellow, with his love of the sea," would run for six months. Then, frankly, I thought he'd tire of the part. I thought the next thing to fill the bill would be the weary man of the world at Monte Carlo, or possibly a laird in the Highlands – he's versatile, Charles is.'

The doctor stopped. It had been a long speech. His eyes were full of affection and amusement as he watched the unconscious man below. In a couple of minutes he would be with them.

'However,' Sir Bartholomew went on, 'it seems we were wrong. The attraction of the simple life holds.'

'A man who dramatises himself is sometimes misjudged,' pointed out Mr Satterthwaite. 'One does not take his sincerities seriously.'

The doctor nodded.

'Yes,' he said thoughtfully. 'That's true.'

With a cheerful halloo Charles Cartwright ran up the steps on to the terrace.

'*Mirabelle* surpassed herself,' he said. 'You ought to have come, Satterthwaite.'

Mr Satterthwaite shook his head. He had suffered too often crossing the Channel to have any illusions about the strength of his stomach afloat. He had observed the *Mirabelle* from his bedroom window that morning. There had been a stiff sailing breeze and Mr Satterthwaite had thanked heaven devoutly for dry land.

Sir Charles went to the drawing-room window and called for drinks.

'You ought to have come, Tollie,' he said to his friend. 'Don't you spend half your life sitting in Harley Street telling your patients how good life on the ocean wave would be for them?'

'The great merit of being a doctor,' said Sir Bartholomew, 'is that you are not obliged to follow your own advice.'

Sir Charles laughed. He was still unconsciously playing his part – the bluff breezy Naval man. He was an extraordinarily good-looking man, beautifully-proportioned, with a lean humorous face, and the touch of grey at his temples gave him a kind of added distinction. He looked what he was – a gentleman first and an actor second.

'Did you go alone?' asked the doctor.

'No,' Sir Charles turned to take his drink from a smart parlourmaid who was holding a tray. 'I had a "hand". The girl Egg, to be exact.'

There was something, some faint trace of self-consciousness in his voice which made Mr Satterthwaite look up sharply.

'Miss Lytton Gore? She knows something about sailing, doesn't she?'

Sir Charles laughed rather ruefully.

'She succeeds in making me feel a complete landlubber; but I'm coming on – thanks to her.'

Thoughts slipped quickly in and out of Mr Satterthwaite's mind.

'I wonder – Egg Lytton Gore – perhaps that's why he hasn't tired – the age – a dangerous age – it's always a young girl at that time of life . . .'

Sir Charles went on: 'The sea – there's nothing like it – sun and wind and sea – and a simple shanty to come home to.'

And he looked with pleasure at the white building behind him, equipped with three bathrooms, hot and cold water in all the bedrooms, the latest system of central heating, the newest electrical fittings and a staff of parlourmaid, housemaid, chef, and kitchenmaid. Sir Charles's interpretation of simple living was, perhaps, a trifle exaggerated.

A tall and exceedingly ugly woman issued from the house and bore down upon them.

'Good morning, Miss Milray.'

'Good morning, Sir Charles. Good morning' (a slight inclination of the head towards the other two). 'This is the menu for dinner. I don't know whether you would like it altered in any way?'

Sir Charles took it and murmured:

'Let's see. Melon Cantaloupe, Bortsch Soup, Fresh Mackerel, Grouse, Soufflé Surprise, Canapé Diane . . . No, I think that will do excellently, Miss Milray. Everyone is coming by the four-thirty train.'

'I have already given Holgate his orders. By the way, Sir

Charles, if you will excuse me, it would be better if I dined with you tonight.'

Sir Charles looked startled, but said courteously:

'Delighted, I am sure, Miss Milray – but – er –'

Miss Milray proceeded calmly to explain.

'Otherwise, Sir Charles, it would make thirteen at table; and so many people are superstitious.'

From her tone it could be gathered that Miss Milray would have sat down thirteen to dinner every night of her life without the slightest qualm. She went on:

'I think everything is arranged. I have told Holgate the car is to fetch Lady Mary and the Babbingtons. Is that right?'

'Absolutely. Just what I was going to ask you to do.'

With a slightly superior smile on her rugged countenance, Miss Milray withdrew.

'That,' said Sir Charles reverently, 'is a very remarkable woman. I'm always afraid she'll come and brush my teeth for me.'

'Efficiency personified,' said Strange.

'She's been with me for six years,' said Sir Charles. 'First as my secretary in London, and here, I suppose, she's a kind of glorified housekeeper. Runs this place like clockwork. And now, if you please, she's going to leave.'

'Why?'

'She says' – Sir Charles rubbed his nose dubiously – 'she *says* she's got an invalid mother. Personally I don't believe it. That kind of woman never had a mother at all. Spontaneously generated from a dynamo. No, there's something else.'

'Quite probably,' said Sir Bartholomew, 'people have been talking.'

'Talking?' The actor stared. 'Talking – what about?'

'My dear Charles. You know what talking means.'

'You mean talking about her – and me? With that face? And at her age?'

'She's probably under fifty.'

'I suppose she is,' Sir Charles considered the matter. 'But seriously, Tollie, have you *noticed* her face? It's got two eyes, a nose and a mouth, but it's not what you would call a *face* – not a *female* face. The most scandal-loving old cat in the neighbourhood couldn't seriously connect sexual passion with a face like that.'

'You underrate the imagination of the British spinster.'

Sir Charles shook his head.

'I don't believe it. There's a kind of hideous respectability about Miss Milray that even a British spinster must recognize. She is virtue and respectability personified – and a damned useful woman. I always choose my secretaries plain as sin.'

'Wise man.'

Sir Charles remained deep in thought for some minutes. To distract him, Sir Bartholomew asked: 'Who's coming this afternoon?'

'Angie, for one.'

'Angela Sutcliffe? That's good.'

Mr Satterthwaite leaned forward interestedly, keen to know the composition of the house-party. Angela Sutcliffe was a well-known actress, no longer young, but with a strong hold on the public and celebrated for her wit and charm. She was sometimes spoken of as Ellen Terry's successor.

'Then there are the Dacres.'

Again Mr Satterthwaite nodded to himself. Mrs Dacres was Ambrosine Ltd, that successful dressmaking establishment. You saw it on programmes – 'Miss Blank's dresses in the first act by Ambrosine Ltd, Brook Street.' Her husband, Captain Dacres, was a dark horse in his own racing parlance. He spent a lot of time on racecourses – had ridden himself in the Grand National in years gone by. There had been some trouble – nobody knew exactly – though rumours had been spread about. There had been no inquiry – nothing overt, but somehow at mention of Freddie Dacres people's eyebrows went up a little.

'Then there's Anthony Astor, the playwright.'

'Of course,' said Mr Satterthwaite. 'She wrote *One-Way Traffic*. I saw it twice. It made a great hit.'

He rather enjoyed showing that he knew that Anthony Astor was a woman.

'That's right,' said Sir Charles. 'I forget what her real name is – Wills, I think. I've only met her once. I asked her to please Angela. That's the lot – of the house-party, I mean.'

'And the locals?' asked the doctor.

'Oh, the locals! Well, there are the Babbingtons – he's the parson, quite a good fellow, not too parsonical, and his wife's a really nice woman. Lectures me on gardening. They're coming – and Lady Mary and Egg. That's all. Oh, yes, there's a young fellow called Manders, he's a journalist, or something. Good-looking young fellow. That completes the party.'

Mr Satterthwaite was a man of methodical nature. He counted heads.

'Miss Sutcliffe, one, the Dacres, three, Anthony Astor, four, Lady Mary and her daughter, six, the parson and his wife, eight, the young fellow nine, ourselves twelve. Either you or Miss Milray must have counted wrong, Sir Charles.'

'It couldn't be Miss Milray,' said Sir Charles with assurance. 'That woman's never wrong. Let me see: Yes, by Jove, you're right. I *have* missed out one guest. He'd slipped my memory.'

He chuckled. 'Wouldn't be best pleased at that, either. The fellow is the most conceited little devil I ever met.'

Mr Satterthwaite's eyes twinkled. He had always been of the opinion that the vainest men in creation were actors. He did not exempt Sir Charles Cartwright. This instance of the pot calling the kettle black amused him.

'Who is the egoist?' he asked.

'Rum little beggar,' said Sir Charles. 'Rather a celebrated little beggar, though. You may have heard of him. Hercule Poirot. He's a Belgian.'

'The detective,' said Mr Satterthwaite. 'I have met him. Rather a remarkable personage.'

'He's a character,' said Sir Charles.

'I've never met him,' said Sir Bartholomew, 'but I've heard a good deal about him. He retired some time ago, though, didn't he? Probably most of what I've heard is legend. Well, Charles, I hope we shan't have a crime this weekend.'

'Why? Because we've got a detective in the house? Rather putting the cart before the horse, aren't you, Tollie?'

'Well, it's by way of being a theory of mine.'

'What is your theory, doctor?' asked Mr Satterthwaite.

'That events come to people – not people to events. Why do some people have exciting lives and other people dull ones? Because of their surroundings? Not at all. One man may travel to the ends of the earth and nothing will happen to him. There will be a massacre a week before he arrives, and an earthquake the day after he leaves, and the boat that he nearly took will be shipwrecked. And another man may live at Balham and travel to the City every day, and things will happen to him. He will be mixed up with blackmailing gangs and beautiful girls and motor bandits. There are people with a tendency to shipwrecks – even if they go on a boat on an ornamental lake something will happen to it. In the same way men like your Hercule Poirot don't have to look for crime – it comes to them.'

'In that case,' said Mr Satterthwaite, 'perhaps it is as well that Miss Milray is joining us, and that we are not sitting down thirteen to dinner.'

'Well,' said Sir Charles handsomely, 'you can have your murder, Tollie, if you're so keen on it. I make only one stipulation – that I shan't be the corpse.'

And, laughing, the three men went into the house.

CHAPTER 2

Incident Before Dinner

The principal interest of Mr Satterthwaite's life was people.

He was on the whole more interested in women than men. For a manly man, Mr Satterthwaite knew far too much about women. There was a womanish strain in his character which lent him insight into the feminine mind. Women all his life had confided in him, but they had never taken him seriously. Sometimes he felt a little bitter about this. He was, he felt, always in the stalls watching the play, never on the stage taking part in the drama. But in truth the rôle of onlooker suited him very well.

This evening, sitting in the large room giving on to the terrace, cleverly decorated by a modern firm to resemble a ship's cabin *de luxe*, he was principally interested in the exact shade of hair dye attained by Cynthia Dacres. It was an entirely new tone – straight from Paris, he suspected – a curious and rather pleasing effect of greenish bronze. What Mrs Dacres really looked like it was impossible to tell. She was a tall woman with a figure perfectly disciplined to the demands of the moment. Her neck and arms were her usual shade of summer tan for the country – whether naturally or artificially produced it was impossible to tell. The greenish bronze hair was set in a clever and novel style that only London's best hairdresser could achieve. Her plucked eyebrows, darkened lashes, exquisitively made-up face, and mouth lip-sticked to a curve that its naturally straight line did not possess, seemed all adjuncts to the perfection of her evening gown of a deep and unusual blue, cut very simply it seemed (though this was ludicrously far from the case) and of an unusual material – dull, but with hidden lights in it.

'That's a clever woman,' said Mr Satterthwaite, eyeing her with approval. 'I wonder what she's really like.'

But this time he meant in mind, not in body.

Her words came drawlingly, in the mode of the moment.

'My dear, it wasn't possible. I mean, things either are possible or they're not. This wasn't. It was simply penetrating.'

That was the new word just now – everything was 'penetrating'.

Sir Charles was vigorously shaking cocktails and talking to Angela Sutcliffe, a tall, grey-haired woman with a mischievous mouth and fine eyes.

Dacres was talking to Bartholomew Strange.

'Everyone knows what's wrong with old Ladisbourne. The whole stable knows.'

He spoke in a high clipped voice – a little red, foxy man with a short moustache and slightly shifty eyes.

Beside Mr Satterthwaite sat Miss Wills, whose play, *One-Way Traffic*, had been acclaimed as one of the most witty and daring seen in London for some years. Miss Wills was tall and thin, with a receding chin and very badly waved fair hair. She wore pince-nez, and was dressed in exceedingly limp green chiffon. Her voice was high and undistinguished.

'I went to the South of France,' she said. 'But, really, I didn't enjoy it very much. Not friendly at all. But of course it's useful to me in my work – to see all the goings-on, you know.'

Mr Satterthwaite thought: 'Poor soul. Cut off by success from her spiritual home – a boarding-house in Bournemouth. That's where she'd like to be.' He marvelled at the difference between written works and their authors. That cultivated 'man-of-the-world' tone that Anthony Astor imparted to his plays – what faintest spark of it could be perceived in Miss Wills? Then he noticed that the pale-blue eyes behind the pince-nez were singularly intelligent. They were turned on him now with an appraising look that slightly disconcerted him. It was as though Miss Wills were painstakingly learning him by heart.

Sir Charles was just pouring out the cocktails.

'Let me get you a cocktail,' said Mr Satterthwaite, springing up.

Miss Wills giggled.

'I don't mind if I do,' she said.

The door opened and Temple announced Lady Mary Lytton Gore and Mr and Mrs Babbington and Miss Lytton Gore.

Mr Satterthwaite supplied Miss Wills with her cocktail and then sidled into the neighbourhood of Lady Mary Lytton Gore. As has been stated before, he had a weakness for titles.

Also, apart from snobbishness, he liked a gentlewoman, and that Lady Mary most undeniably was.

Left as a widow very badly off with a child of three, she had come to Loomouth and taken a small cottage where she had lived with one devoted maid ever since. She was a tall thin woman, looking older than her fifty-five years. Her expression was sweet and rather timid. She adored her daughter, but was a little alarmed by her.

Hermione Lytton Gore, usually known for some obscure reason as Egg, bore little resemblance to her mother. She was of a more energetic type. She was not, Mr Satterthwaite decided, beautiful, but she was undeniably attractive. And the cause of that attraction, he thought, lay in her abounding vitality. She seemed twice as alive as anyone in that room. She had dark hair, and grey eyes and was of medium height. It was something in the way the hair curled crisply in her neck, in the straight glance of the grey eyes, in the curve of the cheek, in the infectious laugh that gave one that impression of riotous youth and vitality.

She stood talking to Oliver Manders, who had just arrived.

'I can't think why sailing bores you so much. You used to like it.'

'Egg – my dear. One grows up.'

He drawled the words, raising his eyebrows.

A handsome young fellow, twenty-five at a guess. Something, perhaps, a little sleek about his good looks. Something else – something – was it foreign? Something unEnglish about him.

Somebody else was watching Oliver Manders. A little man with an egg-shaped head and very foreign-looking moustaches. Mr Satterthwaite had recalled himself to M. Hercule Poirot's memory. The little man had been very affable. Mr Satterthwaite suspected him of deliberately exaggerating his foreign mannerisms. His small twinkly eyes seemed to say, 'You expect me to be the buffoon? To play the comedy for you? *Bien* – it shall be as you wish!'

But there was no twinkle now in Hercule Poirot's eyes. He looked grave and a little sad.

The Rev. Stephen Babbington, rector of Loomouth, came and joined Lady Mary and Mr Satterthwaite. He was a man of sixty odd, with kind faded eyes and a disarming diffident manner. He said to Mr Satterthwaite:

'We are very lucky to have Sir Charles living among us. He has been most kind – most generous. A very pleasant neighbour to have. Lady Mary agrees, I am sure.'

Lady Mary smiled.

'I like him very much. His success hasn't spoilt him. In many ways he is,' her smile deepened, 'a child still.'

The parlourmaid approached with the tray of cocktails as Mr Satterthwaite reflected how unendingly maternal women were. Being of the Victorian generation, he approved that trait.

'You can have a cocktail, Mums,' said Egg, flashing up to them, glass in hand. 'Just one.'

'Thank you, dear,' said Lady Mary meekly.

'I think,' said Mr Babbington, 'that my wife would allow me to have one.'

And he laughed a little gentle clerical laugh.

Mr Satterthwaite glanced over at Mrs Babbington, who was talking earnestly to Sir Charles on the subject of manure.

'She's got fine eyes,' he thought.

Mrs Babbington was a big untidy woman. She looked full of energy and likely to be free from petty mindedness. As Charles Cartwright had said – a nice woman.

'Tell me,' Lady Mary leaned forward. 'Who is the young woman you were talking to when we came in – the one in green?'

'That's the playwright – Anthony Astor.'

'What? That – that anaemic-looking young woman? Oh!' She caught herself up. 'How dreadful of me. But it was a surprise. She doesn't look – I mean she looks exactly like an inefficient nursery governess.'

It was such an apt description of Miss Wills' appearance that Mr Satterthwaite laughed. Mr Babbington was peering across the room with amiable short-sighted eyes. He took a sip of his cocktail and choked a little. He was unused to cocktails, thought Mr Satterthwaite amusedly – probably they represented modernity to his mind – but he didn't like them. Mr Babbington took another determined mouthful with a slightly wry face and said:

'Is it the lady over there? Oh dear –'

His hand went to his throat.

Egg Lytton Gore's voice rang out:

'Oliver – you slippery Shylock –'

'Of course,' thought Mr Satterthwaite, 'that's it – not foreign – Jew!'

What a handsome pair they made. Both so young and good-looking . . . and quarrelling, too – always a healthy sign . . .

He was distracted by a sound at his side. Mr Babbington had risen to his feet and was swaying to and fro. His face was convulsed.

It was Egg's clear voice that drew the attention of the room, though Lady Mary had risen and stretched out an anxious hand.

'Look,' said Egg's voice. 'Mr Babbington is ill.'

Sir Bartholomew Strange came forward hurriedly, supporting the stricken man and half lifting him to a couch at one side of the room. The others crowded round, anxious to help, but impotent . . .

Two minutes later Strange straightened himself and shook his head. He spoke bluntly, aware that it was no use to beat about the bush.

'I'm sorry,' he said. 'He's dead . . .'

CHAPTER 3

Sir Charles Wonders

'Come in here a minute, Satterthwaite, will you?'

Sir Charles poked his head out of the door.

An hour and a half had passed. To confusion had succeeded peace. Lady Mary had led the weeping Mrs Babbington out of the room and had finally gone home with her to the vicarage. Miss Milray had been efficient with the telephone. The local doctor had arrived and taken charge. A simplified dinner had been served, and by mutual consent the house-party had retired to their rooms after it. Mr Satterthwaite had been making his own retreat when Sir Charles had called to him from the door of the Ship-room where the death had taken place.

Mr Satterthwaite passed in, repressing a slight shiver as he did so. He was old enough not to like the sight of death . . . For soon, perhaps, he himself . . . But why think of that?

'I'm good for another twenty years,' said Mr Satterthwaite robustly to himself.

The only other occupant of the Ship-room was Bartholomew Strange. He nodded approval at the sight of Mr Satterthwaite.

'Good man,' he said. 'We can do with Satterthwaite. He knows life.'

A little surprised, Mr Satterthwaite sat down in an armchair near the doctor. Sir Charles was pacing up and down. He had forgotten the semi-clenching of his hands and looked definitely less naval.

'Charles doesn't like it,' said Sir Bartholomew. 'Poor old Babbington's death, I mean.'

Mr Satterthwaite thought the sentiment ill expressed. Surely nobody could be expected to 'like' what had occurred. He realized that Strange had quite another meaning from the bald one the words conveyed.

'It was very distressing,' said Mr Satterthwaite, cautiously feeling his way. 'Very distressing indeed,' he added with a reminiscent shiver.

'H'm, yes, it was rather painful,' said the physician, the professional accent creeping for a moment into his voice.

Cartwright paused in his pacing.

'Ever see anyone die quite like that before, Tollie?'

'No,' said Sir Bartholomew thoughtfully. 'I can't say that I have.

'But,' he added in a moment or two, 'I haven't really seen as many deaths as you might suppose. A nerve specialist doesn't kill off many of his patients. He keeps 'em alive and makes his income out of them. MacDougal has seen far more deceases than I have, I don't doubt.'

Dr MacDougal was the principal doctor in Loomouth, whom Miss Milray had summoned.

'MacDougal didn't see this man die. He was dead when he arrived. There was only what we could tell him, what you could tell him. He said it was some kind of seizure, said Babbington was elderly, and his health was none too good. That doesn't satisfy me.'

'Probably didn't satisfy him,' grunted the other. 'But a doctor has to say something. Seizure is a good word – means nothing at all, but satisfies the lay mind. And, after all, Babbington *was* elderly, and his health *had* been giving him trouble lately; his wife told us so. There may have been some unsuspected weakness somewhere.'

'Was that a typical fit or seizure, or whatever you call it?'

'Typical of what?'

'Of any known disease?'

'If you'd ever studied medicine,' said Sir Bartholomew, 'you'd know that there is hardly any such thing as a typical case.'

'What, precisely, are you suggesting, Sir Charles?' asked Mr Satterthwaite.

Cartwright did not answer. He made a vague gesture with his hand. Strange gave a slight chuckle.

'Charles doesn't know himself,' he said. 'It's just his mind turning naturally to the dramatic possibilities.'

Sir Charles made a reproachful gesture. His face was absorbed

– thoughtful. He shook his head slightly in an abstracted manner.

An elusive resemblance teased Mr Satterthwaite – then he got it. Aristide Duval, the head of the Secret Service, unravelling the tangled plot of 'Underground Wires'. In another minute he was sure. Sir Charles was limping unconsciously as he walked. Aristide Duval had been known as The Man With a Limp.

Sir Bartholomew continued to apply ruthless common sense to Sir Charles's unformulated suspicions.

'Yes, what do you suspect, Charles? Suicide? Murder? Who wants to murder a harmless old clergyman? It's fantastic. Suicide? Well, I suppose that is a point. One might perhaps imagine a reason for Babbington wanting to make away with himself –'

'What reason?'

Sir Bartholomew shook his head gently.

'How can we tell the secrets of the human mind? Just one suggestion – suppose that Babbington had been told he suffered from an incurable disease – such as cancer. Something of that kind might supply a motive. He might wish to spare his wife the pain of watching his own long-drawn-out suffering. That's only a suggestion, of course. There's nothing on earth to make us think that Babbington did want to put an end to himself.'

'I wasn't thinking so much of suicide,' began Sir Charles.

Bartholomew Strange again gave his low chuckle.

'Exactly. You're not out for probability. You want sensation – new and untraceable poison in the cocktails.'

Sir Charles made an expressive grimace.

'I'm not so sure I do want that. Damn it all, Tollie, remember *I* mixed those cocktails.'

'Sudden attack of homicidal mania, eh? I suppose the symptoms are delayed in our case, but we'll all be dead before morning.'

'Damn it all, you joke, but –' Sir Charles broke off irritably.

'I'm not really joking,' said the physician.

His voice had altered. It was grave, and not unsympathetic.

'I'm not joking about poor old Babbington's death. I'm casting fun at your suggestions, Charles, because – well – because I don't want you, thoughtlessly, to do harm.'

'Harm?' demanded Sir Charles.

'Perhaps you understand what I'm driving at, Mr Satterthwaite?'

'I think, perhaps, I can guess,' said Mr Satterthwaite.

'Don't you see, Charles,' went on Sir Bartholomew, 'that those idle suspicions of yours might be definitely harmful? These things get about. A vague suggestion of foul play, totally unfounded, might cause serious trouble and pain to Mrs Babbington. I've known things of that kind happen once or twice. A sudden death – a few idle tongues wagging – rumours flying all round the place – rumours that go on growing – and *that no one can stop*. Damn it all, Charles, don't you see how cruel and unnecessary it would be? You're merely indulging your vivid imagination in a gallop over a wholly speculative course.'

A look of irresolution appeared on the actor's face.

'I hadn't thought of it like that,' he admitted.

'You're a thundering good chap, Charles, but you *do* let your imagination run away with you. Come now: do you seriously believe anyone, *anyone at all*, would want to murder that perfectly harmless old man?'

'I suppose not,' said Sir Charles. 'No, as you say, it's ridiculous. Sorry, Tollie, but it wasn't really a mere "stunt" on my part. I did genuinely have a "hunch" that something was wrong.'

Mr Satterthwaite gave a little cough.

'May I make a suggestion? Mr Babbington was taken ill a very few moments after entering the room and just after drinking his cocktail. Now, I did happen to notice he made a wry face when drinking. I imagined because he was unused to the taste. But supposing that Sir Bartholomew's tentative suggestion is correct – that Mr Babbington may for some reason have wished to commit suicide. That does strike me as just possible, whereas the suggestion of murder seems quite ridiculous.

'I feel that it is possible, though not probable, that Mr Babbington introduced something into that glass unseen by us.

'Now I see that nothing has yet been touched in this room. The cocktail glasses are exactly where they were. This is Mr Babbington's. I know, because I was sitting here talking to him. I suggest that Sir Bartholomew should get the glass analysed – that can be done quite quietly and without causing any "talk".'

Sir Bartholomew rose and picked up the glass.

'Right,' he said. 'I'll humour you so far, Charles, and I'll bet you ten pounds to one that there's nothing in it but honest-to-God gin and vermouth.'

'Done,' said Sir Charles.

Then he added with a rueful smile:

'You know, Tollie, *you* are partly responsible for my flights of fancy.'

'I?'

'Yes, with your talk of crime this morning. You said this man, Hercule Poirot, was a kind of stormy petrel, that where he went crimes followed. No sooner does he arrive than we have a suspiciously sudden death. Of course my thoughts fly to murder at once.'

'I wonder,' said Mr Satterthwaite, and stopped.

'Yes,' said Charles Cartwright. 'I'd thought of that. What do you think, Tollie? Could we ask him what he thinks of it all? Is it etiquette, I mean?'

'A nice point,' murmured Mr Satterthwaite.

'I know medical etiquette, but I'm hanged if I know anything about the etiquette of detection.'

'You can't ask a professional singer to sing,' murmured Mr Satterthwaite. 'Can one ask a professional detective to detect? Yes, a very nice point.'

'Just an opinion,' said Sir Charles.

There was a gentle tap on the door, and Hercule Poirot's face appeared, peering in with an apologetic expression.

'Come in, man,' cried Sir Charles, springing up. 'We were just talking of you.'

'I thought perhaps I might be intruding.'

'Not at all. Have a drink.'

'I thank you, no. I seldom drink the whisky. A glass of sirop, now –'

But sirop was not included in Sir Charles's conception of drinkable fluids. Having settled his guest in a chair, the actor went straight to the point.

'I'm not going to beat about the bush,' he said. 'We were just talking of you, M. Poirot, and – and – of what happened tonight. Look here, do you think there's anything wrong about it?'

Poirot's eyebrows rose. He said:

'Wrong? How do you mean that – wrong?'

Bartholomew Strange said, 'My friend has got an idea into his head that old Babbington was murdered.'

'And you do not think so – eh?'

'We'd like to know what you think.'

Poirot said thoughtfully:

'He was taken ill, of course, very suddenly – very suddenly indeed.'

'Just so.'

Mr Satterthwaite explained the theory of suicide and his own suggestion of having a cocktail glass analysed.

Poirot nodded approval.

'That, at any rate, can do no harm. As a judge of human nature, it seems to me unlikely in the extreme that anyone could wish to do away with a charming and harmless old gentleman. Still less does the solution of suicide appeal to me. However, the cocktail glass will tell us one way or another.'

'And the result of the analysis, you think, will be – what?'

Poirot shrugged his shoulders.

'Me? I can only guess. You ask me to guess what will be the result of the analysis?'

'Yes –?'

'Then I guess that they will find only the remains of a very excellent dry Martini.' (He bowed to Sir Charles.) 'To poison a man in a cocktail, one of many handed round on a tray – well, it would be a technique very – very – difficult. And if that charming old clergyman wanted to commit suicide, I do not think he would do it at a party. That would show a very decided lack of consideration for others, and Mr Babbington struck me as a very considerate person.' He paused. 'That, since you ask me, is my opinion.'

There was a moment's silence. Then Sir Charles gave a deep sigh. He opened one of the windows and looked out.

'Wind's gone round a point,' he said.

The sailor had come back and the Secret Service detective had disappeared.

But to the observant Mr Satterthwaite it seemed as though Sir Charles hankered slightly after the part he was not, after all, to play.

CHAPTER 4

A Modern Elaine

'Yes, but what do you think, Mr Satterthwaite? Really *think*?'

Mr Satterthwaite looked this way and that. There was no escape. Egg Lytton Gore had got him securely cornered on the fishing quay. Merciless, these modern young women – and terrifyingly alive.

'Sir Charles has put this idea into your head,' he said.

'No, he hasn't. It was there already. It's been there from the beginning. It was so frightfully sudden.'

'He was an old man, and his health wasn't very good –'

Egg cut the recital short.

'That's all tripe. He had neuritis and a touch of rheumatoid arthritis. That doesn't make you fall down in a fit. He never had fits. He was the sort of gentle creaking gate that would have lived to be ninety. What did you think of the inquest?'

'It all seemed quite – er – normal.'

'What did you think of Dr MacDougal's evidence? Frightfully technical, and all that – close description of the organs – but didn't it strike you that behind all that bombardment of words he was hedging? What he said amounted to this: that there was nothing to show death had not arisen from natural causes. He didn't say it was the result of natural causes.'

'Aren't you splitting hairs a little, my dear?'

'The point is that *he* did – he was puzzled, but he had nothing to go upon, so he had to take refuge in medical caution. What did Sir Bartholomew Strange think?'

Mr Satterthwaite repeated some of the physician's dictums.

'Pooh-poohed it, did he?' said Egg thoughtfully. 'Of course, he's a cautious man – I suppose a Harley Street big bug has to be.'

'There was nothing in the cocktail glass but gin and vermouth,' Mr Satterthwaite reminded her.

'That seems to settle it. All the same, something that happened after the inquest made me wonder –'

'Something Sir Bartholomew said to you?'

Mr Satterthwaite began to feel a pleasant curiosity.

'Not to me – to Oliver. Oliver Manders – he was at dinner that night, but perhaps you don't remember him.'

'Yes, I remember him very well. Is he a great friend of yours?'

'Used to be. Now we scrap most of the time. He's gone into his uncle's office in the city, and he's getting – well, a bit oily, if you know what I mean. Always talks of chucking it and being a journalist – he writes rather well. But I don't think it's any more than talk now. He wants to get rich. I think everybody is rather disgusting about money, don't you, Mr Satterthwaite?'

Her youth came home to him then – the crude, arrogant childishness of her.

'My dear,' he said, 'so many people are disgusting about so many things.'

'Most people are swine, of course,' agreed Egg cheerfully. 'That's why I'm really cut up about old Mr Babbington. Because you see, he really was rather a pet. He prepared me for confirmation and all that, and though of course a lot of that business is all bunkum, he really was rather sweet about it. You see, Mr Satterthwaite, I really believe in Christianity – not like Mother does, with little books and early service, and things – but intelligently and as a matter of history. The Church is all clotted up with the Pauline tradition – in fact the Church is a mess – but Christianity itself is all right. That's why I can't be a communist like Oliver. In practice our beliefs would work out much the same, things in common and ownership by all, but the difference – well, I needn't go into that. But the Babbingtons really *were* Christians; they didn't poke and pry and condemn, and they were never unkind about people or things. They were pets – and there was Robin . . .'

'Robin?'

'Their son . . . He was out in India and got killed . . . I – I had rather a pash on Robin . . .'

Egg blinked. Her gaze went out to sea . . .

Then her attention returned to Mr Satterthwaite and the present.

'So, you see, I feel rather strongly about this. Supposing it wasn't a natural death . . .'

'My dear child!'

'Well, it's damned odd! You must admit it's damned odd.'

'But surely you yourself have just practically admitted that the Babbingtons hadn't an enemy in the world.'

'That's what's so queer about it. I can't think of any conceivable motive . . .'

'Fantastic! There was nothing in the cocktail.'

'Perhaps someone jabbed him with a hypodermic.'

'Containing the arrow poison of the South American Indians,' suggested Mr Satterthwaite, gently ridiculing.

Egg grinned.

'That's it. The good old untraceable stuff. Oh, well, you're all very superior about it. Some day, perhaps, you'll find out we are right.'

'We?'

'Sir Charles and I.' She flushed slightly.

Mr Satterthwaite thought in the words and metre of his generation when *Quotations for All Occasions* was to be found in every bookcase.

'Of more than twice her years,
Seam'd with an ancient swordcut on the cheek,
And bruised and bronzed, she lifted up her eyes
And loved him, with that love which was her doom.'

He felt a little ashamed of himself for thinking in quotations – Tennyson, too, was very little thought of nowadays. Besides, though Sir Charles was bronzed, he was not scarred, and Egg Lytton Gore, though doubtless capable of a healthy passion, did not look at all likely to perish of love and drift about rivers on a barge. There was nothing of the lily maid of Astolat about her.

'Except,' thought Mr Satterthwaite, 'her youth . . .'

Girls were always attracted to middle-aged men with interesting pasts. Egg seemed to be no exception to this rule.

'Why hasn't he ever married?' she asked abruptly.

'Well . . .' Mr Satterthwaite paused. His own answer, put bluntly, would have been, 'Caution,' but he realized that such a word would be unacceptable to Egg Lytton Gore.

Sir Charles Cartwright had had plenty of affairs with women, actresses and others, but he had always managed to steer clear of matrimony. Egg was clearly seeking for a more romantic explanation.

'That girl who died of consumption – some actress, name began with an M – wasn't he supposed to be very fond of her?'

Mr Satterthwaite remembered the lady in question. Rumour had coupled Charles Cartwright's name with hers, but only very slightly, and Mr Satterthwaite did not for a moment believe that Sir Charles had remained unmarried in order to be faithful to her memory. He conveyed as much tactfully.

'I suppose he's had lots of affairs,' said Egg.

'Er – h'm – probably,' said Mr Satterthwaite, feeling Victorian.

'I like men to have affairs,' said Egg. 'It shows they're not queer or anything.'

Mr Satterthwaite's Victorianism suffered a further pang. He was at a loss for a reply. Egg did not notice his discomfiture. She went on musingly.

'You know, Sir Charles is really cleverer than you'd think. He poses a lot, of course, dramatises himself; but behind all that he's got brains. He's far better sailing a boat than you'd ever think, to hear him talk. You'd think, to listen to him, that it was all pose, but it isn't. It's the same about this business. You think it's all done for effect – that he wants to play the part of the great detective. All I say is: I think he'd play it rather well.'

'Possibly,' agreed Mr Satterthwaite.

The inflection of his voice showed his feelings clearly enough. Egg pounced on them and expressed them in words.

'But your view is that "Death of a Clergyman" isn't a thriller. It's merely "Regrettable Incident at a Dinner Party". Purely a social catastrophe. What did M. Poirot think? *He* ought to know.'

'M. Poirot advised us to wait for the analysis of the cocktail; but in his opinion everything was quite all right.'

'Oh, well,' said Egg, 'he's getting old. He's a back number.' Mr Satterthwaite winced. Egg went on, unconscious of brutality: 'Come home and have tea with Mother. She likes you. She said so.'

Delicately flattered, Mr Satterthwaite accepted the invitation.

On arrival Egg volunteered to ring up Sir Charles and explain the non-appearance of his guest.

Mr Satterthwaite sat down in the tiny sitting-room with its faded chintzes and its well-polished pieces of old furniture. It was a Victorian room, what Mr Satterthwaite called in his own mind a lady's room, and he approved of it.

His conversation with Lady Mary was agreeable, nothing brilliant, but pleasantly chatty. They spoke of Sir Charles. Did Mr Satterthwaite know him well? Not intimately, Mr Satterthwaite said. He had a financial interest in one of Sir Charles's plays some years ago. They had been friends ever since.

'He has great charm,' said Lady Mary, smiling. 'I feel it as well as Egg. I suppose you've discovered that Egg is suffering badly from hero worship?'

Mr Satterthwaite wondered if, as a mother, Lady Mary was not made slightly uneasy by that hero worship. But it did not seem so.

'Egg sees so little of the world,' she said, sighing. 'We are so badly off. One of my cousins presented her and took her to a few things in town, but since then she has hardly been away from here, except for an occasional visit. Young people, I feel, should see plenty of people and places – especially people. Otherwise – well, propinquity is sometimes a dangerous thing.'

Mr Satterthwaite agreed, thinking of Sir Charles and the sailing, but that this was not what was in Lady Mary's mind, she showed a moment or two later.

'Sir Charles's coming has done a lot for Egg. It has widened her horizon. You see, there are very few young people down here – especially men. I've always been afraid that Egg might marry someone simply from being thrown with one person only and seeing no one else.'

Mr Satterthwaite had a quick intuition.

'Are you thinking of young Oliver Manders?'

Lady Mary blushed in ingenuous surprise.

'Oh, Mr Satterthwaite, I don't know how you knew! I *was* thinking of him. He and Egg were together a lot at one time, and I know I'm old-fashioned, but I don't like some of his ideas.'

'Youth must have its fling,' said Mr Satterthwaite.

Lady Mary shook her head.

'I've been so afraid – it's quite suitable, of course, I know all about him, and his uncle, who has recently taken him into his firm, is a very rich man; it's not that – it's silly of me – but –'

She shook her head, unable to express herself further.

Mr Satterthwaite felt curiously intimate. He said quietly and plainly:

'All the same, Lady Mary, you wouldn't like your girl to marry a man twice her own age.'

Her answer surprised him.

'It might be safer so. If you do that, at least you know where you are. At that age a man's follies and sins are definitely behind him; they are not – still to come . . .'

Before Mr Satterthwaite could say any more, Egg rejoined them.

'You've been a long time, darling,' said her mother.

'I was talking to Sir Charles, my sweet. He's all alone in his glory.' She turned reproachfully to Mr Satterthwaite. 'You didn't tell me the house-party had flitted.'

'They went back yesterday – all but Sir Bartholomew Strange. He was staying till tomorrow, but he was recalled to London by an urgent telegram this morning. One of his patients was in a critical condition.'

'It's a pity,' said Egg. 'Because I meant to study the house-party. I might have got a clue.'

'A clue to what, darling?'

'Mr Satterthwaite knows. Oh, well, it doesn't matter. Oliver's still here. We'll rope him in. He's got brains when he likes.'

When Mr Satterthwaite arrived back at Crow's Nest he found his host sitting on the terrace overlooking the sea.

'Hullo, Satterthwaite. Been having tea with the Lytton Gores?'

'Yes. You don't mind?'

'Of course not. Egg telephoned . . . Odd sort of girl, Egg . . .'

'Attractive,' said Mr Satterthwaite.

'H'm, yes, I suppose she is.'

He got up and walked a few aimless steps.

'I wish to God,' he said suddenly and bitterly, 'that I'd never come to this cursed place.'

CHAPTER 5

Flight From A Lady

Mr Satterthwaite thought to himself: 'He's got it badly.'

He felt a sudden pity for his host. At the age of fifty-two, Charles Cartwright, the gay debonair breaker of hearts, had fallen in love. And, as he himself realized, his case was doomed to disappointment. Youth turns to youth.

'Girls don't wear their hearts on their sleeves,' thought Mr Satterthwaite. 'Egg makes a great parade of her feeling for Sir Charles. She wouldn't if it really meant anything. Young Manders is the one.'

Mr Satterthwaite was usually fairly shrewd in his assumptions.

Still, there was probably one factor that he did not take into account, because he was unaware of it himself. That was the enhanced value placed by age on youth. To Mr Satterthwaite, an elderly man, the fact that Egg might prefer a middle-aged man to a young one was frankly incredible. Youth was to him so much the most magical of all gifts.

He felt strengthened in his beliefs when Egg rang up after dinner and demanded permission to bring Oliver along and 'have a consultation'.

Certainly a handsome lad, with his dark, heavy-lidded eyes and easy grace of movement. He had, it seemed, permitted himself to be brought – a tribute to Egg's energy; but his general attitude was lazily sceptical.

'Can't you talk her out of it, sir?' he said to Sir Charles. 'It's this appallingly healthy bucolic life she leads that makes her so energetic. You know, Egg, you really are detestably hearty. And your tastes are childish – crime – sensation – and all that bunk.'

'You're a sceptic, Manders?'

'Well, sir, really. That dear old bleating fellow. It's fantastic to think of anything else but natural causes.'

'I expect you're right,' said Sir Charles.

Mr Satterthwaite glanced at him. What part was Charles Cartwright playing tonight. Not the ex-Naval man – not the international detective. No, some new and unfamiliar rôle.

It came as a shock to Mr Satterthwaite when he realized what that rôle was. Sir Charles was playing second fiddle. Second fiddle to Oliver Manders.

He sat back with his head in shadow watching those two, Egg and Oliver, as they disputed – Egg hotly, Oliver languidly.

Sir Charles looked older than usual – old and tired.

More than once Egg appealed to him – hotly and confidently – but his response was lacking.

It was eleven o'clock when they left. Sir Charles went out on the terrace with them and offered the loan of an electric torch to help them down the stony path.

But there was no need of a torch. It was a beautiful moonlit night. They set off together, their voices growing fainter as they descended.

Moonlight or no moonlight, Mr Sattherthwaite was not going to risk a chill. He returned to the Ship-room. Sir Charles stayed out on the terrace a little while longer.

When he came in he latched the window behind him, and striding to a side table poured himself out a whisky and soda.

'Satterthwaite,' he said, 'I'm leaving here tomorrow for good.'

'What?' cried Mr Satterthwaite, astonished.

A kind of melancholy pleasure at the effect he had produced showed for a minute on Charles Cartwright's face.

'It's the Only Thing To Do,' he said, obviously speaking in capital letters. 'I shall sell this place. What it has meant to me no one will ever know.' His voice dropped, lingeringly . . . effectively.

After an evening of second fiddle, Sir Charles's egoism was taking its revenge. This was the great Renunciation Scene, so often played by him in sundry and divers dramas. Giving Up the Other Man's Wife, Renouncing the Girl he Loved.

There was a brave flippancy in his voice as he went on.

'Cut your losses – it's the only way . . . Youth to youth . . . They're made for each other, those two . . . I shall clear out . . .'

'Where to?' asked Mr Satterthwaite.

The actor made a careless gesture.

'Anywhere. What does it matter?' He added with a slight change of voice, 'Probably Monte Carlo.' And then, retrieving what his sensitive taste could not but feel to be a slight anticlimax, 'In the heart of the desert or the heart of the crowd – what does it matter? The inmost core of man is solitary – alone. I have always been – a lonely soul . . .'

It was clearly an exit line.

He nodded to Mr Satterthwaite and left the room.

Mr Satterthwaite got up and prepared to follow his host to bed.

'But it won't be the heart of a desert,' he thought to himself with a slight chuckle.

On the following morning Sir Charles begged Mr Satterthwaite to forgive him if he went up to town that day.

'Don't cut your visit short, my dear fellow. You were staying till tomorrow, and I know you're going on to the Harbertons at Tavistock. The car will take you there. What I feel is that, having come to my decision, I mustn't look back. No, I mustn't look back.'

Sir Charles squared his shoulders with manly resolution, wrung Mr Satterthwaite's hand with fervour and delivered him over to the capable Miss Milray.

Miss Milray seemed prepared to deal with the situation as she had dealt with any other. She expressed no surprise or emotion at Sir Charles's overnight decision. Nor could Mr Satterthwaite draw her out on the point. Neither sudden deaths nor sudden changes of plan could excite Miss Milray. She accepted whatever happened as a fact and proceeded to cope with it in an efficient way. She telephoned to the house agents, despatched wires abroad, and wrote busily on her typewriter. Mr Satterthwaite escaped from the depressing spectacle of so much efficiency by strolling down to the quay. He was walking aimlessly along when he was seized by the arm from behind, and turned to confront a white-faced girl.

'What's all this?' demanded Egg fiercely.

'All what?' parried Mr Satterthwaite.

'It's all over the place that Sir Charles is going away – that he's going to sell Crow's Nest.'

'Quite true.'

'He is going away?'

'He's gone.'

'Oh!' Egg relinquished his arm. She looked suddenly like a very small child who has been cruelly hurt.

Mr Satterthwaite did not know what to say.

'Where has he gone?'

'Abroad. To the South of France.'

'Oh!'

Still he did not know what to say. For clearly there was more than hero worship here . . .

Pitying her, he was turning over various consolatory words in his mind when she spoke again – and startled him.

'Which of those damned bitches is it?' asked Egg fiercely.

Mr Satterthwaite stared at her, his mouth fallen open in surprise. Egg took him by the arm again and shook him violently.

'You must know,' she cried. 'Which of them? The grey-haired one or the other?'

'My dear, I don't know what you're talking about.'

'You do. You must. Of course it's some woman. He liked me – I know he liked me. One of those women the other night must have seen it, too, and determined to get him away from me. I hate women. Lousy cats. Did you see her clothes – that one with the green hair? They made me gnash my teeth with envy. A woman who has clothes like that has a pull – you can't deny it. She's quite old and ugly as sin, really, but what does it matter. She makes everyone else look like a dowdy curate's wife. Is it her? Or is it the other one with the grey hair? She's amusing – you can see that. She's got masses of S.A. And he called her Angie. It can't be the one like a wilted cabbage. Is it the smart one or is it Angie?'

'My dear, you've got the most extraordinary ideas into your head. He – er – Charles Cartwright isn't the least interested in either of those women.'

'I don't believe you. They're interested in him, anyway . . .'

'No, no, no, you're making a mistake. This is all imagination.'

'Bitches,' said Egg. 'That's what they are!'

'You mustn't use that word, my dear.'

'I can think of a lot worse things to say than that.'

'Possibly, possibly, but pray don't do so. I can assure you that you are labouring under a misapprehension.'

'Then why has he gone away – like this?'

Mr Satterthwaite cleared his throat.

'I fancy he – er – thought it best.'

Egg stared at him piercingly.

'Do you mean – because of *me*?'

'Well – something of the kind, perhaps.'

'And so he's legged it. I suppose I did show my hand a bit plainly . . . Men do hate being chased, don't they? Mums is right, after all . . . You've no idea how sweet she is when she talks about men. Always in the third person – so Victorian and polite. "A man hates being run after; a girl should always let the man make the running." Don't you think it's a sweet expression – make the running? Sounds the opposite of what it means. Actually that's just what Charles has done – made the running. He's running away from me. He's afraid. And the devil of it is, I can't go after him. If I did I suppose he'd take a boat to the wilds of Africa or somewhere.'

'Hermione,' said Mr Satterthwaite, 'are you serious about Sir Charles?'

The girl flung him an impatient glance.

'Of course I am.'

'What about Oliver Manders?'

Egg dismissed Oliver Manders with an impatient whisk of the head. She was following out a train of thought of her own.

'Do you think I might write to him? Nothing alarming. Just chatty girlish stuff . . . you know, put him at his ease, so that he'd get over his scare?'

She frowned.

'What a fool I've been. Mums would have managed it much better. They knew how to do the trick, those Victorians. All blushing retreat. I've been all wrong about it. I actually thought he needed encouraging. He seemed – well, he seemed to need a bit of help. Tell me,' she turned abruptly on Mr Satterthwaite, 'did he see me do my kissing act with Oliver last night?'

'Not that I know of. When –?'

'All in the moonlight. As we were going down the path. I thought he was still looking from the terrace. I thought perhaps if he saw me and Oliver – well, I thought it might wake him up a bit. Because he did like me. I could swear he liked me.'

'Wasn't that a little hard on Oliver?'

Egg shook her head decisively.

'Not in the least. Oliver thinks it's an honour for any girl to be kissed by him. It was damned bad for his conceit, of course; but one can't think of everything. I wanted to ginger up Charles. He's been different lately – more standoffish.'

'My dear child,' said Mr Satterthwaite, 'I don't think you realize quite why Sir Charles went away so suddenly. He thought that you cared for Oliver. He went away to save himself further pain.'

Egg whisked round. She caught hold of Mr Satterthwaite by the shoulders and peered into his face.

'Is that true? Is that really true? The mutt! The boob! Oh –!'

She released Mr Satterthwaite suddenly and moved along beside him with a skipping motion.

'Then he'll come back,' she said. 'He'll come back. If he doesn't –'

'Well, if he doesn't?'

Egg laughed.

'I'll get him back somehow. You see if I don't.'

It seemed as though allowing for difference of language Egg and the lily maid of Astolat had much in common, but Mr Satterthwaite felt that Egg's methods would be more practical than those of Elaine, and that dying of a broken heart would form no part of them.

Second Act

CERTAINTY

CHAPTER 1

Sir Charles Receives A Letter

Mr Satterthwaite had come over for the day to Monte Carlo. His round of house-parties was over, and the Riviera in September was rather a favourite haunt of his.

He was sitting in the gardens enjoying the sun and reading a two-days-old *Daily Mail.*

Suddenly a name caught his attention. *Strange. Death of Sir Bartholomew Strange.* He read the paragraph through:

> *We much regret having to announce the death of Sir Bartholomew Strange, the eminent nerve specialist. Sir Bartholomew was entertaining a party of friends at his house in Yorkshire. Sir Bartholomew appeared to be in perfect health and spirits, and his demise occurred quite suddenly at the end of dinner. He was chatting with his friends and drinking a glass of port when he had a sudden seizure and died before medical aid could be summoned. Sir Bartholomew will be deeply regretted. He was . . .*

Here followed a description of Sir Bartholomew's career and work.

Mr Satterthwaite let the paper slip from his hand. He was very disagreeably impressed. A vision of the physician as he had seen him last flashed across his mind – big, jocund, in the pink of condition. And now – dead. Certain words detached themselves from their context and floated about disagreeably in Mr Satterthwaite's mind. 'Drinking a glass of port.' 'Sudden seizure . . . Died before medical aid could be summoned . . .'

Port, not a cocktail, but otherwise curiously reminiscent of that death in Cornwall. Mr Satterthwaite saw again the convulsed face of the mild old clergyman . . .

Supposing that after all . . .

He looked up to see Sir Charles Cartwright coming towards him across the grass.

'Satterthwaite, by all that's wonderful! Just the man I'd have chosen to see. Have you seen about poor old Tollie?'

'I was just reading it now.'

Sir Charles dropped into a chair beside him. He was immaculately got up in yachting costume. No more grey flannels and old sweaters. He was the sophisticated yachtsman of the South of France.

'Listen, Satterthwaite, Tollie was as sound as a bell. Never had anything wrong with him. Am I being a complete fanciful ass, or does this business remind you of – of –?'

'Of that business at Loomouth? Yes, it does. But of course we may be mistaken. The resemblance may be only superficial. After all, sudden deaths occur the whole time from a variety of causes.'

Sir Charles nodded his head impatiently. Then he said:

'I've just got a letter – from Egg Lytton Gore.'

Mr Satterthwaite concealed a smile.

'The first you've had from her?'

Sir Charles was unsuspecting.

'No. I had a letter soon after I got here. It followed me about a bit. Just giving me the news and all that. I didn't answer it . . . Dash it all, Satterthwaite, I didn't dare answer it . . . The girl had no idea, of course, but I didn't want to make a fool of myself.'

Mr Satterthwaite passed his hand over his mouth where the smile still lingered.

'And this one?' he asked.

'This is different. It's an appeal for help . . .'

'Help?' Mr Satterthwaite's eyebrows went up.

'She was there – you see – in the house – when it happened.'

'You mean she was staying with Sir Bartholomew Strange at the time of his death?'

'Yes.'

'What does she say about it?'

Sir Charles had taken a letter from his pocket. He hesitated for a moment, then he handed it to Mr Satterthwaite.

'You'd better read it for yourself.'

Mr Satterthwaite opened out the sheet with lively curiosity.

'Dear Sir Charles, – I don't know when this will get to you. I do hope soon. I'm so worried, I don't know what to do. You'll have seen, I expect, in the papers that Sir Bartholomew Strange is dead. Well, he died just the same way as Mr Babbington. It can't be a coincidence – it can't – it can't *. . . I'm worried to death . . .*

'Look here, can't you come home and do something? It sounds a bit crude put like that, but you did have suspicions before, and nobody would listen to you, and now it's your own friend who's been killed; and perhaps if you don't come back nobody will ever find out the truth, and I'm sure you could. I feel it in my bones . . .

'And there's something else. I'm worried, definitely, about someone . . . He had absolutely nothing to do with it, I know that, but things might look a bit odd. Oh, I can't explain in a letter. But won't you come back? You could find out the truth. I know you could.

'Yours in haste,

'EGG.'

'Well?' demanded Sir Charles impatiently. 'A bit incoherent of course; she wrote it in a hurry. But what about it?'

Mr Satterthwaite folded the letter slowly to give himself a minute or two before replying.

He agreed that the letter was incoherent, but he did not think it had been written in a hurry. It was, in his view, a very careful production. It was designed to appeal to Sir Charles's vanity, to his chivalry, and to his sporting instincts.

From what Mr Satterthwaite knew of Sir Charles, that letter was a certain draw.

'Who do you think she means by "someone", and "he"?' he asked.

'Manders, I suppose.'

'Was he there, then?'

'Must have been. I don't know why. Tollie never met him except on that one occasion at my house. Why he should ask him to stay, I can't imagine.'

'Did he often have those big house-parties?'

'Three or four times a year. Always one for the St Leger.'

'Did he spend much time in Yorkshire?'

'Had a big sanatorium – nursing home, whatever you like to

call it. He bought Melfort Abbey (it's an old place), restored it and built a sanatorium in the grounds.'

'I see.'

Mr Satterthwaite was silent for a minute or two. Then he said:

'I wonder who else there was in the house-party?'

Sir Charles suggested that it might be in one of the other newspapers, and they went off to institute a newspaper hunt.

'Here we are,' said Sir Charles.

He read aloud:

'Sir Bartholomew Strange is having his usual house-party for the St Leger. Amongst the guests are Lord and Lady Eden, Lady Mary Lytton Gore, Sir Jocelyn and Lady Campbell, Captain and Mrs Dacres, and Miss Angela Sutcliffe, the well-known actress.'

He and Mr Satterthwaite looked at each other.

'The Dacres and Angela Sutcliffe,' said Sir Charles. 'Nothing about Oliver Manders.'

'Let's get today's *Continental Daily Mail,*' said Mr Satterthwaite. 'There might be something in that.'

Sir Charles glanced over the paper. Suddenly he stiffened.

'My God, Satterthwaite, listen to this:

'SIR BARTHOLOMEW STRANGE.

'At the inquest today on the late Sir Bartholomew Strange, a verdict of Death by Nicotine Poisoning was returned, there being no evidence to show how or by whom the poison was administered.'

He frowned.

'Nicotine poisoning. Sounds mild enough – not the sort of thing to make a man fall down in a fit. I don't understand all this.'

'What are you going to do?'

'Do? I'm going to book a berth on the Blue Train tonight.'

'Well,' said Mr Satterthwaite, 'I might as well do the same.'

'You?' Sir Charles wheeled round on him, surprised.

'This sort of thing is rather in my line,' said Mr Satterthwaite modestly. 'I've – er – had a little experience. Besides, I know the Chief Constable in that part of the world rather well – Colonel Johnson. That will come in useful.'

'Good man,' cried Sir Charles. 'Let's go round to the Wagon Lits offices.'

Mr Satterthwaite thought to himself:

'The girl's done it. She's got him back. She said she would. I wonder just exactly how much of her letter was genuine.'

Decidedly, Egg Lytton Gore was an opportunist.

When Sir Charles had gone off to the Wagon Lits offices, Mr Satterthwaite strolled slowly through the gardens. His mind was still pleasantly engaged with the problem of Egg Lytton Gore. He admired her resource and her driving power, and stifled that slightly Victorian side of his nature which disapproved of a member of the fairer sex taking the initiative in affairs of the heart.

Mr Satterthwaite was an observant man. In the midst of his cogitations on the female sex in general, and Egg Lytton Gore in particular, he was unable to resist saying to himself:

'Now where have I seen that particular shaped head before?'

The owner of the head was sitting on a seat gazing thoughtfully ahead of him. He was a little man whose moustaches were out of proportion to his size.

A discontented-looking English child was standing nearby, standing first on one foot, then the other, and occasionally meditatively kicking the lobelia edging.

'Don't do that, darling,' said her mother, who was absorbed in a fashion paper.

'I haven't anything to do,' said the child.

The little man turned his head to look at her, and Mr Satterthwaite recognized him.

'M. Poirot,' he said. 'This is a very pleasant surprise.'

M. Poirot rose and bowed.

'*Enchanté, monsieur.*'

They shook hands, and Mr Satterthwaite sat down.

'Everyone seems to be in Monte Carlo. Not half an hour ago I ran across Sir Charles Cartwright, and now you.'

'Sir Charles, he also is here?'

'He's been yachting. You know that he gave up his house at Loomouth?'

'Ah, no, I did not know it. I am surprised.'

'I don't know that I am. I don't think Cartwright is really the kind of man who likes to live permanently out of the world.'

'Ah, no, I agree with you there. I was surprised for another reason. It seemed to me that Sir Charles had a particular reason for staying in Loomouth – a very charming reason, eh? Am I not right? The little demoiselle who calls herself, so amusingly, the egg?'

His eyes were twinkling gently.

'Oh, so you noticed that?'

'Assuredly I noticed. I have the heart very susceptible to lovers – you too, I think. And *la jeunesse*, it is always touching.'

He sighed.

'I think,' said Mr Satterthwaite, 'that actually you have hit on Sir Charles's reason for leaving Loomouth. He was running away.'

'From Mademoiselle Egg? But it is obvious that he adores her. Why, then, run?'

'Ah,' said Mr Satterthwaite, 'you don't understand our Anglo-Saxon complexes.'

M. Poirot was following his own line of reasoning.

'Of course,' he said, 'it is a good move to pursue. Run from a woman – immediately she follows. Doubtless Sir Charles, a man of much experience, knows that.'

Mr Satterthwaite was rather amused.

'I don't think it was quite that way,' he said. 'Tell me, what are you doing out here? A holiday?'

'My time is all holidays nowadays. I have succeeded. I am rich. I retire. Now I travel about seeing the world.'

'Splendid,' said Mr Satterthwaite.

'*N'est-ce pas?*'

'Mummy,' said the English child, 'isn't there anything to *do*?'

'Darling,' said her mother reproachfully, 'isn't it lovely to have come abroad and to be in the beautiful sunshine?'

'Yes, but there's nothing to do.'

'Run about – amuse yourself. Go and look at the sea.'

'*Maman*, said a French child, suddenly appearing. '*Joue avec moi.*'

A French mother looked up from her book.

'*Amuse toi avec ta balle, Marcelle.*'

Obediently the French child bounced her ball with a gloomy face.

'*Je m'amuse*,' said Hercule Poirot; and there was a very curious expression on his face.

Then, as if in answer to something he read in Mr Satterthwaite's face, he said:

'But yet, you have the quick perceptions. It is as you think –'

He was silent for a minute or two, then he said:

'See you, as a boy I was poor. There were many of us. We had to get on in the world. I entered the Police Force. I worked hard. Slowly I rose in that Force. I began to make a name for myself. I made a name for myself. I began to acquire an international reputation. At last, I was due to retire. There came the War. I was injured. I came, a sad and weary refugee, to England. A kind lady gave me hospitality. She died – not naturally; no, she was killed. *Eh bien*, I set my wits to work. I employed my little grey cells. I discovered her murderer. I found that I was not yet finished. No, indeed, my powers were stronger than ever. Then began my second career, that of a private inquiry agent in England. I have solved many fascinating and baffling problems. Ah, monsieur, I have lived! The psychology of human nature, it is wonderful. I grew rich. Some day, I said to myself, I will have all the money I need. I will realize all my dreams.'

He laid a hand on Mr Satterthwaite's knee.

'My friend, *beware of the day when your dreams come true*. That child near us, doubtless she too has dreamt of coming abroad – of the excitement – of how different everything would be. You understand?'

'I understand,' said Mr Satterthwaite, 'that you are *not* amusing yourself.'

Poirot nodded.

'Exactly.'

There were moments when Mr Satterthwaite looked like Puck. This was one of them. His little wrinkled face twitched impishly. He hesitated. Should he? Should he not?

Slowly he unfolded the newspaper he was still carrying.

'Have you seen this, M. Poirot?'

With his forefinger he indicated the paragraph he meant.

The little Belgian took the paper. Mr Satterthwaite watched

him as he read. No change came over his face, but the Englishman had the impression that his body stiffened, as does that of a terrier when it sniffs a rathole.

Hercule Poirot read the paragraph twice, then he folded the paper and returned it to Mr Satterthwaite.

'That is interesting,' he said.

'Yes. It looks, does it not, as though Sir Charles Cartwright had been right and we had been wrong.'

'Yes,' said Poirot. 'It seems as though we had been wrong . . . I will admit it, my friend, I could not believe that so harmless, so friendly an old man could have been murdered . . . Well, it may be that I was wrong . . . Although, see you, this other death may be coincidence. Coincidences do occur – the most amazing coincidences. I, Hercule Poirot, have known coincidences that would surprise you . . .'

He paused, and went on:

'Sir Charles Cartwright's instinct may have been right. He is an artist – sensitive – impressionable – he feels things, rather than reasons about them . . . Such a method in life is often disastrous – but it is sometimes justified. I wonder where Sir Charles is now.'

Mr Satterthwaite smiled.

'I can tell you that. He is in the office of the Wagon Lits Co. He and I are returning to England tonight.'

'Aha!' Poirot put immense meaning into the exclamation. His eyes, bright, inquiring, roguish, asked a question. 'What zeal he has, our Sir Charles. He is determined, then, to play this rôle, the rôle of the amateur policeman? Or is there another reason?'

Mr Satterthwaite did not reply, but from his silence Poirot seemed to deduce an answer.

'I see,' he said. 'The bright eyes of Mademoiselle are concerned in this. It is not only crime that calls?'

'She wrote to him,' said Mr Satterthwaite, 'begging him to return.'

Poirot nodded.

'I wonder now,' he said. 'I do not quite understand –'

Mr Satterthwaite interrupted.

'You do not understand the modern English girl? Well, that is not surprising. I do not always understand them myself. A girl like Miss Lytton Gore –'

In his turn Poirot interrupted.

'Pardon. You have misunderstood me. I understand Miss Lytton Gore very well. I have met such another – many such others. You call the type modern; but it is – how shall I say? – age-long.'

Mr Satterthwaite was slightly annoyed. He felt that he – and only he – understood Egg. This preposterous foreigner knew nothing about young English womanhood.

Poirot was still speaking. His tone was dreamy – brooding.

'A knowledge of human nature – what a dangerous thing it can be.'

'A useful thing,' corrected Mr Satterthwaite.

'Perhaps. It depends upon the point of view.'

'Well –' Mr Satterthwaite hesitated – got up. He was a little disappointed. He had cast the bait and the fish had not risen. He felt that his own knowledge of human nature was at fault. 'I will wish you a pleasant holiday.'

'I thank you.'

'I hope that when you are next in London you will come and see me.' He produced a card. 'This is my address.'

'You are most amiable, Mr Satterthwaite. I shall be charmed.'

'Goodbye for the present, then.'

'Goodbye, and *bon voyage*.'

Mr Satterthwaite moved away. Poirot looked after him for a moment or two, then once more he stared straight ahead of him, looking out over the blue Mediterranean.

So he sat for at least ten minutes.

The English child reappeared.

'I've looked at the sea, Mummy. What shall I do next?'

'An admirable question,' said Hercule Poirot under his breath.

He rose and walked slowly away – in the direction of the Wagon Lits offices.

CHAPTER 2

The Missing Butler

Sir Charles and Mr Satterthwaite were sitting in Colonel Johnson's study. The chief constable was a big red-faced man with a barrack-room voice and a hearty manner.

He had greeted Mr Satterthwaite with every sign of pleasure and was obviously delighted to make the acquaintance of the famous Charles Cartwright.

'My missus is a great playgoer. She's one of your – what do the Americans call it? – fans. That's it – fans. I like a good play myself – good clean stuff that is, some of the things they put on the stage nowadays – faugh!'

Sir Charles, conscious of rectitude in this respect – he had never put on 'daring' plays, responded suitably with all his easy charm of manner. When they came to mention the object of their visit Colonel Johnson was only too ready to tell them all he could.

'Friend of yours, you say? Too bad – too bad. Yes, he was very popular round here. That sanatorium of his is very highly spoken of, and by all accounts Sir Bartholomew was a first-rate fellow, as well as being at the top of his profession. Kind, generous, popular all round. Last man in the world you'd expect to be murdered – and murder is what it looks like. There's nothing to indicate suicide, and anything like accident seems out of the question.'

'Satterthwaite and I have just come back from abroad,' said Sir Charles. 'We've only seen snippets here and there in the papers.'

'And naturally you want to know all about it. Well, I'll tell you exactly how the matter stands. I think there's no doubt the butler's the man we've got to look for. He was a new man – Sir Bartholomew had only had him a fortnight, and the moment after the crime he disappears – vanishes into thin air. That looks a bit fishy, doesn't it? Eh, what?'

'You've no notion where he went?'

Colonel Johnson's naturally red face got a little redder.

'Negligence on our part, you think. I admit it damn' well looks like it. Naturally the fellow was under observation – just the same as everyone else. He answered our questions quite satisfactorily – gave the London agency which obtained him the place. Last employer, Sir Horace Bird. All very civil spoken, no signs of panic. Next thing was he'd gone – and the house under observation. I've hauled my men over the coals, but they swear they didn't bat an eyelid.'

'Very remarkable,' said Mr Satterthwaite.

'Apart from everything else,' said Sir Charles thoughtfully, 'it seems a damn' fool thing to do. As far as he knew, the man wasn't suspected. By bolting he draws attention to himself.'

'Exactly. And not a hope of escape. His description's been circulated. It's only a matter of days before he's pulled in.'

'Very odd,' said Sir Charles. 'I don't understand it.'

'Oh, the reason's clear enough. He lost his nerve. Got the wind up suddenly.'

'Wouldn't a man who had the nerve to commit murder have the nerve to sit still afterward?'

'Depends. Depends. I know criminals. Chicken-livered, most of them. He thought he was suspected, and he bolted.'

'Have you verified his own account of himself?'

'Naturally, Sir Charles. That's plain routine work. London Agency confirms his story. He had a written reference from Sir Horace Bird, recommending him warmly. Sir Horace himself is in East Africa.'

'So the reference might have been forged?'

'Exactly,' said Colonel Johnson, beaming upon Sir Charles, with the air of a schoolmaster congratulating a bright pupil. 'We've wired to Sir Horace, of course, but it may be some little time before we get a reply. He's on safari.'

'When did the man disappear?'

'Morning after the death. There was a doctor present at the dinner – Sir Jocelyn Campbell – bit of a toxicologist, I understand; he and Davis (local man) agreed over the case, and our people were called in immediately. We interviewed everybody that night. Ellis (that's the butler) went to his room as usual and was missing in the morning. His bed hadn't been slept in.'

'He slipped away under cover of the darkness?'

'Seems so. One of the ladies staying there, Miss Sutcliffe, the actress – you know her, perhaps?'

'Very well, indeed.'

'Miss Sutcliffe has made a suggestion to us. She suggested that the man had left the house through a secret passage.' He blew his nose apologetically. 'Sounds rather Edgar Wallace stuff, but it seems there was such a thing. Sir Bartholomew was rather proud of it. He showed it to Miss Sutcliffe. The end of it comes out among some fallen masonry about half a mile away.'

'That would be a possible explanation, certainly,' agreed Sir Charles. 'Only – would the butler know of the existence of such a passage?'

'That's the point, of course. My missus always says servants know everything. Daresay she's right.'

'I understand the poison was nicotine,' said Mr Satterthwaite.

'That's right. Most unusual stuff to use, I believe. Comparatively rare. I understand if a man's a heavy smoker, such as the doctor was, it would tend to complicate matters. I mean, he might have died of nicotine poisoning in a natural way. Only, of course, this business was too sudden for that.'

'How was it administered?'

'We don't know,' admitted Colonel Johnson. 'That's going to be the weak part of the case. According to medical evidence, it could only have been swallowed a few minutes previous to death.'

'They were drinking port, I understand?'

'Exactly. Seems as though the stuff was in the port; but it wasn't. We analysed his glass. That glass had contained port, and nothing but port. The other wine glasses had been cleared, of course, but they were all on a tray in the pantry, unwashed, and not one of them contained anything it shouldn't. As for what he ate, it was the same as everybody else had. Soup, grilled sole, pheasant and chipped potatoes, chocolate soufflé, soft roes on toast. His cook's been with him fifteen years. No, there doesn't seem to be any way he could have been given the stuff, and yet there it is in the stomach. It's a nasty problem.'

Sir Charles wheeled round on Mr Satterthwaite.

'The same thing,' he said excitedly. 'Exactly the same as before.'

He turned apologetically to the chief constable.

'I must explain. A death occurred at my house in Cornwall –'

Colonel Johnson looked interested.

'I think I've heard about that. From a young lady – Miss Lytton Gore.'

'Yes, she was there. She told you about it?'

'She did. She was very set on her theory. But, you know, Sir Charles, I can't believe there's anything in that theory. It doesn't explain the flight of the butler. Your man didn't disappear by any chance?'

'Haven't got a man – only a parlourmaid.'

'She couldn't have been a man in disguise?'

Thinking of the smart and obviously feminine Temple, Sir Charles smiled.

Colonel Johnson also smiled apologetically.

'Just an idea,' he said. 'No, I can't say I put much reliance in Miss Lytton Gore's theory. I understand the death in question was an elderly clergyman. Who would want to put an old clergyman out of the way?'

'That's just the puzzling part of it,' said Sir Charles.

'I think you'll find it's just coincidence. Depend on it, the butler's our man. Very likely he's a regular criminal. Unluckily we can't find any of his fingerprints. We had a fingerprint expert go over his bedroom and the butler's pantry, but he had no luck.'

'If it was the butler, what motive can you suggest?'

'That, of course, is one of our difficulties,' admitted Colonel Johnson. 'The man might have been there with intent to steal, and Sir Bartholomew might have caught him out.'

'Both Sir Charles and Mr Satterthwaite remained courteously silent. Colonel Johnson himself seemed to feel that the suggestion lacked plausibility.

'The fact of the matter is, one can only theorize. Once we've got John Ellis under lock and key and have found out who he is, and whether he's ever been through our hands before – well, the motive may be as clear as day.'

'You've been through Sir Bartholomew's papers, I suppose?'

'Naturally, Sir Charles. We've given that side of the case every attention. I must introduce you to Superintendent Crossfield, who has charge of the case. A most reliable man. I pointed out to him, and he was quick to agree with me, that Sir Bartholomew's profession might have had something to do with the crime. A doctor knows many professional secrets. Sir Bartholomew's papers were all neatly filed and docketed – his secretary, Miss Lyndon, went through them with Crossfield.'

'And there was nothing?'

'Nothing at all suggestive, Sir Charles.'

'Was anything missing from the house – silver, jewellery, anything like that?'

'Nothing whatsoever.'

'Who exactly was staying in the house?'

'I've got a list – now where is it? Ah, I think Crossfield has it. You must meet Crossfield; as a matter of fact, I'm expecting him any minute now to report' – as a bell went – 'that's probably the man now.'

Superintendent Crossfield was a large, solid-looking man, rather slow of speech, but with a fairly keen blue eye.

He saluted his superior officer, and was introduced to the two visitors.

It is possible that had Mr Satterthwaite been alone he would have found it hard to make Crossfield unbend. Crossfield didn't hold with gentlemen from London – amateurs coming down with 'ideas'. Sir Charles, however, was a different matter. Superintendent Crossfield had a childish reverence for the glamour of the stage. He had twice seen Sir Charles act, and the excitement and rapture of seeing this hero of the footlights in a flesh-and-blood manner made him as friendly and loquacious as could be wished.

'I saw you in London, sir, I did. I was up with the wife. *Lord Aintree's Dilemma* – that's what the play was. In the pit, I was – and the house was crowded out – we had to stand two hours beforehand. But nothing else would do for the wife. "I must see Sir Charles Cartwright in *Lord Aintree's Dilemma*," she said. At the Pall Mall Theatre, it was.'

'Well,' said Sir Charles, 'I've retired from the stage now, as you know. But they still know my name at the Pall Mall.' He took out a card and wrote a few words on it. 'You give this to the people at the box office next time you and Mrs Crossfield are having a jaunt to town, and they'll give you a couple of the best seats going.'

'I take that very kindly of you, Sir Charles – very kindly, indeed. My wife will be all worked up when I tell her about this.'

After this Superintendent Crossfield was as wax in the ex-actor's hands.

'It's an odd case, sir. Never come across a case of nicotine poisoning before in all my experience. No more has our Doctor Davis.'

'I always thought it was a kind of disease you got from over-smoking.'

'To tell the truth, so did I, sir. But the doctor says that the pure alkaloid is an odourless liquid, and that a few drops of it are enough to kill a man almost instantaneously.'

Sir Charles whistled.

'Potent stuff.'

'As you say, sir. And yet it's in common use, as you might say. Solutions are used to spray roses with. And of course it can be extracted from ordinary tobacco.'

'Roses,' said Sir Charles. 'Now, where have I heard –?'

He frowned, then shook his head.

'Anything fresh to report, Crossfield?' asked Colonel Johnson.

'Nothing definite, sir. We've had reports that our man Ellis has been seen at Durham, at Ipswich, at Balham, at Land's End, and a dozen other places. That's all got to be sifted out for what it's worth.' He turned to the other two. 'The moment a man's description is circulated as wanted, he's seen by someone all over England.'

'What is the man's description?' asked Sir Charles.

Johnson took up a paper.

'John Ellis, medium height, say five-foot seven, stoops slightly, grey hair, small side whiskers, dark eyes, husky voice, tooth missing in upper jaw, visible when he smiles, no special marks or characteristics.'

'H'm,' said Sir Charles. 'Very nondescript, bar the side whiskers and the tooth, and the first will be off by now, and you can't rely on his smiling.'

'The trouble is,' said Crossfield, 'that nobody observes anything. The difficulty I had in getting anything but the vaguest description out of the maids at the Abbey. It's always the same. I've had descriptions of one and the same man, and he's been called tall, thin, short, stout, medium height, thickset, slender – not one in fifty really uses their eyes properly.'

'You're satisfied in your own mind, Superintendent, that Ellis is the man? . . .'

'Why else did he bolt, sir? You can't get away from that.'

'That's the stumbling block,' said Sir Charles thoughtfully.

Crossfield turned to Colonel Johnson and reported the measures that were being taken. The Colonel nodded approval and then asked the Superintendent for the list of inmates of the Abbey on the night of the crime. This was handed to the two new inquirers. It ran as follows:

MARTHA LECKIE, cook.
BEATRICE CHURCH, upper-housemaid.
DORIS COKER, under-housemaid.
VICTORIA BALL, between-maid.
ALICE WEST, parlourmaid.
VIOLET BASSINGTON, kitchenmaid.
(Above have all been in service of deceased for some time and bear good character. Mrs Leckie has been there for fifteen years.)
GLADYS LYNDON – secretary, thirty-three, has been secretary to Sir Bartholomew Strange for three years, can give no information as to likely motive.
Guests:
LORD AND LADY EDEN, 187 Cadogan Square.
SIR JOCELYN and LADY CAMPBELL, 1256 Harley Street.
MISS ANGELA SUTCLIFFE, 28 Cantrell Mansions, S.W.3.
CAPTAIN and MRS DACRES, 3 St John's House, W.1. (Mrs Dacres carries on business as Ambrosine, Ltd, Brook Street.)
LADY MARY and MISS HERMIONE LYTTON GORE, Rose Cottage, Loomouth.
MISS MURIEL WILLS, 5 Upper Cathcart Road, Tooting.
MR OLIVER MANDERS, Messrs Speier & Ross, Old Broad Street, E.C.2.

'H'm,' said Sir Charles. 'The Tooting touch was omitted by the papers. I see young Manders was there, too.'

'That's by way of being an accident, sir,' said Superintendent Crossfield. 'The young gentleman ran his car into a wall just by the Abbey, and Sir Bartholomew, who I understood was slightly acquainted with him, asked him to stay the night.'

'Careless thing to do,' said Sir Charles cheerfully.

'It was that, sir,' said the Superintendent. 'In fact, I fancy myself the young gentleman must have had one over the eight, as the saying goes. What made him ram the wall just where he did I can't imagine, if he was sober at the time.'

'Just high spirits, I expect,' said Sir Charles.

'Spirits it was, in my opinion, sir.'

'Well, thank you very much, Superintendent. Any objection to our going and having a look at the Abbey, Colonel Johnson?'

'Of course not, my dear sir. Though I'm afraid you won't learn much more there than I can tell you.'

'Anybody there?'

'Only the domestic staff, sir,' said Crossfield. 'The house-party left immediately after the inquest, and Miss Lyndon has returned to Harley Street.'

'We might, perhaps, see Dr – er – Davis, too?' suggested Mr Satterthwaite.

'Good idea.'

They obtained the doctor's address, and having thanked Colonel Johnson warmly for his kindness, they left.

CHAPTER 3

Which Of Them?

As they walked along the street, Sir Charles said:

'Any ideas, Satterthwaite?'

'What about you?' asked Mr Satterthwaite. He liked to reserve judgment until the last possible moment.

Not so Sir Charles. He spoke emphatically:

'They're wrong, Satterthwaite. They're all wrong. They've got the butler on the brain. The butler's done a bunk – ergo, the butler's the murderer. It doesn't fit. No, it doesn't fit. You can't leave that other death out of account – the one down at my place.'

'You're still of the opinion that the two are connected?'

Mr Satterthwaite asked the question, though he had already answered it in the affirmative in his own mind.

'Man, they *must* be connected. Everything points to it . . . We've got to find the common factor – someone who was present on both occasions –'

'Yes,' said Mr Satterthwaite. 'And that's not going to be as simple a matter as one might think, on the face of it. We've got too many common factors. Do you realize, Cartwright, that practically every person who was present at the dinner at your house was present here?'

Sir Charles nodded.

'Of course I've realized that – but do you realize what deduction one can draw from it?'

'I don't quite follow you, Cartwright?'

'Dash it all, man, do you suppose that's coincidence? No, it was *meant*. Why are all the people who were at the first death present at the second? Accident? Not on your life. It was plan – design – Tollie's plan.'

'Oh!' said Mr Satterthwaite. 'Yes, it's possible . . .'

'It's certain. You didn't know Tollie as well as I did, Satterthwaite. He was a man who kept his own counsel, and a very patient man. In all the years I've known him I've never known Tollie give utterance to a rash opinion or judgment.

'Look at it this way: Babbington's murdered – yes, *murdered* – I'm not going to hedge, or mince terms – murdered one evening in my house. Tollie ridicules me gently for my suspicions in the matter, but all the time he's got suspicions of his own. He doesn't talk about them – that's not his way. But quietly, in his own mind, he's building up a case. I don't know what he had to build upon. It can't, I think, be a case against any one particular person. He believed that one of those people was responsible for the crime, and he made a plan, a test of some kind to find out which person it was.'

'What about the other guests, the Edens and the Campbells?'

'Camouflage. It made the whole thing less obvious.'

'What do you think the plan was?'

'Sir Charles shrugged his shoulders – an exaggerated foreign gesture. He was Aristide Duval, that master mind of the Secret Service. His left foot limped as he walked.

'How can we know? I am not a magician. I cannot guess. But there *was* a plan . . . It went wrong, because the murderer was just one degree cleverer than Tollie thought . . . He struck first . . .'

'He?'

'Or she. Poison is as much a woman's weapon as a man's – more so.'

Mr Satterthwaite was silent. Sir Charles said:

'Come now, don't you agree? Or are you on the side of public opinion? "*The butler's the man. He done it.*"'

'What's your explanation of the butler?'

'I haven't thought about him. In my view he doesn't matter . . . I could suggest an explanation.'

'Such as?'

'Well, say that the police are right so far – Ellis is a professional criminal, working in, shall we say, with a gang of burglars. Ellis obtains this post with false credentials. Then Tollie is murdered. What is Ellis's position? A man is killed, and in the house is a man whose fingerprints are at Scotland Yard, and who is known to the police. Naturally he gets the wind up and bolts.'

'By the secret passage?'

'Secret passage be damned. He dodged out of the house while one of the fat-headed constables who were watching the house was taking forty winks.'

'It certainly seems more probable.'

'Well, Satterthwaite, what's your view?'

'Mine?' said Mr Satterthwaite. 'Oh, it's the same as yours. It has been all along. The butler seems to me a very clumsy red herring. I believe that Sir Bartholomew and poor old Babbington were killed by the same person.'

'One of the house-party?'

'One of the house-party.'

There was silence for a minute or two, and then Mr Satterthwaite asked casually:

'Which of them do you think it was?'

'My God, Satterthwaite, how can I tell?'

'You can't tell, of course,' said Mr Satterthwaite mildly. 'I just thought you might have some idea – you know, nothing scientific or reasoned. Just an ordinary guess.'

'Well, I haven't . . .' He thought for a minute and then burst out: 'You know, Satterthwaite, the moment you begin to *think* it seems impossible that any of them did it.'

'I suppose your theory is right,' mused Mr Satterthwaite. 'As to the assembling of the suspects, I mean. We've got to take it into account that there were certain definite exclusions. Yourself and myself and Mrs Babbington, for instance. Young Manders, too, he was out of it.'

'Manders?'

'Yes, his arrival on the scene was an accident. He wasn't asked or expected. That lets him out of the circle of suspects.'

'The dramatist woman, too – Anthony Astor.'

'No, no, she was there. Miss Muriel Wills of Tooting.'

'So she was – I'd forgotten the woman's name was Wills.'

He frowned. Mr Satterthwaite was fairly good at reading people's thoughts. He estimated with fair accuracy what was passing through the actor's mind. When the other spoke, Mr Satterthwaite mentally patted himself on the back.

'You know, Satterthwaite, you're right. I don't think it was definitely suspected people that he asked – because, after all,

Lady Mary and Egg were there . . . No, he wanted to stage some reproduction of the first business, perhaps . . . He suspected someone, but he wanted other eye-witnesses there to confirm matters. Something of that kind . . .'

'Something of the kind,' agreed Mr Satterthwaite. 'One can only generalize at this stage. Very well, the Lytton Gores are out of it, you and I and Mrs Babbington and Oliver Manders are out of it. Who is left? Angela Sutcliffe?'

'Angie? My dear fellow. She's been a friend of Tollie's for years.'

'Then it boils down to the Dacres . . . In fact, Cartwright, you suspect the Dacres. You might just as well have said so when I asked you.'

Sir Charles looked at him. Mr Satterthwaite had a mildly triumphant air.

'I suppose,' said Cartwright slowly, 'that I do. At least, I don't suspect them . . . They just seem rather more possible than anyone else. I don't know them very well, for one thing. But for the life of me, I can't see why Freddie Dacres, who spends his life on the racecourse, or Cynthia, who spends her time designing fabulously expensive clothes for women, should have any desire to remove a dear, insignificant old clergyman . . .'

He shook his head, then his face brightened.

'There's the Wills woman. I forgot her again. What is there about her that continually makes you forget her? She's the most damnably nondescript creature I've ever seen.'

Mr Satterthwaite smiled.

'I rather fancy she might embody Burns's famous line – "A chiel's amang ye takin' notes." I rather fancy that Miss Wills spends her time taking notes. There are sharp eyes behind that pair of glasses. I think you'll find that anything worth noticing in this affair has been noticed by Miss Wills.'

'Do you?' said Sir Charles doubtfully.

'The next thing to do,' said Mr Satterthwaite, 'is to have some lunch. After that, we'll go out to the Abbey and see what we can discover on the spot.'

'You seem to be taking very kindly to this, Satterthwaite,' said Sir Charles, with a twinkle of amusement.

'The investigation of crime is not new to me,' said Mr

Satterthwaite. 'Once when my car broke down and I was staying at a lonely inn –'

He got no further.

'I remember,' said Sir Charles, in his high, clear carrying actor's voice, 'when I was touring in 1921 . . .'

Sir Charles won.

CHAPTER 4

The Evidence Of The Servants

Nothing could have been more peaceful than the grounds and building of Melfort Abbey as the two men saw it that afternoon in the September sunshine. Portions of the Abbey were fifteenth century. It had been restored and a new wing added on to it. The new Sanatorium was out of sight of the house, with grounds of its own.

Sir Charles and Mr Satterthwaite were received by Mrs Leckie, the cook, a portly lady, decorously gowned in black, who was tearful and voluble. Sir Charles she already knew, and it was to him she addressed most of her conversation.

'You'll understand, I'm sure, sir, what it's meant to me. The master's death and all. Policemen all over the place, poking their noses here and there – would you believe it, even the dusbins they had to have their noses in, and questions! – they wouldn't have done with asking questions. Oh, that I should have lived to see such a thing – the doctor, such a quiet gentleman as he always was, and made Sir Bartholomew, too, which a proud day it was to all of us, as Beatrice and I well remember, though she's been here two years less than I have. And such questions as that police fellow (for gentleman I will not call him, having been accustomed to gentlemen and their ways and knowing what's what), fellow, I say, whether or not he is a superintendent –' Mrs Leckie paused, took breath and extricated herself from the somewhat complicated conversational morass into which she had fallen. 'Questions, that's what I say, about all the maids in the house, and good girls they are, every one of them – not that I'd say that Doris gets up when she should do in the morning. I have to speak about it at least once a week, and Vickie, she's inclined to be impertinent, but, there, with the young ones you can't expect the training – their mothers don't give it to them nowadays – but good girls they are, and no police superintendent shall make me say otherwise. "Yes," I said to him, "you needn't think I'm going to say anything against my girls. They're good girls, they are, and as to having anything to do with murder, why it's right-down wicked to suggest such a thing."'

Mrs Leckie paused.

'Mr Ellis, now – that's different. I don't know anything about Mr Ellis, and couldn't answer for him in any way, he having been brought from London, and strange to the place, while Mr Baker was on holiday.'

'Baker?' asked Mr Satterthwaite.

'Mr Baker had been Sir Bartholomew's butler for the last seven years, sir. He was in London most of the time, in Harley Street. You'll remember him, sir?' She appealed to Sir Charles, who nodded. 'Sir Bartholomew used to bring him up here when he had a party. But he hadn't been so well in his health, so Sir Bartholomew said, and he gave him a couple of months' holiday, paid for him, too, in a place near the sea down near Brighton – a real kind gentleman the doctor was – and he took Mr Ellis on temporary for the time being, and so, as I said to that superintendent, I can't say anything about Mr Ellis, though, from all he said himself, he seems to have been with the best families, and he certainly had a gentlemanly way with him.'

'You didn't find anything – unusual about him?' asked Sir Charles hopefully.

'Well, it's odd your saying that, sir, because, if you know what I mean, I did and I didn't.'

Sir Charles looked encouraging, and Mrs Leckie went on:

'I couldn't exactly say what it was, sir, but there was *some*thing –'

There always is – after the event – thought Mr Satterthwaite to himself grimly. However much Mrs Leckie had despised the police, she was not proof against suggestion. If Ellis turned out to be the criminal, well, Mrs Leckie would have noticed *something*.

'For one thing, he was standoffish. Oh, quite polite, quite the gentleman – as I said, he'd been used to good houses. But he kept himself to himself, spent a lot of time in his own room; and he was – well, I don't know how to describe it, I'm sure – he was, well, there was *something* –'

'You didn't suspect he wasn't – not really a butler?' suggested Mr Satterthwaite.

'Oh, he'd been in service, right enough, sir. The things he knew – and about well-known people in society, too.'

'Such as?' suggested Sir Charles gently.

But Mrs Leckie became vague, and non-committal. She was not going to retail servants' hall gossip. Such a thing would have offended her sense of fitness.

To put her at her ease, Mr Satterthwaite said:

'Perhaps you can describe his appearance.'

Mrs Leckie brightened.

'Yes, indeed, sir. He was a very respectable-looking man – side-whiskers and grey hair, stooped a little, and he was growing stout – it worried him, that did. He had a rather shaky hand, too, but not from the cause you might imagine. He was a most abstemious man – not like many I've known. His eyes were a bit weak, I think, sir, the light hurt them – especially a bright light, used to make them water something cruel. Out with us he wore glasses, but not when he was on duty.'

'No special distinguishing marks?' asked Sir Charles. 'No scars? Or broken fingers? Or birth marks?'

'Oh, no, sir, nothing of that kind.'

'How superior detective stories are to life,' sighed Sir Charles. 'In fiction there is always some distinguishing characteristic.'

'He had a tooth missing,' said Mr Satterthwaite.

'I believe so, sir; I never noticed it myself.'

'What was his manner on the night of the tragedy?' asked Mr Satterthwaite in a slightly bookish manner.

'Well, really, sir, I couldn't say. I was busy, you see, in my kitchen. I hadn't time for noticing things.'

'No, no, quite so.'

'When the news came out that the master was dead we were struck all of a heap. I cried and couldn't stop, and so did Beatrice. The young ones, of course, were excited like, though very upset. Mr Ellis naturally wasn't so upset as we were, he being new, but he behaved very considerate, and insisted on Beatrice and me taking a little glass of port to counteract the shock. And to think that all the time it was he – the villain –'

Words failed Mrs Leckie, her eyes shone with indignation.

'He disappeared that night, I understand?'

'Yes, sir, went to his room like the rest of us, and in the morning he wasn't there. That's what set the police on him, of course.'

'Yes, yes, very foolish of him. Have you any idea how he left the house?'

'Not the slightest. It seems the police were watching the house all night, and they never saw him go – but, there, that's what the police are, human like anyone else, in spite of the airs they give themselves, coming into a gentleman's house and nosing round.'

'I hear there's some question of a secret passage,' Sir Charles said.

Mrs Leckie sniffed.

'That's what the police say.'

'Is there such a thing?'

'I've heard mention of it,' Mrs Leckie agreed cautiously.

'Do you know where it starts from?'

'No, I don't, sir. Secret passages are all very well, but they're not things to be encouraged in the servants' hall. It gives the girls ideas. They might think of slipping out that way. My girls go out by the back door and in by the back door, and then we know where we are.'

'Splendid, Mrs Leckie. I think you're very wise.'

Mrs Leckie bridled in the sun of Sir Charles's approval.

'I wonder,' he went on, 'if we might just ask a few questions of the other servants?'

'Of course, sir; but they can't tell you anything more than I can.'

'Oh, I know. I didn't mean so much about Ellis as about Sir Bartholomew himself – his manner that night, and so on. You see, he was a friend of mine.'

'I know, sir. I quite understand. There's Beatrice, and there's Alice. She waited at table, of course.'

'Yes, I'd like to see Alice.'

Mrs Leckie, however, had a belief in seniority. Beatrice Church, the upper-housemaid, was the first to appear.

She was a tall thin woman, with a pinched mouth, who looked aggressively respectable.

After a few unimportant questions, Sir Charles led the talk to the behaviour of the house-party on the fatal evening. Had they all been terribly upset? What had they said or done?

A little animation entered into Beatrice's manner. She had the usual ghoulish relish for tragedy.

'Miss Sutcliffe, she quite broke down. A very warm-hearted lady, she's stayed here before. I suggested bringing her a little drop of brandy, or a nice cup of tea, but she wouldn't hear of it. She took some aspirin, though. Said she was sure she couldn't sleep. But she was sleeping like a little child the next morning when I brought her her early tea.'

'And Mrs Dacres?'

'I don't think anything would upset that lady much.'

From Beatrice's tone, she had not liked Cynthia Dacres.

'Just anxious to get away, she was. Said her business would suffer. She's a big dressmaker in London, so Mr Ellis told us.'

A big dressmaker, to Beatrice, meant 'trade', and trade she looked down upon.

'And her husband?'

Beatrice sniffed.

'Steadied his nerves with brandy, he did. Or unsteadied them, some would say.'

'What about Lady Mary Lytton Gore?'

'A very nice lady,' said Beatrice, her tone softening. 'My great aunt was in service with her father at the Castle. A pretty young girl she was, so I've always heard. Poor she may be, but you can see she's someone – and so considerate, never giving trouble and always speaking so pleasant. Her daughter's a nice young lady, too. They didn't know Sir Bartholomew well, of course, but they were very distressed.'

'Miss Wills?'

Some of Beatrice's rigidity returned.

'I'm sure I couldn't say, sir, what Miss Wills thought about it.'

'Or what you thought about her?' asked Sir Charles. 'Come now, Beatrice, be human.'

An unexpected smile dinted Beatrice's wooden cheeks. There was something appealingly schoolboyish in Sir Charles's manner. She was not proof against the charm that nightly audiences had felt so strongly.

'Really, sir, I don't know what you want me to say.'

'Just what you thought and felt about Miss Wills.'

'Nothing, sir, nothing at all. She wasn't, of course –'

Beatrice hesitated.

'Go on, Beatrice.'

'Well, she wasn't quite the "class" of the others, sir. She couldn't help it, I know,' went on Beatrice kindly. 'But she did things a real lady wouldn't have done. She pried, if you know what I mean, sir, poked and pried about.'

Sir Charles tried hard to get this statement amplified, but Beatrice remained vague. Miss Wills had poked and pried, but asked to produce a special instance of the poking, Beatrice seemed unable to do so. She merely repeated that Miss Wills pried into things that were no business of hers.

They gave it up at last, and Mr Satterthwaite said:

'Young Mr Manders arrived unexpectedly, didn't he?'

'Yes, sir, he had an accident with his car – just by the lodge gates, it was. He said it was a bit of luck its happening just here. The house was full, of course, but Miss Lyndon had a bed made up for him in the little study.'

'Was everyone very surprised to see him?'

'Oh, yes, sir, naturally, sir.'

Asked her opinion of Ellis, Beatrice was non-committal. She'd seen very little of him. Going off the way he did looked bad, though why he should want to harm the master she couldn't imagine. Nobody could.

'What was he like, the doctor, I mean? Did he seem to be looking forward to the house-party? Had he anything on his mind?'

'He seemed particularly cheerful, sir. Smiled to himself, he did, as though he had some joke on. I even heard him make a joke with Mr Ellis, a thing he'd never done with Mr Baker. He was usually a bit brusque with the servants, kind always, but not speaking to them much.'

'What did he say?' asked Mr Satterthwaite eagerly.

'Well, I forget exactly now, sir. Mr Ellis had come up with a telephone message, and Sir Bartholomew asked him if he was sure he'd got the names right, and Mr Ellis said quite sure – speaking respectful, of course. And the doctor he laughed and said, "You're a good fellow, Ellis, a first-class butler. Eh, Beatrice, what do you think?" And I was so surprised, sir, at the master speaking like that – quite unlike his usual self – that I didn't know what to say.'

'And Ellis?'

'He looked kind of disapproving, sir, as though it was the kind of thing he hadn't been used to. Stiff like.'

'What was the telephone message?' asked Sir Charles.

'The message, sir? Oh, it was from the Sanatorium – about a patient who had arrived there and had stood the journey well.'

'Do you remember the name?'

'It was a queer name, sir.' Beatrice hesitated. 'Mrs de Rushbridger – something like that.'

'Ah, yes,' said Sir Charles soothingly. 'Not an easy name to get right on the telephone. Well, thank you very much, Beatrice. Perhaps we could see Alice now.'

When Beatrice had left the room Sir Charles and Mr Satterthwaite compared notes by an interchange of glances.

'Miss Wills poked and pried, Captain Dacres got drunk, Mrs Dacres displayed no emotion. Anything there? Precious little.'

'Very little indeed,' agreed Mr Satterthwaite.

'Let's pin our hopes on Alice.'

Alice was a demure, dark-eyed young woman of thirty. She was only too pleased to talk.

She herself didn't believe Mr Ellis had anything to do with it. He was too much the gentleman. The police had suggested he was just a common crook. Alice was sure he was nothing of the sort.

'You're quite certain he was an ordinary honest-to-God butler?' asked Sir Charles.

'Not ordinary, sir. He wasn't like any butler I've ever worked with before. He arranged the work different.'

'But you don't think he poisoned your master.'

'Oh, sir, I don't see how he could have done. I was waiting at table with him, and he couldn't have put anything in the master's food without my seeing him.'

'And the drink?'

'He went round with the wine, sir. Sherry first, with the soup, and then hock and claret. But what could he have done, sir? If there'd been anything in the wine he'd have poisoned everybody – or all those who took it. It's not as though the master had anything that nobody else had. The same thing with the port. All the gentlemen had port, and some of the ladies.'

'The wine glasses were taken out on a tray?'

'Yes, sir, I held the tray and Mr Ellis put the glasses on it, and I carried the tray out to the pantry, and there they were, sir, when the police came to examine them. The port glasses were still on the table. And the police didn't find anything.'

'You're quite sure that the doctor didn't have anything to eat or drink at dinner that nobody else had?'

'Not that I saw, sir. In fact, I'm sure he didn't.'

'Nothing that one of the guests gave him –'

'Oh, no, sir.'

'Do you know anything about a secret passage, Alice?'

'One of the gardeners told me something about it. Comes out in the wood where there's some old walls and things tumbled down. But I've never seen any opening to it in the house.'

'Ellis never said anything about it?'

'Oh, no, sir, he wouldn't know anything about it, I'm sure.'

'Who do you really think killed your master, Alice?'

'I don't know, sir. I can't believe anyone did . . . I feel it must have been some kind of accident.'

'H'm. Thank you, Alice.'

'If it wasn't for the death of Babbington,' said Sir Charles as the girl left the room, 'we could make her the criminal. She's a good-looking girl . . . And she waited at table . . . No, it won't do. Babbington was murdered; and anyway Tollie never noticed good-looking girls. He wasn't made that way.'

'But he was fifty-five,' said Mr Satterthwaite thoughtfully.

'Why do you say that?'

'It's the age a man loses his head badly about a girl – even if he hasn't done so before.'

'Dash it all, Satterthwaite, *I'm* – er – getting on for fifty-five.'

'I know,' said Satterthwaite.

And before his gentle twinkling gaze Sir Charles's eyes fell.

Unmistakably he blushed . . .

CHAPTER 5

In The Butler's Room

'How about an examination of Ellis's room?' asked Mr Satterthwaite, having enjoyed the spectacle of Sir Charles's blush to the full.

The actor seized at the diversion.

'Excellent, excellent. Just what I was about to suggest myself.'

'Of course the police have already searched it thoroughly.'

'The police –'

Aristide Duval waved the police away scornfully. Anxious to forget his momentary discomfiture, he flung himself with renewed vigour into his part.

'The police are blockheads,' he said sweepingly. 'What have they looked for in Ellis's room? Evidences of his guilt. We shall look for evidences of his innocence – an entirely different thing.'

'You're completely convinced of Ellis's innocence?'

'If we're right about Babbington, he *must* be innocent.'

'Yes, besides –'

Mr Satterthwaite did not finish his sentence. He had been about to say that if Ellis was a professional criminal who had been detected by Sir Bartholomew and had murdered him in consequence the whole affair would become unbearably dull. Just in time he remembered that Sir Bartholomew had been a friend of Sir Charles Cartwright's and was duly appalled by the callousness of the sentiments he had nearly revealed.

At first sight Ellis's room did not seem to offer much promise of discovery. The clothes in the drawers and hanging in the cupboard were all neatly arranged. They were well cut, and bore different tailors' marks. Clearly cast-offs given him in different situations. The underclothing was on the same scale. The boots were neatly polished and arranged on trees.

Mr Satterthwaite picked up a boot and murmured, 'Nines, just so, nines.' But, since there were no footprints in the case, that didn't seem to lead anywhere.

It seemed clear from its absence that Ellis had departed in his butler's kit, and Mr Satterthwaite pointed out to Sir Charles that that seemed rather a remarkable fact.

'Any man in his senses would have changed into an ordinary suit.'

'Yes, it's odd that . . . Looks almost, though that's absurd, as if he *hadn't* gone at all . . . Nonsense, of course.'

They continued their search. No letters, no papers, except a cutting from a newspaper regarding a cure for corns, and a paragraph relating to the approaching marriage of a duke's daughter.

There was a small blotting-book and a penny bottle of ink on a side table – no pen. Sir Charles held up the blotting-book to the mirror, but without result. One page of it was very much used – a meaningless jumble, and the ink looked to both men old.

'Either he hasn't written any letters since he was here, or he hasn't blotted them,' deduced Mr Satterthwaite. 'This is an old blotter. Ah, yes –' With some gratification he pointed to a barely decipherable 'L. Baker' amidst the jumble.

'I should say Ellis hadn't used this at all.'

'That's rather odd, isn't it?' said Sir Charles slowly.

'What do you mean?'

'Well, a man usually writes letters . . .'

'Not if he's a criminal.'

'No, perhaps you're right . . . There must have been something fishy about him to make him bolt as he did . . . All we say is that he didn't murder Tollie.'

They hunted round the floor, raising the carpet, looking under the bed. There was nothing anywhere, except a splash of ink beside the fireplace. The room was disappointingly bare.

They left it in a somewhat disconcerted fashion. Their zeal as detectives was momentarily damped.

Possibly the thought passed through their minds that things were arranged better in books.

They had a few words with the other members of the staff, scared-looking juniors in awe of Mrs Leckie and Beatrice Church, but they elicited nothing further.

Finally they took their leave.

'Well, Satterthwaite,' said Sir Charles as they strolled across the park (Mr Satterthwaite's car had been instructed to pick them up at the lodge) 'anything strike you – anything at all?'

Mr Satterthwaite thought. He was not to be hurried into an answer – especially as he felt something *ought* to have struck him. To confess that the whole expedition had been a waste of time was an unwelcome idea. He passed over in his mind the evidence of one servant after another – the information was extraordinarily meagre.

As Sir Charles had summed it up just now, Miss Wills had poked and pried, Miss Sutcliffe had been very upset, Mrs Dacres had not been upset at all, and Captain Dacres had got drunk. Very little there, unless Freddie Dacres's indulgence showed the deadening of a guilty conscience. But Freddie Dacres, Mr Satterthwaite knew, quite frequently got drunk.

'Well?' repeated Sir Charles impatiently.

'Nothing,' confessed Mr Satterthwaite reluctantly. 'Except – well, I think we are entitled to assume from the clipping we found that Ellis suffered from corns.'

Sir Charles gave a wry smile.

'That seems quite a reasonable deduction. Does it – er – get us anywhere?'

Mr Satterthwaite confessed that it did not.

'The only other thing—' he said and then stopped.

'Yes? Go on, man. Anything may help.'

'It struck me as a little odd the way that Sir Bartholomew chaffed his butler – you know what the housemaid told us. It seems somehow uncharacteristic.'

'It *was* uncharacteristic,' said Sir Charles with emphasis. 'I knew Tollie well – better than you did – and I can tell you that he wasn't a facetious sort of man. He'd never have spoken like that unless – well, unless for some reason he wasn't quite normal at the time. You're right, Satterthwaite, that is a point. Now where does it get us?'

'Well,' began Mr Satterthwaite; but it was clear that Sir Charles's question had been merely a rhetorical one. He was anxious, not to hear Mr Satterthwaite's views, but to air his own.

'You remember when that incident occurred, Satterthwaite?

Just after Ellis had brought him a telephone message. I think it's a fair deduction to assume that it was that telephone message which was the cause of Tollie's sudden unusual hilarity. You may remember I asked the housemaid woman what that message had been.'

Mr Satterthwaite nodded.

'It was to say that a woman named Mrs de Rushbridger had arrived at the Sanatorium,' he said, to show that he, too, had paid attention to the point. 'It doesn't sound particularly thrilling.'

'It doesn't sound so, certainly. But, if our reasoning is correct, *there must be some significance in that message*.'

'Ye-es,' said Mr Satterthwaite doubtfully.

'Indubitably,' said Sir Charles. 'We've got to find out what that significance was. It just crosses my mind that it may have been a code message of some kind – a harmless sounding natural thing, but which really meant something entirely different. If Tollie had been making inquiries into Babbington's death, this may have had something to do with those inquiries. Say, even, that he employed a private detective to find out a certain fact. He may have told him in the event of this particular suspicion being justified to ring up and use that particular phrase which would convey no hint of the truth to anyone taking it. That would explain his jubilation, it might explain his asking Ellis if he was sure of the name – he himself knowing well there was no such person, really. In fact, the slight lack of balance a person shows when they have brought off what can be described as a long shot.'

'You think there's no such person as Mrs de Rushbridger?'

'Well, I think we ought to find out for certain.'

'How?'

'We might run along to the Sanatorium now and ask the Matron.'

'She may think it rather odd.'

Sir Charles laughed.

'You leave it to me,' he said.

They turned aside from the drive and walked in the direction of the Sanatorium.

Mr Satterthwaite said:

'What about you, Cartwright? Does anything strike you at all? Arising out of our visit to the house, I mean.'

Sir Charles answered slowly.

'Yes, there is something – the devil of it is, I can't remember what.'

Mr Satterthwaite stared at him in surprise. The other frowned.

'How can I explain? There was something – something which at the moment struck me as wrong – as unlikely – only – I hadn't the time to think about it then. I put it aside in my own mind.'

'And now you can't remember what it was?'

'No – only that at some moment I said to myself, "That's odd."'

'Was it when we were questioning the servants? Which servant?'

'I tell you I can't remember. And the more I think the less I shall remember . . . If I leave it alone, it may come back to me.'

They came into view of the Sanatorium, a big white modern building, divided from the park by palings. There was a gate through which they passed, and they rang the front-door bell and asked for the Matron.

The Matron, when she came, was a tall, middle-aged woman, with an intelligent face and a capable manner. Sir Charles she clearly knew by name as a friend of the late Sir Bartholomew Strange.

Sir Charles explained that he had just come back from abroad, had been horrified to hear of his friend's death and of the terrible suspicions entertained, and had been up to the house to learn as many details as he could. The Matron spoke in moving terms of the loss Sir Bartholomew would be to them, and of his fine career as a doctor. Sir Charles professed himself anxious to know what was going to happen to the Sanatorium. The Matron explained that Sir Bartholomew had had two partners, both capable doctors, one was in residence at the Sanatorium.

'Bartholomew was very proud of this place, I know,' said Sir Charles.

'Yes, his treatments were a great success.'

'Mostly nerve cases, isn't it?'

'Yes.'

'That reminds me – fellow I met out at Monte had some kind of relation coming here. I forget her name now – odd sort of name – Rushbridger – Rusbrigger – something like that.'

'Mrs de Rushbridger, you mean?'

'That's it. Is she here now?'

'Oh, yes. But I'm afraid she won't be able to see you – not for some time yet. She's having a very strict rest cure.' The Matron smiled just a trifle archly. 'No letters, no exciting visitors . . .'

'I say, she's not very bad, is she?'

'Rather a bad nervous breakdown – lapses of memory, and severe nervous exhaustion. Oh, we shall get her right in time.'

The Matron smiled reassuringly.

'Let me see, haven't I heard Tollie – Sir Bartholomew – speak of her? She was a friend of his as well as a patient, wasn't she?'

'I don't think so, Sir Charles. At least the doctor never said so. She has recently arrived from the West Indies – really, it was very funny, I must tell you. Rather a difficult name for a servant to remember – the parlourmaid here is rather stupid. She came and said to me, "Mrs West India has come," and of course I suppose Rushbridger *does* sound rather like West India – but it was rather a coincidence her having just come from the West Indies.'

'Rather – rather – most amusing. Her husband over, too?'

'He's still out there.'

'Ah, quite – quite. I must be mixing her up with someone else. It was a case the doctor was specially interested in?'

'Cases of amnesia are fairly common, but they're always interesting to a medical man – the variations, you know. Two cases are seldom alike.'

'Seems all very odd to me. Well, thank you, Matron, I'm glad to have had a little chat with you. I know how much Tollie thought of you. He often spoke about you,' finished Sir Charles mendaciously.

'Oh, I'm glad to hear that.' The Matron flushed and bridled. 'Such a splendid man – such a loss to us all. We were absolutely shocked – well, stunned would describe it better. Murder! Who ever would murder Dr Strange, I said. It's incredible. That awful butler. I hope the police catch him. And no motive or anything.'

Sir Charles shook his head sadly and they took their departure, going round by the road to the spot where the car awaited them.

In revenge for his enforced quiescence during the interview with the Matron, Mr Satterthwaite displayed a lively interest in the scene of Oliver Manders' accident, plying the lodge keeper, a slow-witted man of middle age, with questions.

Yes, that was the place, where the wall was broken away. On a motor cycle the young gentleman was. No, he didn't see it happen. He heard it, though, and come out to see. The young gentleman was standing there – just where the other gentleman was standing now. He didn't seem to be hurt. Just looking rueful-like at his bike – and a proper mess that was. Just asked what the name of the place might be, and when he heard it was Sir Bartholomew Strange's he said, 'That's a piece of luck,' and went on up to the house. A very calm young gentleman he seemed to be – tired like. How he come to have such an accident, the lodge keeper couldn't see, but he supposed them things went wrong sometimes.

'It was an odd accident,' said Mr Satterthwaite thoughtfully.

He looked at the wide straight road. No bends, no dangerous crossroads, nothing to cause a motor cyclist to swerve suddenly into a ten-foot wall. Yes, an odd accident.

'What's in your mind, Satterthwaite?' asked Sir Charles curiously.

'Nothing,' said Mr Satterthwaite, 'nothing.'

'It's odd, certainly,' said Sir Charles, and he, too, stared at the scene of the accident in a puzzled manner.

They got into the car and drove off.

Mr Satterthwaite was busy with his thoughts. Mrs de Rushbridger – Cartwright's theory wouldn't work – it wasn't a code message – there *was* such a person. But could there be something about the woman herself? Was she perhaps a witness of some kind, or was it just because she was an interesting case that Bartholomew Strange had displayed this unusual elation? Was she, perhaps, an attractive woman? To fall in love at the age of fifty-five did (Mr Satterthwaite had observed it many a time) change a man's character completely. It might, perhaps, make him facetious, where before he had been aloof –

His thoughts were interrupted. Sir Charles leant forward.

'Satterthwaite,' he said, 'do you mind if we turn back?'

Without waiting for a reply, he took up the speaking tube and gave the order. The car slowed down, stopped, and the chauffeur began to reverse into a convenient lane. A minute or two later they were bowling along the road in the opposite direction.

'What is it?' asked Mr Satterthwaite.

'I've remembered,' said Sir Charles, 'what struck me as odd. It was the ink-stain on the floor in the butler's room.'

CHAPTER 6

Concerning An Ink-Stain

Mr Satterthwaite stared at his friend in surprise.

'The ink-stain? What do you mean, Cartwright?'

'You remember it?'

'I remember there was an ink-stain, yes.'

'You remember its position?'

'Well – not exactly.'

'It was close to the skirting board near the fireplace.'

'Yes, so it was. I remember now.'

'How do you think that stain was caused, Satterthwaite?'

'It wasn't a big stain,' he said at last. 'It couldn't have been an upset ink-bottle. I should say in all probability that the man dropped his fountain pen there – there was no pen in the room, you remember.' (He shall see I notice things just as much as he does, thought Mr Satterthwaite.) 'So it seems clear the man must have had a fountain pen if he ever wrote at all – and there's no evidence that he ever did.'

'Yes, there is, Satterthwaite. There's the ink-stain.'

'He mayn't have been writing,' snapped Satterthwaite. 'He may have just dropped the pen on the floor.'

'But there wouldn't have been a stain unless the top had been off the pen.'

'I daresay you're right,' said Mr Satterthwaite. 'But I can't see what's odd about it.'

'Perhaps there isn't anything odd,' said Sir Charles. 'I can't tell till I get back and see for myself.'

They were turning in at the lodge gates. A few minutes later they had arrived at the house and Sir Charles was allaying the curiosity caused by his return by inventing a pencil left behind in the butler's room.

'And now,' said Sir Charles, shutting the door of Ellis's room behind them, having with some skill shaken off the helpful Mrs Leckie, 'let's see if I'm making an infernal fool of myself, or whether there's anything in my idea.'

In Mr Satterthwaite's opinion the former alternative was by far the more probable, but he was much too polite to say so. He sat down on the bed and watched the other.

'Here's our stain,' said Sir Charles, indicating the mark with his foot. 'Right up against the skirting board at the opposite side of the room to the writing-table. Under what circumstances would a man drop a pen just there?'

'You can drop a pen anywhere,' said Mr Satterthwaite.

'You can hurl it across the room, of course,' agreed Sir Charles. 'But one doesn't usually treat one's pen like that. I don't know, though. Fountain pens are damned annoying things. Dry up and refuse to write just when you want them to. Perhaps that's the solution of the matter. Ellis lost his temper, said, "Damn the thing," and hurled it across the room.'

'I think there are plenty of explanations,' said Mr Satterthwaite. 'He may have simply laid the pen on the mantelpiece and it rolled off.'

Sir Charles experimented with a pencil. He allowed it to roll off the corner of the mantelpiece. The pencil struck the ground at least a foot from the mark and rolled inwards towards the gas fire.

'Well,' said Mr Satterthwaite. 'What's your explanation?'

'I'm trying to find one.'

From his seat on the bed Mr Satterthwaite now witnessed a thoroughly amusing performance.

Sir Charles tried dropping the pencil from his hand as he walked in the direction of the fireplace. He tried sitting on the edge of the bed and writing there and then dropping the pencil. To get the pencil to fall on the right spot it was necessary to stand or sit jammed up against the wall in a most unconvincing attitude.

'That's impossible,' said Sir Charles aloud. He stood considering the wall, the stain and the prim little gas fire.

'If he were burning papers, now,' he said thoughtfully. 'But one doesn't burn papers in a gas fire –'

Suddenly he drew in his breath.

A minute later Mr Satterthwaite was realizing Sir Charles's profession to the full.

Charles Cartwright had become Ellis the butler. He sat writing at the writing-table. He looked furtive, every now and then he raised his eyes, shooting them shiftily from side to side. Suddenly he seemed to hear something – Mr Satterthwaite could even guess what that something was – footsteps along the passage. The man had a guilty conscience. He attached a certain meaning to those footsteps. He sprang up, the paper on which he had been writing in one hand, his pen in the other. He darted across the room to the fireplace, his head half turned, still alert – listening – afraid. He tried to shove the papers under the gas fire – in order to use both hands he cast down the pen impatiently. Sir Charles's pencil, the 'pen' of the drama, fell accurately on the ink-stain . . .

'Bravo,' said Mr Satterthwaite, applauding generously.

So good had the performance been that he was left with the impression that so and only so could Ellis have acted.

'You see?' said Sir Charles, resuming his own personality and speaking with modest elation. 'If the fellow heard the police or what he thought was the police coming and had to hide what he was writing – well, where could he hide it? Not in a drawer or under the mattress – if the police searched the room, that would be found at once. He hadn't time to take up a floor board. No, behind the gas fire was the only chance.'

'The next thing to do,' said Mr Satterthwaite, 'is to see whether there *is* anything hidden behind the gas fire.'

'Exactly. Of course, it may have been a false alarm, and he may have got the things out again later. But we'll hope for the best.'

'Removing his coat and turning up his shirt sleeves, Sir Charles lay down on the floor and applied his eye to the crack under the gas fire.

'There's something under there,' he reported. 'Something white. How can we get it out? We want something like a woman's hatpins.'

'Women don't have hatpins any more,' said Mr Satterthwaite sadly. 'Perhaps a penknife.'

But a penknife proved unavailing.

In the end Mr Satterthwaite went out and borrowed a knitting needle from Beatrice. Though extremely curious to know what he wanted it for, her sense of decorum was too great to permit her to ask.

The knitting needle did the trick. Sir Charles extracted half a dozen sheets of crumpled writing-paper, hastily crushed together and pushed in.

With growing excitement he and Mr Satterthwaite smoothed them out. They were clearly several different drafts of a letter – written in a small, neat clerkly handwriting.

This is to say (began the first) *that the writer of this does not wish to cause unpleasantness, and may possibly have been mistaken in what he thought he saw tonight, but –*

Here the writer had clearly been dissatisfied, and had broken off to start afresh.

John Ellis, butler, presents his compliments, and would be glad of a short interview touching the tragedy tonight before going to the police with certain information in his possession –

Still dissatisfied, the man had tried again.

John Ellis, butler, has certain facts concerning the death of the doctor in his possession. He has not yet given these facts to the police –

In the next one the use of the third person had been abandoned.

I am badly in need of money. A thousand pounds would make all the difference to me. There are certain things I could tell the police, but do not want to make trouble –

The last one was even more unreserved.

I know how the doctor died. I haven't said anything to the police – yet. If you will meet me –

This letter broke off in a different way – after the 'me' the pen had tailed off in a scrawl, and the last five words were all blurred and blotchy. Clearly it was when writing this that Ellis had heard something that alarmed him. He had crumpled up the papers and dashed to conceal them.

Mr Satterthwaite drew a deep breath.

'I congratulate you, Cartwright,' he said. 'Your instinct about that ink-stain was right. Good work. Now let's see exactly where we stand.'

He paused a minute.

'Ellis, as we thought, is a scoundrel. He wasn't the murderer, but he knew who the murderer was, and he was preparing to blackmail him or her –'

'Him or her,' interrupted Sir Charles. 'Annoying we don't know which. Why couldn't the fellow begin one of his effusions Sir or Madam, then we'd know where we are. Ellis seems to have been an artistic sort of fellow. He was taking a lot of trouble over his blackmailing letter. If only he'd given us one clue – as to whom that letter was addressed.'

'Never mind,' said Mr Satterthwaite. 'We are getting on. You remember you said that what we wanted to find in this room was a proof of Ellis's innocence. Well, we've found it. These letters show that he was innocent – of the murder, I mean. He was a thorough-paced scoundrel in other ways. But he didn't murder Sir Bartholomew Strange. Somebody else did that. Someone who murdered Babbington also. I think even the police will have to come round to our view now.'

'You're going to tell them about this?'

Sir Charles's voice expressed dissatisfaction.

'I don't see that we can do otherwise. Why?'

'Well –' Sir Charles sat down on the bed. His brow furrowed itself in thought. 'How can I put it best? At the moment we know something that nobody else does. The police are looking for Ellis. They think he's the murderer. Everyone knows that they think he's the murderer. So the real criminal must be feeling pretty good. He (or she) will be not exactly off his or her guard, but feeling – well, comfortable. Isn't it a pity to upset that state of things? Isn't that just our chance? I mean our chance of finding a connection between Babbington and one of these people. They don't know that anyone has connected this death with Babbington's death. They'll be unsuspicious. It's a chance in a hundred.'

'I see what you mean,' said Mr Satterthwaite. 'And I agree with you. It is a chance. But, all the same, I don't think we can take it. It is our duty as citizens to report this discovery of ours to the police at once. We have no right to withhold it from them.'

Sir Charles looked at him quizzically.

'You're the pattern of a good citizen, Satterthwaite. I've no doubt the orthodox thing must be done – but I'm not nearly such a good citizen as you are. I should have no scruples in keeping this find to myself for a day or two – only a day or two – eh? No? Well, I give in. Let us be pillars of law and order.'

'You see,' explained Mr Satterthwaite, 'Johnson is a friend of mine, and he was very decent about it all – let us into all the police were doing – gave us full information, and all that.'

'Oh, you're right,' sighed Sir Charles. 'Quite right. Only, after all, no one but me thought of looking under that gas stove. The idea never occurred to one of those thick-headed policemen . . . But have it your own way. I say, Satterthwaite, where do you think Ellis is now?'

'I presume,' said Mr Satterthwaite, 'that he got what he wanted. He was paid to disappear, and he did disappear – most effectually.'

'Yes,' said Sir Charles. 'I suppose that is the explanation.'

He gave a slight shiver.

'I don't like this room, Satterthwaite. Come out of it.'

CHAPTER 7

Plan Of Campaign

Sir Charles and Mr Satterthwaite arrived back in London the following evening.

The interview with Colonel Johnson had had to be very tactfully conducted. Superintendent Crossfield had not been too pleased that mere 'gentlemen' should have found what he and his assistants had missed. He was at some pains to save his face.

'Very creditable, indeed, sir. I confess I never thought of looking under the gas fire. As a matter of fact, it beats me what set you looking there.'

The two men had not gone into a detailed account of how theorizing from an ink-blot had led to the discovery. 'Just nosing around,' was how Sir Charles had put it.

'Still, look you did,' continued the Superintendent, 'and were justified. Not that what you've found is much surprise to me. You see, it stands to reason that if Ellis wasn't the murderer, he must have disappeared for some reason or other, and it's been in the back of my mind all along that blackmail might have been his line of business.'

One thing did arise from their discovery. Colonel Johnson was going to communicate with the Loomouth police. The death of Stephen Babbington ought certainly to be investigated.

'And if they find he died from nicotine poisoning, even Crossfield will admit the two deaths are connected,' said Sir Charles when they were speeding towards London.

He was still a little disgruntled at having had to hand over his discovery to the police.

Mr Satterthwaite had soothed him by pointing out that the information was not to be made public or given to the press.

'The guilty person will have no misgivings. The search for Ellis will still be continued.'

Sir Charles admitted that that was true.

On arrival in London, he explained to Mr Satterthwaite, he proposed to get in touch with Egg Lytton Gore. Her letter had been written from an address in Belgrave Square. He hoped that she might still be there.

Mr Satterthwaite gravely approved this course. He himself was anxious to see Egg. It was arranged that Sir Charles should ring her up as soon as they reached London.

Egg proved to be still in town. She and her mother were staying with relatives and were not returning to Loomouth for about a week. Egg was easily prevailed upon to come out and dine with the two men.

'She can't come here very well, I suppose,' said Sir Charles, looking round his luxurious flat. 'Her mother mightn't like it, eh? Of course we could have Miss Milray, too – but I'd rather not. To tell the truth, Miss Milray cramps my style a bit. She's so efficient that she gives me an inferiority complex.'

Mr Satterthwaite suggested his house. In the end it was arranged to dine at the Berkeley. Afterwards, if Egg liked, they could adjourn elsewhere.

Mr Satterthwaite noticed at once that the girl was looking thinner. Her eyes seemed larger and more feverish, her chin more decided. She was pale and had circles under her eyes. But her charm was as great as ever, her childish eagerness just as intense.

She said to Sir Charles, 'I knew you'd come . . .'

Her tone implied: 'Now that you've come everything will be all right . . .'

Mr Satterthwaite thought to himself: 'But she wasn't sure he'd come – she wasn't sure at all. She's been on tenterhooks. She's been fretting herself to death.' And he thought: 'Doesn't the man realize? Actors are usually vain enough . . . Doesn't he know the girl's head over ears in love with him?'

It was, he thought, an odd situation. That Sir Charles was overwhelmingly in love with the girl, he had no doubt whatever. She was equally in love with him. And the link between them – the link to which each of them clung frenziedly – was a crime – a double crime of a revolting nature.

During dinner little was said. Sir Charles talked about his

experiences abroad. Egg talked about Loomouth. Mr Satterthwaite encouraged them both whenever the conversation seemed likely to flag. When dinner was over they went to Mr Satterthwaite's house.

Mr Satterthwaite's house was on Chelsea Embankment. It was a large house, and contained many beautiful works of art. There were pictures, sculpture, Chinese porcelain, prehistoric pottery, ivories, miniatures and much genuine Chippendale and Hepplewhite furniture. It had an atmosphere about it of mellowness and understanding.

Egg Lytton Gore saw nothing, noticed nothing. She flung off her evening coat on to a chair and said:

'At last. Now tell me all about it.'

She listened with vivid interest whilst Sir Charles narrated their adventures in Yorkshire, drawing in her breath sharply when he described the discovery of the blackmailing letters.

'What happened after that we can only conjecture,' finished Sir Charles. 'Presumably Ellis was paid to hold his tongue and his escape was facilitated.'

But Egg shook her head.

'Oh, no,' she said. 'Don't you see? *Ellis is dead.*'

Both men were startled, but Egg reiterated her assertion.

'Of course he's dead. That's why he's disappeared so successfully that no one can find a trace of him. He knew too much, and so he was killed. Ellis is the third murder.'

Although neither of the two men had considered the possibility before, they were forced to admit that it did not entirely ring false.

'But look here, my dear girl,' argued Sir Charles, 'it's all very well to say Ellis is dead. Where's the body? There's twelve stone or so of solid butler to be accounted for.'

'I don't know where the body is,' said Egg. 'There must be lots of places.'

'Hardly,' murmured Mr Satterthwaite. 'Hardly . . .'

'Lots,' reiterated Egg. 'Let me see . . .' She paused for a moment. 'Attics, there are masses of attics that no one ever goes into. He's probably in a trunk in the attic.'

'Rather unlikely,' said Sir Charles. 'But possible, of course. It might evade discovery – for – er – a time.'

It was not Egg's way to avoid unpleasantness. She dealt immediately with the point in Sir Charles's mind.

'Smell goes up, not down. You'd notice a decaying body in the cellar much sooner than in the attic. And, anyway, for a long time people would think it was a dead rat.'

'If your theory were correct, it would point definitely to a man as the murderer. A woman couldn't drag a body round the house. In fact, it would be a pretty good feat for a man.'

'Well, there are other possibilities. There's a secret passage there, you know. Miss Sutcliffe told me so, and Sir Bartholomew told me he would show it to me. The murderer might have given Ellis the money and shown him the way to get out of the house – gone down the passage with him and killed him there. A woman could do that. She could stab him, or something, from behind. Then she'd just leave the body there and go back, and no one would ever know.'

Sir Charles shook his head doubtfully, but he no longer disputed Egg's theory.

Mr Satterthwaite felt sure that the same suspicion had come to him for a moment in Ellis's room when they had found the letters. He remembered Sir Charles's little shiver. The idea that Ellis might be dead had come to him then . . .

Mr Satterthwaite thought: 'If Ellis is dead, then we're dealing with a very dangerous person . . . Yes, a very dangerous person . . .' And suddenly he felt a cold chill of fear down his spine . . .

A person who had killed three times wouldn't hesitate to kill again . . .

They were in danger, all three of them – Sir Charles, and Egg, and he . . .

If they found out too much . . .

He was recalled by the sound of Sir Charles's voice.

'There's one thing I didn't understand in your letter, Egg. You spoke of Oliver Manders being in danger – of the police suspecting him. I can't see that they attach the least suspicion to him.'

It seemed to Mr Satterthwaite that Egg was very slightly discomposed. He even fancied that she blushed.

'Aha,' said Mr Satterthwaite to himself. 'Let's see how you get out of this, young lady.'

'It was silly of me,' said Egg. 'I got confused. I thought that Oliver arriving as he did, with what might have been a trumped-up excuse – well, I thought the police were sure to suspect him.'

Sir Charles accepted the explanation easily enough.

'Yes,' he said. 'I see.'

Mr Satterthwaite spoke.

'Was it a trumped-up excuse?' he said.

Egg turned on him.

'What do you mean?'

'It was an odd sort of accident,' said Mr Satterthwaite. 'I thought if it was a trumped-up excuse you might know.'

Egg shook her head.

'I don't know. I never thought about it. But why should Oliver pretend to have an accident if he didn't?'

'He might have had reasons,' said Sir Charles. 'Quite natural ones.'

He was smiling at her. Egg blushed crimson.

'Oh, no,' she said. '*No.*'

Sir Charles sighed. It occurred to Mr Satterthwaite that his friend had interpreted that blush quite wrongly. Sir Charles seemed a sadder and older man when he spoke again.

'Well,' he said, 'if our young friend is in no danger, where do I come in?'

Egg came forward quickly and caught him by the coat sleeve.

'You're not going away again. You're not going to give up? You're going to find out the truth – *the truth.* I don't believe anybody but you could find out the truth. You can. You will.'

She was tremendously in earnest. The waves of her vitality seemed to surge and eddy in the old-world air of the room.

'You believe in me?' said Sir Charles. He was moved.

'Yes, yes, yes. We're going to get at the truth. You and I together.'

'And Satterthwaite.'

'Of course, and Mr Satterthwaite,' said Egg without interest.

Mr Satterthwaite smiled covertly. Whether Egg wanted to include him or not, he had no intention of being left out. He was fond of mysteries, and he liked observing human nature, and he had a soft spot for lovers. All three tastes seemed likely to be gratified in this affair.

Sir Charles sat down. His voice changed. He was in command, directing a production.

'First of all we've got to clarify the situation. Do we, or do we not, believe that the same person killed Babbington and Bartholomew Strange?'

'Yes,' said Egg.

'Yes,' said Mr Satterthwaite.

'Do we believe that the second murder sprang directly from the first? I mean, do we believe that Bartholomew Strange was killed in order to prevent his revealing the facts of the first murder, or his suspicion about it?'

'Yes,' said Egg and Mr Satterthwaite again, but in unison this time.

'Then it is the *first* murder we must investigate, not the second –'

Egg nodded.

'In my mind, until we discover the *motive* for the first murder, we can hardly hope to discover the murderer. The motive presents extraordinary difficulty. Babbington was a harmless, pleasant, gentle old man without, one would say, an enemy in the world. Yet he was killed – and there must have been some *reason* for the killing. We've got to find that reason.'

He paused and then said in his ordinary everyday voice:

'Let's get down to it. What reasons are there for killing people? First, I suppose, gain.'

'Revenge,' said Egg.

'Homicidal mania,' said Mr Satterthwaite. 'The *crime passionel* would hardly apply in this case. But there's fear.'

Charles Cartwright nodded. He was scribbling on a piece of paper.

'That about covers the ground,' he said. 'First, *Gain*. Does anyone gain by Babbington's death? Has he any money – or expectation of money?'

'I should think it very unlikely,' said Egg.

'So should I, but we'd better approach Mrs Babbington on the point.'

'Then there's revenge. Did Babbington do any injury to anyone – perhaps in his young days? Did he marry the girl that some other man wanted? We'll have to look into that, too.'

'Then homicidal mania. Were both Babbington and Tollie killed by a lunatic? I don't think that theory will hold water. Even a lunatic has some kind of reasonableness in his crimes. I mean a lunatic might think himself divinely appointed to kill doctors, or to kill clergymen, but not to kill both. I think we can wash out the theory of homicidal mania. There remains *fear*.

'Now, frankly, that seems to me far the most likely solution. Babbington knew something about somebody – or he recognized somebody. He was killed to prevent him telling what that something was.'

'I can't see what someone like Mr Babbington could know that was damaging about anybody who was there that night.'

'Perhaps,' said Sir Charles, 'it was something that he didn't know that he knew.'

He went on, trying to make his meaning clear.

'It's difficult to say just what I mean. Suppose, for instance (this is only an instance) that Babbington saw a certain person in a certain place at a certain time. As far as he knows, there's no reason why that person shouldn't be there. But suppose also that that person had concocted a very clever alibi for some reason showing that at that particular time he was somewhere else a hundred miles away. Well, at any minute old Babbington, in the most innocent way in the world, might give the show away.'

'*I* see,' said Egg. 'Say there's a murder committed in London, and Babbington sees the man who did it at Paddington Station, but the man has proved that he didn't do it by having an alibi showing that he was at Leeds at the time. Then Babbington might give the whole show away.'

'That's what I mean exactly. Of course that's only an instance. It might be anything. Someone he saw that evening whom he'd known under a different name –'

'It might be something to do with a marriage,' said Egg. 'Clergymen do lots of marriages. Somebody who'd committed bigamy.'

'Or it might have to do with a birth or a death,' suggested Mr Satterthwaite.

'It's a very wide field,' said Egg, frowning. 'We'll have to get at it the other way. Work back from the people who were there.

Let's make a list. Who was at your house, and who was at Sir Bartholomew's.'

She took the paper and pencil from Sir Charles.

'The Dacres, they were at both. That woman like a wilted cabbage, what's her name – Wills. Miss Sutcliffe.'

'You can leave Angela out of it,' said Sir Charles. 'I've known her for years.'

Egg frowned mutinously.

'We can't do that sort of thing,' she said. 'Leave people out because we know them. We've got to be business-like. Besides, *I* don't know anything about Angela Sutcliffe. She's just as likely to have done it as anyone else, so far as I can see – more likely. All actresses have pasts. I think, on the whole, she's the most likely person.'

She gazed defiantly at Sir Charles. There was an answering spark in his eyes.

'In that case we mustn't leave out Oliver Manders.'

'How could it be Oliver? He'd met Mr Babbington ever so many times before.'

'He was at both places, and his arrival is a little – open to suspicion.'

'Very well,' said Egg. She paused, and then added: 'In that case I'd better put down Mother and myself as well . . . That makes six suspects.'

'I don't think –'

'We'll do it properly, or not at all.' Her eyes flashed.

Mr Satterthwaite made peace by offering refreshment. He rang for drinks.

Sir Charles strolled off into a far corner to admire a head of Negro sculpture. Egg came over to Mr Satterthwaite and slipped a hand through his arm.

'Stupid of me to have lost my temper,' she murmured. 'I *am* stupid – but why should the woman be excepted? Why is he so keen she should be? Oh, dear, why the devil am I so disgustingly jealous?'

Mr Satterthwaite smiled and patted her hand.

'Jealousy never pays, my dear,' he said. 'If you feel jealous, don't show it. By the way, did you really think young Manders might be suspected?'

Egg grinned – a friendly childish grin.

'Of course not. I put that in so as not to alarm the man.' She turned her head. Sir Charles was still moodily studying Negro sculpture. 'You know – I didn't want him to think I really have a pash for Oliver – because I haven't. How difficult everything is! He's gone back now to his "Bless you, my children," attitude. I don't want that at all.'

'Have patience,' counselled Mr Satterthwaite. 'Everything comes right in the end, you know.'

'I'm not patient,' said Egg. 'I want to have things at once, or even quicker.'

Mr Satterthwaite laughed, and Sir Charles turned and came towards them.

As they sipped their drinks, they arranged a plan of campaign. Sir Charles should return to Crow's Nest, for which he had not yet found a purchaser. Egg and her mother would return to Rose Cottage rather sooner than they had meant to do. Mrs Babbington was still living in Loomouth. They would get what information they could from her and then proceed to act upon it.

'We'll succeed,' said Egg. 'I know we'll succeed.'

She leaned forward to Sir Charles, her eyes glowing. She held out her glass to touch his.

'Drink to our success,' she commanded.

Slowly, very slowly, his eyes fixed on hers, he raised his glass to his lips.

'To success,' he said, 'and to the Future . . .'

Third Act

DISCOVERY

CHAPTER 1

Mrs Babbington

Mrs Babbington had moved into a small fisherman's cottage not far from the harbour. She was expecting a sister home from Japan in about six months. Until her sister arrived she was making no plans for the future. The cottage chanced to be vacant, and she took it for six months. She felt too bewildered by her sudden loss to move away from Loomouth. Stephen Babbington had held the living of St Petroch, Loomouth, for seventeen years. They had been, on the whole, seventeen happy and peaceful years, in spite of the sorrow occasioned by the death of her son Robin. Of her remaining children, Edward was in Ceylon, Lloyd was in South Africa, and Stephen was third officer on the *Angolia*. They wrote frequently and affectionately, but they could offer neither a home nor companionship to their mother.

Margaret Babbington was very lonely . . .

Not that she allowed herself much time for thinking. She was still active in the parish – the new vicar was unmarried, and she spent a good deal of time working in the tiny plot of ground in front of the cottage. She was a woman whose flowers were part of her life.

She was working there one afternoon when she heard the latch of the gate click, and looked up to see Sir Charles Cartwright and Egg Lytton Gore.

Margaret was not surprised to see Egg. She knew that the girl and her mother were due to return shortly. But she was surprised to see Sir Charles. Rumour had insisted that he had left the neighbourhood for good. There had been paragraphs copied from other papers about his doings in the South of France. There had been a board 'TO BE SOLD' stuck up in the garden of Crow's Nest. No one had expected Sir Charles to return. Yet return he had.

Mrs Babbington shook the untidy hair back from her hot forehead and looked ruefully at her earth-stained hands.

'I'm not fit to shake hands,' she said. 'I ought to garden in gloves, I know. I do start in them sometimes; but I always tear them off sooner or later. One can feel things so much better with bare hands.'

She led the way into the house. The tiny sitting-room had been made cosy with chintz. There were photographs and bowls of chrysanthemums.

'It's a great surprise seeing you, Sir Charles. I thought you had given up Crow's Nest for good.'

'I thought I had,' said the actor frankly. 'But sometimes, Mrs Babbington, our destiny is too strong for us.'

Mrs Babbington did not reply. She turned towards Egg, but the girl forestalled the words on her lips.

'Look here, Mrs Babbington. This isn't just a call. Sir Charles and I have got something very serious to say. Only – I – I should hate to upset you.'

Mrs Babbington looked from the girl to Sir Charles. Her face had gone rather grey and pinched.

'First of all,' said Sir Charles, 'I would like to ask you if you have had any communication from the Home Office?'

Mrs Babbington bowed her head.

'I see – well, perhaps that makes what we are about to say easier.'

'Is that what you have come about – this exhumation order?'

'Yes. Is it – I'm afraid it must be – very distressing to you.'

She softened to the sympathy in his voice.

'Perhaps I do not mind as much as you think. To some people the idea of exhumation is very dreadful – not to me. It is not the dead clay that matters. My dear husband is elsewhere – at peace – where no one can trouble his rest. No, it is not that. It is the idea that is a shock to me – the idea, a terrible one, that Stephen did not die a natural death. It seems so impossible – utterly impossible.'

'I'm afraid it must seem so to you. It did to me – to us – at first.'

'What do you mean by at first, Sir Charles?'

'Because the suspicion crossed my mind on the evening of your husband's death, Mrs Babbington. Like you, however, it seemed to me so impossible that I put it aside.'

'I thought so, too,' said Egg.

'You too,' Mrs Babbington looked at her wonderingly. 'You thought someone could have killed – Stephen?'

The incredulity in her voice was so great that neither of her visitors knew quite how to proceed. At last Sir Charles took up the tale.

'As you know, Mrs Babbington, I went abroad. When I was in the South of France I read in the paper of my friend Bartholomew Strange's death in almost exactly similar circumstances. I also got a letter from Miss Lytton Gore.'

Egg nodded.

'I was there, you know, staying with him at the time. Mrs Babbington, it was exactly the same – *exactly*. He drank some port and his face changed, and – and – well, it was just the same. He died two or three minutes later.'

Mrs Babbington shook her head slowly.

'I can't understand it. Stephen! Sir Bartholomew – a kind and clever doctor! Who could want to harm either of them? It must be a mistake.'

'Sir Bartholomew was proved to have been poisoned, remember,' said Sir Charles.

'Then it must have been the work of a lunatic.'

Sir Charles went on:

'Mrs Babbington, I want to get to the bottom of this. I want to find out the truth. And I feel there is no time to lose. Once the news of the exhumation gets about our criminal will be on the alert. I am assuming, for the sake of saving time, what the result of the autopsy on your husband's body will be. I am taking it that he, too, died of nicotine poisoning. To begin with, did you or he know anything about the use of pure nicotine?'

'I always use a solution of nicotine for spraying roses. I didn't know it was supposed to be poisonous.'

'I should imagine (I was reading up the subject last night) that in both cases the pure alkaloid must have been used. Cases of poisoning by nicotine are most unusual.'

Mrs Babbington shook her head.

'I really don't know anything about nicotine poisoning – except that I suppose inveterate smokers might suffer from it.'

'Did your husband smoke?'

'Yes.'

'Now tell me, Mrs Babbington, you have expressed the utmost surprise that anyone should want to do away with your husband. Does that mean that as far as you know he had no enemies?'

'I am sure Stephen had no enemies. Everyone was fond of him. People tried to hustle him sometimes,' she smiled a little tearfully. 'He was getting on, you know, and rather afraid of innovations, but everybody liked him. You couldn't dislike Stephen, Sir Charles.'

'I suppose, Mrs Babbington, that your husband didn't leave very much money?'

'No. Next to nothing. Stephen was not good at saving. He gave away far too much. I used to scold him about it.'

'I suppose he had no expectations from anyone? He wasn't the heir to any property?'

'Oh, no. Stephen hadn't many relations. He has a sister who is married to a clergyman in Northumberland, but they are very badly off, and all his uncles and aunts are dead.'

'Then it does not seem as though there were anyone who could benefit by Mr Babbington's death?'

'No, indeed.'

'Let us come back to the question of enemies for a minute. Your husband had no enemies, you say; but he may have had as a young man.'

Mrs Babbington looked sceptical.

'I should think it very unlikely. Stephen hadn't a quarrelsome nature. He always got on well with people.'

'I don't want to sound melodramatic,' Sir Charles coughed a little nervously. 'But – er – when he got engaged to you, for instance, there wasn't any disappointed suitor in the offing?'

A momentary twinkle came into Mrs Babbington's eyes.

'Stephen was my father's curate. He was the first young man I saw when I came home from school. I fell in love with him and he with me. We were engaged for four years, and then he got a living down in Kent, and we were able to get married. Ours was a very simple love story, Sir Charles – and a very happy one.'

Sir Charles bowed his head. Mrs Babbington's simple dignity was very charming.

Egg took up the rôle of questioner.

'Mrs Babbington, do you think your husband had met any of the guests at Sir Charles's that night before?'

Mrs Babbington looked slightly puzzled.

'Well, there were you and your mother, my dear, and young Oliver Manders.'

'Yes, but any of the others?'

'We had both seen Angela Sutcliffe in a play in London five years ago. Both Stephen and I were very excited that we were actually going to meet her.'

'You had never actually met her before?'

'No. We've never met any actresses – or actors, for the matter of that – until Sir Charles came to live here. And that,' added Mrs Babbington, 'was a great excitement. I don't think Sir Charles knows what a wonderful thing it was to us. Quite a breath of romance in our lives.'

'You hadn't met Captain and Mrs Dacres?'

'Was he the little man, and the woman with the wonderful clothes?'

'Yes.'

'No. Nor the other woman – the one who wrote plays. Poor thing, she looked rather out of it, I thought.'

'You're sure you'd never seen any of them before?'

'I'm quite sure I hadn't – and so I'm fairly sure Stephen hadn't, either. You see, we do everything together.'

'And Mr Babbington didn't say anything to you – anything at all,' persisted Egg, 'about the people you were going to meet, or about them, when he saw them?'

'Nothing beforehand – except that he was looking forward to an interesting evening. And when we got there – well, there wasn't much time –' Her face twisted suddenly.

Sir Charles broke in quickly.

'You must forgive us badgering you like this. But, you see, we feel that there must be *something*, if only we could get at it. There must be some *reason* for an apparently brutal and meaningless murder.'

'I see that,' said Mrs Babbington. 'If it was murder, there must be some reason . . . But I don't know – I can't imagine – what that reason could be.'

There was silence for a minute or two, then Sir Charles said:

'Can you give me a slight biographical sketch of your husband's career?'

Mrs Babbington had a good memory for dates. Sir Charles's final notes ran thus:

'Stephen Babbington, born Islington, Devon, 1868. Educated St Paul's School and Oxford. Ordained Deacon and received a title to the Parish of Hoxton, 1891. Priested 1892. Was Curate Eslington, Surrey, to Rev. Vernon Lorrimer, 1894–1899. Married Margaret Lorrimer, 1899, and presented to the living of Gilling, Kent. Transferred to living of St Petroch, Loomouth, 1916.'

'That gives us something to go upon,' said Sir Charles. 'Our best chance seems to me the time during which Mr Babbington was Vicar of St Mary's, Gilling. His earlier history seems rather far back to concern any of the people who were at my house that evening.'

Mrs Babbington shuddered.

'Do you really think – that one of them –?'

'I don't know what to think,' said Sir Charles. 'Bartholomew saw something or guessed something, and Bartholomew Strange died the same way, and five –'

'Seven,' said Egg.

'– of these people were also present. One of them must be guilty.'

'But why?' cried Mrs Babbington. 'Why? What motive could there be for anyone killing Stephen?'

'That,' said Sir Charles, 'is what we are going to find out.'

CHAPTER 2

Lady Mary

Mr Satterthwaite had come down to Crow's Nest with Sir Charles. Whilst his host and Egg Lytton Gore were visiting Mrs Babbington, Mr Satterthwaite was having tea with Lady Mary.

Lady Mary liked Mr Satterthwaite. For all her gentleness of manner, she was a woman who had very definite views on the subject of whom she did or did not like.

Mr Satterthwaite sipped China tea from a Dresden cup, and ate a microscopic sandwich and chatted. On his last visit they had found many friends and acquaintances in common. Their talk today began on the same subject, but gradually drifted into more intimate channels. Mr Satterthwaite was a sympathetic person – he listened to the troubles of other people and did not intrude his own. Even on his last visit it had seemed natural to Lady Mary to speak to him of her preoccupation with her daughter's future. She talked now as she would have talked to a friend of many years' standing.

'Egg is so headstrong,' she said. 'She flings herself into a thing heart and soul. You know, Mr Satterthwaite, I do not like the way she is – well, mixing herself up in this distressing business. It – Egg would laugh at me, I know – but it doesn't seem to be ladylike.'

She flushed as she spoke. Her brown eyes, gentle and ingenuous, looked with childish appeal at Mr Satterthwaite.

'I know what you mean,' he said. 'I confess that I don't quite like it myself. I know that it's simply an old-fashioned prejudice, but there it is. All the same,' he twinkled at her, 'we can't expect young ladies to sit at home and sew and shudder at the idea of crimes of violence in these enlightened days.'

'I don't like to think of murder,' said Lady Mary. 'I never, never dreamed that I should be mixed up in anything of that kind. It was dreadful.' She shivered. 'Poor Sir Bartholomew.'

'You didn't know him very well?' hazarded Mr Satterthwaite.

'I think I'd only met him twice. The first time about a year ago, when he came down to stay with Sir Charles for a weekend, and the second time was on that dreadful evening when poor Mr Babbington died. I was really most surprised when his invitation arrived. I accepted because I thought Egg would enjoy it. She hasn't many treats, poor child, and – well, she had seemed a little down in the mouth, as though she didn't take any interest in anything. I thought a big house-party might cheer her up.'

Mr Satterthwaite nodded.

'Tell me something about Oliver Manders,' he said. 'The young fellow rather interests me.'

'I think he's clever,' said Lady Mary. 'Of course, things have been difficult for him . . .'

She flushed, and then in answer to the plain inquiry of Mr Satterthwaite's glance she went on.

'You see, his father wasn't married to his mother . . .'

'Really? I had no idea of that.'

'Everyone knows about it down here, otherwise I wouldn't have said anything about it. Old Mrs Manders, Oliver's grandmother, lives at Dunboyne, that biggish house on the Plymouth road. Her husband was a lawyer down here. Her son went into a city firm and did very well. He's quite a rich man. The daughter was a good-looking girl, and she became absolutely infatuated with a married man. I blame him very much indeed. Anyway, in the end, after a lot of scandal, they went off together. His wife wouldn't divorce him. The girl died not long after Oliver was born. His uncle in London took charge of him. He and his wife had no children of their own. The boy divided his time between them and his grandmother. He always came down here for his summer holidays.'

She paused and then went on:

'I always felt sorry for him. I still do. I think that terribly conceited manner of his is a good deal put on.'

'I shouldn't be surprised,' said Mr Satterthwaite. 'It's a very common phenomenon. If I ever see anyone who appears to think a lot of themselves and boasts unceasingly, I always know that there's a secret sense of inferiority somewhere.'

'It seems very odd.'

'An inferiority complex is a very peculiar thing. Crippen, for instance, undoubtedly suffered from it. It's at the back of a lot of crimes. The desire to assert one's personality.'

'It seems very strange to me,' murmured Lady Mary.

She seemed to shrink a little. Mr Satterthwaite looked at her with an almost sentimental eye. He liked her graceful figure with the sloping shoulders, the soft brown of her eyes, her complete absence of make-up. He thought:

'She must have been a beauty when she was young . . .'

Not a flaunting beauty, not a rose – no, a modest, charming violet, hiding its sweetness . . .

His thoughts ran serenely in the idiom of his young days . . .

He remembered incidents in his own youth.

Presently he found himself telling Lady Mary about his own love affair – the only love affair he had ever had. Rather a poor love affair by the standards of today, but very dear to Mr Satterthwaite.

He told her about the Girl, and how pretty she was, and of how they had gone together to see the bluebells at Kew. He had meant to propose to her that day. He had imagined (so he put it) that she reciprocated his sentiments. And then, as they were standing looking at the bluebells, she had confided in him . . . He had discovered that she loved another. And he had hidden the thoughts surging in his breast and had taken up the rôle of the faithful Friend.

It was not, perhaps, a very full-blooded romance, but it sounded well in the dim-faded chintz and egg-shell china atmosphere of Lady Mary's drawing-room.

Afterwards Lady Mary spoke of her own life, of her married life, which had not been very happy.

'I was such a foolish girl – girls are foolish, Mr Satterthwaite. They are so sure of themselves, so convinced they know best. People write and talk a lot of a "woman's instinct". I don't believe, Mr Satterthwaite, that there is any such thing. There doesn't seem to be anything that warns girls against a certain type of man. Nothing in themselves, I mean. Their parents warn them, but that's no good – one doesn't believe. It seems dreadful to say so, but there is something attractive to a girl in being told anyone is a bad man. She thinks at once that her love will reform him.'

Mr Satterthwaite nodded gently.

'One knows so little. When one knows more, it is too late.'

She sighed.

'It was all my own fault. My people didn't want me to marry Ronald. He was well born, but he had a bad reputation. My father told me straight out that he was a wrong 'un. I didn't believe it. I believed that, for my sake, he would turn over a new leaf . . .'

She was silent a moment or two, dwelling on the past.

'Ronald was a very fascinating man. My father was quite right about him. I soon found that out. It's an old-fashioned thing to say – but he broke my heart. Yes, he broke my heart. I was always afraid – of what might come out next.'

Mr Satterthwaite, always intensely interested in other people's lives, made a cautious sympathetic noise.

'It may seem a very wicked thing to say, Mr Satterthwaite, but it was a relief when he got pneumonia and died . . . Not that I didn't care for him – I loved him up to the end – but I had no illusions about him any longer. And there was Egg –'

Her voice softened.

Such a funny little thing she was. A regular little roly-poly, trying to stand up and falling over – just like an egg; that's how that ridiculous nickname started . . .'

She paused again.

'Some books that I've read these last few years have brought a lot of comfort to me. Books on psychology. It seems to show that in many ways people can't help themselves. A kind of kink. Sometimes, in the most carefully brought-up families you get it. As a boy Ronald stole money at school – money that he didn't need. I can feel now that he couldn't help himself . . . He was born with a kink . . .'

Very gently, with a small handkerchief, Lady Mary wiped her eyes.

'It wasn't what I was brought up to believe,' she said apologetically. 'I was taught that everyone knew the difference between right and wrong. But somehow – I don't always think that is so.'

'The human mind is a great mystery,' said Mr Satterthwaite gently. 'As yet, we are going groping our way to understanding.

Without acute mania it may nevertheless occur that certain natures lack what I should describe as braking power. If you or I were to say, "I hate someone – I wish he were dead," the idea would pass from our minds as soon as the words were uttered. The brakes would work automatically. But, in some people the idea, or obsession, holds. They see nothing but the immediate gratification of the idea formed.'

'I'm afraid,' said Lady Mary, 'that that's rather too clever for me.'

'I apologize. I was talking rather bookishly.'

'Did you mean that young people have too little restraint nowadays? It sometimes worries me.'

'No, no, I didn't mean that at all. Less restraint is, I think, a good thing – wholesome. I suppose you are thinking of Miss – er – Egg.'

'I think you'd better call her Egg,' said Lady Mary, smiling.

'Thank you. Miss Egg does sound rather ridiculous.'

'Egg's very impulsive, and once she has set her mind on a thing nothing will stop her. As I said before, I hate her mixing herself up in all this, but she won't listen to me.'

Mr Satterthwaite smiled at the distress in Lady Mary's tone. He thought to himself:

'I wonder if she realizes for one minute that Egg's absorption in crime is neither more nor less than a new variant of that old, old game – the pursuit of the male by the female? No, she'd be horrified at the thought.'

'Egg says that Mr Babbington was poisoned also. Do you think that is true, Mr Satterthwaite? Or do you think it is just one of Egg's sweeping statements?'

'We shall know for certain after the exhumation.'

'There is to be an exhumation, then?' Lady Mary shivered. 'How terrible for poor Mrs Babbington. I can imagine nothing more awful for any woman.'

'You knew the Babbingtons fairly intimately, I suppose, Lady Mary?'

'Yes, indeed. They are – were – very dear friends of ours.'

'Do you know of anyone who could possibly have had a grudge against the vicar?'

'No, indeed.'

'He never spoke of such a person?'

'No.'

'And they got on well together?'

'They were perfectly mated – happy in each other and in their children. They were badly off, of course, and Mr Babbington suffered from rheumatoid arthritis. Those were their only troubles.'

'How did Oliver Manders get on with the vicar?'

'Well –' Lady Mary hesitated, 'they didn't hit it off very well. The Babbingtons were sorry for Oliver, and he used to go to the vicarage a good deal in the holidays to play with the Babbington boys – though I don't think he got on very well with them. Oliver wasn't exactly a popular boy. He boasted too much of the money he had and the tuck he took back to school, and all the fun he had in London. Boys are rather merciless about that sort of thing.'

'Yes, but later – since he's been grown up?'

'I don't think he and the vicarage people have seen much of each other. As a matter of fact Oliver was rather rude to Mr Babbington one day here, in my house. It was about two years ago.'

'What happened?'

'Oliver made a rather ill-bred attack on Christianity. Mr Babbington was very patient and courteous with him. That only seemed to make Oliver worse. He said, "All you religious people look down your noses because my father and mother weren't married. I suppose you'd call me the child of sin. Well, I admire people who have the courage of their convictions and don't care what a lot of hypocrites and parsons think." Mr Babbington didn't answer, but Oliver went on: "You won't answer that. It's ecclesiasticism and supersitition that's got the whole world into the mess it's in. I'd like to sweep away the churches all over the world." Mr Babbington smiled and said, "And the clergy, too?" I think it was his smile that annoyed Oliver. He felt he was not being taken seriously. He said, "I hate everything the Church stands for. Smugness, security and hypocrisy. Get rid of the whole canting tribe, I say!" And Mr Babbington smiled – he had a very sweet smile – and he said, "My dear boy, if you were to sweep away all the churches ever built or planned, you would still have to reckon with God."'

'What did young Manders say to that?'

'He seemed taken aback, and then he recovered his temper and went back to his usual sneering tired manner.

'He said, "I'm afraid the things I've been saying are rather bad form, padre, and not very easily assimilated by your generation."'

'You don't like young Manders, do you, Lady Mary?'

'I'm sorry for him,' said Lady Mary defensively.

'But you wouldn't like him to marry Egg.'

'Oh, no.'

'I wonder why, exactly?'

'Because – because, he isn't *kind* . . . and because –'

'Yes?'

'Because there's something in him, somewhere, that I don't understand. Something *cold* –'

Mr Satterthwaite looked at her thoughtfully for a minute or two, then he said:

'What did Sir Bartholomew Strange think of him? Did he ever mention him?'

'He said, I remember, that he found young Manders an interesting study. He said that he reminded him of a case he was treating at the moment in his nursing home. I said that I thought Oliver looked particularly strong and healthy, and he said, "Yes, his health's all right, but he's riding for a fall."'

She paused and then said:

'I suppose Sir Bartholomew was a very clever nerve specialist.'

'I believe he was very highly thought of by his own colleagues.'

'I liked him,' said Lady Mary.

'Did he ever say anything to you about Babbington's death?'

'No.'

'He never mentioned it at all?'

'I don't think so.'

'Do you think – it's difficult for you to tell, not knowing him well – but do you think he had anything on his mind?'

'He seemed in very good spirits – even amused by something – some private joke of his own. He told me at dinner that night that he was going to spring a surprise on me.'

'Oh, he did, did he?'

On his way home, Mr Satterthwaite pondered that statement.

What had been the surprise Sir Bartholomew had intended to spring on his guests?

Would it, when it came, have been as amusing as he pretended?

Or did that gay manner mask a quiet but indomitable purpose? Would anyone ever know?

CHAPTER 3

Re-Enter Hercule Poirot

'Frankly,' said Sir Charles, 'are we any forrader?'

It was a council of war. Sir Charles, Mr Satterthwaite and Egg Lytton Gore were sitting in the Ship-room. A fire burned in the grate, and outside an equinoctial gale was howling.

Mr Satterthwaite and Egg answered the question simultaneously.

'No,' said Mr Satterthwaite.

'Yes,' said Egg.

Sir Charles looked from one to the other of them. Mr Satterthwaite indicated gracefully that the lady should speak first.

Egg was silent a moment or two, collecting her ideas.

'We *are* further on,' she said at last. 'We are further on because we haven't found out anything. That sounds nonsense, but it isn't. What I mean is that we had certain vague sketchy ideas; we know now that certain of those ideas are definitely washouts.'

'Progress by elimination,' said Sir Charles.

'That's it.'

Mr Satterthwaite cleared his throat. He liked to define things.

'The idea of gain we can now put definitely away,' he said. 'There does not seem to be anybody who (in detective story parlance) could benefit by Stephen Babbington's death. Revenge seems equally out of the question. Apart from his naturally amiable and peace-loving disposition, I doubt if he were *important* enough to make enemies. So we are back at our last rather sketchy idea – fear. By the death of Stephen Babbington, someone gains security.'

'That's rather well put,' said Egg.

Mr Satterthwaite looked modestly pleased with himself. Sir Charles looked a little annoyed. His was the star part, not Satterthwaite's.

'The point is,' said Egg, 'what are we going to do next – actually *do*, I mean. Are we going to sleuth people, or what? Are we going to disguise ourselves and follow them?'

'My dear child,' said Sir Charles, 'I always did set my face against playing old men in beards, and I'm not going to begin now.'

'Then what –?' began Egg.

But she was interrupted. The door opened, and Temple announced:

'Mr Hercule Poirot.'

M. Poirot walked in with a beaming face and greeted three highly astonished people.

'It is permitted,' he said with a twinkle, 'that I assist at this conference? I am right, am I not – it is a conference?'

'My dear fellow, we're delighted to see you.' Sir Charles, recovering from his surprise, shook his guest warmly by the hand and pushed him into a large armchair. 'Where have you sprung from so suddenly?'

'I went to call upon my good friend Mr Satterthwaite in London. They tell me he is away – in Cornwall. *Eh bien*, it leaps to the eye where he has gone. I take the first train to Loomouth, and here I am.'

'Yes,' said Egg. 'But why have you come?'

'I mean,' she went on, flushing a little as she realized the possible discourtesy of her words, 'you have come for some particular reason?'

'I have come,' said Hercule Poirot, 'to admit an error.'

With an engaging smile he turned to Sir Charles and spread out his hands in a foreign gesture.

'Monsieur, it was in this very room that you declared yourself not satisfied. And I – I thought it was your dramatic instinct – I said to myself, he is a great actor, at all costs he must have drama. It seemed, I will admit it, incredible that a harmless old gentleman should have died anything but a natural death. Even now I do not see how poison could have been administered to him, nor can I guess at any motive. It seems absurd – fantastic. And yet – since then, there has been another death, a death under similar circumstances. One cannot attribute it to coincidence. No, there must be a link between the two. And so, Sir Charles, I have come to you to apologize – to say I, Hercule Poirot, was wrong, and to ask you to admit me to your councils.'

Sir Charles cleared his throat rather nervously. He looked a little embarrassed.

'That's extraordinarily handsome of you, M. Poirot. I don't know – taking up a lot of your time – I –'

He stopped, somewhat at a loss. His eyes consulted Mr Satterthwaite.

'It is very good of you—' began Mr Satterthwaite.

'No, no, it is not good of me. It is the curiosity – and, yes, the hurt to my pride. I must repair my fault. My time – that is nothing – why voyage after all? The language may be different, but everywhere human nature is the same. But of course if I am not welcome, if you feel that I intrude –'

Both men spoke at once.

'No, indeed.'

'Rather not.'

Poirot turned his eyes to the girl.

'And Mademoiselle?'

For a minute or two Egg was silent, and on all three men the same impression was produced. *Egg did not want the assistance of M. Poirot . . .*

Mr Satterthwaite thought he knew why. This was the private ploy of Charles Cartwright and Egg Lytton Gore. Mr Satterthwaite had been admitted – on sufferance – on the clear understanding that he was a negligible third party. But Hercule Poirot was different. His would be the leading rôle. Perhaps, even, Sir Charles might retire in his favour. And then Egg's plans would come to naught.

He watched the girl, sympathizing with her predicament. These men did not understand, but he, with his semi-feminine sensitiveness, realized her dilemma. Egg was fighting for her happiness . . .

What would she say?

After all what could she say? How could she speak the thoughts in her mind? '*Go away – go away – your coming may spoil everything – I don't want you here . . .*'

Egg Lytton Gore said the only thing she could say.

'Of course,' she said with a little smile. 'We'd love to have you.'

CHAPTER 4

A Watching Brief

'Good,' said Poirot. 'We are colleagues. *Eh bien*, you will put me, if you please, *au courant* of the situation.'

He listened with close attention whilst Mr Satterthwaite outlined the steps they had taken since returning to England. Mr Satterthwaite was a good narrator. He had the faculty of creating an atmosphere, of painting a picture. His description of the Abbey, of the servants, of the Chief Constable was admirable. Poirot was warm in his appreciation of the discovery by Sir Charles of the unfinished letters under the gas fire.

'*Ah, mais c'est magnifique, ça!*' he exclaimed ecstatically. 'The deduction, the reconstruction – perfect! You should have been a great detective, Sir Charles, instead of a great actor.'

Sir Charles received these plaudits with becoming modesty – his own particular brand of modesty. He had not received compliments on his stage performances for many years without perfecting a manner of acknowledging them.

'Your observation, too, it was very just,' said Poirot, turning to Mr Satterthwaite. 'That point of yours about his sudden familiarity with the butler.'

'Do you think there is anything in this Mrs de Rushbridger idea?' asked Sir Charles eagerly.

'It is an idea. It suggests – well, it suggests several things, does it not?'

Nobody was quite sure about the several things, but nobody liked to say so, so there was merely an assenting murmur.

Sir Charles took up the tale next. He described his and Egg's visit to Mrs Babbington and its rather negative result.

'And now you're up to date,' he said. 'You know what we do. Tell us: how does it all strike you?'

He leaned forward, boyishly eager.

Poirot was silent for some minutes. The other three watched him.

He said at last:

'Can you remember at all, mademoiselle, what type of port glass Sir Bartholomew had on his table?'

Sir Charles interposed just as Egg was shaking her head vexedly.

'I can tell you that.'

He got up and went to a cupboard, where he took out some heavy cut-glass sherry glasses.

'They were a slightly different shape, of course – more rounded – proper port shape. He got them at old Lammersfield's sale – a whole set of table glass. I admired them, and as there were more than he needed, he passed some of them on to me. They're good, aren't they?'

Poirot took the glass and turned it about in his hand.

'Yes,' he said. 'They are fine specimens. I thought something of that kind had been used.'

'Why?' cried Egg.

Poirot merely smiled at her.

'Yes,' he went on, 'the death of Sir Bartholomew Strange could be explained easily enough; but the death of Stephen Babbington is more difficult. Ah, if only it had been the other way about!'

'What do you mean, the other way about?' asked Mr Satterthwaite.

Poirot turned to him.

'Consider, my friend. Sir Bartholomew is a celebrated doctor. There might be many reasons for the death of a celebrated doctor. A doctor knows secrets, my friend, important secrets. A doctor has certain powers. Imagine a patient on the border line of sanity. A word from the doctor, and he will be shut away from the world – what a temptation to an unbalanced brain! A doctor may have suspicions about the sudden death of one of his patients – oh, yes, we can find plenty of motives for the death of a doctor.

'Now, as I say, if only it had been the other way about. If Sir Bartholomew Strange had died *first* and then Stephen Babbington. For Stephen Babbington might have seen something – might have suspected something about the first death.'

He sighed and then resumed.

'But one cannot have a case as one would like to have it. One must take a case as it is. Just one little idea I should like to suggest. I suppose it is not possible that Stephen Babbington's death was an accident – that the poison (if poison there was) was intended for Sir Bartholomew Strange, and that, by mistake, the wrong man was killed.'

'That's an ingenious idea,' said Sir Charles. His face, which had brightened, fell again. 'But I don't believe it will work. Babbington came into this room about four minutes before he was taken ill. During that time the only thing that passed his lips was half a cocktail – there was nothing in that cocktail –'

Poirot interrupted him.

'That you have already told me – but suppose, for the sake of argument, that there was something in that cocktail. Could it have been intended for Sir Bartholomew Strange and did Mr Babbington drink it by mistake?'

Sir Charles shook his head.

'Nobody who knew Tollie at all well would have tried poisoning him in a cocktail.'

'Why?'

'Because he never drank them.'

'Never?'

'Never.'

Poirot made a gesture of annoyance.

'Ah – this business – it goes all wrong. It does not make sense . . .'

'Besides,' went on Sir Charles, 'I don't see how any one glass could have been mistaken for another – or anything of that kind. Temple carried them round on a tray and everyone helped themselves to any glass they fancied.'

'True,' murmured Poirot. 'One cannot force a cocktail like one forces a card. What is she like, this Temple of yours? She is the maid who admitted me tonight – yes?'

'That's right. I've had her three or four years – nice steady girl – knows her work. I don't know where she came from – Miss Milray would know all about that.'

'Miss Milray, that is your secretary? The tall woman – somewhat of the Grenadier?'

'Very much of the Grenadier,' agreed Sir Charles.

'I have dined with you before on various occasions, but I do not think I met her until that night.'

'No, she doesn't usually dine with us. It was a question of thirteen, you see.'

Sir Charles explained the circumstances, to which Poirot listened very attentively.

'It was her own suggestion that she should be present? I see.'

He remained lost in thought a minute, then he said:

'Might I speak to this parlourmaid of yours, this Temple?'

'Certainly, my dear fellow.'

Sir Charles pressed a bell. It was answered promptly.

'You rang, sir?'

Temple was a tall girl of thirty-two or three. She had a certain smartness – her hair was well brushed and glossy, but she was not pretty. Her manner was calm and efficient.

'M. Poirot wants to ask you a few questions,' said Sir Charles.

Temple transferred her superior gaze to Poirot.

'We are talking of the night when Mr Babbington died here,' said Poirot. 'You remember that night?'

'Oh, yes, sir.'

'I want to know exactly how cocktails were served.'

'I beg your pardon, sir.'

'I want to know about the cocktails. Did you mix them?'

'No, sir, Sir Charles likes doing that himself. I brought in the bottles – the vermouth, the gin, and all that.'

'Where did you put them?'

'On the table there, sir.'

She indicated a table by the wall.

'The tray with the glasses stood here, sir. Sir Charles, when he had finished mixing and shaking, poured out the cocktails into the glasses. Then I took the tray round and handed it to the ladies and gentlemen.'

'Were all the cocktails on the tray you handed?'

'Sir Charles gave one to Miss Lytton Gore, sir; he was talking to her at the time, and he took his own. And Mr Satterthwaite' – her eyes shifted to him for a moment – 'came and fetched one for a lady – Miss Wills, I think it was.'

'Quite right,' said Mr Satterthwaite.

'The others I handed, sir; I think everyone took one except Sir Bartholomew.'

'Will you be so very obliging, Temple, as to repeat the performance. Let us put cushions for some of the people. I stood here, I remember – Miss Sutcliffe was there.'

With Mr Satterthwaite's help, the scene was reconstructed. Mr Satterthwaite was observant. He remembered fairly well where everyone had been in the room. Then Temple did her round. They ascertained that she had started with Mrs Dacres, gone on to Miss Sutcliffe and Poirot, and had then come to Mr Babbington, Lady Mary and Mr Satterthwaite, who had been sitting together.

This agreed with Mr Satterthwaite's recollection.

Finally Temple was dismissed.

'Pah,' cried Poirot. 'It does not make sense. Temple is the last person to handle those cocktails, but it was impossible for her to tamper with them in any way, and, as I say, one cannot force a cocktail on a particular person.'

'It's instinctive to take the one nearest to you,' said Sir Charles.

'Possibly that might work by handing the tray to the person first – but even then it would be very uncertain. The glasses are close together; one does not look particularly nearer than another. No, no, such a haphazard method could not be adopted. Tell me, Mr Satterthwaite, did Mr Babbington put his cocktail down, or did he retain it in his hand?'

'He put it down on this table.'

'Did anyone come near that table after he had done so?'

'No. I was the nearest person to him, and I assure you I did not tamper with it in any way – even if I could have done so unobserved.'

Mr Satterthwaite spoke rather stiffly. Poirot hastened to apologize.

'No, no, I am not making an accusation – *quelle idée*! But I want to be very sure of my facts. According to the analysis there was nothing out of the way in that cocktail – now it seems that, apart from that analysis there *could* have been nothing put in it. The same results from two different tests. But Mr Babbington ate or drank nothing else, and if he was poisoned by pure nicotine, death would have resulted very rapidly. You see where that leads us?'

'Nowhere, damn it all,' said Sir Charles.

'I would not say that – no, I would not say that. It suggests a very monstrous idea – which I hope and trust cannot be true. No, of course it is not true – the death of Sir Bartholomew proves that . . . And yet –'

He frowned, lost in thought. The others watched him curiously. He looked up.

'You see my point, do you not? Mrs Babbington was not at Melfort Abbey, therefore Mrs Babbington is cleared of suspicion.'

'Mrs Babbington – but no one has even dreamed of suspecting her.'

Poirot smiled beneficently.

'No? It is a curious thing that. The idea occurred to me at once – but at once. If the poor gentleman is not poisoned by the cocktail, then he must have been poisoned a very few minutes before entering the house. What way could there be? A capsule? Something, perhaps, to prevent indigestion. But who, then, could tamper with that? Only a wife. Who might, perhaps, have a motive that no one outside could possibly suspect? Again a wife.'

'But they were devoted to each other,' cried Egg indignantly. 'You don't understand a bit.'

Poirot smiled kindly at her.

'No. That is valuable. You know, but I do not. I see the facts unbiased by any preconceived notions. And let me tell you something, mademoiselle – in the course of my experience I have known five cases of wives murdered by devoted husbands, and twenty-two of husbands murdered by devoted wives. *Les femmes*, they obviously keep up appearances better.'

'I think you're perfectly horrid,' said Egg. 'I know the Babbingtons are not like that. It's – it's monstrous!'

'Murder is monstrous, mademoiselle,' said Poirot, and there was a sudden sternness in his voice.

He went on in a lighter tone.

'But I – who see only the facts – agree that Mrs Babbington did not do this thing. You see, she was not at Melfort Abbey. No, as Sir Charles has already said, the guilt must lie on a person who was present on both occasions – one of the seven on your list.'

There was a silence.

'And how do you advise us to act?' asked Satterthwaite.

'You have doubtless already your plan?' suggested Poirot.

Sir Charles cleared his throat.

'The only feasible thing seems to be a process of elimination,' he said. 'My idea was to take each person on that list and consider them guilty until they are proved innocent. I mean that we are to feel convinced ourselves that there *is* a connection between that person and Stephen Babbington, and we are to use all our ingenuity to find out what that connection can be. If we find no connection, then we pass on to the next person.'

'It is good psychology, that,' approved Poirot. 'And your methods?'

'That we have not yet had time to discuss. We should welcome your advice on that point, M. Poirot. Perhaps you yourself –'

Poirot held up a hand.

'My friend, do not ask me to do anything of an active nature. It is my lifelong conviction that any problem is best solved by thought. Let me hold what is called, I believe, the watching brief. Continue your investigations which Sir Charles is so ably directing –'

'And what about me?' thought Mr Satterthwaite. 'These actors! Always in the limelight playing the star part!'

'You will, perhaps, from time to time require what we may describe as Counsel's opinion. Me, I am the Counsel.'

He smiled at Egg.

'Does that strike you as the sense, mademoiselle?'

'Excellent,' said Egg. 'I'm sure your experience will be very useful to us.'

Her face looked relieved. She glanced at her watch and gave an exclamation.

'I must go home. Mother will have a fit.'

'I'll drive you home,' said Sir Charles.

They went out together.

CHAPTER 5

Division of Labour

'So you see, the fish has risen,' said Hercule Poirot.

Mr Satterthwaite, who had been looking at the door which had just closed behind the other two, gave a start as he turned to Poirot. The latter was smiling with a hint of mockery.

'Yes, yes, do not deny it. Deliberately you showed me the bait that day in Monte Carlo. Is it not so? You showed me the paragraph in the paper. You hoped that it would arouse my interest – that I should occupy myself with the affair.'

'It is true,' confessed Mr Satterthwaite. 'But I thought that I had failed.'

'No, no, you did not fail. You are a shrewd judge of human nature, my friend. I was suffering from ennui – I had – in the words of the child who was playing near us – "nothing to do". You came at the psychological moment. (And, talking of that, how much crime depends, too, on that psychological moment. The crime, the psychology, they go hand in hand.) But let us come back to our muttons. This is a crime very intriguing – it puzzles me completely.'

'Which crime – the first or the second?'

'There is only one – what you call the first and second murder are only the two halves of the same crime. The second half is simple – the motive – the means adopted –'

Mr Satterthwaite interrupted.

'Surely the means present an equal difficulty. There was no poison found in any of the wine, and the food was eaten by everybody.'

'No, no, it is quite different. In the first case it does not seem as though *anybody* could have poisoned Stephen Babbington. Sir Charles, if he had wanted to, could have poisoned *one* of his guests, but not any particular guest. Temple might possibly have slipped something into the last glass on the tray – but Mr Babbington's was not the last glass. No, the murder of Mr Babbington seems so impossible that I still feel that perhaps it *is* impossible – that he died a natural death after all . . . But that we shall soon know. The second case is different. Any one of the guests present, or the butler or parlourmaid, could have poisoned Bartholomew Strange. That presents no difficulty whatever.'

'I don't see –' began Mr Satterthwaite.

Poirot swept on:

'I will prove that to you some time by a little experiment. Let us pass on to another and most important matter. It is vital, you see (and you *will* see, I am sure, you have the sympathetic heart and the delicate understanding), that I must not play the part of what you call the spoilsport.'

'You mean –' began Mr Satterthwaite with the beginning of a smile.

'That Sir Charles must have the star part! He is used to it. And, moreover, it is expected of him by someone else. Am I not right? It does not please mademoiselle at all that I come to concern myself in this matter.'

'You are what we call "quick in the uptake", M. Poirot.'

'Ah, that, it leaps to the eye! I am of a very susceptible nature – I wish to assist a love affair – not to hinder it. You and I, my friend, must work together in this – to the honour and glory of Charles Cartwright; is it not so? When the case is solved –'

'If –' said Mr Satterthwaite mildly.

'When! I do not permit myself to fail.'

'Never?' asked Mr Satterthwaite searchingly.

'There have been times,' said Poirot with dignity, 'when for a short time, I have been what I suppose you would call slow in the take-up. I have not perceived the truth as soon as I might have done.'

'But you've never failed altogether?'

The persistence of Mr Satterthwaite was curiosity, pure and simple. He wondered . . .

'*Eh bien*,' said Poirot. 'Once. Long ago, in Belgium. We will not talk of it . . .'

Mr Satterthwaite, his curiosity (and his malice) satisfied, hastened to change the subject.

'Just so. You were saying that when the case is solved –'

'Sir Charles will have solved it. That is essential. I shall have been a little cog in the wheel,' he spread out his hands. 'Now and then, here and there, I shall say a little word – just one little word – a hint, no more. I desire no honour – no renown. I have all the renown I need.'

Mr Satterthwaite studied him with interest. He was amused by the naïve conceit, the immense egoism of the little man. But he did not make the easy mistake of considering it mere empty boasting. An Englishman is usually modest about what he does well, sometimes pleased with himself over something he does badly; but a Latin has a truer appreciation of his own powers. If he is clever he sees no reason for concealing the fact.

'I should like to know,' said Mr Satterthwaite, 'it would interest me very much – just what do you yourself hope to get out of this business? Is it the excitement of the chase?'

Poirot shook his head.

'No – no – it is not that. Like the *chien de chasse*, I follow the scent, and I get excited, and once on the scent I cannot be called off it. All that is true. But there is more . . . It is – how shall I put it? – a passion for getting at the *truth*. In all the world there is nothing so curious and so interesting and so beautiful as truth . . .'

There was silence for a little while after Poirot's words.

Then he took up the paper on which Mr Satterthwaite had carefully copied out the seven names, and read them aloud.

'Mrs Dacres, Captain Dacres, Miss Wills, Miss Sutcliffe, Lady Mary Lytton Gore, Miss Lytton Gore, Oliver Manders.

'Yes,' he said, 'suggestive, is it not?'

'What is suggestive about it?'

'The order in which the names occur.'

'I don't think there is anything suggestive about it. We just wrote the names down without any particular order about it.'

'Exactly. The list is headed by Mrs Dacres. I deduce from that that she is considered the most likely person to have committed the crime.'

'Not the most likely,' said Mr Satterthwaite. 'The least unlikely would express it better.'

'And a third phrase would express it better still. She is perhaps the person you would all *prefer* to have committed the crime.'

Mr Satterthwaite opened his lips impulsively, then met the gentle quizzical gaze of Poirot's shining green eyes, and altered what he had been about to say.

'I wonder – perhaps, M. Poirot, you are right – unconsciously that may be true.'

'I would like to ask you something, Mr Satterthwaite.'

'Certainly – certainly,' Mr Satterthwaite answered complacently.

'From what you have told me, I gather that Sir Charles and Miss Lytton Gore went together to interview Mrs Babbington.'

'Yes.'

'You did not accompany them?'

'No. Three would have been rather a crowd.'

Poirot smiled.

'And also, perhaps, your inclinations led you elsewhere. You had, as they say, different fish to fry. Where did you go, Mr Satterthwaite?'

'I had tea with Lady Mary Lytton Gore,' said Mr Satterthwaite stiffly.

'And what did you talk about?'

'She was so good as to confide in me some of the troubles of her early married life.'

He repeated the substance of Lady Mary's story. Poirot nodded his head sympathetically.

'That is so true to life – the idealistic young girl who marries the bad hat and will listen to nobody. But did you talk of nothing else? Did you, for instance, not speak of Mr Oliver Manders?'

'As a matter of fact we did.'

'And you learnt about him – what?'

Mr Satterthwaite repeated what Lady Mary had told him. Then he said:

'What made you think we had talked of him?'

'Because you went there for that reason. Oh, yes, do not protest. You may *hope* that Mrs Dacres or her husband committed the crime, but you *think* that young Manders did.'

He stilled Mr Satterthwaite's protests.

'Yes, yes, you have the secretive nature. You have your ideas, but you like keeping them to yourself. I have sympathy with you. I do the same myself . . .'

'I don't suspect him – that's absurd. But I just wanted to know more about him.'

'That is as I say. He is your instinctive choice. I, too, am interested in that young man. I was interested in him on the night of the dinner here, because I saw –'

'What did you see?' asked Mr Satterthwaite eagerly.

'I saw that there were two people at least (perhaps more) who were playing a part. One was Sir Charles.' He smiled. 'He was playing the naval officer, am I not right? That is quite natural. A great actor does not cease to act because he is not on the stage any more. But young Manders, he too was acting. He was playing the part of the bored and blasé young man – but in reality he was neither bored nor blasé – he was very keenly alive. And therefore, my friend, I noticed him.'

'How did you know I'd been wondering about him?'

'In many little ways. You had been interested in that accident of his that brought him to Melfort Abbey that night. You had not gone with Sir Charles and Miss Lytton Gore to see Mrs Babbington. Why? Because you wanted to follow out some line of your own unobserved. You went to Lady Mary's to find out about someone. Who? It could only be someone local. Oliver Manders. And then, most characteristic, you put his name at the bottom of the list. Who are really the least likely suspects in your mind – Lady Mary and Mademoiselle Egg – but you put his name after theirs, because he is your dark horse, and you want to keep him to yourself.'

'Dear me,' said Mr Satterthwaite. 'Am I really that kind of man?'

'*Précisément.* You have shrewd judgment and observation, and you like keeping its results to yourself. Your opinions of people are your private collection. You do not display them for all the world to see.'

'I believe,' began Mr Satterthwaite, but he was interrupted by the return of Sir Charles.

The actor came in with a springing buoyant step.

'Brrr,' he said. 'It's a wild night.'

He poured himself out a whisky and soda.

Mr Satterthwaite and Poirot both declined.

'Well,' said Sir Charles, 'let's map out our plan of campaign.

Where's that list, Satterthwaite? Ah, thanks. Now M. Poirot, Counsel's opinion, if you please. How shall we divide up the spadework?'

'How would you suggest yourself, Sir Charles?'

'Well, we might divide these people up – division of labour – eh? First, there's Mrs Dacres. Egg seems rather keen to take her on. She seems to think that anyone so perfectly turned out won't get impartial treatment from mere males. It seems quite a good idea to approach her through the professional side. Satterthwaite and I might work the other gambit as well if it seemed advisable. Then there's Dacres. I know some of his racing pals. I daresay I could pick up something that way. Then there's Angela Sutcliffe.'

'That also seems to be your work, Cartwright,' said Mr Satterthwaite. 'You know her pretty well, don't you?'

'Yes. That's why I'd rather somebody else tackled her . . . Firstly,' he smiled ruefully, 'I shall be accused of not putting my back into the job, and secondly – well – she's a friend – you understand?'

'*Parfaitement, parfaitement* – you feel the natural delicacy. It is most understandable. This good Mr Satterthwaite – he will replace you in the task.'

'Lady Mary and Egg – they don't count, of course. What about young Manders? His presence on the night of Tollie's death was an accident; still, I suppose we ought to include him.'

'Mr Satterthwaite will look after young Manders,' said Poirot. 'But I think, Sir Charles, you have missed out a name on your list. You have passed over Miss Muriel Wills.'

'So I have. Well, if Satterthwaite takes on Manders, I'll take on Miss Wills. Is that settled? Any suggestions, M. Poirot?'

'No, no – I do not think so. I shall be interested to hear your results.'

'Of course – that goes without saying. Another idea: If we procured photographs of these people we might use them in making inquiries in Gilling.'

'Excellent,' approved Poirot. 'There was something – ah, yes, your friend, Sir Bartholomew, he did not drink cocktails, but he did drink the port?'

'Yes, he had a particular weakness for port.'

'It seems odd to me that he did not taste anything unusual. Pure nicotine has a most pungent and unpleasant taste.'

'You've got to remember,' said Sir Charles, 'that there probably wasn't any nicotine in the port. The contents of the glass were analysed, remember.'

'Ah, yes – foolish of me. But, however it was administered – nicotine has a very disagreeable taste.'

'I don't know that that would matter,' said Sir Charles slowly. 'Tollie had a very bad go of influenza last spring, and it left him with his sense of taste and smell a good deal impaired.'

'Ah, yes,' said Poirot thoughtfully. 'That might account for it. That simplifies things considerably.'

Sir Charles went to the window and looked out.

'Still blowing a gale. I'll send for your things, M. Poirot. The Rose and Crown is all very well for enthusiastic artists, but I think you'd prefer proper sanitation and a comfortable bed.'

'You are extremely amiable, Sir Charles.'

'Not at all. I'll see to it now.'

He left the room.

Poirot looked at Mr Satterthwaite.

'If I may permit myself a suggestion.'

'Yes?'

Poirot leaned forward, and said in a low voice:

'*Ask young Manders why he faked an accident.* Tell him the police suspect him – and see what he says.'

CHAPTER 6

Cynthia Dacres

The showrooms of Ambrosine Ltd were very pure in appearance. The walls were a shade just off white – the thick pile carpet was so neutral as to be almost colourless – so was the upholstery. Chromium gleamed here and there, and on one wall was a gigantic geometric design in vivid blue and lemon yellow. The room had been designed by Mr Sydney Sandford – the newest and youngest decorator of the moment.

Egg Lytton Gore sat in an arm-chair of modern design – faintly reminiscent of a dentist's chair, and watched exquisite snake-like young women with beautiful bored faces pass sinuously before her. Egg was principally concerned with endeavouring to appear as though fifty or sixty pounds was a mere bagatelle to pay for a dress.

Mrs Dacres, looking as usual marvellously unreal, was (as Egg put it to herself) doing her stuff.

'Now, do you like this? Those shoulder knots – rather amusing, don't you think? And the waistline's rather penetrating. I shouldn't have the red lead colour, though – I should have it in the new colour – Espanol – most attractive – like mustard, with a dash of cayenne in it. How do you like Vin Ordinaire? Rather absurd, isn't it? Quite penetrating and ridiculous. Clothes simply must not be serious nowadays.'

'It's very difficult to decide,' said Egg. 'You see' – she became confidential – 'I've never been able to afford any clothes before. We were always so dreadfully poor. I remembered how simply marvellous you looked that night at Crow's Nest, and I thought, "Now that I've got money to spend, I shall go to Mrs Dacres and ask her to advise me." I did admire you so much that night.'

'My dear, how charming of you. I simply adore dressing a

young girl. It's so important that girls shouldn't look raw – if you know what I mean.'

'Nothing raw about you,' thought Egg ungratefully. 'Cooked to a turn, you are.'

'You've got so much personality,' continued Mrs Dacres. 'You mustn't have anything at all ordinary. Your clothes must be simple and penetrating – and just faintly visible. You understand? Do you want several things?'

'I thought about four evening frocks, and a couple of day things, and a sports suit or two – that sort of thing.'

The honey of Mrs Dacres's manner became sweeter. It was fortunate that she did not know that at that moment Egg's bank balance was exactly fifteen pounds twelve shillings, and that the said balance had got to last her until December.

More girls in gowns filed past Egg. In the intervals of technical conversation, Egg interspersed other matters.

'I suppose you've never been to Crow's Nest since?' she said.

'No. My dear, I couldn't. It was *so* upsetting – and, anyway, I always think Cornwall is rather terribly artisty . . . I simply cannot bear artists. Their bodies are always such a curious shape.'

'It was a shattering business, wasn't it?' said Egg. 'Old Mr Babbington was rather a pet, too.'

'Quite a period piece, I should imagine,' said Mrs Dacres.

'You'd met him before somewhere, hadn't you?'

'That dear old dug-out? Had I? I don't remember.'

'I think I remember his saying so,' said Egg. 'Not in Cornwall, though. I think it was at a place called Gilling.'

'Was it?' Mrs Dacres's eyes were vague. 'No, Marcelle – *Petite Scandale* is what I want – the Jenny model – and after that blue Patou.'

'Wasn't it extraordinary,' said Egg, 'about Sir Bartholomew being poisoned?'

'My dear, it was too penetrating for words! It's done me a world of good. All sorts of dreadful women come and order frocks from me just for the sensation. Now this Patou model would be perfect for you. Look at that perfectly useless and ridiculous frill – it makes the whole thing adorable. Young without being tiresome. Yes, poor Sir Bartholomew's death has been rather a godsend to me. There's just an off-chance, you see, that I might have murdered him. I've rather played up to that. Extraordinary fat women come and positively goggle at me. Too penetrating. And then, you see –'

But she was interrupted by the advent of a monumental American, evidently a valued client.

While the American was unburdening herself of her requirements, which sounded comprehensive and expensive, Egg managed to make an unobtrusive exit, telling the young lady who had succeeded Mrs Dacres that she would think it over before making a final choice.

As she emerged into Bruton Street, Egg glanced at her watch. It was twenty minutes to one. Before very long she might be able to put her second plan into operation.

She walked as far as Berkeley Square, and then slowly back again. At one o'clock she had her nose glued to a window displaying Chinese *objets d'art*.

Miss Doris Sims came rapidly out into Bruton Street and turned in the direction of Berkeley Square. Just before she got there a voice spoke at her elbow.

'Excuse me,' said Egg, 'but can I speak to you a minute?'

The girl turned, surprised.

'You're one of the mannequins at Ambrosine's, aren't you? I noticed you this morning. I hope you won't be frightfully offended if I say I think you've got simply the most perfect figure I've ever seen.'

Doris Sims was not offended. She was merely slightly confused.

'It's very kind of you, I'm sure, madam,' she said.

'You look frightfully good-natured, too,' said Egg. 'That's why I'm going to ask you a favour. Will you have lunch with me at the Berkeley or the Ritz and let me tell you about it?'

After a moment's hesitation Doris Sims agreed. She was curious and she liked good food.

Once established at a table and lunch ordered, Egg plunged into explanations.

'I hope you'll keep this to yourself,' she said. 'You see, I've got a job – writing up various professions for women. I want you to tell me all about the dressmaking business.'

Doris looked slightly disappointed, but she complied amiably enough, giving bald statements as to hours, rates of pay, conveniences and inconveniences of her employment. Egg entered particulars in a little note-book.

'It's awfully kind of you,' she said. 'I'm very stupid at this. It's quite new to me. You see I'm frightfully badly off, and this little bit of journalistic work will make all the difference.'

She went on confidentially.

'It was rather nerve on my part, walking into Ambrosine's and pretending I could buy lots of your models. Really, I've got just a few pounds of my dress allowance to last me till Christmas. I expect Mrs Dacres would be simply wild if she knew.'

Doris giggled.

'I should say she would.'

'Did I do it well?' asked Egg. 'Did I look as though I had money?'

'You did it splendidly, Miss Lytton Gore. Madam thinks you're going to get quite a lot of things.'

'I'm afraid she'll be disappointed,' said Egg.

Doris giggled more. She was enjoying her lunch, and she felt attracted to Egg. 'She may be a Society young lady,' she thought to herself, 'but she doesn't put on airs. She's as natural as can be.'

These pleasant relations once established, Egg found no difficulty in inducing her companion to talk freely on the subject of her employer.

'I always think,' said Egg, 'that Mrs Dacres looks a frightful cat. Is she?'

'None of us like her, Miss Lytton Gore, and that's a fact. But she's clever, of course, and she's got a rare head for business. Not like some Society ladies who take up the dressmaking business and go bankrupt because their friends get clothes and don't pay. She's as hard as nails, Madam is – though I will say she's fair enough – and she's got real taste – she knows what's what, and she's clever at getting people to have the style that suits them.'

'I suppose she makes a lot of money?'

A queer knowing look came into Doris's eye.

'It's not for me to say anything – or to gossip.'

'Of course not,' said Egg. 'Go on.'

'But if you ask me – the firm's not far off Queer Street. There was a Jewish gentleman came to see Madam, and there have been one or two things – it's my belief she's been borrowing to keep going in the hope that trade would revive, and that she's got in deep. Really, Miss Lytton Gore, she looks terrible sometimes. Quite desperate. I don't know what she'd look like without her make-up. I don't believe she sleeps of nights.'

'What's her husband like?'

'He's a queer fish. Bit of a bad lot, if you ask me. Not that we ever see much of him. None of the other girls agree with me, but I believe she's very keen on him still. Of course a lot of nasty things have been said –'

'Such as?' asked Egg.

'Well, I don't like to repeat things. I never have been one for that.'

'Of course not. Go on, you were saying –?'

'Well, there's been a lot of talk among the girls. About a young fellow – very rich and very soft. Not exactly balmy, if you know what I mean – sort of betwixt and between. Madam's been running him for all she was worth. He might have put things right – he was soft enough for anything – but then he was ordered on a sea voyage – suddenly.'

'Ordered by whom – a doctor?'

'Yes, someone in Harley Street. I believe now that it was the same doctor who was murdered up in Yorkshire – poisoned, so they said.'

'Sir Bartholomew Strange?'

'That was the name. Madam was at the house-party, and we girls said among ourselves – just laughing, you know – well, we said, supposing Madame did him in – out of revenge, you know! Of course it was just *fun* –'

'Naturally,' said Egg. 'Girlish fun. I quite understand. You know, Mrs Dacres is quite my idea of a murderess – so hard and remorseless.'

'She's ever so hard – and she's got a wicked temper! When she lets go, there's not one of us dares to come near her. They say her husband's frightened of her – and no wonder.'

'Have you ever heard her speak of anyone called Babbington or of a place in Kent – Gilling?'

'Really, now, I can't call to mind that I have.'

Doris looked at her watch and uttered an exclamation.

'Oh, dear, I must hurry. I shall be late.'

'Goodbye, and thanks so much for coming.'

'It's been a pleasure, I'm sure. Goodbye, Miss Lytton Gore, and I hope the article will be a great success. I shall look out for it.'

'You'll look in vain, my girl,' thought Egg, as she asked for her bill.

Then, drawing a line through the supposed jottings for the article, she wrote in her little note-book:

'Cynthia Dacres. Believed to be in financial difficulties. Described as having a "wicked temper". Young man (rich) with whom she was believed to be having an affair was ordered on sea voyage by Sir Bartholomew Strange. Showed no reaction at mention of Gilling or at statement that Babbington knew her.'

'There doesn't seem much there,' said Egg to herself. 'A possible motive for the murder of Sir Bartholomew, but very thin. M. Poirot may be able to make something of that. I can't.'

CHAPTER 7

Captain Dacres

Egg had not yet finished her programme for the day. Her next move was to St John's House, in which building the Dacres had a flat. St John's House was a new block of extremely expensive flats. There were sumptuous window-boxes and uniformed porters of such magnificence that they looked like foreign generals.

Egg did not enter the building. She strolled up and down on the opposite side of the street. After about an hour of this she calculated that she must have walked several miles. It was half-past five.

Then a taxi drew up at the Mansions, and Captain Dacres alighted from it. Egg allowed three minutes to elapse, then she crossed the road and entered the building.

Egg pressed the door-bell of No. 3. Dacres himself opened the door. He was still engaged in taking off his overcoat.

'Oh,' said Egg. 'How do you do? You do remember me, don't you? We met in Cornwall, and again in Yorkshire.'

'Of course – of course. In at the death both times, weren't we? Come in, Miss Lytton Gore.'

'I wanted to see your wife. Is she in?'

'She's round in Bruton Street – at her dressmaking place.'

'I know. I was there today. I thought perhaps she'd be back by now, and that she wouldn't mind, perhaps, if I came here – only, of course, I suppose I'm being a frightful bother –'

Egg paused appealingly.

Freddie Dacres said to himself:

'Nice looking filly. Damned pretty girl, in fact.'

Aloud he said:

'Cynthia won't be back till well after six. I've just come back from Newbury. Had a rotten day and left early. Come round to the Seventy-Two Club and have a cocktail?'

Egg accepted, though she had a shrewd suspicion that Dacres had already had quite as much alcohol as was good for him.

Sitting in the underground dimness of the Seventy-Two Club, and sipping a Martini, Egg said: 'This is great fun. I've never been here before.'

Freddie Dacres smiled indulgently. He liked a young and pretty girl. Not perhaps as much as he liked some other things – but well enough.

'Upsettin' sort of time, wasn't it?' he said. 'Up in Yorkshire, I mean. Something rather amusin' about a doctor being poisoned – you see what I mean – wrong way about. A doctor's a chap who poisons other people.'

He laughed uproariously at his own remark and ordered another pink gin.

'That's rather clever of you,' said Egg. 'I never thought of it that way before.'

'Only a joke, of course,' said Freddie Dacres.

'It's odd, isn't it,' said Egg, 'that when we meet it's always at a death.'

'Bit odd,' admitted Captain Dacres. 'You mean the old clergyman chap at what's his name's – the actor fellow's place?'

'Yes. It was very queer the way he died so suddenly.'

'Damn' disturbin',' said Dacres. 'Makes you feel a bit gruey, fellows popping off all over the place. You know, you think "my turn next", and it gives you the shivers.'

'You knew Mr Babbington before, didn't you, at Gilling?'

'Don't know the place. No, I never set eyes on the old chap before. Funny thing is he popped off just the same way as old Strange did. Bit odd, that. Can't have been bumped off, too, I suppose?'

'Well, what do you think?'

Dacres shook his head.

'Can't have been,' he said decisively. 'Nobody murders parsons. Doctors are different.'

'Yes,' said Egg. 'I suppose doctors are different.'

''Course they are. Stands to reason. Doctors are interfering devils.' He slurred the words a little. He leant forward. 'Won't let well alone. Understand?'

'No,' said Egg.

'They monkey about with fellows' lives. They've got a damned sight too much power. Oughtn't to be allowed.'

'I don't quite see what you mean.'

'M' dear girl, I'm *telling* you. Get a fellow shut up – that's what I mean – put him in hell. God, they're cruel. Shut him up and keep the stuff from him – and however much you beg and pray they won't give it you. Don't care a damn what torture you're in. That's doctors for you. I'm telling you – and I *know*.'

His face twitched painfully. His little pinpoint pupils stared past her.

'It's hell, I tell you – hell. And they call it curing you! Pretend they're doing a decent action. Swine!'

'Did Sir Bartholomew Strange –?' began Egg cautiously.

He took the words out of her mouth.

'Sir Bartholomew Strange. Sir Bartholomew Humbug. I'd like to know what goes on in that precious Sanatorium of his. Nerve cases. That's what they say. You're in there and you can't get out. And they say you've gone of your own free will. Free will! Just because they get hold of you when you've got the horrors.'

He was shaking now. His mouth drooped suddenly.

'I'm all to pieces,' he said apologetically. 'All to pieces.' He called to the waiter, pressed Egg to have another drink, and when she refused, ordered one himself.

'That's better,' he said as he drained the glass. 'Got my nerve back now. Nasty business losing your nerve. Mustn't make Cynthia angry. She told me not to talk.' He nodded his head once or twice. 'Wouldn't do to tell the police all this,' he said. 'They might think I'd bumped old Strange off. Eh? You realize, don't you, that someone must have done it? One of us must have killed him. That's a funny thought. Which of us? That's the question.'

'Perhaps *you* know which,' said Egg.

'What d'you say that for? Why should I know?'

He looked at her angrily and suspiciously.

'I don't know anything about it, I tell you. I wasn't going to take that damnable "cure" of his. No matter what Cynthia said – I wasn't going to take it. He was up to something – they were both up to something. But they couldn't fool me.'

He drew himself up.

'I'm a shtrong man, Mish Lytton Gore.'

'I'm sure you are,' said Egg. 'Tell me, do you know anything of a Mrs de Rushbridger who is at the Sanatorium?'

'Rushbridger? Rushbridger? Old Strange said something about her. Now what was it? Can't remember anything.'

He sighed, shook his head.

'Memory's going, that's what it is. And I've got enemies – a lot of enemies. They may be spying on me now.'

He looked round uneasily. Then he leant across the table to Egg.

'What was that woman doing in my room that day?'

'What woman?'

'Rabbit-faced woman. Writes plays. It was the morning after – after he died. I'd just come up from breakfast. She came out of my room and went through the baize door at the end of the passage – went through into the servants' quarters. Odd, eh? Why did she go into my room? What did she think she'd find there? What did she want to go nosing about for, anyway? What's it got to do with her?' He leaned forward confidentially. 'Or do you think it's true what Cynthia says?'

'What does Mrs Dacres say?'

'Says I imagined it. Says I was "seeing things".' He laughed uncertainly. 'I do see things now and again. Pink mice – snakes – all that sort of thing. But seein' a woman's different . . . I *did* see her. She's a queer fish, that woman. Nasty sort of eye she's got. Goes through you.'

He leaned back on the soft couch. He seemed to be dropping asleep.

Egg got up.

'I must be going. Thank you very much, Captain Dacres.'

'Don't thank me. Delighted. Absolutely delighted . . .'

His voice tailed off.

'I'd better go before he passes out altogether,' thought Egg.

She emerged from the smoky atmosphere of the Seventy-Two Club into the cool evening air.

Beatrice, the housemaid, had said that Miss Wills poked and pried. Now came this story from Freddie Dacres. What *had* Miss Wills been looking for? What had she found? Was it possible that Miss Wills *knew* something?

Was there anything in this rather muddled story about Sir

Bartholomew Strange? Had Freddie Dacres secretly feared and hated him?

It seemed possible.

But in all this no hint of any guilty knowledge in the Babbington case.

'How odd it would be,' said Egg to herself, 'if he wasn't murdered after all.'

And then she caught her breath sharply as she caught sight of the words on a newspaper placard a few feet away:

'CORNISH EXHUMATION CASE – RESULT.'

Hastily she held out a penny and snatched a paper. As she did so she collided with another woman doing the same thing. As Egg apologized she recognized Sir Charles's secretary, the efficient Miss Milray.

Standing side by side, they both sought the stop-press news. Yes, there it was.

'RESULT OF CORNISH EXHUMATION.'

The words danced before Egg's eyes. Analysis of the organs . . . Nicotine . . .

'So he *was* murdered,' said Egg.

'Oh, dear,' said Miss Milray. 'This is terrible – terrible –'

Her rugged countenance was distorted with emotion. Egg looked at her in surprise. She had always regarded Miss Milray as something less than human.

'It upsets me,' said Miss Milray, in explanation. 'You see, I've known him all my life.'

'Mr Babbington?'

'Yes. You see, my mother lives at Gilling, where he used to be vicar. Naturally it's upsetting.'

'Oh, of course.'

'In fact,' said Miss Milray, 'I don't know what to do.'

She flushed a little before Egg's look of astonishment.

'I'd like to write to Mrs Babbington,' she said quickly. 'Only it doesn't seem quite – well, quite . . . I don't know what I had better do about it.'

Somehow, to Egg, the explanation was not quite satisfying.

CHAPTER 8

Angela Sutcliffe

'Now, are you a friend or are you a sleuth? I simply must know.'

Miss Sutcliffe flashed a pair of mocking eyes as she spoke. She was sitting in a straight-backed chair, her grey hair becomingly arranged, her legs were crossed and Mr Satterthwaite admired the perfection of her beautifully shod feet and her slender ankles. Miss Sutcliffe was a very fascinating woman, mainly owing to the fact that she seldom took anything seriously.

'Is that quite fair?' asked Mr Satterthwaite.

'My dear man, of course it's fair. Have you come here for the sake of my beautiful eyes, as the French say so charmingly, or have you, you nasty man, come just to pump me about murders?'

'Can you doubt that your first alternative is the correct one?' asked Mr Satterthwaite with a little bow.

'I can and I do,' said the actress with energy. 'You are one of those people who look so mild, and really wallow in blood.'

'No, no.'

'Yes, yes. The only thing I can't make up my mind about is whether it is an insult or a compliment to be considered a potential murderess. On the whole, I think it's a compliment.'

She cocked her head a little on one side and smiled that slow bewitching smile that never failed.

Mr Satterthwaite thought to himself:

'Adorable creature.'

Aloud he said, 'I will admit, dear lady, that the death of Sir Bartholomew Strange has interested me considerably. I have, as you perhaps know, dabbled in such doings before . . .'

He paused modestly, perhaps hoping that Miss Sutcliffe would show some knowledge of his activities. However, she merely asked:

'Tell me one thing – is there anything in what that girl said?'

'Which girl, and what did she say?'

'The Lytton Gore girl. The one who is so fascinated by Charles. (What a wretch Charles is – he will do it!) She thinks that that nice old man down in Cornwall was murdered, too.'

'What do you think?'

'Well, it certainly happened just the same way . . . She's an intelligent girl, you know. Tell me – is Charles serious?'

'I expect your views on the subject are likely to be much more valuable than mine,' said Mr Satterthwaite.

'What a tiresomely discreet man you are,' cried Miss Sutcliffe. 'Now I' – she sighed – 'am appallingly indiscreet . . .'

She fluttered an eyelash at him.

'I know Charles pretty well. I know men pretty well. He seems to me to display all the signs of settling down. There's an air of virtue about him. He'll be handing round the plate and founding a family in record time – that's my view. How dull men are when they decide to settle down! They lose all their charm.'

'I've often wondered why Sir Charles has never married,' said Mr Satterthwaite.

'My dear, he never showed any signs of wanting to marry. He wasn't what they call a marrying man. But he was a very attractive man . . .' She sighed. A slight twinkle showed in her eyes as she looked at Mr Satterthwaite. 'He and I were once – well, why deny what everybody knows? It was very pleasant while it lasted . . . and we're still the best of friends. I suppose that's the reason the Lytton Gore child looks at me so fiercely. She suspects I still have a *tendresse* for Charles. Have I? Perhaps I have. But at any rate I haven't yet written my memoirs describing all my affairs in detail as most of my friends seem to have done. If I did, you know, the girl wouldn't like it. She'd be shocked. Modern girls are easily shocked. Her mother wouldn't be shocked at all. You can't really shock a sweet mid-Victorian. They say so little, but always think the worst . . .'

Mr Satterthwaite contented himself with saying:

'I think you are right in suspecting that Egg Lytton Gore mistrusts you.'

Miss Sutcliffe frowned.

'I'm not at all sure that I'm not a little jealous of her . . . we women are such cats, aren't we? Scratch, scratch, miauw, miauw, purr, purr . . .'

She laughed.

'Why didn't Charles come and catechize me on this business? Too much nice feeling, I suppose. The man must think me guilty . . . Am I guilty, Mr Satterthwaite? What do you think now?'

She stood up and stretched out a hand.

'All the perfumes of Arabia will not sweeten this little hand –'

She broke off.

'No, I'm not Lady Macbeth. Comedy's my line.'

'There seems also a certain lack of motive,' said Mr Satterthwaite.

'True. I liked Bartholomew Strange. We were friends. I had no reason for wishing him out of the way. Because we were friends I'd rather like to take an active part in hunting down his murderer. Tell me if I can help in any way.'

'I suppose, Miss Sutcliffe, you didn't see or hear anything that might have a bearing on the crime?'

'Nothing that I haven't already told the police. The house-party had only just arrived, you know. His death occurred on that first evening.'

'The butler?'

'I hardly noticed him.'

'Any peculiar behaviour on the part of the guests?'

'No. Of course that boy – what's his name? Manders turned up rather unexpectedly.'

'Did Sir Bartholomew Strange seemed surprised?'

'Yes, I think he was. He said to me just before we went in to dinner that it was an odd business, "a new method of gate crashing", he called it. "Only," he said, "it's my wall he's crashed, not my gate."'

'Sir Bartholomew was in good spirits?'

'Very good spirits!'

'What about this secret passage you mentioned to the police?'

'I believe it led out of the library. Sir Bartholomew promised to show it to me – but of course the poor man died.'

'How did the subject come up?'

'We were discussing a recent purchase of his – an old walnut bureau. I asked if it had a secret drawer in it. I told him I adored secret drawers. It's a secret passion of mine. And he said, "No, there wasn't a secret drawer that he knew of – but he had got a secret passage in the house."'

'He didn't mention a patient of his, a Mrs de Rushbridger?'

'No.'

'Do you know a place called Gilling, in Kent?'

'Gilling? Gilling, no, I don't think I do. Why?'

'Well, you knew Mr Babbington before, didn't you?'

'Who is Mr Babbington?'

'The man who died, or who was killed, at the Crow's Nest.'

'Oh, the clergyman. I'd forgotten his name. No, I'd never seen him before in my life. Who told you I knew him?'

'Someone who ought to know,' said Mr Satterthwaite boldly.

Miss Sutcliffe seemed amused.

'Dear old man, did they think I'd had an affair with him? Archdeacons are sometimes very naughty, aren't they? So why not vicars? There's the man in the barrel, isn't there? But I must clear the poor man's memory. I'd never seen him before in my life.'

And with that statement Mr Satterthwaite was forced to rest content.

CHAPTER 9

Muriel Wills

Five Upper Cathcart Road, Tooting, seemed an incongruous home for a satiric playwright. The room into which Sir Charles was shown had walls of a rather drab oatmeal colour with a frieze of laburnum round the top. The curtains were of rose-coloured velvet, there were a lot of photographs and china dogs, the telephone was coyly hidden by a lady with ruffled skirts, there were a great many little tables and some suspicious-looking brasswork from Birmingham via the Far East.

Miss Wills entered the room so noiselessly that Sir Charles, who was at the moment examining a ridiculously elongated pierrot doll lying across the sofa, did not hear her. Her thin voice saying, 'How d'you do, Sir Charles. This is really a great pleasure,' made him spin round.

Miss Wills was dressed in a limp jumper suit which hung disconsolately on her angular form. Her stockings were slightly wrinkled, and she had on very high-heeled patent leather slippers.

Sir Charles shook hands, accepted a cigarette, and sat down on the sofa by the pierrot doll. Miss Wills sat opposite him. The light from the window caught her pince-nez and made them give off little flashes.

'Fancy you finding me out here,' said Miss Wills. 'My mother will be ever so excited. She just adores the theatre – especially anything romantic. That play where you were a Prince at a University – she's often talked of it. She goes to matinées, you know, and eats chocolates – she's one of that kind. And she does love it.'

'How delightful,' said Sir Charles. 'You don't know how charming it is to be remembered. The public memory is short!' He sighed.

'She'll be thrilled at meeting you,' said Miss Wills. 'Miss

Sutcliffe came the other day, and Mother was thrilled at meeting her.'

'Angela was here?'

'Yes. She's putting on a play of mine, you know: *Little Dog Laughed*.'

'Of course,' said Sir Charles. 'I've read about it. Rather intriguing title.'

'I'm so glad you think so. Miss Sutcliffe likes it, too. It's a kind of modern version of the nursery rhyme – a lot of froth and nonsense – Hey diddle diddle and the dish and the spoon scandal. Of course, it all revolves round Miss Sutcliffe's part – everyone dances to her fiddling – that's the idea.'

Sir Charles said:

'Not bad. The world nowadays is rather like a mad nursery rhyme. And the little dog laughed to see such sport, eh?' And he thought suddenly: 'Of course this woman's the Little Dog. She looks on and laughs.'

The light shifted from Miss Wills' pince-nez, and he saw her pale-blue eyes regarding him intelligently through them.

'This woman,' thought Sir Charles, 'has a fiendish sense of humour.'

Aloud he said:

'I wonder if you can guess what errand has brought me here?'

'Well,' said Miss Wills archly, 'I don't suppose it was only to see poor little me.'

Sir Charles registered for a moment the difference between the spoken and the written word. On paper Miss Wills was witty and cynical, in speech she was arch.

'It was really Satterthwaite put the idea into my head,' said Sir Charles. 'He fancies himself as being a good judge of character.'

'He's very clever about people,' said Miss Wills. 'It's rather his hobby, I should say.'

'And he is strongly of opinion that if there were anything worth noticing that night at Melfort Abbey you would have noticed it.'

'Is that what he said?'

'Yes.'

'I was very interested, I must admit,' said Miss Wills slowly. 'You see, I'd never seen a murder at close hand before. A writer's got to take everything as copy, hasn't she?'

'I believe that's a well-known axiom.'

'So naturally,' said Miss Wills, 'I tried to notice everything I could.'

This was obviously Miss Wills' version of Beatrice's 'poking and prying.'

'About the guests?'

'About the guests.'

'And what exactly did you notice?'

The pince-nez shifted.

'I didn't really find out anything – if I had I'd have told the police, of course,' she added virtuously.

'But you noticed things.'

'I always do notice things. I can't help it. I'm funny that way.' She giggled.

'And you noticed – what?'

'Oh, nothing – that is – nothing that you'd call anything, Sir Charles. Just little odds and ends about people's characters. I find people so very interesting. So typical, if you know what I mean.'

'Typical of what?'

'Of themselves. Oh, I can't explain. I'm ever so silly at saying things.'

She giggled again.

'Your pen is deadlier than your tongue,' said Sir Charles, smiling.

'I don't think it's very nice of you to say deadlier, Sir Charles.'

'My dear Miss Wills, admit that with a pen in your hand you're quite merciless.'

'I think you're horrid, Sir Charles. It's *you* who are merciless to *me*.'

'I must get out of this bog of badinage,' said Sir Charles to himself. He said aloud:

'So you didn't find out anything concrete, Miss Wills?'

'No – not exactly. At least, there was one thing. Something I noticed and ought to have told the police about, only I forgot.'

'What was that?'

'The butler. He had a kind of strawberry mark on his left wrist. I noticed it when he was handing me vegetables. I suppose that's the sort of thing which might come in useful.'

'I should say very useful indeed. The police are trying hard to track down that man Ellis. Really, Miss Wills, you are a very remarkable woman. Not one of the servants or guests mentioned such a mark.'

'Most people don't use their eyes much, do they?' said Miss Wills.

'Where exactly was the mark? And what size was it?'

'If you'll just stretch out your own wrist –' Sir Charles extended his arm. 'Thank you. It was here.' Miss Wills placed an unerring finger on the spot. 'It was about the size, roughly, of a sixpence, and rather the shape of Australia.'

'Thank you, that's very clear,' said Sir Charles, removing his hand and pulling down his cuffs again.

'You think I ought to write to the police and tell them?'

'Certainly I do. It might be most valuable in tracing the man. Dash it all,' went on Sir Charles with feeling, 'in detective stories there's always some identifying mark on the villain. I thought it was a bit hard that real life should prove so lamentably behindhand.'

'It's usually a scar in stories,' said Miss Wills thoughtfully.

'A birthmark's just as good,' said Sir Charles.

He looked boyishly pleased.

'The trouble is,' he went on, 'most people are so indeterminate. There's nothing about them to take hold of.'

Miss Wills looked inquiringly at him.

'Old Babbington, for instance,' went on Sir Charles, 'he had a curiously vague personality. Very difficult to lay hold of.'

'His hands were very characteristic,' said Miss Wills. 'What I call a scholar's hands. A little crippled with arthritis, but very refined fingers and beautiful nails.'

'What an observer you are. Ah, but – of course, you knew him before.'

'Knew Mr Babbington?'

'Yes, I remember his telling me so – where was it he said he had known you?'

Miss Wills shook her head decisively.

'Not me. You must have been mixing me up with someone else – or he was. I'd never met him before.'

'It must be a mistake. I thought – at Gilling –'

He looked at her keenly. Miss Wills appeared quite composed.

'No,' she said.

'Did it ever occur to you, Miss Wills, that he might have been murdered, too?'

'I know you and Miss Lytton Gore think so – or rather *you* think so.'

'Oh – and – er – what do *you* think?'

'It doesn't seem likely,' said Miss Wills.

A little baffled by Miss Wills's clear lack of interest in the subject Sir Charles started on another tack.

'Did Sir Bartholomew mention a Mrs de Rushbridger at all?'

'No, I don't think so.'

'She was a patient in his Home. Suffering from nervous breakdown and loss of memory.'

'He mentioned a case of lost memory,' said Miss Wills. 'He said you could hypnotize a person and bring their memory back.'

'Did he, now? I wonder – could that be significant?'

Sir Charles frowned and remained lost in thought. Miss Wills said nothing.

'There's nothing else you could tell me? Nothing about any of the guests?'

It seemed to him there was just the slightest pause before Miss Wills answered.

'No.'

'About Mrs Dacres? Or Captain Dacres? Or Miss Sutcliffe? Or Mr Manders?'

He watched her very intently as he pronounced each name.

Once he thought he saw the pince-nez flicker, but he could not be sure.

'I'm afraid there's nothing I can tell you, Sir Charles.'

'Oh, well!' He stood up. 'Satterthwaite will be disappointed.'

'I'm so sorry,' said Miss Wills primly.

'I'm sorry, too, for disturbing you. I expect you were busy writing.'

'I was, as a matter of fact.'

'Another play?'

'Yes. To tell you the truth, I thought of using some of the characters at the house-party at Melfort Abbey.'

'What about libel?'

'That's quite all right, Sir Charles, I find people never recognize themselves.' She giggled. 'Not if, as you said just now, one is really merciless.'

'You mean,' said Sir Charles, 'that we all have an exaggerated idea of our own personalities and don't recognize the truth if it's sufficiently brutally portrayed. I was quite right, Miss Wills, you *are* a cruel woman.'

Miss Wills tittered.

'You needn't be afraid, Sir Charles. Women aren't usually cruel to men – unless it's some particular man – they're only cruel to other women.'

'Meaning you've got your analytical knife into some unfortunate female. Which one? Well, perhaps I can guess. Cynthia's not beloved by her own sex.'

Miss Wills said nothing. She continued to smile – rather a catlike smile.

'Do you write your stuff or dictate it?'

'Oh, I write it and send it to be typed.'

'You ought to have a secretary.'

'Perhaps. Have you still got that clever Miss – Miss Milray, wasn't it?'

'Yes, I've got Miss Milray. She went away for a time to look after her mother in the country, but she's back again now. Most efficient woman.'

'So I should think. Perhaps a little impulsive.'

'Impulsive? Miss Milray?'

Sir Charles stared. Never in his wildest flights of fancy had he associated impulse with Miss Milray.

'Only on occasions, perhaps,' said Miss Wills.

Sir Charles shook his head.

'Miss Milray's the perfect robot. Goodbye, Miss Wills. Forgive me for bothering you, and don't forget to let the police know about that thingummybob.'

'The mark on the butler's right wrist? No, I won't forget.'

'Well, goodbye – half a sec. – did you say right wrist? You said left just now.'

'Did I? How stupid of me.'

'Well, which was it?'

Miss Wills frowned and half closed her eyes.

'Let me see. I was sitting so – and he – would you mind, Sir Charles, handing me that brass plate as though it was a vegetable dish. Left side.'

Sir Charles presented the beaten brass atrocity as directed.

'Cabbage, madam?'

'Thank you,' said Miss Wills, 'I'm quite sure now. It was the left wrist, as I said first. Stupid of me.'

'No, no,' said Sir Charles. 'Left and right are always puzzling.'

He said goodbye for the third time.

As he closed the door he looked back. Miss Wills was not looking at him. She was standing where he had left her. She was gazing at the fire, and on her lips was a smile of satisfied malice.

Sir Charles was startled.

'That woman knows something,' he said to himself. 'I'll swear she knows something. And she won't say . . . But what the devil is it she knows?'

CHAPTER 10

Oliver Manders

At the office of Messrs Speier & Ross, Mr Satterthwaite asked for Mr Oliver Manders and sent in his card.

Presently he was ushered into a small room, where Oliver was sitting at a writing-table.

The young man got up and shook hands.

'Good of you to look me up, sir,' he said.

His tone implied:

'I have to say that, but really it's a damned bore.'

Mr Satterthwaite, however, was not easily put off. He sat down, blew his nose thoughtfully, and, peering over the top of his handkerchief, said:

'Seen the news this morning?'

'You mean the new financial situation? Well, the dollar –'

'Not dollars,' said Mr Satterthwaite. 'Death. The result of the Loomouth exhumation. Babbington was poisoned – by nicotine.'

'Oh, that – yes, I saw that. Our energetic Egg will be pleased. She always insisted it was murder.'

'But it doesn't interest you?'

'My tastes aren't so crude. After all, murder –' he shrugged his shoulders. 'So violent and inartistic.'

'Not always inartistic,' said Mr Satterthwaite.

'No? Well, perhaps not.'

'It depends, does it not, on who commits the murder. You, for instance, would, I am sure, commit a murder in a very artistic manner.'

'Nice of you to say so,' drawled Oliver.

'But frankly, my dear boy, I don't think much of the accident you faked. No more do the police, I understand.'

There was a moment's silence – then a pen dropped to the floor.

Oliver said:

'Excuse me, I don't quite understand you.'

'That rather inartistic performance of yours at Melfort Abbey. I *should* be interested to know – just why you did it.'

There was another silence, then Oliver said:

'You say the police – suspect?'

Mr Satterthwaite nodded.

'It looks a little suspicious, don't you think?' he asked pleasantly. 'But perhaps you have a perfectly good explanation.'

'I've got an explanation,' said Oliver slowly. 'Whether it's a good one or not, I don't know.'

'Will you let me judge?'

There was a pause, then Oliver said:

'I came there – the way I did – at Sir Bartholomew's own suggestion.'

'What?' Mr Satterthwaite was astonished.

'A bit odd, isn't it? But it's true. I got a letter from him suggesting that I should have a sham accident and claim hospitality. He said he couldn't put his reasons in writing, but he would explain them to me at the first opportunity.'

'And did he explain?'

'No, he didn't . . . I got there just before dinner. I didn't see him alone. At the end of dinner he – he died.'

The weariness had gone out of Oliver's manner. His dark eyes were fixed on Mr Satterthwaite. He seemed to be studying attentively the reactions aroused by his words.

'You've got this letter?'

'No, I tore it up.'

'A pity,' said Mr Satterthwaite dryly. 'And you said nothing to the police?'

'No, it all seemed – well, rather fantastic.'

'It is fantastic.'

Mr Satterthwaite shook his head. Had Bartholomew Strange written such a letter? It seemed highly uncharacteristic. The story had a melodramatic touch most unlike the physician's cheerful common sense.

He looked up at the young man. Oliver was still watching him. Mr Satterthwaite thought: 'He's looking to see if I swallow this story.'

He said, 'And Sir Bartholomew gave absolutely no reason for his request?'

'None whatever.'

'An extraordinary story.'

Oliver did not speak.

'Yet you obeyed the summons?'

Something of the weary manner returned.

'Yes, it seemed refreshingly out of the way to a somewhat jaded palate. I was curious, I must confess.'

'Is there anything else?' asked Mr Satterthwaite.

'What do you mean, sir, anything else?'

Mr Satterthwaite did not really know what he meant. He was led by some obscure instinct.

'I mean,' he said, 'is there anything else that might tell – against you?'

There was a pause. Then the young man shrugged his shoulders.

'I suppose I might as well make a clean breast of it. The woman isn't likely to hold her tongue about it.'

Mr Satterthwaite looked a question.

'It was the morning after the murder stuff. I was talking to the Anthony Armstrong woman. I took out my pocket-book and something fell out of it. She picked it up and handed it back to me.'

'And this something?'

'Unfortunately she glanced at it before returning it to me. It was a cutting from a newspaper about nicotine – what a deadly poison it was, and so on.'

'How did you come to have such an interest in the subject?'

'I didn't. I suppose I must have put that cutting in my wallet sometime or other, but I can't remember doing so. Bit awkward, eh?'

Mr Satterthwaite thought: 'A thin story.'

'I suppose,' went on Oliver Manders, 'she went to the police about it?'

Mr Satterthwaite shook his head.

'I don't think so. I fancy she's a woman who likes – well, to keep things to herself. She's a collector of knowledge.'

Oliver Manders leaned forward suddenly.

'I'm innocent, sir, absolutely innocent.'

'I haven't suggested that you are guilty,' said Mr Satterthwaite mildly.

'But someone has – someone must have done. Someone has put the police on to me.'

Mr Satterthwaite shook his head.

'No, no.'

'Then why did you come here today?'

'Partly as the result of my – er – investigations on the spot.' Mr Satterthwaite spoke a little pompously. 'And partly at the suggestion of – a friend.'

'What friend?'

'Hercule Poirot.'

'That man!' The expression burst from Oliver. 'Is he back in England?'

'Yes.'

'Why has he come back?'

Mr Satterthwaite rose.

'Why does a dog go hunting?' he inquired.

And, rather pleased with his retort, he left the room.

CHAPTER 11

Poirot Gives A Sherry Party

I

Sitting in a comfortable arm-chair in his slightly florid suite at the Ritz, Hercule Poirot listened.

Egg was perched on the arm of a chair, Sir Charles stood in front of the fireplace, Mr Satterthwaite sat a little farther away observing the group.

'It's failure all along the line,' said Egg.

Poirot shook his head gently.

'No, no, you exaggerate. As regards a link with Mr Babbington, you have drawn the blank – yes; but you have collected other suggestive information.'

'The Wills woman knows something,' said Sir Charles. 'I'll swear she knows something.'

'And Captain Dacres, he too has not the clear conscience. And Mrs Dacres was desperately in want of money, and Sir Bartholomew spoilt her chance of laying hold of some.'

'What do you think of young Manders's story?' asked Mr Satterthwaite.

'It strikes me as peculiar and as being highly uncharacteristic of the late Sir Bartholomew Strange.'

'You mean it's a lie?' asked Sir Charles bluntly.

'There are so many kinds of lies,' said Hercule Poirot.

He was silent for a minute or two, then he said:

'This Miss Wills, she has written a play for Miss Sutcliffe?'

'Yes. The first night is Wednesday next.'

'Ah!'

He was silent again. Egg said:

'Tell us: What shall we do now?'

The little man smiled at her.

'There is only one thing to do – think.'

'Think?' cried Egg. Her voice was disgusted.

Poirot beamed on her.

'But yes, exactly that. *Think*! With thought, all problems can be solved.'

'Can't we do something?'

'For you the action, eh, mademoiselle? But certainly, there are still things you can do. There is, for instance, this place, Gilling, where Mr Babbington lived for so many years. You can make inquiries there. You say that this Miss Milray's mother lives at Gilling and is an invalid. An invalid knows everything. She hears everything and forgets nothing. Make your inquiries of her, it may lead to something – who knows?'

'Aren't *you* going to do anything?' demanded Egg persistently.

Poirot twinkled.

'You insist that I, too, shall be active? *Eh bien*. It shall be as you wish. Only me, I shall not leave this place. I am very comfortable here. But I will tell you what I will do: I will give the party – the Sherry Party – that is fashionable, is it not?'

'A Sherry Party?'

'*Précisément*, and to it I will ask Mrs Dacres, Captain Dacres, Miss Sutcliffe, Miss Wills, Mr Manders and your charming mother, mademoiselle.'

'And me?'

'Naturally, and you. The present company is included.'

'Hurrah,' said Egg. 'You can't deceive me, M. Poirot. Something will happen at that party. It will, won't it?'

'We shall see,' said Poirot. 'But do not expect too much, mademoiselle. Now leave me with Sir Charles, for there are a few things about which I want to ask his advice.'

As Egg and Mr Satterthwaite stood waiting for the lift, Egg said ecstatically:

'It's lovely – just like detective stories. All the people will be there, and then he'll tell us *which* of them did it.'

'I wonder,' said Mr Satterthwaite.

II

The Sherry Party took place on Monday evening. The invitation had been accepted by all. The charming and indiscreet Miss Sutcliffe laughed mischievously as she glanced round.

'Quite the spider's parlour, M. Poirot. And here all we poor little flies have walked in. I'm sure you're going to give us the most marvellous résumé of the case and then suddenly you'll point at me and say, "Thou art the woman", and everyone will say, "She done it", and I shall burst into tears and confess because I'm too terribly suggestible for words. Oh, M. Poirot, I'm so frightened of you.'

'*Quelle histoire*,' cried Poirot. He was busy with a decanter and glasses. He handed her a glass of sherry with a bow. 'This is a friendly little party. Do not let us talk of murders and bloodshed and poison. *Là, là*! these things, they spoil the palate.'

He handed a glass to the grim Miss Milray, who had accompanied Sir Charles and was standing with a forbidding expression on her face.

'*Voilà*,' said Poirot as he finished dispensing hospitality. 'Let us forget the occasion on which we first met. Let us have the party spirit. Eat, drink and be merry, for tomorrow we die. *Ah, malheur*, I have again mentioned death. Madame,' he bowed to Mrs Dacres, 'may I be permitted to wish you good luck and congratulate you on your very charming gown.'

'Here's to you, Egg,' said Sir Charles.

'Cheerio,' said Freddie Dacres.

Everybody murmured something. There was an air of forced gaiety about the proceedings. Everyone was determined to appear gay and unconcerned. Only Poirot himself seemed naturally so. He rambled on happily . . .

'The sherry, I prefer it to the cocktail – and a thousand times to the whisky. Ah, *quel horreur*, the whisky. By drinking the whisky, you ruin, absolutely ruin, the palate. The delicate wines of France, to appreciate them, you must never never – ah *qu'est-ce qu'il y a* –?'

A strange sound had interrupted him – a kind of choking cry. Every eye went to Sir Charles as he stood swaying, his face convulsed. The glass dropped from his hand on to the carpet, he took a few steps blindly, then collapsed.

There was a moment's stupefied silence, then Angela Sutcliffe screamed and Egg started forward.

'Charles,' cried Egg. 'Charles.'

She fought her way blindly forward. Mr Satterthwaite gently held her back.

'Oh, dear God,' cried Lady Mary. '*Not another*!'

Angela Sutcliffe cried out:

'He's been poisoned, too . . . This is awful. Oh, my God, this is too awful . . .'

And suddenly collapsing on to a sofa, she began to sob and laugh – a horrible sound.

Poirot had taken charge of the situation. He was kneeling by the prostrate man. The others drew back while he made his examination. He rose to his feet, mechanically dusting the knees of his trousers. He looked round at the assembly. There was complete silence, except for the smothered sobs of Angela Sutcliffe.

'My friends,' began Poirot.

He got no further, for Egg spat out at him:

'You fool. You absurd play-acting little fool! Pretending to be so great and so wonderful, and to know all about everything. And now you let this happen. Another murder. Under your very nose . . . If you'd let the whole thing alone this wouldn't have happened . . . It's you who have murdered Charles – you – you – you . . .'

She stopped, unable to get out the words.

Poirot nodded his head gravely and sadly.

'It is true, mademoiselle. I confess it. It is I who have murdered Sir Charles. But I, mademoiselle, am a very special kind of murderer. I can kill – and I can restore to life.' He turned and in a different tone of voice, an apologetic everyday voice, he said:

'A magnificent performance, Sir Charles, I congratulate you. Perhaps you would now like to take your curtain.'

With a laugh the actor sprang to his feet and bowed mockingly.

Egg gave a great gasp.

'M. Poirot, you – you *beast*.'

'Charles,' cried Angela Sutcliffe. 'You complete devil . . .'

'But why –?'

'How –?'

'What on earth –?'

By means of his upraised hand, Poirot obtained silence.

'Messieurs, mesdames. I demand pardon of you all. This little farce was necessary to prove to you all, and incidentally, to prove to myself a fact which my reason already told me is true.

'Listen. On this tray of glasses I placed in one glass a teaspoonful of plain water. That water represented pure nicotine. These glasses are of the same kind as those possessed by Sir Charles Cartwright and by Sir Bartholomew Strange. Owing to the heavy cut glass, a small quantity of a colourless liquid is quite undetectable. Imagine, then, the port glass of Sir Bartholomew Strange. After it was put on the table somebody introduced into it a sufficient quantity of pure nicotine. That might have been done by anybody. The butler, the parlour-maid, or one of the guests who slipped into the dining-room on his or her way downstairs. Dessert arrived, the port is taken round, the glass is filled. Sir Bartholomew drinks – and dies.

'Tonight we have played a third tragedy – a sham tragedy – I asked Sir Charles to play the part of the victim. This he did magnificently. Now suppose for a minute that this was not a farce, but truth. *Sir Charles is dead.* What will be the steps taken by the police?'

Miss Sutcliffe cried:

'Why, the glass, of course.' She nodded to where the glass lay on the floor as it had fallen from Sir Charles's hand. 'You only put water in, but if it had been nicotine –'

'Let us suppose it was nicotine.' Poirot touched the glass gently with his toe. 'You are of opinion that the police would analyse the glass, and that traces of nicotine would be found?'

'Certainly.'

Poirot shook his head gently.

'You are wrong. No nicotine would be found.'

They stared at him.

'You see,' he smiled, '*that* is not the glass from which Sir Charles drank.' With an apologetic grin he extended a glass from the tail pocket of his coat. '*This* is the glass he used.'

He went on:

'It is, you see, the simple theory of the conjuring trick. The attention cannot be in two places at once. To do my conjuring trick I need the attention focused elsewhere. Well, there is a moment, a psychological moment. When Sir Charles falls – dead – every eye in the room is on his dead body. Everyone crowds forward to get near him, and no one, no one at all, looks at Hercule Poirot, and in that moment I exchange the glasses and no one sees . . .

'So you see, I prove my point . . . There was such a moment at Crow's Nest, there was such a moment at Melfort Abbey – and so, there was nothing in the cocktail glass and nothing in the port glass . . .'

Egg cried:

'Who changed them?'

Looking at her, Poirot replied:

'That, we have still to find out . . .'

'You don't know?'

Poirot shrugged his shoulders.

Rather uncertainly, the guests made signs of departure. Their manner was a little cold. They felt they had been badly fooled.

With a gesture of the hand, Poirot arrested them.

'One little moment, I pray of you. There is one thing more that I have to say. Tonight, admittedly, we have played the comedy. But the comedy may be played in earnest – it may become a tragedy. Under certain conditions the murderer may strike a third time . . . I speak now to all of you here present. *If anyone of you knows something – something that may bear in any way on this crime, I implore that person to speak now.* To keep knowledge to oneself at this juncture may be dangerous – so dangerous that death may be the result of silence. Therefore I beg again – *if anyone knows anything, let that person speak now . . .*'

It seemed to Sir Charles that Poirot's appeal was addressed especially to Miss Wills. If so, it had no result. Nobody spoke or answered.

Poirot sighed. His hand fell.

'Be it so, then. I have given warning. I can do no more. Remember, to keep silence is dangerous . . .'

But still nobody spoke.

Awkwardly the guests departed.

Egg, Sir Charles and Mr Satterthwaite were left.

Egg had not yet forgiven Poirot. She sat very still, her cheeks flushed and her eyes angry. She wouldn't look at Sir Charles.

'That was a damned clever bit of work, Poirot,' said Sir Charles appreciatively.

'Amazing,' said Mr Satterthwaite with a chuckle. 'I wouldn't have believed that I wouldn't have seen you do that exchange.'

'That is why,' said Poirot, 'I could take no one into any confidence. The experiment could only be fair this way.'

'Was that the only reason you planned this – to see whether it could be done unnoticed?'

'Well, not quite, perhaps. I had one other aim.'

'Yes?'

'I wanted to watch the expression on one person's face when Sir Charles fell dead.'

'Which person's?' said Egg sharply.

'Ah, that is my secret.'

'And you did watch that person's face?' asked Mr Satterthwaite.

'Yes.'

'Well?'

Poirot did not reply. He merely shook his head.

'Won't you tell us what you saw there?'

Poirot said slowly:

'I saw an expression of the utmost surprise . . .'

Egg drew her breath in sharply.

'You mean,' she said, '*that you know who the murderer is*?'

'You can put it that way if you like, mademoiselle.'

'But then – but then – you know everything?'

Poirot shook his head.

'No; on the contrary I know nothing at all. For, you see, I do not know *why* Stephen Babbington was killed. Until I know that I can prove nothing, I can know nothing . . . It all hinges on that – the motive for Stephen Babbington's death . . .'

There was a knock at the door and a page entered with a telegram on a tray.

Poirot opened it. His face changed. He handed the telegram to Sir Charles. Leaning over Sir Charles's shoulder, Egg read it aloud:

'Please come and see me at once can give you valuable information as to Bartholomew Strange's death – Margaret Rushbridger.'

'Mrs de Rushbridger!' cried Sir Charles. 'We were right after all. She *has* got something to do with the case.'

CHAPTER 12

Day At Gilling

I

At once an excited discussion sprang up. An A.B.C. was produced. It was decided that an early train would be better than going by car.

'At last,' said Sir Charles, 'we're going to get that particular part of the mystery cleared up.'

'What do you think the mystery is?' asked Egg.

'I can't imagine. But it can't fail to throw some light on the Babbington affair. If Tollie got those people together on purpose, as I feel pretty sure he did, then the "surprise" he talked of springing on them had something to do with this Rushbridger woman. I think we can assume that, don't you, M. Poirot?'

Poirot shook his head in a perplexed manner.

'This telegram complicates the affair,' he murmured. 'But we must be quick – extremely quick.'

Mr Satterthwaite did not see the need for extreme haste, but he agreed politely.

'Certainly, we will go by the first train in the morning. Er – that is to say, is it necessary for us all to go?'

'Sir Charles and I had arranged to go down to Gilling,' said Egg.

'We can postpone that,' said Sir Charles.

'I don't think we ought to postpone anything,' said Egg. 'There is no need for all four of us to go to Yorkshire. It's absurd. Mass formation. M. Poirot and Mr Satterthwaite go to Yorkshire and Sir Charles and I go to Gilling.'

'I'd rather like to look into this Rushbridger business,' said Sir Charles with a trace of wistfulness. 'You see, I – er – talked to the Matron before – got my foot in, so to speak.'

'That's just why you'd better keep away,' said Egg. 'You involved yourself in a lot of lies, and now this Rushbridger woman has come to herself you'll be exposed as a thorough-paced liar. It's far far more important that you should come to Gilling. If we want to see Miss Milray's mother she'll open out to you much more than she would to anyone else. You're her daughter's employer, and she'll have confidence in you.'

Sir Charles looked into Egg's glowing, earnest face.

'I'll come to Gilling,' he said. 'I think you're quite right.'

'I know I'm right,' said Egg.

'In my opinion an excellent arrangement,' said Poirot briskly. 'As mademoiselle says, Sir Charles is pre-eminently the person to interview this Mrs Milray. Who knows, you may learn from her facts of much more importance than those we shall learn in Yorkshire.'

Matters were arranged on this basis, and the following morning Sir Charles picked up Egg in his car at a quarter to ten. Poirot and Mr Satterthwaite had already left London by train.

It was a lovely crisp morning, with just a touch of frost in the air. Egg felt her spirits rising as they turned and twisted through the various short cuts which Sir Charles's experience had discovered south of the Thames.

At last, however, they were flying smoothly along the Folkestone road. After passing through Maidstone, Sir Charles consulted a map, and they turned off from the main road and were shortly winding through country lanes. It was about a quarter to twelve when they at last reached their objective.

Gilling was a village which the world had left behind. It had an old church, a vicarage, two or three shops, a row of cottages, three or four new council houses and a very attractive village green.

Miss Milray's mother lived in a tiny house on the other side of the green to the church.

As the car drew up Egg asked:

'Does Miss Milray know you are going to see her mother?'

'Oh, yes. She wrote to prepare the old lady.'

'Do you think that was a good thing?'

'My dear child, why not?'

'Oh, I don't know . . . You didn't bring her down with you, though.'

'As a matter of fact, I thought she might cramp my style. She's so much more efficient than I am – she'd probably try to prompt me.'

Egg laughed.

Mrs Milray turned out to be almost ludicrously unlike her daughter. Where Miss Milray was hard, she was soft, where Miss Milray was angular, she was round. Mrs Milray was an immense dumpling of a woman immovably fixed in an armchair conveniently placed so that she could, from the window, observe all that went on in the world outside.

She seemed pleasurably excited by the arrival of her visitors.

'This is very nice of you, I'm sure, Sir Charles. I've heard so much about you from my Violet.' (Violet! Singularly incongruous name for Miss Milray.) 'You don't know how much she admires you. It's been most interesting for her working with you all these years. Won't you sit down, Miss Lytton Gore? You'll excuse my not getting up. I've lost the use of my limbs for many years now. The Lord's will, and I don't complain, and what I say is one can get used to anything. Perhaps you'd like a little refreshment after your drive down?'

Both Sir Charles and Egg disclaimed the need of refreshment, but Mrs Milray paid no attention. She clapped her hands in an Oriental manner, and tea and biscuits made their appearance. As they nibbled and sipped, Sir Charles came to the object of their visit.

'I expect you've heard, Mrs Milray, all about the tragic death of Mr Babbington who used to be vicar here?'

The dumpling nodded its head in vigorous assent.

'Yes, indeed. I've read all about the exhumation in the paper. And whoever can have poisoned him I can't imagine. A very nice man, he was, everyone liked him here – and her, too. And their little children and all.'

'It is indeed a great mystery,' said Sir Charles. 'We're all in despair about it. In fact, we wondered if you could possibly throw any light upon the matter.'

'Me? But I haven't seen the Babbingtons – let me see – it must be over fifteen years.'

'I know, but some of us have the idea that there might be something in the past to account for his death.'

'I'm sure I don't know what there could be. They led very quiet lives – very badly off, poor things, with all those children.'

Mrs Milray was willing enough to reminisce, but her reminiscences seemed to shed little light on the problem they had set out to solve.

Sir Charles showed her the enlargement of a snapshot which included the Dacres, also an early portrait of Angela Sutcliffe and a somewhat blurred reproduction of Miss Wills cut from a newspaper. Mrs Milray surveyed them all with great interest, but with no signs of recognition.

'I can't say I remember any of them – of course it's a long time ago. But this is a small place. There's not much coming and going. The Agnew girls, the doctor's daughters – they're all married and out in the world, and our present doctor's a bachelor – he's got a new young partner. Then there were the old Miss Cayleys – sat in the big pew – they're all dead many years back. And the Richardsons – he died and she went to Wales. And the village people, of course. But there's not much change there. Violet, I expect, could tell you as much as I could. She was a young girl then and often over at the Vicarage.'

Sir Charles tried to envisage Miss Milray as a young girl and failed.

He asked Mrs Milray if she remembered anyone of the name of Rushbridger, but the name failed to evoke any response.

Finally they took their leave.

Their next move was a scratch lunch in the baker's shop. Sir Charles had hankerings for fleshpots elsewhere, but Egg pointed out that they might get hold of some local gossip.

'And boiled eggs and scones will do you no harm for once,' she said severely. 'Men are so fussy about their food.'

'I always find eggs so depressing,' said Sir Charles meekly.

The woman who served them was communicative enough. She, too, had read of the exhumation in the paper and had been proportionately thrilled by its being 'old vicar'. 'I were a child at the time,' she explained. 'But I remember him.'

She could not, however, tell them much about him.

After lunch they went to the church and looked through the register of births, marriages and deaths. Here again there seemed nothing hopeful or suggestive.

They came out into the churchyard and lingered. Egg read the names on the tombstones.

'What queer names there are,' she said. 'Listen, here's a whole family of Stavepennys and here's a Mary Ann Sticklepath.'

'None of them so queer as mine,' murmured Sir Charles.

'Cartwright? I don't think that's a queer name at all.'

'I didn't mean Cartwright. Cartwright's my acting name, and I finally adopted it legally.'

'What's your real name?'

'I couldn't possibly tell you. It's my guilty secret.'

'Is it as terrible as all that?'

'It's not so much terrible as humorous.'

'Oh – tell it me.'

'Certainly not,' said Sir Charles firmly.

'Please.'

'No.'

'Why not?'

'You'd laugh.'

'I wouldn't.'

'You wouldn't be able to help laughing.'

'Oh, please tell me. Please, please, please.'

'What a persistent creature you are, Egg. Why do you want to know?'

'Because you won't tell me.'

'You adorable child,' said Sir Charles a little unsteadily.

'I'm not a child.'

'Aren't you? I wonder.'

'Tell me,' whispered Egg softly.

A humorous and rueful smile twisted Sir Charles's mouth.

'Very well, here goes. My father's name was Mugg.'

'Not really?'

'Really and truly.'

'H'm,' said Egg. 'That is a bit catastrophic. To go through life as Mugg –'

'Wouldn't have taken me far in my career, I agree. I remember,' went on Sir Charles dreamily, 'I played with the idea (I was young then) of calling myself Ludovic Castiglione – but I eventually compromised on British alliteration as Charles Cartwright.'

'Are you really Charles?'

'Yes, my godfathers and godmothers saw to that.' He hesitated, then said, 'Why don't you say Charles – and drop the Sir?'

'I might.'

'You did yesterday. When – when – you thought I was dead.'

'Oh, then.' Egg tried to make her voice nonchalant.

Sir Charles said abruptly: 'Egg, somehow or other this murder business doesn't seem real any more. Today especially, it seems fantastic. I meant to clear the thing up before – before anything else. I've been superstitious about it. I've associated success in solving problems with – with another kind of success. Oh, damn, why do I beat about the bush? I've made love on the stage so often that I'm diffident about it in real life . . . Is it me or is it young Manders, Egg? I must know. Yesterday I thought it was me . . .'

'You thought right . . .'

'You incredible angel,' cried Sir Charles.

'Charles, Charles, you can't kiss me in a churchyard . . .'

'I shall kiss you anywhere I please . . .'

II

'We've found out nothing,' said Egg later, as they were speeding back to London.

'Nonsense, we've found out the only thing worth finding out . . . What do I care about dead clergymen or dead doctors? You're the only thing that matters . . . You know, my dear, I'm thirty years older than you – are you sure it doesn't matter?'

Egg pinched his arm gently.

'Don't be silly . . . I wonder if the others have found out anything?'

'They're welcome to it,' said Sir Charles generously.

'Charles – you used to be so keen.'

But Sir Charles was no longer playing the part of the great detective.

'Well, it was my own show. Now I've handed over to Moustachios. It's his business.'

'Do you think he really knows who committed the crimes? He said he did.'

'Probably hasn't the faintest idea, but he's got to keep up his professional reputation.'

Egg was silent. Sir Charles said:

'What are you thinking about, darling?'

'I was thinking about Miss Milray. She was so odd in her manner that evening I told you about. She had just bought the paper about the exhumation, and she said she didn't know what to do.'

'Nonsense,' said Sir Charles cheerfully. 'That woman always knows what to do.'

'Do be serious, Charles. She sounded – worried.'

'Egg, my sweet, what do I care for Miss Milray's worries? What do I care for anything but you and me?'

'You'd better pay some attention to the trams!' said Egg. 'I don't want to be widowed before I'm a wife.'

They arrived back at Sir Charles's flat for tea. Miss Milray came out to meet them.

'There is a telegram for you, Sir Charles.'

'Thank you, Miss Milray.' He laughed, a nervous boyish laugh. 'Look here, I must tell you our news. Miss Lytton Gore and I are going to get married.'

There was a moment's pause, and then Miss Milray said:

'Oh! I'm sure – I'm sure you'll be very happy.'

There was a queer note in her voice. Egg noticed it, but before she could formulate her impression Charles Cartwright had swung round to her with a quick exclamation.

'My God, Egg, look at this. It's from Satterthwaite.'

He shoved the telegram into her hands. Egg read it, and her eyes opened wide.

CHAPTER 13

Mrs De Rushbridger

Before catching their train Hercule Poirot and Mr Satterthwaite had had a brief interview with Miss Lyndon, the late Sir Bartholomew Strange's secretary. Miss Lyndon had been very willing to help, but had had nothing of importance to tell them. Mrs de Rushbridger was only mentioned in Sir Bartholomew's case book in a purely professional fashion. Sir Bartholomew had never spoken of her save in medical terms.

The two men arrived at the Sanatorium about twelve o'clock. The maid who opened the door looked excited and flushed. Mr Satterthwaite asked first for the Matron.

'I don't know whether she can see you this morning,' said the girl doubtfully.

Mr Satterthwaite extracted a card and wrote a few words on it.

'Please take her this.'

They were shown into a small waiting-room. In about five minutes the door opened and the Matron came in. She was looking quite unlike her usual brisk efficient self.

Mr Satterthwaite rose.

'I hope you remember me' he said. 'I came here with Sir Charles Cartwright just after the death of Sir Bartholomew Strange.'

'Yes, indeed, Mr Satterthwaite, of course I remember; and Sir Charles asked after poor Mrs de Rushbridger then, and it seems such a coincidence.'

'Let me introduce M. Hercule Poirot.'

Poirot bowed and the Matron responded absently. She went on:

'I can't understand how you can have had a telegram as you say. The whole thing seems most mysterious. Surely it can't be connected with the poor doctor's death in any way? There must be some madman about – that's the only way I can account for it. Having the police here and everything. It's really been terrible.'

'The police?' said Mr Satterthwaite, surprised.

'Yes, since ten o'clock they've been here.'

'The police?' said Hercule Poirot.

'Perhaps we could see Mrs de Rushbridger now,' suggested Mr Satterthwaite. 'Since she asked us to come –'

The Matron interrupted him.

'Oh, Mr Satterthwaite, then you don't know!'

'Know what?' demanded Poirot sharply.

'Poor Mrs de Rushbridger. She's dead.'

'Dead?' cried Poirot. '*Mille Tonnerres*! That explains it. Yes, that explains it. I should have seen—' He broke off. 'How did she die?'

'It's most mysterious. A box of chocolates came for her – liqueur chocolates – by post. She ate one – it must have tasted horrible, but she was taken by surprise, I suppose, and she swallowed it. One doesn't like spitting a thing out.'

'*Oui, oui*, and if a liquid runs suddenly down your throat, it is difficult.'

'So she swallowed it and called out and Nurse came rushing, but we couldn't do anything. She died in about two minutes. Then doctor sent for the police, and they came and examined the chocolates. All the top layer had been tampered with, the underneath ones were all right.'

'And the poison employed?'

'They think it's nicotine.'

'Yes,' said Poirot. 'Again nicotine. What a stroke! What an audacious stroke!'

'We are too late,' said Mr Satterthwaite. 'We shall never know now what she had to tell us. Unless – unless – she confided in someone?' He glanced interrogatively at the Matron.

Poirot shook his head.

'There will have been no confidences, you will find.'

'We can ask,' said Mr Satterthwaite. 'One of the nurses, perhaps?'

'By all means ask,' said Poirot; but he did not sound hopeful.

Mr Satterthwaite turned to the Matron who immediately sent for the two nurses, on day and night duty respectively, who had been in attendance on Mrs de Rushbridger, but neither of them could add any information to that already given. Mrs de Rushbridger had never mentioned Sir Bartholomew's death, and they did not even know of the despatching of the telegram.

On a request from Poirot, the two men were taken to the dead woman's room. They found Superintendent Crossfield in charge, and Mr Satterthwaite introduced him to Poirot.

Then the two men moved over to the bed and stood looking down on the dead woman. She was about forty, dark-haired and pale. Her face was not peaceful – it still showed the agony of her death.

Mr Satterthwaite said slowly:

'Poor soul . . .'

He looked across at Hercule Poirot. There was a strange expression on the little Belgian's face. Something about it made Mr Satterthwaite shiver . . .

Mr Satterthwaite said:

'Someone knew she was going to speak, and killed her . . . She was killed in order to prevent her speaking . . .'

Poirot nodded.

'Yes, that is so.'

'She was murdered to prevent her telling us what she knew.'

'Or what she did not know . . . But let us not waste time . . . There is much to be done. *There must be no more deaths*. We must see to that.'

Mr Satterthwaite asked curiously:

'Does this fit in with your idea of the murderer's identity?'

'Yes, it fits . . . But I realize one thing: The murderer is more dangerous than I thought . . . We must be careful.'

Superintendent Crossfield followed them out of the room and learnt from them of the telegram which had been received by them. The telegram had been handed in at Melfort Post Office, and on inquiry there it was elicited that it had been handed in by a small boy. The young lady in charge remembered it, because the message had excited her very much, mentioning, as it did, Sir Bartholomew Strange's death.

After some lunch in company with the superintendent, and after despatching a telegram to Sir Charles, the quest was resumed.

At six o'clock that evening the small boy who had handed in the telegram was found. He told his story promptly. He had been given the telegram by a man dressed in shabby clothes. The man told him that the telegram had been given him by a 'loony lady' in the 'House in the Park'. She had dropped it out of the window wrapped round two half-crowns. The man was afraid to be mixed up in some funny business, and was tramping in the other direction, so he had given the boy two and six and told him to keep the change.

A search would be instituted for the man. In the meantime there seemed nothing more to be done, and Poirot and Mr Satterthwaite returned to London.

It was close on midnight when the two men arrived back in town. Egg had gone back to her mother, but Sir Charles met them, and the three men discussed the situation.

'*Mon ami*,' said Poirot, 'be guided by me. Only one thing will solve this case – the little grey cells of the brain. To rush up and down England, to hope that this person and that will tell us what we want to know – all such methods are amateurish and absurd. The truth can only be seen from within.'

Sir Charles looked slightly sceptical.

'What do you want to do, then?'

'I want to think. I ask of you twenty-four hours – in which to think.'

Sir Charles shook his head with a slight smile.

'Will thinking tell you what it was this woman could have said if she lived?'

'I believe so.'

'It hardly seems possible. However, M. Poirot, you must have it your own way. If you can see through this mystery, it's more than I can. I'm beaten, and I confess it. In any case, I've other fish to fry.'

Perhaps he hoped to be questioned, but if so his expectation was disappointed. Mr Satterthwaite did indeed look up alertly, but Poirot remained lost in thought.

'Well, I must be off,' said the actor. 'Oh, just one thing. I'm rather worried about – Miss Wills.'

'What about her?'

'She's gone.'

Poirot stared at him.

'Gone? Gone where?'

'Nobody knows . . . I was thinking things over after I got your telegram. As I told you at the time, I felt convinced that that woman knew something she hadn't told us. I thought I'd have a last shot at getting it out of her. I drove out to her house – it was about half-past nine when I got there – and asked for her. It appears she left home this morning – went up to London for the day – that's what she said. Her people got a telegram in the evening saying she wasn't returning for a day or so and not to worry.'

'And were they worrying?'

'I gather they were, rather. You see, she hadn't taken any luggage with her.'

'Odd,' murmured Poirot.

'I know. It seems as though – I don't know. I feel uneasy.'

'I warned her,' said Poirot. 'I warned everyone. You remember I said to them, "Speak now."'

'Yes, yes. Do you think that she, too –?'

'I have my ideas,' said Poirot. 'For the moment I prefer not to discuss them.'

'First, the butler – Ellis – then Miss Wills. Where is Ellis? It's incredible that the police have never been able to lay hands on him.'

'They have not looked for his body in the right place,' said Poirot.

'Then you agree with Egg. You think he is dead?'

'Ellis will never be seen alive again.'

'My God,' burst out Sir Charles. 'It's a nightmare – the whole thing is utterly incomprehensible.'

'No, no. It is sane and logical, on the contrary.'

Sir Charles stared at him.

'You say that?'

'Certainly. You see, I have the orderly mind.'

'I don't understand you.'

Mr Satterthwaite, too, looked curiously at the little detective.

'What kind of a mind have I?' demanded Sir Charles, slightly hurt.

'You have the actor's mind, Sir Charles, creative, original, seeing always dramatic values. Mr Satterthwaite here, he has the playgoer's mind, he observes the characters, he has the sense of atmosphere. But me, I have the prosaic mind. I see only the facts without any dramatic trappings or footlights.'

'Then we're to leave you to it?'

'That is my idea. For twenty-four hours.'

'Good luck to you, then. Goodnight.'

As they went away together Sir Charles said to Mr Satterthwaite:

'That chap thinks a lot of himself.'

He spoke rather coldly.

Mr Satterthwaite smiled. The star part! So that was it. He said:

'What did you mean by saying you had other fish to fry, Sir Charles?'

On Sir Charles's face appeared the sheepish expression that Mr Satterthwaite knew so well from attending weddings in Hanover Square.

'Well, as a matter of fact, I – er – well, Egg and I –'

'I'm delighted to hear it,' said Mr Satterthwaite. 'My best congratulations.'

'Of course I'm years too old for her.'

'She doesn't think so – and she's the best judge.'

'That's very nice of you, Satterthwaite. You know, I'd got it into my head she was fond of young Manders.'

'I wonder what made you think that,' said Mr Satterthwaite innocently.

'Anyway,' said Sir Charles firmly, 'she isn't . . .'

CHAPTER 14

Miss Milray

Poirot did not have quite the uninterrupted twenty- four hours for which he had stipulated.

At twenty minutes past eleven on the following morning Egg walked in unannounced. To her amazement she found the great detective engaged in building card houses. Her face showed such lively scorn that Poirot was impelled to defend himself.

'It is not, mademoiselle, that I have become childish in my old age. No. But the building of card houses, I have always found it most stimulating to the mind. It is an old habit of mine. This morning, first thing, I go out and buy the pack of cards. Unfortunately I make an error, they are not real cards. But they do just as well.'

Egg looked more closely at the erection on the table.

She laughed.

'Good heavens, they've sold you Happy Families.'

'What is that you say, the Happy Family?'

'Yes, it's a game. Children play it in the nursery.'

'Ah, well, one can compose the houses just in the same manner.'

Egg had picked up some of the cards from the table and was looking at them affectionately.

'Master Bun, the baker's son – I always loved him. And here's Mrs Mug, the milkman's wife. Oh, dear, I suppose that's me.'

'Why is that funny picture you, mademoiselle?'

'Because of the name.'

Egg laughed at his bewildered face and then began explaining. When she had finished he said:

'Ah, it was that that Sir Charles meant last night. I wondered . . . Mugg – ah, yes, one says in slang, does one not, you are a *mug* –

a fool? Naturally you would change your name. You would not like to be the Lady Mugg, eh?'

Egg laughed. She said:

'Well, wish me happiness.'

'I do wish you happiness, mademoiselle. Not the brief happiness of youth, but the happiness that endures – the happiness that is built upon a rock.'

'I'll tell Charles you call him a rock,' said Egg. 'And now for what I came to see you about. I've been worrying and worrying about that cutting from the paper that Oliver dropped from his wallet. You know, the one Miss Wills picked up and handed back to him. It seems to me that either Oliver is telling a downright lie when he says he doesn't remember its being there, *or else it never was there.* He dropped some odd bit of paper, and that woman pretended it was the nicotine cutting.'

'Why should she have done that, mademoiselle?'

'Because she wanted to get rid of it. She planted it on Oliver.'

'You mean she is the criminal?'

'Yes.'

'What was her motive?'

'It's no good asking me that. I can only suggest that she's a lunatic. Clever people often are rather mad. I can't see any other reason – in fact I can't see any motive anywhere.'

'Decidedly, that is the *impasse.* I should not ask *you* to guess at a motive. It is of myself that I ask that question without ceasing. *What was the motive behind Mr Babbington's death*? When I can answer that the case will be solved.'

'You don't think just madness –?' suggested Egg.

'No, mademoiselle – not madness in the sense you mean. There is a *reason.* I must find that reason.'

'Well, goodbye,' said Egg. 'I'm sorry to have disturbed you, but the idea just occurred to me. I must hurry. I'm going with Charles to the dress rehearsal of *Little Dog Laughed* – you know, the play Miss Wills has written for Angela Sutcliffe. It's the first night tomorrow.'

'*Mon dieu*!' cried Poirot.

'What is it? Has anything happened?'

'Yes, indeed something has happened. An idea. A superb idea. Oh, but I have been blind – blind –'

Egg stared at him. As though realizing his eccentricity, Poirot took a hold on himself. He patted Egg on the shoulder.

'You think I am mad. Not at all. I heard what you said. You go to see '*The Little Dog Laughed*, and Miss Sutcliffe acts in it. Go then, and pay no attention to what I have said.'

Rather doubtfully Egg departed. Left to himself, Poirot strode up and down the room muttering under his breath. His eyes shone green as any cat's.

'*Mais oui* – that explains everything. A curious motive – a very curious motive – such a motive as I have never come across before, and yet it is reasonable, and, given the circumstances, natural. Altogether a very curious case.'

He passed the table where his card house still reposed. With a sweep of his hands he swept the cards from the table.

'The happy family, I need it no longer,' he said. 'The problem is solved. It only remains to act.'

He caught up his hat and put on his overcoat. Then he went downstairs and the commissionaire called him a taxi. Poirot gave the address of Sir Charles's flat.

Arrived there, he paid off the taxi, and stepped into the hall. The porter was absent taking up the lift. Poirot walked up the stairs. Just as he arrived on the second floor the door of Sir Charles's flat opened and Miss Milray came out.

She started when she saw Poirot.

'You!'

Poirot smiled.

'Me! Or is it I? *Enfin, moi*!'

Miss Milray said:

'I'm afraid you won't find Sir Charles. He's gone to the Babylon Theatre with Miss Lytton Gore.'

'It is not Sir Charles I seek. It is my stick that I think I have left behind one day.'

'Oh, I see. Well, if you'll ring, Temple will find it for you. I'm sorry I can't stop. I'm on my way to catch a train. I'm going down to Kent – to my mother.'

'I comprehend. Do not let me delay you, mademoiselle.'

He stood aside and Miss Milray passed rapidly down the stairs. She was carrying a small attaché case.

But when she had gone Poirot seemed to forget the purpose

for which he had come. Instead of going on up to the landing, he turned and made his way downstairs again. He arrived at the front door just in time to see Miss Milray getting into a taxi. Another taxi was coming slowly along the kerb. Poirot raised a hand and it came to rest. He got in and directed the driver to follow the other taxi.

No surprise showed on his face when the first taxi went north and finally drew up at Paddington Station, though Paddington is an odd station from which to proceed to Kent. Poirot went to the first-class booking window and demanded a return ticket to Loomouth. The train was due to depart in five minutes. Pulling up his overcoat well about his ears, for the day was cold, Poirot ensconced himself in the corner of a first-class carriage.

They arrived at Loomouth about five o'clock. It was already growing dark. Standing back a little, Poirot heard Miss Milray being greeted by the friendly porter at the little station.

'Well, now, miss, we didn't expect you. Is Sir Charles coming down?'

Miss Milray replied:

'I've come down here unexpectedly. I shall be going back tomorrow morning. I've just come to fetch some things. No, I don't want a cab, thank you. I'll walk up by the cliff path.'

The dusk had deepened. Miss Milray walked briskly up the steep zigzag path. A good way behind came Hercule Poirot. He trod softly like a cat. Miss Milray, on arrival at Crow's Nest, produced a key from her bag and passed through the side door, leaving it ajar. She reappeared a minute or two later. She had a rusty door key and an electric torch in her hand. Poirot drew back a little behind a convenient bush.

Miss Milray passed round behind the house and up a scrambling overgrown path. Hercule Poirot followed. Up and up went Miss Milray until she came suddenly to an old stone tower such as is found often on that coast. This one was of humble and dilapidated appearance. There was, however, a curtain over the dirty window, and Miss Milray inserted her key in the big wooden door.

The key turned with a protesting creak. The door swung with a groan on its hinges. Miss Milray and her torch passed inside.

With an increase of pace Poirot caught up. He passed, in his turn, noiselessly through the door. The light of Miss Milray's torch gleamed fitfully on glass retorts, a bunsen burner – various apparatus.

Miss Milray had picked up a crowbar. She had raised it and was holding it over the glass apparatus when a hand caught her by the arm. She gasped and turned.

The green, catlike eyes of Poirot looked into hers.

'You cannot do that, mademoiselle,' he said. 'For what you seek to destroy is evidence.'

CHAPTER 15

Curtain

Hercule Poirot sat in a big arm-chair. The wall lights had been turned out. Only a rose-shaded lamp shed its glow on the figure in the arm-chair. There seemed something symbolic about it – he alone in the light – and the other three, Sir Charles, Mr Satterthwaite and Egg Lytton Gore – Poirot's audience – sitting in the outer darkness.

Hercule Poirot's voice was dreamy. He seemed to be addressing himself to space rather than to his listeners.

'To reconstruct the crime – that is the aim of the detective. To reconstruct a crime you must place one fact upon another just as you place one card on another in building a house of cards. And if the facts will not fit – if the card will not balance – well – you must start your house again, or else it will fall . . .

'As I said the other day, there are three different types of mind: There is the dramatic mind – the producer's mind, which sees the effect of reality that can be produced by mechanical appliances – there is also the mind that reacts easily to dramatic appearances – and there is the young romantic mind – and finally, my friends, there is the prosaic mind – the mind that sees not blue sea and mimosa trees, but the painted backcloth of stage scenery.

'So I come, *mes amis*, to the murder of Stephen Babbington in August last. On that evening Sir Charles Cartwright advanced the theory that Stephen Babbington had been murdered. I did not agree with that theory. I could not believe (a) that such a man as Stephen Babbington was likely to have been murdered, and (b) that it was possible to administer poison to a particular person under the circumstances that had obtained that evening.

'Now here I admit that Sir Charles was right and I was wrong. I was wrong because I was looking at the crime from an entirely false angle. It is only twenty-four hours ago that I suddenly perceived the proper angle of vision – and let me say that from that angle of vision the murder of Stephen Babbington is both *reasonable* and *possible*.

'But I will pass from that point for the moment and take you step by step along the path I myself have trodden. The death of Stephen Babbington I may call the first act of our drama. The curtain fell on that act when we all departed from Crow's Nest.

'What I might call the second act of the drama began in Monte Carlo when Mr Satterthwaite showed me the newspaper account of Sir Bartholomew's death. It was at once clear that I had been wrong and Sir Charles had been right. Both Stephen Babbington and Sir Bartholomew Strange had been murdered and the two murders formed part of one and the same crime. Later a third murder completed the series – the murder of Mrs de Rushbridger. What we need, therefore, is a reasonable common-sense theory which will link those three deaths together – in other words those three crimes were committed by one and the same person, and were to the advantage and benefit of that particular person.

'Now I may say at once that the principal thing that worried me was the fact that the murder of Sir Bartholomew Strange came *after* that of Stephen Babbington. Looking at those three murders without distinction of time and place the probabilities pointed to the murder of Sir Bartholomew Strange being what one might call the central or principal crime, and the other two murders as secondary in character – that is, arising from the connection of those two people with Sir Bartholomew Strange. However, as I remarked before – one cannot have one's crime as one would like to have it. Stephen Babbington had been murdered first and Sir Bartholomew Strange some time later. It seemed, therefore, as though the second crime must necessarily arise out of the first and that accordingly it was the first crime we must examine for the clue to the whole.

'I did indeed so far incline to the theory of probability that I seriously considered the idea of a *mistake* having arisen. Was it possible that Sir Bartholomew Strange was intended as the first victim, and that Mr Babbington was poisoned by mistake? I was forced, however, to abandon that idea. Anybody who knew Sir Bartholomew Strange with any degree of intimacy knew that he disliked the cocktail habit.

'Another suggestion: Had Stephen Babbington been poisoned in mistake for any other member of the original party? I could not find any evidence of such a thing. I was therefore forced back to the conclusion that the murder of Stephen Babbington had been definitely *intended* – and at once I came up against a complete stumbling block – the apparent *impossibility* of such a thing having happened.

'One should always start an investigation with the simplest and most obvious theories. Granting that Stephen Babbington had drunk a poisoned cocktail, who had had the opportunity of poisoning that cocktail? At first sight, it seemed to me that the only two people who could have done so (e.g., who handled the drinks) were Sir Charles Cartwright himself and the parlourmaid Temple. But though either of them could presumably have introduced the poison into the glass, *neither of them had had any opportunity of directing that particular glass into Mr Babbington's hand.* Temple might have done so by adroit handing of the tray so as to offer him the one remaining glass – (not easy, but it might have been done). Sir Charles could have done so by deliberately picking up the particular glass and handing it to him. But neither of these things had occurred. It looked as though *chance* and *chance* alone directed that particular glass to Stephen Babbington.

'Sir Charles Cartwright and Temple had the handling of the cocktails. Were either of those two at Melfort Abbey? They were not. Who had the best chance of tampering with Sir Bartholomew's port glass? The absconding butler, Ellis, and his helper, the parlourmaid. But here, however, the possibility that one of the guests had done so could not be laid aside. It was risky, but it was possible, for any of the house-party to have slipped into the dining-room and put the nicotine into the port glass.

'When I joined you at Crow's Nest you already had a list drawn up of the people who had been at Crow's Nest and at Melfort Abbey. I may say now that the four names which headed the list – Captain and Mrs Dacres, Miss Sutcliffe and Miss Wills – I discarded immediately.

'It was *impossible* that any of those four people should have known *beforehand* that they were going to meet Stephen Babbington at dinner. The employment of nicotine as a poison showed a carefully thought-out plan, not one that could be put into operation on the spur of the moment. There were three other names on that list – Lady Mary Lytton Gore, Miss Lytton Gore and Mr Oliver Manders. Although not probable, those three were *possible*. They were local people, they might conceivably have motives for the removal of Stephen Babbington, and have chosen the evening of the dinner-party for putting their plans into operation.

'On the other hand, I could find no evidence whatsoever that any of them had actually done such a thing.

'Mr Satterthwaite, I think, reasoned on much the same lines as I had done, and he fixed his suspicions on Oliver Manders. I may say that young Manders was by far the most possible suspect. He displayed all the signs of high nervous tension on that evening at Crow's Nest – he had a somewhat distorted view of life owing to his private troubles – he had a strong inferiority complex, which is a frequent cause of crime, he was at an unbalanced age, he had actually had a quarrel, or shall we say had displayed animosity against Mr Babbington. Then there were the curious circumstances of his arrival at Melfort Abbey. And later we had his somewhat incredible story of the letter from Sir Bartholomew Strange and the evidence of Miss Wills as to his having a newspaper cutting on the subject of nicotine poisoning in his possession.

'Oliver Manders, then, was clearly the person who should be placed at the head of the list of those seven suspects.

'But then, my friends, I was visited by a curious sensation. It seemed clear and logical enough that the person who had committed the crimes *must have been a person who had been present on both occasions*; in other words *a person on that list of seven – but I had the feeling that that obviousness was an arranged obviousness*. It was what any sane and logical person would be *expected* to think. I felt that I was, in fact, looking not at reality but at an artfully painted bit of scenery. A really clever criminal would have realized that *anyone whose name was on that list would necessarily be suspect*, and therefore he or she would arrange for it not to be there.

'In other words, the murderer of Stephen Babbington and Sir Bartholomew Strange *was* present on both occasions – but was not *apparently* so.

'Who had been present on the first occasion and not on the second? Sir Charles Cartwright, Mr Satterthwaite, Miss Milray and Mr Babbington.

'Could any of those four have been present on the second occasion in some capacity other than their own? Sir Charles and Mr Satterthwaite had been in the South of France, Miss Milray had been in London, Mrs Babbington had been in Loomouth. Of the four, then, Miss Milray and Mrs Babbington seemed indicated. But could Miss Milray have been present at Melfort Abbey unrecognized by any of the company? Miss Milray has very striking features not easily disguised and not easily forgotten. I decided that it was impossible that Miss Milray could have been at Melfort Abbey unrecognized. The same applied to Mrs Babbington.

'For the matter of that could Mr Satterthwaite or Sir Charles Cartwright have been at Melfort Abbey and not been recognized? Mr Satterthwaite just possibly; but when we come to Sir Charles Cartwright we come to a very different matter. Sir Charles is an actor accustomed to playing a part. But what part could he have played?

'And then I came to the consideration of the butler Ellis.

'A very mysterious person, Ellis. A person who appears from nowhere a fortnight before the crime and vanishes afterwards with complete success. Why was Ellis so successful? *Because Ellis did not really exist.* Ellis, again, was a thing of pasteboard and paint and stagecraft – Ellis was not *real.*

'But was it *possible*? After all, the servants at Melfort Abbey knew Sir Charles Cartwright, and Sir Bartholomew Strange was an intimate friend of his. The servants I got over easily enough. The impersonation of the butler risked nothing – if the servants recognized him – why, no harm would be done – the whole thing could be passed off as a joke. If, on the other hand, a fortnight passed without any suspicion being aroused, well, the thing was safe as houses. And I recalled what I had been told of the servants' remarks about the butler. He was "quite the gentleman", and had been "in good houses", and knew several interesting scandals. That was easy enough. But a very significant statement was made by the parlourmaid Alice. She said, "He arranged the work different from any butler I ever knew before." When that remark was repeated to me, it became a confirmation of my theory.

'But Sir Bartholomew Strange was another matter. It is hardly to be supposed that his friend could take him in. He must have known of the impersonation. Had we any evidence of that? Yes. The acute Mr Satterthwaite pounced on one point quite early in the proceedings – the facetious remark of Sir Bartholomew (totally uncharacteristic of his manner to servants) – "You're a first-class butler, aren't you, Ellis?" *A perfectly understandable remark if the butler were Sir Charles Cartwright and Sir Bartholomew was in on the joke.*

'Because that is undoubtedly how Sir Bartholomew saw the matter. The impersonation of Ellis was a joke, possibly even a wager, its culmination was designed to be the successful spoofing of the house-party – hence Sir Bartholomew's remark about a surprise and his cheerful humour. Note, too, that there was still time to draw back. If any of the house-party had spotted Charles Cartwright that first evening at the dinner-table, nothing irrevocable had yet occurred. The whole thing could have been passed off as a joke. But nobody noticed the stooping middle-aged butler, with his belladonna darkened eyes, and his whiskers, and the painted birthmark on his wrist. A very subtle identifying touch that – which completely failed, owing to the lack of observation of most human beings! The birthmark was intended to bulk largely in the description of Ellis – and in all that fortnight no one noticed it! The only person who did was the sharp-eyed Miss Wills, to whom we shall come presently.

'What happened next? Sir Bartholomew died. This time the death was not put down to natural causes. The police came. They questioned Ellis and the others. Later that night "Ellis" left by the secret passage, resumed his own personality, and two days later was strolling about the gardens at Monte Carlo ready to be shocked and surprised by the news of his friend's death.

'This, mind you, was all theory. I had no actual proof, but everything that arose supported that theory. My house of cards was well and truly built. The blackmailing letters discovered in Ellis's room? But it was Sir Charles himself who discovered them!

'And what of the supposed letter from Sir Bartholomew Strange asking young Manders to arrange an accident? Well, what could be easier than for Sir Charles to write that letter in Sir Bartholomew's name? If Manders had not destroyed that letter himself, Sir Charles in the rôle of Ellis can easily do so when he valets the young gentleman. In the same way the newspaper cutting is easily introduced by Ellis into Oliver Manders's wallet.

'And now we come to the third victim – Mrs de Rushbridger. When do we first hear of Mrs de Rushbridger? Immediately after that very awkward chaffing reference to Ellis being the perfect butler – that extremely uncharacteristic utterance of Sir Bartholomew Strange. At all costs attention must be drawn away from Sir Bartholomew's manner to his butler. Sir Charles quickly asks what was the message the butler had brought. It is about this woman – this patient of the doctor's. And immediately Sir Charles throws all his personality into directing attention to this unknown woman and away from the butler. He goes to the Sanatorium and questions the Matron. He runs Mrs de Rushbridger for all he is worth as a red herring.

'We must now examine the part played by Miss Wills in the drama. Miss Wills has a curious personality. She is one of those people who are quite unable to impress themselves on their surroundings. She is neither good-looking nor witty nor clever, not even particularly sympathetic. She is nondescript. But she is extremely observant and extremely intelligent. She takes her revenge on the world with her pen. She has the great art of being able to reproduce character on paper. I do not know if there was anything about the butler that struck Miss Wills as unusual, but I do think that she was the only person at the table who noticed him at all. On the morning after the murder her insatiable curiosity led her to poke and pry, as the housemaid put it. She went into Dacres's room, she went through the baize door into the servants' quarters, led, I think, by the mongoose instinct for finding out.

'She was the only person who occasioned Sir Charles any uneasiness. That is why he was anxious to be the one to tackle her. He was fairly reassured by his interview and distinctly gratified that she had noticed the birthmark. But after that came catastrophe. I don't think that until that minute Miss Wills had connected Ellis the butler with Sir Charles Cartwright. I think she had only been vaguely struck by some resemblance to someone in Ellis. But she was an observer. When dishes were handed to her she had automatically noted – not the face – but the hands that held the dishes.

'It did not occur to her that *Ellis was Sir Charles*. But when Sir Charles was talking to her it did suddenly occur to her that *Sir Charles was Ellis*! And so she asked him to pretend to hand her a dish of vegetables. But it was not whether the birthmark was on the right or left wrist that interested her. She wanted a pretext to study his *hands* – hands held in the same position as those of Ellis the butler.

'And so she leaped to the truth. But she was a peculiar woman. She enjoyed knowledge for its own sake. Besides, she was by no means sure that Sir Charles had murdered his friend. He had masqueraded as a butler, yes – but that did not necessarily make him a murderer. Many an innocent man has kept silence because speech would place him in an awkward position.

'So Miss Wills kept her knowledge to herself – and enjoyed it. But Sir Charles was worried. He did not like that expression of satisfied malice on her face that he saw as he left the room. She knew something. What? Did it affect him? He could not be sure. But he felt that it was something connected with Ellis the butler. First Mr Satterthwaite – now Miss Wills. Attention *must* be drawn away from that vital point. It *must* be focused definitely elsewhere. And he thought of a plan – simple, audacious and, as he fancied, definitely mystifying.

'On the day of my Sherry Party I imagine Sir Charles rose very early, went to Yorkshire and, disguised in shabby clothes, gave the telegram to a small boy to send off. Then he returned to town in time to act the part I had indicated in my little drama. He did one more thing. *He posted a box of chocolates to a woman he had never seen and of whom he knew nothing . . .*

'You know what happened that evening. From Sir Charles's uneasiness I was fairly sure that Miss Wills had certain suspicions. When Sir Charles did his "death scene" I watched Miss Wills's face. I saw the look of astonishment that showed on it. I knew then that *Miss Wills definitely suspected Sir Charles of being the murderer*. When he appeared to die poisoned like the other two she thought her deductions must be wrong.

'But if Miss Wills suspected Sir Charles, then Miss Wills was in serious danger. A man who has killed twice will kill again. I uttered a very solemn warning. Later that night I communicated with Miss Wills by telephone, and on my advice she left home suddenly the next day. Since then she has been living here in this hotel. That I was wise is proved by the fact that Sir Charles went out to Tooting on the following evening after he had returned from Gilling. He was too late. The bird had flown.

'In the meantime, from his point of view, the plan had worked well. Mrs de Rushbridger had something of importance to tell us. Mrs de Rushbridger was killed before she could speak. How dramatic! How like the detective stories, the plays, the films! Again the cardboard and the tinsel and the painted cloth.

'But I, Hercule Poirot, was not deceived. Mr Satterthwaite said to me she was killed in order that she should not speak. I agreed. He went on to say she was killed before she could tell us what she knew. I said, "*Or what she did* NOT *know.*" I think he was puzzled. But he should have seen then the truth. Mrs de Rushbridger was killed because she could, in actual fact, have told us *nothing at all.* Because she had no connection with the crime. If she were to be Sir Charles's successful red herring – she could only be so *dead.* And so Mrs de Rushbridger, a harmless stranger, was murdered . . .

'Yet even in that seeming triumph Sir Charles made a colossal – a childish – error! The telegram was addressed to me, Hercule Poirot, at the Ritz Hotel. But Mrs de Rushbridger had never heard of my connection with the case! No one up in that part of the world knew of it. It was an unbelievably childish error.

'*Eh bien*, then I had reached a certain stage. I knew the identity of the murderer. But I did not know the motive for the original crime.

'I reflected.

'And once again, more clearly than ever, I saw the death of Sir Bartholomew Strange as the original and purposeful murder. What reason could Sir Charles Cartwright have for the murder of his friend? Could I imagine a motive? I thought I could.'

There was a deep sigh. Sir Charles Cartwright rose slowly to his feet and strolled to the fireplace. He stood there, his hand on his hip, looking down at Poirot. His attitude (Mr Satterthwaite could have told you) was that of Lord Eaglemount as he looks scornfully at the rascally solicitor who has succeeded in fastening an accusation of fraud upon him. He radiated nobility and disgust. He was the aristocrat looking down at the ignoble canaille.

'You have an extraordinary imagination, M. Poirot,' he said. 'It's hardly worth while saying that there's not one single word of truth in your story. How you have the damned impertinence to dish up such an absurd fandangle of lies I don't know. But go on, I am interested. What was my motive for murdering a man whom I had known ever since boyhood?'

Hercule Poirot, the little bourgeois, looked up at the aristocrat. He spoke quickly but firmly.

'Sir Charles, we have a proverb that says, "*Cherchez la femme.*" It was *there* that I found my motive. I had seen you with Mademoiselle Lytton Gore. It was clear that you loved her – loved her with that terrible absorbing passion that comes to a middle-aged man and which is usually inspired by an innocent young girl.

'You loved her. She, I could see, had the hero worship for you. You had only to speak and she would fall into your arms. But you did not speak. Why?

'You pretended to your friend, Mr Satterthwaite, that you were the dense lover who cannot recognize his mistress's answering passion. You pretended to think that Miss Lytton Gore was in love with Oliver Manders. But I say, Sir Charles, that you are a man of the world. You are a man with a great experience of women. *You cannot have been deceived.* You knew perfectly well that Miss Lytton Gore cared for you. Why, then, did you not marry her? You wanted to do so.

'It must be that there was some obstacle. What could that obstacle be? It could only be the fact that you already had a wife. But nobody ever spoke of you as a married man. You passed always as a bachelor. The marriage, then, had taken place when you were very young – before you became known as a rising young actor.

'What had happened to your wife? If she were still alive, why did nobody know about her? If you were living apart there was the remedy of divorce. If your wife was a Catholic, or one who disapproved of divorce, she would still be known as living apart from you.

'But there are two tragedies where the law gives no relief. The woman you married might be serving a life sentence in some prison, or she might be confined in a lunatic asylum. *In neither case could you obtain a divorce*, and if it had happened while you were still a boy nobody might know about it.

'If nobody knew, you might marry Miss Lytton Gore without telling her the truth. *But supposing one person knew* – a friend who had known you all your life? Sir Bartholomew Strange was an honourable, upright physician. He might pity you deeply, he might sympathize with a liaison or an irregular life, but he would not stand by silent and see you enter into a bigamous marriage with an unsuspecting young girl.

'Before you could marry Miss Lytton Gore, Sir Bartholomew Strange must be removed . . .'

Sir Charles laughed.

'And dear old Babbington? Did he know all about it, too?'

'I fancied so at first. But I soon found that there was no evidence to support that theory. Besides, my original stumbling block remained. *Even if it was you who put the nicotine into the cocktail glass, you could not have ensured its reaching one particular person.*

'That was my problem. And suddenly a chance word from Miss Lytton Gore showed me light.

'The poison was not intended especially for Stephen Babbington. It was intended for *any one* of those present, with three exceptions. These exceptions were Miss Lytton Gore, to whom you were careful to hand an innocent glass, yourself, and Sir Bartholomew Strange, who, you knew, did not drink cocktails.'

Mr Satterthwaite cried out:

'But that's nonsense! What's the point of it? There isn't any.'

Poirot turned towards him. Triumph came into his voice.

'Oh, yes, there is. A queer point – a very queer point. The only time I have come across such a motive for murder. The murder of Stephen Babbington was neither more nor less than a *dress rehearsal*.'

'*What*?'

'Yes, Sir Charles was an actor. He obeyed his actor's instinct. He tried out his murder before committing it. No suspicion could possibly attach to him. Not one of those people's deaths could benefit him in any way, and, moreover, as everyone has found, *he could not have been proved to have poisoned any particular person*. And, my friends, the dress rehearsal went well. Mr Babbington dies, and foul play is not even suspected. It is left to Sir Charles to urge that suspicion and he is highly gratified at our refusal to take it seriously. The substitution of the glass, too, that has gone without a hitch. In fact, he can be sure that, when the real performance comes, it will be "all right on the night".

'As you know, events took a slightly different turn. On the second occasion a doctor was present who immediately suspected poison. It was then to Sir Charles's interests to stress the death of Babbington. Sir Bartholomew's death must be presumed to be the outcome of the earlier death. Attention must be focused on the motive for Babbington's murder, not on any motive that might exist for Sir Bartholomew's removal.

'But there was one thing that Sir Charles failed to realize – the efficient watchfulness of Miss Milray. Miss Milray knew that her employer dabbled in chemical experiments in the tower in the garden. Miss Milray paid bills for rose spraying solution, and realized that quite a lot of it had unaccountably disappeared. When she read that Mr Babbington had died of nicotine poisoning, her clever brain leaped at once to the conclusion that Sir Charles had extracted the pure alkaloid from the rose solution.

'And Miss Milray did not know what to do, for she had known Mr Babbington as a little girl, and she was in love, deeply and devotedly as an ugly woman can be, with her fascinating employer.

'In the end she decided to destroy Sir Charles's apparatus. Sir Charles himself had been so cocksure of his success that he had never thought it necessary. She went down to Cornwall, and I followed.'

Again Sir Charles laughed. More than ever he looked a fine gentleman disgusted by a rat.

'Is some old chemical apparatus all your evidence?' he demanded contemptuously.

'No,' said Poirot. 'There is your passport showing the dates when you returned to and left England. And there is the fact that in the Harverton County Asylum there is a woman, Gladys Mary Mugg, the wife of Charles Mugg.'

Egg had so far sat silent – a frozen figure. But now she stirred. A little cry – almost a moan – came from her.

Sir Charles turned superbly.

'Egg, you don't believe a word of this absurd story, do you?'

He laughed. His hands were outstretched.

Egg came slowly forward as though hypnotized. Her eyes, appealing, tortured, gazed into her lover's. And then, just before she reached him, she wavered, her glance fell, went this way and that as though seeking for reassurance.

Then with a cry she fell on her knees by Poirot.

'Is this true? Is this true?'

He put both hands on her shoulders, a firm, kindly touch.

'It is true, mademoiselle.'

There was no sound then but Egg's sobs.

Sir Charles seemed suddenly to have aged. It was an old man's face, a leering satyr's face.

'God damn you,' he said.

And never, in all his acting career, had words come with such utter and compelling malignancy.

Then he turned and went out of the room.

Mr Satterthwaite half sprang up from his chair, but Poirot shook his head, his hand still gently stroking the sobbing girl.

'He'll escape,' said Mr Satterthwaite.

Poirot shook his head.

'No, he will only choose his exit. The slow one before the eyes of the world, or the quick one off stage.'

The door opened softly and someone came in. It was Oliver Manders. His usual sneering expression was gone. He looked white and unhappy.

Poirot bent over the girl.

'See, mademoiselle,' he said gently. 'Here is a friend come to take you home.'

Egg rose to her feet. She looked uncertainly towards Oliver then made a step stumblingly towards him.

'Oliver . . . Take me to Mother. Oh, take me to Mother.'

He put an arm round her and drew her towards the door.

'Yes, dear, I'll take you. Come.'

Egg's legs were trembling so that she could hardly walk. Between them Oliver and Mr Satterthwaite guided her footsteps.

At the door she took a hold upon herself and threw back her head.

'I'm all right.'

Poirot made a gesture, and Oliver Manders came back into the room.

'Be very good to her,' said Poirot.

'I will, sir. She's all I care about in the world – you know that. Love for her made me bitter and cynical. But I shall be different now. I'm ready to stand by. And some day, perhaps –'

'I think so,' said Poirot. 'I think she was beginning to care for you when he came along and dazzled her. Hero worship is a real and terrible danger to the young. Some day Egg will fall in love with a friend, and build her happiness upon rock.'

He looked kindly after the young man as he left the room.

Presently Mr Satterthwaite returned.

'M. Poirot,' he said. 'You have been wonderful – absolutely wonderful.'

Poirot put on his modest look.

'It is nothing – nothing. A tragedy in three acts – and now the curtain has fallen.'

'You'll excuse me –' said Mr Satterthwaite.

'Yes, there is some point you want explained to you?'

'There is one thing I want to know.'

'Ask then.'

'Why do you sometimes speak perfectly good English and at other times not?'

Poirot laughed.

'Ah, I will explain. It is true that I can speak the exact, the idiomatic English. But, my friend, to speak the broken English is an enormous asset. It leads people to despise you. They say – a foreigner – he can't even speak English properly. It is not my policy to terrify people – instead I invite their gentle ridicule. Also I boast! An Englishman he says often, "A fellow who thinks as much of himself as that cannot be worth much." That is the English point of view. It is not at all true. And so, you see, I put people off their guard. Besides,' he added, 'it has become a habit.'

'Dear me,' said Mr Satterthwaite, 'quite the cunning of the serpent.'

He was silent for a moment or two, thinking over the case.

'I'm afraid I have not shone over this matter,' he said vexedly.

'On the contrary. You appreciated that important point – Sir Bartholomew's remark about the butler – you realized the astute observation of Miss Wills. In fact, you could have solved the whole thing but for your playgoer's reaction to dramatic effect.'

Mr Satterthwaite looked cheerful.

Suddenly an idea struck him. His jaw fell.

'My goodness,' he cried, 'I've only just realized it. That rascal, with his poisoned cocktail! Anyone might have drunk it. It might have been *me*.'

'There is an even more terrible possibility that you have not considered,' said Poirot.

'Eh?'

'It might have been ME,' said Hercule Poirot.

DEAD MAN'S MIRROR

CHAPTER 1

I

The flat was a modern one. The furnishings of the room were modern, too. The armchairs were squarely built, the upright chairs were angular. A modern writing-table was set squarely in front of the window, and at it sat a small, elderly man. His head was practically the only thing in the room that was not square. It was egg-shaped.

M. Hercule Poirot was reading a letter:

Station: Whimperley.
Telegrams:
Hamborough St. John.

Hamborough Close,
Hamborough St Mary
Westshire.

September 24th, 1936.

M. Hercule Poirot.

Dear Sir, – A matter has arisen which requires handling with great delicacy and discretion. I have heard good accounts of you, and have decided to entrust the matter to you. I have reason to believe that I am the victim of fraud, but for family reasons I do not wish to call in the police. I am taking certain measures of my own to deal with the business, but you must be prepared to come down here immediately on receipt of a telegram. I should be obliged if you will not answer this letter.

Yours faithfully,
Gervase Chevenix-Gore.

The eyebrows of M. Hercule Poirot climbed slowly up his forehead until they nearly disappeared into his hair.

'And who, then,' he demanded of space, 'is this Gervase Chevenix-Gore?'

He crossed to a bookcase and took out a large, fat book.

He found what he wanted easily enough.

Chevenix-Gore, Sir Gervase Francis Xavier, 10th Bt. cr. 1694; formerly Captain 17th Lancers; b. 18th May, 1878; e.s. of Sir Guy Chevenix-Gore, 9th Bt., and Lady Claudia Bretherton, 2nd. d. of 8th Earl of Wallingford. S. father, 1911; m. 1912, Vanda Elizabeth, e.d. of Colonel Frederick Arbuthnot, q.v.; educ. Eton. Served European War, 1914–18. Recreations: travelling, big-game hunting. Address: Hamborough St Mary, Westshire, and 218 Lowndes Square, S.W.1. Clubs: Cavalry. Travellers.

Poirot shook his head in a slightly dissatisfied manner. For a moment or two he remained lost in thought, then he went to the desk, pulled open a drawer and took out a little pile of invitation cards.

His face brightened.

'*A la bonne heure!* Exactly my affair! He will certainly be there.'

II

A duchess greeted M. Hercule Poirot in fulsome tones.

'So you could manage to come after all, M. Poirot! Why, that's splendid.'

'The pleasure is mine, madame,' murmured Poirot, bowing.

He escaped from several important and splendid beings – a famous diplomat, an equally famous actress and a well-known sporting peer – and found at last the person he had come to seek, that invariably 'also present' guest, Mr Satterthwaite.

Mr Satterthwaite twittered amiably.

'The dear duchess – I always enjoy her parties . . . Such a *personality*, if you know what I mean. I saw a lot of her in Corsica some years ago . . .'

Mr Satterthwaite's conversation was apt to be unduly burdened by mentions of his titled acquaintances. It is possible that he *may* sometimes have found pleasure in the company of Messrs. Jones, Brown or Robinson, but, if so, he did not mention the fact. And yet, to describe Mr Satterthwaite as a mere snob and leave it at that would have been to do him an injustice. He was a keen observer of human nature, and if it is true that the looker-on knows most of the game, Mr Satterthwaite knew a good deal.

'You know, my dear fellow, it is really ages since I saw you. I always feel myself privileged to have seen you work at close quarters in the Crow's Nest business. I feel since then that I am in the know, so to speak. I saw Lady Mary only last week, by the way. A charming creature – pot-pourri and lavender!'

After passing lightly on one or two scandals of the moment – the indiscretions of an earl's daughter, and the lamentable conduct of a viscount – Poirot succeeded in introducing the name of Gervase Chevenix-Gore.

Mr Satterthwaite responded immediately.

'Ah, now, there *is* a character, if you like! The Last of the Baronets – that's his nickname.'

'*Pardon*, I do not quite comprehend.'

Mr Satterthwaite unbent indulgently to the lower comprehension of a foreigner.

'It's a joke, you know – a *joke*. Naturally, he's not *really* the last baronet in England – but he *does* represent the end of an era. The Bold Bad Baronet – the mad harum-scarum baronet so popular in the novels of the last century – the kind of fellow who laid impossible wagers and won 'em.'

He went on to expound what he meant in more detail. In younger years, Gervase Chevenix-Gore had sailed round the world in a windjammer. He had been on an expedition to the Pole. He had challenged a racing peer to a duel. For a wager he had ridden his favourite mare up the staircase of a ducal house. He had once leapt from a box to the stage and carried off a well-known actress in the middle of her rôle.

The anecdotes of him were innumerable.

'It's an old family,' went on Mr Satterthwaite. 'Sir Guy de Chevenix went on the first crusade. Now, alas, the line looks like coming to an end. Old Gervase is the last Chevenix-Gore.'

'The estate, it is impoverished?'

'Not a bit of it. Gervase is fabulously wealthy. Owns valuable house property – coalfields – and in addition he staked out a claim to some mine in Peru or somewhere in South America, when he was a young man, which has yielded him a fortune. An amazing man. Always lucky in everything he's undertaken.'

'He is now an elderly man, of course?'

'Yes, poor old Gervase.' Mr Satterthwaite sighed, shook his head. 'Most people would describe him to you as mad as a hatter. It's true, in a way. He *is* mad – not in the sense of being certifiable or having delusions – but mad in the sense of being abnormal. He's always been a man of great originality of character.'

'And originality becomes eccentricity as the years go by?' suggested Poirot.

'Very true. That's exactly what's happened to poor old Gervase.'

'He has perhaps, a swollen idea of his own importance?'

'Absolutely. I should imagine that, in Gervase's mind, the world has always been divided into two parts – there are the Chevenix-Gores, and the other people!'

'An exaggerated sense of family!'

'Yes. The Chevenix-Gores are all arrogant as the devil – a law unto themselves. Gervase, being the last of them, has got it badly. He is – well, really, you know, to hear him talk, you might imagine him to be – er, the Almighty!'

Poirot nodded his head slowly and thoughtfully.

'Yes, I imagined that. I have had, you see, a letter from him. It was an unusual letter. It did not demand. It summoned!'

'A royal command,' said Mr Satterthwaite, tittering a little.

'Precisely. It did not seem to occur to this Sir Gervase that I, Hercule Poirot, am a man of importance, a man of infinite affairs! That it was extremely unlikely that I should be able to fling everything aside and come hastening like an obedient dog – like a mere nobody, gratified to receive a commission!'

Mr Satterthwaite bit his lip in an effort to suppress a smile. It may have occurred to him that where egoism was concerned, there was not much to choose between Hercule Poirot and Gervase Chevenix-Gore.

He murmured:

'Of course, if the cause of the summons was urgent –?'

'It was not!' Poirot's hands rose in the air in an emphatic

gesture. 'I was to hold myself at his disposition, that was all, *in case* he should require me! *Enfin, je vous demande!*'

Again the hands rose eloquently, expressing better than words could do M. Hercule Poirot's sense of utter outrage.

'I take it,' said Mr Satterthwaite, 'that you refused?'

'I have not yet had the opportunity,' said Poirot slowly.

'But you will refuse?'

A new expression passed over the little man's face. His brow furrowed itself perplexedly.

He said:

'How can I express myself? To refuse – yes, that was my first instinct. But I do not know . . . One has, sometimes, a feeling. Faintly, I seem to smell the fish . . .'

Mr Satterthwaite received this last statement without any sign of amusement.

'Oh?' he said. 'That is interesting . . .'

'It seems to me,' went on Hercule Poirot, 'that a man such as you have described might be very vulnerable –'

'Vulnerable?' queried Mr Satterthwaite. For the moment he was surprised. The word was not one that he would naturally have associated with Gervase Chevenix-Gore. But he was a man of perception, quick in observation. He said slowly:

'I think I see what you mean.'

'Such a one is encased, is he not, in an armour – such an armour! The armour of the crusaders was nothing to it – an armour of arrogance, of pride, of complete self-esteem. This armour, it is in some ways a protection, the arrows, the everyday arrows of life glance off it. But there is this danger; *Sometimes a man in armour might not even know he was being attacked.* He will be slow to see, slow to hear – slower still to feel.'

He paused, then asked with a change of manner:

'Of what does the family of this Sir Gervase consist?'

'There's Vanda – his wife. She was an Arbuthnot – very handsome girl. She's still quite a handsome woman. Frightfully vague, though. Devoted to Gervase. She's got a leaning towards the occult, I believe. Wears amulets and scarabs and gives out that she's the reincarnation of an Egyptian Queen . . . Then there's Ruth – she's their adopted daughter. They've no children of their own. Very attractive girl in the modern style. That's all the family. Except, of course, for Hugo Trent. He's Gervase's nephew. Pamela Chevenix-Gore married Reggie Trent and Hugo was their only child. He's an orphan. He can't inherit the title, of course, but I imagine he'll come in for most of Gervase's money in the end. Good-looking lad, he's in the Blues.'

Poirot nodded his head thoughtfully. Then he asked:

'It is a grief to Sir Gervase, yes, that he has no son to inherit his name?'

'I should imagine that it cuts pretty deep.'

'The family name, it is a passion with him?'

'Yes.'

Mr Satterthwaite was silent a moment or two. He was very intrigued. Finally he ventured:

'You see a definite reason for going down to Hamborough Close?'

Slowly, Poirot shook his head.

'No,' he said. 'As far as I can see, there is no reason at all. But, all the same, I fancy I shall go.'

CHAPTER 2

Hercule Poirot sat in the corner of a first-class carriage speeding through the English countryside.

Meditatively he took from his pocket a neatly-folded telegram, which he opened and re-read:

Take four-thirty from St Pancras instruct guard have express stopped at Whimperley.
Chevenix-Gore.

He folded up the telegram again and put it back in his pocket.

The guard on the train had been obsequious. The gentleman was going to Hamborough Close? Oh, yes, Sir Gervase Chevenix-Gore's guests always had the express stopped at Whimperley. 'A special kind of prerogative, I think it is, sir.'

Since then the guard had paid two visits to the carriage – the first in order to assure the traveller that everything would be done to keep the carriage for himself, the second to announce that the express was running ten minutes late.

The train was due to arrive at 7.50, but it was exactly two minutes past eight when Hercule Poirot descended on to the platform of the little country station and pressed the expected half-crown into the attentive guard's hand.

There was a whistle from the engine, and the Northern Express began to move once more. A tall chauffeur in dark green uniform stepped up to Poirot.

'Mr Poirot? For Hamborough Close?'

He picked up the detective's neat valise and led the way out of the station. A big Rolls was waiting. The chauffeur held the door open for Poirot to get in, arranged a sumptuous fur rug over his knees, and they drove off.

After some ten minutes of cross-country driving, round sharp corners and down country lanes, the car turned in at a wide gateway flanked with huge stone griffons.

They drove through a park and up to the house. The door of it was opened as they drew up, and a butler of imposing proportions showed himself upon the front step.

'Mr Poirot? This way, sir.'

He led the way along the hall and threw open a door half-way along it on the right.

'Mr Hercule Poirot,' he announced.

The room contained a number of people in evening dress, and as Poirot walked in his quick eyes perceived at once that his appearance was not expected. The eyes of all present rested on him in unfeigned surprise.

Then a tall woman, whose dark hair was threaded with grey, made an uncertain advance towards him.

Poirot bowed over her hand.

'My apologies, madame,' he said. 'I fear that my train was late.'

'Not at all,' said Lady Chevenix-Gore vaguely. Her eyes still stared at him in a puzzled fashion. 'Not at all, Mr – er – I didn't quite hear –'

'Hercule Poirot.'

He said the name clearly and distinctly.

Somewhere behind him he heard a sudden sharp intake of breath.

At the same time he realized that clearly his host could not be in the room. He murmured gently:

'You knew I was coming, madame?'

'Oh – oh, yes . . .' Her manner was not convincing. 'I think – I mean I suppose so, but I am so terribly impractical, M. Poirot. I forget everything.' Her tone held a melancholy pleasure in the fact. 'I am told things. I appear to take them in – but they just pass through my brain and are gone! Vanished! As though they had never been.'

Then, with a slight air of performing a duty long overdue, she glanced round her vaguely and murmured:

'I expect you know everybody.'

Though this was patently not the case, the phrase was clearly a well-worn formula by means of which Lady Chevenix-Gore spared herself the trouble of introduction and the strain of remembering people's right names.

Making a supreme effort to meet the difficulties of this particular case, she added:

'My daughter – Ruth.'

The girl who stood before him was also tall and dark, but she was of a very different type. Instead of the flattish, indeterminate features of Lady Chevenix-Gore, she had a well-chiselled nose, slightly aquiline, and a clear, sharp line of jaw. Her black hair swept back from her face into a mass of little tight curls. Her colouring was of carnation clearness and brilliance, and owed little to make-up. She was, so Hercule Poirot thought, one of the loveliest girls he had seen.

He recognized, too, that she had brains as well as beauty, and guessed at certain qualities of pride and temper. Her voice, when she spoke, came with a slight drawl that struck him as deliberately put on.

'How exciting,' she said, 'to entertain M. Hércule Poirot! The old man arranged a little surprise for us, I suppose.'

'So you did not know I was coming, mademoiselle?' he said quickly.

'I hadn't an idea of it. As it is, I must postpone getting my autograph book until after dinner.'

The notes of a gong sounded from the hall, then the butler opened the door and announced:

'Dinner is served.'

And then, almost before the last word, 'served', had been uttered, something very curious happened. The pontifical domestic figure became, just for one moment, a highly-astonished human being . . .

The metamorphosis was so quick and the mask of the well-trained servant was back again so soon, that anyone who had not happened to be looking would not have noticed the change. Poirot, however, *had* happened to be looking. He wondered.

The butler hesitated in the doorway. Though his face was again correctly expressionless, an air of tension hung about his figure.

Lady Chevenix-Gore said uncertainly:

'Oh, dear – this is most extraordinary. Really, I – one hardly knows what to do.'

Ruth said to Poirot:

'This singular consternation, M. Poirot, is occasioned by the fact that my father, for the first time for at least twenty years, is late for dinner.'

'It is most extraordinary –' wailed Lady Chevenix-Gore. 'Gervase never –'

An elderly man of upright soldierly carriage came to her side. He laughed genially.

'Good old Gervase! Late at last! Upon my word, we'll rag him over this. Elusive collar-stud, d'you think? Or is Gervase immune from our common weaknesses?'

Lady Chevenix-Gore said in a low, puzzled voice:

'But Gervase is *never* late.'

It was almost ludicrous, the consternation caused by this simple *contretemps*. And yet, to Hercule Poirot, it was *not* ludicrous . . . Behind the consternation he felt uneasiness – perhaps even apprehension. And he, too, found it strange that Gervase Chevenix-Gore should not appear to greet the guest he had summoned in such a mysterious manner.

In the meantime, it was clear that nobody knew quite what to do. An unprecedented situation had arisen with which nobody knew how to deal.

Lady Chevenix-Gore at last took the initiative, if initiative it can be called. Certainly her manner was vague in the extreme.

'Snell,' she said, 'is your master –?'

She did not finish the sentence, merely looked at the butler expectantly.

Snell, who was clearly used to his mistress's methods of seeking information, replied promptly to the unspecified question:

'Sir Gervase came downstairs at five minutes to eight, m'lady, and went straight to the study.'

'Oh, I see –' Her mouth remained open, her eyes seemed far away. 'You don't think – I mean – he heard the gong?'

'I think he must have done so, m'lady, the gong being immediately outside the study door. I did not, of course, know that Sir Gervase was still in the study, otherwise I should have announced to him that dinner was ready. Shall I do so now, m'lady?'

Lady Chevenix-Gore seized on the suggestion with manifest relief.

'Oh, thank you, Snell. Yes, please do. Yes, certainly.'

She said, as the butler left the room:

'Snell is such a treasure. I rely on him absolutely. I really don't know what I should *do* without Snell.'

Somebody murmured a sympathetic assent, but nobody spoke. Hercule Poirot, watching that room full of people with suddenly sharpened attention, had an idea that one and all were in a state of tension. His eyes ran quickly over them, tabulating them roughly. Two elderly men, the soldierly one who had spoken just now, and a thin, spare, grey-haired man with closely pinched legal lips. Two youngish men – very different in type from each other. One with a moustache and an air of modest arrogance, he guessed to be possibly Sir Gervase's nephew, the one in the Blues. The other, with sleek brushed-back hair and a rather obvious style of good looks, he put down as of a definitely inferior social class. There was a small middle-aged woman with pince-nez and intelligent eyes, and there was a girl with flaming red hair.

Snell appeared at the door. His manner was perfect, but once again the veneer of the impersonal butler showed signs of the perturbed human being beneath the surface.

'Excuse me, m'lady, the study door is locked.'

'Locked?'

It was a man's voice – young, alert, with a ring of excitement in it. It was the good-looking young man with the slicked-back hair who had spoken. He went on, hurrying forward:

'Shall I go and see –?'

But very quietly Hercule Poirot took command. He did it so naturally that no one thought it odd that this stranger, who had just arrived, should suddenly assume charge of the situation.

'Come,' he said. 'Let us go to the study.'

He continued, speaking to Snell:

'Lead the way, if you please.'

Snell obeyed. Poirot followed close behind him, and, like a flock of sheep, everyone else followed.

Snell led the way through the big hall, past the great branching curve of the staircase, past an enormous grandfather clock and

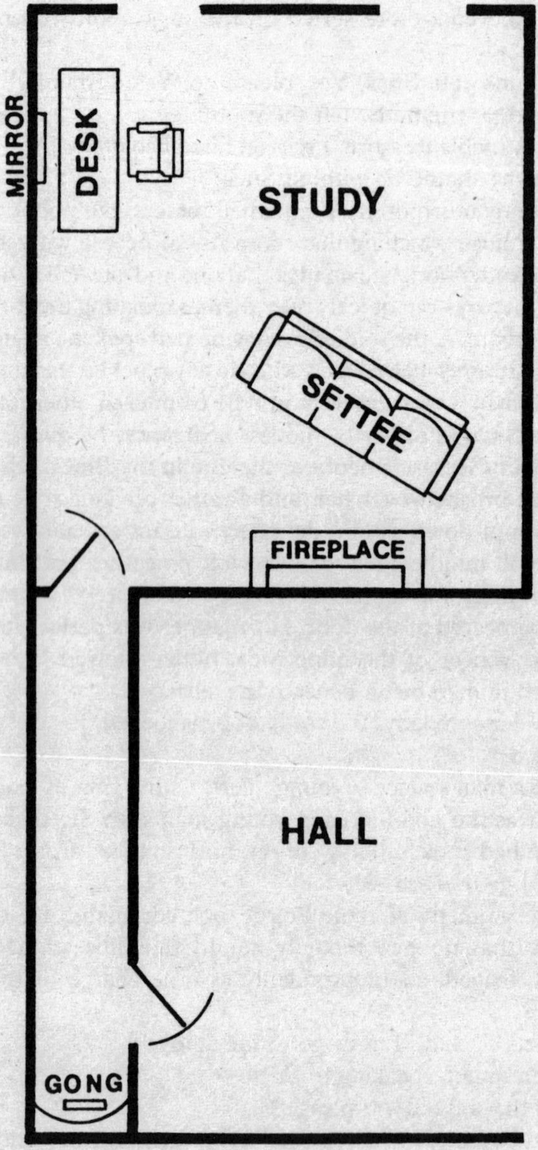
MIRROR
DESK
STUDY
SETTEE
FIREPLACE
HALL
GONG

a recess in which stood a gong, along a narrow passage which ended in a door.

Here Poirot passed Snell and gently tried the handle. It turned, but the door did not open. Poirot rapped gently with his knuckles on the panel of the door. He rapped louder and louder. Then, suddenly desisting, he dropped to his knees and applied his eye to the keyhole.

Slowly he rose to his feet and looked round. His face was stern.

'Gentlemen!' he said. 'This door must be broken open immediately!'

Under his direction the two young men, who were both tall and powerfully built, attacked the door. It was no easy matter. The doors of Hamborough Close were solidly built.

At last, however, the lock gave, and the door swung inwards with a noise of splintering, rending wood.

And then, for a moment, everyone stood still, huddled in the doorway looking at the scene inside. The lights were on. Along the left-hand wall was a big writing-table, a massive affair of solid mahogany. Sitting, not at the table, but sideways to it, so that his back was directly towards them, was a big man slouched down in a chair. His head and the upper part of his body hung down over the right side of the chair, and his right hand and arm hung limply down. Just below it on the carpet was a small, gleaming pistol . . .

There was no need of speculation. The picture was clear. Sir Gervase Chevenix-Gore had shot himself.

CHAPTER 3

For a moment or two the group in the doorway stood motionless, staring at the scene. Then Poirot strode forward.

At the same moment Hugo Trent said crisply:

'My God, the Old Man's shot himself!'

And there was a long, shuddering moan from Lady Chevenix-Gore.

'Oh, Gervase – Gervase!'

Over his shoulder Poirot said sharply:

'Take Lady Chevenix-Gore away. She can do nothing here.'

The elderly soldierly man obeyed. He said:

'Come, Vanda. Come, my dear. You can do nothing. It's all over. Ruth, come and look after your mother.'

But Ruth Chevenix-Gore had pressed into the room and stood close by Poirot's side as he bent over the dreadful sprawled figure in the chair – the figure of a man of Herculean build with a Viking beard.

She said in a low, tense voice, curiously restrained and muffled:

'You're quite sure he's – dead?'

Poirot looked up.

The girl's face was alive with some emotion – an emotion sternly checked and repressed – that he did not quite understand. It was not grief – it seemed more like a kind of half-fearful excitement.

The little woman in the pince-nez murmured:

'Your mother, my dear – don't you think –?'

In a high, hysterical voice the girl with the red hair cried out:

'Then it *wasn't* a car or a champagne cork! It was a *shot* we heard . . .'

Poirot turned and faced them all.

'Somebody must communicate with the police –'

Ruth Chevenix-Gore cried out violently:

'No!'

The elderly man with the legal face said:

'Unavoidable, I am afraid. Will you see to that, Burrows? Hugo –'

Poirot said:

'You are Mr Hugo Trent?' to the tall young man with the moustache. 'It would be well, I think, if everyone except you and I were to leave this room.'

Again his authority was not questioned. The lawyer shepherded the others away. Poirot and Hugo Trent were left alone.

The latter said, staring:

'Look here – who *are* you? I mean, I haven't the foggiest idea. What are you doing here?'

Poirot took a card-case from his pocket and selected a card.

Hugo Trent said, staring at it:

'Private detective – eh? Of course, I've heard of you . . . But I still don't see what you are doing *here*.'

'You did not know that your uncle – he was your uncle, was he not –?'

Hugo's eyes dropped for a fleeting moment to the dead man.

'The Old Man? Yes, he was my uncle all right.'

'You did not know that he had sent for me?'

Hugo shook his head. He said slowly:

'I'd no idea of it.'

There was an emotion in his voice that was rather hard to classify. His face looked wooden and stupid – the kind of expression, Poirot thought, that made a useful mask in times of stress.

Poirot said quietly:

'We are in Westshire, are we not? I know your Chief Constable, Major Riddle, very well.'

Hugo said:

'Riddle lives about half a mile away. He'll probably come over himself.'

'That,' said Poirot, 'will be very convenient.'

He began prowling gently round the room. He twitched aside

the window curtain and examined the french windows, trying them gently. They were closed.

On the wall behind the desk there hung a round mirror. The mirror was shivered. Poirot bent down and picked up a small object.

'What's that?' asked Hugo Trent.

'The bullet.'

'It passed straight through his head and struck the mirror?'

'It seems so.'

Poirot replaced the bullet meticulously where he had found it. He came up to the desk. Some papers were arranged neatly stacked in heaps. On the blotting-pad itself there was a loose sheet of paper with the word SORRY printed across it in large, shaky handwriting.

Hugo said: 'He must have written that just before he – did it.'

Poirot nodded thoughtfully.

He looked again at the smashed mirror, then at the dead man. His brow creased itself a little as though in perplexity. He went over to the door, where it hung crookedly with its splintered lock. There was no key in the door, as he knew – otherwise he would not have been able to see through the keyhole. There was no sign of it on the floor. Poirot leaned over the dead man and ran his fingers over him.

'Yes,' he said. 'The key is in his pocket.'

Hugo drew out a cigarette-case and lighted a cigarette. He spoke rather hoarsely.

'It seems all quite clear,' he said. 'My uncle shut himself up in here, scrawled that message on a piece of paper, and then shot himself.'

Poirot nodded meditatively. Hugo went on:

'But I don't understand why he sent for you. What was it all about?'

'That is rather more difficult to explain. While we are waiting, Mr Trent, for the authorities to take charge, perhaps you will tell me exactly who all the people are whom I saw tonight when I arrived?'

'Who they are?' Hugo spoke almost absently. 'Oh, yes, of course. Sorry. Shall we sit down?' He indicated a settee in the farthest corner of the room from the body. He went on, speaking jerkily: 'Well, there's Vanda – my aunt, you know. And Ruth, my cousin. But you know them. Then the other girl is Susan Cardwell. She's just staying here. And there's Colonel Bury. He's an old friend of the family. And Mr Forbes. He's an old friend, too, besides being the family lawyer and all that. Both the old boys had a passion for Vanda when she was young, and they still hang round in a faithful, devoted sort of way. Ridiculous, but rather touching. Then there's Godfrey Burrows, the Old Man's – I mean my uncle's – secretary, and Miss Lingard, who's here to help him write a history of the Chevenix-Gores. She mugs up historical stuff for writers. That's the lot, I think.'

Poirot nodded. Then he said:

'And I understand you actually heard the shot that killed your uncle?'

'Yes, we did. Thought it was a champagne cork – at least, I did. Susan and Miss Lingard thought it was a car backfiring outside – the road runs quite near, you know.'

'When was this?'

'Oh, about ten past eight. Snell had just sounded the first gong.'

'And where were you when you heard it?'

'In the hall. We – we were laughing about it – arguing, you know, as to where the sound came from. I said it came from the dining-room, and Susan said it came from the direction of the drawing-room, and Miss Lingard said it sounded like upstairs, and Snell said it came from the road outside, only it came through the upstairs windows. And Susan said, 'Any more theories?' And I laughed and said there was always murder! Seems pretty rotten to think of it now.'

His face twitched nervously.

'It did not occur to anyone that Sir Gervase might have shot himself?'

'No, of course not.'

'You have, in fact, no idea why he should have shot himself?'

Hugo said slowly:

'Oh, well, I shouldn't say that –'

'You *have* an idea?'

'Yes – well – it's difficult to explain. Naturally I didn't expect him to commit suicide, but all the same I'm not frightfully surprised. The truth of it is that my uncle was as mad as a hatter, M. Poirot. Everyone knew that.'

'That strikes you as a sufficient explanation?'

'Well, people do shoot themselves when they're a bit barmy.'

'An explanation of an admirable simplicity.'

Hugo stared.

Poirot got up again and wandered aimlessly round the room. It was comfortably furnished, mainly in a rather heavy Victorian style. There were massive bookcases, huge arm-chairs, and some upright chairs of genuine Chippendale. There were not many ornaments, but some bronzes on the mantel-piece attracted Poirot's attention and apparently stirred his admiration. He picked them up one by one, carefully examining them before replacing them with care. From the one on the extreme left he detached something with a fingernail.

'What's that?' asked Hugo without much interest.

'Nothing very much. A tiny sliver of looking-glass.'

Hugo said:

'Funny the way that mirror was smashed by the shot. A broken mirror means bad luck. Poor old Gervase . . . I suppose his luck had held a bit too long.'

'Your uncle was a lucky man?'

Hugo gave a short laugh.

'Why, his luck was proverbial! Everything he touched turned to gold! If he backed an outsider, it romped home! If he invested in a doubtful mine, they struck a vein of ore at once! He's had the most amazing escapes from the tightest of tight places. His life's been saved by a kind of miracle more than once. He was rather a fine old boy, in his way, you know. He'd certainly "been places and seen things" – more than most of his generation.'

Poirot murmured in a conversational tone:

'You were attached to your uncle, Mr Trent?'

Hugo Trent seemed a little startled by the question.

'Oh – er – yes, of course,' he said rather vaguely. 'You know, he was a bit difficult at times. Frightful strain to live with, and all that. Fortunately I didn't have to see much of him.'

'*He* was fond of *you*?'

'Not so that you'd notice it! As a matter of fact, he rather resented my existence, so to speak.'

'How was that, Mr Trent?'

'Well, you see, he had no son of his own – and he was pretty sore about it. He was mad about family and all that sort of thing. I believe it cut him to the quick to know that when he died the Chevenix-Gores would cease to exist. They've been going ever since the Norman Conquest, you know. The Old Man was the last of them. I suppose it *was* rather rotten from his point of view.'

'You yourself do not share that sentiment?'

Hugo shrugged his shoulders.

'All that sort of thing seems to me rather out of date.'

'What will happen to the estate?'

'Don't really know. I might get it. Or he may have left it to Ruth. Probably Vanda has it for her lifetime.'

'Your uncle did not definitely declare his intentions?'

'Well, he had his pet idea.'

'And what was that?'

'His idea was that Ruth and I should make a match of it.'

'That would doubtless have been very suitable.'

'Eminently suitable. But Ruth – well, Ruth has very decided views of her own about life. Mind you, she's an extremely attractive young woman, and she knows it. She's in no hurry to marry and settle down.'

Poirot leaned forward.

'But you yourself would have been willing, M. Trent?'

Hugo said in a bored tone of voice:

'I really can't see it makes a ha'p'orth of difference who you marry nowadays. Divorce is so easy. If you're not hitting it off, nothing is easier than to cut the tangle and start again.'

The door opened and Forbes entered with a tall, spruce-looking man.

The latter nodded to Trent.

'Hallo, Hugo. I'm extremely sorry about this. Very rough on all of you.'

Hercule Poirot came forward.

'How do you do, Major Riddle? You remember me?'

'Yes, indeed.' The chief constable shook hands. 'So *you're* down here?'

There was a meditative note in his voice. He glanced curiously at Hercule Poirot.

CHAPTER 4

'Well?' said Major Riddle.

It was twenty minutes later. The chief constable's interrogative 'Well?' was addressed to the police surgeon, a lank elderly man with grizzled hair.

The latter shrugged his shoulders.

'He's been dead over half an hour – but not more than an hour. You don't want technicalities, I know, so I'll spare you them. The man was shot through the head, the pistol being held a few inches from the right temple. Bullet passed right through the brain and out again.'

'Perfectly compatible with suicide?'

'Oh, perfectly. The body then slumped down in the chair, and the pistol dropped from his hand.'

'You've got the bullet?'

'Yes.' The doctor held it up.

'Good,' said Major Riddle. 'We'll keep it for comparison with the pistol. Glad it's a clear case and no difficulties.'

Hercule Poirot asked gently:

'You are sure there *are* no difficulties, Doctor?'

The doctor replied slowly:

'Well, I suppose you might call one thing a little odd. When he shot himself he must have been leaning slightly over to the right. Otherwise the bullet would have hit the wall *below* the mirror, instead of plumb in the middle.'

'An uncomfortable position in which to commit suicide,' said Poirot.

The doctor shrugged his shoulders.

'Oh, well – comfort – if you're going to end it all–' He left the sentence unfinished.

Major Riddle said:

'The body can be moved now?'

'Oh, yes. I've done with it until the P.-M.'

'What about you, Inspector?' Major Riddle spoke to a tall impassive-faced man in plain clothes.

'O.K., sir. We've got all we want. Only the deceased's fingerprints on the pistol.'

'Then you can get on with it.'

The mortal remains of Gervase Chevenix-Gore were removed. The chief constable and Poirot were left together.

'Well,' said Riddle, 'everything seems quite clear and above-board. Door locked, window fastened, key of door in dead man's pocket. Everything according to Cocker – but for one circumstance.'

'And what is that, my friend?' inquired Poirot.

'*You*!' said Riddle bluntly. 'What are *you* doing down here?'

By way of reply, Poirot handed to him the letter he had received from the dead man a week ago, and the telegram which had finally brought him there.

'Humph,' said the chief constable. 'Interesting. We'll have to get to the bottom of this. I should say it had a direct bearing upon his suicide.'

'I agree.'

'We must check up on who is in the house.'

'I can tell you their names. I have just been making inquiries of Mr Trent.'

He repeated the list of names.

'Perhaps you, Major Riddle, know something about these people?'

'I know something of them, naturally. Lady Chevenix-Gore is quite as mad in her own way as old Sir Gervase. They were devoted to each other – and both quite mad. She's the vaguest creature that ever lived, with an occasional uncanny shrewdness that strikes the nail on the head in the most surprising fashion. People laugh at her a good deal. I think she knows it, but she doesn't care. She's absolutely no sense of humour.'

'Miss Chevenix-Gore is only their adopted daughter, I understand?'

'Yes.'

'A very handsome young lady.'

'She's a devilishly attractive girl. Has played havoc with most of the young fellows round here. Leads them all on and then turns round and laughs at them. Good seat on a horse, and wonderful hands.'

'That, for the moment, does not concern us.'

'Er – no, perhaps not . . . Well, about the other people. I know old Bury, of course. He's here most of the time. Almost a tame cat about the house. Kind of A.D.C. to Lady Chevenix-Gore. He's a very old friend. They've known him all their lives. I think he and Sir Gervase were both interested in some company of which Bury was a director.'

'Oswald Forbes, do you know anything of him?'

'I rather believe I've met him once.'

'Miss Lingard?'

'Never heard of her.'

'Miss Susan Cardwell?'

'Rather a good-looking girl with red hair? I've seen her about with Ruth Chevenix-Gore the last few days.'

'Mr Burrows?'

'Yes, I know him. Chevenix-Gore's secretary. Between you and me, I don't take to him much. He's good-looking, and knows it. Not quite out of the top drawer.'

'Had he been with Sir Gervase long?'

'About two years, I fancy.'

'And there is no one else –?'

Poirot broke off.

A tall, fair-haired man in a lounge suit came hurrying in. He was out of breath and looked disturbed.

'Good evening, Major Riddle. I heard a rumour that Sir Gervase had shot himself, and I hurried up here. Snell tells me it's true. It's incredible! I can't believe it!'

'It's true enough, Lake. Let me introduce you. This is Captain Lake, Sir Gervase's agent for the estate. M. Hercule Poirot, of whom you may have heard.'

Lake's face lit up with what seemed a kind of delighted incredulity.

'M. Hercule Poirot? I'm most awfully pleased to meet you. At least –' He broke off, the quick charming smile vanished – he looked disturbed and upset. 'There isn't anything – fishy – about this suicide, is there, sir?'

'Why should there be anything "fishy," as you call it?' asked the chief constable sharply.

'I mean, because M. Poirot is here. Oh, and because the whole business seems so incredible!'

'No, no,' said Poirot quickly. 'I am not here on account of the death of Sir Gervase. I was already in the house – as a guest.'

'Oh, I see. Funny, he never told me you were coming when I was going over accounts with him this afternoon.'

Poirot said quietly:

'You have twice used the word "incredible," Captain Lake. Are you, then, so surprised to hear of Sir Gervase commiting suicide?'

'Indeed I am. Of course, he was mad as a hatter; everyone would agree about that. But all the same, I simply can't imagine his thinking the world would be able to get on without him.'

'Yes,' said Poirot. 'It is a point, that.' And he looked with appreciation at the frank, intelligent countenance of the young man.

Major Riddle cleared his throat.

'Since you are here, Captain Lake, perhaps you will sit down and answer a few questions.'

'Certainly, sir.'

Lake took a chair opposite the other two.

'When did you last see Sir Gervase?'

'This afternoon, just before three o'clock. There were some accounts to be checked, and the question of a new tenant for one of the farms.'

'How long were you with him?'

'Perhaps half an hour.'

'Think carefully, and tell me whether you noticed anything unusual in his manner.'

The young man considered.

'No, I hardly think so. He was, perhaps, a trifle excited – but that wasn't unusual with him.'

'He was not depressed in any way?'

'Oh, no, he seemed in good spirits. He was enjoying himself very much just now, writing up a history of the family.'

'How long had he been doing this?'

'He began it about six months ago.'

'Is that when Miss Lingard came here?'

'No. She arrived about two months ago when he had discovered that he could not manage the necessary research work by himself.'

'And you consider he was enjoying himself?'

'Oh, simply enormously! He really didn't think that anything else mattered in the world except his family.'

There was a momentary bitterness in the young man's tone.

'Then, as far as you know, Sir Gervase had no worries of any kind?'

There was a slight – a very slight – pause before Captain Lake answered.

'No.'

Poirot suddenly interposed a question:

'Sir Gervase was not, you think, worried about his daughter in any way?'

'His daughter?'

'That is what I said.'

'Not as far as I know,' said the young man stiffly.

Poirot said nothing further. Major Riddle said:

'Well, thank you, Lake. Perhaps you'd stay around in case I might want to ask you anything.'

'Certainly, sir.' He rose. 'Anything I can do?'

'Yes, you might send the butler here. And perhaps you'd find out for me how Lady Chevenix-Gore is, and if I could have a few words with her presently, or if she's too upset.'

The young man nodded and left the room with a quick, decisive step.

'An attractive personality,' said Hercule Poirot.

'Yes, nice fellow, and good at his job. Everyone likes him.'

CHAPTER 5

'Sit down, Snell,' said Major Riddle in a friendly tone. 'I've a good many questions to ask you, and I expect this has been a shock to you.'

'Oh, it has indeed, sir. Thank you, sir.' Snell sat down with such a discreet air that it was practically the same as though he had remained on his feet.

'Been here a good long time, haven't you?'

'Sixteen years, sir, ever since Sir Gervase – er – settled down, so to speak.'

'Ah, yes, of course, your master was a great traveller in his day.'

'Yes, sir. He went on an expedition to the Pole and many other interesting places.'

'Now, Snell, can you tell me when you last saw your master this evening?'

'I was in the dining-room, sir, seeing that the table arrangements were all complete. The door into the hall was open, and I saw Sir Gervase come down the stairs, cross the hall and go along the passage to the study.'

'That was at what time?'

'Just before eight o'clock. It might have been as much as five minutes before eight.'

'And that was the last you saw of him?'

'Yes, sir.'

'Did you hear a shot?'

'Oh, yes, indeed, sir; but of course I had no idea at the time – how should I have had?'

'What did you think it was?'

'I thought it was a car, sir. The road runs quite near the park wall. Or it might have been a shot in the woods – a poacher, perhaps. I never dreamed –'

Major Riddle cut him short.

'What time was that?'

'It was exactly eight minutes past eight, sir.'

The chief constable said sharply:

'How is it you can fix the time to a minute?'

'That's easy, sir. I had just sounded the first going.'

'The first gong?'

'Yes, sir. By Sir Gervase's orders, a gong was always to be sounded seven minutes before the actual dinner gong. Very particular he was, sir, that everyone should be assembled ready in the drawing-room when the second gong went. As soon as I had sounded the second gong, I went to the drawing-room and announced dinner, and everyone went in.'

'I begin to understand,' said Hercule Poirot, 'why you looked so surprised when you announced dinner this evening. It was usual for Sir Gervase to be in the drawing-room?'

'I'd never known him not be there before, sir. It was quite a shock. I little thought –'

Again Major Riddle interrupted adroitly:

'And were the others also usually there?'

Snell coughed.

'Anyone who was late for dinner, sir, was never asked to the house again.'

'H'm, very drastic.'

'Sir Gervase, sir, employed a chef who was formerly with the Emperor of Moravia. He used to say, sir, that dinner was as important as a religious ritual.'

'And what about his own family?'

'Lady Chevenix-Gore was always very particular not to upset him, sir, and even Miss Ruth dared not be late for dinner.'

'Interesting,' murmured Hercule Poirot.

'I see,' said Riddle. 'So, dinner being at a quarter past eight, you sounded the first gong at eight minutes past as usual?'

'That is so, sir – but it wasn't as usual. Dinner was usually at eight. Sir Gervase gave orders that dinner was to be a quarter of an hour later this evening, as he was expecting a gentleman by the late train.'

Snell made a little bow towards Poirot as he spoke.

'When your master went to the study, did he look upset or worried in any way?'

'I could not say, sir. It was too far for me to judge of his expression. I just noticed him, that was all.'

'Was he left alone when he went to the study?'

'Yes, sir.'

'Did anyone go to the study after that?'

'I could not say, sir. I went to the butler's pantry after that, and was there until I sounded the first gong at eight minutes past eight.'

'That was when you heard the shot?'

'Yes, sir.'

Poirot gently interposed a question.

'There were others, I think, who also heard the shot?'

'Yes, sir. Mr Hugo and Miss Cardwell. And Miss Lingard.'

'These people were also in the hall?'

'Miss Lingard came out from the drawing-room, and Miss Cardwell and Mr Hugo were just coming down the stairs.'

Poirot asked:

'Was there any conversation about the matter?'

'Well, sir, Mr Hugo asked if there was champagne for dinner. I told him that sherry, hock and burgundy were being served.'

'He thought it was a champagne cork?'

'Yes, sir.'

'But nobody took it seriously?'

'Oh, no, sir. They all went into the drawing-room talking and laughing.'

'Where were the other members of the household?'

'I could not say, sir.'

Major Riddle said:

'Do you know anything about this pistol?' He held it out as he spoke.

'Oh, yes, sir. That belonged to Sir Gervase. He always kept it in the drawer of his desk in here.'

'Was it usually loaded?'

'I couldn't say, sir.'

Major Riddle laid down the pistol and cleared his throat.

'Now, Snell, I'm going to ask you a rather important question. I hope you will answer it as truthfully as you can. *Do you know of any reason which might lead your master to commit suicide?*'

'No, sir. I know of nothing.'

'Sir Gervase had not been odd in his manner of late? Not depressed? Or worried?'

Snell coughed apologetically.

'You'll excuse my saying it, sir, but Sir Gervase was always what might have seemed to strangers a little odd in his manner. He was a highly original gentleman, sir.'

'Yes, yes, I am quite aware of that.'

'Outsiders, sir, did not always Understand Sir Gervase.'

Snell gave the phrase a definite value of capital letter.

'I know. I know. But there was nothing that *you* would have called unusual?'

The butler hesitated.

'I think, sir, that Sir Gervase was worried about something,' he said at last.

'Worried and depressed?'

'I shouldn't say depressed, sir. But worried, yes.'

'Have you any idea of the cause of that worry?'

'No, sir.'

'Was it connected with any particular person, for instance?'

'I could not say at all, sir. In any case, it is only an impression of mine.'

Poirot spoke again.

'You were surprised at his suicide?'

'Very surprised, sir. It has been a terrible shock to me. I never dreamed of such a thing.'

Poirot nodded thoughtfully.

Riddle glanced at him, then he said:

'Well, Snell, I think that is all we want to ask you. You are quite sure that there is nothing else you can tell us – no unusual incident, for instance, that has happened in the last few days?'

The butler, rising to his feet, shook his head.

'There is nothing, sir, nothing whatever.'

'Then you can go.'

'Thank you, sir.'

Moving towards the doorway, Snell drew back and stood aside. Lady Chevenix-Gore floated into the room.

She was wearing an oriental-looking garment of purple and orange silk wound tightly round her body. Her face was serene and her manner collected and calm.

'Lady Chevenix-Gore.' Major Riddle sprang to his feet.

She said:

'They told me you would like to talk to me, so I came.'

'Shall we go into another room? This must be painful for you in the extreme.'

Lady Chevenix-Gore shook her head and sat down on one of the Chippendale chairs. She murmured:

'Oh, no, what does it matter?'

'It is very good of you, Lady Chevenix-Gore, to put your feelings aside. I know what a frightful shock this must have been and –'

She interrupted him.

'It was rather a shock at first,' she admitted. Her tone was easy and conversational. 'But there is no such thing as Death, really, you know, only Change.' She added: 'As a matter of fact, Gervase is standing just behind your left shoulder now. I can see him distinctly.'

Major Riddle's left shoulder twitched slightly. He looked at Lady Chevenix-Gore rather doubtfully.

She smiled at him, a vague, happy smile.

'You don't believe, of course! So few people will. To me, the spirit world is quite as real as this one. But please ask me anything you like, and don't worry about distressing me. I'm not in the least distressed. Everything, you see, is Fate. One cannot escape one's Karma. It all fits in – the mirror – everything.'

'The mirror, madame?' asked Poirot.

She nodded her head towards it vaguely.

'Yes. It's splintered, you see. A symbol! You know Tennyson's poem? I used to read it as a girl – though, of course, I didn't realise then the esoteric side of it. "*The mirror cracked from side to side. 'The curse is come upon me!' cried the Lady of Shalott.*" That's what happened to Gervase. The Curse came upon him suddenly. I think, you know, most very old families have a curse . . . the mirror cracked. He knew that he was doomed! *The Curse had come!*'

'But, madame, it was not a curse that cracked the mirror – it was a bullet!'

Lady Chevenix-Gore said, still in the same sweet vague manner:

'It's all the same thing, really . . . It was Fate.'

'But your husband shot himself.'

Lady Chevenix-Gore smiled indulgently.

'He shouldn't have done that, of course. But Gervase was always impatient. He could never wait. His hour had come – he went forward to meet it. It's all so simple, really.'

Major Riddle, clearing his throat in exasperation, said sharply:

'Then you weren't surprised at your husband's taking his own life? Had you been expecting such a thing to happen?'

'Oh, no.' Her eyes opened wide. 'One can't always foresee the future. Gervase, of course, was a very strange man, a very unusual man. He was quite unlike anyone else. He was one of the Great Ones born again. I've known that for some time. I think he knew it himself. He found it very hard to conform to the silly little standards of the everyday world.' She added, looking over Major Riddle's shoulder, 'He's smiling now. He's thinking how foolish we all are. So we are really. Just like children. Pretending that life is real and that it matters . . . Life is only one of the Great Illusions.'

Feeling that he was fighting a losing battle, Major Riddle asked desperately:

'You can't help us at all as to *why* your husband should have taken his life?'

She shrugged her thin shoulders.

'Forces move us – they move us . . . You cannot understand. You move only on the material plane.'

Poirot coughed.

'Talking of the material plane, have you any idea, madame, as to how your husband has left his money?'

'Money?' she stared at him. 'I never think of money.'

Her tone was disdainful.

Poirot switched to another point.

'At what time did you come downstairs to dinner tonight?'

'Time? What is Time? Infinite, that is the answer. Time is infinite.'

Poirot murmured:

'But your husband, madame, was rather particular about time – especially, so I have been told, as regards the dinner hour.'

'Dear Gervase,' she smiled indulgently. 'He was very foolish about that. But it made him happy. So we were never late.'

'Were you in the drawing-room, madame, when the first gong went?'

'No, I was in my room then.'

'Do you remember who was in the drawing-room when you did come down?'

'Nearly everybody, I think,' said Lady Chevenix-Gore vaguely. 'Does it matter?'

'Possibly not,' admitted Poirot. 'Then there is something else. Did your husband ever tell you that he suspected he was being robbed?'

Lady Chevenix-Gore did not seem much interested in the question.

'Robbed? No, I don't think so.'

'Robbed, swindled – victimized in some way –?'

'No – no – I don't think so . . . Gervase would have been very angry if anybody had dared to do anything like that.'

'At any rate he said nothing about it to you?'

'No – no.' Lady Chevenix-Gore shook her head, still without much real interest. 'I should have remembered . . .'

'When did you last see your husband alive?'

'He looked in, as usual, on his way downstairs before dinner. My maid was there. He just said he was going down.'

'What has he talked about most in the last few weeks?'

'Oh, the family history. He was getting on so well with it. He found that funny old thing, Miss Lingard, quite invaluable. She looked up things for him in the British Museum – all that sort of thing. She worked with Lord Mulcaster on his book, you know. And she was tactful – I mean, she didn't look up the wrong things. After all, there are ancestors one doesn't want raked up. Gervase was very sensitive. She helped me, too. She got a lot of information for me about Hatshepsut. I am a reincarnation of Hatshepsut, you know.'

Lady Chevenix-Gore made this announcement in a calm voice.

'Before that,' she went on, 'I was a Priestess in Atlantis.'

Major Riddle shifted a little in his chair.

'Er – er – very interesting,' he said. 'Well, really, Lady Chevenix-Gore, I think that will be all. Very kind of you.'

Lady Chevenix-Gore rose, clasping her oriental robes about her.

'Goodnight,' she said. And then, her eyes shifting to a point behind Major Riddle. 'Goodnight, Gervase dear. I wish you could come, but I know you have to stay here.' She added in an explanatory fashion, 'You have to stay in the place where you've passed over for at least twenty-four hours. It's some time before you can move about freely and communicate.'

She trailed out of the room.

Major Riddle wiped his brow.

'Phew,' he murmured. 'She's a great deal madder than I ever thought. Does she really believe all that nonsense?'

Poirot shook his head thoughtfully.

'It is possible that she finds it helpful,' he said. 'She needs, at this moment, to create for herself a world of illusion so that she can escape the stark reality of her husband's death.'

'She seems almost certifiable to me,' said Major Riddle. 'A long farrago of nonsense without one word of sense in it.'

'No, no, my friend. The interesting thing is, as Mr Hugo Trent casually remarked to me, that amidst all the vapouring there is an occasional shrewd thrust. She showed it by her remark about Miss Lingard's tact in not stressing undesirable ancestors. Believe me, Lady Chevenix-Gore is no fool.'

He got up and paced up and down the room.

'There are things in this affair that I do not like. No, I do not like them at all.'

Riddle looked at him curiously.

'You mean the motive for his suicide?'

'Suicide – suicide! It is all wrong, I tell you. *It is wrong psychologically*. How did Chevenix-Gore think of himself? As a Colossus, as an immensely important person, as the centre of the universe! Does such a man destroy himself? Surely not. He is far more likely to destroy someone else – some miserable crawling ant of a human being who had dared to cause him annoyance . . . Such an act he might regard as necessary – as sanctified! But self-destruction? The destruction of such a Self?'

'It's all very well, Poirot. But the evidence is clear enough. Door locked, key in his own pocket. Window closed and fastened. I know these things happen in books – but I've never come across them in real life. Anything else?'

'But yes, there is something else.' Poirot sat down in the chair.

'Here I am. I am Chevenix-Gore. I am sitting at my desk. I am determined to kill myself – because, let us say, I have made a discovery concerning some terrific dishonour to the family name. It is not very convincing, that, but it must suffice.

'*Eh bien*, what do I do? I scrawl on a piece of paper the word *SORRY*. Yes, that is quite possible. Then I open a drawer of the desk, take out the pistol which I keep there, load it, if it is not loaded, and then – do I proceed to shoot myself? No, I first turn my chair round – so, and I lean over a little to the right – so – and then I put the pistol to my temple and fire!'

Poirot sprang up from his chair, and wheeling round, demanded:

'I ask you, does that make sense? *Why* turn the chair round? If, for instance, there had been a picture on the wall there, then, yes, there might be an explanation. Some portrait which a dying man might wish to be the last thing on earth his eyes would see, but a window-curtain – *ah non*, that does not make sense.'

'He might have wished to look out of the window. Last view out over the estate.'

'My dear friend, you do not suggest that with any conviction. In fact, you know it is nonsense. At eight minutes past eight it was dark, and in any case the curtains are drawn. No, there must be some other explanation . . .'

'There's only one as far as I can see. Gervase Chevenix-Gore was mad.'

Poirot shook his head in a dissatisfied manner.

Major Riddle rose.

'Come,' he said. 'Let us go and interview the rest of the party. We may get at something that way.'

CHAPTER 6

After the difficulties of getting a direct statement from Lady Chevenix-Gore, Major Riddle found considerable relief in dealing with a shrewd lawyer like Forbes.

Mr Forbes was extremely guarded and cautious in his statements, but his replies were all directly to the point.

He admitted that Sir Gervase's suicide had been a great shock to him. He should never have considered Sir Gervase the kind of man who would take his own life. He knew nothing of any cause for such an act.

'Sir Gervase was not only my client, but was a very old friend. I have known him since boyhood. I should say that he had always enjoyed life.'

'In the circumstances, Mr Forbes, I must ask you to speak quite candidly. You did not know of any secret anxiety or sorrow in Sir Gervase's life?'

'No. He had minor worries, like most men, but there was nothing of a serious nature.'

'No illness? No trouble between him and his wife?'

'No. Sir Gervase and Lady Chevenix-Gore were devoted to each other.'

Major Riddle said cautiously:

'Lady Chevenix-Gore appears to hold somewhat curious views.'

Mr Forbes smiled – an indulgent, manly smile.

'Ladies,' he said, 'must be allowed their fancies.'

The chief constable went on:

'You managed all Sir Gervase's legal affairs?'

'Yes, my firm, Forbes, Ogilvie and Spence, have acted for the Chevenix-Gore family for well over a hundred years.'

'Were there any – scandals in the Chevenix-Gore family?'

Mr Forbes's eyebrows rose.

'Really, I fail to understand you?'

'M. Poirot, will you show Mr Forbes the letter you showed me?'

In silence Poirot rose and handed the letter to Mr Forbes with a little bow.

Mr Forbes read it and his eyebrows rose still more.

'A most remarkable letter,' he said. 'I appreciate your question now. No, so far as my knowledge went, there was nothing to justify the writing of such a letter.'

'Sir Gervase said nothing of this matter to you?'

'Nothing at all. I must say I find it very curious that he should not have done so.'

'He was accustomed to confide in you?'

'I think he relied on my judgment.'

'And you have no idea as to what this letter refers?'

'I should not like to make any rash speculations.'

Major Riddle appreciated the subtlety of this reply.

'Now, Mr Forbes, perhaps you can tell us how Sir Gervase has left his property.'

'Certainly. I see no objection to such a course. To his wife, Sir Gervase left an annual income of six thousand pounds chargeable on the estate, and the choice of the Dower House or the town house in Lowndes Square, whichever she should prefer. There were, of course, several legacies and bequests, but nothing of an outstanding nature. The residue of his property was left to his adopted daughter, Ruth, on condition that, if she married, her husband should take the name of Chevenix-Gore.'

'Was nothing left to his nephew, Mr Hugo Trent?'

'Yes. A legacy of five thousand pounds.'

'And I take it that Sir Gervase was a rich man?'

'He was extremely wealthy. He had a vast private fortune apart from the estate. Of course, he was not quite so well-off as in the past. Practically all invested incomes have felt the strain. Also, Sir Gervase had dropped a good deal of money over a certain company – the Paragon Synthetic Rubber Substitute in which Colonel Bury persuaded him to invest a good deal of money.'

'Not very wise advice?'

Mr Forbes sighed.

'Retired soldiers are the worst sufferers when they engage in financial operations. I have found that their credulity far exceeds that of widows – and that is saying a good deal.'

'But these unfortunate investments did not seriously affect Sir Gervase's income?'

'Oh, no, not seriously. He was still an extremely rich man.'

'When was this will made?'

'Two years ago.'

Poirot murmured:

'This arrangement, was it not possibly a little unfair to Mr Hugo Trent, Sir Gervase's nephew? He is, after all, Sir Gervase's nearest blood relation.'

Mr Forbes shrugged his shoulders.

'One has to take a certain amount of family history into account.'

'Such as –?'

Mr Forbes seemed slightly unwilling to proceed.

Major Riddle said:

'You mustn't think we're unduly concerned with raking up old scandals or anything of that sort. But this letter of Sir Gervase's to M. Poirot has got to be explained.'

'There is certainly nothing scandalous in the explanation of Sir Gervase's attitude to his nephew,' said Mr Forbes quickly. 'It was simply that Sir Gervase always took his position as head of the family very seriously. He had a younger brother and sister. The brother, Anthony Chevenix-Gore, was killed in the war. The sister, Pamela, married, and Sir Gervase disapproved of the marriage. That is to say, he considered that she ought to obtain his consent and approval before marrying. He thought that Captain Trent's family was not of sufficient prominence to be allied with a Chevenix-Gore. His sister was merely amused by his attitude. As a result, Sir Gervase has always been inclined to dislike his nephew. I think that dislike may have influenced him in deciding to adopt a child.'

'There was no hope of his having children of his own?'

'No. There was a still-born child about a year after his marriage. The doctors told Lady Chevenix-Gore that she would never be able to have another child. About two years later he adopted Ruth.'

'And who *was* Mademoiselle Ruth? How did they come to settle upon her?'

'She was, I believe, the child of a distant connection.'

'That I had guessed,' said Poirot. He looked up at the wall which was hung with family portraits. 'One can see that she was of the same blood – the nose, the line of the chin. It repeats itself on these walls many times.'

'She inherits the temper too,' said Mr Forbes dryly.

'So I should imagine. How did she and her adopted father get on?'

'Much as you might imagine. There was a fierce clash of wills more than once. But in spite of these quarrels I believe there was also an underlying harmony.'

'Nevertheless, she caused him a good deal of anxiety?'

'Incessant anxiety. But I can assure you not to the point of causing him to take his own life.'

'Ah, that, no,' agreed Poirot. 'One does not blow one's brains out because one has a headstrong daughter! And so mademoiselle inherits! Sir Gervase, he never thought of altering his will?'

'Ahem!' Mr Forbes coughed to hide a little discomposure. 'As a matter of fact, I took instructions from Sir Gervase on my arrival here (two days ago, that is to say) as to the drafting of a new will.'

'What's this?' Major Riddle hitched his chair a little closer. 'You didn't tell us this.'

Mr Forbes said quickly:

'You merely asked me what the terms of Sir Gervase's will were. I gave you the information for which you asked. The new will was not even properly drawn up – much less signed.'

'What were its provisions? They may be some guide to Sir Gervase's state of mind.'

'In the main, they were the same as before, but Miss Chevenix-Gore was only to inherit on condition that she married Mr Hugo Trent.'

'Aha,' said Poirot. 'But there is a very decided difference there.'

'I did not approve of the clause,' said Mr Forbes. 'And I felt bound to point out that it was quite possible it might be contested successfully. The Court does not look upon such conditional bequests with approval. Sir Gervase, however, was quite decided.'

'And if Miss Chevenix-Gore (or, incidentally, Mr Trent) refused to comply?'

'If Mr Trent was not willing to marry Miss Chevenix-Gore, then the money went to her unconditionally. But if *he* was willing and *she* refused, then the money went to him instead.'

'Odd business,' said Major Riddle.

Poirot leaned forward. He tapped the lawyer on the knee.

'But what is behind it? What was in the mind of Sir Gervase when he made that stipulation? There must have been something very definite . . . There must, I think, have been the image of another man . . . a man of whom he disapproved. I think, Mr Forbes, that *you* must know who that man was?'

'Really, M. Poirot, I have no information.'

'But you could make a guess.'

'I never guess,' said Mr Forbes, and his tone was scandalized.

Removing his pince-nez, he wiped them with a silk handkerchief and inquired:

'Is there anything else that you desire to know?'

'At the moment, no,' said Poirot. 'Not, that is, as far as I am concerned.'

Mr Forbes looked as though, in his opinion, that was not very far, and bent his attention on the chief constable.

'Thank you, Mr Forbes. I think that's all. I should like, if I may, to speak to Miss Chevenix-Gore.'

'Certainly. I think she is upstairs with Lady Chevenix-Gore.'

'Oh, well, perhaps I'll have a word with – what's his name? – Burrows, first, and the family-history woman.'

'They're both in the library. I will tell them.'

CHAPTER 7

'Hard work, that,' said Major Riddle, as the lawyer left the room. 'Extracting information from these old-fashioned legal wallahs takes a bit of doing. The whole business seems to me to centre about the girl.'

'It would seem so – yes.'

'Ah, here comes Burrows.'

Godfrey Burrows came in with a pleasant eagerness to be of use. His smile was discreetly tempered with gloom and showed only a fraction too much teeth. It seemed more mechanical than spontaneous.

'Now, Mr Burrows, we want to ask you a few questions.'

'Certainly, Major Riddle. Anything you like.'

'Well, first and foremost, to put it quite simply, have you any ideas of your own about Sir Gervase's suicide?'

'Absolutely none. It was the greatest shock to me.'

'You heard the shot?'

'No; I must have been in the library at the time, as far as I can make out. I came down rather early and went to the library to look up a reference I wanted. The library's right the other side of the house from the study, so I shouldn't hear anything.'

'Was anyone with you in the library?' asked Poirot.

'No one at all.'

'You've no idea where the other members of the household were at that time?'

'Mostly upstairs dressing, I should imagine.'

'When did you come to the drawing-room?'

'Just before M. Poirot arrived. Everybody was there then – except Sir Gervase, of course.'

'Did it strike you as strange that he wasn't there?'

'Yes, it did, as a matter of fact. As a rule he was always in the drawing-room before the first gong sounded.'

'Have you noticed any difference in Sir Gervase's manner lately? Has he been worried? Or anxious? Depressed?'

Godfrey Burrows considered.

'No – I don't think so. A little – well, preoccupied, perhaps.'

'But he did not appear to be worried about any one definite matter?'

'Oh, no.'

'No – financial worries of any kind?'

'He was rather perturbed about the affairs of one particular company – the Paragon Synthetic Rubber Company to be exact.'

'What did he actually say about it?'

Again Godfrey Burrows' mechanical smile flashed out, and again it seemed slightly unreal.

'Well – as a matter of fact – what he said was, "Old Bury's either a fool or a knave. A fool, I suppose. I must go easy with him for Vanda's sake."'

'And why did he say that – *for Vanda's sake*?' inquired Poirot.

'Well, you see, Lady Chevenix-Gore was very fond of Colonel Bury, and he worshipped her. Followed her about like a dog.'

'Sir Gervase was not – jealous at all?'

'Jealous?' Burrows stared and then laughed. 'Sir Gervase jealous? He wouldn't know how to set about it. Why, it would never have entered his head that anyone could ever prefer another man to him. Such a thing couldn't be, you understand.'

Poirot said gently:

'You did not, I think, like Sir Gervase Chevenix-Gore very much?'

Burrows flushed.

'Oh, yes, I did. At least – well, all that sort of thing strikes one as rather ridiculous nowadays.'

'All what sort of thing?' asked Poirot.

'Well, the feudal motif, if you like. This worship of ancestry and personal arrogance. Sir Gervase was a very able man in many ways, and had led an interesting life, but he would have been more interesting if he hadn't been so entirely wrapped up in himself and his own egoism.'

'Did his daughter agree with you there?'

Burrows flushed again – this time a deep purple.

He said:

'I should imagine Miss Chevenix-Gore is quite one of the moderns! Naturally, I shouldn't discuss her father with her.'

'But the moderns *do* discuss their fathers a good deal!' said Poirot. 'It is entirely in the modern spirit to criticize your parents!'

Burrows shrugged his shoulders.

Major Riddle asked:

'And there was nothing else – no other financial anxiety? Sir Gervase never spoke of having been *victimized*?'

'Victimized?' Burrows sounded very astonished. 'Oh, no.'

'And you yourself were on quite good terms with him?'

'Certainly I was. Why not?'

'I am asking you, Mr Burrows.'

The young man looked sulky.

'We were on the best of terms.'

'Did you know that Sir Gervase had written to M. Poirot asking him to come down here?'

'No.'

'Did Sir Gervase usually write his own letters?'

'No, he nearly always dictated them to me.'

'But he did not do so in this case?'

'No.'

'Why was that, do you think?'

'I can't imagine.'

'You can suggest no reason why he should have written this particular letter himself?'

'No, I can't.'

'Ah!' said Major Riddle, adding smoothly, 'Rather curious. When did you last see Sir Gervase?'

'Just before I went to dress for dinner. I took him some letters to sign.'

'What was his manner then?'

'Quite normal. In fact I should say he was feeling rather pleased with himself about something.'

Poirot stirred a little in his chair.

'Ah?' he said. 'So that was your impression, was it? That he was pleased about something. And yet, not so very long afterwards, he shoots himself. It is odd, that!'

Godfrey Burrows shrugged his shoulders.

'I'm only telling you my impressions.'

'Yes, yes, they are very valuable. After all, you are probably one of the last people who saw Sir Gervase alive.'

'Snell was the last person to see him.'

'To see him, yes, but not to speak to him.'

Burrows did not reply.

Major Riddle said:

'What time was it when you went up to dress for dinner?'

'About five minutes past seven.'

'What did Sir Gervase do?'

'I left him in the study.'

'How long did he usually take to change?'

'He usually gave himself a full three-quarters of an hour.'

'Then, if dinner was at a quarter-past eight, he would probably have gone up at half-past seven at the latest?'

'Very likely.'

'You yourself went to change early?'

'Yes, I thought I would change and then go to the library and look up the references I wanted.'

Poirot nodded thoughtfully. Major Riddle said:

'Well, I think that's all for the moment. Will you send Miss What's-her-name along?'

Little Miss Lingard tripped in almost immediately. She was wearing several chains which tinkled a little as she sat down and looked inquiringly from one to the other of the two men.

'This is all very – er – sad, Miss Lingard,' began Major Riddle.

'Very sad indeed,' said Miss Lingard decorously.

'You came to this house – when?'

'About two months ago. Sir Gervase wrote to a friend of his in the Museum – Colonel Fotheringay it was – and Colonel Fotheringary recommended me. I have done a good deal of historical research work.'

'Did you find Sir Gervase difficult to work for?'

'Oh, not really. One had to humour him a little, of course. But then I always find one has to do that with men.'

With an uneasy feeling that Miss Lingard was probably humouring him at this moment, Major Riddle went on:

'Your work here was to help Sir Gervase with the book he was writing?'

'Yes.'

'What did it involve?'

For a moment, Miss Lingard looked quite human. Her eyes twinkled as she replied:

'Well, actually, you know, it involved writing the book! I looked up all the information and made notes, and arranged the material. And then, later, I revised what Sir Gervase had written.'

'You must have had to exercise a good deal of tact, mademoiselle,' said Poirot.

'Tact and firmness. One needs them both,' said Miss Lingard.

'Sir Gervase did not resent your – er – firmness?'

'Oh not at all. Of course I put it to him that he mustn't be bothered with all the petty detail.'

'Oh, yes, I see.'

'It was quite simple, really,' said Miss Lingard. 'Sir Gervase was perfectly easy to manage if one took him the right way.'

'Now, Miss Lingard, I wonder if you know anything that can throw light on this tragedy?'

Miss Lingard shook her head.

'I'm afraid I don't. You see, naturally he wouldn't confide in me at all. I was practically a stranger. In any case I think he was far too proud to speak to anyone of family troubles.'

'But you think it *was* family troubles that caused him to take his life?'

Miss Lingard looked rather surprised.

'But of course! Is there any other suggestion?'

'You feel sure that there were family troubles worrying him?'

'I know that he was in great distress of mind.'

'Oh, you know that?'

'Why, of course.'

'Tell me, mademoiselle, did he speak to you of the matter?'

'Not explicitly.'

'What did he say?'

'Let me see. I found that he didn't seem to be taking in what I was saying –'

'One moment. *Pardon*. When was this?'

'This afternoon. We usually worked from three to five.'

'Pray go on.'

'As I say, Sir Gervase seemed to be finding it hard to concentrate – in fact, he said as much, adding that he had several grave matters preying on his mind. And he said – let me see – something like this – (of course, I can't be sure of the exact words): "*It's a terrible thing, Miss Lingard, when a family has been one of the proudest in the land, that dishonour should be brought on it.*"'

'And what did you say to that?'

'Oh, just something soothing. I think I said that every generation had its weaklings – that that was one of the penalties of greatness – but that their failings were seldom remembered by posterity.'

'And did that have the soothing effect you hoped?'

'More or less. We got back to Sir Roger Chevenix-Gore. I had found a most interesting mention of him in a contemporary manuscript. But Sir Gervase's attention wandered again. In the end he said he would not do any more work that afternoon. He said he had had a shock.'

'A shock?'

'That is what he said. Of course, I didn't ask any questions. I just said, "I am sorry to hear it, Sir Gervase." And then he asked me to tell Snell that M. Poirot would be arriving and to put off dinner until eight-fifteen, and send the car to meet the seven-fifty train.'

'Did he usually ask you to make these arrangements?'

'Well – no – that was really Mr Burrows's business. I did nothing but my own literary work. I wasn't a secretary in any sense of the word.'

Poirot asked:

'Do you think Sir Gervase had a definite reason for asking you to make these arrangements, instead of asking Mr Burrows to do so?'

Miss Lingard considered.

'Well, he may have had . . . I did not think of it at the time. I thought it was just a matter of convenience. Still, it's true now I come to think of it, that he *did* ask me not to tell anyone that M. Poirot was coming. It was to be a surprise, he said.'

'Ah! he said that, did he? Very curious, very interesting. And *did* you tell anyone?'

'Certainly not, M. Poirot. I told Snell about dinner and to send the chauffeur to meet the seven-fifty as a gentleman was arriving by it.'

'Did Sir Gervase say anything else that may have had a bearing on the situation?'

Miss Lingard thought.

'No – I don't think so – he was very much strung-up – I do remember that just as I was leaving the room, he said, "*Not that it's any good his coming now. It's too late.*"'

'And you have no idea at all what he meant by that?'

'N – no.'

Just the faintest suspicion of indecision about the simple negative. Poirot repeated with a frown:

'"*Too late.*" That is what he said, is it? "*Too late.*"'

Major Riddle said:

'You can give us no idea, Miss Lingard, as to the nature of the circumstance that so distressed Sir Gervase?'

Miss Lingard said slowly:

'I have an idea that it was in some way connected with Mr Hugo Trent.'

'With Hugo Trent? Why do you think that?'

'Well, it was nothing definite, but yesterday afternoon we were just touching on Sir Hugo de Chevenix (who, I'm afraid, didn't bear too good a character in the Wars of the Roses), and Sir Gervase said, "My sister *would* choose the family name of Hugo for her son! It's always been an unsatisfactory name in our family. She might have known no Hugo would turn out well."'

'What you tell us there is suggestive,' said Poirot. 'Yes, it suggests a new idea to me.'

'Sir Gervase said nothing more definite than that?' asked Major Riddle.

Miss Lingard shook her head.

'No, and of course it wouldn't have done for me to say anything. Sir Gervase was really just talking to himself. He wasn't really speaking to me.'

'Quite so.'

Poirot said:

'Mademoiselle, you, a stranger, have been here for two months.

It would be, I think, very valuable if you were to tell us quite frankly your impressions of the family and household.'

Miss Lingard took off her pince-nez and blinked reflectively.

'Well, at first, quite frankly, I felt as though I'd walked straight into a madhouse! What with Lady Chevenix-Gore continually seeing things that weren't there, and Sir Gervase behaving like – like a king – and dramatizing himself in the most extraordinary way – well, I really did think they were the queerest people I had ever come across. Of course, Miss Chevenix-Gore was perfectly normal, and I soon found that Lady Chevenix-Gore was really an extremely kind, nice woman. Nobody could be kinder and nicer to me than she has been. Sir Gervase – well, I really think he *was* mad. His egomania – isn't that what you call it? – was getting worse and worse every day.'

'And the others?'

'Mr Burrows had rather a difficult time with Sir Gervase, I should imagine. I think he was glad that our work on the book gave him a little more breathing space. Colonel Bury was always charming. He was devoted to Lady Chevenix-Gore and he managed Sir Gervase quite well. Mr Trent, Mr Forbes and Miss Cardwell have only been here a few days, so of course I don't know much about them.'

'Thank you, mademoiselle. And what about Captain Lake, the agent?'

'Oh, he's very nice. Everybody liked him.'

'Including Sir Gervase?'

'Oh, yes. I've heard him say Lake was much the best agent he'd had. Of course, Captain Lake had his difficulties with Sir Gervase, too – but he managed pretty well on the whole. It wasn't easy.'

Poirot nodded thoughtfully. He murmured, 'There was something – something – that I had in mind to ask you – some little thing . . . What was it now?'

Miss Lingard turned a patient face towards him.

Poirot shook his head vexedly.

'Tchah! It is on the tip of my tongue.'

Major Riddle waited a minute or two, then as Poirot continued to frown perplexedly, he took up the interrogation once more.

'When was the last time you saw Sir Gervase?'

'At tea-time, in this room.'

'What was his manner then? Normal?'

'As normal as it ever was.'

'Was there any sense of strain among the party?'

'No, I think everybody seemed quite ordinary.'

'Where did Sir Gervase go after tea?'

'He took Mr Burrows with him into the study, as usual.'

'That was the last time you saw him?'

'Yes. I went to the small morning-room where I worked, and typed a chapter of the book from the notes I had gone over with Sir Gervase, until seven o'clock, when I went upstairs to rest and dress for dinner.'

'You actually heard the shot, I understand?'

'Yes, I was in this room. I heard what sounded like a shot and I went out into the hall. Mr Trent was there, and Miss Cardwell. Mr Trent asked Snell if there was champagne for dinner, and made rather a joke of it. It never entered our heads to take the matter seriously, I'm afraid. We felt sure it must have been a car back-firing.'

Poirot said:

'Did you hear Mr Trent say, "*There's always murder*"?'

'I believe he did say something like that – joking, of course.'

'What happened next?'

'We all came in here.'

'Can you remember the order in which the others came down to dinner?'

'Miss Chevenix-Gore was the first, I think, and then Mr Forbes. Then Colonel Bury and Lady Chevenix-Gore together, and Mr Burrows immediately after them. I think that was the order, but I can't be quite sure because they more or less came in all together.'

'Gathered by the sound of the first gong?'

'Yes. Everyone always hustled when they heard that gong. Sir Gervase was a terrible stickler for punctuality in the evening.'

'What time did he himself usually come down?'

'He was nearly always in the room before the first gong went.'

'Did it surprise you that he was not down on this occasion?'

'Very much.'

'Ah, I have it!' cried Poirot.

As the other two looked inquiringly at him he went on:

'I have remembered what I wanted to ask. This evening, mademoiselle, as we all went along to the study on Snell's reporting it to be locked, you stooped and picked something up.'

'I did?' Miss Lingard seemed very surprised.

'Yes, just as we turned into the straight passage to the study. Something small and bright.'

'How extraordinary – I don't remember. Wait a minute – yes, I do. Only I wasn't thinking. Let me see – it must be in here.'

Opening her black satin bag, she poured the contents on a table.

Poirot and Major Riddle surveyed the collection with interest. There were two handkerchiefs, a powder-compact, a small bunch of keys, a spectacle-case and one other object on which Poirot pounced eagerly.

'A bullet, by jove!' said Major Riddle.

The thing was indeed shaped like a bullet, but it proved to be a small pencil.

'That's what I picked up,' said Miss Lingard. 'I'd forgotten all about it.'

'Do you know who this belongs to, Miss Lingard?'

'Oh, yes, it's Colonel Bury's. He had it made out of a bullet that hit him – or rather, didn't hit him, if you know what I mean – in the South African War.'

'Do you know when he had it last?'

'Well, he had it this afternoon when they were playing bridge, because I noticed him writing with it on the score when I came in to tea.'

'Who was playing bridge?'

'Colonel Bury, Lady Chevenix-Gore, Mr Trent and Miss Cardwell.'

'I think,' said Poirot gently, 'we will keep this and return it to the colonel ourselves.'

'Oh, please do. I am so forgetful, I might not remember to do so.'

'Perhaps, mademoiselle, you would be so good as to ask Colonel Bury to come here now?'

'Certainly. I will go and find him at once.'

She hurried away. Poirot got up and began walking aimlessly round the room.

'We begin,' he said, 'to reconstruct the afternoon. It is interesting. At half-past two Sir Gervase goes over accounts with Captain Lake. *He is slightly preoccupied.* At three, he discusses the book he is writing with Miss Lingard. *He is in great distress of mind.* Miss Lingard associates that distress of mind with Hugo Trent on the strength of a chance remark. At teatime *his behaviour is normal.* After tea, Godfrey Burrows tells us *he was in good spirits over something.* At five minutes to eight he comes downstairs, goes to his study, scrawls "*Sorry*" on a sheet of paper, and shoots himself!'

Riddle said slowly:

'I see what you mean. It isn't consistent.'

'Strange alteration of moods in Sir Gervase Chevenix-Gore! He is preoccupied – he is seriously upset – he is normal – he is in high spirits! There is something very curious here! And then that phrase he used, "*Too late.*" That I should get here "Too late." Well, it is true that. I *did* get here too late – *to see him alive.*'

'I see. You really think –?'

'I shall never know now why Sir Gervase sent for me! That is certain!'

Poirot was still wandering round the room. He straightened one or two objects on the mantelpiece; he examined a card-table that stood against a wall, he opened the drawer of it and took out the bridge-markers. Then he wandered over to the writing-table and peered into the wastepaper basket. There was nothing in it but a paper bag. Poirot took it out, smelt it, murmured 'Oranges' and flattened it out, reading the name on it. 'Carpenter and Sons, Fruiterers, Hamborough St Mary.' He was just folding it neatly into squares when Colonel Bury entered the room.

CHAPTER 8

The Colonel dropped into a chair, shook his head, sighed and said:

'Terrible business, this, Riddle. Lady Chevenix-Gore is being wonderful – wonderful. Grand woman! Full of courage!'

Coming softly back to his chair, Poirot said:

'You have known her very many years, I think?'

'Yes, indeed, I was at her coming-out dance. Wore rosebuds in her hair, I remember. And a white, fluffy dress . . . Wasn't anyone to touch her in the room!'

His voice was full of enthusiasm. Poirot held out the pencil to him.

'This is yours, I think?'

'Eh? What? Oh, thank you, had it this afternoon when we were playing bridge. Amazing, you know, I held a hundred honours in spades three times running. Never done such a thing before.'

'You were playing bridge before tea, I understand?' said Poirot. 'What was Sir Gervase's frame of mind when he came in to tea?'

'Usual – quite usual. Never dreamed he was thinking of making away with himself. Perhaps he was a little more excitable than usual, now I come to think of it.'

'When was the last time you saw him?'

'Why, then! Tea-time. Never saw the poor chap alive again.'

'You didn't go to the study at all after tea?'

'No, never saw him again.'

'What time did you come down to dinner?'

'After the first gong went.'

'You and Lady Chevenix-Gore came down together?'

'No, we – er – met in the hall. I think she'd been into the dining-room to see to the flowers – something like that.'

Major Riddle said:

'I hope you won't mind, Colonel Bury, if I ask you a somewhat personal question. Was there any trouble between you and Sir Gervase over the question of the Paragon Synthetic Rubber Company?'

Colonel Bury's face became suddenly purple. He spluttered a little.

'Not at all. Not at all. Old Gervase was an unreasonable sort of fellow. You've got to remember that. He always expected everything he touched to turn out trumps! Didn't seem to realize that the whole world was going through a period of crisis. All stocks and shares bound to be affected.'

'So there *was* a certain amount of trouble between you?'

'No trouble. Just damned unreasonable of Gervase!'

'He blamed you for certain losses he had sustained?'

'Gervase wasn't normal! Vanda knew that. But she could always handle him. I was content to leave it all in her hands.'

Poirot coughed and Major Riddle, after glancing at him, changed the subject.

'You are a very old friend of the family, I know, Colonel Bury. Had you any knowledge as to how Sir Gervase had left his money?'

'Well, I should imagine the bulk of it would go to Ruth. That's what I gathered from what Gervase let fall.'

'You don't think that was at all unfair on Hugo Trent?'

'Gervase didn't like Hugo. Never could stick him.'

'But he had a great sense of family. Miss Chevenix-Gore was, after all, only his adopted daughter.'

Colonel Bury hesitated, then after humming and hawing a moment, he said:

'Look here, I think I'd better tell you something. Strict confidence, and all that.'

'Of course – of course.'

'Ruth's illegitimate, but she's a Chevenix-Gore all right. Daughter of Gervase's brother, Anthony, who was killed in the war. Seemed he'd had an affair with a typist. When he was killed, the girl wrote to Vanda. Vanda went to see her – girl was expecting a baby. Vanda took it up with Gervase, she'd just been told that she herself could never have another child. Result was they took over the child when it was born, adopted it legally. The mother renounced all rights in it. They've brought Ruth up as their own daughter and to all intents and purposes, she *is* their own daughter, and you've only got to look at her to realise she's a Chevenix-Gore all right!'

'Aha,' said Poirot. 'I see. That makes Sir Gervase's attitude very much clearer. But if he did not like Mr Hugo Trent, why was he so anxious to arrange a marriage between him and Mademoiselle Ruth?'

'To regularize the family position. It pleased his sense of fitness.'

'Even though he did not like or trust the young man?'

Colonel Bury snorted.

'You don't understand old Gervase. He couldn't regard people as human beings. He arranged alliances as though the parties were royal personages! He considered it fitting that Ruth and Hugo should marry, Hugo taking the name of Chevenix-Gore. What Hugo and Ruth thought about it didn't matter.'

'And was Mademoiselle Ruth willing to fall in with this arrangement?'

Colonel Bury chuckled.

'Not she! She's a tartar!'

'Did you know that shortly before his death Sir Gervase was drafting a new will by which Miss Chevenix-Gore would inherit only on condition that she should marry Mr Trent?'

Colonel Bury whistled.

'Then he really *had* got the wind-up about her and Burrows –'

As soon as he had spoken, he bit the words off, but it was too late. Poirot had pounced upon the admission.

'There was something between Mademoiselle Ruth and young Monsieur Burrows?'

'Probably nothing in it – nothing in it at all.'

Major Riddle coughed and said:

'I think, Colonel Bury, that you must tell us all you know. It might have a direct bearing on Sir Gervase's state of mind.'

'I suppose it might,' said Colonel Bury, doubtfully. 'Well, the truth of it is, young Burrows is not a bad-looking chap – at least, women seem to think so. He and Ruth seem to have got as thick as thieves just lately, and Gervase didn't like it – didn't like it at all. Didn't like to sack Burrows for fear of precipitating matters. He knows what Ruth's like. She won't be dictated to in any way. So I suppose he hit on this scheme. Ruth's not the sort of girl to sacrifice everything for love. She's fond of the fleshpots and she likes money.'

'Do you yourself approve of Mr Burrows?'

The colonel delivered himself of the opinion that Godfrey Burrows was slightly hairy at the heel, a pronouncement which baffled Poirot completely, but made Major Riddle smile into his moustache.

A few more questions were asked and answered, and then Colonel Bury departed.

Riddle glanced over at Poirot who was sitting absorbed in thought.

'What do you make of it all, M. Poirot?'

The little man raised his hands.

'I seem to see a pattern – a purposeful design.'

Riddle said, 'It's difficult.'

'Yes, it is difficult. But more and more one phrase, lightly uttered, strikes me as significant.'

'What was that?'

'That laughing sentence spoken by Hugo Trent: "*There's always murder*" . . .'

Riddle said sharply:

'Yes, I can see that you've been leaning that way all along.'

'Do you not agree, my friend, that the more we learn, the less and less motive we find for suicide? But for murder, we begin to have a surprising collection of motives!'

'Still, you've got to remember the facts – door locked, key in dead man's pocket. Oh, I know there are ways and means. Bent pins, strings – all sorts of devices. It would, I suppose, be *possible* . . . But do those things really work? That's what I very much doubt.'

'At all events, let us examine the position from the point of view of murder, not of suicide.'

'Oh, all right. As *you* are on the scene, it probably *would* be murder!'

For a moment Poirot smiled.

'I hardly like that remark.'

Then he became grave once more.

'Yes, let us examine the case from the standpoint of murder. The shot is heard, four people are in the hall, Miss Lingard, Hugo Trent, Miss Cardwell and Snell. Where are all the others?'

'Burrows was in the library, according to his own story. No one to check that statement. The others were presumably in their rooms, but who is to know if they were really there? Everybody seems to have come down separately. Even Lady Chevenix-Gore and Bury only met in the hall. Lady Chevenix-Gore came from the dining-room. Where did Bury come from? Isn't it possible that he came, not from upstairs, but *from the study*? There's that pencil.'

'Yes, the pencil is interesting. He showed no emotion when I produced it, but that might be because he did not know where I found it and was unaware himself of having dropped it. Let us see, who else was playing bridge when the pencil was in use? Hugo Trent and Miss Cardwell. They're out of it. Miss Lingard and the butler can vouch for their alibis. The fourth was Lady Chevenix-Gore.'

'You can't seriously suspect her.'

'Why not, my friend? I tell you, me, I can suspect everybody! Supposing that, in spite of her apparent devotion to her husband, it is the faithful Bury she really loves?'

'H'm,' said Riddle. 'In a way it has been a kind of *ménage à trois* for years.'

'And there is some trouble about this company between Sir Gervase and Colonel Bury.'

'It's true that Sir Gervase might have been meaning to turn really nasty. We don't know the ins-and-outs of it. It might fit in with that summons to you. Say Sir Gervase suspects that Bury has deliberately fleeced him, but he doesn't want publicity because of a suspicion that his wife may be mixed up in it. Yes, that's possible. That gives either of those two a possible motive. And it *is* a bit odd really that Lady Chevenix-Gore should take her husband's death so calmly. All this spirit business may be acting!'

'Then there is the other complication,' said Poirot. 'Miss Chevenix-Gore and Burrows. It is very much to their interest that Sir Gervase should not sign the new will. As it is, she gets everything on condition that her husband takes the family name –'

'Yes, and Burrows's account of Sir Gervase's attitude this evening is a bit fishy. High spirits, pleased about something! That doesn't fit with anything else we've been told.'

'There is, too, Mr Forbes. Most correct, most severe, of an old and well-established firm. But lawyers, even the most respectable, have been known to embezzle their client's money when they themselves are in a hole.'

'You're getting a bit too sensational, I think, Poirot.'

'You think what I suggest is too like the pictures? But life, Major Riddle, is often amazingly like the pictures.'

'It has been, so far, in Westshire,' said the chief constable. 'We'd better finish interviewing the rest of them, don't you think? It's getting late. We haven't seen Ruth Chevenix-Gore yet, and she's probably the most important of the lot.'

'I agree. There is Miss Cardwell, too. Perhaps we might see her first, since that will not take long, and interview Miss Chevenix-Gore last.

'Quite a good idea.'

CHAPTER 9

That evening Poirot had only given Susan Cardwell a fleeting glance. He examined her now more attentively. An intelligent face, he thought, not strictly good-looking, but possessing an attraction that a merely pretty girl might envy. Her hair was magnificent, her face skilfully made-up. Her eyes, he thought, were watchful.

After a few preliminary questions, Major Riddle said:

'I don't know how close a friend you are of the family, Miss Cardwell?'

'I don't know them at all. Hugo arranged that I should be asked down here.'

'You are, then, a friend of Hugo Trent's?'

'Yes, that's my position. Hugo's girl-friend.' Susan Cardwell smiled as she drawled out the words.

'You have known him a long time?'

'Oh, no, just a month or so.'

She paused and then added:

'I'm by way of being engaged to him.'

'And he brought you down here to introduce you to his people?'

'Oh, dear no, nothing like that. We were keeping it very hush-hush. I just came down to spy out the land. Hugo told me the place was just like a madhouse. I thought I'd better come and see for myself. Hugo, poor sweet, is a perfect pet, but he's got absolutely no brains. The position, you see, was rather critical. Neither Hugo nor I have any money, and old Sir Gervase, who was Hugo's main hope, had set his heart on Hugo making a match of it with Ruth. Hugo's a bit weak, you know. He might agree to this marriage and count on being able to get out of it later.'

'That idea did not commend itself to you, mademoiselle?' inquired Poirot gently.

'Definitely not. Ruth might have gone all peculiar and refused to divorce him or something. I put my foot down. No trotting off to St Paul's, Knightsbridge, until I could be there dithering with a sheaf of lilies.'

'So you came down to study the situation for yourself?'

'Yes.'

'*Eh bien!*' said Poirot.

'Well, of course, Hugo was right! The whole family were bughouse! Except Ruth, who seems perfectly sensible. She'd got her own boy-friend and wasn't any keener on the marriage idea than I was.'

'You refer to M. Burrows?'

'Burrows? Of course not. Ruth wouldn't fall for a bogus person like that.'

'Then who was the object of her affection?'

Susan Cardwell paused, stretched for a cigarette, lit it, and remarked:

'You'd better ask her that. After all, it isn't my business.'

Major Riddle asked:

'When was the last time you saw Sir Gervase?'

'At tea.'

'Did his manner strike you as peculiar in any way?'

The girl shrugged her shoulders.

'Not more than usual.'

'What did you do after tea?'

'Played billiards with Hugo.'

'You didn't see Sir Gervase again?'

'No.'

'What about the shot?'

'That was rather odd. You see, I thought the first gong had gone, so I hurried up with my dressing, came dashing out of my room, heard, as I thought, the second gong and fairly raced down the stairs. I'd been one minute late for dinner the first night I was here and Hugo told me it had about wrecked our chances with the old man, so I fairly hared down. Hugo was just ahead of me and then there was a queer kind of pop-bang and Hugo said it was a champagne cork, but Snell said "No" to that and, anyway, I didn't think it had come from the dining-room. Miss Lingard thought it came from upstairs, but anyway we agreed it was a back-fire and we trooped into the drawing-room and forgot about it.'

'It did not occur to you for one moment that Sir Gervase might have shot himself?' asked Poirot.

'I ask you, should I be likely to think of such a thing? The Old Man seemed to enjoy himself throwing his weight about. I never imagined he'd do such a thing. I can't think why he did it. I suppose just because he was nuts.'

'An unfortunate occurrence.'

'Very – for Hugo and me. I gather he's left Hugo nothing at all, or practically nothing.'

'Who told you that?'

'Hugo got it out of old Forbes.'

'Well, Miss Cardwell –' Major Riddle paused a moment, 'I think that's all. Do you think Miss Chevenix-Gore is feeling well enough to come down and talk to us?'

'Oh, I should think so. I'll tell her.'

Poirot intervened.

'A little moment, mademoiselle. Have you seen this before?'

He held out the bullet pencil.

'Oh, yes, we had it at bridge this afternoon. Belongs to old Colonel Bury, I think.'

'Did he take it when the rubber was over?'

'I haven't the faintest idea.'

'Thank you, mademoiselle. That is all.'

'Right, I'll tell Ruth.'

Ruth Chevenix-Gore came into the room like a queen. Her colour was vivid, her head held high. But her eyes, like the eyes of Susan Cardwell, were watchful. She wore the same frock she had had on when Poirot arrived. It was a pale shade of apricot. On her shoulder was pinned a deep, salmon-pink rose. It had been fresh and blooming an hour earlier, now it drooped.

'Well?' said Ruth.

'I'm extremely sorry to bother you,' began Major Riddle.

She interrupted him.

'Of course you have to bother me. You have to bother everyone. I can save you time, though. I haven't the faintest idea why the Old Man killed himself. All I can tell you is that it wasn't a bit like him.'

'Did you notice anything amiss in his manner today? Was he depressed, or unduly excited – was there anything at all abnormal?'

'I don't think so. I wasn't noticing –'

'When did you see him last?'

'Tea-time.'

Poirot spoke:

'You did not go to the study – later?'

'No. The last I saw of him was in this room. Sitting there.'

She indicated a chair.

'I see. Do you know this pencil, mademoiselle?'

'It's Colonel Bury's.'

'Have you seen it lately?'

'I don't really remember.'

'Do you know anything of a – disagreement between Sir Gervase and Colonel Bury?'

'Over the Paragon Rubber Company, you mean?'

'Yes.'

'I should think so. The Old Man was rabid about it!'

'He considered, perhaps, that he had been swindled?'

Ruth shrugged her shoulders.

'He didn't understand the first thing about finance.'

Poirot said:

'May I ask you a question, mademoiselle – a somewhat impertinent question?'

'Certainly, if you like.'

'It is this – are you sorry that your – father is dead?'

She stared at him.

'Of course I'm sorry. I don't indulge in sob-stuff. But I shall miss him . . . I was fond of the Old Man. That's what we called him, Hugo and I, always. The "Old Man" – you know – something of the primitive – anthropoid-ape-original-Patriarch-of-the-tribe business. It sounds disrespectful, but there's really a lot of affection behind it. Of course, he was really the most complete, muddle-headed old ass that ever lived!'

'You interest me, mademoiselle.'

'The Old Man had the brains of a louse! Sorry to have to say it, but it's true. He was incapable of any kind of headwork. Mind you, he was a character. Fantastically brave and all that! Could go careering off to the Pole, or fighting duels. I always think that he blustered such a lot because he really knew that his brains weren't up to much. Anyone could have got the better of him.'

Poirot took the letter from his pocket.

'Read this, mademoiselle.'

She read it through and handed it back to him.

'So that's what brought you here!'

'Does it suggest anything to you, that letter?'

She shook her head.

'No. It's probably quite true. Anyone could have robbed the poor old pet. John says the last agent before him swindled him right and left. You see, the Old Man was so grand and so pompous that he never really condescended to look into details! He was an invitation to crooks.'

'You paint a different picture of him, mademoiselle, from the accepted one.'

'Oh, well – he put up a pretty good camouflage. Vanda (my mother) backed him for all she was worth. He was so happy stalking round pretending he was God Almighty. That's why, in a way, I'm glad he's dead. It's the best thing for him.'

'I do not quite follow you, mademoiselle.'

Ruth said broodingly:

'It was growing on him. One of these days he would have had to be locked up . . . People were beginning to talk as it was.'

'Did you know, mademoiselle, that he was contemplating a will whereby you could only inherit his money if you married Mr Trent?'

She cried:

'How absurd! Anyway, I'm sure that could be set aside by law . . . I'm sure you can't dictate to people about whom they shall marry.'

'If he had actually signed such a will, would you have complied with its provisions, mademoiselle?'

She stared.

'I – I –'

She broke off. For two or three minutes she sat irresolute,

looking down at her dangling slipper. A little piece of earth detached itself from the heel and fell on the carpet.

Suddenly Ruth Chevenix-Gore said:

'Wait!'

She got up and ran out of the room. She returned almost immediately with Captain Lake by her side.

'It's got to come out,' she said rather breathlessly. 'You might as well know now. John and I were married in London three weeks ago.'

CHAPTER 10

Of the two of them, Captain Lake looked far the more embarrassed.

'This is a great surprise, Miss Chevenix-Gore – Mrs Lake, I should say,' said Major Riddle. 'Did no one know of this marriage of yours?'

'No, we kept it quite dark. John didn't like that part of it much.'

Lake said, stammering a little:

'I – I know that it seems rather a rotten way to set about things. I ought to have gone straight to Sir Gervase –'

Ruth interrupted:

'And told him you wanted to marry his daughter, and have been kicked out on your head and he'd probably have disinherited me, raised hell generally in the house, and we could have told each other how beautifully we'd behaved! Believe me, my way was better! If a thing's done, it's done. There would still have been a row – but he'd have come round.'

Lake still looked unhappy. Poirot asked:

'When did you intend to break the news to Sir Gervase?'

Ruth answered:

'I was preparing the ground. He'd been rather suspicious about me and John, so I pretended to turn my attentions to Godfrey. Naturally, he was ready to go quite off the deep-end about that. I figured it out that the news I was married to John would come almost as a relief!'

'Did anybody at all know of this marriage?'

'Yes, I told Vanda in the end. I wanted to get her on my side.'

'And you succeeded in doing so?'

'Yes. You see, she wasn't very keen about my marrying Hugo

– because he was a cousin, I think. She seemed to think the family was so batty already that we'd probably have completely batty children. That was probably rather absurd, because I'm only adopted, you know. I believe I'm some quite distant cousin's child.'

'You are sure Sir Gervase had no suspicion of the truth?'

'Oh, no.'

Poirot said:

'Is that true, Captain Lake? In your interview with Sir Gervase this afternoon, are you quite sure the matter was not mentioned?'

'No, sir. It was not.'

'Because, you see, Captain Lake, there is certain evidence to show that Sir Gervase was in a highly-excitable condition after the time he spent with you, and that he spoke once or twice of family dishonour.'

'The matter was not mentioned,' Lake repeated. His face had gone very white.

'Was that the last time you saw Sir Gervase?'

'Yes, I have already told you so.'

'Where were you at eight minutes past eight this evening?'

'Where was I? In my house. At the end of the village, about half a mile away.'

'You did not come up to Hamborough Close round about that time?'

'No.'

Poirot turned to the girl.

'Where were you, mademoiselle, when your father shot himself?'

'In the garden.'

'In the garden? You heard the shot?'

'Oh, yes. But I didn't think about it particularly. I thought it was someone out shooting rabbits, although now I remember I did think it sounded quite close at hand.'

'You returned to the house – which way?'

'I came in through this window.'

Ruth indicated with a turn of her head the window behind her.

'Was anyone in here?'

'No. But Hugo and Susan and Miss Lingard came in from the hall almost immediately. They were talking about shooting and murders and things.'

'I see,' said Poirot. 'Yes, I think I see now . . .'

Major Riddle said rather doubtfully:

'Well – er – thank you. I think that's all for the moment.'

Ruth and her husband turned and left the room.

'What the devil—' began Major Riddle, and ended rather hopelessly: 'It gets more and more difficult to keep track of this business.'

Poirot nodded. He had picked up the little piece of earth that had fallen from Ruth's shoe and was holding it thoughtfully in his hand.

'It is like the mirror smashed on the wall,' he said. 'The dead man's mirror. Every new fact we come across shows us some different angle of the dead man. He is reflected from every conceivable point of view. We shall have soon a complete picture . . .'

He rose and put the little piece of earth tidily in the waste-paper basket.

'I will tell you one thing, my friend. The clue to the whole mystery is the mirror. Go into the study and look for yourself, if you do not believe me.'

Major Riddle, said decisively:

'If it's murder, it's up to you to prove it. If you ask me, I say it's definitely suicide. Did you notice what the girl said about a former agent having swindled old Gervase? I bet Lake told that tale for his own purposes. He was probably helping himself a bit, Sir Gervase suspected it, and sent for you because he didn't know how far things had gone between Lake and Ruth. Then this afternoon Lake told him they were married. That broke Gervase up. It was "too late" now for anything to be done. He determined to get out of it all. In fact his brain, never very well balanced at the best of times, gave way. In my opinion that's what happened. What have you got to say against it?'

Poirot stood still in the middle of the room.

'What have I to say? This: I have nothing to say against your theory – but it does not go far enough. There are certain things it does not take into account.'

'Such as?'

'The discrepancies in Sir Gervase's moods today, the finding of Colonel Bury's pencil, the evidence of Miss Cardwell (which is very important), the evidence of Miss Lingard as to the order in which people came down to dinner, the position of Sir Gervase's chair when he was found, the paper bag which had held oranges and, finally, the all-important clue of the broken mirror.'

Major Riddle stared.

'Are you going to tell me that that rigmarole makes *sense*?' he asked.

Hercule Poirot replied softly:

'I hope to make it do so – by tomorrow.'

CHAPTER 11

It was just after dawn when Hercule Poirot awoke on the following morning. He had been given a bedroom on the east side of the house.

Getting out of bed, he drew aside the window-blind and satisfied himself that the sun had risen, and that it was a fine morning.

He began to dress with his usual meticulous care. Having finished his toilet, he wrapped himself up in a thick overcoat and wound a muffler round his neck.

Then he tiptoed out of his room and through the silent house down to the drawing-room. He opened the french windows noiselessly and passed out into the garden.

The sun was just showing now. The air was misty, with the mist of a fine morning. Hercule Poirot followed the terraced walk round the side of the house till he came to the windows of Sir Gervase's study. Here he stopped and surveyed the scene.

Immediately outside the windows was a strip of grass that ran parallel with the house. In front of that was a wide herbaceous border. The michaelmas daisies still made a fine show. In front of the border was the flagged walk where Poirot was standing. A strip of grass ran from the grass walk behind the border to the terrace. Poirot examined it carefully, then shook his head. He turned his attention to the border on either side of it.

Very slowly he nodded his head. In the right-hand bed, distinct in the soft mould, there were footprints.

As he stared down at them, frowning, a sound caught his ears and he lifted his head sharply.

Above him a window had been pushed up. He saw a red head of hair. Framed in an aureole of golden red he saw the intelligent face of Susan Cardwell.

'What on earth are you doing at this hour, M. Poirot? A spot of sleuthing?'

Poirot bowed with the utmost correctitude.

'Good morning, mademoiselle. Yes, it is as you say. You now behold a detective – a great detective, I may say – in the act of detecting!'

The remark was a little flamboyant. Susan put her head on one side.

'I must remember this in my memoirs,' she remarked. 'Shall I come down and help?'

'I should be enchanted.'

'I thought you were a burglar at first. Which way did you get out?'

'Through the drawing-room window.'

'Just a minute and I'll be with you.'

She was as good as her word. To all appearances Poirot was exactly in the same position as when she had first seen him.

'You are awake very early, mademoiselle?'

'I haven't been to sleep really properly. I was just getting that desperate feeling that one does get at five in the morning.'

'It's not quite so early as that!'

'It feels like it! Now then, my super-sleuth, what are we looking at?'

'But observe, mademoiselle, footprints.'

'So they are.'

'Four of them,' continued Poirot. 'See, I will point them out to you. Two going towards the window, two coming from it.'

'Whose are they? The gardener's?'

'Mademoiselle, mademoiselle! Those footmarks are made by the small dainty high-heeled shoes of a woman. See, convince yourself. Step, I beg of you, in the earth here beside them.'

Susan hesitated a minute, then placed a foot gingerly on to the mould in the place indicated by Poirot. She was wearing small high-heeled slippers of dark brown leather.

'You see, yours are nearly the same size. Nearly, but not quite. These others are made by a rather longer foot than yours. Perhaps Miss Chevenix-Gore's – or Miss Lingard's – or even Lady Chevenix-Gore's.'

'Not Lady Chevenix-Gore – she's got tiny feet. People did

in those days – manage to have small feet, I mean. And Miss Lingard wears queer flat-heeled things.'

'Then they are the marks of Miss Chevenix-Gore. Ah, yes, I remember she mentioned having been out in the garden yesterday evening.'

He led the way back round the house.

'Are we still sleuthing?' asked Susan.

'But certainly. We will go now to Sir Gervase's study.'

He led the way. Susan Cardwell followed him.

The door still hung in a melancholy fashion. Inside, the room was as it had been last night. Poirot pulled the curtains and admitted the daylight.

He stood looking out at the border a minute or two, then he said:

'You have not, I presume, mademoiselle, much acquaintance with burglars?'

Susan Cardwell shook her red head regretfully.

'I'm afraid not, M. Poirot.'

'The chief constable, he, too, has not had the advantages of a friendly relationship with them. His connection with the criminal clases has always been strictly official. With me that is not so. I had a very pleasant chat with a burglar once. He told me an interesting thing about french windows – a trick that could sometimes be employed if the fastening was sufficiently loose.'

He turned the handle of the left-hand window as he spoke, the middle shaft came up out of the hole in the ground, and Poirot was able to pull the two doors of the window towards him. Having opened them wide, he closed them again – closed them without turning the handle, so as not to send the shaft down into its socket. He let go of the handle, waited a moment, then struck a quick, jarring blow high up on the centre of the shaft. The jar of the blow sent the shaft down into the socket in the ground – the handle turned of its own accord.

'You see, mademoiselle?'

'I think I do.'

Susan had gone rather pale.

'The window is now closed. It is impossible to *enter* a room when the window is closed, but it *is* possible to *leave* a room, pull the doors to from outside, then hit it as I did, and the bolt goes down into the ground, turning the handle. The window then is firmly closed, and anyone looking at it would say it had been closed from the *inside*.'

'Is that' – Susan's voice shook a little – 'is that what happened last night?'

'I think so, yes, mademoiselle.'

Susan said violently:

'I don't believe a word of it.'

Poirot did not answer. He walked over to the mantelpiece. He wheeled sharply round.

'Mademoiselle, I have need of you as a witness. I have already one witness, Mr Trent. He saw me find this tiny sliver of looking-glass last night. I spoke of it to him. I left it where it was for the police. I even told the chief constable that a valuable clue was the broken mirror. But he did not avail himself of my hint. Now you are a witness that I place this sliver of looking-glass (to which, remember, I have already called Mr Trent's attention) into a little envelope – so.' He suited the action to the word. 'And I write on it – so – and seal it up. You are a witness, mademoiselle?'

'Yes – but – but I don't know what it means.'

Poirot walked over to the other side of the room. He stood in front of the desk and stared at the shattered mirror on the wall in front of him.

'I will tell you what it means, mademoiselle. If you had been standing here last night, looking into this mirror, you could have seen in it *murder being committed . . .*'

CHAPTER 12

I

For once in her life Ruth Chevenix-Gore – now Ruth Lake – came down to breakfast in good time. Hercule Poirot was in the hall and drew her aside before she went into the dining-room.

'I have a question to ask you, madame.'

'Yes?'

'You were in the garden last night. Did you at any time step in the flower-bed outside Sir Gervase's study window?'

Ruth stared at him.

'Yes, twice.'

'Ah! *Twice*. How twice?'

'The first time I was picking michaelmas daisies. That was about seven o'clock.'

'Was it not rather an odd time of day to pick flowers?'

'Yes, it was, as a matter of fact. I'd done the flowers yesterday morning, but Vanda said after tea that the flowers on the dinner-table weren't good enough. I had thought they would be all right, so I hadn't done them fresh.'

'But your mother requested you to do them? Is that right?'

'Yes. So I went out just before seven. I took them from that part of the border because hardly anyone goes round there, and so it didn't matter spoiling the effect.'

'Yes, yes, but the *second* time. You went there a *second* time, you said?'

'That was just before dinner. I had dropped a spot of brilliantine on my dress – just by the shoulder. I didn't want to bother to change, and none of my artificial flowers went with the yellow of that dress. I remembered I'd seen a late rose when I was picking the michaelmas daisies, so I hurried out and got it and pinned it on my shoulder.'

Poirot nodded his head slowly.

'Yes, I remember that you wore a rose last night. What time was it, madame, when you picked that rose?'

'I don't really know.'

'But it is *essential*, madame. Consider – reflect.'

Ruth frowned. She looked swiftly at Poirot and then away again.

'I can't say exactly,' she said at last. 'It must have been – oh, of course – it must have been about five minutes past eight. It was when I was on my way back round the house that I heard the gong go, and then that funny bang. I was hurrying because I thought it was the second gong and not the first.'

'Ah, so you thought that – and did you not try the study window when you stood there in the flower-bed?'

'As a matter of fact, I did. I thought it might be open, and it would be quicker to come in that way. But it was fastened.'

'So everything is explained. I congratulate you, madame.'

She stared at him.

'What do you mean?'

'That you have an explanation for everything, for the mould on your shoes, for your footprints in the flower-bed, for your fingerprints on the outside of the window. It is very convenient that.'

Before Ruth could answer, Miss Lingard came hurrying down the stairs. There was a queer purple flush on her cheeks, and she looked a little startled at seeing Poirot and Ruth standing together.

'I beg your pardon,' she said. 'Is anything the matter?'

Ruth said angrily:

'I think M. Poirot has gone mad!'

She swept by them and into the dining-room. Miss Lingard turned an astonished face on Poirot.

He shook his head.

'After breakfast,' he said. 'I will explain. I should like everyone to assemble in Sir Gervase's study at ten o'clock.'

He repeated this request on entering the dining-room.

Susan Cardwell gave him a quick glance, then transferred her gaze to Ruth. When Hugo said:

'Eh? What's the idea?' she gave him a sharp nudge in the side, and he shut up obediently.

When he had finished his breakfast, Poirot rose and walked to the door. He turned and drew out a large old-fashioned watch.

'It is five minutes to ten. In five minutes – in the study.'

II

Poirot looked round him. A circle of interested faces stared back at him. Everyone was there, he noted, with one exception, and at that very moment the exception swept into the room. Lady Chevenix-Gore came in with a soft, gliding step. She looked haggard and ill.

Poirot drew forward a big chair for her, and she sat down.

She looked up at the broken mirror, shivered, and pulled her chair a little way round.

'Gervase is still here,' she remarked in a matter-of-fact tone. 'Poor Gervase . . . He will soon be free now.'

Poirot cleared his throat and announced:

'I have asked you all to come here so that you may hear the true facts of Sir Gervase's suicide.'

'It was Fate,' said Lady Chevenix-Gore. 'Gervase was strong, but his Fate was stronger.'

Colonel Bury moved forward a little.

'Vanda – my dear.'

She smiled up at him, then put up her hand. He took it in his. She said softly: 'You are such a comfort, Ned.'

Ruth said sharply:

'Are we to understand, M. Poirot, that you have definitely ascertained the cause of my father's suicide?'

Poirot shook his head.

'No, madame.'

'Then what is all this rigmarole about?'

Poirot said quietly:

'I do not know the cause of Sir Gervase Chevenix-Gore's suicide, *because Sir Gervase Chevenix-Gore did not commit suicide.* He did not kill himself. *He was killed . . .*'

'Killed?' Several voices echoed the word. Startled faces were turned in Poirot's direction. Lady Chevenix-Gore looked up, said, 'Killed? Oh, no!' and gently shook her head.

'Killed, did you say?' It was Hugo who spoke now. 'Impossible. There was no one in the room when we broke in. The window was fastened. The door was locked on the inside, and the key was in my uncle's pocket. How could he have been killed?'

'Nevertheless, he was killed.'

'And the murderer escaped through the keyhole, I suppose?' said Colonel Bury sceptically. 'Or flew up the chimney?'

'The murderer,' said Poirot, 'went out through the window. I will show you how.'

He repeated his manoeuvres with the window.

'You see?' he said. 'That was how it was done! From the first I could not consider it likely that Sir Gervase had committed suicide. He had pronounced egomania, and such a man does not kill himself.

'And there were other things! Apparently, just before his death, Sir Gervase had sat down at his desk, scrawled the word *SORRY* on a sheet of note-paper and had then shot himself. But before this last action he had, for some reason or other altered the position of his chair, turning it so that it was sideways to the desk. Why? There must be some reason. I began to see light when I found, sticking to the base of a heavy bronze statuette, a tiny sliver of looking-glass . . .

'I asked myself, how does a sliver of broken looking-glass come to be there? – and an answer suggested itself to me. The mirror had been broken, not by a bullet, *but by being struck with the heavy bronze figure.* That mirror had been broken *deliberately.*

'But why? I returned to the desk and looked down at the chair. Yes, I saw now. It was all wrong. No suicide would turn his chair round, lean over the edge of it, and then shoot himself. The whole thing was arranged. The suicide was a fake!

'And now I come to something very important. The evidence of Miss Cardwell. Miss Cardwell said that she hurried downstairs last night because she thought that the *second* gong had sounded. That is to say, she thought that she had already heard the *first* gong.

'Now observe, *if* Sir Gervase was sitting at his desk in the normal fashion when he was shot, where would the bullet go?

Travelling in a straight line, it would pass through the door, if the door were open, and finally *hit the gong*!

'You see now the importance of Miss Cardwell's statement? No one else heard the first gong, but, then, her room is situated immediately above this one, and she was in the best position for hearing it. It would consist of only one single note, remember.

'There could be no question of Sir Gervase's shooting himself. A dead man cannot get up, shut the door, lock it and arrange himself in a convenient position! Somebody else was concerned, and therefore it was not suicide, but murder. Someone whose presence was easily accepted by Sir Gervase, stood by his side talking to him. Sir Gervase was busy writing, perhaps. The murderer brings the pistol up to the right side of his head and fires. The deed is done! Then quick, to work! The murderer slips on gloves. The door is locked, the key put in Sir Gervase's pocket. But supposing that one loud note of the gong has been heard? Then it will be realized that the door was *open*, not *shut*, when the shot was fired. So the chair is turned, the body rearranged, the dead man's fingers pressed on the pistol, the mirror deliberately smashed. Then the murderer goes out through the window, jars it shut, steps, not on the grass, but in the flower-bed where footprints can be smoothed out afterwards; then round the side of the house and into the drawing-room.'

He paused and said:

'*There was only one person who was out in the garden when the shot was fired.* That same person left her footprints in the flower-bed and her fingerprints on the outside of the window.'

He came towards Ruth.

'And there was a motive, wasn't there? Your father had learnt of your secret marriage. He was preparing to disinherit you.'

'It's a lie!' Ruth's voice came scornful and clear. 'There's not a word of truth in your story. It's a lie from start to finish!'

'The proofs against you are very strong, madame. A jury *may* believe you. It may *not*!'

'She won't have to face a jury.'

The others turned – startled. Miss Lingard was on her feet. Her face altered. She was trembling all over.

'*I* shot him. I admit it! I had my reason. I – I've been waiting for some time. M. Poirot is quite right. I followed him in here. I had taken the pistol out of the drawer earlier. I stood beside him talking about the book – and I shot him. That was just after eight. The bullet struck the gong. I never dreamt it would pass right through his head like that. There wasn't time to go out and look for it. I locked the door and put the key in his pocket. Then I swung the chair round, smashed the mirror, and, after scrawling 'Sorry' on a piece of paper, I went out through the window and shut it the way M. Poirot showed you. I stepped in the flower-bed, but I smoothed out the footprints with a little rake I had put there ready. Then I went round to the drawing-room. I had left the window open. I didn't know Ruth had gone out through it. She must have come round the front of the house while I went round the back. I had to put the rake away, you see, in a shed. I waited in the drawing-room till I heard someone coming downstairs and Snell going to the gong, and then –'

She looked at Poirot.

'You don't know what I did then?'

'Oh yes, I do. I found the bag in the wastepaper basket. It was very clever, that idea of yours. You did what children love to do. You blew up the bag and then hit it. It made a satisfactory big bang. You threw the bag into the wastepaper basket and rushed out into the hall. You had established the time of the suicide – and an alibi for yourself. But there was still one thing that worried you. You had not had time to pick up the bullet. It must be somewhere near the gong. It was essential that the bullet should be found in the study somewhere near the mirror. I didn't know when you had the idea of taking Colonel Bury's pencil –'

'It was just then,' said Miss Lingard. 'When we all came in from the hall. I was surprised to see Ruth in the room. I realized she must have come from the garden through the window. Then I noticed Colonel Bury's pencil lying on the bridge table. I slipped it into my bag. If, later, anyone saw me pick up the bullet, I could pretend it was the pencil. As a matter of fact, I didn't think anyone saw me pick up the bullet. I dropped it by the mirror while you were looking at the body. When you tackled me on the subject, I was very glad I had thought of the pencil.'

'Yes, that was clever. It confused me completely.'

'I was afraid someone must hear the real shot, but I knew everyone was dressing for dinner, and would be shut away in their rooms. The servants were in their quarters. Miss Cardwell was the only one at all likely to hear it, and she would probably think it was a backfire. What she did hear was the gong. I thought – I thought everything had gone without a hitch . . .'

Mr Forbes said slowly in his precise tones:

'This is a most extraordinary story. There seems no motive –'

Miss Lingard said clearly: 'There *was* a motive . . .'

She added fiercely:

'Go on, ring up the police! What are you waiting for?'

Poirot said gently:

'Will you all please leave the room? Mr Forbes, ring up Major Riddle. I will stay here till he comes.'

Slowly, one by one, the family filed out of the room. Puzzled, uncomprehending, shocked, they cast abashed glances at the trim, upright figure with its neatly-parted grey hair.

Ruth was the last to go. She stood, hesitating in the doorway.

'I don't understand.' She spoke angrily, defiantly, accusing Poirot. 'Just now, you thought *I* had done it.'

'No, no,' Poirot shook his head. 'No, I never thought that.'

Ruth went out slowly.

Poirot was left with the little middle-aged prim woman who had just confessed to a cleverly-planned and cold-blooded murder.

'No,' said Miss Lingard. 'You didn't think she had done it. You accused *her* to make *me* speak. That's right, isn't it?'

Poirot bowed his head.

'While we're waiting,' said Miss Lingard in a conversational tone, 'you might tell me what made you suspect *me*.'

'Several things. To begin with, your account of Sir Gervase. A proud man like Sir Gervase would never speak disparagingly of his nephew to an outsider, especially someone in your position. You wanted to strengthen the theory of suicide. You also went out of your way to suggest that the cause of the suicide was some dishonourable trouble connected with Hugo Trent. That, again, was a thing Sir Gervase would never have admitted to a stranger. Then there was the object you picked up in the hall, and the very significant fact that you did not mention that Ruth, when she entered the drawing-room, did so *from the garden*. And then I found the paper bag – a most unlikely object to find in the wastepaper basket in the drawing-room of a house like

Hamborough Close! You were the only person who had been in the drawing-room when the "shot" was heard. The paper bag trick was one that would suggest itself to a woman – an ingenious home-made device. So everything fitted in. The endeavour to throw suspicion on Hugo, and to keep it away from Ruth. The mechanism of crime – and its motive.'

The little grey-haired woman stirred.

'You know the motive?'

'I think so. Ruth's happiness – that was the motive! I fancy that you had seen her with John Lake – you knew how it was with them. And then with your easy access to Sir Gervase's papers, you came across the draft of his new will – Ruth disinherited unless she married Hugo Trent. That decided you to take the law into your own hands, using the fact that Sir Gervase had previously written to me. You probably saw a copy of that letter. What muddled feeling of suspicion and fear had caused him to write originally, I do not know. He must have suspected either Burrows or Lake of systematically robbing him. His uncertainty regarding Ruth's feelings made him seek a private investigation. You used that fact and deliberately set the stage for suicide, backing it up by your account of his being very distressed over something connected with Hugo Trent. You sent a telegram to me and reported Sir Gervase as having said I should arrive "too late."'

Miss Lingard said fiercely:

'Gervase Chevenix-Gore was a bully, a snob and a windbag! I wasn't going to have him ruin Ruth's happiness.'

Poirot said gently:

'Ruth is your daughter?'

'Yes – she is my daughter – I've often – thought about her. When I heard Sir Gervase Chevenix-Gore wanted someone to help him with a family history, I jumped at the chance. I was curious to see my – my girl. I knew Lady Chevenix-Gore wouldn't recognize me. It was years ago – I was young and pretty then, and I changed my name after that time. Besides Lady Chevenix-Gore is too vague to know anything definitely. I liked her, but I hated the Chevenix-Gore family. They treated me like dirt. And here was Gervase going to ruin Ruth's life with pride and snobbery. But I determined that she should be happy. And she *will* be happy – *if she never knows about me*!'

It was a plea – not a question.

Poirot bent his head gently.

'No one shall know from me.'

Miss Lingard said quietly:

'Thank you.'

III

Later, when the police had come and gone, Poirot found Ruth Lake with her husband in the garden.

She said challengingly:

'Did you really think that I had done it, M. Poirot?'

'I knew, madame, that you could *not* have done it – because of the michaelmas daisies.'

'The michaelmas daisies? I don't understand.'

'Madame, there were four footprints and four footprints *only* in the border. But if you had been picking flowers there would have been many more. That meant that between your first visit and your second, *someone had smoothed all those footsteps away.* That could only have been done by the guilty person, and since your footprints had *not* been removed, you were *not* the guilty person. You were automatically cleared.'

Ruth's face lightened.

'Oh, I see. You know – I suppose it's dreadful, but I feel rather sorry for that poor woman. After all, she did confess rather than let me be arrested – or at any rate, that is what she thought. That was – rather noble in a way. I hate to think of her going through a trial for murder.'

Poirot said gently:

'Do not distress yourself. It will not come to that. The doctor, he tells me that she has serious heart trouble. She will not live many weeks.'

'I'm glad of that.' Ruth picked an autumn crocus and pressed it idly against her cheek.

'Poor woman. I wonder why she did it . . .'

THE LOVE DETECTIVES

I

Little Mr Satterthwaite looked thoughtfully across at his host. The friendship between these two men was an odd one. The colonel was a simple country gentleman whose passion in life was sport. The few weeks that he spent perforce in London, he spent unwillingly. Mr Satterthwaite, on the other hand, was a town bird. He was an authority on French cooking, on ladies' dress, and on all the latest scandals. His passion was observing human nature, and he was an expert in his own special line – that of an onlooker at life.

It would seem, therefore, that he and Colonel Melrose would have little in common, for the colonel had no interest in his neighbours' affairs and a horror of any kind of emotion. The two men were friends mainly because their fathers before them had been friends. Also they knew the same people and had reactionary views about *nouveaux riches*.

It was about half past seven. The two men were sitting in the colonel's comfortable study, and Melrose was describing a run of the previous winter with a keen hunting man's enthusiasm. Mr Satterthwaite, whose knowledge of horses consisted chiefly of the time-honoured Sunday morning visit to the stables which still obtains in old-fashioned country houses, listened with his invariable politeness.

The sharp ringing of the telephone interrupted Melrose. He crossed to the table and took up the receiver.

'Hello, yes – Colonel Melrose speaking. What's that?' His whole demeanour altered – became stiff and official. It was the magistrate speaking now, not the sportsman.

He listened for some moments, then said laconically, 'Right,

Curtis. I'll be over at once.' He replaced the receiver and turned to his guest. 'Sir James Dwighton has been found in his library – murdered.'

'What?'

Mr Satterthwaite was startled – thrilled.

'I must go over to Alderway at once. Care to come with me?'

Mr Satterthwaite remembered that the colonel was chief constable of the county.

'If I shan't be in the way –' He hesitated.

'Not at all. That was Inspector Curtis telephoning. Good, honest fellow, but no brains. I'd be glad if you would come with me, Satterthwaite. I've got an idea this is going to turn out a nasty business.'

'Have they got the fellow who did it?'

'No,' replied Melrose shortly.

Mr Satterthwaite's trained ear detected a nuance of reserve behind the curt negative. He began to go over in his mind all that he knew of the Dwightons.

A pompous old fellow, the late Sir James, brusque in his manner. A man that might easily make enemies. Veering on sixty, with grizzled hair and a florid face. Reputed to be tight-fisted in the extreme.

His mind went on to Lady Dwighton. Her image floated before him, young, auburn-haired, slender. He remembered various rumours, hints, odd bits of gossip. So that was it – that was why Melrose looked so glum. Then he pulled himself up – his imagination was running away with him.

Five minutes later Mr Satterthwaite took his place beside his host in the latter's little two seater, and they drove off together into the night.

The colonel was a taciturn man. They had gone quite a mile and a half before he spoke. Then he jerked out abruptly. 'You know 'em, I suppose?'

'The Dwightons? I know all about them, of course.' Who was there Mr Satterthwaite didn't know all about? 'I've met him once, I think, and her rather oftener.'

'Pretty woman,' said Melrose.

'Beautiful!' declared Mr Satterthwaite.

'Think so?'

'A pure Renaissance type,' declared Mr Satterthwaite, warming up to his theme. 'She acted in those theatricals – the charity matinee, you know, last spring. I was very much struck. Nothing modern about her – a pure survival. One can imagine her in the doge's palace, or as Lucrezia Borgia.'

The colonel let the car swerve slightly, and Mr Satterthwaite came to an abrupt stop. He wondered what fatality had brought the name of Lucrezia Borgia to his tongue. Under the circumstances –

'Dwighton was not poisoned, was he?' he asked abruptly.

Melrose looked at him sideways, somewhat curiously. 'Why do you ask that, I wonder?' he said.

'Oh, I – I don't know.' Mr Satterthwaite was flustered. 'I – It just occurred to me.'

'Well, he wasn't,' said Melrose gloomily. 'If you want to know, he was crashed on the head.'

'With a blunt instrument,' murmured Mr Satterthwaite, nodding his head sagely.

'Don't talk like a damned detective story, Satterthwaite. He was hit on the head with a bronze figure.'

'Oh,' said Satterthwaite, and relapsed into silence.

'Know anything of a chap called Paul Delangua?' asked Melrose after a minute or two.

'Yes. Good-looking young fellow.'

'I daresay women would call him so,' growled the colonel.

'You don't like him?'

'No, I don't.'

'I should have thought you would have. He rides very well.'

'Like a foreigner at the horse show. Full of monkey tricks.'

Mr Satterthwaite suppressed a smile. Poor old Melrose was so very British in his outlook. Agreeably conscious himself of a cosmopolitan point of view, Mr Satterthwaite was able to deplore the insular attitude toward life.

'Has he been down in this part of the world?' he asked.

'He's been staying at Alderway with the Dwightons. The rumour goes that Sir James kicked him out a week ago.'

'Why?'

'Found him making love to his wife, I suppose. What the hell –'

There was a violent swerve, and a jarring impact.

'Most dangerous crossroads in England,' said Melrose. 'All the same, the other fellow should have sounded his horn. We're on the main road. I fancy we've damaged him rather more than he has damaged us.'

He sprang out. A figure alighted from the other car and joined him. Fragments of speech reached Satterthwaite.

'Entirely my fault, I'm afraid,' the stranger was saying. 'But I do not know this part of the country very well, and there's absolutely no sign of any kind to show you're coming onto the main road.'

The colonel, mollified, rejoined suitably. The two men bent together over the stranger's car, which a chauffeur was already examining. The conversation became highly technical.

'A matter of half an hour, I'm afraid,' said the stranger. 'But don't let me detain you. I'm glad your car escaped injury as well as it did.'

'As a matter of fact –' the colonel was beginning, but he was interrupted.

Mr Satterthwaite, seething with excitement, hopped out of the car with a birdlike action, and seized the stranger warmly by the hand.

'It *is!* I thought I recognized the voice,' he declared excitedly. 'What an extraordinary thing. What a very extraordinary thing.'

'Eh?' said Colonel Melrose.

'Mr Harley Quin. Melrose, I'm sure you've heard me speak many times of Mr Quin?'

Colonel Melrose did not seem to remember the fact, but he assisted politely at the scene while Mr Satterthwaite was chirruping gaily on. 'I haven't seen you – let me see –'

'Since the night at the Bells and Motley,' said the other quietly.

'The Bells and Motley, eh?' said the colonel.

'An inn,' explained Mr Satterthwaite.

'What an odd name for an inn.'

'Only an old one,' said Mr Quin. 'There was a time, remember, when bells and motley were more common in England than they are nowadays.'

'I suppose so, yes, no doubt you are right,' said Melrose

vaguely. He blinked. By a curious effect of light – the headlights of one car and the red tail-light of the other – Mr Quin seemed for a moment to be dressed in motley himself. But it was only the light.

'We can't leave you here stranded on the road,' continued Mr Satterthwaite. 'You must come along with us. There's plenty of room for three, isn't there, Melrose?'

'Oh rather.' But the colonel's voice was a little doubtful. 'The only thing is,' he remarked, 'the job we're on. Eh, Satterthwaite?'

Mr Satterthwaite stood stock-still. Ideas leaped and flashed over him. He positively shook with excitement.

'No,' he cried. 'No, I should have known better! There is no chance where you are concerned, Mr Quin. It was not an accident that we all met tonight at the crossroads.'

Colonel Melrose stared at his friend in astonishment. Mr Satterthwaite took him by the arm.

'You remember what I told you – about our friend Derek Capel? The motive for his suicide, which no one could guess? It was Mr Quin who solved that problem – and there have been others since. He shows you things that are there all the time, but which you haven't seen. He's marvellous.'

'My dear Satterthwaite, you are making me blush,' said Mr Quin, smiling. 'As far as I can remember, these discoveries were all made by you, not by me.'

'They were made because you were there,' said Mr Satterthwaite with intense conviction.

'Well,' said Colonel Melrose, clearing his throat uncomfortably. 'We mustn't waste any more time. Let's get on.'

He climbed into the driver's seat. He was not too well pleased at having the stranger foisted upon him through Mr Satterthwaite's enthusiasm, but he had no valid objection to offer, and he was anxious to get on to Alderway as fast as possible.

Mr Satterthwaite urged Mr Quin in next, and himself took the outside seat. The car was a roomy one and took three without undue squeezing.

'So you are interested in crime, Mr Quin?' said the colonel, doing his best to be genial.

'No, not exactly in crime.'

'What, then?'

Mr Quin smiled. 'Let us ask Mr Satterthwaite. He is a very shrewd observer.'

'I think,' said Satterthwaite slowly, 'I may be wrong, but I think – that Mr Quin is interested in – lovers.'

He blushed as he said the last word, which is one no Englishman can pronounce without self-consciousness. Mr Satterthwaite brought it out apologetically, and with an effect of inverted commas.

'By gad!' said the colonel, startled and silenced.

He reflected inwardly that this seemed to be a very rum friend of Satterthwaite's. He glanced at him sideways. The fellow looked all right – quite a normal young chap. Rather dark, but not at all foreign-looking.

'And now,' said Satterthwaite importantly, 'I must tell you all about the case.'

He talked for some ten minutes. Sitting there in the darkness, rushing through the night, he had an intoxicating feeling of power. What did it matter if he were only a looker-on at life? He had words at his command, he was master of them, he could string them to a pattern – a strange Renaissance pattern composed of the beauty of Laura Dwighton, with her white arms and red hair – and the shadowy dark figure of Paul Delangua, whom women found handsome.

Set that against the background of Alderway – Alderway that had stood since the days of Henry VII and, some said, before that. Alderway that was English to the core, with its clipped yew and its old beak barn and the fishpond, where monks had kept their carp for Fridays.

In a few deft strokes he had etched in Sir James, a Dwighton who was a true descendant of the old De Wittons, who long ago had wrung money out of the land and locked it fast in coffers, so that whoever else had fallen on evil days, the masters of Alderway had never become impoverished.

At last Mr Satterthwaite ceased. He was sure, had been sure all along, of the sympathy of his audience. He waited now the word of praise which was his due. It came.

'You are an artist, Mr Satterthwaite.'

'I – I do my best.' The little man was suddenly humble.

They had turned in at the lodge gates some minutes ago. Now

the car drew up in front of the doorway, and a police constable came hurriedly down the steps to meet them.

'Good evening, sir. Inspector Curtis is in the library.'

'Right.'

Melrose ran up the steps followed by the other two. As the three of them passed across the wide hall, an elderly butler peered from a doorway apprehensively. Melrose nodded to him.

'Evening, Miles. This is a sad business.'

'It is indeed,' the other quavered. 'I can hardly believe it, sir; indeed I can't. To think that anyone should strike down the master.'

'Yes, yes,' said Melrose, cutting him short. 'I'll have a talk with you presently.'

He strode on to the library. There a big, soldierly-looking inspector greeted him with respect.

'Nasty business, sir. I have not disturbed things. No fingerprints on the weapon. Whoever did it knew his business.'

Mr Satterthwaite looked at the bowed figure sitting at the big writing table, and looked hurriedly away again. The man had been struck down from behind, a smashing blow that had crashed in the skull. The sight was not a pretty one.

The weapon lay on the floor – a bronze figure about two feet high, the base of it stained and wet. Mr Satterthwaite bent over it curiously.

'A Venus,' he said softly. 'So he was struck down by Venus.'

He found food for poetic meditation in the thought.

'The windows,' said the inspector, 'were all closed and bolted on the inside.'

He paused significantly.

'Making an inside job of it,' said the chief constable reluctantly. 'Well – well, we'll see.'

The murdered man was dressed in golf clothes, and a bag of golf clubs had been flung untidily across a big leather couch.

'Just come in from the links,' explained the inspector, following the chief constable's glance. 'At five-fifteen, that was. Had tea brought here by the butler. Later he rang for his valet to bring him down a pair of soft slippers. As far as we can tell, the valet was the last person to see him alive.'

Melrose nodded, and turned his attention once more to the writing table.

A good many of the ornaments had been overturned and broken. Prominent among these was a big dark enamel clock, which lay on its side in the very centre of the table.

The inspector cleared his throat.

'That's what you might call a piece of luck, sir,' he said. 'As you see, it's stopped. *At half past six.* That gives us the time of the crime. Very convenient.'

The colonel was staring at the clock.

'As you say,' he remarked. 'Very convenient.' He paused a minute, and then added, 'Too damned convenient! I don't like it, Inspector.'

He looked around at the other two. His eye sought Mr Quin's with a look of appeal in it.

'Damn it all,' he said. 'It's too neat. You know what I mean. Things don't happen like that.'

'You mean,' murmured Mr Quin, 'that clocks don't fall like that?'

Melrose stared at him for a moment, then back at the clock, which had that pathetic and innocent look familiar to objects which have been suddenly bereft of their dignity. Very carefully Colonel Melrose replaced it on its legs again. He struck the table a violent blow. The clock rocked, but it did not fall. Melrose repeated the action, and very slowly, with a kind of unwillingness, the clock fell over on its back.

'What time was the crime discovered?' demanded Melrose sharply.

'Just about seven o'clock, sir.'

'Who discovered it?'

'The butler.'

'Fetch him in,' said the chief constable. 'I'll see him now. Where is Lady Dwighton, by the way?'

'Lying down, sir. Her maid says that she's prostrated and can't see anyone.'

Melrose nodded, and Inspector Curtis went in search of the butler. Mr Quin was looking thoughtfully into the fireplace. Mr Satterthwaite followed his example. He blinked at the smouldering logs for a minute or two, and then something bright lying in the grate caught his eye. He stooped and picked up a little sliver of curved glass.

'You wanted me, sir?'

It was the butler's voice, still quavering and uncertain. Mr Satterthwaite slipped the fragment of glass into his waistcoat pocket and turned round.

The old man was standing in the doorway.

'Sit down,' said the chief constable kindly. 'You're shaking all over. It's been a shock to you, I expect.'

'It has indeed, sir.'

'Well, I shan't keep you long. Your master came in just after five, I believe?'

'Yes, sir. He ordered tea to be brought to him here. Afterward, when I came to take it away, he asked for Jennings to be sent to him – that's his valet, sir.'

'What time was that?'

'About ten minutes past six, sir.'

'Yes – well?'

'I sent word to Jennings, sir. And it wasn't till I came in here to shut the windows and draw the curtains at seven o'clock that I saw –'

Melrose cut him short. 'Yes, yes, you needn't go into all that. You didn't touch the body, or disturb anything, did you?'

'Oh! No indeed, sir! I went as fast as I could go to the telephone to ring up the police.'

'And then?'

'I told Jane – her ladyship's maid, sir – to break the news to her ladyship.'

'You haven't seen your mistress at all this evening?'

Colonel Melrose put the question casually enough, but Mr Satterthwaite's keen ears caught anxiety behind the words.

'Not to speak to, sir. Her ladyship has remained in her own apartments since the tragedy.'

'Did you see her before?'

The question came sharply, and everyone in the room noted the hesitation before the butler replied.

'I – I just caught a glimpse of her, sir, descending the staircase.'

'Did she come in here?'

Mr Satterthwaite held his breath.

'I – I think so, sir.'

'What time was that?'

You might have heard a pin drop. Did the old man know, Mr Satterthwaite wondered, what hung on his answer?

'It was just upon half past six, sir.'

Colonel Melrose drew a deep breath. 'That will do, thank you. Just send Jennings, the valet, to me, will you?'

Jennings answered the summons with promptitude. A narrow-faced man with a catlike tread. Something sly and secretive about him.

A man, thought Mr Satterthwaite, who would easily murder his master if he could be sure of not being found out.

He listened eagerly to the man's answers to Colonel Melrose's questions. But his story seemed straightforward enough. He had brought his master down some soft hide slippers and removed the brogues.

'What did you do after that, Jennings?'

'I went back to the stewards' room, sir.'

'At what time did you leave your master?'

'It must have been just after a quarter past six, sir.'

'Where were you at half past six, Jennings?'

'In the stewards' room, sir.'

Colonel Melrose dismissed the man with a nod. He looked across at Curtis inquiringly.

'Quite correct, sir, I checked that up. He was in the stewards' room from about six-twenty until seven o'clock.'

'Then that lets him out,' said the chief constable a trifle regretfully. 'Besides, there's no motive.'

They looked at each other.

There was a tap at the door.

'Come in,' said the colonel.

A scared-looking lady's maid appeared.

'If you please, her ladyship has heard that Colonel Melrose is here and she would like to see him.'

'Certainly,' said Melrose. 'I'll come at once. Will you show me the way?'

But a hand pushed the girl aside. A very different figure now stood in the doorway. Laura Dwighton looked like a visitor from another world.

She was dressed in a clinging medieval tea gown of dull blue brocade. Her auburn hair was parted in the middle and brought down over her ears. Conscious of the fact she had a style of her own, Lady Dwighton had never had her hair cut. It was drawn back into a simple knot on the nape of her neck. Her arms were bare.

One of them was outstretched to steady herself against the frame of the doorway, the other hung down by her side, clasping a book. *She looks*, Mr Satterthwaite thought, *like a Madonna from an early Italian canvas.*

She stood there, swaying slightly from side to side. Colonel Melrose sprang toward her.

'I've come to tell you – to tell you –'

Her voice was low and rich. Mr Satterthwaite was so entranced with the dramatic value of the scene that he had forgotten its reality.

'Please, Lady Dwighton –' Melrose had an arm round her, supporting her. He took her across the hall into a small anteroom, its walls hung with faded silk. Quin and Satterthwaite followed. She sank down on the low settee, her head resting back on a rust-coloured cushion, her eyelids closed. The three men watched her. Suddenly she opened her eyes and sat up. She spoke very quietly.

'*I killed him*,' she said. 'That's what I came to tell you. *I killed him!*'

There was a moment's agonized silence. Mr Satterthwaite's heart missed a beat.

'Lady Dwighton,' said Melrose. 'You've had a great shock – you're unstrung. I don't think you quite know what you're saying.'

Would she draw back now – while there was yet time?

'I know perfectly what I'm saying. It was I who shot him.'

Two of the men in the room gasped, the other made no sound. Laura Dwighton leaned still farther forward.

'Don't you understand? I came down and shot him. I admit it.'

The book she had been holding in her hand clattered to the floor. There was a paper cutter in it, a thing shaped like a dagger with a jewelled hilt. Mr Satterthwaite picked it up mechanically and placed it on the table. As he did so he thought, *That's a dangerous toy. You could kill a man with that.*

'Well –' Laura Dwighton's voice was impatient. '– what are you going to do about it? Arrest me? Take me away?'

Colonel Melrose found his voice with difficulty.

'What you have told me is very serious, Lady Dwighton. I must ask you to go to your room till I have – er – made arrangements.'

She nodded and rose to her feet. She was quite composed now, grave and cold.

As she turned toward the door, Mr Quin spoke. 'What did you do with the revolver, Lady Dwighton?'

A flicker of uncertainty passed across her face. 'I – I dropped it there on the floor. No, I think I threw it out of the window – oh! I can't remember now. What does it matter? I hardly knew what I was doing. It doesn't matter, does it?'

'No,' said Mr Quin. 'I hardly think it matters.'

She looked at him in perplexity with a shade of something that might have been alarm. Then she flung back her head and went imperiously out of the room. Mr Satterthwaite hastened after her. She might, he felt, collapse at any minute. But she was already halfway up the staircase, displaying no sign of her earlier weakness. The scared-looking maid was standing at the foot of the stairway, and Mr Satterthwaite spoke to her authoritatively.

'Look after your mistress,' he said.

'Yes, sir.' The girl prepared to ascend after the blue-robed figure. 'Oh, please, sir, they don't suspect him, do they?'

'Suspect whom?'

'Jennings, sir. Oh! Indeed, sir, he wouldn't hurt a fly.'

'Jennings? No, of course not. Go and look after your mistress.'

'Yes, sir.'

The girl ran quickly up the staircase. Mr Satterthwaite returned to the room he had just vacated.

Colonel Melrose was saying heavily, 'Well, I'm jiggered. There's more in this than meets the eye. It – it's like those dashed silly things heroines do in many novels.'

'It's unreal,' agreed Mr Satterthwaite. 'It's like something on the stage.'

Mr Quin nodded. 'Yes, you admire the drama, do you not? You are a man who appreciates good acting when you see it.'

Mr Satterthwaite looked hard at him.

In the silence that followed a far-off sound came to their ears.

'Sounds like a shot,' said Colonel Melrose. 'One of the keepers, I daresay. That's probably what she heard. Perhaps she went down to see. She wouldn't go close or examine the body. She'd leap at once to the conclusion –'

'Mr Delangua, sir.' It was the old butler who spoke, standing apologetically in the doorway.

'Eh?' said Melrose. 'What's that?'

'Mr Delangua is here, sir, and would like to speak to you if he may.'

Colonel Melrose leaned back in his chair. 'Show him in,' he said grimly.

A moment later Paul Delangua stood in the doorway. As Colonel Melrose had hinted, there was something un-English about him – the easy grace of his movements, the dark, handsome face, the eyes set a little too near together. There hung about him the air of the Renaissance. He and Laura Dwighton suggested the same atmosphere.

'Good evening, gentlemen,' said Delangua. He made a little theatrical bow.

'I don't know what your business may be, Mr Delangua,' said Colonel Melrose sharply, 'but if it is nothing to do with the matter at hand –'

Delangua interrupted him with a laugh. 'On the contrary,' he said, 'it has everything to do with it.'

'What do you mean?'

'I mean,' said Delangua quietly, 'that I have come to give myself up for the murder of Sir James Dwighton.'

'You know what you are saying?' said Melrose gravely.

'Perfectly.'

The young man's eyes were riveted to the table.

'I don't understand –'

'Why I give myself up? Call it remorse – call it anything you please. I stabbed him, right enough – you may be quite sure of that.' He nodded toward the table. 'You've got the weapon there, I see. A very handy little tool. Lady Dwighton unfortunately left it lying around in a book, and I happened to snatch it up.'

'One minute,' said Colonel Melrose. 'Am I to understand that you admit stabbing Sir James with this?' He held the dagger aloft.

'Quite right. I stole in through the window, you know. He had his back to me. It was quite easy. I left the same way.'

'Through the window?'

'Through the window, of course.'

'And what time was this?'

Delangua hesitated. 'Let me see – I was talking to the keeper fellow – that was at a quarter past six. I heard the church tower chime. It must have been – well, say somewhere about half past.'

A grim smile came to the colonel's lips.

'Quite right, young man,' he said. 'Half past six was the time. Perhaps you've heard that already? But this is altogether a most peculiar murder!'

'Why?'

'So many people confess to it,' said Colonel Melrose.

They heard the sharp intake of the other's breath.

'Who else has confessed to it?' he asked in a voice that he vainly strove to render steady.

'Lady Dwighton.'

Delangua threw back his head and laughed in rather a forced manner. 'Lady Dwighton is apt to be hysterical,' he said lightly. 'I shouldn't pay any attention to what she says if I were you.'

'I don't think I shall,' said Melrose. 'But there's another odd thing about this murder.'

'What's that?'

'Well,' said Melrose, 'Lady Dwighton has confessed to having shot Sir James, and you have confessed to having stabbed him. But luckily for both of you, he wasn't shot or stabbed, you see. His skull was smashed in.'

'My God!' cried Delangua. 'But a woman couldn't possibly do that –'

He stopped, biting his lip. Melrose nodded with the ghost of a smile.

'Often read of it,' he volunteered. 'Never seen it happen.'

'What?'

'Couple of young idiots each accusing themselves because they thought the other had done it,' said Melrose. 'Now we've got to begin at the beginning.'

'The valet,' cried Mr Satterthwaite. 'That girl just now – I wasn't paying any attention at the time.' He paused, striving for coherence. 'She was afraid of our suspecting him. There must be some motive that he had and which we don't know, but she does.'

Colonel Melrose frowned, then he rang the bell. When it was answered, he said, 'Please ask Lady Dwighton if she will be good enough to come down again.'

They waited in silence until she came. At sight of Delangua she started and stretched out a hand to save herself from falling. Colonel Melrose came quickly to the rescue.

'It's quite all right, Lady Dwighton. Please don't be alarmed.'

'I don't understand. What is Mr Delangua doing here?'

Delangua came over to her, 'Laura – Laura – why did you do it?'

'Do it?'

'I know. It was for me – because you thought that – After all, it was natural, I suppose. But, oh! You angel!'

Colonel Melrose cleared his throat. He was a man who disliked emotion and had a horror of anything approaching a 'scene'.

'If you'll allow me to say so, Lady Dwighton, both you and Mr Delangua have had a lucky escape. He had just arrived in his turn to "confess" to the murder – oh, it's quite all right, he didn't do it! But what we want to know is the truth. No more shillyshallying. The butler says you went into the library at half past six – is that so?'

Laura looked at Delangua. He nodded.

'The truth, Laura,' he said. 'That is what we want now.'

She breathed a deep sigh. 'I will tell you.'

She sank down on a chair that Mr Satterthwaite had hurriedly pushed forward.

'I did come down. I opened the library door and I saw –'

She stopped and swallowed. Mr Satterthwaite leaned forward and patted her hand encouragingly.

'Yes,' he said. 'Yes. You saw?'

'My husband was lying across the writing table. I saw his head – the blood – oh!'

She put her hands to her face. The chief constable leaned forward.

'Excuse me, Lady Dwighton. You thought Mr Delangua had shot him?'

She nodded. 'Forgive me, Paul,' she pleaded. 'But you said – you said –'

'That I'd shoot him like a dog,' said Delangua grimly. 'I remember. That was the day I discovered he'd been ill-treating you.'

The chief constable kept sternly to the matter in hand.

'Then I am to understand, Lady Dwighton, that you went upstairs again and – er – said nothing. We needn't go into your reason. You didn't touch the body or go near the writing table?'

She shuddered.

'No, no. I ran straight out of the room.'

'I see, I see. And what time was this exactly? Do you know?'

'It was just half past six when I got back to my bedroom.'

'Then at – say five-and-twenty past six, Sir James was already dead.' The chief constable looked at the others. 'That clock – it was faked, eh? We suspected that all along. Nothing easier than to move the hands to whatever time you wished, but they made a mistake to lay it down on its side like that. Well, that seems to narrow it down to the butler or the valet, and I can't believe it's the butler. Tell me, Lady Dwighton, did this man Jennings have any grudge against your husband?'

Laura lifted her face from her hands. 'Not exactly a grudge, but – well, James told me only this morning that he'd dismissed him. He'd found him pilfering.'

'Ah! Now we're getting at it. Jennings would have been dismissed without a character. A serious matter for him.'

'You said something about a clock,' said Laura Dwighton. 'There's just a chance – if you want to fix the time – James would have been sure to have his little golf watch on him. Mightn't that have been smashed, too, when he fell forward?'

'It's an idea,' said the colonel slowly. 'But I'm afraid – Curtis!'

The inspector nodded in quick comprehension and left the

room. He returned a minute later. On the palm of his hand was a silver watch marked like a golf ball, the kind that are sold for golfers to carry loose in a pocket with balls.

'Here it is, sir,' he said, 'but I doubt if it will be any good. They're tough, these watches.'

The colonel took it from him and held it to his ear.

'It seems to have stopped, anyway,' he observed.

He pressed with his thumb, and the lid of the watch flew open. Inside the glass was cracked across.

'Ah!' he said exultantly.

The hand pointed to exactly a quarter past six.

II

'A very good glass of port, Colonel Melrose,' said Mr Quin.

It was half past nine, and the three men had just finished a belated dinner at Colonel Melrose's house. Mr Satterthwaite was particularly jubilant.

'I was quite right,' he chuckled. 'You can't deny it, Mr Quin. You turned up tonight to save two absurd young people who were both bent on putting their heads into a noose.'

'Did I?' said Mr Quin. 'Surely not. I did nothing at all.'

'As it turned out, it was not necessary,' agreed Mr Satterthwaite. 'But it might have been. It was touch and go, you know. I shall never forget the moment when Lady Dwighton said, "I killed him." I've never seen anything on the stage half as dramatic.'

'I'm inclined to agree with you,' said Mr Quin.

'Wouldn't have believed such a thing could happen outside a novel,' declared the colonel, for perhaps the twentieth time that night.

'Does it?' asked Mr Quin.

The colonel stared at him, 'Damn it, it happened tonight.'

'Mind you,' interposed Mr Satterthwaite, leaning back and sipping his port, 'Lady Dwighton was magnificent, quite magnificent, but she made one mistake. She shouldn't have leaped to the conclusion that her husband had been shot. In the same way Delangua was a fool to assume that he had been stabbed just because the dagger happened to be lying on the table in front of us. It was a mere coincidence that Lady Dwighton should have brought it down with her.'

'Was it?' asked Mr Quin.

'Now if they'd only confined themselves to saying that they'd killed Sir James, without particularizing how –' went on Mr Satterthwaite – 'what would have been the result?'

'They might have been believed,' said Mr Quin with an odd smile.

'The whole thing was exactly like a novel,' said the colonel.

'That's where they got the idea from, I daresay,' said Mr Quin.

'Possibly,' agreed Mr Satterthwaite. 'Things one has read do come back to one in the oddest way.' He looked across at Mr Quin. 'Of course,' he said, 'the clock really looked suspicious from the first. One ought never to forget how easy it is to put the hands of a clock or watch forward or back.'

Mr Quin nodded and repeated the words. 'Forward,' he said, and paused. 'Or back.'

There was something encouraging in his voice. His bright, dark eyes were fixed on Mr Satterthwaite.

'The hands of the clock were put forward,' said Mr Satterthwaite. 'We know that.'

'Were they?' asked Mr Quin.

Mr Satterthwaite stared at him. 'Do you mean,' he said slowly, 'that it was the watch which was put back? But that doesn't make sense. It's impossible.'

'Not impossible,' murmured Mr Quin.

'Well – absurd. To whose advantage could that be?'

'Only, I suppose, to someone who had an *alibi* for that time.'

'By gad!' cried the colonel. 'That's the time young Delangua said he was talking to the keeper.'

'He told us that very particularly,' said Mr Satterthwaite.

They looked at each other. They had an uneasy feeling as of solid ground failing beneath their feet. Facts went spinning round, turning new and unexpected faces. And in the centre of the kaleidoscope was the dark, smiling face of Mr Quin.

'But in that case –' began Melrose '– in that case –'

Mr Satterthwaite, nimble-witted, finished his sentence for him. 'It's all the other way round. A plant just the same – but a plant against the valet. Oh, but it can't be! It's impossible. Why each of them accused themselves of the crime.'

'Yes,' said Mr Quin. 'Up till then you suspected them, didn't you?' His voice went on, placid and dreamy. 'Just like something out of a book, you said, colonel. They got the idea there. It's what the innocent hero and heroine do. Of course it made you think them innocent – there was the force of tradition behind them. Mr Satterthwaite has been saying all along it was like something on the stage. You were both right. It wasn't real. You've been saying so all along without knowing what you were saying. They'd have told a much better story than that if they'd wanted to be believed.'

The two men looked at him helplessly.

'It would be clever,' said Mr Satterthwaite slowly. 'It would be diabolically clever. And I've thought of something else. The butler said he went in at seven to shut the windows – so he must have expected them to be open.'

'That's the way Delangua came in,' said Mr Quin. 'He killed Sir James with one blow, and he and she together did what they had to do –'

He looked at Mr Satterthwaite, encouraging him to reconstruct the scene. He did so, hesitatingly.

'They smashed the clock and put it on its side. Yes. They altered the watch and smashed it. Then he went out of the window, and she fastened it after him. But there's one thing I don't see. Why bother with the watch at all? Why not simply put back the hands of the clock?'

'The clock was always a little obvious,' said Mr Quin.

'Anyone might have seen through a rather transparent device like that.'

'But surely the watch was too far-fetched. Why, it was pure chance that we ever thought of the watch.'

'Oh, no,' said Mr Quin. 'It was the lady's suggestion, remember.'

Mr Satterthwaite stared at him, fascinated.

'And yet, you know,' said Mr Quin dreamily, 'the one person who wouldn't be likely to overlook the watch would be the valet. Valets know better than anyone what their masters carry in their pockets. If he altered the clock, the valet would have altered the watch, too. They don't understand human nature, those two. They are not like Mr Satterthwaite.'

Mr Satterthwaite shook his head.

'I was all wrong,' he murmured humbly. 'I thought that you had come to save them.'

'So I did,' said Mr Quin. 'Oh! Not those two – the others. Perhaps you didn't notice the lady's maid? She wasn't wearing blue brocade, or acting a dramatic part. But she's really a very pretty girl, and I think she loves that man Jennings very much. I think that between you you'll be able to save her man from getting hanged.'

'We've no proof of any kind,' said Colonel Melrose heavily.

Mr Quin smiled. 'Mr Satterthwaite has.'

'I?' Mr Satterthwaite was astonished.

Mr Quin went on. 'You've got a proof that that watch wasn't smashed in Sir James's pocket. You can't smash a watch like that without opening the case. Just try it and see. Someone took the watch out and opened it, set back the hands, smashed the glass, and then shut it and put it back. They never noticed that a fragment of glass was missing.'

'Oh!' cried Mr Satterthwaite. His hand flew to his waistcoat pocket. He drew out a fragment of curved glass.

It was his moment.

'With this,' said Mr Satterthwaite importantly, 'I shall save a man from death.'

THE HARLEQUIN TEA SET

Mr Satterthwaite clucked twice in vexation. Whether right in his assumption or not, he was more and more convinced that cars nowadays broke down far more frequently than they used to do. The only cars he trusted were old friends who had survived the test of time. They had their little idiosyncrasies, but you knew about those, provided for them, fulfilled their wants before the demand became too acute. But new cars! Full of new gadgets, different kinds of windows, an instrument panel newly and differently arranged, handsome in its glistening wood but being unfamiliar, your groping hand hovered uneasily over fog lights, windscreen wipers, the choke, etcetera. All these things with knobs in a place you didn't expect them. And when your gleaming new purchase failed in performance, your local garage uttered the intensely irritating words: 'Teething troubles. Splendid car, sir, these roadsters Super Superbos. All the latest accessories. But bound to have their teething troubles, you know. Ha, ha.' Just as though a car was a baby.

But Mr Satterthwaite, being now of an advanced age, was strongly of the opinion that a new car ought to be fully adult. Tested, inspected, and its teething troubles already dealt with before it came into its purchaser's possession.

Mr Satterthwaite was on his way to pay a weekend visit to friends in the country. His new car had already, on the way from London, given certain symptoms of discomfort, and was now drawn up in a garage waiting for the diagnosis, and how long it would take before he could resume progress towards his destination. His chauffeur was in consultation with a mechanic. Mr Satterthwaite sat, striving for patience. He had assured his hosts, on the telephone the night before, that he would be arriving in good time for tea. He would reach Doverton Kingsbourne, he assured them, well before four o'clock.

He clucked again in irritation and tried to turn his thoughts to something pleasant. It was no good sitting here in a state of acute irritation, frequently consulting his wristwatch, clucking once more and giving, he had to realize, a very good imitation of a hen pleased with its prowess in laying an egg.

Yes. Something pleasant. Yes, now hadn't there been something – something he had noticed as they were driving along. Not very long ago. Something that he had seen through the window which had pleased and excited him. But before he had had time to think about it, the car's misbehaviour had become more pronounced and a rapid visit to the nearest service station had been inevitable.

What was it that he had seen? On the left – no, on the right. Yes, on the right as they drove slowly through the village street. Next door to a post office. Yes, he was quite sure of that. Next door to a post office because the sight of the post office had given him the idea of telephoning to the Addisons to break the news that he might be slightly late in his arrival. The post office. A village post office. And next to it – yes, definitely, next to it, next door or if not next door the door after. Something that had stirred old memories, and he had wanted – just what was it that he had wanted? Oh dear, it would come to him presently. It was mixed up with a colour. Several colours. Yes, a colour or colours. Or a word. Some definite word that had stirred memories, thoughts, pleasures gone by, excitement, recalling something that had been vivid and alive. Something in which he himself had not only seen but observed. No, he had done more. He had taken part. Taken part in what, and why, and where? All sorts of places. The answer came quickly at the last thought. All sorts of places.

On an island? In Corsica? At Monte Carlo watching the croupier spinning his roulette wheel? A house in the country? All sorts of places. And he had been there, and someone else. Yes, someone else. It all tied up with that. He was getting there at last. If he could just . . . He was interrupted at that moment by the chauffeur coming to the window with the garage mechanic in tow behind him.

'Won't be long now, sir,' the chauffeur assured Mr Satterthwaite cheerfully. 'Matter of ten minutes or so. Not more.'

'Nothing seriously wrong,' said the mechanic, in a low, hoarse, country voice. 'Teething troubles, as you might say.'

Mr Satterthwaite did not cluck this time. He gnashed his own teeth. A phrase he had often read in books and which in old age he seemed to have got into the habit of doing himself, due, perhaps, to the slight looseness of his upper plate. Really, teething trouble! Toothache. Teeth gnashing. False teeth. One's whole life centred, he thought, about teeth.

'Doverton Kingsbourne's only a few miles away,' said the chauffeur, 'and they've a taxi here. You could go on in that, sir, and I'd bring the car along later as soon as it's fixed up.'

'No!' said Mr Satterthwaite.

He said the word explosively and both the chauffeur and the mechanic looked startled. Mr Satterthwaite's eyes were sparkling. His voice was clear and decisive. Memory had come to him.

'I propose,' he said, 'to walk along the road we have just come by. When the car is ready, you will pick me up there. The Harlequin Cafe, I think it is called.'

'It's not very much of a place, sir,' the mechanic advised.

'That is where I shall be,' said Mr Satterthwaite, speaking with a kind of regal autocracy.

He walked off briskly. The two men stared after him.

'Don't know what's got into him,' said the chauffeur. 'Never seen him like that before.'

The village of Kingsbourne Ducis did not live up to the old world grandeur of its name. It was a smallish village consisting of one street. A few houses. Shops that were dotted rather unevenly, sometimes betraying the fact that they were houses which had been turned into shops or that they were shops which now existed as houses without any industrial intentions.

It was not particularly old world or beautiful. It was just simple and rather unobtrusive. Perhaps that was why, thought Mr Satterthwaite, that a dash of brilliant colour had caught his eye. Ah, here he was at the post office. The post office was a simply functioning post office with a pillar box outside, a display of some newspapers and some postcards, and surely, next to it, yes there was the sign up above. The Harlequin Cafe. A sudden qualm struck Mr Satterthwaite. Really, he was getting too old. He had fancies. Why should that one word stir his heart? *The Harlequin Cafe.*

The mechanic at the service station had been quite right. It did not look like a place in which one would really be tempted to have a meal. A snack perhaps. A morning coffee. Then why? But he suddenly realized why. Because the cafe, or perhaps one could better put it as the house that sheltered the cafe, was in two portions. One side of it had small tables with chairs round them arranged ready for patrons who came here to eat. But the other side was a shop. A shop that sold china. It was not an antique shop. It had no little shelves of glass vases or mugs. It was a shop that sold modern goods, and the show window that gave on the street was at the present moment housing every shade of the rainbow. A tea set of largish cups and saucers, each one of a different colour. Blue, red, yellow, green, pink, purple. Really, Mr Satterthwaite thought, a wonderful show of colour. No wonder it had struck his eye as the car had passed slowly beside the pavement, looking ahead for any sign of a garage or a service station. It was labelled with a large card as 'A Harlequin Tea Set'.

It was the word 'harlequin' of course which had remained fixed in Mr Satterthwaite's mind, although just far enough back in his mind so that it had been difficult to recall it. The gay colours. The harlequin colours. And he had thought, wondered, had the absurd but exciting idea that in some way here was a call to him. To him specially. Here, perhaps, eating a meal or purchasing cups and saucers might be his own old friend, Mr Harley Quin. How many years was it since he had last seen Mr Quin? A large number of years. Was it the day he had seen Mr Quin walking away from him down a country lane, Lovers' Lane they had called it? He had always expected to see Mr Quin again, once a year at least. Possibly twice a year. But no. That had not happened.

And so today he had had the wonderful and surprising idea that here, in the village of Kingsbourne Ducis, he might once again find Mr Harley Quin.

'Absurd of me,' said Mr Satterthwaite, 'quite absurd of me. Really, the ideas one has as one gets old!'

He had missed Mr Quin. Missed something that had been one of the most exciting things in the late years of his life. Someone who might turn up anywhere and who, if he did turn up, was always an announcement that something was going to happen. Something that was going to happen to him. No, that was not quite right. Not *to* him, but through him. That was the exciting part. Just from the words that Mr Quin might utter. Words. Things he might show him, ideas would come to Mr Satterthwaite. He would see things, he would imagine things, he would find out things. He would deal with something that needed to be dealt with. And opposite him would sit Mr Quin, perhaps smiling approval. Something that Mr Quin said would start the flow of ideas, the active person would be he himself. He – Mr Satterthwaite. The man with so many old friends. A man among whose friends had been duchesses, an occasional bishop, people that counted. Especially, he had to admit, people who had counted in the social world. Because, after all, Mr Satterthwaite had always been a snob. He had liked duchesses, he had liked knowing old families, families who had represented the landed gentry of England for several generations. And he had had, too, an interest in young people not necessarily socially important. Young people who were in trouble, who were in love, who were unhappy, who needed help. Because of Mr Quin, Mr Satterthwaite was enabled to give help.

And now, like an idiot, he was looking into an unprepossessing village cafe and a shop for modern china and tea sets and casseroles no doubt.

'All the same,' said Mr Satterthwaite to himself, 'I must go in. Now I've been foolish enough to walk back here, I must go in just – well, just in case. They'll be longer, I expect, doing the car than they say. It will be more than ten minutes. Just in case there was anything interesting inside.'

He looked once more at the window full of china. He appreciated suddenly that it was good china. Well made. A good modern product. He looked back into the past, remembering. The Duchess of Leith, he remembered. What a wonderful old lady she had been. How kind she had been to her maid on the occasion of a very rough sea voyage to the island of Corsica. She had ministered to her with the kindliness of a ministering angel and only on the next day had she resumed her autocratic, bullying manner which the domestics of those days had seemed able to stand quite easily without any sign of rebellion.

Maria. Yes, that's what the Duchess's name had been. Dear old Maria Leith. Ah well. She had died some years ago. But she had had a harlequin breakfast set, he remembered. Yes. Big round cups in different colours. Black. Yellow, red and a particularly pernicious shade of puce. Puce, he thought, must have been a favourite colour of hers. She had had a Rockingham tea set, he remembered, in which the predominating colour had been puce decorated with gold.

'Ah,' sighed Mr Satterthwaite, 'those were the days. Well, I suppose I'd better go in. Perhaps order a cup of coffee or something. It will be very full of milk, I expect, and possibly already sweetened. But still, one has to pass the time.'

He went in. The cafe side was practically empty. It was early, Mr Satterthwaite supposed, for people to want cups of tea. And anyway, very few people did want cups of tea nowadays. Except, that is, occasionally elderly people in their own homes. There was a young couple in the far window and two women gossiping at a table against the back wall.

'I said to her,' one of them was saying, 'I said you can't do that sort of thing. No, it's not the sort of thing that I'll put up with, and I said the same to Henry and he agreed with me.'

It shot through Mr Satterthwaite's mind that Henry must have rather a hard life and that no doubt he had found it always wise to agree, whatever the proposition put up to him might be. A most unattractive woman with a most unattractive friend. He turned his attention to the other side of the building, murmuring, 'May I just look round?'

There was quite a pleasant woman in charge and she said 'Oh yes, sir. We've got a good stock at present.'

Mr Satterthwaite looked at the coloured cups, picked up one or two of them, examined the milk jug, picked up a china zebra and considered it, examined some ashtrays of a fairly pleasing pattern. He heard chairs being pushed back and turning his head, noted that the two middle-aged women still discussing former grievances had paid their bill and were now leaving the shop. As they went out of the door, a tall man in a dark suit came in. He sat down at the table which they had just vacated. His back was to Mr Satterthwaite, who thought that he had an attractive back. Lean, strong, well-muscled but rather dark and sinister-looking because there was very little light in the shop. Mr Satterthwaite looked back again at the ashtrays. 'I might buy an ashtray so as not to cause a disappointment to the shop owner,' he thought. As he did so, the sun came out suddenly.

He had not realized that the shop had looked dim because of the lack of sunshine. The sun must have been under a cloud for some time. It had clouded over, he remembered, at about the time they had got to the service station. But now there was this sudden burst of sunlight. It caught up the colours of the china and through a coloured glass window of somewhat ecclesiastical pattern which must, Mr Satterthwaite thought, have been left over in the original Victorian house. The sun came through the window and lit up the dingy cafe. In some curious way it lit up the back of the man who had just sat down there. Instead of a dark black silhouette, there was now a festoon of colours. Red and blue and yellow. And suddenly Mr Satterthwaite realized that he was looking at exactly what he had hoped to find. His intuition had not played him false. He knew who it was who had just come in and sat down there. He knew so well that he had no need to wait until he could look at the face. He turned his back on the china, went back into the cafe, round the corner of the round table and sat down opposite the man who had just come in.

'Mr Quin,' said Mr Satterthwaite. 'I knew somehow it was going to be you.'

Mr Quin smiled.

'You always know so many things,' he said.

'It's a long time since I've seen you,' said Mr Satterthwaite.

'Does time matter?' said Mr Quin.

'Perhaps not. You may be right. Perhaps not.'

'May I offer you some refreshment?'

'Is there any refreshment to be had?' said Mr Satterthwaite doubtfully. 'I suppose you must have come in for that purpose.'

'One is never quite sure of one's purpose, is one?' said Mr Quin.

'I am so pleased to see you again,' said Mr Satterthwaite. 'I'd almost forgotten, you know. I mean forgotten the way you talk, the things you say. The things you make me think of, the things you make me do.'

'I – make you do? You are so wrong. You have always known yourself just what you wanted to do and why you want to do them and why you know so well that they have to be done.'

'I only feel that when you are here.'

'Oh no,' said Mr Quin lightly. 'I have nothing to do with it. I am just – as I've often told you – I am just passing by. That is all.'

'Today you are passing by through Kingsbourne Ducis.'

'And you are not passing by. You are going to a definite place. Am I right?'

'I'm going to see a very old friend. A friend I have not seen for a good many years. He's old now. Somewhat crippled. He has had one stroke. He has recovered from it quite well, but one never knows.'

'Does he live by himself?'

'Not now, I am glad to say. His family have come back from abroad, what is left of his family that is. They have been living with him now for some months. I am glad to be able to come and see them again all together. Those, that's to say, that I have seen before, and those that I have not seen.'

'You mean children?'

'Children and grandchildren.' Mr Satterthwaite sighed. Just for a moment he was sad that he had had no children and no grandchildren and no great-grandchildren himself. He did not usually regret it at all.

'They have some special Turkish coffee here,' said Mr Quin. 'Really good of its kind. Everything else is, as you have guessed, rather unpalatable. But one can always have a cup of Turkish coffee, can one not? Let us have one because I suppose you will soon have to get on with your pilgrimage, or whatever it is.'

In the doorway came a small black dog. He came and sat down by the table and looked up at Mr Quin.

'Your dog?' said Mr Satterthwaite.

'Yes. Let me introduce you to Hermes.' He stroked the black dog's head. 'Coffee,' he said. 'Tell Ali.'

The black dog walked from the table through a door at the back of the shop. They heard him give a short, incisive bark. Presently he reappeared and with him came a young man with a very dark complexion, wearing an emerald green pullover.

'Coffee, Ali,' said Mr Quin. 'Two coffees.'

'Turkish coffee. That's right, isn't it, sir?' He smiled and disappeared.

The dog sat down again.

'Tell me,' said Mr Satterthwaite, 'tell me where you've been and what you have been doing and why I have not seen you for so long.'

'I have just told you that time really means nothing. It is clear in my mind and I think it is clear in yours the occasion when we last met.'

'A very tragic occasion,' said Mr Satterthwaite. 'I do not really like to think of it.'

'Because of death? But death is not always a tragedy. I have told you that before.'

'No,' said Mr Satterthwaite, 'perhaps that death – the one we are both thinking of – was not a tragedy. But all the same . . .'

'But all the same it is life that really matters. You are quite right, of course,' said Mr Quin. 'Quite right. It is life that matters. We do not want someone young, someone who is happy, or could be happy, to die. Neither of us want that, do we. That is the reason why we must always save a life when the command comes.'

'Have you got a command for me?'

'Me – command for you?' Harley Quin's long, sad face brightened into its peculiarly charming smile. 'I have no commands for *you*, Mr Satterthwaite. I have never had commands. You yourself know things, see things, know what to do, do them. It has nothing to do with me.'

'Oh yes, it has,' said Mr Satterthwaite. 'You're not going to change my mind on that point. But tell me. Where have you been during what it is too short to call time?'

'Well, I have been here and there. In different countries, different climates, different adventures. But mostly, as usual, just passing by. I think it is more for you to tell me not only what you have been doing but what you are going to do now. More about where you are going. Who you are going to meet. Your friends, what they are like.'

'Of course I will tell you. I should enjoy telling you because I have been wondering, thinking you know about these friends I am going to. When you have not seen a family for a long time, when you have not been closely connected with them for many years, it is always a nervous moment when you are going to resume old friendships and old ties.'

'You are so right,' said Mr Quin.

The Turkish coffee was brought in little cups of oriental pattern. Ali placed them with a smile and departed. Mr Satterthwaite sipped approvingly.

'As sweet as love, as black as night and as hot as hell. That is the old Arab phrase, isn't it?'

Harley smiled over his shoulder and nodded.

'Yes,' said Mr Satterthwaite, 'I must tell you where I am going though what I am doing hardly matters. I am going to renew old friendships, to make acquaintance with the younger generation. Tom Addison, as I have said, is a very old friend of mine. We did many things together in our young days. Then, as often happens, life parted us. He was in the Diplomatic Service, went abroad for several foreign posts in turn. Sometimes I went and stayed with him, sometimes I saw him when he was home in England. One of his early posts was in Spain. He married a Spanish girl, a very beautiful, dark girl called Pilar. He loved her very much.'

'They had children?'

'Two daughters. A fair-haired baby like her father, called Lily, and a second daughter, Maria, who took after her Spanish mother. I was Lily's godfather. Naturally, I did not see either of the children very often. Two or three times a year either I gave a party for Lily or went to see her at her school. She was a sweet and lovely person. Very devoted to her father and he was very devoted to her. But in between these meetings, these revivals of friendship, we went through some difficult times. You will know about it as well as I do. I and my contemporaries had difficulties in meeting through the war years. Lily married a pilot in the Air Force. A fighter pilot. Until the other day I had even forgotten his name. Simon Gilliatt. Squadron Leader Gilliatt.'

'He was killed in the war?'

'No, no. No. He came through safely. After the war he resigned from the Air Force and he and Lily went out to Kenya as so many did. They settled there and they lived very happily. They had a son, a little boy called Roland. Later when he was at school in England I saw him once or twice. The last time, I think, was when he was twelve years old. A nice boy. He had red hair like his father. I've not seen him since so I am looking forward to seeing him today. He is twenty-three – twenty-four now. Time goes on so.'

'Is he married?'

'No. Well, not yet.'

'Ah. Prospects of marriage?'

'Well, I wondered from something Tom Addison said in his letter. There is a girl cousin. The younger daughter Maria married the local doctor. I never knew her very well. It was rather sad. She died in childbirth. Her little girl was called Inez, a family name chosen by her Spanish grandmother. As it happens I have only seen Inez once since she grew up. A dark, Spanish type very much like her grandmother. But I am boring you with all this.'

'No. I want to hear it. It is very interesting to me.'

'I wonder why,' said Mr Satterthwaite.

He looked at Mr Quin with that slight air of suspicion which sometimes came to him.

'You want to know all about this family. Why?'

'So that I can picture it, perhaps, in my mind.'

'Well, this house I am going to, Doverton Kingsbourne it is called. It is quite a beautiful old house. Not so spectacular as to invite tourists or to be open to visitors on special days. Just a quiet country house to live in by an Englishman who has served his country and comes back to enjoy a mellow life when the age of retirement comes. Tom was always fond of country life. He enjoyed fishing. He was a good shot and we had very happy days together in his family home of his boyhood. I spent many of my own holidays as a boy at Doverton Kingsbourne. And all through my life I have had that image in my mind. No place like Doverton Kingsbourne. No other house to touch it. Every time I drove near it I would make a detour perhaps and just pass to see the view through a gap in the trees of the long lane that runs in front of the house, glimpses of the river where we used to fish, and of the house itself. And I would remember all the things that Tom and I did together. He has been a man of action. A man who has done things. And I – I have just been an old bachelor.'

'You have been more than that,' said Mr Quin. 'You have been a man who made friends, who had many friends and who has served his friends well.'

'Well, if I can think that. Perhaps you are being too kind.'

'Not at all. You are very good company besides. The stories you can tell, the things you've seen, the places you have visited.

The curious things that have happened in your life. You could write a whole book on them,' said Mr Quin.

'I should make you the main character in it if I did.'

'No, you would not,' said Mr Quin. 'I am the one who passes by. That is all. But go on. Tell me more.'

'Well, this is just a family chronicle that I'm telling you. As I say, there were long periods, years of time when I did not see any of them. But they have been always my old friends. I saw Tom and Pilar until the time when Pilar died – she died rather young, unfortunately – Lily, my godchild, Inez, the quiet doctor's daughter who lives in the village with her father . . .'

'How old is the daughter?'

'Inez is nineteen or twenty, I think. I shall be glad to make friends with her.'

'So it is on the whole a happy chronicle?'

'Not entirely. Lily, my godchild – the one who went to Kenya with her husband – was killed there in an automobile accident. She was killed outright, leaving behind her a baby of barely a year old, little Roland. Simon, her husband, was quite broken-hearted. They were an unusually happy couple. However, the best thing happened to him that could happen, I suppose. He married again, a young widow who was the widow of a Squadron Leader, a friend of his and who also had been left with a baby the same age. Little Timothy and little Roland had only two or three months in age between them. Simon's marriage, I believe, has been quite happy though I've not seen them, of course, because they continued to live in Kenya. The boys were brought up like brothers. They went to the same school in England and spent their holidays usually in Kenya. I have not seen them, of course, for many years. Well, you know what has happened in Kenya. Some people have managed to stay on. Some people, friends of mine, have gone to Western Australia and have settled again happily there with their families. Some have come home to this country.

'Simon Gilliatt and his wife and their two children left Kenya. It was not the same to them and so they came home and accepted the invitation that has always been given them and renewed every year by old Tom Addison. They have come, his son-in-law, his son-in-law's second wife and the two children, now grown up boys, or rather, young men. They have come to live as a family there and they are happy. Tom's other grandchild, Inez Horton, as I told you, lives in the village with her father, the doctor, and she spends a good deal of her time, I gather, at Doverton Kingsbourne with Tom Addison who is very devoted to his grand-daughter. They sound all very happy together there. He has urged me several times to come there and see. Meet them all again. And so I accepted the invitation. Just for a weekend. It will be sad in some ways to see dear old Tom again, somewhat crippled, with perhaps not a very long expectation of life but still cheerful and gay, as far as I can make out. And to see also the old house again. Doverton Kingsbourne. Tied up with all my boyish memories. When one has not lived a very eventful life, when nothing has happened to one personally, and that is true of me, the things that remain with you are the friends, the houses and the things you did as a child and a boy and a young man. There is only one thing that worries me.'

'You should not be worried. What is it that worries you?'

'That I might be – disappointed. The house one remembers, one has dreams of, when one might come to see it again it would not be as you remembered it or dreamt it. A new wing would have been added, the garden would have been altered, all sorts of things can have happened to it. It is a very long time, really, since I have been there.'

'I think your memories will go with you,' said Mr Quin. 'I am glad you are going there.'

'I have an idea,' said Mr Satterthwaite. 'Come with me. Come with me on this visit. You need not fear that you'll not be welcome. Dear Tom Addison is the most hospitable fellow in the world. Any friend of mine would immediately be a friend of his. Come with me. You must. I insist.'

Making an impulsive gesture, Mr Satterthwaite nearly knocked his coffee cup off the table. He caught it just in time.

At that moment the shop door was pushed open, ringing its old-fashioned bell as it did so. A middle-aged woman came in. She was slightly out of breath and looked somewhat hot. She was good-looking still with a head of auburn hair only just touched here and there with grey. She had that clear ivory-coloured skin that so often goes with reddish hair and blue eyes, and she had kept her figure well. The newcomer swept a quick glance round the cafe and turned immediately into the china shop.

'Oh!' she exclaimed, 'you've still got some of the Harlequin cups.'

'Yes, Mrs Gilliatt, we had a new stock arrived in yesterday.'

'Oh, I'm so pleased. I really have been very worried. I rushed down here. I took one of the boys' motor bikes. They'd gone off somewhere and I couldn't find either of them. But I really had to do something. There was an unfortunate accident this morning with some of the cups and we've got people arriving for tea and a party this afternoon. So if you can give me a blue and a green and perhaps I'd better have another red one as well in case. That's the worst of these different coloured cups, isn't it?'

'Well, I know they do say as it's a disadvantage and you can't always replace the particular colour you want.'

Mr Satterthwaite's head had gone over his shoulder now and he was looking with some interest at what was going on. Mrs Gilliatt, the shop woman had said. But of course. He realized it now. This must be – he rose from his seat, half hesitating, and then took a step or two into the shop.

'Excuse me,' he said, 'but are you – are you Mrs Gilliatt from Doverton Kingsbourne?'

'Oh yes. I am Beryl Gilliatt. Do you – I mean . . . ?'

She looked at him, wrinkling her brows a little. An attractive woman, Mr Satterthwaite thought. Rather a hard face, perhaps, but competent. So this was Simon Gilliatt's second wife. She hadn't got the beauty of Lily, but she seemed an attractive woman, pleasant and efficient. Suddenly a smile came to Mrs Gilliatt's face.

'I do believe . . . yes, of course. My father-in-law, Tom, has got a photograph of you and you must be the guest we are expecting this afternoon. You must be Mr Satterthwaite.'

'Exactly,' said Mr Satterthwaite. 'That is who I am. But I shall have to apologize very much for being so much later in arriving than I said. But unfortunately my car has had a breakdown. It's in the garage now being attended to.'

'Oh, how miserable for you. But what a shame. But it's not tea time yet. Don't worry. We've put it off anyway. As you probably heard, I ran down to replace a few cups which unfortunately got swept off a table this morning. Whenever one has anyone to lunch or tea or dinner, something like that always happens.'

'There you are, Mrs Gilliatt,' said the woman in the shop. 'I'll wrap them up in here. Shall I put them in a box for you?'

'No, if you'll just put some paper around them and put them in this shopping bag of mine, they'll be quite all right that way.'

'If you are returning to Doverton Kingsbourne,' said Mr Satterthwaite, 'I could give you a lift in my car. It will be arriving from the garage any moment now.'

'That's very kind of you. I wish really I could accept. But I've simply got to take the motorbike back. The boys will be miserable without it. They're going somewhere this evening.'

'Let me introduce you,' said Mr Satterthwaite. He turned towards Mr Quin, who had risen to his feet and was now standing quite near. 'This is an old friend of mine, Mr Harley Quin, whom I have just happened to run across here. I've been trying to persuade him to come along to Doverton Kingsbourne. Would it be possible, do you think, for Tom to put up yet another guest for tonight?'

'Oh, I'm sure it would be quite all right,' said Beryl Gilliatt. 'I'm sure he'd be delighted to see another friend of yours. Perhaps it's a friend of his as well.'

'No,' said Mr Quin, 'I've never met Mr Addison though I've often heard my friend, Mr Satterthwaite, speak of him.'

'Well then, do let Mr Satterthwaite bring you. We should be delighted.'

'I am very sorry,' said Mr Quin. 'Unfortunately, I have another engagement. Indeed –' he looked at his watch '– I must start for it immediately. I am late already, which is what comes of meeting old friends.'

'Here you are, Mrs Gilliatt,' said the saleswoman. 'It'll be quite all right, I think, in your bag.'

Beryl Gilliatt put the parcel carefully into the bag she was carrying, then said to Mr Satterthwaite:

'Well, see you presently. Tea isn't until quarter past five, so don't worry. I'm so pleased to meet you at last, having heard so much about you always both from Simon and from my father-in-law.'

She said a hurried goodbye to Mr Quin and went out of the shop.

'Bit of a hurry she's in, isn't she?' said the shop woman, 'but she's always like that. Gets through a lot in a day, I'd say.'

The sound of the bicycle outside was heard as it revved up.

'Quite a character, isn't she?' said Mr Satterthwaite.

'It would seem so,' said Mr Quin.

'And I really can't persuade you?'

'I'm only passing by,' said Mr Quin.

'And when shall I see you again? I wonder now.'

'Oh, it will not be very long,' said Mr Quin. 'I think you will recognize me when you do see me.'

'Have you nothing more – nothing more to tell me? Nothing more to explain?'

'To explain what?'

'To explain why I have met you here.'

'You are a man of considerable knowledge,' said Mr Quin. 'One word might mean something to you. I think it would and it might come in useful.'

'What word?'

'Daltonism,' said Mr Quin. He smiled.

'I don't think –' Mr Satterthwaite frowned for a moment. 'Yes. Yes, I do know only just for the moment I can't remember . . .'

'Goodbye for the present,' said Mr Quin. 'Here is your car.'

At that moment the car was indeed pulling up by the post office door. Mr Satterthwaite went out to it. He was anxious not to waste more time and keep his hosts waiting longer than need be. But he was sad all the same at saying goodbye to his friend.

'There is nothing I can do for you?' he said, and his tone was almost wistful.

'Nothing you can do for *me*.'

'For someone else?'

'I think so. Very likely.'

'I hope I know what you mean.'

'I have the utmost faith in you,' said Mr Quin. 'You always know things. You are very quick to observe and to know the meaning of things. You have not changed, I assure you.'

His hand rested for a moment on Mr Satterthwaite's shoulder, then he walked out and proceeded briskly down the village street in the opposite direction to Doverton Kingsbourne. Mr Satterthwaite got into his car.

'I hope we shan't have any more trouble,' he said.

His chauffeur reassured him.

'It's no distance from here, sir. Three or four miles at most, and she's running beautifully now.'

He ran the car a little way along the street and turned where the road widened so as to return the way he had just come. He said again,

'Only three or four miles.'

Mr Satterthwaite said again, 'Daltonism.' It still didn't mean anything to him, but yet he felt it should. It was a word he'd heard used before.

'Doverton Kingsbourne,' said Mr Satterthwaite to himself. He said it very softly under his breath. The two words still meant to him what they had always meant. A place of joyous reunion, a place where he couldn't get there too quickly. A place where he was going to enjoy himself, even though so many of those whom he had known would not be there any longer. But Tom would be there. His old friend, Tom, and he thought again of the grass and the lake and the river and the things they had done together as boys.

Tea was set out upon the lawn. Steps led out from the French windows in the drawing room and down to where a big copper beech at one side and a cedar of Lebanon on the other made the setting for the afternoon scene. There were two painted and carved white tables and various garden chairs. Upright ones with coloured cushions and lounging ones where you could lean back and stretch your feet out and sleep, if you wished to do so. Some of them had hoods over them to guard you from the sun.

It was a beautiful early evening and the green of the grass was a soft deep colour. The golden light came through the copper beech and the cedar showed the lines of its beauty against a soft pinkish-golden sky.

Tom Addison was waiting for his guest in a long basket chair, his feet up, Mr Satterthwaite noted with some amusement what he remembered from many other occasions of meeting his host, he had comfortable bedroom slippers suited to his slightly swollen gouty feet, and the shoes were odd ones. One red and one green.

Good old Tom, thought Mr Satterthwaite, he hasn't changed. Just the same. And he thought, 'What an idiot I am. Of course I know what that word meant. Why didn't I think of it at once?'

'Thought you were never going to turn up, you old devil,' said Tom Addison.

He was still a handsome old man, a broad face with deep-set twinkling grey eyes, shoulders that were still square and gave him a look of power. Every line in his face seemed a line of good humour and of affectionate welcome. 'He never changes,' thought Mr Satterthwaite.

'Can't get up to greet you,' said Tom Addison. 'Takes two strong men and a stick to get me on my feet. Now, do you know our little crowd, or don't you? You know Simon, of course.'

'Of course I do. It's a good few years since I've seen you, but you haven't changed much.'

Squadron Leader Simon Gilliatt was a lean, handsome man with a mop of red hair.

'Sorry you never came to see us when we were in Kenya,' he said. 'You'd have enjoyed yourself. Lots of things we could have shown you. Ah well, one can't see what the future may bring. I thought I'd lay my bones in that country.'

'We've got a very nice churchyard here,' said Tom Addison. 'Nobody's ruined our church yet by restoring it and we haven't very much new building round about so there's plenty of room in the churchyard still. We haven't had one of these terrible additions of a new intake of graves.'

'What a gloomy conversation you're having,' said Beryl Gilliatt, smiling. 'These are our boys,' she said, 'but you know them already, don't you, Mr Satterthwaite?'

'I don't think I'd have known them now,' said Mr Satterthwaite.

Indeed, the last time he had seen the two boys was on a day when he had taken them out from their prep school. Although there was no relationship between them – they had had different fathers and mothers – yet the boys could have been, and often were, taken for brothers. They were about the same height and they both had red hair. Roland, presumably, having inherited it from his father and Timothy from his auburn-haired mother. There seemed also to be a kind of comradeship between them. Yet really, Mr Satterthwaite thought, they were very different.

The difference was clearer now when they were, he supposed, between twenty-two and twenty-five years old. He could see no resemblance in Roland to his grandfather. Nor apart from his red hair did he look like his father.

Mr Satterthwaite had wondered sometimes whether the boy would look like Lily, his dead mother. But there again he could see little resemblance. If anything, Timothy looked more as a son of Lily's might have looked. The fair skin and the high forehead and a delicacy of bone structure. At his elbow, a soft deep voice said,

'I'm Inez. I don't expect you remember me. It was quite a long time ago when I saw you.'

A beautiful girl, Mr Satterthwaite thought at once. A dark type. He cast his mind back a long way to the days when he had come to be best man at Tom Addison's wedding to Pilar. She showed her Spanish blood, he thought, the carriage of her head and the dark aristocratic beauty. Her father, Dr Horton, was standing just behind her. He looked much older than when Mr Satterthwaite had seen him last. A nice man and kindly. A good general practitioner, unambitious but reliable and devoted, Mr Satterthwaite thought, to his daughter. He was obviously immensely proud of her.

Mr Satterthwaite felt an enormous happiness creeping over him. All these people, he thought, although some of them strange to him, it seemed like friends he had already known. The dark beautiful girl, the two red-haired boys, Beryl Gilliatt, fussing over the tea tray, arranging cups and saucers, beckoning to a maid from the house to bring out cakes and plates of sandwiches. A splendid tea. There were chairs that pulled up to the tables so that you could sit comfortably eating all you wanted to eat. The boys settled themselves, inviting Mr Satterthwaite to sit between them.

He was pleased at that. He had already planned in his own mind that it was the boys he wanted to talk to first, to see how much they recalled to him Tom Addison in the old days, and he thought, 'Lily. How I wish Lily could be here now'. Here he was, thought Mr Satterthwaite, here he was back in his boyhood. Here where he had come and been welcomed by Tom's father and mother, an aunt or so, too, there had been and a great-uncle and cousins. And now, well, there were not so many in this family, but it *was* a family. Tom in his bedroom slippers, one red, one green, old but still merry and happy. Happy in those who were spread round him. And here was Doverton just, or almost just, as it had been. Not quite so well kept up, perhaps, but the lawn was in good condition. And down there he could see the gleam of the river through the trees and the trees, too. More trees than there had been. And the house needing, perhaps, another coat of paint but not too badly. After all, Tom Addison was a rich man. Well provided for, owning a large quantity of land. A man with simple tastes who spent enough to keep his place up but was not a spendthrift in other ways. He seldom travelled or went abroad nowadays, but he entertained. Not big parties, just friends. Friends who came to stay, friends who usually had some connection going back into the past. A friendly house.

He turned a little in his chair, drawing it away from the table and turning it sideways so that he could see better the view down to the river. Down there was the mill, of course, and beyond the other side there were fields. And in one of the fields, it amused him to see a kind of scarecrow, a dark figure on which birds were settling on the straw. Just for a moment he thought it looked like Mr Harley Quin. Perhaps, thought Mr Satterthwaite, it *is* my friend Mr Quin. It was an absurd idea and yet if someone had piled up the scarecrow and tried to make it look like Mr Quin, it could have had the sort of slender elegance that was foreign to most scarecrows one saw.

'Are you looking at our scarecrow?' said Timothy. 'We've got a name for him, you know. We call him Mister Harley Barley.'

'Do you indeed' said Mr Satterthwaite. 'Dear me, I find that very interesting.'

'Why do you find it interesting?' said Roly, with some curiosity.

'Well, because it rather resembles someone that I know, whose name happens to be Harley. His first name, that is.'

The boys began singing, '*Harley Barley, stands on guard, Harley Barley takes things hard. Guards the ricks and guards the hay, Keeps the trespassers away.*'

'Cucumber sandwich, Mr Satterthwaite?' said Beryl Gilliatt, 'or do you prefer a home-made pâté one?'

Mr Satterthwaite accepted the home-made pâté. She deposited

by his side a puce cup, the same colour as he had admired in the shop. How gay it looked, all that tea set on the table. Yellow, red, blue, green and all the rest of it. He wondered if each one had their favourite colour. Timothy, he noticed, had a red cup, Roland had a yellow one. Beside Timothy's cup was an object Mr Satterthwaite could not at first identify. Then he saw it was a meerschaum pipe. It was years since Mr Satterthwaite had thought of or seen a meerschaum pipe. Roland, noticing what he was looking at, said, 'Tim brought that back from Germany when he went. He's killing himself with cancer smoking his pipe all the time.'

'Don't you smoke, Roland?'

'No. I'm not one for smoking. I don't smoke cigarettes and I don't smoke pot either.'

Inez came to the table and sat down the other side of him. Both the young men pressed food upon her. They started a laughing conversation together.

Mr Satterthwaite felt very happy among these young people. Not that they took very much notice of him apart from their natural politeness. But he liked hearing them. He liked, too, making up his judgement about them. He thought, he was almost sure, that both the young men were in love with Inez. Well, it was not surprising. Propinquity brings these things about. They had come to live here with their grandfather. A beautiful girl, Roland's first cousin, was living almost next door. Mr Satterthwaite turned his head. He could just see the house through the trees where it poked up from the road just beyond the front gate. That was the same house that Dr Horton had lived in last time he came here, seven or eight years ago.

He looked at Inez. He wondered which of the two young men she preferred or whether her affections were already engaged elsewhere. There was no reason why she should fall in love with one of these two attractive young specimens of the male race.

Having eaten as much as he wanted, it was not very much, Mr Satterthwaite drew his chair back altering its angle a little so that he could look all round him.

Mrs Gilliatt was still busy. Very much the housewife, he thought, making perhaps rather more of a fuss than she need of domesticity. Continually offering people cakes, taking their cups away and replenishing them, handing things round. Somehow, he thought, it would be more pleasant and more informal if she let people help themselves. He wished she was not so busy a hostess.

He looked up to the place where Tom Addison lay stretched out in his chair. Tom Addison was also watching Beryl Gilliatt. Mr Satterthwaite thought to himself: 'He doesn't like her. No. Tom doesn't like her. Well, perhaps that's to be expected.' After all, Beryl had taken the place of his own daughter, of Simon Gilliatt's first wife, Lily. 'My beautiful Lily,' thought Mr Satterthwaite again, and wondered why for some reason he felt that although he could not see anyone like her, yet Lily in some strange way was here. She was here at this tea party.

'I suppose one begins to imagine these things as one gets old,' said Mr Satterthwaite. 'After all, why shouldn't Lily be here to see her son.'

He looked affectionately at Timothy and then suddenly realized that he was not looking at Lily's son. Roland was Lily's son. Timothy was Beryl's son.

'I believe Lily knows I'm here. I believe she'd like to speak to me,' said Mr Satterthwaite. 'Oh dear, oh dear, I mustn't start imagining foolish things.'

For some reason he looked again at the scarecrow. It didn't look like a scarecrow now. It looked like Mr Harley Quin. Some tricks of the light, of the sunset, were providing it with colour, and there was a black dog like Hermes chasing the birds.

'Colour,' said Mr Satterthwaite, and looked again at the table and the tea set and the people having tea. 'Why am I here?' said Mr Satterthwaite to himself. 'Why am I here and what ought I to be doing? There's a reason . . .'

Now he knew, he felt, there was something, some crisis, something affecting – affecting all these people or only some of them? Beryl Gilliatt, Mrs Gilliatt. She was nervous about something. On edge. Tom? Nothing wrong with Tom. He wasn't affected. A lucky man to own this beauty, to own Doverton and to have a grandson so that when he died all this would come to Roland. All this would be Roland's. Was Tom hoping that Roland would marry Inez? Or would he have a fear of first cousins marrying? Though throughout history, Mr Satterthwaite thought, brothers had married sisters with no ill result. 'Nothing must happen,' said Mr Satterthwaite, 'nothing must happen. I must prevent it.'

Really, his thoughts were the thoughts of a madman. A peaceful scene. A tea set. The varying colours of the Harlequin cups. He looked at the white meerschaum pipe lying against the red of the cup. Beryl Gilliatt said something to Timothy. Timothy nodded, got up and went off towards the house. Beryl removed some empty plates from the table, adjusted a chair or two, murmured something to Roland, who went across and offered a frosted cake to Dr Horton.

Mr Satterthwaite watched her. He had to watch her. The sweep of her sleeve as she passed the table. He saw a red cup get pushed off the table. It broke on the iron feet of a chair. He heard her little exclamation as she picked up the bits. She went to the tea tray, came back and placed on the table a pale blue cup and saucer. She replaced the meerschaum pipe, putting it close against it. She brought the teapot and poured tea, then she moved away.

The table was untenanted now. Inez also had got up and left it. Gone to speak to her grandfather. 'I don't understand,' said Mr Satterthwaite to himself. 'Something's going to happen. What's going to happen?'

A table with different coloured cups round, and – yes, Timothy, his red hair glowing in the sun. Red hair glowing with that same tint, that attractive sideways wave that Simon Gilliatt's hair had always had. Timothy, coming back, standing a moment, looking at the table with a slightly puzzled eye, then going to where the meerschaum pipe rested against the pale blue cup.

Inez came back then. She laughed suddenly and she said, 'Timothy, you're drinking your tea out of the wrong cup. The blue cup's mine. Yours is the red one.'

And Timothy said, 'Don't be silly, Inez, I know my own cup. It's got sugar in it and you won't like it. Nonsense. This is my cup. The meerschaum's up against it.'

It came to Mr Satterthwaite then. A shock. Was he mad? Was he imagining things? Was any of this real?

He got up. He walked quickly towards the table, and as Timothy raised the blue cup to his lips, he shouted.

'Don't drink that!' he called. 'Don't drink it, I say.'

Timothy turned a surprised face. Mr Satterthwaite turned his head. Dr Horton, rather startled, got up from his seat and was coming near.

'What's the matter, Satterthwaite?'

'That cup. There's something wrong about it,' said Mr Satterthwaite. 'Don't let the boy drink from it.'

Horton stared at it. 'My dear fellow –'

'I know what I'm saying. The red cup was his,' said Mr Satterthwaite, 'and the red cup's broken. It's been replaced with a blue one. He doesn't know the red from blue, does he?'

Dr Horton looked puzzled. 'D'you mean – d'you mean – like Tom?'

'Tom Addison. He's colour blind. You know that, don't you?'

'Oh yes, of course. We all know that. That's why he's got odd shoes on today. He never knew red from green.'

'This boy is the same.'

'But – but surely not. Anyway, there's never been any sign of it in – in Roland.'

'There might be, though, mightn't there?' said Mr Satterthwaite. 'I'm right in thinking – Daltonism. That's what they call it, don't they?'

'It was a name they used to call it by, yes.'

'It's not inherited by a female, but it passes through the female. Lily wasn't colour blind, but Lily's son might easily be colour blind.'

'But my dear Satterthwaite, Timothy isn't Lily's son. Roly is Lily's son. I know they're rather alike. Same age, same coloured hair and things, but – well, perhaps you don't remember.'

'No,' said Mr Satterthwaite, 'I shouldn't have remembered. But I know now. I can see the resemblance too. Roland's Beryl's son. They were both babies, weren't they, when Simon re-married. It is very easy for a woman looking after two babies, especially if both of them were going to have red hair. Timothy's Lily's son and Roland is Beryl's son. Beryl's and Christopher Eden's. There is no reason why he should be colour blind. I know it, I tell you. I know it!'

He saw Dr Horton's eyes go from one to the other. Timothy, not catching what they said but standing holding the blue cup and looking puzzled.

'I saw her buy it,' said Mr Satterthwaite. 'Listen to me, man.

You must listen to me. You've known me for some years. You know that I don't make mistakes if I say a thing positively.'

'Quite true. I've never known you make a mistake.'

'Take that cup away from him,' said Mr Satterthwaite. 'Take it back to your surgery or take it to an analytic chemist and find out what's in it. I saw that woman buy that cup. She bought it in the village shop. She knew then that she was going to break a red cup, replace it by a blue and that Timothy would never know that the colours were different.'

'I think you're mad, Satterthwaite. But all the same I'm going to do what you say.'

He advanced on the table, stretched out a hand to the blue cup.

'Do you mind letting me have a look at that?' said Dr Horton.

'Of course,' said Timothy. He looked slightly surprised.

'I think there's a flaw in the china, here, you know. Rather interesting.'

Beryl came across the lawn. She came quickly and sharply.

'What are you doing? What's the matter? What is happening?'

'Nothing's the matter,' said Dr Horton, cheerfully. 'I just want to show the boys a little experiment I'm going to make with a cup of tea.'

He was looking at her very closely and he saw the expression of fear, of terror. Mr Satterthwaite saw the entire change of countenance.

'Would you like to come with me, Satterthwaite? Just a little experiment, you know. A matter of testing porcelain and different qualities in it nowadays. A very interesting discovery was made lately.'

Chatting, he walked along the grass. Mr Satterthwaite followed him and the two young men, chatting to each other, followed him.

'What's the Doc up to now, Roly?' said Timothy.

'I don't know,' said Roland. 'He seems to have got some very extraordinary ideas. Oh well, we shall hear about it later, I expect. Let's go and get our bikes.'

Beryl Gilliatt turned abruptly. She retraced her steps rapidly up the lawn towards the house. Tom Addison called to her:

'Anything the matter, Beryl?'

'Something I'd forgotten,' said Beryl Gilliatt. 'That's all.'

Tom Addison looked inquiringly towards Simon Gilliatt.

'Anything wrong with your wife?' he said.

'Beryl? Oh no, not that I know of. I expect it's some little thing or other that she's forgotten. Nothing I can do for you, Beryl?' he called.

'No. No, I'll be back later.' She turned her head half sideways, looking at the old man lying back in the chair. She spoke suddenly and vehemently. 'You silly old fool. You've got the wrong shoes on again today. They don't match. Do you know you've got one shoe that's red and one shoe that's green?'

'Ah, done it again, have I?' said Tom Addison. 'They look exactly the same colour to me, you know. It's odd, isn't it, but there it is.'

She went past him, her steps quickening.

Presently Mr Satterthwaite and Dr Horton reached the gate that led out into the roadway. They heard a motor bicycle speeding along.

'She's gone,' said Dr Horton. 'She's run for it. We ought to have stopped her, I suppose. Do you think she'll come back?'

'No,' said Mr Satterthwaite, 'I don't think she'll come back. Perhaps,' he said thoughtfully, 'it's best left that way.'

'You mean?'

'It's an old house,' said Mr Satterthwaite. 'And old family. A good family. A lot of good people in it. One doesn't want trouble, scandal, everything brought upon it. Best to let her go, I think.'

'Tom Addison never liked her,' said Dr Horton. 'Never. He was always polite and kind but he didn't like her.'

'And there's the boy to think of,' said Mr Satterthwaite.

'The boy. You mean?'

'The other boy. Roland. This way he needn't know about what his mother was trying to do.'

'Why did she do it? Why on earth did she do it?'

'You've no doubt now that she did,' said Mr Satterthwaite.

'No. I've no doubt now. I saw her face, Satterthwaite, when she looked at me. I knew then that what you'd said was truth. But why?'

'Greed, I suppose,' said Mr Satterthwaite. 'She hadn't any money of her own, I believe. Her husband, Christopher Eden, was a nice chap by all accounts but he hadn't anything in the way of means. But Tom Addison's grandchild has got big money coming to him. A lot of money. Property all around here has appreciated enormously. I've no doubt that Tom Addison will leave the bulk of what he has to his grandson. She wanted it for her own son and through her own son, of course, for herself. She is a greedy woman.'

Mr Satterthwaite turned his head back suddenly.

'Something's on fire over there,' he said.

'Good lord, so it is. Oh, it's the scarecrow down in the field. Some young chap or other's set fire to it, I suppose. But there's nothing to worry about. There are no ricks or anything anywhere near. It'll just burn itself out.'

'Yes,' said Mr Satterthwaite. 'Well, you go on, Doctor. You don't need me to help you in your tests.'

'I've no doubt of what I shall find. I don't mean the exact substance, but I have come to your belief that this blue cup holds death.'

Mr Satterthwaite had turned back through the gate. He was going now down in the direction where the scarecrow was burning. Behind it was the sunset. A remarkable sunset that evening. Its colours illuminated the air round it, illuminated the burning scarecrow.

'So that's the way you've chosen to go,' said Mr Satterthwaite.

He looked slightly startled then, for in the neighbourhood of the flames he saw the tall, slight figure of a woman. A woman dressed in some pale mother-of-pearl colouring. She was walking in the direction of Mr Satterthwaite. He stopped dead, watching.

'Lily,' he said. 'Lily.'

He saw her quite plainly now. It was Lily walking towards him. Too far away for him to see her face but he knew very well who it was. Just for a moment or two he wondered whether anyone else would see her or whether the sight was only for him. He said, not very loud, only in a whisper,

'It's all right, Lily, your son is safe.'

She stopped then. She raised one hand to her lips. He didn't see her smile, but he knew she was smiling. She kissed her hand and waved it to him and then she turned. She walked back towards where the scarecrow was disintegrating into a mass of ashes.

'She's going away again,' said Mr Satterthwaite to himself. 'She's going away with him. They're walking away together. They belong to the same world, of course. They only come – those sort of people – they only come when it's a case of love or death or both.'

He wouldn't see Lily again, he supposed, but he wondered how soon he would meet Mr Quin again. He turned then and went back across the lawn towards the tea table and the Harlequin tea set, and beyond that, to his old friend Tom Addison. Beryl wouldn't come back. He was sure of it. Doverton Kingsbourne was safe again.

Across the lawn came the small black dog in flying leaps. It came to Mr Satterthwaite, panting a little and wagging its tail. Through its collar was twisted a scrap of paper. Mr Satterthwaite stooped and detached it – smoothing it out – on it in coloured letters was written a message:

CONGRATULATIONS! TO OUR NEXT MEETING
H.Q.

'Thank you, Hermes,' said Mr Satterthwaite, and watched the black dog flying across the meadow to rejoin the two figures that he himself knew were there but could no longer see.